FATAL FLAWS

To Kiana
For those
who still
Remember

RAM
7/26/21

FATAL FLAWS

FATAL FLAWS

The Historical Web from WWI to September 11, 2001
Book 2 1945-1975

CAPT RICHARD A. MEO RET.

Copyright © 2017 by Capt Richard A. Meo ret.

ISBN: Softcover   978-1-5245-4260-3
             eBook   978-1-5245-4259-7

All rights reserved. No part of this book may be reproduced or transmitted in any form or by any means, electronic or mechanical, including photocopying, recording, or by any information storage and retrieval system, without permission in writing from the copyright owner.

Any people depicted in stock imagery provided by Thinkstock are models, and such images are being used for illustrative purposes only. Certain stock imagery © Thinkstock.

Print information available on the last page.

Rev. date: 02/24/2017

To order additional copies of this book, contact:
Xlibris
1-888-795-4274
www.Xlibris.com
Orders@Xlibris.com
539699

Book 2 Sections

Introduction vii
Preface ix

Part III

Peace and the Cold War September 1945 1

Part IV

America's Turn To Lead 227

Index 569
References 575
Video Documentaries 581
Source Notes 585
Direct Quotes 613

Introduction

On September 11, 2001 I was the Fire Captain of Engine Co. 34 based on W 38 Street in Manhattan. I was scheduled to work that tour but just before I went in one of my Lieutenants called to make a swap. If not for that last minute call I would have died with the 343 brothers of the FDNY.

On 9/11 I lost 105 of my friends in the FDNY.

Every month more are becoming sick and dying from the illnesses all developed at the toxic site.

(In the FDNY over 190 have died, over 6,000 are sick and another 1400 have confirmed cancers. Over 48,000 worked and volunteered at the WTC. From that total, as of 8/16 1140 have died and over 5400 have cancer.)

In the aftermath of that terrible day numerous books, articles and documentaries have been completed. Some have tried to bring to light what created Islamic Fundamentalism and the terrorism that followed, while others have revealed the failures and even subversive acts that occurred during the Clinton presidency. **During his eight years in office Bill Clinton became the world wide example of appeasement as he placated, assisted and allowed Islamic extremism to fall upon the world.**

(Since he was out of office the mainstream media never fixed the blame upon him.)

My first book *My Turn on the Fire Lines*, came out in 2009 and was updated in 2014. That work dealt with the years from 1980-2003 and is an in depth book describing my years in the FDNY. In those pages I highlighted our operations and some of the civil and social mistakes that contributed to our many problems in NYC.

Also highlighted were dozens of Islamic terrorist attacks, plots and suspicious events that happened during the Clinton Years which culminated in the attacks on 9/11/01.

After that book was published I began researching in detail the history of events that created the attacks of 9/11/01. As a history buff and an avid reader I realized that the story of the last century was intertwined with 9/11.

Within the "Big Picture" of world politics are a continual stream of events and decisions made and unmade by those few in power. Hidden within those details are the real reasons that America and the world are in this turbulent point in history. *And as has happened to every generation, thousands upon thousands of innocents will pay the price for the failures of those few.*

Most of the worlds citizens are not allowed to know of those secrets until years have passed and the guilty are gone. These books which comprise the *Fatal Flaws* series are a historical narrative of our century. By writing these books I hope the reader will be able to visualize and understand how a century of events and decisions created an interconnected web that led to the attacks of September 11, 2001.

Preface

Most people look at history as a boring series of dates and events from the past.

And one of the most common problems when reading or learning about the past is the mistaken belief that history is a linear event with a pre-ordained conclusion. But history is not a predetermined series of events.

There was no guarantee that the allied invasion of France in 1944 would succeed any more than one can guarantee happiness and prosperity for all.

As we live our lives historical events are occurring all around us. The events of today were dictated by decisions, errors and occurrences from yesterday. And those defining proceedings were also shaped by what went before them forming a historical web that never ends.

The books that make up **Fatal Flaws** are meant as a *non-politically correct* history primer of our century. It is not intended to be a deep comprehensive story of that century, or any event, but instead highlights many of the events that occurred in this web of history. All of the events in these pages have been written about by other authors or shown in historical documentaries.

I took sections from those sources and put them together to highlight those truths. And the truth is the one part of the human experience of the utmost importance to mankind. **Those who look to hide or obscure the truth are not to be trusted, ever.**

Our liberal media and educational system have chosen to ignore those hidden truths and discuss only those events that "they felt to be relevant" to advancing their agenda. *But in the "Big Picture of World History" it is those Inconvenient Truths that have brought us to this dangerous point in the human experience.*

Numerous pages in these books describe the many battles and wars that have been fought during the past one hundred years. Some of the battles were highlighted while others were given only a mere mention. These books were not meant to solely explore military history but to give more insight into certain ones that the public needed to explore. Many times there were strategic implications that historians ignored, missed or decided not to bring up. It is not the mission of these books to speculate on their decisions as to why, but it is felt that you the readers needed to learn of those battles to gain a better insight into what has shaped our world.

Rather than write the typical history of one storyline at a time I decided to showcase the events in ***Fatal Flaws*** in a flowing timeline. There are few natural breaks in History, so there are no "chapters" here. Hopefully in this way the reader will understand and see the many events that were occurring at the same time. Often the events were interrelated.

In ***Fatal Flaws Book 1***, I tried to highlight the history from WWI to the end of WWII. The main themes presented were;

1. That History is not a linear line of events that happen one at a time, but rather it is an interconnected web of events and decisions.
2. The collapse of the Old World and its dynastic empires in the fires of WWI.
3. The post-war emergence and growing danger of Communism from Bolshevik Russia as they aggressively expanded their conquests around the world.
4. The failures of the Old World mindsets of the British and French Colonial Ministers who controlled the dispersed territories that once made up the Ottoman Empire. Their repeated mistakes allowed a new entity to emerge, **Islamic Fundamentalism.** It was from that political entity the Islamic Extremists and Terrorists would emerge.
5. The numerous military and political failures that lost the chance to avoid WWII in Asia and in Europe
6. The failures by the Axis partners Germany and Italy to strike the strategic blows that would have knocked Britain out of the war before America entered. Japan made the same mistakes in the Pacific and their repeated failures cost them the victory they had sought and expected.
7. The U.S. and British military and political failures to win the war in Europe faster than it was which resulted in Communist domination of Eastern and Central Europe. Those failures would

then result in the emergence of a dangerous military-political competition which would be known as the **Cold War.**
8. The human disaster and worldwide devastation from WWII.

Never before had a calamity of this magnitude struck the entire globe.
Though the infant United Nations had been approved in the world's capitols their efforts to repair the broken world were only just beginning.
In fact the world on the whole was on the verge of chaos.
Only a revolutionary and monumental effort from America would stop this collapse.
During the WWII there were numerous political/military errors made by Pres. Roosevelt, Pres. Truman, Winston Churchill, George Marshall and numerous others. Those Fatal Flaws were to become grievous as the world separated into two competing and antagonistic political/economic spheres. Most of the people of the world did not recognize the dangers and neither did the world's leaders.
They had local disasters to fix their attention.
But ever so slowly war and turmoil again raised their hydra-like heads.
And all too soon the peace the world sought would be eclipsed,

**For There Are Tigers in This World,
And They Are Always Watching**

Human will can only be effective at the margin of events.

Once the situations have grown in scope, only actions will change the course of those proceedings. Over the millennia much of our history was affected by forces beyond human control, by events from the past, by accidental happenings, or even by chance.

For those who desire it, freedom is not an absolute for the individual or for any nation. At any given moment in time the margin of freedom may end or appear so small as to make any effort to keep it pointless.

But as has happened for eons, even a small chance for freedom can create a broader possibility for tomorrow.

"It is the decisions of today that makes possible or forecloses ten decisions of tomorrow."

(Paul Nitze, *From Hiroshima to Glasnost* pg158)

Part III

Peace and the Cold War September 1945

At the end of WWII a never to be seen again opportunity existed for one nation to control the entire world. For those who are not students or lovers of History, that nation was *The United States of America.*

When the guns of war fell silent America was the owner of the most incredible and powerful military force the World had ever seen or will ever see again.

The U.S. Navy weakened from the post WWI cutbacks and the reduced budgets of the Great Depression, had by September 1945 arisen to an astonishing force of; *100 Aircraft Carriers with over 10,000 aircraft, 23 Battleships, 73 Cruisers, 733 Destroyers and Destroyer Escorts, 234 Submarines, 1200 Patrol Craft, 600 Mine Craft, 1800 Auxiliary ships of all types and over 61,000 Landing Craft.*

Over half of the merchant ships on the oceans flew the stars and stripes.

Had our leaders and people desired it, our Navy could have swept the Seven Seas of all other nation's warships without breaking a sweat. With that accomplished America would have controlled all of the trade that plied the oceans. Any nation that desired to thrive would have had to ask us for permission.

Our Army and Marine Divisions numbered almost one hundred highly trained and battle tested warriors. They were equipped with modern and effective equipment that had assaulted and taken every stronghold Japan and Germany had setup. Though the early equipment and at times the generalship had faltered, the troops carried the day.

By September 1945 only Russia's Armies could have tried to stand in our way.

By the end of the war America's industrial output surpassed all of the other combatants combined. Our mass production techniques and motivated civilians worked nonstop to produce the weapons of war. And unlike the rest of the world America had been untouched by the war, our production was still at top speed.

It may seem impossible, **but in just four years America had produced over 300,000 aircraft of all types.** Our Army Air Force had grown to a mind numbing force of over 15,000 heavy bombers, equal numbers of medium bombers, transports and over 20,000 fighters.

No nation or group of nations could have withstood our aerial capabilities.

And in 1945 only America had Atomic Weapons.

But America and her citizens had no desires for conquest.

Not in 1918, not in 1945, and even now 70 years later there is no thirst for empires.

It is a fortunate thing for the world to have such a benevolent benefactor. There had not been such an entity ever before.

For certain there will not be one after our time as world leader has ended.

And because of the many useless and arrogant politicos and liberal ideologists who are dragging America down, that day draws dangerously near.

One must always remember,

That There Are Tigers in This World, (1)
And They Are Always Watching.

After six ghastly years of war from 1939-1945, did the surrender documents provide peace in Europe? Though the Fascists of Italy and Germany were vanquished and all of their conquered territories freed from their harsh rule, multiple thousands of German soldiers and civilians were set upon by the freed populations and hanged, raped, shot or drowned. In the devastation societies were breaking down and rape and murder became commonplace. Starvation returned to the land.

In Asia fourteen years of brutal war was over, 1931-1945, and the imperialists of Japan were beaten. All across the far Pacific Japanese administrators, soldiers and civilians were suffering the same fates as had the German occupiers in Europe, death and torment. War has that ability to strip away the communal side of humanity.

Among the three surviving Western powers, America, England and France, a great relief had come from their victory. But two of them would soon fall from world influence. Though England had enjoyed their war ending triumph, they were collapsing economically. On December 6,

1945 Pres. Truman authorized a credit line of $3.75 billion dollars, (an incredible sum at that time), to keep them afloat. He also gave the British an additional $650 million in lend lease aid. (That sum was to be repaid in the year 2000.)

France had lost all of their national pride, wealth and power in their rapid defeat in 1940. They were shamed by the collaborationist government of Petain and Vichy, and were hated by many. Their empire had been stripped from their control, and those populations were now demanding freedom. By September 1945 almost all of their military capability was what America provided.

Between those three Western powers were greatly differing views of the world. **And all were far dissimilar from what Josef Stalin had planned.** The Soviets had thanks to Hitler's stupidity, become a massive power in this "Post-war world". *Freed from the confines of the 1917 treaty of Brest-Litosk, and greatly aided by allied mistakes, by September 1945 Soviet Russia had gained control of the Baltic States and all of Eastern and Central Europe.*

And this same misfortune had happened in the Pacific. FDR had recklessly given in to Stalin's demands for concessions in the Pacific. *Freed from the treaty of Portsmouth in 1905, Russia recovered all the territories they had lost to Japan in 1905.*

Wherever they went they took complete control, and the Russians resembled locusts stripping the countryside bare. This unanticipated post-war political change was by far the most important one, for in that reality would come most the trials of the Cold War.

With the fighting ended the Allies were faced with what the war had wrought. The devastation within Europe was difficult to imagine as hundreds of cities and towns were completely destroyed leaving the surviving populations homeless and destitute.

It was felt that it would take 15 years just to remove the rubble from Berlin!

Poland had lost 1/6 of its population with many gone from outright murder.

Over 20 million Russians had died, many because of Stalin and his demented policies.

The holocaust had claimed over 6,500,000 "undesirables, from the European populations of Jews, Gypsies, Christians and non-Aryans."

Millions of *displaced people* (**DPs**), wandered the ravaged European landscape in a hopeless daze. Many thousands of them were ignored as they died along the roads.

Those DP's, were comprised of the war refugees, former POWs, former slave laborers from the Nazi's and Communists, survivors from the death camps and anyone else who just wanted out of Europe.

Hunger was rampant as abandoned fields lay fallow, filled with mines and unexploded ordinance. It was probably just as well as the ruined transport systems were incapable of moving the foods anyway. Judge Samuel Rosenman went on a fact finding trip into Europe similar to the one conducted by former president Herbert Hoover. Both reported back that famine would soon overtake the continent.

Pres. Truman knew we had to help even though our own harvests had been light. In a radio address to the nation he said, "Europe today is hungry, and as the winter comes on their distress will increase. *Unless we do what we can to help, we may lose next winter what we fought so hard for last spring. If we let Europe go cold and hungry, we may lose the foundations for order upon which the hope for worldwide peace rests*" (2)

Asia too was starving. India lost almost an entire crop because of heavy monsoons. China was finally reclaiming thousands of square miles of territory that Japan had long controlled. That land had been abandoned and unproductive, and their remaining harvests were too light to support their population. That same scenario was observed throughout the Pacific Ocean area. There was only one nation that could help.

From 1941 through 1945 America spent the staggering sum of $46 Billion dollars, with $11 Billion going just to the Soviet Union.

On February 6, 1946 Truman announced a nine-part emergency program to prevent worldwide starvation. Once again the cost for that aid would be staggering. But America did the right thing.

In defeated Germany the occupation zones had been organized by the time of the Potsdam meetings. Gen. George Patton was in charge of the province of Bavaria, but his efforts at De-Nazification were lagging. Twice Eisenhower had warned him to speed things up. But Patton claimed he needed the Nazi workers at their jobs to keep vital public services running. (A common problem in all invaded and colonized nations.)

Patton also had a secret reason.

He felt a war was on the horizon against the Russians, and he wanted to be on good terms with the Germans in case we needed their help. (Even before the shooting in Germany had ended Patton and many others were hearing the troubling stories of the Russian occupation in the "liberated countries".)

As always Patton spoke his mind on this subject.

Berlin was located deep inside the Soviet occupation zone. As with their nation, Berlin was carved into four sectors each run by an Allied Power. Gen. Lucius Clay was the first U.S. Military Governor of the American sector of Berlin. "Wherever we looked there was desolation and ruin. It was like a city of the dead. Bodies lay in canals, lakes and in the bombed out buildings". In August of 1945 no less than 4000 Berliners died each day! Only the massive imports of food into the British and U.S. sectors kept anyone alive. Housing was nonexistent and people lived in caves hollowed out of the debris. The black market thrived as those who remained traded away their remaining possessions for a chance to survive one more day.

(Many of the Allied occupation troops profited from this misery, as jobs were few and little was being made in the factories. And the Nazi money was worthless as there were no gold reserves to back up the paper notes.)

When the western allies finally took stock of the conquered nation they realized that Germany was a disaster. Few of the cities had escaped complete destruction, the result of the strategic bombing. Millions of additional DPs had entered western Germany to escape the brutal rule of the communists. That further exacerbated the humanitarian problems for the western allies. *During the first six months of peace America had to spend $1.6 billion to feed these starving masses. Britain spent $700 million more.*

In the Russian occupied zones all of the industrial equipment and anything of value was being dismantled and shipped back to Russia.
And much had already been looted by the Russians from their "Allies" occupation zones before the Allies even got into Berlin! (None of the Allies were allowed into the city for weeks after the war ended, enabling the communist occupiers to do as they pleased.)

There are no concrete reports of post-war civilian deaths behind the Russian lines as no one was around to record the horrors and the communists cared not to write them down.

When the Russians and Germans signed their non-aggression pact on Aug 23, 1939 they divided the areas to be invaded between them.
At that time Russia would take all of the Baltic States, while Germany picked up more of Poland. As he did everywhere they invaded, Stalin had millions of those citizens shipped from the Baltic States deep into Russia to use as slave labor. Most were never seen again.

And to make the carnage against those innocents even worse, after the war ended the Allies forcibly turned over two million Soviet POWs taken by the Germans during the war. Along with those captured troops, non-combatant Soviet exiles who most certainly did not want to go back to Russia were also forced to go.

Many were the surviving Czarist émigrés from 1918!

Naively the Allies thought they could curry favor from Stalin.

Not only did he not reciprocate, most of those "repatriated citizens" also disappeared into the gulags as slave laborers.

Middle East

As shown in *Fatal Flaws Book 1*, Britain had agreed to the Balfour Declaration at the end of WWI to find a Jewish homeland. In 1922 Britain had split the ancient area of Palestine into two sections. Transjordan was an area east of the River Jordan, and Palestine made up the western side. Their plan back then was to turn this new area of Palestine into a Jewish homeland, which was greatly desired by the influential European Jews. Many had already emigrated into Palestine, but the fighting it had caused during the 1920s caused the British to restrict future Jewish immigration. Britain's plan for a Jewish homeland was put on hold. Jewish plans were not.

But during the charged anti-Semitic years of the 1930s over 100,000 additional Jewish immigrants had gone there. With their better financial capabilities those new immigrants/refugees began building up their own cities and towns.

That was something that had never been done for the Arabs who had lived and toiled there for centuries.

In fact, none of the previous Arab rulers had done anything for that area ever. Jealousies sprang up as the newcomers built communities and planned for more Jewish immigrants. More violence ensued.

At that time the Gran Mufti, Haj Amin al-Husseini was the voice of anti-Jewish hatred in the region and he decried any further Jewish immigration. To further inflame the region Hitler's agents worked tirelessly to stoke the flames.

In an effort to appease the Gran Mufti and the growing ranks of Islamists Britain released a report called the *White Paper* on Palestine on May 17, 1939. Within those pages the British insisted that the status quo would be maintained for ten more years and that the Arabs and Jews would form a bi-national state. Jewish immigration would be limited to just 15,000 people per year. After that time frame the Arabs would decide the quota.

During WWII thousands of additional émigrés made it to Palestine.

In late 1944 attempts were made to save 250,000 Hungarian Jews from the death camps. Foreign Minister Anthony Eden and Winston Churchill stopped the effort at the last minute knowing that Palestine would erupt if that many émigrés showed up in such a short time. As it was Jewish refugees were arriving constantly.

After the fighting had ended, among the millions of displaced people were multiple hundreds of thousands of Jews. When those few survivors attempted to return to their former homes they were again brutalized, and hundreds were even murdered! Their "neighbors" had stolen their homes, possessions and businesses when they were hauled off to the death camps. None thought the Jews would return.

Those despicable acts reinforced the beliefs of the Jews that they had to have their own homeland. Having lost everything in their struggle to survive many sought to return to the ancient land of Judea. Britain was still governing Palestine under the old mandate from the League of Nations. Again they feared that another large influx of those post-war Jewish settlers would inflame the region. Britain sought to limit the numbers of immigrants to an impossible quota of just 1500 per month.

Hundreds of thousands of those poor souls were barely existing in neglected refugee camps scattered throughout Europe. (All of the free nations slowed the emigration of these DP's, which included men, women and children from every war torn nation in Europe. Only 400,000 Jews gained entry into the U.S.)

Watching the changing world picture the Arab nations stretching from N. Africa to the Persian Gulf formed the Arab League in March 1945. Those nations were determined to form a unified voice in their efforts to shape their future. In December 1945 they announced that they would fight any Jewish state.

The colonial powers in the region, Britain and France brushed the Arab union aside with total indifference. Tensions continued to rise and in the unstable political climate of post-war 1946 the British continued trying to avoid the troubling issue of Palestine. England desperately needed to hang on to its empire, and creating a Jewish State would only bring them a new dilemma. Their military and police units began clamping down on the incoming Jewish refugees. Fighting intensified.

Freedom

Post-war cries for freedom rang out in Africa, India, Egypt and many other nations including those in Latin America. It was symptomatic of the changing world picture, a future that Britain and the rest of the Europeans tried to ignore.

America however wanted the end of all colonialism and freedom for all nations.

This was the same idealistic but politically naïve ideology Wilson had expressed at Versailles twenty seven years earlier. It had been met with contempt by the imperialistic powers then, and was equally ignored in 1945/46. However the intense fighting that every colonizer faced was a rude awakening that the Old World and its colonizing were over.

(One of the unforeseen effects of the war was the massive amount of weapons and ammunition that was floating around. It was now easy to arm the rebels, and their weapons were modern and effective. The colonial masters would now face a well armed and hostile population.)

Trying to lead by example, America's former territory of Cuba had already been granted their future independence. Movements were under way to do the same in the Philippines and it was hoped in Puerto Rico. As shown in *Fatal Flaws Book 1* it had taken decades of work to undo the damage the Spanish had done in those former colonial holdings. It was hoped that they were ready for self-governing.

We had picked up Cuba, Puerto Rico and the Philippines from Spain in the Spanish-American War. Pres. William McKinley who had fought for four years in the American Civil War was actually against the war with Spain. But the explosion aboard the *USS Maine* and the yellow journalism by the major newspapers had triggered the call to arms. (Many influential people wanted to help the Cubans against the harsh rule of Spain, seeing their quest for freedom in the same light as ours.) To try to heal our nation from the continued agony of the Civil War, Pres. McKinley gave commands to former Confederate commanders/ families. Over time his effort worked, and helped produce our modernized military force that fought in WWI.

Over in the Pacific the freed island chains of the Caroline's, Marshalls and Marianas were to become independent as soon as possible as the overworked Pres. Truman and the isolationist Congress had no desire to keep them.

FDR however had wanted to keep many of those Pacific Islands as forward U.S. bases. And the Navy led by Adm. King was adamant about holding onto them as we had paid a terrible price in blood to advance across the Pacific. (King and many others felt we were entitled to and needed those islands to ensure we could maintain the peace in the Pacific.)

France

After the war ended France was led by the egotistical Charles de Gaulle and his provisional government. Refusing to face reality, he recklessly wanted to keep all of their colonies. (France had colonies in the Caribbean, N. Africa, Syria, Lebanon, Madagascar and Indochina.) As shown in *Fatal Flaws Book 1*, de Gaulle was determined to keep France in the first class of nations even though they had completely fallen from power.

When the Allies met at Potsdam in July 1945, de Gaulle and France were not even invited such was their fall. It was wrong for the western allies not to have him at the meetings for France was supposed to be a major part of the post-war peace.

That calculated insult, (Stalin did not want France there), further infuriated de Gaulle and actually caused great harm to the overall allied cause.

As of that date no arrangements had been made for the handling of the expected Japanese surrender in Indochina. In the rush to come up with a plan the beleaguered and inexperienced Truman and the new liberal British Prime Minister Clement Atlee decided to have the Nationalist Chinese oversee the future surrender of Indochina north of the 16th parallel since they already had large armies nearby. The British would handle the Japanese surrender south of the 16th parallel and be based in Saigon. (France had no military forces in the region.)

Britain's Lord Mountbatten was the overall Commander of the SW Pacific Theatre during the War. (India, Burma and SE Asia) He did not want the separate surrender arrangement instituted, fearing a diversion of effort and of the potential of new problems occurring. Mountbatten wanted total control of the Japanese surrender in all of Indochina. *Like many of the well schooled Europeans, he realized with this uneasy peace starting to settle over the region new and dangerous issues would arise.* And with them would be the expected increase in Nationalism. He knew that that issue could hurt England and the Empire.

When Winston Churchill came to power in those darkest hours in 1940 he swore that the British Empire would go on. He kept England focused and in the war.

But by late 1945 to maintain her empire meant that vast sums of men, material and money were needed. Commodities she no longer had. In fact England was almost bankrupt. Her leaders tried to stay the course, but one by one her colonies became free because England could no longer sustain them.

Since the French had not been invited to any of the post-war talks, France had had no say in addressing or planning for those future problems.

The people of Indochina had been ruled by the French for almost a century. They were a proud people who had defeated the earlier Chinese attempts to control them. But they had fallen to the modern weapons and tactics of colonial France.

As is the case with all forced colonizing efforts, most of the people seethed with hatred for the foreign rulers. Discontent and conflict inevitably followed and aggressive policing, torture and intensive control was used by the colonizer to remain in power.

To keep the people leaderless, education was limited and key positions in government and industry were restricted to a select few, those who had converted to Catholicism.

The only active non-communist guerrilla party in Vietnam was the Kuomintang, and in the 1930's their ranks had been decimated by the French secret police, the Surete` Gene`rale. Rebellions to gain Vietnamese freedom were tried repeatedly but all would fail against the well seasoned French. And then came the Samurai.

With little effort the French rulers were pushed aside, fallout from Vichy's collaboration. But there was a hidden price for their effort, the people saw that the French could be forced out. And it had been done by Asians.

During the 1920s Ho Chi Minh, (Nguyen That Thanh), had organized a secret communist society known as the *Viet Minh*. In time they became the principal rebel group as they had the best funding and organization. As the survivors of the other rebel groups returned from hiding to fight against those brutal Japanese, they also sought to rebuild their movements. It was a fatal error as the Viet Minh had become the dominant faction in the Northern part of Indochina.

Ironically Ho Chi Minh would become the same type of ruler as the French, ruthless. Anyone who became a threat or stood in the way of Ho's programs for his "new freedom" were forced out or killed. During a sixteen month campaign of terror the Viet Minh used selective assassination to get rid of any non-communists who might pose a threat. (One of those men was Ngo Dinh Khoi, eldest brother to Ngo Diem, who would later rule in the Southern part of Vietnam.)

The most vital lesson a potential communist learns when schooled in Russia was how to eliminate any rivals. And Ho Chi Minh had learned his lessons well.

Out in the countryside and jungles away from prying eyes those killings ran into the thousands. Before Japan was even defeated the Viet Minh were organized to take over.

Ho had even sent a message to Pres. Truman asking for his help in obtaining Vietnam's freedom. His wish was that Truman would stand by the Atlantic Charter signed by FDR in August 1941. Wrongly Truman never replied, and the message remained hidden and classified until 1972!

When the French colonial forces returned to Indochina in late September 1945 Gen. Jacques Le Clerc realized from the conditions he found that it would be better to give the Vietnamese more autonomy. He proposed bringing back former Prince Vinh San and allow him to "rule an Independent Federation of Laos, Cambodia and Vietnam." His negotiations and actions were leading to that solution.

De Gaulle may even have agreed with that resolution, for on Dec 14, 1945 he stated that he would accompany the Prince to Vietnam for his coronation.

But once again a potential leader was eliminated when San's airplane flying him back to Saigon "was lost" over N. Africa. (When de Gaulle was fighting for control of the Free French Forces in 1942, his main rival was "killed in a plane crash". Eisenhower reputedly authorized the assassination of Vichy leader Darlan.)

A week later the French people held elections in France, their first since before the war. Almost 51% of the vote went to the Socialist/Communist parties, while de Gaulle's Popular Republican Movement took only 25.6% of the vote.

De Gaulle like Churchill, (who had been voted out of office while at Potsdam), was stunned at the voter discontent.

Always quarrelsome, de Gaulle refused to share power with anyone else, and in Jan 46 he resigned from the presidency.

(In France the Government was a shared body among all of the parties. In that case the Socialists would be number one.)

De Gaulle privately told his aides he would soon be back in power, but he was wrong. *The Socialists held on for over a decade.*

(Out of office de Gaulle undermined all pacification and governing efforts from behind the scenes.)

In January 1946 Socialist Felix Gouin took over aided by Georges Bidault as Foreign Minister. (Five Communists were part of this majority.) It was the start of a long period of governmental instability. With his Socialist/Communist majority Gouin nationalized their coal, gas, electrical and insurance industries. It had an immediate negative impact on their economy, which was weak already.

Similar to de Gaulle, no one in their new government wanted to part with their colonies. Once in office Gouin and Bidault unwisely decided to break off contacts with Ho Chi Minh. (With Japan beaten Ho and his followers had assumed power in the North of Vietnam.) After months of tension Ho went to Paris in May 1946 to try to work out a compromise, but his efforts were again futile. The Gaullists that were still in power worked behind the scenes to stop any compromise, while Bidault and others simply refused the thought of losing control.

After four months of negotiations Ho returned to Hanoi with a weak "agreement for joint rule", but it had no real meaning. To insure their army did what was needed, Gen. Le Clerc was replaced with Gen. E`tienne Valluy, a hard liner who had fought in both World Wars. And so the stage was set for more conflict.

Russia and Communism

During the war "Uncle Joe Stalin" had been propagandized to America by FDR and a few others claiming that he was "on our side". The numerous political problems that appeared between the Allies were not reported on, and the late 1930s brutal Russian transgressions in Poland and Finland were conveniently ignored. Thus no one could have explained a sudden war with the Russians.

(Unknown to most, after WWII had ended in September 1945 twenty Atomic bombs had been prepared for use on Russia in case war did breakout.)

Our "wartime ally" the Soviet Union was still totally committed to the spreading of their communist ideology throughout the world. This time they were not conquering with a force of arms as a colonial power in search of riches, they were expanding quietly to take over the world's political system. Once that was accomplished the riches would follow.

As shown in *Fatal Flaws Book 1,* at the end of WWI Russia had fought and conquered the Ukraine and the Caucasus. They were curtailed from further expansion to the south by Great Britain. Stalin who took over after Lenin died remained patient and worked to consolidate his rule.

By the end of WWII, Stalin's Russia had "re-absorbed" the Baltic states of Latvia, Lithuania and Estonia. Russia had also taken the eastern section of Finland, Romania and Poland. And with their total control over Eastern Europe, they were "converting" this re-designed Poland, Bulgaria, Hungary, Romania, Eastern Germany, and later Czechoslovakia to Communism. *In Poland, Hungary and Romania the communists used election fraud and massive arrests to "win the day". Brutality was commonplace.*

Independent communist states were also forming in Albania and Yugoslavia. Both countries had deposed their monarchs, and in both former partisan leaders had taken over. Josip Broz, known to the West as Marshall Tito seized power in Yugoslavia.

While consolidating his rule Tito executed over 100,000 Croats who had been collaborators with the Axis. He also executed his main rival, Gen. Draza Mihajlovic who had been a leader of the monarchist rebels the Chetniks.

In Albania Gen. Enver Hoxha who had fought in the Spanish Civil War took over in his country. Hoxha had two former reagents and a Prime Minister shot to make sure everyone understood who was now in charge.

In Manchuria and Northern Korea the Soviets were in control. Communist led insurgencies were beginning in Greece, Italy, Iran, and Turkey, and continuing in China and Indochina. The broken world of 1945 had no answers for those losses, and ever so slowly communism seemed to be taking over the globe.

(Like so many naïve liberals, America's Arthur Schlesinger Jr. wrote pages of pro-communist nonsense for Life magazine, not seeing the brutal realities.)

Capitalism and Democracy led by the United States was communism's main enemy, and at that time the western world's only savior.

The ideological differences between those contrary political/economic viewpoints would quickly lead the world into the next war, *"The Cold War"*. (Just as Stalin knew it would when he lectured FDR about the U.N. at Yalta.)

America and Communist Spies

As shown in *Fatal Flaws Book 1*, to keep abreast of the policies and actions of other nations and to try to destabilize them, Bolshevik Russia had undertaken a well designed espionage system that began as soon as they took power. All of the major Western powers had been infiltrated by the flood of Russian refugees, especially England and America. The work by those initial communist spies had been extremely effective in organizing networks, cover fronts and businesses.

When FDR was elected in Nov 1932 he did not share the same fear and hatred of communism as had the three prior Republican Presidents. He actually had leftist leanings, and felt the Russians weren't so bad. *That naïve attitude became one of his great failures.* (Roosevelt berated his naval aide Adm. William Leahy that his anti-Bolshevik political beliefs belonged in the Middle Ages.)

Pres. Roosevelt's first foreign policy directive had been to "renew" relations with communist Russia. Embassies were reopened and dozens of their well trained communist agents entered our country legally. They went to work with a zeal finding hundreds of willing converts and rapidly penetrated the U.S. government.

But in the late 1930s the Russian spy network was beginning to weaken as a few defectors broke ranks. Stalin's "insane purges" were killing hundreds of thousands of senior officials, military men and dozens of Russian agents who had been based throughout the West. Fear was a strong motivator for those who saw the light.

Ignatz Reiss secretly left his position in Paris as the head of the NKVD in 1937. Reiss had been ordered back to Russia and he was certain he would be executed. Instead of returning to Moscow, Reiss went on the run. He was later caught and killed by Russian agents in Switzerland.

Peter Gutzeit the station chief in New York was also recalled back to Russia. He obediently returned and was promptly executed. Watching those uncalled for purges and killings **Walter Krivitsky** and **Whittaker Chambers** defected to the U.S. in 1939. **Krivisky** was eventually found and murdered in 1941. To deter his pursuers, **Chambers** had cagily stashed a cache of damaging information about the Russians. Upon his untimely death, that secret information was to "get out and expose all". Because of his foresight he was not murdered, just belittled and ignored.

When Chambers defected he had tried to warn Pres. Roosevelt about the extensive Soviet spy networks that he had helped setup and operate.

But FDR had condescendingly refused to believe this first hand information, though some members of his Administration most certainly did.

FDR was so pro-Soviet, that in 1939 when his security advisor and Asst. Sec State Adolf Berle went to him with evidence from Chambers that Alger Hiss, and Harry Dexter White at the Treasury Dept., and FDR aide Lauchlin Currie were Soviet spies, FDR became angry and forbade any further mention of the issue!

Part of the fallout from the Chamber's admissions was the secretive formation of the **Venona Project** by the U.S. Army to decipher Russian communications.

The program was begun in 1942 after we became Allies.

Because of his prior intransience, Pres. Roosevelt and those in his Administration were not told of the program!

By 1943 the U.S. Army was uncovering proof of a vast Russian spy network operating within our government. But the Army kept the information a secret because if they had told Roosevelt he would have closed Venona down.

The unhindered work of the Russian spies continued throughout WWII. It helped save Russia from the Germans and kept Stalin informed of FDR's political goals and America's military capabilities. **The zenith of their** spying was stealing the top secret research of the Manhattan Project and getting it back to Russia.

After the war ended **Igor Gouzenko** defected from his Canadian post in September 1945. **Gouzenko's** defection resulted in the arrest and collapse of an entire spy ring in Canada, and increased the dangers to the spies still operating in England and America. Americans **Louis Budenz** and later **Elizabeth Bentley** defected in Nov. 1945. **Bentley** felt betrayed by her confederates in the CPUSA, (Communist Party USA) and by the defection of **Budenz** who personally knew her.

So in early November 1945 she turned herself into the FBI telling all.

The company she "worked for" was Global Tourist corp., a front for deceased spymaster **Jacob Golos**, (1943). *Investigation by the FBI soon revealed that the Golos spy ring had indeed penetrated the U.S. Government with thirty agents.*

Their investigation was hindered by a disinterested Truman Administration. (The Russians finally stopped trying to kill Bentley in 1955, after Stalin's death.)

In early 1946 British MI-6 agent Kim Philby had been brought in to work on the backlog of the still secret Venona Project. **But what the FBI did not know was that Briton Kim Philby was another highly placed Russian spy. He quickly reported in on the extensive breech.** (The Russians had already been warned by another spy and changed their codes so no new cables were being intercepted.)

Philby was yet another Cambridge graduate who had been turned and was a long time Communist spy though at that time no one knew it. He had started spying in 1936, and during his years he had recruited numerous Britons to spy on their homeland.

In mid-1945 Soviet Intelligence officer Konstantin Volkov offered to defect to England. Once safe inside England he would supply MI-6 with the names of British traitors. Philby was the head of the counter-intelligence desk in London. He opened the communiqué and saw his own death. (He was number one on the list.) *A short while later Volkov was "picked up", taken to Moscow and shot.*

While stationed in Istanbul, Philby assigned numerous British agents to infiltrate into the Soviet Union. After they had left the city he alerted his masters in Moscow. All of those British agents were quickly found and "murdered". He coldly did this repeatedly over his career.

Working as the aforementioned liaison officer in Washington D.C. he learned that the Americans were becoming aware of numerous Soviet agents operating inside their government. The prior defections of Gousenko, Budenz and Bentley were unleashing a torrent of information about the

Soviet NKVD spy networks. Upon his reporting in with this bad news the Russians jumped into action and pulled out the vital spy masters, the **Cohen's, Morris and Lona**.

*During their many years in America the **Cohen's** had recruited dozens of new spies. If they had been captured and talked a large part of the remaining Soviet networks would have been in jeopardy.* **Jack Bjoze** was another U.S. traitor-spy, and he was directed to get the crucial couple out. They escaped back into Russia through Canada.

Moscow's leaders wisely recalled all of their people who had had contact with Bentley. (Before they could be arrested.) They also broke off all contacts with the Golos spy ring which effectively shut down the NKVD/KGB activities in Washington D.C. To prevent his potential arrest, they next recalled the KGB chief in Washington, Anatoly Gorsky. By late 1945 all of the strategic military threats to the Soviet Union had been ended, though battles with partisans in the annexed nations continued for years.

Thus their vital need for foreign intelligence had also ended.

With the closing of their most useful U.S. spy rings Russia turned to less active means of spying, they used American citizens as dupes for the communist party. Their efforts were directed to be more subversive than outright spying. In that way they were less visible and non-threatening. Time was on the communist side as all over the world their sympathizers and supporters were undermining the nations of the world.

Post War

As World War II neared its end senior U.S. Military leaders realized that we were now the sole military power in the Western World. Most wanted to keep large forces on hand just in case a new war began. (Presumably one with Russia.) The Army wanted a ground force that was capable of expanding to 4.5 million within a year, while the Navy wanted a force of 600,000 with 371 active combat ships, 5,000 auxiliaries and 8,000 aircraft. The Air Corps wanted to become a separate service, (which happened in 1947), with 70 air groups with 400,000 men and women. Most of the principal political and military leaders knew that the world had changed, and they knew that America could not just close their windows.

President Truman did not heed the advice of those senior Officers, Winston Churchill, Sec-Def. Forrestal, Dean Acheson or any other highly placed officials who warned that the U.S must not disarm.

Truman recklessly decided to follow the expedient political course, he allowed the nation to unilaterally disarm. With the shooting ended the national sentiment was to "bring the boys home". America had always been an isolationist nation, and the citizens wanted to get on with their lives. But the rush to get "the boys home" turned into a route as the 14.3 million men and women in uniform were being demobilized without any thoughts on the effects it would have politically or militarily. Using every ship possible 100,000 troops a week were going home by mid-September 45.

The Russian Armies however stayed at full strength right through 1946, and they remained in the nations they had "liberated".

Moving in tandem with their forces were the political and social police. Russia was in for the long term.

During his time in Germany General George Patton repeatedly chastised the higher ups including Eisenhower and Bradley, that something needed to be done about the Russians. According to the Yalta and Potsdam agreements, every command had to turn over to the Russians all of their POWs, former soldiers, citizens and Germans who had crossed into allied lines! To Patton it made no sense to deliver those souls to a death sentence, so many times he refused.

Lt. Gen. Bishop Gowlina of the Polish Army had personally briefed Patton on the tortures the Russians were doing in Poland. His report also included eye witness accounts of Russians grabbing anyone in their path, DPs, POWs, refugees and even American soldiers and shipping them eastward to use as slave labor. (Gowlina insisted that Washington was kept informed of those issues, but refused to act!)

Those issues came up repeatedly, and at one point Patton yelled into a phone at Ike's Chief of Staff warning that we were going to end up fighting the damn Bolsheviks', let me start it now while we still have an army to do it! Patton was soon relieved from commanding 3d Army. With his relief came the end of any protective details and bodyguards. All Gen. Patton was entitled to was a driver, and the one he was issued was a new private.

Upset at the idiotic and arrogant fools in power, Patton decided to resign from the Army so there would be no constraints upon him in civilian life. He would be free to speak out and tell the truth to the American people.

Patton was "killed in an automotive accident" a month later. Or so we had been told.

Gen. George Patton had been a controversial figure during the war, disliking the British and especially the pompous Montgomery. He was often at odds with Eisenhower, his junior in seniority and another leader who had never had a combat command.

George Marshall was the one who had promoted Ike above dozens of senior generals.

Always quick to speak out Patton even complained about FDR, especially when the president made the foolish proclamation about unconditional surrender. Patton yelled if anything will motivate them to fight on to the end that was it. It will cost us more lives and the Russians will grab more territory because the war will drag on. Sometimes we are so foolish it makes me cry.

Everyone knew he was the best *combat leader* in the U.S. Army. Everyone in the U.S. Army knew it, the Germans knew it, the British knew it, and the Russians knew it. And because of that Patton had been secretly placed on a Soviet list for execution. On the dreary morning of December 9, 1945 Gen. Patton's Cadillac was traveling on an empty road. Riding with him was Gen. Hobart Gay and Pfc. Horace Woodring the new driver. Suddenly a truck driving on the other side of the road turned towards Patton's Cadillac. Only Patton had been injured in the unusual crash, and he was taken to an army hospital in Heidelburg, Germany. He was treated for paralysis from the shoulders down.

Patton had started to recover, so much so he was due to be released and flown home for Christmas. But on the 20th he had a sudden setback, suffering from blood clots and embolisms. He died the next day and was buried with his men in France. No autopsy was performed.

The driver and passengers inside the errant truck curiously disappeared.

One of the original OSS members was a Charles Bazata. He stated in a lie detector test that he was ordered by his boss Gen. William Donovan to take Patton out.

Bazata refused, but was sure someone else had taken the job against Patton. Donovan was a communist sympathizer, a friend of FDR, and a hero in WWI and WWII. But after leading the OSS in WWII, Donovan was unexpectedly "retired" to obscurity.

Soon after trouble followed him as the *Amerasia Scandal* began and his aide **Duncan Lee** was accused of being a Russian agent. **Lee fled and escaped.**
(In the Venona files Lee worked for the NKVD, Russia's spy service)

Donovan would be called in to testify before Congress in 1947 because he had known communists working in his OSS organization. (Donovan had actually lied about their backgrounds in order to hire them. *All four men in question were confirmed communist party members.*) Because of that scandal Truman did not pick Donovan to run the new CIA. Instead Admiral Roscoe Hillenkoetter would become the first Director of the CIA. *He called Donovan a traitor.*

It was more likely that the Russians had murdered Patton. If a war started in Europe he would be their biggest threat. *Russia's NKVD had agents all over the destroyed landscape of Europe in 1945.* It was easy to pose as a DP, (displaced person) to observe and scout. And the NKVD had used truck accidents to kill many targets.

Stalin had his former Ambassador to the U.S. Maxim Litvinov murdered by truck to keep him quite. The Soviet Consul in China Dimitri Apresyan was on vacation in Russia when he had his accident. He too knew too much, and Stalin became nervous. The same was done to Bishop Theodore Romzha in 1947.

And when the accidents failed, NKVD assassins used special poisons to finish the victims off while they were in the hospital, such as when Trotsky's son Sedov died in Paris after a successful appendectomy. *(Gen. George Stratemeyer AAF-USAF was so convinced that Patton and Sec-Def James Forrestal were both assassinated he sent a letter expressing it to the FBI and his attorney. He also stated that if the same fate befell him it was a lie.)*

Before the fighting of WWII had ended Paul Nitze and other senior civilians were directed to get teams together to conduct the U.S. Strategic Bombing Survey, (USSBS). Their mission was to determine with an objective attitude what effect strategic bombing had had on Germany. Their missions involved some danger as the teams moved around most of Nazi Germany, and at times alone.

Nitze and his team observed that the principal damage to the country involved its transportation systems. *As time went on they also realized that not one item of German war production had been affected by the strategic bombing of the ball bearing industry.*

(The AAF Generals insisted that they could cripple German war production by knocking out a few vital primary products, such as ball bearings and oil.)

Their teams realized that although most of the factory buildings had been taken out, the manufacturing machinery was not affected. Their workers simply recovered the equipment and went back to work. Teams also found vast tunnel complexes where the V-1 and V-2 rockets had been manufactured. Nazi Production Minister Albert Speer had been captured and was interviewed by Nitze. He corroborated the team's investigations that German war production had reached its peak in mid-1944, and had not been affected by the allied bombing until the final months of the war. Then the overall reductions in oil, steel and chemicals stopped most production lines.

Nitze's report showed that the air attacks did little to directly defeat Germany, though they tied up thousands of troops in anti-air defenses and reconstruction.

With their work in Germany ended the USSBS traveled to Japan to perform the same task. Their reports on Germany were written up before the A-bomb had been used. They recommended that the bombers concentrate on Japan's transportation systems. With those systems destroyed Japan would like Germany, be unable to move anything around leading to capitulation. Because of the imminent probability of invading Japan and the ghastly losses expected, it was decided to use the atomic bombs.

Unlike Germany, on site inspections in Japan could not occur until the enemy had actually surrendered. Upon their arrival the teams noted the vast destruction of Japan's urban areas by the "barbaric firebombing" that had been used. Nitze and a few others had felt that had the U.S. leaders been willing to wait, it was possible Japan might have surrendered within six months. (However the reader must remember that the longer one waits to invade, the better the defenses and the higher the invaders casualties.)

Moving around the investigating teams could see that Japan's manufacturing capability had been reduced from the repeated fire-bombings, but in the case of Japan the teams felt the loss of their merchant fleet was the major factor that affected production. Raw materials, especially oils were in critically short supply. As a result their production of large weapons and munitions was stopped. A short while later the teams and the U.S. occupation forces discovered that the Japanese had plenty of small arms and defensive ammunition with which to continue resisting. Had it not been for the atomic bombs the close-in fighting would have been brutal.

To end the war the principals had planned to invade Japan's home islands starting in November 1945. But after the horrendous casualties from Pelileu, Leyte, Iwo Jima and Okinawa, Pres. Truman decided to use the atomic bombs in the hope the war would end without having to invade. *He saved well over a million Japanese lives and spared Japan the total destruction they would have endured if we and the Russians had invaded!*

(One example of our humanitarian effort was at Wake Island which was "taken" by the Japanese in early 1942. Wake was heavily fortified by them. It was not assaulted in 1944, instead it was bypassed and cutoff. Our units did not land there until September 4, 1945. Of the 3,000 Japanese troops who had been on the islands, 2,000 had died. The rest were saved and returned to Japan. This happened all across the Pacific Ocean theatre.)

Inspections of the atomic-targeted cities of Hiroshima and Nagasaki noted the limited range and blast radius of the atomic weapons. Civilians in shelters suffered no affect from the blasts, and only those in the open had radiation poisoning.

(Though at that time few knew what that really was.)

Nitze was asked to provide recommendations for the post war military. *He presented a case for a vastly increased intelligence capability, unification of the armed forces, increased research and development of weapons and defenses, and the expectation that our future enemies will get atomic weapons.*

The report from the USSBS was released to the public in July 1946.

Tensions

In late 1945 Stalin made a decision to remain in northern Iran and he refused to remove his troops as had been agreed. (Soviet and British troops had occupied the country jointly in 1942 to protect the oil supplies.) The British had already pulled out, and the Soviets were supposed to do the same by March 2, 1946. But now Stalin demanded that Iran accept the Soviet backed provinces, the Republic of Azerbaijan and a Kurdish People's Republic. Next was a demand to setup a joint company to exploit the oil reserves in the region with 51% to go to Russia. In addition to those issues Soviet Military units were moving closer to Turkey's borders. It was possible that the Russians might decide to invade or just annex the territory Stalin wanted.

The issue went to the U.N. United Nations where the Russians complained loudly and demanded the British remove their troops from Greece. British Foreign Secretary Ernest Bevin was outraged that the Soviets would invoke a claim of Britain threatening world peace when it was the Russian Communists that were threatening a dozen nations.

During WWII the Greek communist party had grown to almost two million members. *In late 1944 Churchill had met with Stalin to discuss the tradeoff of Russian control over the Balkans in exchange for Greece.* Knowing that the nation was in turmoil, the Greek Communists began plotting their control. Dozens of potential enemies were eliminated and as soon as the Germans pulled out the EAM-ELAS began their takeover.

Tensions in the region increased even though WWII had ended. Britain worked out a compromise government between the communists and Royalists. Their effort lasted just a few weeks, and on December 3, 1945 a civil war began. With much effort the British forces regained control of the country, and setup an election.

On March 5, 1946 Churchill gave his famous speech in Fulton, Missouri. On the 6th Truman had the State Dept. send a warning to Russia's Foreign Minister Molotov over Iran. Orders had been given to the U.S. Military to prepare for movement into the area. The Navy was sent in to "show the flag".

Stalin again backed down, but as stated before he could afford to be patient. One of the unstated reasons for Stalin's eventual pull back was that in the time of 1945-49 only America had atomic weapons. And though he may not have thought much of Harry Truman, Stalin understood that Russia could not absorb any further losses.

A week later in mid-March 1946 the Greek rightist candidates won the majority of the Parliamentary seats in their election. Greek Communists claimed the elections were fixed and the Civil War began anew a few months later. British troops and aid were involved helping the nationalists, while the communists received help from Yugoslavia and Albania.

Thus far the Soviet advances had been done with caution, using a *faits accomplis* and subterfuge. Stalin had observed that America had not intervened in the countries where a communist regime had been emplaced by the Soviets, such as in Eastern Europe, Manchuria or N. Korea. He decided not to provoke a fight over a new conquest, not yet. Iran and Greece would be turned slowly, so no one would notice.

In spite of the positive result of this implied threat and show of force, Truman wrongly continued with his near total disarmament of America. **As a result of his policy, during April 1946 the planners for the JCS, Joint Chiefs of Staff estimated that with the present state of our armed forces any Soviet attack into Europe would result in the loss of most of Western Europe.**

Any Russian effort into the southern Mediterranean could result in the loss of Turkey, Iran, Iraq and the Suez Canal.

In mid-1945 the Russians had captured most of the Nazi submarine assembly sites and had taken many of the excellent and updated Type XXI U-boats as reparations.

By mid-46 most of those boats had become operational and put to sea with Russian crews. Our Naval leaders felt that that factor alone could pose a terrible risk if we had to try to repeat Operation Overlord to protect Europe.

For many of the nation's military leaders it was already evident that the weakened state of our armed forces was actually causing the Russians to become more aggressive. Why should they hold back when there was no military force that could stop them.

As shown before, Paul Nitze, James Forrestal and many other mid-level civilian managers had worked for FDR and then the Truman Administration since 1940. Most of those "Republican" outsiders had been brought in because of their business savvy, and because FDR needed to repair the bad feelings generated from many of his New Deal policies.

Without the help from those business leaders, the allies would not have won the war.

With the war fighting over those same administrative units and leaders began realizing that most of the world's nations could not pay for the aid we had given them during the war. And none of them could pay for the aid they would still need. A plan was developed to trade our surplus equipment and prior aid in exchange for long term base rights throughout the world.

Without realizing it, and with no input from the citizens or Congress, those men were changing America from an isolationist nation to a long-term participant in world affairs. But America had never played the major role in world affairs before.

In fact George Washington had stated to his predecessors to avoid Foreign Entanglements. That was the role we were used to having, and best suited to.

Anthropologist Ruth Benedict had done research for the War Dept in WWII. Working from the Office of War Information she had observed our actions and our interference in those "foreign countries" that we had operated in. She tried to warn the national administrators that we were on the wrong path.

"With every occupied country the United States assists in freeing from Axis domination, with every Asiatic country where we operate in cooperation with the existing culture, the need for intelligent understanding of that country and its ways of life will be crucial. The danger, and it will be fatal to world peace, is that in our ignorance of their cultural values and lives we shall meet in head-on collision. And then inexorably we will fall back on the old pattern of simply imposing our values upon them by force." (3) Her warning was of course ignored.

We fell into the same trap as every other strong power and ended up imposing our way of life on others. But this time it was done to those we were trying to save.

China

As shown in *Fatal Flaws Book 1,* Japan had invaded China forcing Chiang's Kuomintang forces to fight the Samurai instead of the Chinese communists. And that same situation forced the communist forces to reluctantly join up with the Nationalists. But the Communists wisely sought not to drive out the foreign devils but to survive. They would let the Nationalists bleed themselves white.

For eight grueling years the Chinese had to fight the forces of Nippon alone.

With the exception of the Flying Tigers and some logistic and commando units, China was fighting the Japanese by themselves. Hundreds of Chinese cities and towns were destroyed and an estimated 15 million perished during their war.

Luckily for the West, like Russia was to Germany, China siphoned off over half of Japan's Army and air units. Had it not been for that vital factor and their mistakes at Pearl Harbor, the Coral Sea and Midway, Japan could have conquered Australia and possibly India in 1942. And that would have changed everything.

All during those years the Nationalists had been bled and grew weary of war. When the Japanese finally departed in late 1945 the Communist Chinese Forces had grown to a force of over 600,000 troops entrenched across northern China.

They had learned much in their battles against the Japanese.

By late 1945 many had thought that Stalin was going to try to simply claim Manchuria as his forces had "liberated" that territory from Japan.

Similar to what Russia had done in Eastern Europe, *everywhere the Russians went they looted the landscape like locusts. In Chinchow two oil refineries were dismantled and sent to Russia, as reparations! They even took the watches and clothing from the Chinese civilians.*

Originally China had been fighting Japan because of their invasion of Manchuria and then northern China. Since the Russian occupation of that vital region in August of 1945, China's communists had been setting up new bases there with Russian help.

There was no way Chiang was going to allow this "second invasion" to occur.

As shown in Fatal Flaws Book 1, at Yalta FDR had wrongly given and Stalin had agreed to secret provisions that gave Russia a privileged administrative and military position in Manchuria. Incredibly there were no references to Chinese sovereignty of Manchuria!

Word of Roosevelt's secret double dealing had finally gotten out and the Nationalist Chinese demanded answers. But only a select few knew of those secret deals, and so the Nationalists were denied the answers they sought or the resolution that was their due. Chiang was preparing to address that problem on his own.

Reprising his great campaign of 1925-28, when Chiang had conquered China by attacking from the south. (He was only the second leader in China's history to accomplish that difficult feat of arms.)

His strategy for reclaiming Manchuria rested on the same concept of assessing the situation, identifying the opportunity and attacking quickly. It took a few months to organize, but in late 1945 Chiang began relocating his best troops from their battlefields in the China-Burma-India sector.

(They had been fighting there to protect the vital supply areas and airfields in India.)

Their new targets were the communist bases that were being setup in Manchuria by the Russians.

But Pres. Harry Truman had imprudently decided in May 1945, (with the negative assessments by the Russian spies inside the State Dept.), that because of his disdain for Chiang and his "corrupt practices" he would limit all U.S. aid.

Truman even eliminated the 14th USAAF in China when he dismissively disbanded it in June 1945! *Gen. Claire Chennault USAAF resigned in disgust at this mindless move just as victory against Japan was getting close.*

There was no militarily justifiable reason for Truman to have disbanded the 14th AAF. The Atomic Bomb had not yet been built, and no one knew what the final strategy would be to finish off Japan. For certain the 14th AAF would have been a part of that effort! There was a huge negative factor resulting from the disbanding of the 14th AAF, their aerial striking power was no longer a part of Chiang's forces. (Was that the surreptitious idea all along.?)

Had the Nationalists still had the tactical striking power of the 14th AAF it was possible the Chinese communists could have been defeated quickly.

And that too would have changed everything.

(The 14th had attained an unbelievable record of damage to the Japanese and was poised for great things in the future. But Gen. Marshall and Gen. Arnold USAAF did not like Gen. Chennault because of his outspokenness and his achievements. *After FDR died they decided to replace and relegate him to obscurity.* The transition of the 14th AAF units to the China Theatre Command was given to Gen. George Stratemeyer, a team player. Under his watch the CTC was broken up.)

Truman also refused to using any U.S. troops, naval or air power in the region to help Chiang and the Nationalists in their pending battles against the Chinese communists.

Though the U.S. Marines had returned to China in late 1945, they were not allowed to fight which would have helped our ally.

Mao however was still being aided by Stalin.

Fifteen years earlier the communists had almost been beaten by Chiang.

The reason the communists had escaped to far off Yenan province in 1929 was that it bordered the Mongolian Peoples Republic. At that time Mongolia was basically a colony of the Soviet Union. And the reprieve given to them because of the war with Japan had allowed the communists to rebuild.

Always skilled at guerrilla tactics, the resurgent forces under Mao Zedong had learned how to fight the larger battles. His forces used captured U.S. supplies meant for Chiang to augment their weapons and supply pipeline. They also used captured Japanese munitions and arms and equipment from Russia.

Just one day after Japan surrendered Mao directed his forces to strike out and disarm every Japanese in every place they could get to. He was determined to extend communist control over as much of China as he could before the Nationalists could react.

(They had a long way to move to reach that part of China.)

Stalin's decision to move the Chinese Communists from Yenan into Manchuria in late 1945 was his secretive way of trying to annex the territory using "proxy troops".

Soviet transport units and railroads moved the Chinese Communist administration and army units deep into Manchuria. The Soviets paid their usual lip-service that Manchuria was legitimately a part of China, and that they did not "recognize" the Chinese Communists. But in 1945 they were all under the same banner as Communists and their plan was to take over the world.

The Red Chinese troops (CCF) were listed as "local defense forces" and given quarters outside of the Manchurian cities. Under the protection of the Russians, the Red Chinese did not expand their military capabilities by building defenses.

Instead they concentrated their efforts on "political indoctrination".

Every Manchurian town and village had a new "party headquarters opened. The plan was to turn Manchuria "peacefully" before the Nationalists could react.

After the Japanese surrender Chiang and the Nationalists were initially concerned with getting the Russians out of their land. They instituted an intense diplomatic effort towards that goal and eventually succeeded. By late 1945 most of the Russians reluctantly pulled out of Manchuria. *The CCF however stayed.*

Chiang began moving his units northward. American advisors still working in China and a few of his own staff tried to talk him out of attacking into Manchuria. They wanted him to concentrate on the myriad problems within China itself and in rebuilding from the war. Many felt that such a campaign was too much of a risk after all of the years of war. For some reason their mindset was to leave Manchuria alone, even if it turned communist.

(It is hard to tell if that was the U.S. advisors true feelings or if they were being told to reign in Chiang. The reader must remember that quite a few high placed communist spies were active inside the U.S. State Dept. They had worked for years to undermine U.S.-China relations.)

But to Chiang the communists were an enemy that had to be vanquished.

Chiang had said the Japanese were a disease of the skin, the communists a disease of the soul. Safe and comfortable in Manchuria the enemy was not expecting his attack.

And with the Russian exit from Manchuria only the Nationalist forces would have heavy weapons.

Chiang planned on using his new but small air transport force to overcome the long distances that had imperiled war in China for centuries. He would use air transport to leapfrog his forces deep behind the communist strongholds. This unexpected multi-faceted campaign would hopefully overwhelm the peasant army of the Chinese communists and end them. The initial battles seemed promising though the U.S. advisors still warned Chiang that his forces would be spread thin.

And then Gen. George Marshall showed up to broker a "peace treaty". *Nowhere in any of the war ending treaties or meetings had it ever been agreed or stated that Chiang would not or could not attack the Chinese Communists.* Why did Pres. Truman interject peace desires into a civil war in which one side was fighting the world's new enemy of communism?

Truman had already prevented Russian expansion into Japan, Southern Korea, Turkey and Iran, and Yugoslavian communist expansion into NE Italy.

Why did he interfere in China?

Gen. Marshall had accomplished miracles in directing the Army that had won WWII, but was completely outclassed in the role as a peace moderator.

That was especially so in the complex politics of China.

He may have intended to bring peace, but what he accomplished was the communist takeover of much of Asia.

When Marshall was appointed as Chief of Staff of the Army on September 1, 1939 Germany had just invaded Poland. Gen. Marshall had fought in WWI and knew in his heart that America would end up fighting in this new war, and he also knew it was woefully unprepared. At that moment the Army had just 197,000 officers and men.

Over the months he began analyzing his service and making deep changes to the senior ranks of the Army. Men who were too old, unfit or out of date tactically were weaned out. Marshall wanted younger bodies and minds, and he wanted *team players*.

Once war came he would use the relief of unfit commanders to try to keep the Army from killing itself as he had witnessed in WWI. (Unfit commanders could not grasp the terrible price of the modern battlefield and adjust their tactics to it. Multiple thousands of needless casualties resulted.)

In prior times elitist and unprofessional policies and attitudes allowed numerous poor men into vital positions of military leadership. Marshall wanted to end that practice with new policies. During WWII two thirds of the officer ranks in the eight million man U.S. Army were promoted from the enlisted men who showed battlefield capabilities. (That one fact showed how poor and antiquated the Army's training and promotional system actually was.)

A few leaders like Generals George Patton, Matt Ridgeway and Terry Allen were adept in making war. They could visualize the battlefield situation and make quick strikes using improvisation. (One of major strengths of the Nazi Army.) But men like Patton and Allen were demanding and prone to stepping on toes as they insisted things get done. Thus they were not looked upon as "team players". (Though the U.S. Army in France learned the true meaning of combined arms team under Patton.)

The new officer mold that Marshall looked for was meant to produce more Eisenhower's' and Bradley's', not the old school hard combat leaders. This decision to promote team players meant slower reactions in most units. As the Army of WWII learned about "modern warfare" advice was sought and meetings were held to determine an action. A commander did not just make a decision, he sought counsel. The Germans knew of this tendency and used it to their advantage throughout the fighting. (German

Commanders were encouraged to react to the battlefield and improvise. That was one of the foundations of Blitzkrieg. They would routinely form Kampfgruppen, battle groups, for adhoc situations.)

As shown earlier and in *Fatal Flaws Book 1*, there was only one senior U.S. general the Germans had worried about, George Patton. Because of that fear one of the most effective deceptions used for Normandy had been the one with Patton in charge of the phantom army that would land at Calais. It tied up the German reserves for weeks and was instrumental in the invasion's success. With the war over, Patton and Terry Allen were gone, and there were few men like them left.

On November 26, 1945 General of the Army George Marshall retired from active service. He and his wife looked forward to a quiet retirement.

Yet a day later President Truman called him.

He wanted Marshall to go to China to replace the "turncoat Ambassador Patrick Hurley and get control of China".

Patrick Hurley had been sent out to China by FDR in early 1945. Hurley was another of those outspoken types and had quickly grown tired of the political subterfuge, (the communist spies and supporters), within the U.S. State Department. His many months in China had revealed serious problems within the personnel assigned to China. He wanted to make major changes, but with FDR's death, Truman and the cabinet refused to listen to Hurley's numerous complaints. After months of trying to get action from this new Administration, Hurley finally decided his complaints had to be made public.

What Hurley had observed and tried to end was that American Communists working in the State Dept. were working tirelessly to stop, weaken and prevent our efforts to shore up Chiang's Chinese Nationalists.

Hurley told the wire service reporters, "A considerable section within State is endeavoring to support Communism generally as well as specifically in China."

Their efforts were designed to help the communists take over! (4)

With that statement Patrick Hurley ended the bipartisan effort that characterized WWII. His "resignation" and aggressive statements condemning the communists within our State Department shot across the wire services. Once again there was talk was of Reds in the government. (As shown earlier, the initial warnings were in 39-40, the latest ones were just occurring with the uncovered spy rings, Bently Budenz and Gouzenko.)

Outraged by Hurley's claims, Pres. Truman and his cabinet struggled to effect damage control. They did not endeavor to stop the communists!

"At a luncheon" the next day Sec. of Agriculture Clinton Anderson suggested using the just retired Gen. Marshall as Hurley's replacement. Sec. of the Navy James Forrestal seconded the pick as they agreed that *Marshall's appointment would quickly steal the headlines from Ambassador Hurley's charges of Reds in the State Dept."* (5)

(No one looked into Hurley's charges.)

But before he could report to China, Marshall had to face the Senate.

And to make things even worse politically for the Democrats, Congress was still looking into the debacle of Pearl Harbor. Secretary of War Henry Stimson had finally released the classified report of the Japanese attack at Pearl Harbor on Aug. 29, 1945.

In the heady moments of the end of WWII the report slipped past most eyes.

But now Congress wanted to hold public hearings on that report, and Gen. Marshall would be one of those called in. Marshall had also been named often in the secret report, and his mistakes had been highlighted. (Many believed that FDR wanted the attack to happen to get us into the war.)

To try to head off this danger to his party Senator Albren Barkley a Kentucky Democrat sponsored a preemptive resolution calling for a "thorough, impartial and fearless inquiry" into the matter. His words were the customary political doublespeak that he was going to bury the matter and no one would get the truth. Since the Democrats ruled the Congress, six of the ten members on the panel were Democrats.

Gen. Marshall was called in on Dec. 6, 1945.

For six days he was questioned. Interest in the proceedings was intense and not everything could be hushed up. The Stimson report highlighted the numerous failures from many of those in the top commands. (As a true leader Marshall accepted responsibility for his.)

It was revealed that Pearl Harbor could have been prevented with more direct and better communication from the senior Commanders and within the separate Commands. *The Republican members reported that the major failures for Pearl Harbor lay with in order, Pres. Roosevelt, Sec. of War Stimson, Sec. of Navy Frank Knox, General Marshall, Admiral Stark, and the former head of the War Plans Division Gen. Leonard Gerow.*

With the war now ended the Senate panel "refused" to recommend any punishments. Soon after General Marshall was accepted by the Senate as the interim Ambassador to China. For George Marshall and the world his coming failures in China would be far worse than the losses at Pearl Harbor.

As shown in *Fatal Flaws Book 1*, FDR had named China as one of the major Allied powers in the War effort. Great amounts of supplies and investments had been made to keep them in place and fighting. Claire Chennault's Flying Tigers had started the initial effort and Col. Joseph Stilwell had been sent over as a military advisor for ground forces. Upon our entry in the war in December 1941 both of the above had been promoted to General Officers, and soon commanded large support forces with the intent to aid the Nationalist efforts against Japan.

Chiang's Nationalists and the Communists under Mao had continued to clash during the long war with Japan. There was no way to rectify their diametrical differences in the same way Russia and the West never would. In early 1945 Gen. Stilwell had been replaced by Gen. Albert Wedemeyer, and the previously mentioned Patrick Hurley had also been sent over by FDR to try to get the Nationalists to final victory.

(Stilwell and Chiang greatly disliked each other and could not cooperate.)

Gen. Wedemeyer had worked with George Marshall planning many of the allied campaigns in Europe, but he was quite unhappy with the "controls" Marshall placed on all of the senior Army officers. *Marshall's controls concerned any reporting or complaining about communists or their activities. No matter how aggressive or sinister Soviet actions were, no one was allowed to discuss them!*

Wedemeyer wrote that he constantly experienced "admonitions from Marshall and Harry Hopkins not to refer to the Russians critically or to speak of the dangerous implications of communism"!

(Strange rules from one of those who approved the Army's Venona Project, the super-secret project to break the Soviet radio codes.)

Back on March 1, 1945 Chiang had invited the Communists to attend a national assembly to draft a constitution for the new Nationalist government. Mao refused the offer claiming his Communists were the real rulers, and he demanded Chiang's ouster. *Because of pressure from Pres. Truman, Chiang and the Nationalists were forced to legalize all of China's political entities, and that included the communists.*

With the war against Japan ending Chiang again invited Mao to attend conferences to work on China's myriad problems. Mao accepted the invitation on Aug. 15, 1945. For six weeks the two men met with Ambassador Hurley to attempt to find common ground. Their amity would not last long.

By early November 1945 fighting between the two groups was raging in 11 of China's 28 provinces. Mao accused the U.S. of using its forces, (Navy&Marines), to help the Nationalists instead of disarming the remaining Japanese. The 7th Fleet and over 50,000 Marines were in

China disarming the Japanese, keeping the peace and helping to move the Nationalists around. *Five armies were moved northward.*

Gen. Wedemeyer knew of those activities, and also admitted that skirmishes were occurring with the communists. That was to be expected with our troops helping our ally. He asked for further mission clarification from Washington and was told to just disarm the Japanese so the Nationalists could take over on their own. *What was happening however was that anytime the U.S. Marines entered an area that Mao's CCF, (Chinese communist forces), troops were in, clashes would break out.* The CCF were determined to control any area they were in.

Gen. Wedemeyer sent additional messages stating that the Nationalists were still unable to occupy the areas in Northern China because of **fighting hostile CCF forces under Mao.** It could take months before the Nationalists actually took over.

Unless a settlement was reached, the fighting in China would continue.

Sec. of State James Byrnes suggested they try to force a settlement in China by denying any further aid to Chiang and the Nationalists. (Truman and his Administration had decided that China should give the communists northern China and Manchuria in order to end the fighting.) His idea became the stick and carrot for George Marshall.

Ambassador Marshall and Undersecretary of State Dean Acheson met repeatedly to try to plan for the mission as Truman's special envoy. Marshall felt the CCF were being used by the Russians, as everywhere the Russians had gone a communist government was installed. He was authorized to use the Navy and Marines to help the Nationalists move into northern China and Manchuria.

They were not authorized to fight, just transport and support.

Marshall's overriding mission statement was to try to join the Communists and the Nationalists into one China! What was Truman and his Administration thinking in issuing those orders? Why would he try to force an ally into a union with an enemy? In his initial meetings with Chiang Kai-shek, George Marshall tried to lay the blame for this new policy on the American citizens. "The American people would strongly disapprove of any action by their government that would involve them in the internal disputes in China. The American people wanted a peaceful world."

Unfazed by the implied threat Chiang stated to Marshall that the CCF and the Russians were behind the ongoing civil conflict. In fact (as stated earlier), the Russians were trying to create a puppet government in Manchuria as they spoke. For days those meetings went on and Marshall succeeded in brokering a conference with himself, Communist leader Chou En-lai, and the Nationalist General Chang Chun.

(Chou En-lai had been a long time communist, and a leader in their Long March. He was well schooled and clever.)

Their first get-together was on Jan. 7, 1946.

To get the meeting to be held a ceasefire had to be arranged. That ceasefire that would prevent any Nationalist attacks, and allow the communists time to move and reinforce.

Among the topics discussed was giving the CCF control of all areas north of the Great Wall and control of Manchuria.

Back in October the CCF 8th route army had taken possession of the province of Jehol from the Japanese. That blocked any Nationalist forces from being able to get into Manchuria. In effect the CCF 8th Army had been acting as a lookout and blocking force so the Russians could finish looting Manchuria and leave supplies and weapons for them.

Neither Chang nor Chou would yield over the issue.

Marshall continued to try to finesse the situation getting a renewal of the token ceasefire on the 10th. Chiang pledged to allow all Chinese a part in his democratic government, but the communists as always gave little.

Chiang would write in his diary on how naïve and foolhardy the Americans were in dealing with the communists.

(Chiang of course was correct. It is hard to fathom how the U.S. leaders consistently fell for the communist siren. Marshall had been with FDR at all of their meetings with Stalin and saw the aftermath from them. Yet here he was making the same mistakes.)

One other interesting note concerned the major wartime leaders. By this point FDR was dead, Hitler was dead, Tojo was imprisoned awaiting execution, Churchill had been voted out of power and de Gaulle had just resigned.

Only Josef Stalin was still in power, with his unwavering sense of purpose.

Inside a great hall in London the first meeting of the *United Nations* was held on January 10, 1946. Fifty one nations joined the organization in the hopes that the established principals of peaceful coexistence and basic human freedoms could be assured. The U.N. was organized into six units; the Economic and Social Council, the Trusteeship Council for countries under trust territories, the International Court of Justice, an Administrative Secretariat, the General assembly and the Security Council.

Each Nation could be heard in the General Assembly, but the Security Council was tasked with decisions on international peace and security. There were five permanent members, Nationalist China, England, France, the Soviet Union and the United States.

There were also six rotating seats of two year duration.

Despite all of the ideals for peace, a no vote by any of the permanent members could stop any U.N. action. (Stalin's insistence)

Pres. Truman had written in his notes in January 1946;

"At Potsdam we were faced with an accomplished fact and were by circumstances forced to agree to the Russian occupation of Eastern Poland and that part of Germany east of the Oder River. It was a high handed outrage!

There isn't a doubt in my mind that Russia intends to invade Turkey and seize the Sea Straits to the Mediterranean." (Stalin however was just trying to adhere to FDR's secret promise to gain control of the Straits.)

Russia next tried to force their hand in Iran and were turned back by our actions there too.

"Unless Russia is faced with an iron fist and strong language, another war is in the making. They, (Communists), understand only one language, how many divisions do you have. I do not think that we should compromise any longer."

We should refuse to recognize the governments of Bulgaria and Rumania until they comply with our requirements for free elections. We must make our position in Iran be known in no uncertain terms and we should maintain complete control of Japan and the Pacific." (Russia was not allowed in on the occupation of Japan.)

"We must rehabilitate China and create a strong central government.

And we should do the same for Korea as I'm tired of babying the Soviets"! (6)

This call for action became some of Truman's greatest thoughts, and some of his worst failures. He did not follow up his righteous words with deeds in China or Korea.

In fact he did just the opposite.

Following the trials above, on February 9, 1946 Stalin gave a speech outlining Russia's five year rearmament goals. It was meant to warn the U.S. that any comity the world had known during the war was ended. Around the Western world alarm bells began going off. (Supreme Court Justice William O. Douglas termed the speech the Declaration of WWIII.)

Nine days later the Soviet defector, (Gouzenko), from the Soviet embassy in Ottawa finally disclosed the details of the well placed spy ring that had targeted the U.S., specifically the atomic research.

Sec. of State Byrnes demanded to know what was happening.

George Keenan our Ambassador to Russia was admonished about the turn of relations between the former allies. On the 22nd he sent a harsh signal back to the State Department; *"For two years I have been trying to persuade the people in Washington that Josef Stalin and his regime are the same one that was in power before the war.*

This is the same regime that conducted the purges in the 1930s, the Non-aggression pact with Hitler, and invaded non-threatening Poland and Finland!

They are no friends of ours.

I have tried to persuade those in Washington that the dreams of a happy postwar world with this Soviet government are quite unreal, that our problems with them are deeper than you realize. Capitalism is their enemy, and they are determined to enact world domination of communism. Stalin and his associates are elated with their recent military and political successes.

They see favorable prospects for extending their politics throughout Europe using the devices of infiltration and subversion!"

America must take a hard-line foreign policy to counter this Soviet aggression.

Still Pres. Harry Truman directed George Marshall to stay the course in China and reach an agreement with the Communists!

On February 25, 1946 a military compact was signed in China. George Marshall was able to get an "agreement", but even as the signatories were penning the papers, fighting was flaring up again in Manchuria. As always any treaty with the communists was folly.

The Russians were still refusing to pull back to Mongolia and they continued to strip the countryside. The Soviet Ambassador would not cooperate or coordinate any pullbacks or even the repatriation of the 800,000 Japanese still there. (They were being used as slave labor.)

Those planned delays allowed the CCF more time to organize and control the area. *Though the signed treaty returned sovereignty of Manchuria back to China, access to it was still blocked by the CCF. And the Russians denied any U.S. ships from docking at the port of Darien slowing the landing of Nationalist troops.*

On February 28 Sec. Byrnes gave a speech in New York warning the West it had to stick together and face this new threat. "If we are to be a great power, we must act like one not only to ensure our own safety, but to preserve peace in the world!"

Six days later Winston Churchill gave his famous speech in Fulton, Missouri.

By the time the Russians began their pullback from Manchuria in late March 1946 the CCF had settled in and setup communist party headquarters in every village. The Russians had conveniently left behind vast stores of captured Japanese ammunition and weapons and left some of their own. By April 1946 the CCF was in an entrenched position throughout Manchuria. (This was the same time as Truman's threatening letter to Stalin over Iran.)

Gen. Marshall was sent back a month later to ameliorate the continued problems. While flying over the Pacific another disaster occurred.
In the Manchurian capitol city of Changchun two CCF armies launched an attack upon the small Nationalist garrison, a clear violation of the treaty.

All of the communist advances and actions over the past weeks had highlighted the futility of any compromise with them, and strengthened the position of the conservatives among the Nationalists. Chiang refused any additional compromises as long as the Americans were appeasing the communists.

And the more Marshall pressed, the more convinced Chiang became that the U.S. was trying to give China away.

Chiang's forces were finally striking out strongly. As stated earlier, he had relocated his best forces from their victorious southern battles against Japan with help from the U.S. Navy and Marines. The troops were well led by Gen. Sun Lijen, and had been reequipped with surplus U.S. weapons. (USMC)

The CCF units comprised of light infantry were not prepared for the heavier battles that came, and they lost their forward positions. At Sipingjie, a vital junction about midway inside Manchuria a pitched battle was fought for weeks.

CCF commander Lin Biao repeatedly sent human wave assaults against the Nationalists, *even forcing 100,000 factory workers from Changchun to fight*. By May 18 with almost half his force killed the CCF fled north.

With their successes against the Communists in the north the Nationalists did not want a truce. And as they lost more and more battles, the Communists needed a truce to survive.

Just as victory was within reach, Gen. Marshall again forced Chiang to order a halt.

Marshall had worked hard to get millions in aid for Chiang and he threatened to withhold it if a ceasefire was not arranged. (Marshall did refuse to give any more money to Chiang.) Mao demanded that all U.S. aid be stopped, while his communists received untold amounts of support from Russia. (It was the usual communist scam.)

Marshall brought intense pressure on our wartime ally to stop his Manchurian offensive in late May 1946.

Since America was the only western power left in the ruined world, and because America had been such a staunch ally during WWII, Chiang Kai-shek listened and stopped his forces. *"Chiang's generals begged him to reconsider, for if they took the city of Harbin the communist forces in Manchuria would be defeated!"* (7)

This erroneous decision to halt their attacks prevented the Nationalists from completing the destruction of the communist forces. (Similar to Hitler's call to stop the panzers outside of Dunkirk.)

Into June the negotiations continued trying to force Chiang to join a coalition government with the communists! On the 30th Marshall worked on Chiang for so long it drove him to tears. Chiang issued orders not to fire on the reds unless fired upon.

Throughout the summer of 1946 the CCF units repeatedly attacked the U.S. Marines as they assisted the Nationalist movements and logistical needs. Chou En-lai knew of those CCF attacks, but communist propaganda turned the story completely around. *Truman directly threatened Chiang and any aid for the Nationalists if he did not negotiate with the communists!??* In August all military aid was stopped.

As always the truce broke down quickly and the communists used Gen. Marshall to do what their army could not, stop the Nationalists.

Chiang's forces lost their "battlefield momentum" and were never able to get it back!

The reprieve they had received because of Pres. Truman and Gen. Marshall's unwarranted and imprudent actions enabled the Red Chinese to re-group, re-supply and rebuild. By the middle of August the constant skirmishes prompted Chiang to again attack. On the first anniversary of VJ Day Chiang issued a public statement lamenting the Communist tricks and tactics. His Nationalist units went back on the offensive.

On October 10, 1946 the Nationalists captured *Kalgan*, and with that city came all of the land routes into Manchuria. The CCF retreated quickly to avoid being cutoff.

But without an Air Force to stop them, large units of the CCF escaped north and west into Russian held areas. Still Marshall counseled a truce not understanding that the communists would never give up.

On Oct. 11 Chiang tried to convene a national assembly which would include communist seats. It was ignored. On the 16th Chiang proposed a ceasefire, but it too was rejected by the Communists. After a year of failed diplomacy George Marshall returned to the U.S.

Gen. Marshall had wanted Chiang to give up their Northern provinces and Manchuria to the communists in exchange for a peace treaty.
Chiang had refused.

There is no proof that his peace deal would have been adhered to, as every treaty made with the Communists was broken before the ink was dry.

As the war dragged on the Nationalists began to grow weary.

Then their supplies dried up.

Infused with fresh troops from N. Korea and new armaments the communists fought on.

Korea

As shown in *Fatal Flaws Book 1*, for three years after Pearl Harbor FDR desperately worked to get Russian help against Japan. In 1941/42 Russia had been on the brink of collapse and Stalin did not want to fight anyone except the Germans. Thanks to lend-lease aid, Stalin's draconian rule and Hitler's many mistakes, the Eastern Front became a killing field for Germany. By 1943 the tide had turned and Russia was winning. At the meeting in Yalta in early 1945 Stalin promised FDR that within three months of the end of war in Europe he would fight the Japanese.

Secretly he had already begun moving supplies eastward. During late June 1945 Russian units began the long and difficult move to the east. Japan was already reeling from constant U.S. strategic aerial bombardments and naval air and sea attacks. The defensive chain of islands that had protected Japan was long gone and U.S. might was destroying Japan's cities blocks at a time.

After the meetings in Potsdam had ended, and seeing that the tide had turned against Japan, Stalin was satisfied that the Allies would not threaten his new empire in Eastern Europe. (As FDR had promised at Yalta, U.S. forces were leaving Europe in large numbers. They were going to fight Japan.)

Stalin increased his forces relocating to the east and plotted their moves. *By this point all of the Russian supply needs had already been moved east. Most of it was U.S. Lend-Lease aid that Stalin had squirreled away in secret. He then demanded and received more aid to "fight Japan".*

On August 6 the Atomic bomb was used on Hiroshima. One bomb was dropped, one Japanese city was destroyed. Pres. Truman who was returning from Europe and the Potsdam Conference sent the Japanese warlords an ultimatum; Surrender or face complete destruction.

Reading the tea leaves correctly Stalin ordered his units to attack. On August 8th over 1,200,000 Russians began an offensive against the remnants of the once mighty Kwantang Army of Japan. This was a greatly improved Russian Army than the one Japan had fought and lost to in 1937. Russian armored units easily pushed the Imperial forces back and began to conquer all of Manchuria.

After Manchuria was subdued, *Korea* would be the next place the Russians armored forces would strike. *Close by Russian amphibious landing forces were being readied for their upcoming invasion of Japan's northern island of Hokkaido! Stalin saw opportunity like no other.*

Then the second A-bomb fell, and on August 15 the Japanese reluctantly surrendered.

In Washington a group of men known as SWINK, (SWNCC, State Dept, War Dept, Navy Coordinating Committee), were directed to come up with a solution to the impending problem of where the U.S. and Russian forces would meet up in Asia.

Since the Cairo Declaration of 1943, the Allies had agreed on a free Korea.

The follow up conferences at Tehran, Yalta and Potsdam had also agreed on a "Trusteeship for Korea", consisting of members from the U.S., Britain, China and Russia. They were to guide the provisional government of *Chosun* until such time that it could take over and rule on their own.

But the military leaders in America were growing weary of Russia duplicity.

The proceeding months had shown them that Stalin's efforts and attitude in Europe was not like a benevolent freedom fighter. No the Russians were acting more like conquerors. So these men in *SWINK* had to quickly find a Demarcation line somewhere in *Korea* before the Russians overran the entire peninsula. The Russians would disarm the Japanese on their side, and the Americans would do the same on ours.

In mid-August U.S. forces had landed in southern Chosun. But their movements northward were slow. The country had few good roads and was a backwater to the modern world. The Yalu River which separated Korea from China/Manchuria had been the preferred boundary to separate the allied forces. But the Russians had already crossed it on Aug 12 and the idea was scrapped. A new line would have to be found and quickly.

The vital decision for this boundary line was debated and passed around from one command to the next. And then a low ranking staff member suggested the 38th parallel.

In typical American mentality the thought was for a boundary that would "evenly split Korea between the two Allies". (This would be another one of those overlooked minor decisions that would be the source of so much grief.)

No thought was given to the future or to military or political considerations. The line basically cut Korea in two almost equal parts, almost. Everyone in the group liked the pick and their decision was passed up the chain of command from Col. Dean Rusk's office. (Future Sec. State.)

Every person in the respective Departments agreed with the pick, though more than likely very few actually questioned the idea. It quickly became the final order which was passed on to the British and to Russia. The British reply was a "Good Show", and for once the Russians did not argue. "Da" was cabled back.

(The Russians did not argue because the choice was a good deal for them.)
But these men of influence had failed everyone.

The highest circles of our Government are supposed to anticipate and plan. They had seen four months of Russian peace overwhelm Eastern and Central Europe.

And yet in Korea they did not look to 1958, or even to 1948.

And so the land of Chosun would be doomed to be the site of the first major war between the West and Communism.

In the Land of the Morning Calm the U.S. troops that landed were handed a daunting mission. They were tasked to restore a war and colonial oppressed, ravaged country into a functioning society. Lt Col William Jones of the 1108th Engineer combat group arrived at Pusan, the main Port in southern Korea. *They had been redeployed from Leghorn Italy.*

These were the men who would serve as occupation troops and engineers in the rebirth of Korea. They were part of Lt. Gen. John R. Hodge's XXIV Corps, a corps that was quickly being dismantled as whole units were suddenly being sent home.

Those remaining troops were in for a rude awakening.

Work in the American zone encompassed all of the country south of the 38th parallel, and all of it was bad. Western societies do not produce many citizens who can accept the stench and squalor in the lands of the abject poor. In Korea there were no toilets, for human waste was used in the fields as fertilizer.

And just as the rebuilding of this land was beginning our government made a disastrous mistake. The complete demobilization and discharge of the servicemen and women began. *No thought was given to the world situation, its needs or its threats.*

The most powerful military machine ever created did not melt away in an orderly fashion. No, it was disintegrated within months.

Battle hardened Infantry, Armor, Artillery and Engineer units were discharged as fast as ships and planes could be rounded up to take them home. Well seasoned commanders at all levels and ranks were slipping away. And with them went all of the hard learned lessons of combat. The ranks that remained were mostly comprised of career staff officers and those few committed to the uniform.

Mighty Air Corps units simply left their hundreds of "unneeded" planes on the airfields, for no one knew what to do with them.

Navy task forces were tied up at wharves and left empty.

And thousands upon thousands upon thousands of tons of spare parts, foods, supplies, weapons, vehicles and ammunition were simply dumped at sea.

Vehicles, tanks, and artillery were left unattended at the unneeded bases along with all manner of support and construction equipment. Any replacement troops that did arrive in the occupation units were 18 year old draftees who knew little and cared less.

The war was over, and now they were stuck in these various hell holes.

And the worst of all was in *Korea.*

Few of our national leaders realized that winning the peace was just as important as winning the battles.
(And in our time that failure is still evident.)

Safe behind her ocean moats Americans had never felt the need to think about the world as a "Big Picture". There had not been an enemy upon our shores since the war of 1812, hence we were "safe".

Another fault in the American experience is that our land and people are so young. There is no collective memory, or pattern or purpose.

All of the lands in Europe could count their histories in multiple centuries. China and Japan in millennia.

America however was founded by those seeking a better way of life and those seeking freedoms. Other than that America is simply a collection of immigrant groups who left their "Old World" and its problems behind. The national psyche is to be left in peace.

But this was no longer the "Old World" that those immigrants had left.

This was a broken world, one that was ripe for malevolent change from those who saw opportunity. And because of her safe existence Americans had never learned that most vital lesson;

"That There Are Tigers In The World". (8)
And They Are Always Watching.

And so by the millions, U.S. Personnel were shipped home, shed their military OD's and slipped on suits, dresses and work clothes. It was time to get on with living.

But the communists of Russia, China, Yugoslavia and Vietnam did not change their uniforms or their goals. They had a broken world to conquer.

(John Adams, the second President of the United States was quoted over two centuries ago, "I must study politics and war, so that our sons may have the liberty to study mathematics and philosophy.")

Back in Korea the understaffed U.S. units used Japanese Officers and soldiers to keep the country functioning. (The same way Gen. Patton did with the Nazi's in Germany). Eventually all of the Japanese who had been in other countries were repatriated. When they left those war torn lands there was not a skilled worker to be found. Typical of all colonial powers, Japanese rule was assisted by keeping the ruled people ignorant and dependent. Korea was a hell of a mess.

Appalling poverty, squalor, dust, dirt and filth filled the streets. Orphans wandered aimlessly, and it became a common sight to see women and children fall along the roads and die in place. All were ignored.
Forty years of Japanese slavery and brutality could not be brushed aside.

There were no trained administrators to run the government or businesses, so nothing functioned. The black market was rampant here too. Scores from old feuds had to be settled, and food was scarce as was any semblance of a functioning society.

Morale among the U.S. troops which was low to begin with disappeared.

A large part of that problem was caused by the loss of all of the war vets at the same time. In early 1946, Col. Jones the first military commander in his sector also rotated back to the states. He too never looked back.
And to add to the problems in Korea, communist subversives were hard at work.

Gen. Hodge notified Douglas MacArthur, the overall commander of the Western Pacific that he was declaring war upon those communists. Hodge realized he had to stamp out those insidious enemies quickly, before they took over in the power vacuum in Korea. MacArthur readily agreed, and left all of those tactical decisions to Hodge. Being so far from home MacArthur was sure that word of their "anti-communist transgressions" would never reach Washington.

Vietnam

For almost a century Indochina had been under the oppressive rule of France. As shown earlier, numerous rebel groups had tried to fight the French but none had succeeded in defeating them. During the treaty conferences at Versailles in 1919, Ho Chi Minh had gone to France hoping to speak with America's Pres. Wilson. As the spokesman for a free world, Ho wanted Wilson's support in ending French Rule. Naturally the French could not allow that, and Ho was not permitted to see Wilson.

As a Socialist and Nationalist, Ho traveled to Russia soon after the peace of WWI had been completed. While in Moscow he attended the University of Oriental Workers, an academy for Asian insurgents. He was impressed with Lenin's main dictum, that revolution must be launched only under "favorable circumstances". In that insidious environment Ho Chi Minh remained, and he became an ardent communist trained in Bolshevik techniques and ideology.

After his lessons ended, in 1924 Ho traveled to Canton, China where he worked with Chiang Kai-shek and his Russian advisor Mikhail Borodin. Ho worked as an interpreter and met up with other disenchanted Vietnamese. Ho formed a Revolutionary Youth League and taught his Vietnamese students to form small secure cells to spread the word of communism. They were to learn about their audience and write passages tailored to that audience. He urged them to be generous, and to be concrete.

"Peasants believe in facts, not theories."

In 1927 Chiang Kai-shek turned against the growing movement of the communists and went to war against them. Faced with prison Ho Chi Minh escaped back into Russia, finding his way to Paris. After spreading his new philosophy there he eventually ended up in Bangkok, Thailand. Slowly he made his way to northern Siam disguised as a monk. He joined up with a community of Vietnamese expatriates and taught and published a newspaper under various pseudonyms. (He was a wanted man.)

French repressions and Vietnamese rebellions continued throughout those years, especially in the hard times of the 1930s. Relocating to Hong Kong, Ho and some other rebellious leaders formed their Indochinese Communist Party. They wanted to rule all of Indochina under a proletarian government. (A far cry from Ho's desires in 1919.)

Back in Indochina sweeps by the French police picked him and his followers up, with Pham Van Dong and Le Duc Tho spending years in prison. Ho always seemed to get away, and that time he talked a hospital employee to report him dead. His file in Paris was closed, as he melted away.

Reacting to their recurring troubles in Indochina the French decided to allow some loosening of the reigns on Emperor Bo Dai. The eighteen year old Emperor wanted to make reforms but was politically incapable. His lack of effort caused another intense nationalist to leave, Ngo Dinh Diem.

Ho Chi Minh continued his wanderings, returning to Moscow, then China and back to Russia. Ho trekked into the Chinese Communist stronghold in central China staying in the caves of Yenan. All through those years he thought of Vietnam, and of making it his. Then in 1940 a tidal wave swept over Asia, the Samurai.

Many of the native nationalists in those colonial lands embraced the Japanese, but not Ho. He allied himself with the allied powers believing that they would eventually evict the Japanese. Then the discredited French would also leave and he could gain independence for Vietnam. His Russians masters were not happy with his political alignment, but then it was not yet June 1941.

Sometime in early 1941 Ho Chi Minh snuck back into Vietnam. He had been gone over twenty years! In a cave near Pac Bo, Ho met like minded thinkers Pham Van Dong and Vo Nguyen Giap. They called him uncle Ho, the respected elder.

Their movement was called the *Viet Nam Doc Lap Dong Minh*, the Vietnamese Independence League. It was shortened to Viet Minh, and their fight soon began.

Giap showed his military side by organizing small military units and using hit and run tactics. Because of the immense size of Vietnam the Viet Minh activities in the south were not as well organized as those in the north. But they were still there and did what they could. As WWII continued the Japanese were slowly being beaten back and it was clear that they would not last.

During March 1945 the Japanese ordered the Vichy French Colonial forces to assist them in fighting the allies. They refused, and most surrendered to the Japanese.

A few fought against the Japanese, and those that did were slaughtered and the local civilians tortured. The stage was being set for the collapse of all French influence, and the Viet Minh were ready to step in.

In June 1945 Ho had gone back into China to speak with the American consulate in Kunming to get U.S. assistance for Vietnam. During July American OSS agents parachuted into North Vietnam to assist in the guerrilla actions against the Japanese.

French intelligence officers tried to warn the Americans not to underestimate the sly, and cunning Ho. (Afraid that America would interfere with France's colonies, de Gaulle secreted French agents and commandos into Vietnam to stay abreast of any U.S. activity.)

Upon meeting and working with Ho the OSS officers came away impressed with the small and wiry middle aged man his followers called Ho Chi Minh.

Major Patti was the senior OSS agent and he became close to Ho, and his operations messages stated that Ho was a nationalist first. Major Patti felt that we could moderate and work with Ho, and even pull him away from his communist ideology.

Ho Chi Minh was indeed a nationalist first, but as a longtime communist he met with and formed a collection of like minded men. Using his prior training and aid from other communist groups, Ho's communist led Viet Minh became the strongest of the rebel groups. When Ho went to Russia he was trained in the fine art of communism, became a fervent believer, and by 1945 had been a convert for almost 25 years. All of the senior leaders of the *Vietminh* were also communists, and all of Ho's practices followed the standard communist line. (There was little hope that he would change.)

Ho's intelligence organization astonished the OSS officers. His Vietminh knew everything that was going on in the region and were able to convey the messages needed to operate with impunity. The Americans were also impressed with his guerrilla fighters whom they supplied with mortars, rifles and ammunition. They learned quickly and could adapt easily to any new technique or weaponry.

From August 45 into September 1946, Ho appealed to the United States on numerous occasions to help them attain independence from the hated French.

As stated before America was the only country able to help the Vietnamese. But once again Ho was turned away due to the West's need of French help in containing communism in Europe. *(Ho told one of the OSS officers they would welcome a million American soldiers, but not a single French one.)*

This is a clear example of how bad decisions in the past cause additional ones later. The numerous military and political failures by the Allies aided the communist takeover of all of Eastern Europe. By the time that Ho Chi Minh was asking for U.S. help against France, Pres. Truman was forced to have France's help in trying to stabilize Europe despite the fact that the desired U.S. position was freedom for all nations.

As stated earlier, on September 2, 1945 Ho had brazenly declared Vietnamese independence using quotes from America's Declaration of Independence. By the time of Japan's surrender in mid- September Ho and his followers had won control of most of Northern Vietnam and established their own provisional government in Hanoi. (It is doubtful that Ho would have been able to get so far without the cataclysm of WWII. The rapid defeat of France by the Germans and the occupation by the Japanese signaled the rebels in Vietnam that they too could defeat the French.)

As shown earlier, to try to make the disarmament easier, at Potsdam the allies split Vietnam into two parts. South of the 16th parallel the British would disarm the Japanese. North of it the Nationalists from China would. French picked Emperor Bo Dai cabled de Gaulle and warned him that the Vietnamese could feel that their independence is at hand. If you try to come back your soldiers and rulers will not be obeyed.

De Gaulle dismissed his warning.

(Emperor Bo Dai was ordered by the Vietminh to resign, which he wisely did.)

In the south chaos reigned as multiple groups now vied for power. French authorities sat in the background watching and learning who the main threats were. Strikes were held crippling the nation as communist atrocities increased in an effort to scare the French out. During October 1945 Gen. Jacques Le Clerc had arrived with strong forces determined to restore order and drive the Vietminh out. Their initial attacks drove through the vital Mekong Delta area, Vietnam's breadbasket. From there they cleared the Vietminh stranglehold on Saigon and then moved northward into the Central Highlands. As they retreated the Vietminh burned villages, destroyed roads and bridges and terrorized everyone.

As soon as Le Clerc's units moved out of an area the Vietminh returned.

It became apparent that to defeat these communists the French would have to establish fortified positions all over the country, patrol out from them, and train and equip the villagers to help. *The 35,000 men originally sent in would have to be increased to over 100,000, and Le Clerc felt that would only pacify the South.*

He warned his government that the situation was dire and should be negotiated.

De Gaulle was again unmoved.

In the North Ho Chi Minh and "his party" ruled. They cleverly added Chinese, Catholics and socialists to his interim government as they began "reforming their country". The elections for Ho's government in the north were held in January 1946 and complied with the usual communist dogma. *The citizens in the North were forced to vote but there was only one slate of candidates, those from Ho's party. The polls were watched by armed guards and Ho's party won with 99% of the vote.*

To placate the Nationalist Chinese commander Lu Han, "Ho dissolved the communist party". Both leaders were adamant about keeping the French out, but both knew they were coming.

In a secret agreement reached in December 45, De Gaulle and Chiang had agreed to remove Chiang's occupying forces allowing French Army units to return to the North. Chiang needed his troops to fight the communists in China.

To get something in return for helping the French, Chiang was able to get all French interests in China ended. The agreement was signed in Feb 1946.

During March 1946 Ho and his followers who were still in charge in the North began liquidating rival political parties and personnel.
Over 5,000 rivals were executed, 25,000 went to labor camps and 6,000 were exiled.

Ho was carefully following the normal communist routine of eliminating any potential risks. The Vietminh even used criminals to "mask the intentions of their efforts".

Soon after additional French forces returned to Indochina with orders to take back control of their colonies. As stated above they accomplished their goals in the Southern part of the country, but in the North they faced Ho and his organized fighters.
Numerous battles and routine sabotage alerted the French that in the North they would have a tough task.

Ho lamented that even though they had declared their independence in September 1945, none of the Western Nations had recognized them, not even America.

Ho travelled to France to work out an agreement, and in conferences with the French they arrived at a reluctant accord. France would recognize the Hanoi regime as an association of the French Union, similar to the British Commonwealth system.

Only "15,000" French troops would enter N. Vietnam, and each year 3,000 were supposed to leave. By the end of 1951 N. Vietnam would be a free state.

Pragmatically Ho and his followers would allow the French to rule in the hopes of gaining independence. (It was better to smell the French for five more years than take a chance that the Chinese would stay forever.)

But the manipulative French were only playing for time. Their October 1946 constitutional reforms made no mention of the prior agreement or of any provisions for creating independent nations. Tensions heightened, and Gen. Le Clerc was replaced by the aggressive Gen. Valluy. His French forces were increased to 100,000 troops of various nationalities. Valluy attacked near Hanoi, and his paratroops almost landed on Ho Chi Minh and Gen. Giap in their jungle headquarters. They had escaped by the smallest of margins, and who could say what would have been. The Vietminh encircled the paratroops and harassed them and a relief column for days.

On November 20th, 1946 a French gunboat opened fire on a crowd in the northern city of Haiphong. Over 6,000 civilians were killed. Ho's *Vietminh* forces retaliated on the French troops and on French civilians. The second battle between the west and communism had begun. (Greece was the first.)

Throughout November and December attacks and retaliatory attacks went on. France sent in larger forces, now over 115,000, but the modern army that France used could not win in the heavy jungles of Vietnam against the guerrilla tactics used by these communists. Dozens of battles were being waged across northern Vietnam and as each month went by the Vietminh became more proficient and organized.

Vietnam was bordered by China, Laos and Cambodia. When things turned against them on the battlefield, Ho's forces would melt away into the jungles, hide over the borders, or disperse themselves among the turned populace.

They avoided fighting in large stand up battles.

Europe and America

Inside devastated Europe strong communist movements began to take hold. As stated before the Monarchies with their imperialism, and Democracy and capitalism with their boom and bust business cycles had many strong detractors in the world of yesterday. Their history of economic turmoil, colonialism and war had convinced much of the world that a political change was needed. That was one reason why Marxism gained so many new disciples in the years after WWI.

During 1946-1947 after another and worse cataclysm had devastated the earth, more and more of the worlds people were turning to the "workers paradise" myth.

When communist states were forced on the nations of Eastern Europe the world did not give universal condemnation. And in France sympathetic communists staged crippling strikes to help their brethren in Vietnam. Even the Labour Party in England had become a socialist leaning entity. Since the 1930s, America too had an active communist party.

In Greece an attempted coup against the monarchy in late 1945 had nearly succeeded. As had happened in every country that had partisans fighting in WWII, many of them were communists. They were well led and motivated to win. The political turmoil in Greece was so bad that the Monarchists and communists began fighting a civil war over which political philosophy would take over.

And Stalin was only too happy to send arms to the embattled lands.

(Ironically the British had been aiding the Balkan partisans in the fight against the Germans. About half of the fighters had been communists and the weapons and training given to them was now being used to fight against Democracy and the British.)

Back in America the end of the war unleashed a pent up demand for fair wages and prices. Businesses demanded and received the end of wartime price controls. Inflation began to rise so the workers wanted increased wages. Job actions began as unions insisted that the workers demands be heard.

On top of those economic issues, the returning war veterans needed housing.

Most had left the home of their parents to serve during the war. They did not want to go home to ma and pa. Rents increased as the housing demands quickly outstripped supply.

And because of government controls foods were still high priced and hard to find.

Most of the vets and the defense workers had amassed nest eggs during the years of war. (Few goods to buy at home and most of the vets sent their meager pay home.) They were now capable of independence and desired just that. Weddings that had been postponed because of the war occurred by the hundreds each week.

And that resulted in the beginning of the Baby-boom, a nation altering event. Hundreds of thousands of babies were being born in rapid succession. That further increased the need for housing. Caught flat by the rush to demobilize the Democrats in power had no solutions to the civilian-social problems that were being created. Fortunately many dozens of thousands of those vets had years of service in engineer units. They were well trained in the building trades and were disciplined to work. Infrastructure and housing projects seemed to burst from the ground as the nation underwent a building boom. Factories turned over to making civilian goods and found a willing work force.

One of the greatest benefits given to the returning veterans, (and the nation), was the passage of the GI Bill of Rights. This bill gave all of the vets a free education in a secondary school or a vocational school. Those vets had suffered the privations of the Great Depression, and then the horrors of WWII. They were extremely motivated to having a better life and they set out to make it happen. And their work ethic and values would propel America into an economic powerhouse that was the envy of the world.

In July 1941 the U.S. Ambassador to Russia Averill Harriman had received a gift from the "Russian Boy Scouts." The "gift" was an elegant wood carving that he happily placed inside his office in Moscow.

Hidden inside the wood was a sophisticated listening device that was cleverly activated by radio waves generated and directed at the carving from outside of the building!

For seven years the Russians heard every conversation in the Ambassador's office!

As stated earlier, George Keenan was the subsequent Ambassador at the Embassy in Moscow and in February 1946 he issued a famous 5500 word telegram describing the evil intentions of the Russians. *In summation he explained how the Bolsheviks would do anything to set nations against each other in order to tear down a country's will, strength and character to advance Soviet control.*

The telegram caused an uproar in diplomatic circles.

(Already the "enlightened liberals" of the world were on the side of mankind's greatest enemy.)

During March 1946 Winston Churchill met with Pres. Truman to concur with Keenan's view. Days later in his famous publicized speech Churchill would again state a phrase that would become symbolic of this new crisis;

"From Stettin in the Baltic to Trieste in the Adriatic, **an Iron Curtain** *has descended across the continent. Behind that line lie all of the capitals of the ancient states of Central and Eastern Europe, Warsaw, Berlin, Budapest, Vienna, Belgrade, Prague, Sofia, and Bucharest.*
All of the famous cities and their populations now lie within the Soviet sphere.

Far from the frontiers of Russia, and throughout the world, Communist fifth columns are established and work in complete obedience to the directions they receive from the Communists center. Except in the British Commonwealth and in the United States, where communism is in it's infancy, the Communist party and their fifth columns constitute a growing challenge and peril to Christian civilization"!

Nowhere in those words was there a cry for war.

No, it was a call for the world to wake up and see its future destruction.

Incredibly Truman was upset over the speech and told Asst. Sec. of State Dean Acheson not to attend a reception for Churchill in NYC.

Stalin was invited for a rebuttal, but he refused.

(We face a similar threat from Islamic Extremists. Yet our politicos downplay the peril in the foolish thought that it will go away.)

With all of the above problems on the minds of the voters, in the November 1946 mid-term elections the people had grown tired of Truman the Democrats. The average citizen clearly saw that the world they had fought to save was in turmoil, with communist movements and insurgent fighting occurring all over the globe.

In the largest reversal of political fortunes ever seen the Democrats were thrown out of office in a Republican tidal-wave. The Republicans now controlled the Congress. So serious was the decline of the Democrats, that all of California went to the Republicans. One of their new Congressmen was former Lt. Commander Richard Nixon who took the seat of a liberal New Dealer that all thought was unbeatable.

Like fellow new Congressman John Kennedy from Massachusetts, Nixon had served in the Navy in the Solomon Islands until 1944. Almost all of the vets from that generation felt it was time for new ideas.

John Kennedy, (also a future president) was the son of wealthy bootlegger and Wall Street speculator Joseph Kennedy. John had been turned down for service by the Army because of a chronically bad back. His father was very active in the Democratic Party, (Ambassador to England), and pulled strings to get John into the Navy where he became the commander of PT109. Hollywood and propaganda has built up the incident in which PT 109 was run over by a Japanese destroyer. In most cases the Officer in command of the fastest and most maneuverable boat in the navy would have been disciplined, especially for having it sunk in that way. But John was given a commendation and the incident was used to promote his political career which was just starting.

As shown in *Fatal Flaws Book 1*, Truman and the Democrats had lost the support of labor and the New Dealers. Those losses weakened them greatly, and a center-piece of the Republican election effort was the linkage of the aggressive spread of communism to the failed policies of FDR and now Truman.

Pres. Truman, his Administration and the Western World had seen what the Russians had done in Eastern Europe, and what they were trying to do in China, Indochina, western Europe, Turkey, Greece and Iran. *During the previous eighteen months that Truman had been in office, from April 45-Nov 46, there had been no ideas or initiatives to stop the communist organism.*

Faced with an incoming hostile Congress and electorate Truman and his Administration had to come up with a way to stop the communist spread.

After his second trip to China, George Marshall had been approved as the next Secretary of State by the post election lame duck Senate. (Truman did not like Byrnes's hard line attitude against the communists.) Marshall took over in the fallout from the midterm election loss. One of his first initiatives in early 1947 was to create a Policy Planning Staff to try to pre-plan for long range issues. **George Kennan** was selected to head that group, which included many well known and traveled civilian administrators such as Paul Nitze.

As shown earlier a flood of Russian refugees hit the West right after the Bolsheviks took over. Many of them were Bolshevik agents, and in 1919 and 1920 *the Palmer Raids* were directed to find them in America. *Thousands of those refugees were interrogated and hundreds of suspects were rightfully deported!* **But not everyone was caught.**

After WWI George Keenan had originally served in the State Department listening post that had been installed in Riga, Latvia. *Their mission for more than a decade had been to keep tabs on the post WWI Bolsheviks.* All of the Western World was at risk for communist subversion, hence the Palmer Raids.

That listening post was closed by FDR in 1933 after he was sworn in. FDR then wrongly reopened the Russian embassies by recognizing Communist Russia.

After the Latvia Post was closed Keenan worked at other diplomatic positions in Europe and spent a total of five years in Moscow as Ambassador. He was a learned man on all things Russian, and had even witnessed the purges of the 1930s. He was deeply suspicious of Stalin and his post-war plans.

Europe

On February 21, 1947 the British sent a secret message to Sec. Marshall.

The two part message detailed a new crisis; the British were almost bankrupt and could no longer support (fight for), the Grecian Monarchy. A second part of the message warned that Greece was also bankrupt and needed an immediate infusion of $240 million dollars with more to follow to have any chance at defeating the growing communist inspired civil war. Turkey also desperately needed aid.

America would have to step in and step up, or both nations would be lost to Russia and that would have dire strategic consequences worldwide.

On the 24th Marshall met with Dean Acheson and George Keenan. His committee had prepared a summery of the situation, and again it was tragically ironic. **During WWII General of the Army George Marshall had successfully fought against all of Winston Churchill's Mediterranean operations, and his actions kept America out of the Balkan region during the war.**

But now that the war was over and the communists had taken control of the region, Marshall was forced to recommend U.S. action far above anything that Churchill had ever wanted or dreamed.

On the 27th Truman and his team met with the incoming Congressional leaders to explain the problems and their thoughts. Marshall spoke of the clear and present danger to the region and to Europe. "No other nation could take up the slack, nor could he say that $400 million would be enough. The choice was between acting with energy, or losing by default". (9)

Acheson added that the Soviets could well break into three continents if Greece and Turkey fell. *The President ended the talk with a dire warning that we were now caught up in a global struggle, between two divergent ways of life.*

He asked Congress to appropriate the money and the authority to send civil and military aid. With these new developments Truman was ending FDR's forlorn and naïve hope for a cooperating world.

(Once again this illustrated the flawed and racist Euro-centrist thinking that colored western governments. The Japanese began to wage war in the Pacific in 1931 with almost no reaction from the West. In 1946 almost no thought was being given to Asia's needs from the war's devastation. That same thinking prevented our leaders from realizing the dire threat to the world should the Communists takeover in China.)

Attempts to finalize a German peace treaty in March 1947 were again met with great trepidation. France wanted no part of a revived Germany. Great Britain wanted to join its German Zone with America's to save money, while the Soviets wanted a strong Central Government, one that was socialist.

The winter of 46/47 had been another brutal one that caused much suffering and death. Almost two years after the fighting, nothing in Germany had been rebuilt.

For the German people starvation had been averted only because of another $450 million in aid from America and England. Life in the rubble centered on mere survival. ("In a gallows humor the Germans rated which zone was best to dwell in; The Russians promised everything but did nothing, America promised nothing but did everything, while the British promised nothing and did less.") (10)

Marshall and his planning staff realized that Germany was so ruined it was possible that the burden of trying to keep them alive could actually bring down all of Western Europe. Because of Europe's severe war devastation its economic and political stability was falling apart. He and many others in our government realized that Germany must be restored for its recovery to commence. Almost all of its needs were being provided by tax dollars from America and England.

Germany was not paying for its defeat in the war, the taxpayers were.

On April 15 Marshall met with Stalin in Moscow to try to break the continuing deadlock over Germany. Stalin spoke with him for an hour, and unknowingly convinced Marshall that the Russians did not want a solution to the problems in Europe.
The worse things became the easier it would be for the communists to win converts.

This Moscow Conference had been yet another failure in the diplomacy between the West and Communism.
But that should not have been a surprise after the failures at Yalta, Potsdam and China.

On April 29, 1947 Sec. Marshall returned home and met with George Keenan to describe his trip. "Europe is a hell of a mess. Something will have to be done".

Marshall was certain the Russians were doing everything possible to allow Europe to collapse. Keenan and his group were directed to produce recommendations on what to do. Meanwhile the Republican led Congress was still debating Truman's foreign aid package for Greece and Turkey. Marshall lamented on how the isolationists in our government could not see that the world had completely changed.
What affected Europe, would soon affect America.

As the days went by the State Dept. continued its investigations of Europe. In mid-May business leader William Clayton returned with a warning that Europe could collapse economically at any time.

During August 1947 Sec. Marshall went to Rio de Janiero to try to arrange a multi-nation defense treaty for Latin America. Initial outlines had begun on the Economic Rescue Plan for Europe, but the Truman Administration had no plan to assist the nations to our south. Marshall was well known to the nations in the America's, having worked hard to get their help in WWII. This time his visit did not succeed, for there would be no American money given to start the defensive and economic pact.

Soon after another attempt at finalizing the peace treaties with Germany and Austria was attempted in London. The ministers were the same as those who had met in Moscow, Sec. Marshall, Russia's Molotov, France's Georges Bidault and Britain's Ernest Bevin. As before, Molotov and the Russians demanded multiple concessions and $10 Billion in reparations before they would agree to any peace with Germany! And the Russians most definitely did not want to pull their troops out of Austria.

They controlled all of the Danube River and its navigation, thus all of the nations on that river were beholden to Russia for trade and food.

In 1941 Russia had been invaded from its neighbors. Stalin insisted it would never happen again, and to make it so those governments would stay communist. Facing that feeling Marshall refused to give any more ground to the Russians. He finally realized that the war-time allies were done.

Marshall met privately with Bidault and later Bevin, and discussed joining their three western zones to make a new and separate Germany. Bevin was worried over the Russian reaction to any attempt to reform Germany. Russia still had large forces in their sector, while the allies had almost none.

Marshall then suggested a possible military association among the former allies. It was to be the initial idea of what would become NATO.

As more time went by a fundamental change occurred within the Administration. The policy that would emerge from "that awakening" would be called *"Containment"*. And the idea was based on the post-WWI French model of *"Cordon Sanitaire"*. (11)

This "novel policy of containment" was the result of an article written by George Keenan. **His strategy would be centered on an economic and military policy that recognized that though the World had to co-exist with communism, it could also try to arrest it.** (Conservatives ridiculed the policy as weak, but what was their alternative?)

This American led effort would involve vast expenditures of money and men. Not a sought after venture to a land that had just demobilized and was enjoying some peace. But the world's problems would not go away, and someone had to guard the far frontier,
"For There Are Tigers in this World". (12)
And They Are Always Watching.

Two major foreign policy decisions would be born, the *Truman Doctrine* of trying to stem the spread of this vile degradation to humanity in Turkey and Greece with economic and military aid, and the *1947 Marshall Plan*, which called for nothing less than the American financed reconstruction of Europe.

Truman's first steps at containment were directed to giving $400 million dollars of aid to Greece and Turkey. His main problem was in trying to convince the isolationist and hostile Republicans that such aid was desperately needed. He had George Marshall and Under Secretary of State Dean Acheson go to the Congress and explain the military and political realities to the Congress. The Congressional leaders became convinced but told the Administration that they had to convince the American people.

Truman and his Administration finally began painting the Russians as a grave danger to the world. "Twice we had tried to avoid the horrors of war, and yet both times we were forced to fight. America can no longer isolate ourselves from the world's problems." (13)
Truman also desired to bring another 200,000 war refugees into our country.

Marshall warned the Congress that if we do not help Europe now, we will have to face dictatorships or police states. Their alarmist measures worked to get the 1947 Truman Doctrine started, and this aid from America bought time for the hardy Greeks and Turks to save their nations.

Initially the communist subversives had been hitting Greece non-stop by going through Yugoslavia and Albania. The Greeks were becoming disheartened because the communists they continuously battled would escape back over the borders to safety and security. *While hiding over the borders of Yugoslavia and Albania the communists would rebuild and resupply. They would reenter Greece only when they were ready.*

Stalin had backed Marshall Tito's earlier claim that the port city of Trieste should be given to Yugoslavia. (Tito had also tried to seize territory from Austria in May-45 but was forced out by the British.) Britain and America refused his latest claim for spoils, and U.S. troops would remained in the Trieste area for nine years.

Unhappy with Russia's weakness, Tito had also watched the trials with Russia along his borders and his neighbors. He decided without any warning to quietly aide Greece's effort, he withdrew his support for the Russian inspired communist rebels. Tito was a smart, tough, self-made entity who even though he had fought with and been trained in Russia, had recognized that the Soviets were not to be trusted.

Yugoslavia would defect from the Soviet sphere in early 1948. Tito decided to form his own Balkan Communist entity, and he refused to allow any insurgent troops or Russian advisors into his country. That greatly reduced the overall communist effort in Greece and helped bring the West's first victory against communism.

(All had seen the takeover of Eastern and Central Europe by Russia. All feared the Russian Bear, and that helped Tito unify the various nationalities existing within Yugoslavia. Unite under him or face the Russians on your own.)

Stalin and the Kremlin were stunned at Tito's move and became resolved to prevent that type of nationalistic idea from reoccurring! Stalin went on a merciless campaign to eliminate any revisionist elements from all communist governments.

(Tito was the only communist ruler who stood up to Russia and survived.)

Stalin used the Tito incident to expand his ongoing post-war purge. Initially anyone who had been captured during the war had been sent to the gulags.

In 1946 he had included all artists, intellectuals, Jews, students, writers and even musicians. After that was over anyone who had had contact with a westerner was suspect. A year later most of the Party officials in Leningrad were executed or imprisoned.

Over 300,000 Crimean Tartars were disappeared, just because.

And the list went on and on.

The second part of the Administration's effort to stop the Communists was the *Marshall Plan*. One of the worst winters in memory had added to the world's graveyards and crushed the will of the struggling European people. The Continent was falling into the abyss.
Winston Churchill would write, *"What is Europe now?*
It is a rubble heap, a charnel house, and a breeding ground of pestilence and hate."

From the work sessions with George Keenan and staff, Sec. of State George Marshall promoted an economic rebuilding plan that provided aid to Europe.

Marshall included the Soviets plus Central and Eastern Europe in the program!

Poland and Czechoslovakia wanted our help, while Russia and most of Eastern Europe "did not". Stalin ordered all of the satellite leaders to refuse the aid, claiming it was a capitalist trick to enslave them.

Incredibly Pres. Truman did not want anything included in the aid package for Nationalist China, even though they were fighting communists!

The Republican led Congress refused to fund the aid for Russia or its satellites, and they insisted that our ally China receive our help.

Marshall who had been primarily involved in Europe during WWII seemed strangely blinded when it came to the threat from Chinese Communists.

One of the requirements for getting aid from this program which Truman named the *Marshall Plan*, was the provision that the nation in need had to list their requirements and assets. No nation liked that provision, as Britain's Foreign Minister Bevin reluctantly relented while France's Bidault complained loudly and often.

Russia's Molotov tried to delay the reconstruction conference with endless talks and "proposed" that Italy and Germany could not take part. His stated purpose was to punish the transgressors who had started the war in Europe.

(Their unstated objective was to allow both nations to collapse into anarchy.)

On July 2, 1947 Russia left the proceedings and the Czechs and Poles were told to withdraw. With the exit of the Communist states Congress worked on passage of the rescue plan. *Averill Harriman would later remark, the Russians could have killed the Marshall Plan had they just joined it.*

Worried by the potential effectiveness of the "Marshall Plan" Stalin responded to the American led efforts by forming the "Communist Information Bureau", or Cominform. (See how Politically Correct they were. Remind you of anybody?)

The **Cominform** and its agents were directed to foment unrest and mobilize labor strikes in France and Italy, the two western nations most in peril. Their actions succeeded in causing multiple problems in those two nations, but their actions backfired.

Alarmed at how quickly the fragile democracies could be destabilized, Truman had the CIA formed. The *Central Intelligence Agency's* mission was to gather all manner of information in an attempt to plan ahead, control and cutoff the communists and their agents.

(America had avoided any foreign entanglements until WWI. At that time Pres. Wilson refused to allow any spying, relying on the intelligence services of other nations, especially Britain and France.) The former OSS leaders and agents were the starting team of the CIA. (But as shown earlier William Donovan was not invited.)

During the earlier time *When the sun never set on the British Empire*, Britain's efficient Foreign Service saw to it that all of the worlds events were under their watchful eyes. The Empire had to be protected and the best way to do so was to *nip any problem in the bud*. For that reason the large Royal Navy was established and stood watch across the globe. In step the Kings Regiments would police the trouble spots with boots on the ground. *But with the British leaving the world stage, America by default would be tasked with those endeavors.*

British Prime Minister Clement Atlee had lamented that change of fortunes in 1946. "The conditions which made it possible to defend an empire across five continents and every ocean was gone. Our empire can no longer take care of itself."

During WWII Great Britain had lost over 1500 ships of all types. *Their nation was almost bankrupt and owed America over six hundred million pounds!* The sum was so vast that most of their administrators doubted it could ever be repaid.

And with those clear dangers Truman also created the National Security Council, (NSC), to look at strategic threats, and had the military reorganized under the Dept. of Defense with James Forrestal as the first Sec-Defense. His hope was that the power brokers in the War Dept. would be streamlined and more efficient than under the old War Dept. (During the war Chief of Staff of the Navy Admiral Ernest King had sardonically stated that the War Department was like the alimentary canal. You feed it well in the front but nothing but crap comes out of the other end.)

Additional talks were held in Paris on the reconstruction from the Marshall Plan. Stalin still forbade any of his puppet rulers from attending the new meetings, while Russian Foreign Minister Molotov dismissed the plan as an attempt at Anglo-American domination of Europe. Undeterred by the Communist leader's words, administrators from Czechoslovakia attended the latest conferences.

On February 23, 1948 the talks to unify the western zones of Germany began.

It was also the day Edward Bene's coalition government in Czechoslovakia was overthrown in the communist coup led by "police and paramilitary committees". Because of those recent events renewed fears of war sprang up in Europe.

The four-part zoning of Germany was to be ended to form one large united country from the English, French and American zones. All of the European countries could feel the hot breath of the Russian Bear close upon them, especially after what had just happened in Bulgaria and Czechoslovakia.

On March 6 the three allies were joined by representatives from Belgium, Luxemburg and the Netherlands to issue a statement calling for the unification of the western zones of Germany. *Less than three years after the end of the brutal war in Europe the Western nations were listening to Gen. Patton's 1945 warning, that you would need the Germans to fight off the Russians.*

(As always Stalin knew in advance of the allies plan. He had told representatives from Yugoslavia that it would happen, and that the

Communists would simply keep their eastern zone and form it into a new communist state.)

On March 10, 1948 Czech Foreign Minister Jan Masaryk "fell" from a window into his courtyard and died during the communist-led takeover.

Within a month the communists had total control of the Czech government too.

Stalin's Machiavellian usurping of power in Czechoslovakia also convinced the U.S. legislators of the dire need for American action. In record time the Marshall Plan was passed in both houses, though the Republican led Congress set strict limits on the U.S. financed reconstruction plan. *British historian H.G. Nicholas realized that he was witnessing a great reversal in American Foreign Policy.*

But the world was still uneasy. On March 16 many newspapers were warning of a war between Russia and America. The next day Pres. Truman appeared before Congress and publicly stated that the Soviet Union was the great obstacle to world peace.

He wanted a return of the military draft, and universal military training for all Americans. Truman warned that the Soviet Union and its agents have taken the independence from the nations of Europe. Tyranny has throughout history assumed many disguises and relied on numerous falsehoods to justify attacks on human freedom.

Communism masquerades as a doctrine of progress, but it is nothing of the kind. It is a movement that denies mankind's right to govern himself or to even believe in God. We must be prepared to meet this danger with calm restraint and judicious action if we are to be successful in having any peace. He ended with a summation, *"We must be prepared to pay the price for peace, or assuredly we will surly pay the price of war."* The mood before his speech was of the victorious postwar outlook.

After his talk it was of a prewar atmosphere. (14)

(Truman wanted the speech to motivate the Congress to finish work on the Marshall Plan, to extend the selective service bill, and for universal military training for all young men over 18. The first two went ahead, unfortunately the third did not.)

On the 21st the Europeans and the U.S. signed a fifty year mutual defensive pact.

This was the precursor agreement to the formation of NATO.

Once again Truman had allowed the idea to progress without any input from the citizens!

Those decisions he was making were a fundamental change to America's isolationist mindset, we were joining into foreign entanglements based on Truman's foreign policy program of Containment.

The Russians retaliated a week later by imposing strict regulations on any allied movement of personnel or goods traveling to West Berlin. (Berlin was 110 miles inside the Soviet zone of Germany.) Naturally the Allies refused to abide by those rules and the tensions increased. And as the days went by the Russians increased the restrictions.

To highlight the dangerous mindset of Stalin, that period of time when America had a monopoly on atomic weapons was actually the time of greatest aggression from Russia's foreign policy.

They were moving forward with rapid "communist development" across all of Eastern Europe, they controlled Manchuria following their attacks in 1945, had supported and supplied the communists in China in their fight to take over, and had just setup a communist state in N. Korea. Russia was still trying to force communism into Greece, Italy and Turkey, and though they were unsuccessful in their attempt to stay in Iran, they were actively assisting the communist movements there and those developing in South America, and Indochina. Stalin was unimpressed with the meager militaries of the West, and sought whatever easy gains he could take.

With no warning on Sept. 23 the head of the Bulgarian opposition party was executed.
The next day Bulgaria became a one party communist state aligned with Moscow.

When Congress passed and funded the Marshall Plan, they stipulated that only $17 Billion could be spent over the following four years.
The anxious people of Europe would only need half the time and less of the money to get themselves on track.

Most of the those who were against the program missed the fact that the majority of the funds that were to be spent in the Marshall Plan were actually spent in the U.S.

The broken nations of Europe purchased vast amounts of American foods, clothing, machinery and building materials, thus providing jobs in America.

Though most of this American aid **was again never paid back**, the returns of unity and friendship came back four-fold.

France would describe the plan as one of the most decisive events in world history.
The London Economist praised the Marshall Plan as "the most generous thing any country has ever done for others".

So effective was this American financed and supervised effort that by 1952 Europe was producing twice as many motor vehicles as they had before the war. Their transportation systems, farming and industrial bases were all restored, as was their morale.

None of the threatened countries of Western Europe turned communist.

And an isolationist nation was now embroiled in world affairs.

(I wonder what Truman would have come up with without George Marshall, George Keenan or Dean Acheson? And why did he interfere in China and then let it fall?)

To insure that the Soviets would understand just how he felt Pres. Truman had the Navy organize and equip the Sixth Task Force. This would be the forerunner of the 6th Fleet that would operate in and keep the Mediterranean Sea safe and the Russians out.

The recently created U.S. Air Force was split off from the Army and had strategic forward airbases situated in friendly Libya, Turkey and Saudi Arabia.

Sec. Def. Forrestal and the forward thinkers in the military had warned that; "Without the vital oil in the Middle East any European recovery will fail."

Such was the world's dependency on this recently exploited energy source.

And as each strategic situation became clearer, America was forced to begin policing the far off frontier with ships and planes and with her sons.

The Strategic Air Command, SAC, had been formed in 1946.

In October 1948 Gen. Curtis LeMay took over, improving training, maintenance, performance and incentives. He also started the unique concept of aerial refueling, where old B-29 bombers were fitted with internal fuel tanks to supply our atomic bomb carrying bombers with fuel in mid-air. That would ensure our bombers could reach Russia.

Latin America

With the increase in world tension, in the spring of 1948 another allied conference was held in Bogota', Columbia in an effort to create a similar multi-nation defense treaty. Secretary of State Marshall warned the ministers that they needed to band together for their mutual protection as had just been done in Europe.

At that time Argentina was still led by the popular Col. Juan Peron.

He had gained power via a coup in 1946, and was quickly destroying his vibrant nation's economy. (This was a common effect with every country that turned socialist or communist.) *During the Latin Defense minister's meeting in Bogota, Peron was busy hosting a revolutionary conference of Latin American students. One of the supportive Cuban students present was*

Fidel Castro Ruz. Peron used the common time frame of the meetings in an effort to show contempt for the current governments of S. America and the Yankees.

During that same time Columbia was undergoing a tough fight with their own communist rebels who were making inroads among the nations eternally poor. While Sec. Marshall was there violence exploded on April 9 when a popular Columbian politician was assassinated. Squads of rebels raced through the under-defended capitol torching building after building. Mobs of thugs which included Fidel Castro were soon roaming the streets attacking all in their path. Not until the following day was order restored. Their lovely capitol city was ruined.

The conference delegates repeatedly asked Marshall to have the U.S. intercede. Marshall refused citing that the events in Bogota were the same as those seen in France and Italy, and must be solved by the nation's themselves.

(Strange that Marshall ignored the fact that American personnel, arms and aid were helping those European nations survive.)

Despite Marshall's refusal to get America directly involved, the delegates approved the reconstitution of the Pan American Union and renamed it the Organization of American States. (OAS) Their stated goal was to settle all disputes peacefully, and to condemn all forms of totalitarian governments.

(Argentina however was becoming a terrible dictatorship under Peron')

None of those former colonial ruled countries had the schooled and trained civil and governmental leaders necessary for running a country. Their occupiers did not want them to be able to make it on their own, so many times the only organized and learned men were in the military. As a result many of these countries would be run by their Generals because their was no one else. But that caused their own problems as the generals ruled because of their military force, not the consent of the ruled.

Middle East

Throughout 1946 violence against British authorities increased as they tried to stop Jewish immigration into Palestine. Hundreds had been killed in bombings, ambushes and outright battles. By 1947 the illegal entry of Jewish refugees flourished undeterred by the British rules and troops. Every month thousands went around the small British quotas, and many thousands of those illegal's were caught and forcibly returned to Europe or to camps on Cyprus. But all the while efforts were being made to create the Jewish homeland from within. Arabs throughout the area wondered why they had to pay for Hitler's crimes. (Conveniently forgetting that the Jews had lived there first and many still lived there as did Christians and others.)

The proposed solution of simply sharing the land was impossible to implement among the growing religious hatred. In Syria the Baa'thist Party had gained many converts, led by Michel 'Aflaq. He was a Syrian who was a Christian, and he dreamed of a single Arab nation across all of the Arab states recapturing the glory of the Ottoman Empire. His movement respected Islamic tenets, but his agenda was secular and socialist. And he was against the western occupiers and all they stood for.

In the U.S. Sec. Marshall and most of the JCS were against any effort to create a Jewish Homeland. Clark Clifford, a long time Democratic advisor argued with Sec. Def. Forrestal over the desired partition. Forrestal was convinced the forty million Arabs in the region would revolt and overrun the area killing everyone. Like the military minds and those in the CIA, he too valued the oil over the unfortunate displaced Jewish people.

Truman however was in favor of partition of Palestine and he instructed our U.N. delegate to support it too. Truman also pressed the British to allow 100,000 DP's to enter Palestine. It would relieve the overcrowded camps and reduce the trials those people faced every day.

Sec. Marshall met with the Foreign minister of the Jewish agency Moshe Shertok on May 8, 1947. Marshall tried to dissuade the Jewish movement with a lecture on the military realities. Shertok was unmoved. The Arab armies of Egypt and Trans-Jordan had been trained by the British. Thus far, the Jewish fighters had won every fight.

The *Haganah*, the Jewish underground army became well equipped and effective in freeing penned up immigrants, sinking British patrol boats and raiding radar and guard stations. Similar to the Vietminh, the Haganah was implementing a low level guerrilla war. They moved up in sophistication and became a guerrilla army, mining roads, blowing up bridges and aircraft, cutting oil deliveries and killing more and more of the British soldiers and Arab fighters who tried to stop them.

The infant United Nations had discussed the many problems there and decided on November 27, 1947 that the best way for peace was to partition the country into Arab and Jewish sectors. (The same plan Britain had proposed years ago.)

This was one of the few times that the Soviets and Americans agreed on anything. Britain abstained from voting, but was for the resolution in the hope that peace could be attained. All of the Arab nations were against the resolution as expected.

With the vote completed and passed the Jewish activists declared the nation of Israel was born in their section of the U.N. partition mandate. And in the strange world of politics Jewish pilots learned to fly from communist instructors in Czechoslovakia, and the Czechs provided major arms supplies to them too.

As the fighting continued Britain decided they could tolerate no more casualties or costs in trying to maintain order. They announced that as of May 14, 1948 they were completely pulling out of Palestine. It was a bitter end to the thirty years of British rule in which they had tried to work with the Arabs, but had created more problems than they solved. (As shown in *Fatal Flaws Book 1*, it was the British and French Colonial Governors that had alienated and usurped the power and daily lives of those in the region. Their failures resulted in the formation of the Muslim Brotherhood and the tensions that followed.)

As the British departed on schedule, Jewish leaders in Tel Aviv announced that the State of Israel was proclaimed. With the next presidential election on the horizon, and hoping to stabilize the area before the fighting broke out, Pres. Harry Truman recognized the new Israeli State, despite the objections of many in his administration.

Truman wrote to Chaim Weizman then the president of Israel, that what the world has tried to give your people is far less than was your due. (The Holocaust.)

Almost one million European DP's wanted to emigrate to Israel in the hope of finding a new life. But among the Arab nations no regional organization existed to help them turn the Arab sector into a nation.

During the many previous centuries the Arabs had lived in Palestine, no Arab nation ever planned for or helped them to become a nation. They were simply a poor people who lived in a territory that was a part of the Ottoman Empire.

The only goal of the Arab League nations was to prevent an Israeli state from existing. Terrorist acts occurred daily, on both sides.

Though the Arab League had taken over the anti-Israeli movement, it took time to organize for war. During the past months their casualties had increased as did the hatred.

As soon as Israel was proclaimed war finally broke out.

Arab fighters had been trained in Syria, and Syrian and Lebanese guerillas were crossing the borders to attack the Jewish settlements in an effort to terrorize the people. Arab Legion artillery in Jordan bombarded Jerusalem, a city that had been predominately Jewish for over a century. In the center of the country fighters from Iraq attacked, and planes from

Egypt bombed Tel Aviv. The Soviets eagerly supplied the Arabs states with weapons to promote the fighting. (Which was probably their plan all along.)

Arabs throughout the Middle East called for a Jihad against the Jews, though infighting among them weakened their efforts. During the yearlong war the killings became savage and each side was guilty of inhuman practices.

Fighters from five Arab nations could not defeat the small Jewish Army, and the U.N. finally brokered an armistice in 1949. Despite their humanitarian efforts, thousands of Palestinians fled from the country resulting in another terrible refugee crisis.

Again the nearby Arab nations took no actions to help those displaced souls.

In fact, Jordan and Egypt annexed the territory that the U.N. had decreed to belong to the Palestinians! Jordan took over the West Bank area which had been the main section for Arab-Palestine, and Egypt took the Gaza area.

In reality the countries of the West did not want large numbers of Jewish refugee/immigrants flooding their shores. Like Truman, they too quickly recognized the new State of Israel in a forlorn hope that the fighting would end over time. The borders created in the U.N. ceasefire became defacto national boundaries. Ceasefires came and went, battles continued to be fought, and Jewish immigration continued despite attempts to stop it. Israel was the first Jewish homeland in 1800 years.

(During and after the war almost one million Jews emigrated to Israel. Only 160,000 Arabs returned, but they became citizens and voted in the national elections.)

All of the Arab rulers who had been in power during the war over Israel's formation would be killed or exiled by dissidents within their countries.
New and more repressive Autocracies were formed.

The only common feature among the new rulers was that all hated Israel.

None of those new rulers worked to improve their own nations or to accept and help the Palestinian refugees that had been created in the war.

Those refugees were used as pawns to continue the status quo.

With everyone fighting the Jews, no one would fight the new rulers.

Europe

On June 7, 1948 the Western Nations of Europe announced the assembly of delegates to draft a constitution that would transform "Trizonia" into an independent and unoccupied West Germany. The powers also announced the creation of a separate currency, the Deutsche mark. That proposal would naturally mean currency reform, and economic competition between the east and west.

The Russians again retaliated, and on June 19, 1948 they closed Berlin's barge, rail and road access. Berlin, located deep inside the Russian zone was now cutoff from all commercial traffic but air. Even the electricity was cutoff. Gen. Lucius Clay the Military Governor wanted to force an armed convoy into Berlin, but the two battalions of troops would have been vaporized by the divisions the Russians had nearby. Using his initiative Clay ordered his air transport units to plan an operation for flying supplies into the city.

Another glaring failure by the Western Powers at Yalta and Potsdam was in not getting concrete guarantees of unlimited access to their rightful sectors of Berlin.

That terrible failure was why the Russians were able to loot everything of value, murder and rape at will, and keep the allies out until they were ready to let us in.

(And if the war on the Western Front been won in August/September 1945 like it could have been, this crisis and the future problems would not have occurred.)

This unexpected situation in Berlin produced another emergency in the capitols of the Western Powers. In Washington the Congress called for immediate evacuation of all non-military personnel. Some of the principals which included Gen. Bradley, the Army Chief of Staff called for the withdrawal from Berlin in total. They felt that militarily we could not stay in Berlin if the Russians surrounded it, not unless we were prepared for WWIII.

Gen. Clay felt that the Russian action was a show a force to instill panic and trick the Allies into the abandonment of Berlin. He and his advisor Robert Murphy warned that the allies had to stay. Should Berlin fall, the new state of Germany would collapse.

"If we intend to defend Europe from communism we have to start here!" (15)

(Berlin itself may not have been significant militarily, but it was vital politically. A pullout by the Western Powers would have weakened any allied efforts at anti-communism worldwide.)

The Allies had to face a grave situation; they could abandon Berlin to the communists or force the issue and risk war. Truman agreed fully with Gen Clay's position, stating that we were going to stay in Berlin, period. Robert Murphy suggested that some of our B-29 bombers be transferred into Europe as a show of force and as a warning to the Russians.

Atomic capable aircraft were soon staged in Britain and Western Germany. All could reach Moscow.

(In its never ending turf war, the Air Force wanted to have control over the atomic weapons. Truman disdained the bomber glamour boys and refused their request.)

Soviet harassment of Berlin continued as they next stopped the city's water supply. On June 24 the Russians completely sealed Berlin off to all land based imports.

On June 25 the first U.S. C-47 cargo planes of the airlift landed at Templehof Airport. Gen. Clay and his staff were joined by USAF Gen. Turner who had commanded the flights over the Burma Hump in WWII. Those Commanders, staffs and crews pulled off a logistical miracle as they organized a non-stop airlift to continually fly in everything including coal. Over two hundred aircraft, (C-47 & C-54s), flew in each day to provide the material needs of the ravaged city. A third airfield was actually built in the French sector by flying everything in to build it!

On April 16, 1949 the airlift brought in a record 13,000 tons of supplies in one day. *The Berlin Airlift would last fifteen months, with over 270,000 flights into the city.* Gen. Clay reported that he could see the spirit and soul of the German people reborn. Sec. Marshall worked to keep the military tension levels down as their efforts at containment had appeared (by July 1948) to have been successful in Greece, Italy, Turkey and France.

(Little however was ever mentioned about the fact that China was falling, though the Republican presidential candidates tried to bring it up.)

Even Josef Stalin knew that had the Soviets attacked the airlift WWIII would have commenced. The only incident involved a Russian fighter plane that buzzed too close to a British transport plane causing a crash. The Russian pilot died along with fourteen on the transport plane. There were no more incidents, though the Russians held air maneuvers over Berlin as a show of force.

USAF Gen. Curtis LeMay had the Air Force Staff organize retaliatory bomber strikes on all of the Russian airfields in Europe as their first attacks in the coming war. With the airfields gone the flyers were directed to savage the Russian formations.

In addition to the Berlin airlift, the Allies also imposed a trade blockade upon Russia and Central Europe. Only Stalin knew how bad his economy was, and the disruption in commerce had a noticeable impact on the inefficient communist economies.

(After the war and our aid ended Stalin issued forced work rules on everyone to try to rebuild his war ravaged nation.)

On May 12th 1949 the Russians reluctantly reopened the roads to Berlin.

In reaction to the success in Berlin, the Federal Republic of Germany was formed.

Pres. Truman and the hard allied stance had saved Berlin, allowed the creation of a free Germany and stopped the bullying effort of the Soviets. It is a sorrowful problem that this vital and incredibly accurate lesson is forgotten by every generation that follows.

The only way to prevent a war is to be so powerful that no nation would dare to attack you.

The reader must also analyze the incredible psychology of this event.

The Western nations that had been Germany's mortal enemy just three years ago were now risking war with the massive Russian Military just to keep this prior enemy free.

I know it is difficult for the later generations to understand these historical events, but this one deserves special attention.

(These examples of the extreme tensions and potential war with the Soviets are ignored or played down in most textbooks as the liberal whitewash of history continues.)

Because of Stalin, tensions between the West and the Communists were at an all time high and remained that way for over a year. Each day the headlines and bylines spoke of the struggle to save Berlin and of how the communists were our new enemy. Sec. Marshall spoke of the struggle at the United Nations in the fall of 1948 highlighting the reign of fear and terror in the communist nations. *(Even so China was allowed to fall.)*

Asia

As the work of our Korean Occupation troops continued into 1947 attempts were made to explain to the Koreans why they needed democracy. The Koreans asked many questions, such as why the Americans refused to have anything to do with the Korean people? Why do the Americans throw Koreans out of their train compartments?

Why do you try to recreate America here?

And most importantly, why do your allies the Russians keep Korea separated?

Within weeks of the demarcation line being established, Communist cadres led by Kim il Sung took over in the North. **Kim had also been trained in Russia**, and he was well schooled in taking control. Military conscription in the North became mandatory.

The hurried disarmament line at the 38th parallel became a de-facto border, and with all of the troubles Truman faced Korea was way down on his list.

That border line became an armed separation and no one was allowed to cross it.

By the summer of 1947 all of the original U.S. troops had rotated out, replaced by another group of disheartened American draftees. The complete chaos that was Korea was gone, but conditions were only a little better. The U.S. Military Government concluded that with the partition it may never be possible to restore the Korean economy.

In the time since the SWINK decision a major problem had come to light. Over 2/3ds of the Korean population lived south of the 38th parallel, but 90% of its resources and industry were north of it, in the Russian Zone. Left to themselves it was possible that in fifty years Korea might have recovered.

But with the Russian factor dividing the nation the situation had already been lost.

By late 1947 Korea could only be rejoined on communist terms.

Stalin and his people used every argument and delaying tactic they could to keep the land separated. The longer it was, the less a chance it ever would be reunited by the West.

Long before the liberals of today thought of "Politically Correct terms", the Communists of the "New World Order" saw the value in those lies of language.

The Russians insisted that Korea had to have a "Democratic Communist Government" for the entire peninsula. Until that day occurred, no Korean or American was allowed across the 38th parallel. As a result the West had no idea what had occurred or what was going on across that line and the Russians refused any cooperative effort between the two Koreas.

They actively fomented economic and political instability as was their usual plan.

Their ploy was to demand incessant conferences and commissions and then make ceaseless claims and demands for givebacks. And when that was over they repeated the process time and again. Soon the U.S. Military Gov. in Korea stopped even trying to work with the Russians. This same blueprint had been used at Tehran, Yalta and Potsdam, and then again with all of the countries of Eastern Europe.

The world had not yet learned that it was impossible to do business with these Communists, except from a position of power.

And so with little fanfare the 1st Domino in Asia had fallen to the communists.

China

In China Communist Commander Gen. Lin Biao sacrificed tens of thousands more of his troops in the attrition battles of 46-47 that followed the "failed peace".

Assisted by the Russians, the Chinese Communists learned how to use artillery and anti-aircraft weapons. They were able to stay even with the Nationalist forces, and their anti-aircraft fire was finally able to shut down Chiang's air-transport system that had worked so well in the initial battles.

And to guarantee their success, the Chinese were also aided by tens of thousands of Communist soldiers from N. Korea who had been rushed into the breech.

(Once the North was turned, a large army was created to insure they remained in power.)

To disperse the Nationalist effort Communist incursions began in other areas of China tying up needed units. Instead of attacking, the Nationalist forces found themselves trying to hold onto their gains inside Manchuria. Losses and fatigue began to whittle down the best of Chiang's forces while the Reds had safe sanctuary in northern Manchuria. Supplies continued to dwindle as Truman had stopped all aid. However the Communists were well supplied by Russia and had shorter and more dependable supply lines.

Mao and the Communists cleverly drew strength from the peasants in the countryside. His forces were taught to respect all civilians, in contrast to Chiang's forces heavy handed tactics. Promising a peoples war, Mao and his followers skillfully attracted the peasants to their cause. *Those who have little in life are easily seduced by the voices that promise change. Only later do they realize the change is renewed slavery to a new master.*

The Communists also motivated their followers to fight a guerrilla war everywhere they could, similar to what the Russian and Yugoslavian partisans had done to Germany when they invaded in 1941. That further depleted the Nationalist forces and used up their supplies as they found themselves fighting all over northern China.

In Washington the Administration was coming under increasing fire from the conservatives who led the China Lobby. They demanded Truman do more to help our failing ally. Marshall had given up on Chiang, and felt that any further aid was a waste. *To hold off his critics, Truman suggested a "fact finding mission".*

It would buy them some time, while postponing any further aid.

However the JCS had been adamant that America had to get into China.

Marshall called upon Gen. Wedemeyer, who in late 1947 was working for the Defense Department. Wedemeyer was still a fervent anti-communist and had serious reservations about any dealings with Russia. For the Administration he was the perfect political choice and scapegoat to head the mission. Wedemeyer was honest and forthright and would give them the real story. It would also silence the critics and buy Truman some time as the next election was coming up.

After his month long mission the general recommended that despite the Nationalist's shortcomings, we had to stand by them. He recommended the United Nations get involved in Manchuria and that America had to come up with a five year plan to save China! (Similar to the Marshall Plan in Europe.)

Gen. Wedemeyer met briefly with Pres. Truman who asked few questions. Later he spent the day with Sec. Marshall giving him the same news. His report was not well received by the Sec. of State, who decided to embargo the report!

Within a month the battlefield reports showed a dire direction in the war in China. Reluctantly Marshall decided to send advisors to Formosa to train the Nationalists.?

Logistic personnel also went to China to help their supply problems, but that was the extent of American military help. Partisan fighting within the Congress further delayed any aid, and by the time it was decided and approved, the Communists had advanced into central China.

By the spring of 1948 Manchuria was lost trapping tens of thousands of Chiang's troops. The loss of almost all of the best of the Nationalist forces enabled the Communists to strike out in a series of crushing blows. Quickly the Nationalist Army began to fold. They continued to lose territories to Mao and the communists, and finally in 1949 the defeated Nationalists fled to Taiwan as the communists claimed the most populous country on earth.

This loss of China to communism was by far Truman's worst mistake.

Six hundred million people were about to be added to the roles of the devil. China is also a huge and strategically placed nation.

With China as an ally the Soviets would have been hemmed in along the Pacific.

With China as a communist enemy all of Asia was now at risk.

The Marxist imperialists of China would continue the exportation of this poison to new areas. They would become a second communist superpower and enemy to America and the West. **Communist China would actively support the Marxist movements in Indo-China, Burma, Malaya and of course Korea!**

Millions would die in the coming wars, with millions more becoming prisoners of Communism. But Pres. Truman and his cabinet were "preoccupied" with the growing communist menace in Europe to give much thought to the calamity they were allowing across the Pacific. And besides, Asia was full of Orientals.

Like most of the Western leaders of that time Truman was Euro-centrist in his thinking and his earlier remarks about stopping the Chinese communists were not backed up with deeds. (Marshall Plan, aid to Greece etc.)

As stated previously, Truman despised Generalissimo Chiang Kai-shek because he was corrupt. A suitable feeling for a common man like Truman, but a short sighted and sanctimonious ideal when one contemplates what would replace Chiang and the Nationalists. This inconsistent ideal became one of the most important factors which prevented Pres. Truman from giving any direct U.S. military assistance to the Nationalists.

(That ridiculous idea of who constitutes a "worthy" leader became a constant and flawed premise that would affect the thinking of every Democratic president who followed. Ironically most of those "Democratic Presidents" were far from being worthy themselves. Their repetitive and critical failures added greatly to the death rolls and dangers all of us would and still face. And the Obama failures are soon to show themselves.)

As stated before most of America's political leaders were indifferent to foreign policy. Because of our isolated nation, almost all of American politics is local or regional. *Most of our politicos have only dealt with other Americans who think and act like them. (Unlike the leaders in Europe or Asia who always had to deal with other nations.)*

By training and inclination our politicians and administrators were unfit for this "New World Order" and America's place in it.
As a result of their failures the second and most important Domino in Asia had fallen.

It is probable that had Chiang won against the communists in China, there would not have been a war in Korea.

The French would have been able to defeat the communists in N. Vietnam with help from the Nationalist Chinese.

And that would have meant that Laos, Cambodia and S. Vietnam would also have avoided war.

Even Tibet would have stayed free.
This was the price for Truman's failure in China, but few know of this truth.

America - More Spies

When FDR created the OSS, Office of Strategic Services, (the forerunner to the CIA) he cautioned his friend Gen. William Donovan not to spy on Russia. It was best if we could work together.

In secret, FDR had released as a gesture of goodwill to Stalin, one Gaik Ovakimyan. He was a productive NKVD agent who had been jailed by the FBI in 1941. Stalin gave his thanks to FDR's naive offer by sending Ovakimyan back to America to run NKVD spying in all of N. America!

William Donovan, Chip Bolen and Ambassador Harriman met in secret at the Lubyanka prison with NKVD Chief Lt. Gen. Paval Fitin, Russian Foreign Minister Molotov and Gaik Ovakimyan on Dec. 27, 1943 to "work out our joint spying".

In reality though the Russians used the meeting to pre-plan inserting their best agents and sympathizers within the OSS! Included among their agents were "secretaries, translators, researchers, managers, economists" and operatives.

Venona Project transcripts placed the numbers of Russian agents installed within the OSS at double figures!

After he took over in April 1945 Pres. Harry Truman was like FDR, warned numerous times about Soviet spies operating here. He too callously dismissed the warnings. By late 1946 (after the previously listed defections had occurred), it had become clear to the FBI and some in the Congress that potentially hundreds of American Communists, (CPUSA) could actually be spies.

(This problem is similar to the predicament we now face with Muslims in the West. Though only a small percentage of them actually pose a threat, the key was and still is in finding who they are. *To accomplish that end proper investigations were and are required. And if the proven method of profiling is needed to separate the threats so be it. As the attacks of September 11, 2001 clearly show, it is better to make a few mistakes arresting the innocent than losing thousands because you did not!*)

This visible rise of the worldwide communist tide was spawning a wakeup call in the halls of power. America's citizens became anxious, and showed it by giving the Republicans an election landslide in November of 1946. *That voter discontent convinced Truman that he needed to act against communism.*

Not until 1947 did he and his Administration began implementing any anti-communist foreign policy actions, (Marshall Plan etc). Everything his Administration proposed was enacted and/or improved by the Republican led Congress.

Those same legislators also demanded that the President address their decade old claim of Communists operating inside the Government itself! Reluctantly Truman signed Executive Order 9835, which required a loyalty check of all two million plus federal employees. *Any derogatory evidence could be grounds for dismissal from their jobs.*

On March 21, 1947 Pres. Truman created the *Loyalty-Security Program,* to head off the "claims of collusion by the other party". All government employees could be investigated by the FBI over their political beliefs. (Truman referred to the "other side" as animals, while Dean Acheson called Republicans the "primitives". In our time the Democrats still refer to anyone who does not agree with them as racists, far-right wing extremists and other derogatory comments. *It is illustrative that the Republicans always seem to be correct.*)

On June 10, 1947 Senate Republican Styles Bridges who headed the Senate Appropriations Committee wrote to Sec. State Marshall complaining on how the State Dept. was not only trying to protect Communist personnel who were in high places, but trying to reduce our security and intelligence protection to nullity.

His letter named nine employees in State who the Senators felt were a "hazard to National Security." Bridges wanted them dismissed as per the new rules, but Marshall refused claiming the State Dept. had already screened them. However on June 27 Marshall suddenly reversed his decision and ten "potential security risks" were dismissed. None had received the required hearing the security ruling required because the damaging information on them was considered highly classified.

That damaging information had come from the FBI.

(Presumably from the prior communist defections and investigations.)

As shown earlier, as the Cold War grew worse, Truman ordered the CIA, (Central Intelligence Agency) be organized on September 18, 1947. *Their mission was to provide all types of information about the world around us, but it's main goal was to keep tabs on the communists.*

In January and February 1948 the House Appropriations Committee directed their own investigation into the State Department. Sec. Marshall reluctantly handed over the files they requested and the Committee exposed dozens of additional potential security risks. Those files were opened to public record, though the names had rightfully been erased. (Innocent until proven guilty.)

This move by the Committee was a deliberate effort to highlight to the public just how many, (600), potential risks were working in the State Department.

How many more security risks worked in other federal agencies?

The next Administration attempt at addressing the public's anger over American Communists led to the 1948 Justice Dept. prosecution of American Communists, (CPUSA), for sedition under the *Alien Registration Act*. That law had been passed in 1940 for all resident aliens to register with the government. It also made it illegal to advocate the overthrow of the U.S. Government.

(During its use at trial 215 communists, anarchists and fascists were prosecuted. The Supreme Court would later throw out the law.)

Republicans in the Congress rightfully wanted to find out who the American Communists actually were. *As our agencies tried to investigate and enact the necessary solutions, it became a huge problem because of liberal intransience and obstruction.* (The same game the Democrats would play with the many Clinton scandals, Obama's hidden past, the IRS scandals, Obamacare, Hillary's E-mail scandal and the attack in Benghazi on our Embassy.)

In the spring of 1948 they Republicans held the Congressional hearings called *HUAC, House Un-American Activities Hearings*. Dozens of people were called in to testify, and during those hearings many Hollywood workers were among those questioned. *Ten* of them refused to say if they were members of the Communist Party in the U.S. (CPUSA). They would be fined, and some imprisoned for failing to cooperate with Congress. *But while the liberal propagandists try to portray the Hearings as a witch hunt, or communist baiting, it was a legal procedure used to answer legitimate concerns.*

Actor Ronald Reagan was a Democrat in 1948, a member of the Screen Actors Guild and many other civic organizations. As was happening all across America, CPUSA members and sympathizers were also members of many civic and social organizations, which included the Screen Actors Guild. In reaction to the Congressional Hearings the hostile leaders of the Screen Actors Guild and other groups called for strikes and wholesale refusals to cooperate. Unafraid to testify, Reagan crossed the striker's picket lines and was physically threatened and verbally abused by his colleagues and sympathizers. Being over six feet tall and in good shape, Reagan was not intimidated by the mob. On the contrary, their repeated threats that he was subjected to stiffened his resolve and he willingly testified before the Congress. He had nothing to hide.

Those same threats also galvanized him to strike back at the ones hostile to him and the investigations that were going on. His hard fought efforts removed many of the communists from the SA Guild, but it also cost him his marriage. Like many of us Ronald Reagan would eventually leave the Democratic Party. He had awoken to their failures.

Whittaker Chambers, *the original communist whistle-blower from 1939 was called in to testify at the HUAC hearings after a decade of being conveniently ignored by the Democrats who had controlled all aspects of our government.*

At that time (1948), Chambers worked for *Time Magazine*, and he again named *Alger Hiss* as a Soviet agent.

As shown earlier, back in 1939 Chambers had originally spoke with Asst. Sec State Adolph Berle who was a member of FDR's "brain trust". Upset with this dire warning about Hiss, Berle reported back to the president. But FDR blew him off and Hiss stayed in FDR's inner circle. **When FDR was planning his strategies for the summit meetings with Stalin, Hiss was at his side.**

Alger Hiss was a polished "Harvard" man, where as Chambers was a rumpled, squalid figure. *The elitist Ivy Leaguers quickly went on the attack.* How dare any mere civilian attack one of their people? To assist the "elites and their efforts" their friends in the media turned against the hearings and Whittaker Chambers. He was profiled as unstable and branded as a homosexual. Truman sanctimoniously denounced the hearings as cheap politics. *To try to stop the investigation Pres. Truman even used the FBI to investigate Chambers!* But the American people of 1948 knew what was right.

A poll showed that 4 out of 5 voters were for the HUAC hearings, and even 71% of registered Democrats favored the hearings! Zero percent of the media did!
(Even back then the mainstream media was against saving our nation.)

On the radio program called Meet the Press, Chambers was publicly vilified. *The media pursued a strategy that is still used by them today, they attack anyone that they are against or who pose a threat to their agenda or ideals.*

Chambers was libeled and maligned repeatedly, and a civil suit against him was started. In an illegal effort to discredit his testimony the Truman Justice Dept. was about to indict him. Lawyers for Hiss attacked Chambers brother and concocted a story of how all of the proceedings was like a book Whittaker had read years before. The liberal claim was that "He was unstable and could not be trusted to tell the truth."

A first term Congressman from California was not snowed by those "elites" or the media. *Richard Nixon* refused to let the matter drop and he continued the investigation.

Nixon had heard from the FBI that Hiss had actually been under suspicions for a decade!

But in all of that time nothing was ever done. He was sure that Pres. Truman was attempting to close off the investigations to keep the truth of Communist operations in America a secret.

Nixon had joined Congressman Mundt to sponsor a bill which would outlaw the CPUSA. FBI's Hoover was actually against the bill because he felt that it would be harder to find the communists if they went underground. Hoover had also testified at the HUAC Committee, but he gave guarded testimony. **Hoover knew of the secret Venona Project, and that spies were operating in the U.S. Government. But he could not publicly say so.**

(Around this same time Democratic Congressman Lyndon Johnson was working hard fixing his senate election in Texas. Johnson was behind the conservative Coke Stevenson in the polls, and knew that if he lost he was finished in politics.)

On Dec 12, 1948 Chambers and two HUAC investigators went out to his farm and retrieved a micro-film that was hidden inside a pumpkin. This was Chambers secret cache that had kept him alive through all of the past years. *The film contained many classified documents from the State Dept and the Navy.*

At least three of the secret documents had come from Hiss's own office typewriter.

The proof of Hiss's spying was delivered to the committee, but even with this damning evidence *Hiss would only be convicted of perjury.*

(Sec. State Dean Acheson illegally backed Alger Hiss right through 1949 by providing secret documents to his lawyers in an effort to bolster the defense.)

Whittaker Chambers, *the one man who had tried to warn the U.S. Government about the threat of communist spies in America in 1939 and again in 1948 would be blacklisted and become virtually unemployable.*

When the decoded Soviet cables of the **Venona Project** were released for publication in 1995, **Alger Hiss** was listed as a Soviet agent. **When FDR was at Yalta handing Poland and Eastern Europe over to their doom, Alger Hiss was at his side feeding the Russians vital information.**

So was presidential aide **Harry Hopkins** who was also on the list.

Hopkins worked behind the scenes to remove anti-communist officials from important posts. He even warned Soviet Ambassador Litvinov that the FBI had bugged his phone lines! Hopkins also tried to get uranium sent to Russia via Lend-Lease aid.

As stated earlier, **Whittaker Chambers** was not the only ex-communist who had come forward. Canadian **Igor Gouzenko** had defected in late 1945. He was quickly followed by Americans **Louis Budenz** and then **Elizabeth Bentley.**

Gouzenko's defection brought down over twenty spies operating in Canada.

Budenz had been a spy and member in the CPUSA and editor of the *Dailey Worker.*

Bentley was used as a courier, and named over 50 agents to the FBI. Because of her testimony, other "defectors" brought out more documents naming names.

Victor Kravchenko was a rare Soviet Officer who had also defected.

In 1946 he published a book called *I Chose Freedom,* an expose of Soviet use of starvation, slave labor and murder, especially in his homeland of Ukraine.

It was Harry Hopkins who tried to have Kravchenko returned to Russia and certain execution. When that failed, the recently married defector "died from a supposed self-inflicted gunshot" in 1948. Kravchenko had just started a new life and family in this country. It is doubtful he would have shot himself.

With those major defections listed above there was no longer any doubt that there was a serious problem of Russian spies operating in America.

But no investigations were started by the 1945-46 Truman Administration or the Democratic run Congress. (Why?)

Not until this Republican effort was any investigation started.

Harry Dexter White was an Assistant Sec. of the Treasury and Sec. Treasury Henry Morgenthau's closest aide. *Like many of the active agents he was able to secure positions for eleven additional spies.* To help his masters in Moscow, White worked tirelessly to increase the friction between Japan and America. It was White who proposed the U.S. demands for Japan to leave Manchuria, and his actions on the pending embargos may have created the impetus for the attack on Pearl Harbor.

In 1945 the Allies were planning on a currency reform to help Germany recover from the war. White passed on copies of the printing plates to the Russians "to help their part of Germany too." The Russians then printed up billions of the reformed currency causing a terrible inflation which naturally hurt Germany's recovery and cost the U.S. taxpayers hundreds of millions of dollars. At the urging of White, Sec. Morgenthau recommended that Germany be turned into a toothless agrarian society, so they could never recover from the war.

Pres. Truman was first warned about White back in 1946, but like FDR he refused to believe the information. Soviet defector Igor Gouzenko had left the Soviet's Canadian Embassy with dozens of documents detailing their spy network. With those papers in hand, the Canadians arrested 22 Soviet agents that week.

White's name was in the documents!

For years FBI director Hoover repeatedly warned Truman and Dean Acheson about White. *The Canadian Prime Minister even flew down to Washington to personally warn Pres. Truman about White! Still Truman refused to believe the information.*

Incredulously Truman promoted Dexter White into the International Monetary Fund to get him away from "the Republican scrutiny".

At the HUAC hearings White continually took the 5th amendment.

Harry Dexter White was also named in the Venona Project.

He died of "heart failure" in 1948.

Frank Coe and **Solomon Alder** were two of White's most important confederates. *They worked tirelessly to stop aid and loans to Nationalist China*, while helping their Soviet masters obtain one for $10 Billion dollars.

Frank Coe had to appear at the HUAC hearings and he too continually pleaded the 5th Amendment when asked if he was a Soviet agent.

Somehow he escaped to Red China!

Until his death Coe worked as a top advisor to the Chinese communists.

Ducan Lee a descendant of Robert E. Lee worked with William Donovan in NYC. Lee had also become the *Chief of Staff in the OSS* under Gen. William Donovan and had access to almost everything Donovan did. Two of the super-secrets he sent to his handlers was the time and date of D-Day, and the atomic work going on at Oak Ridge, Tennessee. Other information he passed along concerned anti-communist Russians that had come forward to work with the OSS.

All were hunted down and killed by the NKVD.

Lee had been identified as a Soviet NKVD agent by ex-spy Elizabeth Bentley.

He too was confirmed in Venona.

Lauchlin Currie was another top White House official and close confidant to FDR. *He was the agent who tried to shut down the Venona Project in late 1944 and then warned the Soviets of the breech.*

Currie was called to testify at the HUAC hearings and like Hiss, had Dean Acheson at his side. Currie was another "Harvard man" and was being protected.

Soon after the hearings Currie fled to Columbia and escaped!

He too was named in Venona.

Laurence Duggan worked in the State Dept. in the S. American section.

He was also called in to testify. After being questioned by the FBI about Alger Hiss, Duggan "fell" from a sixteenth floor window. His death was another improbable suicide that many believe was the work of the NKVD.

The liberals of the day which included Eleanor Roosevelt were crestfallen over his death. *(Acheson had also been defending Duggan at the hearings.)*

Duggan had worked for the Soviets since the mid-30s and had passed hundreds of classified documents to Moscow.

Helen Silvermaster, her husband **Gregory**, and **their son** worked for an active spy ring. When she was questioned in 1947 by the FBI she sanctimoniously claimed that it seemed that all liberals are under suspicion. (Sound familiar.)

Gregory Silvermaster worked in the Board of Economic Warfare and the Treasury Dept. under FDR. He was being paid by Moscow while he worked for Uncle Sam. This family team smuggled out "huge quantities" of data on weapons, aircraft, tanks etc. *Their grade school son was even used as a courier!*

During the hearings White and Currie vouched for the Gregory's!

The family trio were also listed in the decoded Venona cables.
And the Soviets gave Gregory Silvermaster a medal for his fine work.

Owen Lattimore was picked for his Foreign Affairs post by FDR on the recommendation of, **Currie.**

Lattimore was assigned to the Far East Office to work with Chiang Kai-Shek.

It was he who had accompanied Vice President Wallace to China in 1944.

It was his recommendations to Truman to end all aid for Chiang and the Nationalists.

Lattimore later worked at the Institute of Pacific Relations.

*During the HUAC hearings **forty six** of his co-workers had been named as members of the Communist Party, and eight had been active agents!*

Maurice Halperin ran OSS's Latin American Division. His NKVD codename was "Hare".

Franz Neumann ran OSS's German Division. His NKVD codename was "Ruff".

Michael Straight was another personal friend of the Roosevelt's'.

Eleanor Roosevelt got him a job in the State Dept., where he provided the NKVD with armaments reports and promising spy recruits.

Samuel Dickstein was a NY Congressman. His code name was "Crook", and he was paid a lot of money to provide information about fascist groups, and to steer Congressional inquiries away from communists.

Harold Glasser was a confederate of White who also worked on Morgenthau's staff.

His work was so vital that seventy-four of his reports went directly to Josef Stalin.

General Fitin who personally ran the OSS-NKVD pipeline insisted that Glasser be awarded the Order of the Red Star for his service to Russia!

His code name was "Ruble".

Carl Marzani was a secret member of the CPUSA, and yet another NKVD agent who worked in the OSS during the war. Venona decryptions and evidence from Soviet archives proved he too was a valued agent. He wrote a book called *We Can Be Friends* (from his Soviet subsidized company) in an effort to weaken the increasing Cold War rhetoric and give disinformation about why the Cold War had begun. (His book claimed Truman started it.)

Not all of the HUAC hearings were directed at senior governmental officials. Herbert Philbrick was a normal idealistic young American who had been active in civil groups. In his 1952 biography, *I Led Three Lives*, he details the nine years of struggles he found himself in when he realized his Boston civic group was actually a communist spy ring.

In his testimony he shed light on the extensive Soviet Spy Networks operating in the U.S. There were four major networks that he knew of. Each was independent of the other and were well disciplined. His group was subdivided into separate cells, and each was given assignments to assist in undermining our government.

His group and his cell were composed of well educated and affluent people who were active in civil affairs. Cell members were eventually to be the leaders of the CPUSA, and direct the thinking and activities of the party members. Herb's cell was tasked to promote American disarmament, and assist the Soviet Union in anyway possible. *(Stalin feared that war with America could come soon, and he directed all of the western based communist parties to ready themselves and try to split the "old coalitions".)*

In 1948 Philbrick's group and the CPUSA (Communist Party USA), were actively working to help former Vice President Henry Wallace get elected. Wallace's friend and chief advisor was C.B. Baldwin, another secret member of the CPUSA. So was John Abt, John Gates, Eugene Dennis, Al Blumberg and William Foster. During that time they gave talks, printed flyers and worked behind the scenes to promote Wallace and try to stop the Marshall Plan from being implemented. In addition they also provided the Soviets with all manor of information on U.S. Corporations' and economic activity.

Philbrick's testimony highlighted on the secret dealings of the Communists and that they used four types of Front Groups to hide in plain sight.

The first front was the Communist Front in which the CPUSA was directed by longtime Russian master spies. Their training and direction enabled them to remain hidden from view, and only the American citizens were noticed.

The second one was the Coalition Front in which the CPUSA members join up with established civil groups and work to turn their members.

Front number three involved organizations of humanitarian and civil needs. This front gave the appearance of being good citizens trying to help. As always the cell members were to convert any unfortunates to the new cause.

The last Front was organized to using any type of civic group available as a way of building up the members resume of civic organizations. In this way the CPUSA member had access to new faces and targets and was able to join previously unavailable social or civic circles.

In mid-48 Philbrick told the HUAC Committee that the CPUSA was beginning to preach for armed insurrection and revolutionary struggle.

Russia's Cominform had tried to bring about an economic disaster in the West by their subversive activities in France and Italy. Had their plan worked, the Soviets expected another economic depression similar to the 1930s.

They wanted the "workers" to be armed and ready to strike.

On July 20, 1948 a Federal Grand Jury indicted the top 12 leaders of the CPUSA.

As stated earlier in an effort to start damage control the surprised Russians wisely closed up all of the spy rings that could have been compromised by those defections.

All of their people were recalled to prevent any arrests, and no contacts were to be made with any of their turncoat Americans who could be a potential threat. It was more important for them to protect the main agents they still had. And with the war won and the atomic secrets stolen, there was no need to continue such dangerous operations. *Ironically by the time the HUAC hearings begun the Russian spy networks had closed down.*

Truman and his Administration tried to stop the Republican led effort. In 1950 the House and Senate had to override Truman's veto of the McCarran Act. That law imposed restrictions against communists who were in sensitive positions, required registration of all those groups and individuals, and forbid entry into the U.S. of any such person. *Yet the Democrats were against the law.(??)*

The next U.S. presidential election of November 1948 was fast approaching. The Republicans had re-nominated Thomas Dewey, who had done well against FDR in 1944. (One of the unstated reasons the Democrats needed the dying FDR to run back in 1944 was the serious threat Dewey posed to their party and continued control of the White House. Other than Wallace there were no big name Democrats who could have run and won against Dewey.)

This time the Democrats were being torn apart as many did not want Truman to run. As stated earlier Truman gave quick recognition to Israel, and was urging the desegregation of the U.S. military. Both moves went against many in his Administration and the Democratic Party. Labor was still against him for what he had done during the railroad strikes in 1946, and the liberal side of the party was throwing their support behind former Vice-President Henry Wallace and his Progressive Party.

Henry Wallace had been a long time New Dealer and a longtime leftist. *Even in 1940 he had promoted the idea that the radical left was the political wave of the future.* As the Sec. of Agriculture he pushed for U.S. support for the leftist radicals in Latin America, to stay on the political forefront.

Wallace was also a longtime Soviet sympathizer and had pledged more cooperation with Russia. His idol was Russian emigr`e and theosophist Nicholas Roerich, a communist conman. As shown in *Fatal Flaws Book 1* Wallace had gone to Russia in May 1944 visiting 22 Siberian cities. The NKVD setup elaborate hoaxes to fool Wallace into thinking the Gulags were simply workers camps. Wallace accepted all of the Soviet lies and propaganda that everything there was wonderful. His passion for the Russians became a warning sign that worried many in the Democratic Party. *Wallace also wanted an alliance between the Democrats, the CPUSA and Socialists so they could continue FDR's expanding welfare state and have peace with the Russians.*

In reaction to his actions and beliefs the Democratic party leaders removed Wallace from the 1944 presidential ticket and replaced him with party faithful Harry Truman. If not for that one decision, America would have been run from Moscow in 1945!

(After FDR won in 1944 Wallace was moved over to run the Commerce Department. He was fired by Truman on September 20, 1946 for his public advocacy of conciliation towards the Soviets. This episode hopefully highlights just how fragile our security really is.)

With the recent Congressional hearings on Russian spies and the many communist subversions occurring across the globe Wallace was out of touch with the nation's political reality. As stated above the CPUSA was actively helping his election as a way to destroy America from within. *Wallace told his supporters that if he was elected, Laurence Duggan would be his Sec. State and Harry Dexter White his Sec. Treasury!*

The conservative Southern Democrats were seething over Truman's recent Civil Rights stance. Many of those delegates walked out and formed the Dixiecrat Party.

The Dixiecrats then nominated a segregationist for president.

This multi-candidate ticket promised to erode the support for Truman, and hand the election to Dewey.

As such, Dewey's campaign believed in their polls and ran a quiet race that took no risks, offered no surprises, didn't say anything controversial and didn't antagonize anyone. When Truman went to sleep on election night even the head of the Secret Service left for NYC to stay with Dewey.

But the next morning it appeared as if Truman had pulled off the greatest upset in our political history. No one in radio, the news or in politics had thought Harry could win. Truman had made a last minute train tour of the country stopping everywhere.

He even implied that Dewey was supported by Nazi's. (But as shown in *Fatal Flaws Book 1, Truman's 1934 Senate election had been fixed.* Was something done here?)

Elated over his victory Truman got in a few licks at his detractors.

But it was a hollow victory as the mistakes he made in his first term would come back ten-fold. **The next day Sec. of State George Marshall was told "he was retiring".**

With all of the scrutiny and admissions from the HUAC hearings it is hard to understand how Truman was re-elected in November 1948. Incredulously the Democrats also took back the Congress. The Republicans had erroneously waited until 1948 to start their investigations. They were incomplete by the time of the election in November.

Once the Democrats got back into power in January 1949 all of the hearings on Communist agents in the U.S. were conveniently stopped.

Russia and Europe

As 1949 began Stalin and his cronies were continuing to torment all who crossed their path. Over 43,000 Latvians were herded onto trains bound for Siberia. They would join the 5,000,000 plus who were recently imprisoned for slights as small as complaining about waiting in line to buy food. (A common and recurring issue.) All of those souls were used as slave labor in Siberia or Central Asia, far from prying eyes. Most worked until the day they died.

Victor Kravchenko's book, *I Chose Freedom* was being highlighted in a trial against the Soviets and Communism. Testimony from multiple sources had ended the shroud of secrecy that covered communism. Their crimes against humanity could no longer be denied. But still thousands of foolish minds ignored the truth and continued their spying on the West.

On April 4, 1949 the Washington Treaty was signed and NATO officially began. America was now allied with Canada, Great Britain, Norway, Iceland, France, Italy, Denmark, Belgium, Portugal, Luxemburg and the Netherlands. Germany was no longer the feared enemy, Russia and the communists were.

This large number of nations allowed for allied air bases to ring the communist Soviet Empire, and gave the allied navies unhindered access to ports all over Europe.

(This was the first peace time defense treaty ever signed by America.)

One of the reasons this military/political organization came about was a reaction to the communist takeover of Czechoslovakia mentioned earlier. Armed forces from the member nations were formed into a common force under a joint command.

Their purpose was committing all of the signatories to fight the Soviets should the Russians or their satellites attack one of the member nations. This treaty was exactly like the prior pacts of mutual defense that led to WWI.

But in the time of the late 1940s there was no one nation that could face the massed Soviet forces alone. Even though the Soviet land army had been reduced, it was believed to be over 2.5 million strong with almost half of them stationed in or near Eastern Europe. NATO planners also had to add in the troops from the Eastern European countries too. All of those units were trained in the Russian army model and supplied with Russian weapon systems. (Large formations of artillery and tanks.)

Against this steamroller the NATO nations could muster just sixteen divisions stationed in Britain, Italy, Germany, Austria, France and the low countries.

Because of the rapid demobilization and the following budget assaults on the military the U.S. units were under strength, poorly equipped and poorly trained. Most of the U.S. Divisions did not have good leadership as the changes enacted in the post-war Army first by General Eisenhower and then by Bradley had eliminated many of the true fighters. More and more of the senior officers were simply staff and support managers who were trained in the Marshall system "to work together".

Our weakened Navy was faced with multiple tasks in NATO such as resupply, convoys and patrolling/protecting the sea lanes. But it too was critically under-strength having been decimated in the post-war demobilization. *Most of our remaining naval assets were centered on the Atlantic and the Mediterranean as part of NATO.*

Our allies fared even worse.

The British as already noted were collapsing financially, and could only afford a limited number of military units. Forces from Holland and Belgium were considered as practically useless in conventional fighting. And the French forces were overcommitted in fighting their many wars as they tried to hold on to their colonies.

(A lot of the Marshall Plan aid was diverted by them to fight those wars.)

Scandinavia and Denmark wanted to remain neutral and committed little to the defensive efforts.

Those problems were a primary reason the senior U.S. planners wanted to rebuild and rearm Germany. All knew that they were good fighters. However most of the Europeans were loathe to see Germany rearmed, though secretly all realized that without them it would be impossible to fight off the Russians. And no one knew what reaction would be had in Russia should Germany rearm.

Among many in high positions it was felt that the Russians could reach the English Channel in two weeks. Under Secretary of State Robert Lovett stated,

"All the Russians need to reach the Rhine is a sturdy set of shoes."

Winston Churchill succinctly warned that the only thing that kept the Russians from the English Channel were the American atomic bombs. (That was true.)

In reaction to the blatant conventional military weakness in NATO the original planners were prepared to rely upon tactical atomic weapons against the forward enemy units. If for some reason the Russians continued attacking the planners would then send bomber formations to destroy Russia's cities.

This tragic but essential planning for atomic war in Europe would by necessity result in the destruction of large areas of the continent. And that fact fueled the "Better Red than Dead" mindset that became prevalent in post-war Europe.

In Germany the dark joke was that the Allies intended to fight WWIII to the last German.

(In trying to "contain Soviet Communism" President Truman and the U.S. policy makers had to make nice with all of the remaining free countries, no matter who was in charge or what they were doing. This included many less than perfect despots and dictators, as long as they were anti-communist. But that alignment would eventually come back to haunt us.)

After the war France's economy was in awful shape with food and jobs scarce. The French communist party had 900,000 dues paying members and was well schooled in playing on the people's anger and fear. After the war Stalin expected another depression to come on as had happened after WWI. He directed the Communist Party members in France and Italy to keep a low profile and not antagonize England of America.

But no economic depression occurred, and in 1948 Moscow had directed their cadres to foment strikes and a general uprising. Industrial sabotage, train derailments and violence ensued. Troops had to be called out for security, but more importantly the people of France realized that the communists were crippling the nation in order to take over. In a stunning backlash on election day, the French voters gave de Gaulle's anti-communist party their votes. *Violence and strife began to decline and France was renewed with the incoming aid from the Marshall Plan.*

Given some time, their economy began to restore. (Stalin remarked after their political efforts had failed, "The only reason France is not now a communist state is because our armies had not reached her.")

Italy was going through the same scenario, as their communists tried to push for power. Realizing that they had to act fast to counter the Marshall Plan, the Italian communists rushed their plots forward and were again seen as the enemy.

In the 1948 Italian elections the communists were also voted out as the Christian Democrats and the Catholic Church, (helped by U.S. funds), won a landslide victory.

Italy too began to recover.

In Greece the communists had not given up from the early battles with the British in the 1945 attempted coup or after their "Civil War" began in 46. They fought on right through 1948, and only the aid from the Truman Doctrine kept the communists at bay.

They followed Stalin's philosophy that in chaos there is opportunity, and those power hungry ideologists would continue to fight for control until

1949 when they were finally defeated. An additional 160,000 Greeks were killed during the post-war strife. U.S. aid under the Truman Doctrine (and the loss of Tito's support), enabled the country to restore order and stability. *Greece also remained free.*

(Sadly the surviving Greek government became more like a military dictatorship than a democracy, but that was what was required to defeat the communists and their sympathizers.)

Unfortunately the Western powers and leaders, especially those in the U.S., drew the wrong conclusions from those initial victories. They thought that sending money and some local fighting could stop the communists. The more important lesson was missed. **Communism could not come to power in a previously free country where it had not "turned the population to its cause".**

Eastern Europe had been "liberated" by the Russian Armies, which was the same as having been invaded by them. They were lost because the Russians had the time and capability to "turn them".

The communist efforts in Greece, Turkey, Italy and France were still in the early stages when the West, (U.S.) interfered. Awash with American money, material aid, and some fighting, those countries were able to turn away from communism and remain free.

But in Asia that vital lesson went unnoticed. Except for the imperialistic fixation of the Europeans in regaining their colonies, the Western World especially America turned away from most of Asia after the war ended. *Because of Truman's policies the Communists were given the time and access they needed to win in China.* As time went by "turning the population" to his side was exactly what Mao and his communists were doing in China, and what Ho Chi Minh was doing in Northern Vietnam. To accomplish their "golden rule" the communists needed *unhindered access and time* to "convince the people" that communism was the way. Then the "communist magic" was wielded over the captive populations and they were turned. Or else they were eliminated.

Nations that were physically cutoff and / or isolated from the West and their aid were all coerced into communism, such as those in Eastern Europe, China and North Korea.

Even Australia was falling under the communist spell. Working through socialist groups and the trade unions, the communists began exerting great influence on the Australian Labor Party. Their communists needed to hide their work under the guise of innocent sounding groups, because Australia like America was a conservative nation. (France, Italy, Spain and some other nations that were more liberalized, and their communist parties operated out in the open. They sought open alliances with the labor unions and political parties.)

By 1945 the CPA, Communist Party of Australia had over 20,000 members.

All during 45-48 Moscow was covertly obtaining dozens of crucial documents from spies within their Foreign Ministry. It was later revealed that numerous Soviet spies worked for Herbert Evatt the Australian Foreign Minister from that time.

They almost succeeded in crippling the nation.

Asia

The old colonial powers had profited greatly from their empires of unfortunate peoples. In Asia, Britain and the Netherlands had had the largest holdings by far, with France grabbing Indochina. But since fellow Asian Japan had forced all of them out in record time, those hardy people had had enough of their slavery, and began to rebel.

Some of the rebellions were based on religious influences, some from communist partisans who now desired their own power, but most were from indigenous people lusting for freedom. The returning Europeans conceitedly wrote off all of these movements, particularly the French. They misjudged the strengths of their foes and overvalued themselves in the typical and monumental arrogance of the colonial mindset.

As stated before, in Burma the British quickly realized their shortcomings and granted them independence in 1948 along with Ceylon, (Sri Lanka).

They had also wanted to shed Malaya in 1948 but were faced with a growing communist insurgency that was being aided from China. The factions that had wanted to take over and run the country were facing a determined communist insurgency. Hundreds of their people had died already, and the road ahead promised more suffering.

Malaya had never known a history as an independent country. It was a collection of twelve states that had been held together by the British Colonial rulers. Their rich land stretched south from Thailand and included the island city of Singapore. Three main populations predominated, Chinese, Malay and Indian, and all were at odds with the others. Thus the communists found fertile ground to foment their revolution. *To their credit the British did not cut and run.*

They stayed and successfully fought the communists for nine years.

Fatal Flaws | 91

Because they had been involved in the country for so long they understood what they were up against. In combating the rebels the British used small infantry units.

Sir Robert Thompson led the British-Malay anti-communist effort.

Their committed and eventually victorious effort was predicated on separating the communists from their suppliers among the populace, and in getting to know the area intimately. Thompson instituted a *Strategic Hamlet Program* in which the villagers were protected behind defenses and barbed wire. If the communist insurgents wanted to interact with the people they had to face armed forces. Over the years of their deployment the British infantry and SAS commandos knew who belonged in an area and who did not.

The latter were killed.

Thanks to their unswerving and focused effort Malaya would become a vibrant, stable country and has continued to prosper.

(The communists were never given the chance to "turn the population".)

In keeping with our original plan for freedom, on July 4, 1946 the United States granted the Philippines their independence. Manuel Roxas became the first president of the independent Philippines. But even with this milestone discontent still raged.

A guerilla war began with the Hukbalahaps, a leftist/communist movement that saw a chance to take over. The Filipino government with help from the CIA was forced to fight a multi-year battle against these communist insurgents. The hundreds of islands that constituted the Philippines proved ideal in hiding this new enemy.

(And this geography would become a perfect breeding ground for the next enemy of free nations, the Muslim Extremists of Abu Zayef.)

On August 17, 1945 while Japanese troops still occupied Djakarta, Indonesian nationalist leader Raden Sukarno announced that "We the people of Indonesia declare our independence". Merdeka, (Freedom) was their call and spoken as a greeting with one hand raised the fingers spread apart. For more than 300 years the Dutch had controlled this immense archipelago.

Upon the end of the fighting against Japan they too pompously "assumed" their colonial control would be reinstated. The imperious Dutch asked the British forces under Mountbatten to "hold European order" until their forces could get back there.

(Due to their rapid defeats on land and at sea the Dutch had almost no military left.)

Sukarno worked to organize the people into forming a stable government that would be able to "stand up" to the returning Dutch. He also tried to maintain control of the multiple freedom factions, some of whom wanted a civil war.

In November 1945 heavy fighting finally broke out at Surabaya and it took the British three bloody weeks to restore order. Stunned by the will of these people, the British authorities pressed the Dutch to negotiate a settlement. However the arrogant Dutch refused and they returned in force armed to the teeth with U.S. made weapons.

Though the Dutch tried to return to their former time of a police state, the Indonesians resisted fiercely and a "treaty arrangement" was finally made. As in Indochina, the treaty was just a lie as the Dutch tried to reinstate their control over the lands. The Indonesian people justifiably fought their oppressors and even practiced a scorched earth policy rather than have the Dutch get anything.

Communist agents had been active throughout the decade of the 40s, and with the defeat of Japan they had eagerly helped the Indonesian Republicans in their quest for freedom. Naturally the communist insurgents joined the fighting in the hope that they could gain from the continued losses to the other two sides. (For in chaos there is always profit.)

In 1947 the U.N. tried to broker a peace, but again it proved futile. Then the communists rebelled openly, fearing that the nation would slip from their grasp.

Their insurgency was poorly planned and was not welcomed by the people. The Republican-Nationalists quickly fought back and captured or killed every communist that was known. Their civil war continued for more than a year.

Finally on December 27, 1949 the Dutch turned sovereignty over to the *Republic of the United States of Indonesia*. President Sukarno and his nation rejoiced in a sea of people, yelling, "We are free"!

(America was and is the hallmark for freedom to the world, and let none doubt how our country has benefited the world.)

In India their people had demanded and worked for twenty years to become free. They had been led by Mahatma Gandhi and his non-violent protests. Their efforts were finally rewarded as the British rule ended in 1947. But the country faced partition and savage communal riots as the nations 250 million Hindu's clashed with the 90 million Muslims and 6 million Sikhs. Lord Mountbatten was directed to come up with a solution.

Consulting with Nehru, Mohammed Jinnah and Ghandi, Mountbatten recommended the great nation of India would have to be partitioned. He saw no way to negotiate a compromise.

Sectional fighting began when the Muslim leader Ali Jinnah demanded a separate state, to be called Pakistan. To Prime Minister Nehru and the Hindus this would be a sacrilege to their sacred homeland. Fighting and murders intensified until Nehru reluctantly gave in. Two Muslim states 1000 miles apart were allowed to break off, Pakistan and East Pakistan. (E Pakistan-Bengal would later be renamed Bangladesh.)

Two other provinces that were of mixed populations, Punjab and Bengal would be arbitrarily divided between them, (similar to what was tried in Palestine). Like Palestine, peace was never obtained.

In the northern province of Kashmir the ruling Maharajah refused to join either nation. War again broke out as the troops from Pakistan fought their former brothers from India. A U.N. ceasefire could not end the strife there either.

The infighting continues to this day.

Bloody cross-migrations ensued throughout the region as each religious group sought safety among their own. By 1948 when the fighting and relocation process had ended over a million people had died, and over 16 million had been relocated. Even with their separation those nations still harbor deep resentments.

Thousands of miles away in Korea still more problems simmered and never seemed to end. *The U.S. Military and Government leaders wanted to leave Korea far behind.* It was nothing but a stinking rat-hole. Gen. Douglas MacArthur, Commander of our Far East Forces had been responsible for the disarmament of Japan and her reconstruction, as well as those in NE Asia. His efforts in Japan were inspired, while in Korea the effort was marginal.

South Korea was only slowly returning to life.

The JCS had done a military assessment on Korea and realized that it would take hundreds of millions of dollars to restore the nation. Russia still would not assist any of the post-war rebuilding efforts, and in reality they wanted the status quo.

Those leaders also knew that if war returned to Europe, any forces we had in Korea would be tied up and wasted.

According to those senior leaders we had "No strategic need of Korea."

Eisenhower and most of the Army leaders felt our troops needed to be redeployed even though it could look like American was withdrawing from Korea.

Many were aware that if the U.S. simply abandoned Korea to its fate, Japan might fall to the communist siren, but all eyes were fixed on Europe. Sec. State Dean Acheson had replaced George Marshall after "his sudden retirement", and he too viewed the world from a European mindset. Asia had nothing worth fighting for.

Even after having lost China to the communists, Truman and now Acheson were about to give another nation away. Seeing no way out of this political quagmire in Asia, Pres. Truman turned to the United Nations. He felt the unyielding problems of Korea should be "turned over to them".

Harry Truman whose mantra was "The Buck Stops Here," had just passed the buck.

The United Nations leaders jumped at a chance to promote a peaceful settlement. Korea became a United Nations ward with a U.N. mandate over the divided nation.

On the surface it looked to be a good paper solution, but between the lines it was still an American withdrawal. The U.S. had handed the ball off to the United Nations which had no army, it had nothing but words.

With the communist menace still fomenting trouble in Greece, Italy, Turkey, Iran, Albania, Indochina and China, all U.S. forces still in uniform began to be redeployed to Europe. And so the 45,000 U.S. troops that had been working in *Chosun* were needed elsewhere. Within the year they would be gone.

Only two hundred advisors were left to create South Korea's defense force.

Political organizations slowly began to take shape in Korea. Most were fringe movements, but the conservative group led by the just returned Dr. Syngman Rhee seemed to be consolidating power. The choices available to the people were not akin to Rhee, or a middle of the road party. It was turning into a clear choice between the communist left and the conservative right.

Rhee was an acceptable conservative who held a doctorate from Princeton. (He had studied there when Woodrow Wilson had been the president at the college.)

In 1944 he succinctly warned the State Dept. that America's only hope of avoiding war with Russia was to install Democracy everywhere they could!

Above the 38th parallel the Russian installation of the Communist Regime of Kim Il Sung had been completed. *Like Ho Chi Minh, Kim had gone to Russia during the 1920's and been trained in the fine art of communist power.* His rule was absolute and brutal.

During 1948 the newly formed United Nations tried to enter into the communist ruled and sealed off North to supervise their "required elections". They were refused entry.

In a no surprise ending, Kim was "elected" in a landslide. Despair quickly set in at the U.N. and in South Korea over the closed door policy in effect in the North.

The nation and its people had been separated by a piece of paper framed in the rush at SWINK. It seemed for all intents and purposes that the separation had become permanent. And no one in the West would advocate any action to end the stalemate.

Stalin was pleased.

The U.N. had also proposed and supervised the free elections in the south. When the final count was in, the conservatives under Rhee had won.

Naturally Russia protested the outcome at each U.N. forum and proceeding.

When all was said and done the Republic of Korea was established in the south.

Russia then recognized the "Korean Democratic People's Republic" in the north under Kim Il Sung. The conquest was completed and not a shot had been fired.

(As stated earlier, N. Korea was the first domino in Asia.)

In Asia only Japan remained above the communist fray as 450,000 U.S. troops initially stayed on in occupation duties. Gen. Douglas MacArthur had been left in command in the Pacific, and *he shrewdly* ensured that the Japanese Emperor would stay in power. This one act convinced the Japanese people of the friendly peace they had made and they obediently complied with Mac's disarmament and reconstruction demands. (MacArthur had ordered that any GI who even slapped a Japanese citizen would get five years in prison!)

The Japanese shared America's passion for baseball, and it became a common sight to see friendly games played between such bitter enemies.

Prewar Japan had been Asia's most industrialized nation, partly due to the adaptability of their people, and partly because they had not been placed under the colonial yoke like most of Asia. They had been the masters in Korea and Manchuria.

After WWII ended, Japan like Germany was shattered.

All of her cities, ports and industries were in ruins. The country's transportation systems had to be rebuilt and farm production renewed.

The devastated nation required $400 million a year in U.S. aid to remain viable.

But their people were highly motivated to rebuild, and with their homogenous population everyone worked for the common good.

(One of the understated problems in America is that we are a nation of a hundred nationalities. Common ground is found only when a catastrophe strikes or there is a common danger. Other than that America is always at war with itself.)

Japan's textile industry had been the prewar star of its industries, and with U.S. help was the first to recover. With assistance from MacArthur's staff, the Japanese Diet, (Congress), passed farm reform measures that gave the land to those who farmed it. Harvests quickly increased and food became plentiful.

Protected from aggression by the U.S. forces, Japan could devote all of its revenue, resources and energy to rebuilding. By 1952 Japan was producing and exporting autos. **By 1954 no further U.S. aid was needed as Japan's GDP and personal income had recovered to prewar figures.** (That is how you win the peace.)

After four years of watching the growing menace of communism initially in Manchuria and North Korea and then in China, Gen. MacArthur was asked at a press conference about our security concerns in Asia. He made a short public statement saying that, *"The Pacific is now an Anglo-Saxon lake. Our line of Defense runs from the Philippines to the Ryukyu archipelago, through Japan to the Aleutians Islands and Alaska.* **For some reason he did not mention Formosa or Korea.**

The article appeared in the New York Times on March 12, 1949.
(Like so many innocuous decisions this one would have a far reaching impact.)

As the threat of confrontation with Russia was increasing the West either had to ease the tension by giving up, or re-arm and prepare for the coming storm.

In Europe the West began to organize for the storm with the creation of NATO.

Asia, well it was full of Asians.

Stalin was not unhappy with recent events as Communism was gaining in many areas, especially Asia. He had once asked a diplomat how many divisions did the Pope have? The answer was NONE. (A clear warning of how Stalin's mind worked.)

He knew that the U.N. had no military forces of their own. With the power of a veto in the Security Council the Soviets could shut down any potential U.N. action.

NATO was militarily weak and so were all of the countries in the West. It would soon be time to test the waters.

America

In the U.S. Pres. Truman and many of our military leaders clung to the belief that since only we had the "bomb" any Soviet led war would mean massive destruction to Russia. As a follow up to this reasoning only the budget for the newly created U.S. Air Force was increased. Led by the "Bomber Generals", in the same way the Navy had been led by the "Gun Admirals", the Air Force was organized for having large forces of strategic bombers. Their parochial thoughts were based on their incredibly flawed presumption, "That the bomber commands had won WWII".

Thus all that was needed to beat the Soviets were large numbers of bombers.

Little attention was directed to having a balanced Air Force of fighters, fighter-bombers and heavy bombers. So extreme was their self-delusion the senior Air Force commanders actually wanted the navy to be disbanded!

They truly felt that "squadrons of bombers could control every situation. (Since the atomic weapons remained large, only their bombers could deliver them.)

But their irrational line of thinking went against the proven premise of a balanced military machine.

Gen. Doolittle who had been given the Medal of Honor for flying the mission over Japan in 1942, and was their trademark spokesman. He led their absurd claim that the Air Forces had won the wars. As tough as that one mission was, it was flown by over a hundred airmen, yet he was the only one to get that award. It is hard to understand how someone who was awarded a medal for one mission carried more weight in the realm of ideas than those who had fought for years in direct combat.

After the total disarmament of the U.S. Military the services were floundering. Severe budget cuts had been enacted stripping them of most of their funding.

By late 1946 the Navy could barely keep its few remaining ships at sea! The Army had been cut to the bone, and training was virtually stopped because "we had the bomb."

In addition to the new Air Force, the 1948 U.S. Armed Forces Unification Act had created a new position, Chairman of the Joint Chiefs of Staff. Gen. Eisenhower was the first chairman and he readily agreed with Truman's stated position that the U.S. Marine Corps was to be kept at minimum levels and was to be an adjunct of the fleet only.

No Marine Corps unit was to be larger than a regiment, and total strength was to be kept below 50,000. This was 1/10 of the Marines WWII peak.

At that time each military service was trying to survive the budget chainsaw, so no one would speak up for the USMC. The Marine Corps senior leaders struggled through their restricted budgets and looked to the problems America would face in the next possible war. They ran experiments with helicopters, improved their close-in air support tactics and designed a force in readiness concept.

As the cuts in manpower worsened the Corps was required to maintain a well trained *reserve force* as the only way to man its units in the event of a war.

Due to the hatchet job done to the Marines, only the very best of the mid-level and senior leaders and commanders were kept on. Proven war veterans like Generals Harris, Shepperd and Oliver Smith ran constant war problems and brain storming sessions.

Their forward thinking would save the day in Korea.

But you will never read that in the history books.

(The out of touch Democrats had missed a major political sore point in the homefront of 1946 and again in 1949. By a margin of 3-1 the citizens would rather have a strong military than the weak one Truman had created. They also preferred the military over spending programs like the Marshall Plan.)

Another terrible failure that was forced onto our nation and its Army was enacted by the political leaders who convened the *Doolitle Board*. The board was headed by USAF General James Doolittle, and it was convened after the war to examine the Army's caste system. This *Doolittle Board* examined the rank structure of the Army as a "right", that all were equal. The members examined 100 written complaints that the Army was too tough on its soldiers. In typical foolish liberal style this board determined that the present Military Rank system was too "hard", for the soft American kids to deal with. Military discipline and punishments were reduced and the power of the unit leaders was greatly restricted.

Payback for this absurdity was to increase by a factor of 20, the number of headstones America would soon build.

Communist Advances

In the summer of 1949 evidence was gathered that the Russians had exploded their own Atomic bomb, shaking the West to its core.
Scientists and the politicians had felt it would be years before the Soviets could get an Atomic bomb. Our security and planning had rested on that simple fact.

U.S. Gen. Leslie Groves who had run the Manhattan Project had boasted that the Russians were fifteen years from producing a bomb.

(All those years of work by the dozens of discovered Soviet agents had been "conveniently ignored".)

As soon as the stolen information landed in Russia, Stalin had directed a crash program to build their atomic bomb based on the American effort. Over 37,000 prisoners had been used to begin the project deep in Siberia! They built the infrastructure to begin the program and hundreds of imprisoned scientists were told to get to work. Their "efforts" quickly paid off, for in December 1946 the Russians achieved their first atomic chain reaction.

Truman's public announcement of a Russian bomb caused an uproar in political and military circles. *Fear now ruled, with the outcome being an arms race and the realization that a real Cold War had begun between the previous wartime allies.* From that point on U.S. policy and actions would be tempered to avoid war with the Russians.

In Czechoslovakia communist control was imposed at all levels of society. Men were taken in forced labor projects, women were forced to work in factories, re-education camps were established, and all manner of their goods were "exported" to Russia. The same thing was happening in Poland, Bulgaria and Hungary. Religion was banned as communism was the new faith. Imprisonments and executions of undesirables continued, and trumped up charges were the norm. It seemed as if the purges of the 1930s were back in spades.

Then on October 1, 1949 more disastrous bad news arrived. Mao Tse-tung proclaimed the formation of the PRC, Peoples Republic of China.

Nine weeks later Chiang and just 300,000 Nationalists escaped from the mainland to Formosa, (Taiwan), with help from the U.S. 7th Fleet. It was a bitter defeat.

The Nationalist's supporters in the U.S. were crestfallen that this had been allowed to happen, and they demanded Truman take all steps to return them to China.

Truman's popularity continued to fall.

During WWII U.S. diplomat George Abbott worked in Indochina and had gotten to know Ho Chi Minh and his Viet Minh movement. He had felt and reported that Ho's brand of communism was akin to Tito's, and had little anti-American propaganda. Abbott also felt that we might have been able to work with the Ho and the Viet Minh, but by 1946 communism was quickly becoming the new enemy.

In 1947 a Vietnamese delegation visited Stalin in Moscow. He was pleased with their progress and promised them aid and weapons to insure their survival against the French. As stated earlier, the Viet Minh which had fought and recruited during the Japanese occupation returned to the fight. Their initial battles against the French were along the northern border of Vietnam adjacent to China. The French won most of those fights forcing the communist leaders to escape into the jungles to rebuild their forces.

And just as it had happened in China twenty years earlier, the resilient communists survived. By April 1949 they had rebuilt their forces to almost 300,000 guerrilla fighters. In the quite interim period it appeared to the French that they might have succeeded in their policy of strict policing and establishing outposts throughout the affected area. But soon after Communist commander Gen. Giap finally felt confident that his forces could begin attacking the French outposts along the Red River. Success followed success as the limited Viet Minh attacks continued to cause casualties to the French and large stores of weapons and supplies were being captured.

To try to appease the Americans and get more aid the French signed the Elysee' Agreement which purported to confirm Vietnam's independence, even though the French retained control. Ho asked for more and insisted that he would stay neutral in the conflict between the West and Communism. Ho's offer was refused by the French.

(Mao and Stalin were communists first and foremost. Ho was a nationalist first, who used communism to get what he needed to drive the French out.)

Ho's next step was to get help from Red China and Russia. Both countries recognized his regime, the Democratic Republic of Vietnam. It was a clear warning to the West, especially France.

Dean Acheson responded that those events should remove any illusions about Ho Chi Minh and his true goals. (Many in the State Dept. were furious that the French had refused to see the light and grant Indochina their independence.)

Then the biggest triumph for Ho and the Viet Minh appeared, the fall of China to Mao and the communists.

Help was just across the border.

With the loss of China, George Keenan suggested that containment against mainland Asia was now out of the question. We were already overextended because of Europe, so Keenan recommended that sea-bound Japan and the Philippines be the cornerstones of our Pacific security plans. Acheson and the JCS agreed. With China lost there was no way to hold onto the land mass of Asia.

(And that set the stage for the potential abandonment of Korea.)

With China lost the Vietminh had a safe haven to hide in and unlimited supplies to draw from. And with a hostile Communist government across the large northern border of Vietnam the French were forced to build more and larger outposts.

That reduced the forces that were patrolling the countryside searching for the communist insurgents. It also provided the Vietminh with fixed targets to attack.

A month after Red China and the Soviet Union recognized Ho's N. Vietnamese government, the recently returned Emperor Bo Dai and S. Vietnam were given diplomatic recognition by America. That weak response was all we did.

As shown above, with his communist expansion was being blocked in Europe and the Middle East by U.S. and British actions and policies, Stalin had looked to Asia.

Two dominoes had already fallen in N. Korea and China, and Indochina was being threatened as the Vietminh were effectively fighting the French.

Communists in Burma, Malaya and Indonesia were now fighting against the Western backed governments, while in the Philippines the Hukbalahap communists were just getting started. (Stalin had given up on the Japanese communists.)

Burma was also beset with rebellions as various groups vied for power.

Naturally communists were in the fight, but strangely there were two separate groups, The White Flag and The Red Flags. The fledgling Burmese government was beleaguered with fighting so many enemies at one time. Luckily they did not cooperate with each other. Naturally the fighting was wrecking their economy, and Britain was forced to extend them and the neighboring nations large loans to keep them going.

America

After months of repeated setbacks to Communism the national mood was turning grim. The U.S. failure to assist Chiang in China was having political repercussions back home. (As well it should have.) The Democrats were accused of being "soft on communism", and the loss of China was causing the people of Asia to become unsettled. The largest nation in Asia was now a communist giant that had borders with almost a dozen nations. *At this time Sen. Joseph McCarthy warned Pres. Truman that the State Dept. was riddled with Communists and their sympathizers.*

Six former Communist intellectuals cooperated on a book highlighting their disillusionment with communism. The work was titled, *The God that Failed,* and it highlighted the barbarism that communism was. Their words were a chilling call to arms for the rest of the world, if you wanted to be free. All anyone needed to do was observe what was happening in Eastern Europe.

On January 21, 1950 **Alger Hiss** was finally convicted of perjury in his trial of espionage. (Dean Acheson the Sec. of State was still defending him four days later.)

Then on February 3, 1950 **Klaus Fuchs** the German born physicist who had come over from Great Britain to work on the Manhattan Project confessed that he too had passed classified information on the project to the Russians.

His American confederate **Harry Gold** would be convicted and sentenced to thirty years in prison for his spying for Russia. It seemed every place you turned Russian spies and Russian activities were working against the West.

A week later Senator Joseph McCarthy gave his first speech highlighting that communist agents were at work inside the U.S. government.
He also claimed that Sec. Acheson knew that it was true and that he knew many of them.

That was why the world was turning out the way it was.

On March 10, 1950 Pres. Truman approved the startup of a crash program to try to build a hydrogen bomb ahead of the Russians. (This was the beginning of the arms race.)

With all of the negative situations occurring in the world a group of high level National Security Officials headed by Paul Nitze completed a review of U.S. defense policies. National Security Council report NSC-68 was begun in early 1950 and completed in April 1950. It was listed as top secret and reflected the anti-communist attitude of that time.

"The Soviet Union has armed forces far in excess of what is needed for defense. They are developing the military capability to support its design for world domination. Should a major war occur in 1950, the JCS, (Joint Chiefs of Staff), feel that Russia and its satellites are in such an advanced state of preparation that they are capable of the following campaigns: To overrun Western Europe, To launch air attacks against Britain, and to attack selected targets with atomic weapons such as Alaska, Canada, the Continental United States etc". (16)

According to NSC 68, the CIA felt that by 1954 the Soviet atomic stockpile could reach 200 bombs. They had enough strategic bombers on line that they could deliver 100 atomic bombs upon America. That number of strikes would seriously damage the country. *The Nitze group recommended "immediate and substantial increases in military spending and warned that sacrifice and discipline would be required of the American people. Costs were expected to be in the range of $35-40 billion per year, and the American people will have to give up some of their freedoms."*

Not long after the completion of NSC 68 Paul Nitze met up with Alexander Sachs. Sachs had been a friend from their Wall Street Days, an economist for the New Deal programs, and the bearer of that vital letter from Albert Einstein, Edward Teller and Leo Szilard to FDR in 1940. (Like those named physicists', Sachs had been born in Europe and emigrated to America to escape the trials and terrors of the 1930s.)

His spring 1950 meeting with Nitze had a similar urgent purpose. Sachs and his staff had prepared three research papers on Soviet Russia.

The first concerned the compellation of their military forces, the second one on possible actions now that they had atomic weapons and that China had become communist, and the third paper analyzed what they might do with their new power.

Their workup predicted that North Korea would attack South Korea in the late summer of 1950!

A week later an alarmed Paul Nitze met with John Muccio our Ambassador to South Korea. Muccio was in Washington trying to get more military aid for South Korea.

Nitze showed him the secret reports from Sachs, and the Ambassador agreed that trouble was brewing. *For the past year attacks from the North had been occurring all over the border. Most were quick hit and run attacks, but the feeling was that a larger one was coming.* Muccio was not able to impress upon Acheson that Korea was in danger.

Until the recommendations of NSC 68 was approved by the Congress, all Nitze could get for the Muccio and South Korea were fast patrol boats.

Four days after the Senate approved the NATO Treaty Truman sent in a request for a peacetime military assistance program. Congress passed with large majorities a $1.4 billion dollar Foreign Military Assistance package to provide NATO with the military capability it would need to stand up to the Russians. Gen. Eisenhower was asked to become its first commander.

Small amounts of additional aid were to be provided to Greece, Turkey, Iran, the Philippines and Korea. Despite the growing Cold War and NSC-68, Pres. Truman's budgets for defense had remained small. In 1948 it had been just $10.9 billion. In 1949 $11.9, and projected for 1950 it was just $14.2, billion, (which now included the NATO funding). Pres. Truman was still not planning ahead for the coming storms.

As before the Air Force was given much of the funding for their super-bomber the B-36. (It was a dud that tied up a billion dollars.) Because of that project and the costs of NATO the Navy was unable to get the funding for the first of their next generation of aircraft carriers. In just a short while the issue would return to the forefront.

Asia

Despite what had just happened in China our government was again losing focus and turning away from events it felt wasn't threatening us directly. *Pres. Truman publicly stated on January 5, 1950 that the U.S had no predatory designs for Formosa, and that we had no intentions of utilizing our armed forces to interfere in their present situation. (China was preparing to invade the island.)*

"America will not pursue a course which would lead to our involvement in the civil conflict in China".

Truman was basically telling the Communists to invade Formosa. Secretary of State Dean Acheson repeated this same idea at a speech before the National Press Club on January 12. And Acheson's speech had mirrored the earlier one MacArthur recently made in that Korea and Formosa were omitted from our protection.

Again the content of those speeches was overlooked by our "leaders" and in the western press, but not by the communists. With the obvious lack of U.S. interest in mainland Asia, Stalin and the communists felt **that a third country** could be taken quickly and easily. And that third one sat alone and unprepared just below the porous 38th parallel.

Back on January 1, 1949 the United States had officially recognized the New Republic in the southern half of Korea and Ambassadors were exchanged. The State Dept. was placed in charge of our efforts in Korea and kept about 300-500 U.S military advisors to train the "army" of South Korea. They did not allow any heavy or crew served weapons to be brought in to keep to the notion that this army was for defense only.

As shown earlier, through 1949 **over 300 communist attacks** had occurred in the South killing more than 2,000 communist infiltrators and dozens of Republic of Korea (ROK) troops. During early 1950 **another 600 attacks** by communist guerilla fighters and saboteurs occurred, with even more losses. Despite their losses, enemy troops repeatedly landed, observed and fought in South Korea. *They were actually there to test and* *to learn, and they realized that the South had almost no heavy weapons or tanks.*

Added to those border raids were large doses of communist propaganda and economic pressures. Anything that could be done by the Northern communists to destabilize and destroy the South was done. But one irrefutable fact remained, despite their massive problems and the imperfect regime of President Rhee the Republic of Korea did not turn. Its citizens wanted no part of a united Korea that would be a tool of a harsh new ruler. That tragic pastime had been played before by many prior conquerors.

The people of S. Korea had freedom, and they would not yield.

Backed by Josef Stalin, Kim Il Sung the well trained communist leader of the North called upon all of the "Korean Volunteers" who had fought with the CCF, (Chinese Communist Forces) in China. It was time to return home. It was time to move south.

During the past two years over 100,000 communist Koreans had fought against Chiang and the Nationalists. (Even that did not inspire Truman to help out.)

Those surviving 30,000 battle hardened troops would form the nucleus of the *Inmun Gun*, as the North Korean People's Army was being born. (NKPA)

From its inception North Korea had a cohesion that the south lacked.

Ruled with the usual motivating tool of all communist states, a pistol placed at the back of one's head, it's "citizens worked with a "renewed determination" to accomplish the "Party's goals and reforms".

Assisted with Russian support and military supplies, the North Koreans trained and prepared for war. North of the impassible border hundreds of Soviet military specialists worked closely with Kim's forces to create a well trained modern military based on the Russian model. Unneeded tanks and heavy armaments that had been stockpiled to invade Japan were given to Kim's forces, and they were expertly trained in their use.

Hundreds of Russian "advisors" would be near the front fighting, directing and coaching during the initial battles as the North invaded the South.

However in neighboring China Chairman Mao was not happy with those events. He had wanted to attack Formosa quickly and crush the remaining Nationalists.

But to do so he needed Russian help and weapons.

Mao had visited Stalin on Dec. 16, 1949 and asked for "volunteer pilots and naval specialists" to get him to the island that Chiang now "occupied". Mao waited in Moscow for 17 days, but Stalin cagily promised little.

Mao returned in February 1950 and finally came away with a "treaty of friendship". In outward appearances all seemed well. But Mao was still upset over the locust like activity the Russians had done to Manchuria, and the fact that Mongolia was still in dispute between them. In reality Mao could not protest too much for China was wrecked from twenty years of war. He needed Russia's help.

One vital thing Mao did not know, was that N. Korea's Kim Il Sung had also been in Moscow. But weeks earlier. According to Nikita Khrushchev's memoirs Kim had convinced Stalin to help him in Korea first. (Who can say what would have happened had Formosa been invaded in 1950 instead of South Korea.)

On January 28th 1950 Stalin was given a final update from Russian Intelligence.

They reported that South Korea had little hope of getting any U.S. military assistance, and that Truman would give up Korea as he had China. America was transfixed on Europe. (Those speeches.)

Based on their intelligence, on January 30, 1950 Stalin made up his mind that Korea would be taken next. Stalin felt that with the Koreans fighting each other in a *"Civil War"*, the U.S. would not interfere. China would just have to be patient.

Stalin signaled the Russian units assigned to Pyongyang, N. Korea that it was right to help the North as long as surrogates were involved. China owed many favors to Stalin, and thousands of their support troops would be needed to cross into Korea to help the NKPA succeed with their battle plan. China was informed.

To get ready for the project Kim had all civilians removed from a two mile strip near the frontier. Pres. Rhee and MacArthur's intelligence people knew about the forced relocations, but missed the significance of the directive and movements.

With their planned blitzkrieg type use of Russian tanks Kim felt the reunification would take just three to four weeks. (The South had no tanks.) His well trained NKPA saboteurs and fifth columnists would work behind the lines preventing reinforcements and disrupting all communications and transportation. They would strike hard and fast before the dazed and confused puppets knew what was happening. It was a fine plan.

Stalin insisted that Kim had to work with Comrade Mao and win him over. Russia would aid Korea and China logistically and diplomatically, while China would aid Korea directly. Stalin wanted this arrangement to avoid a direct conflict with the West, to keep Mao's China dependent upon him, and because Stalin feared that China could become a rival for power.

(Milovan Djilas a Yugoslavian leader and ally to Marshall Tito met with Stalin often. To Stalin's warped mind any new communist entity was a potential rival and threat to his and Russia's supremacy. (As had happened when Tito rebelled.) This was particularly true of China, because of its size and population. Like many, Djilas would become disillusioned with the corruption among the Belgrade communists and he was forced out in 1954.)

After taking over in China the CCF forces moved throughout the country reaching and threatening all of the borders of their neighbors. As shown above, Red China and Russia had both recognized the regime of Ho Chi Minh, a clear warning to the French that they would aid the communists in Vietnam.

Communist China's Premier and Foreign Minister was Chou En-lai.

He and the other senior leaders agreed that Korea had the right to try to move south. Mao reluctantly agreed to their attack, but only wanted to give them support units. Any actions by them was dependent that China received the two hundred combat aircraft and pilots that Stalin had "approved" at their last meeting. After four days of hard talks with Kim, Mao relented. *The Chairman also decided,"If the Americans cross the 38th parallel we will come in fighting".*

Despite being in command of all of the Far Pacific area, Gen. MacArthur had visited Korea only once since the war had ended, back in 1948. He gave a speech promising to fight for the fledgling nation, but privately wanted nothing to do with it. "Korea belongs to the State Dept, they wanted it and they got it".

All of the aid and upgrades to the South were being administered by the Dept. of State and overseen by the United Nations. The U.S. Armed Forces simply provided military training personnel.

Even up to May 18, 1950 MacArthur believed the Russians were defensive minded, concentrating on Europe. His intelligence network consisted of the military advisors, the ROK personnel and patrol reports from within the South.

No one could operate in or above the 38th parallel.

His intelligence chief was Gen. Charles Willoughby a MacArthur loyalist. He was more interested in keeping the Boss happy than in providing accurate information. Willoughby actually worked to keep the hard running CIA "out of his area" as much as possible. *And Willoughby arrogantly placed no credence in their reports that the North was preparing to attack.*

(British Foreign Officer Major J.R. Fergusson had also warned that the North was getting dangerous. He stated the North would trample the South if it did attack. He and his staff doubted the Americans would intercede as Korea was not considered essential for the West's security.)

MacArthur had given another press interview with NY Times reporter Cyrus Sulzberger on May 18. Mac had stated that he felt warfare was changed with the development of atomic weapons, and that even the Russians would avoid it.

In the five years he had been in command in Japan, no serious military training or war gaming had been done by any of the units or staffs assigned to him.
They were involved in friendly occupation duty, and war was far from anyone's mind.

Back in the Pentagon Gen. Bradley the new Chairman of the JCS, (Ike had gone to NATO), was getting worried. None of the JCS requests for heavy weapons or reinforcements for the Pacific had been approved from Washington yet. (Just like in 1941.)

Because of Russia, Europe had been the focal point for the West's limited military buildup. But lately they were hearing rumors of war in the Pacific. *During this time the CIA's chief Admiral Roscoe Hillenkoetter repeatedly warned of the coming Communist attack. And he insisted it was going to be in Korea.*

He was so sure of it, he directed that hand delivered copies of the CIA reports were to be brought to all of the principals, including the President!
No one listened.

Those frequent border and guerilla raids from North Korea suddenly stopped in May 1950, suggesting an easing of tensions. But the *NKPA* had actually used the spring raids for intelligence gathering and to secret their commando forces south of the border. *They were in their advance positions hiding and waiting.*

On June 1, 1950 Bradley became so fearful about the CIA's repeated reports that S. Korea was in danger he sent a query to Gen. MacArthur at his headquarters in Japan. For the past two years there had been numerous skirmishes along the border, with almost all of the attacks occurring in South Korea. Bradley wanted to know if MacArthur felt an invasion was coming.

The CIA had initially warned everyone in March that the North would invade in June 1950. They had repeated the warning in April, and again in May! Bradley was starting to panic.

Truman's hatchet man in the military was Sec. of Def. Louis Johnson, a long serving Democrat. Since he had come aboard after Sec. Forrestal's "suicide",

Johnson was adamant about hacking the defense budget to ribbons. With the release of the earlier mentioned NSC-68 in March 1950 Johnson had exploded. According to that report the required increases to the defense budget meant the Army would grow from 10 Divisions to 18. The Navy would increase from 281 ships to 397, the Air Force from 58 air wings to 95. If it was passed, the increased defense budget would create a large and permanent military establishment instead of the usual succession of feasts and famine. (At this point it was deep famine as the NSC- 68 warning and rearming was begun too late to stop Kim.)

On June 8, 1950 an announcement had appeared in the Pyongyang Press of North Korea that the "Central Committee of the United Democratic Front" had called for an August 15 meeting in Seoul, South Korea. This meeting would be a parliamentary assembly representing both North and South. The date given was the 5th anniversary of the Japanese surrender, and thus Korean independence from colonialism.

(Asian people are very date conscious).

There was no doubt that Pres. Rhee would reject any coalition with the communists. *But since 1917 the Communists had a long history of insinuating a minority party into power, usually from the barrel of a gun.*

From their viewpoint, Stalin and Kim felt the time to act had arrived.

On June 10th the same story appeared in Moscow in *Izvestia* their state controlled paper. The intelligence officers in the West again missed the significance of this *empty offer*, as did General MacArthur's people at the Dai Ichi, (His HQ), in Tokyo. And once again America was to be caught unprepared.

A week later John Foster Dulles, advisor on Far Eastern Affairs was at the border frontier taking a look for himself at the ghostly landscape of the Korean DMZ.

Dulles felt that Korea would be a big part in this growing Cold War, and the next day he joined MacArthur and other guests in Tokyo. Like the General, Dulles wanted to use Chiang's extra Divisions to help defend Korea. That would tie them up and save the U.S. the expense of shipping our troops in.

Then Gen. Bradley also showed up in Japan, for an "inspection trip". Bradley did not trust MacArthur's messages, and went to speak with him directly. Even after hearing straight from America's Caesar, Bradley decided to speak to the head of KMAG. (Korean military Advisory Group) The head of KMAG was Gen. William Roberts, who also believed that nothing was afoot. He proudly told Bradley that his forces could handle the North Koreans if they attacked, just as they had been doing for the last two years.

Korea, Land of the Morning Calm

Around 5am on June 25th, 1950 *a South Korean fast patrol boat* intercepted a blacked out transport ship sailing a ways south of their border with North Korea. The only port the ship could have used was Pusan on the southern coast. After many attempts to identify the ship the South Koreans attacked and drove the craft back to the north.

Soon after South Korean Navy patrol craft *PC-701* found another similar innocuous vessel also sailing towards the port of Pusan. After waiting for a few minutes of unanswered challenges, *PC-701* fired on and sank the craft.

Packed aboard was a second group of 600 commando troops from the NKPA, the North Korean Peoples Army. They were heavily armed and highly trained for their mission, to destroy the port of Pusan. (Joined by that second transport.)

Unknown to the South Korean crews, they had just saved their nation.

All along the 38th parallel battles were breaking out.

Previously placed commandos from the *NKPA* had secretly scouted out the locations of all of the South's border posts. Most of those posts were at reduced staffing, and their officers and U.S. advisors were away for the normal Sunday - day of rest.

(How many times does history need to be repeated, the Wehrmacht invasion of Russia, Pearl Harbor etc.)

Major communist border attacks had been a routine occurrence on Sunday's, including the larger battle that had been fought just a year ago on the Ongjin peninsula. By attacking repeatedly in that way the American advisors and the South's border forces had become acclimated to the "normal weekend attack". But this one was far different.

Claiming that the South was trying to invade the North, the communist papers quickly spun propaganda to try to create the illusion that the fighting was caused by unprovoked attacks by ROK, (Republic of Korea), and U.S troops.

(Kang Sangho the Communist Party Chief for Kangwon Province was sent to the Chunchon area and observed that there was no evidence of aggression from the South.)

Lenin had called propaganda the communist party's main weapon. Lies, deceit and censorship were to be used to distort any and all information that arose from the communists.
In that way they could control the knowledge, thoughts and discussions of the masses. (Sound familiar.)

When Stalin took over in Russia he elevated propaganda and control to new levels, going so far as rewriting history books and having people removed from photos.

Every residence in Russia had a radio hard wired to the state radio station, and the masses were subjected to nonstop lies and propaganda all day every day.

By 1950, almost every person in Russia had been raised under the communist indoctrination program. It started when they were small and continued until death.

And if the party line failed, the KGB were everywhere listening and watching. Those who missed the point were quickly arrested.

Throughout that first night the border battles continued and then became worse.

Communist trucks and tanks had quietly moved up to the border as did their artillery units. Working by dimmed lights the *NKPA* were also re-laying the railway tracks down to the border. This railroad line used to connect Pyongyang with Seoul and was an efficient way to move commerce. Now it would make history as a new way to attack a non-threatening nation. *It would be sadly satirical that these invading Korean communists were riding to war in the same old Japanese rail carriages that had been used against them.*

All along the eastern coast sampans and junks had sailed unseen and unheard below the 38th parallel to beach themselves on unpatrolled shore areas. Thousands more NKPA troops fanned out. In next to no time their well conceived plan was succeeding at all points, **except at the port at Pusan.**

Under equipped and poorly led, the ROK units along the border began to fall back. Never having had an army of their own, (since Japan had taken over), the commanders in the South failed their units with poor commands and decisions. Word began to filter back that this was not just a series of raids.

President Rhee wisely began to move his government south to the city of Suwon and he called MacArthur's HQ in Tokyo. Yelling into the phone Rhee scolded MacArthur, *"Had your country been more concerned about us this could have been prevented. We've warned you many times that the North would attack"!*

General MacArthur had no authority to intervene, but he promised to send fighter planes to assist in the evacuation. Almost two thousand American non-military personnel were at risk in the embattled nation.

Nearly nine years ago MacArthur had received a similar call while based in Manila. He had failed to act decisively, losing the Philippines and all of America's military strength in the far Western Pacific.
Years of conflict were needed for MacArthur to "Return", and had resulted in over 100,000 casualties in the Philippines loss alone.

MacArthur's Chief of Staff Gen. Ned Almond asked for orders, but Mac needed time to think. In his mind MacArthur was trying to convince himself that this was just a small fight. He boasted that the Koreans could handle it just fine.

But inside his office the aging general was locked in indecision.

News reports began coming in bringing Washington to life.

America's political leaders needed to give Gen. MacArthur instructions, the world was finally being overtly threatened by the communists in an invasion. President Truman who had been resting in Missouri boarded a plane to return to Washington D.C. *Just a few months ago he had denied the requests to increase the defense budgets of the Armed Forces.* Now the unprepared U.S. military was facing a new war.
(His denial was to the Nitze group report, NSC-68.)

While flying back to Washington Truman looked back a few years and realized that the pattern of Communist subversive efforts was the same scam Germany and Japan had used in the 1930s. He knew that if he did not act now, more aggression would follow. And he knew that Russia was behind this invasion.

When Truman received the call from Sec. of State Acheson that the North Koreans had invaded he directed him to call the United Nations and speak directly to Secretary General Trygvie Lie of Norway. Like many from that time, Lie knew all too well about unprovoked invasions.
(Ironically Lie had been nominated for the post by Russia's Andrei Gromyko.)

Sec. Lie quickly responded that "This is a war against the United Nations" and he called for an emergency session of the U.N. Security Council.
By a fortunate twist of fate Russia was boycotting the United Nations over their refusal to admit Red China.

(FDR's vision of the United Nations expected that China, the one ruled by Chiang would be the one in place on the Security Council. Now that the communists had won Russia wanted them to be admitted into the United

Nations and take the spot on the Security Council. In 1950 America and the West refused.)

Within hours of the U.N. meeting a resolution was approved blaming North Korea for breaching the peace; calling for a cessation of hostilities and a return to the border of all of their forces. Kim Il Sung was making his own statements on Pyongyang radio.

In his high pitched voice he claimed that the "Puppet Regime in the South had rejected all methods for a peaceful reunification proposed by the communist DPRK.

He had ordered his forces to counter-attack and repel the invaders from the south". Kim's claim was that the South had assaulted his forces on the Ongjin peninsula and must be held responsible. (Militarily this was ridiculous. The peninsula was completely cutoff from the South and an attack there would accomplish nothing of value.)

Meanwhile Gen. MacArthur continued to downplay the disturbing reports giving different stories to each group he met. "If Washington will not hobble me, I can handle this with one arm tied behind my back".

Since the end of the Berlin Blockade and the inception of NATO tensions in Europe had actually decreased. Everyone had grown hopeful. But now the politicians in Washington were stunned and furious. There had been no overt warning signs or threats. *What those bureaucrats forgot, was this is just what happened in Dec. 1941.*

(America did not have spies hidden in Tokyo to warn them of what the Tojo Government was thinking. *However our Ambassador in Japan had learned of the plot and sent a warning to Sec. State Hull. As always no intelligent action was taken by those in power.* And the world paid a terrible price for those failures. *Fatal Flaws Book 1*)

In 1950 we had no agents inside Moscow, Peking or Pyongyang.

As with Ambassador Hull in Japan, the CIA did learn of the threat, but all of their warnings were ignored. And as usual, no one would ever be held accountable.

Many national leaders in D.C. began expressing the idea that the U.S. must intervene militarily even if it brings in the Russians. To sit by while a free nation was overrun in an unprovoked invasion could start a dangerous chain of events, most likely leading to another world war".

Fighting to maintain any non-communist government was worth the risk.
(This same thinking occurred a decade later in Vietnam.)

To those emerging Cold War Warriors this new war went far beyond the boundaries of *Chosun*. And all agreed that it would be impossible to try to bargain this conflict away. (This was the start of the Cold War-Domino theory for Asia, a theory I believe had already begun with the theft of N. Korea and the loss of China.)

Gen. Bradley chairman of the JCS agreed that we had to draw the line, but it was still unclear if the Russian's were simply using Korea as a smokescreen to get us to commit to Asia, while they invaded Europe.

After 24 hours had passed the battlefield situation was becoming clearer, and much worse. Everywhere along the border the ROK forces were being pushed back or chewed up. The communists had advanced deep into the South. At one point the ROK 6th Division had actually stopped the *Inmun Gun* in man-to man combat. (Some of the ROK units were as good at infantry fighting as the communists.)

But once the Russian built T-34 tanks arrived, the *NKPA* always won.

America had supplied the ROK army with our old 2.36 inch rocket launcher which was used at the start of WWII. It was incapable of stopping the Russian built T-34 tank. **This was a vital failure that the U.S. military should have known about.**

(Since Russia was supplying the North with weapons, the U.S. should have ensured that our equipment would be effective against theirs. But only the leftovers were given away.)

As the well coordinated NKPA attacks continued the ROK's fell back further, and lost more and more of their bravest fighters. President Rhee then decided to move his government further south to the city of *Taejon*. Many members of the Korean National Assembly decided to remain in Seoul as a show of will. All were soon captured and murdered by the advancing North Koreans.

On Tuesday the 27th MacArthur went to see John Dulles and his aide John Allison as they were preparing to fly back to D.C. He told them privately that Korea was lost.

All that remains is to get our people out. The general looked despondent.

(MacArthur had ignored all of the recent reports from the CIA and Ambassador Muccio that trouble was coming.)

Dulles and Allison rushed a memo to Sec. Acheson and his Far Eastern assistant Dean Rusk, (SWINK). Their report stated that if they were needed, U.S. forces would have to be used even if the Russians caused trouble elsewhere. Later that afternoon Pres. Truman had made his decision, "By God I'm going to let them have it"!

Gen MacArthur was directed to provide U.S. air and naval support for now.

The Republic of Korea's capitol was in Seoul close to the indefensible 38th parallel. With the proximity of the fighting the city was wisely being evacuated.

But the British Embassy staff also decided to stay in place despite their fine analysis of the bleak military situation. Britain had already recognized Red China, (in an effort to save Hong Kong and Macao), and it was felt that they would have "Diplomatic Immunity". Like most of the world, the British did not understand the communist foe.

Many of their embassy personnel would be captured and murdered in *Chosun*.

The American consul since 1948 was John Muccio a veteran of assignments in China. He initially downplayed the attacks to prevent panic, but his staff and the KMAG officers pleaded with him to evacuate their dependents. Initially he refused them, still not wanting to appear to panic. But after the first 24 hrs had passed he realized their position was untenable. Russian made YAK fighters had already strafed the roads and airport.

Prudently he decided to force the civilians onto any ship in the harbors headed for Japan.

He also decided to have the Embassy staff flee to the south.

But to his and the embassy personnel's ever lasting shame, they left the files of over 5000 South Korean agents and employees in the embassy. The files were found intact by the North Korean's, and none of those individuals who stayed behind would survive the month's long communist purge.

(As stated many times, the universal and effective tactic of the communist animal is that any time they entered a location all of the "undesirables" were quickly found and murdered. Any potential threats were thus removed and an effective message was displayed to the survivors. And dead men tell no tales.)

A second major and also inexcusable failure at the Embassy was the abandonment of tons of supplies and over 1400 vehicles.
The ROK forces desperately needed supplies and transportation, but it was the *Inmun Gun* who would benefit and use the abandoned U.S. equipment.

NKPA forces were soon attacking just across the Han River. Thousands of the South's best fighting men and thousands upon thousands of fleeing civilians were left to their fate when the bridges over the Han River were blown up prematurely. Desperate soldiers and civilians tried all manor of movement in an effort to cross the wide flowing river. Thousands more would needlessly die.

(Trapped by the blown bridges, over 44,000 S. Korean troops and all of their equipment were lost!)

By nightfall on the 27th communist advance parties and their sympathizers were entering Seoul itself. Their execution squads quickly moved through the city eliminating all trapped soldiers, police or governmental officials.

On Truman's orders the 7th fleet was moved north from the Philippines to take a position between mainland China and Formosa to "prevent the war from spreading." What the president's action actually accomplished was to make the leaders in Red China nervous about U.S. intentions. Once they realized the navy's mission, it freed up many Red Chinese Divisions that had been protecting China's coast from a possible Nationalist invasion. Those CCF (Communist Chinese Forces), units would reappear all too soon.

On June 29th the U.N. passed a momentous resolution that put the United Nations into a war against the communists of North Korea.

The U.N. wanted all of its member nations to heed the call to help South Korea. Visually seeing the threat, many did.

Naturally the Soviets dismissed the calls for help, as this was a "Civil War". (The same mendacious lie was used in China and repeated in Vietnam.)

Russia was still boycotting the U.N. over the refusal to admit Red China.

Had the Russians been present on the Security Council it is doubtful the resolution could have been passed. In that case the U.N. would probably have failed to survive the war itself as the West had to act against this aggression.

Truman spoke to his press assistant George Elsey, "Iran is the place I believe they will start trouble next". (As stated before Russia had long coveted the Persian basin, especially after oil was found. Their efforts there had not stopped in the past five years.)

"Korea is the Greece of the Far East. If we stand up to the Russians like we did in Greece three years ago, they won't take any further steps. There's no telling what they'll do if we don't put up a fight now".

Pres. Truman had made a correct political call, but he committed another serious shortfall. He did not explain to the American people what was happening to their world. During WWII FDR and many of his people had portrayed Josef Stalin as "Uncle Joe", a good friend who was fighting with the same pure heart and motives as ours.

Nothing could have been more wrong, for Stalin had only one motive, Power.

(He once told the head of his secret police, "That Power is the one element in the human condition that you can't fake".) No he was not like any American.

FDR's first Ambassador to Russia, Joseph E. Davies was a shameless Stalin supporter. He even refused to condemn Stalin's maniacal purges. Even the NY Times Moscow correspondents actively worked to suppress the reports of the famines, purges and gulags that were the hallmark of the Bolsheviks. In that way the secrets of the communists were hidden from view.

The United States had fought WWII war as a crusade, while Russia fought first for survival, and then for power.

It was no wonder that Stalin and the communists were winning the "peace".

As a consequence of all of the prior years of secret deals and subterfuge that FDR and his cabinet had started, Truman and his Administration had begun to isolate all foreign policy decisions from the American public.

It was a terrible mistake for the governed not to be aware of what their government was doing and dealing with. The Marshall Plan and Truman Doctrine were not overly popular programs in America. Few understood what the world's problems were, or why we had to be involved.

It was significant that every historic decision made by the Truman Administration was debated in the Congress only after the programs had become irreversible. Under Harry Truman the executive branch was making national policy that was not of the popular will. It was the start of a failed notion of executive power that would cause America to fight herself as she became engaged in more of the world's affairs and wars.

The next Fatal Flaw that Pres. Truman made was committing U.S. forces into Korea without having a Declaration of War from the Congress. Asking your citizen soldiers to die in a distant land must always be approved in the Congress. Granted in Korea we were caught completely unprepared, and any debate would have prevented quick action which was what was needed there, but the debate was and should be required for any potential long term conflict.

With the start of hostilities MacArthur and his staff turned to the only force they had that was capable of interfering with the NKPA attack, the Far Eastern Air Force, (FEAF). On his own MacArthur had already given the USAF commander permission to attack North Korean aircraft, and to destroy NK airfields and convoys. By the next day the highly skilled USAF pilots flying F-80 and F-82 jets were attacking and beating the N. Koreans in the air.

FEAF was also flying missions to try to support the ROK infantry. But without air-ground control parties operating with the ROK units, the

FEAF pilots in their jets attacked anyone they saw. This caused even more confusion and losses to the ROK units. Other FEAF units were flying support missions for the few ships that had escaped with the refugees. By the next day the harbors in the Seoul/Inchon area had emptied, and all Americans exited safely.

With Truman's initial war orders in hand Gen. MacArthur had boldly flown in for a recon tour of South Korea. His team landed at Suwon Airfield south of Seoul on the 29th. Around his entourage burning planes flamed and hissed. Communist planes (Yak fighter-bombers of Soviet design) had just made an attack and FEAF fighters had shot down two of them. Mac was taken by car to Gen. Church's Administrative HQ to check the maps and dispositions of units. (Another attack by enemy planes was made and two more went down.) MacArthur also met with Ambassador Muccio and Pres. Rhee. They watched from a small hill as the shattered remnants of ROK units ran past.

America's senior General (who was most definitely not of George Marshall's school), noted that there were few wounded troops, no defensive preparations and no leadership. The evidence was clear, the communists would win and soon. (The panicked loss of those troops trapped north of the Han River was a major contributor.) As he watched the scenes around him it became evident to MacArthur that U.S. ground forces were needed now if any chance to save Korea was to be made.

The first ground unit in country was an antiaircraft team from the 507th. Their mission was to defend the Suwon airfield which was now the only way out of this northern sector. (This type of defensive operation does not need Congressional approval.) After observing and giving his initial orders to his survey group Mac and his staff flew off. Just after his plane the *Bataan* took off to return to Japan, four more communist Yak fighters showed up. They had just missed their big prize.

(I wonder if they had shot MacArthur down if it would have galvanized the American effort or if it would have ended before it begun.)

There were numerous seasoned war reporters in the battle area. They too witnessed the panicked evacuation by the ROK units and the plight of the desperate civilians. They did not like what they saw. Like Mac's survey group they were subjected to enemy air attacks, and were soon fighting to escape from the advancing NKPA ground forces.

Before noon on the 29th Secretary of Defense Louis Johnson telephoned Pres Truman to give him the basic Army battle plan. Of all of Truman's cabinet, Johnson was the most shocked by these events. He had not only cut the U.S. Army down, he had made it almost impossible for it to fight.

The rule changes and reductions in training and equipment budgets had destroyed the Army's morale as well as its effectiveness.

And recent changes in personnel management created even more problems.

To round out the "education" of its members, all ranks were rotated through assignments. Prior to 1945 if someone was in the infantry, that was were they stayed for their career. But in 1948 a rotation had been setup so that all ranks rotated through units every two years. No one had a chance to get to know anyone or to really learn their trade.

This Army was staffed at the lower ranks with draftees. They were the ones who had to do the actual fighting, but most were clueless on what to do and with these rotation changes so were their leaders.

After having been told repeatedly that because of the Atomic Bomb there were no more wars to fight, the weakened U.S. Army would now have to be sent in.

None of the ten standing Army Divisions were at full strength. Incredibly and sadly our Navy had fewer ships in 1950, than before WWII!

Never before had a nation that was so involved in world affairs been so unprepared for the task. *(It is hard to understand why Truman was committing America to fight communists in Korea, when he had refused to do so with a vital ally in China.)*

Late on the 29th the following directive was issued to MacArthur;

He was authorized to use U.S. forces to maintain communications and supply to ROK units; To employ U.S. combat units to ensure an air and naval base was maintained near Pusan. All U.S. ground operations were limited to S. Korea.

He was to use both air and naval units against military targets in N. Korea, but they must stay away from border areas affecting China or Russia.

He was to also to defend Formosa from an attack by Red China, and to keep the Nationalists from attacking Red China.

He was to provide supplies and munitions to ROK units and to give whatever support he could to the South Korean government.

A final note on the orders ended with a clear statement that no decision had been made to engage in ground combat with Russian forces even if they intervene.

Already a determination had been made to "limit this fight" if possible.

Naturally MacArthur was quite unhappy with any limits on his power. He had already sent USAF planes into North Korea *before* he had received this authorization, and now Washington was telling him who he could fight.

Hours later Mac's report on his personal recon into South Korea arrived in Washington, and with it his recommendations for immediately using U.S. ground forces.

It landed like a bomb.

Washington was not yet committed to using U.S. ground troops in a fight for Korea. The only fighting authorized was in the air or at sea, where the U.S. could win and keep the casualties down. When the Navy was directed to blockade Korea, Chief of Naval Operations *Adm. Sherman insisted our allies had to help as our navy did not have enough ships. Only one third of our total number was on duty in the vast Pacific, and of that only seven percent were near Korea!*

Gen. MacArthur's inspection report clearly stated that air and naval attacks could not be decisive. Only U.S. troops could drive out the invaders and restore order.

His plan was to commit a Regimental Combat Team, (RCT), initially, and build up to two Army Divisions. Pres. Truman was brought up to speed on the requests and approved sending the RCT. Using any additional units needed to be discussed.

Mac was notified immediately.

(Truman was unhappy that he was sending America's sons and daughters to fight. But again it was his failures that had allowed this to happen.)

Less than five years after the most horrific event in Human History had ended America's sons and daughters were again being sent off to war to rescue a faraway land from conquest. But they were not spiritually, physically or mentally prepared or equipped for the task, as no one had taught them that vital lesson,

"*That There Were Tigers in the World*". (17)

On the midmorning of June 30th Truman again met with his staff. It was agreed to send in the two Divisions that Mac had requested. In using the American military to stem the communist invasion Pres. Truman acted in the best interests of the world as a whole. His failure was that he had committed America to war by executive action.

After the meeting was over and the decision had been made and issued Truman met with the entire cabinet and congressional leaders. Some of them were completely shaken when they were informed of his actions.
America was again going to war to protect someone else's freedom, not it's own.

American citizens were being sent to fight this new war on the rushed order of the President based on the urging of an aged pro-Asian general who had not been in the United States in fifteen years.

In actuality though they would fight and die for a strange and obscure idea, to maintain the balance of power.

That was something Her Majesty's Regiments or the Legion's of Rome had done.

But America had no more Legions for they had been chopped into pieces and what was left was sent out to "peacefully occupy the war torn lands". *Because of the Doolittle Board the U.S. Army units on duty had been civilianized and were as unfit for war as was most of their equipment.*

Our forces were comprised of normal American youth, not the tough and battle hardened tribunes of Rome or the Kings Regiments.

They may have worn a uniform, but our troops were innocent civilians inside. Citizen soldiers will fight to preserve their homes, or to go on a crusade.

But a frontier cannot be maintained using the citizens in a republic.

They have better things to do.

And President Truman did not ring the bells, nor blow the trumpet.

He was sending America's sons and daughters off to war and few understood why. (18)

Back in Korea MacArthur was happily surprised. Most of the restrictions on him had been lifted and he was free to fight below the 38th parallel. If he could he was to clear all of South Korea of the communist invaders. He was in effect the United Nations Commander in Chief, and was told not to issue any public statements.

Mac's suspicions that Truman was weak concerning Asia vanished for now.

Having spent most of his years in the Pacific Gen. MacArthur believed that the fulcrum of the world lay there. *MacArthur had been a large voice in the call to deny the Russians a seat in drafting the peace treaty with Japan. He had also fought to keep Russia out of the occupation of Japan.* (Both actions had been correct.)

MacArthur despised the communists and knew that any Russian presence in Japan was a call for trouble. He was certain that the Soviets were behind this invasion.

He would make a battle plan that would spin their heads.

At a Washington press conference Pres. Truman was asked what was going on.

One reporter asked if this was like a "police action against a criminal?"

Jumping onto the benign idea, "Yes, "said Truman, We are not at War".

The action that we are taking is a police action against a violator of the law of nations, and the Charter of the U.N.

Truman and many others naively hoped that with the show of force by our air and naval forces that the North Koreans would back down. But despite taking some losses from our planes and ships the NKPA continued on as victory was near.

Then Truman and company forlornly hoped for the same ending when our ground forces arrived. The NKPA would brush them aside in an unrelenting tide.

A day later MacArthur cabled the JCS that he had to have **4 full divisions from the States,** or the war would be over in 10 days! Task Force Smith, the initial Regimental Combat Team, RCT was still being organized from the 24th Division. They had not even moved from Japan into Korea yet MacArthur was claiming the sky was falling before a shot had been fired. Those in power were stunned at the news.

Deviously MacArthur was setting up the pieces for his secret battle plan.

Task Force Smith was hurriedly and haphazardly organized and sent over to S. Korea. It consisted of a mere 406 men from the 21st Regiment. They were to try to stop the North Korean Army that had just overrun seven ROK Divisions. And those U.S. troops had nothing to stop the T-34 tanks.

But the military's nightmare was just starting. Organizing the movement of complete Army Divisions from comfortable occupation bases to a war setting fell completely apart. One of the last remaining amphibious commanders, Adm. James Doyle was in the command based in Japan.

His amphibious fleet consisted of one attack transport, one attack cargo ship, one LST (landing ship-tank), and one fleet tugboat!

That was all that was left of the far Pacific amphibious fleets that had won WWII.

The Navy base in Yokosuka, Japan had almost no staff, no workshops, only a 100 bed hospital and three aircraft. At Sasebo, Japan the closest seaport to Pusan, South Korea, only two dilapidated rust buckets were in the harbor.

Neither had been used since 1946.

Anything seaworthy was hastily rounded up as were any crews that could be found. It almost reached the point of using "press gangs" to round up sailors.

Warehoused foods were non-existent. Some old WWII K-rations were found and sent over, but in the ham and egg ration the egg portions had turned black.

It was loaded and shipped anyway.

There were no tents, rope, tools, radios, batteries nor communication wire. Clothing, combat boots, spare parts for the thousands of pieces of equipment, all types of weapons and ammunition were all in drastically short supply.

(Remember the thousands upon thousands of tons of supplies, equipment, weapons and ammo that had been dumped at sea or left abandoned when the WWII ended.)

The small port at Pusan was so ill equipped even Jeeps could not be offloaded because the gantry cranes were too light to lift them. Rope was hard to come by and troops turned to Japanese rice-straw ropes to try to secure equipment. Since no one had expected a ground war the litany of inadequacies was overwhelming.

Neglect and failure was the hallmark of those occupation forces.

And MacArthur as the Commander in Chief was just as much responsible as Sec. of Defense Johnson for this ridiculous state of affairs.

From the third day of the communist invasion all of the Army, Navy and Air Force units in Japan should have been preparing and equipping themselves for possible battle. It is hard to fathom why they waited until the last minute.

Desperate to turn his weakened military around Harry Truman called upon George Marshall to save the day. (As stated before, the day after he was elected in Nov. 48 Truman dumped Marshall as Sec. State.)

Now Truman decided to dump Sec. Johnson and use him as the "Administration Scapegoat". Strangely Marshall again left his retirement to do Truman's bidding.

(Upon taking over George Marshall told a reporter that the U.S. military was in worse shape in 1950, than it had been in 1942!)

Among the many who were against Marshall's return was Admiral Arthur Radford. Radford was one of the most vocal critics to Truman's wanton and foolish destruction of our military forces. He was shocked that Marshall sat on the sidelines saying nothing and doing less as he watched the destruction unfold.

Sec-Def. Louis Johnson had been the hatchet man extreme as he savaged the budgets of the services, except for the Air Force. Radford spoke up to remind all that the former Chief of Staff of the Army, Presidential Envoy to China and then Sec. of State had ignored the draconian and drastic cuts to the military that Truman ordered.

Marshall knew that the consequences of those cuts would be dire.

After hearing the complaints Marshall was sworn in anyway.

At the dawn of July 5th Task Force Smith was ashore and dug in amid a series of rolling hills near the town of *Osan, S. Korea*. They had been reinforced by a battery of six light artillery guns. This small unit was up to 504 men.

They had a total of *six rounds of anti-tank ammo.* **And that was 1/3 of the supply of anti-tank rounds in all of Japan!!**

As expected the NKPA troops and tanks soon appeared. Within a few brief hours the front line group of Task Force Smith was gone. This first U.S. combat unit had been shattered because of poor equipment, no training, little ammo and no discipline.
Survivors of the battle left their weapons, their wounded and ran south.

The next American unit in line was few miles further south.

They too quickly fell apart and were overrun.

Gen. Walton Walker, (a corps commander under Patton), was C in C of the U.S. 8th Army in Japan. (He too was at fault for not training and preparing.) On July 8th he met with the shaken Gen. William Dean of the 24th Division which had just been shipped to Korea. Walker explained to Dean that help was coming, and what was left of his division was to hold at the city of Taejon. MacArthur had just asked for the entire 8th Army from Japan in addition to a RCT from the 82nd Airborne, the 2nd Div from Ft Lewis in the states, army engineers, three tank battalions and a fully equipped Marine Corps regiment. This last unit would include Beach and Shore parties and a Marine Air Wing.

Unknown to the world, MacArthur had spotted a weakness when he had visited Korea in late June. This weakness he planned to exploit. But to do so required him having the U.S. Marine Corps onboard. What Mac hadn't realized, was how hard it would be to stop the *Inmun Gun.*

Thus far the KNPA was winning and it sent shock waves throughout the world. Those nations closest to the main aggressors of Russia and China feared greatly. No one knew who would be next. In fact Truman was warned of a possible move by Russia into Yugoslavia and then possibly Greece. High level warnings were sent to Moscow, not to attempt entry into those countries. Truman gave his first press conference since the war started, telling the world that we were in Korea to stay.

George Keenan observed our recent and terrible trials and wrote; **Today we have fallen heir to the problems and responsibilities that the Japanese had borne those past decades, trying to keep the communists out of Korea.** It is a perverse justice that we discounted their work then, but find ourselves in the same position now.

Gen. Dean's 24th Div was like all of the 8th Army, under-strength and inexperienced. It was also the closest one to Korea, so they were sent in first. Units tried to fight together and were told to hold the line at *Taejon* which was on the river Kum. Dean's men attempted to stop the well trained and led communists, but they were chewed up and spit out by July 17. Gen. Dean was captured inside the city.

The Pentagon tried to put on a smile and say that everything was fine.

But all was not well.

This first U.S. Army Division involved in the fight had been broken and quickly.

On July 14th Pres Rhee's wife had written to Robert Oliver an American speechwriter, and complained about the poor quality of the American soldiers. Word began to quickly circulate about the U.S. troop's poor showing in the first fights. Meanwhile the 25th Div would be assembled and ready in a few days, and the 1st Cavalry Div within a week.

As stated before many seasoned American reporters from WWII were at the front lines like Maggie Higgins (again), Keyes Beach, James Michener and Carl Mydans.

They had seen first hand the casualties caused by the lack of U.S. combat readiness and were appalled. In spite of what they witnessed, they tried to report on the bravery and not the negatives. Since all had covered WWII they knew not to give aid and comfort to the enemy. All knew what war was like and how good units were supposed to fight.

(Higgins should have been the role model for all future women correspondents. She was tough, dedicated and brave. At times the combat was so close she became an adhoc medic. She was also anti-communist, which probably explains why she was ignored by the liberals that compiled and wrote on feminist history.)

In addition to their superior tactics the NKPA routinely shelled or machine gunned any vehicles, tents or buildings that displayed a Red Cross. For them nothing was sacred or considered off limits. Time and again U.S. troops would patrol a battle site and find medical personnel wounded and murdered.

They also saw first hand how the communists would use human shields of women and children to protect their troops as they advanced.

This enemy knew that the Americans would not shoot into crowds of innocents.

As this vial practice continued and U.S. losses rose, American boys had no choice but to fire into the civilians. They had to understand, that this was war against communists.

FEAF – Far Eastern Air Force jets and planes continued their erratic air support by bombing the NKPA, ROK and U.S. units. Gen. John Church the assistant commander of the 25th angrily complained about this to Gen. Stratemeyer in Tokyo. Because they were so inconsistent, Church wanted the FEAF planes to attack only in the north, far away from his men. (At that time the Air Force did not use ground controllers the way the Marines did to coordinate air support. Thus it was easy to attack the wrong unit or site, especially in the fast moving jets.

During those first weeks the Air Force had only a limited number of planes to send to Korea, and most were jet aircraft. They were gas guzzlers and could spend only a few minutes over the battle areas after flying over from Japan. Thus their air support was sporadic at best.

Our Navy had only one aircraft carrier in the western Pacific, the *Valley Forge*. She was an updated Essex class ship and carried 86 aircraft, 30 of the F9F Panther jets, 40 F4U Corsair fighters of WWII fame and 26 of the post war propeller driven attack planes the AD4 Skyraiders. While the AF jets could do some damage, they always had to fly back to Japan to refuel and rearm. It would be hours before they could return.

However aircraft carriers could stay offshore and send continual relays of aircraft to hurt the enemy. And with their prior experience from attacking land targets and shipping, their sorties were better aimed and more effective. On July 3 the carrier pilots attacked and shut down a North Korean airfield. The next day a railroad yard was blasted, and during July the navy fliers shot down over 35 NKPA aircraft. This was naval air warfare at its finest. Capable of going anywhere it wanted, striking repeatedly and moving away for safety. But at that time their numbers were too few to be decisive. And so the armored forces of the NKPA continued their advances.

Taejon finally fell to the NKPA, and the disheartened U.S. troops fell back again. In three weeks of fighting, the 24th Div had lost over 30% of its men. Next in line was the 25th division, and despite directives to integrate the military their 24th Regiment was still an all black outfit with white officers. Because of that segregationist attitude the 24th also performed poorly. As with its predecessor, the 25 Division fell back losing tons of equipment and many poorly trained men. Many of their senior officers had no combat experience!

Then the NKPA made a huge strategic error which may have cost them the war. **Instead of attacking at the disorganized U.S. forces and trying to reach and shut down the Port of Pusan where our units were landing, they moved much of their men southward to capture the large but unimportant territory to the south.**

Those areas could have been taken after the Americans had been crushed.

Back at home no one in the Government would explain what was happening or why. It was all peaches and cream, and even the latest batch of troops landing in Korea had no idea why they were there. But they needed to learn and fast.

(Air transport was flying soldiers into the country as fast as they could.)

Already pictures and reports were coming in showing and describing how captured GI's fared. Many had been found with their hands bound behind them and they were executed with a bullet to the back of the head.

Unlike WWII, the U.S. troops in 1950 were not motivated to fight this enemy. America had years to watch as the Germans crushed Europe, and Japan savaged China. Then we had been backstabbed by Japan at Pearl Harbor.

But in Korea the communists were fighting their own kind, and to many the ROK's were not putting up much of a fight. In some cases the ROK's were still running away. As the days and weeks went by the poorly trained U.S. units lost fight after fight.

But they did trade their lives to gain some time for reinforcements to arrive.

The last natural defensible terrain in Korea was the Naktong River. The area behind this river became a pocket of approximately 100x50 miles around the S/E coast of *Chosun*, centered on the port city of Pusan. This pocket became known as the **Pusan Perimeter.**

(Pusan was the southern city that was saved by the crew of PC-701 that first night. Had the NKPA commandos landed successfully and been reinforced by the follow on transport, the port would have been destroyed and any chance at U.S. help stopped dead in its tracks.)

Gen. Walker had eight weak divisions at his disposal in the pocket. On the north side of his perimeter was the ROK 3d, Capital, 8th, 6th and 1st Divisions. Along the western side were the American 1st Cavalry, the remains of the 24th, 25th and the 5th RCT from Hawaii. Within the semi-confined Pusan Perimeter fields of fire could be better organized, defensive lines were setup and communications were better.

Each unit knew that another friendly unit was on each side. (Allied units began arriving too.) Supply problems were eased since the distances to be covered were less. And air support could also be better coordinated since the good guys were on one side of the Naktong River and the bad guys were on the other.

It was hoped that even the FEAF pukes could figure that one out.

On July 27 Generals Walker and Almond got into another heated exchange about tactics. Almond had little command or battlefield experience, but he constantly questioned Walker's decisions. To clear things up MacArthur went to Korea and met with the 8th Army Commander.

He insisted that Walker had to hold the line at Pusan, there was no place left to go. (Mac did not tell Walker about his secret plan.)

It was then that Gen. Walker told the 8th Army to make their stand at the Pusan Perimeter or die. There would be no Dunkirk here he told them. Navy commanders felt that even if the NKPA broke through they could hold onto the many accessible coastal areas around the retreating troops and prevent any slaughter. MacArthur agreed, there was no need to panic. If the troops looked upon their orders as grim there was some bright news too. Battle ready reinforcements were due to land on Aug 2.

Over the past weeks Gen. MacArthur had been analyzing the war effort and knew the time was fast approaching to formulate his secret plan, a seaborne assault behind the Inmun Gun. But to do this he needed for Walker's forces to hold at Pusan to keep the NKPA occupied, and he would need the experienced U.S. Marines for the amphibious invasion.

But implausibly there were none to be called.

With consent from above the six US Marine Corps Divisions that had been built up and trained to perfection in WWII had been cut, disbanded and chopped up. What was left sent to the seven seas in small groups. **At this point in time there were less than 55,000 Marines worldwide!** Pres. Truman, Generals Marshall, Eisenhower, Bradley and many others felt the USMC were not needed. Truman in fact had blasted a reporter who had complained at a press conference about the reduced state of the Corps.

"He deridingly referred to the Marine Corps as the Navy's police force, and as long as I am President that is what it will remain! They have a press machine that is almost equal to Stalin!"

Truman, Marshall, Eisenhower and Bradley all resented the good press the Corps had received from their many brutal victories going back to WWI. George Marshall had even retorted in 1946 that the Marines had won their last war.

Sec of Def. Louis Johnson, (had also served in the Army in WWI), despised the Marines so much he banned them from celebrating the traditional November 10, Marine Corps birthday. Before he was fired he had vowed to cut another 10,000 by years end.

There were other reasons for the reduction of the Marine Corps.

The Army was trying to save themselves from the budget cuts and saw a way by agreeing to the elimination of the USMC. Their offspring the Air Force wanted the USMC aircraft assignments. And in incredible arrogance and idiocy the Air Force Brass had even been fighting to take over the Navy's carrier plane assignments by eliminating the carriers!

During the cutback years the Air Force had somehow bamboozled the civilians into believing that "they had won" WWII. It was conveniently forgotten that the Army Air Corps did nothing in Europe until 1943, when the Navy bested the U-boats and was able to transport the planes and their supplies to England and North Africa.

It is seldom reported though stated earlier here that German war production actually increased throughout the war in spite of the strategic attacks from the bombers.

Not until 1945 did German war production actually start to drop.

In the Pacific the Air Corps accomplished nothing in their attacks on the Japanese ships in the Philippines or at Midway in 1942. Their strategic fliers sat on the sidelines until the Navy/Marines and MacArthur's forces fought their way into the Central Pacific.

The first big bomber attacks finally hit Japan in September of 1944, but accomplished little until the Marines took Iwo Jima in Feb-45. (Some attacks were also made from China by Chennault's 14th AAF, but then Truman irrationally disbanded them.)

Though the big bombers destroyed the cities of the Axis enemies, until the ground units actually took the positions and territory, the enemy still fought on. Only the atomic bomb had prevented the multi-year long invasions of Japan.

Marine Corps Commandant, Gen. Vandergrift, (Guadalcanal), had appeared before the Congress in 1948 to plead the case for the Marines to remain a viable part of the nation's military. (Lobbying efforts by the others undercut his speech.)

And as stated earlier the Marine Corps looked at themselves to see how they could best serve the nation. They knew the time honored techniques of storm landings had to be changed in this atomic world, so the Corps began experimenting with ship to shore assaults using helicopters from their old mainstays the escort carriers. (Col. Krulak who ultimately would bear a share of the blame for Vietnam had even *prepared a helicopter field manual in 1948.)*

After the NKPA invasion began in late June USMC Commandant Clifton Cates ordered the "1st Marine Division" to get ready to deploy within a week!

Even though no such entity actually existed, the assorted staffs and logistic people began to organize and find the units and supplies they would need to try to reconstitute the 1st Marine Division. (This is what the 8th Army should also have done in Japan.)

Gen. Cates also contacted Gen. MacArthur in Tokyo and told him that he had a provisional air-ground Brigade fully armed and ready to go.

(One Marine Brigade was always kept on stand-by, ready to deploy upon notification.)

With that information in hand Gen. MacArthur then contacted the JCS at the Pentagon and requested the Marines be sent promptly.

The JCS replied that no Marine units were available.

Gen. Cates actually had to personally report to the JCS, (the Marine Corps was not a member of the JCS), *and convince those ill advised senior officers that yes, the 5th Marines were indeed equipped and ready to go to war.*

(This was in keeping with the mantra of First to Fight.)

Meeting with Gen. Lem Shepard and Col. Victor Krulak at his Tokyo HQ in mid-July, MacArthur and the Marine commanders were completely in sync on how to fight this latest war. *Mac promised to keep the Marine Air Wing under USMC command, and away from FEAF. He then secretly told them that if he had a full Marine Division he would land them at Inchon, deep behind the communist lines.*

Knowing that those organization efforts were already happening back in the states, Gen. Shepherd smiled and promised MacArthur that the 1st Division would be ready by September. But again they would have to be requested directly by MacArthur.

A day later the request for the 1st Marine Division was sent in by MacArthur. (It took a day for the JCS to comprehend that the Marines were almost finished organizing for the mission.) Then they approved the request.

Their initial Marine Brigade was activated and staffed from Camp Pendleton in California. *They were actually the first intact military unit to leave the continental U.S., because they were always ready to "Ship Out".*

They sailed out on schedule and were commanded by Gen. Craig, a veteran of *Bougainville, Guam and Iwo Jima.*

The 5th Marine Regiment was the ground component of that provisional Brigade, and was commanded by Col. Ray Murray, another well seasoned commander who had fought at *Guadalcanal, Tarawa, and Saipan.* Included in the Brigade were their organic engineer, logistic, tank, tractor and artillery units. (Which made the unit self sufficient.)

The Marine Air Wing component of the Brigade was commanded by Gen. Cushman, who had fought in the "Banana wars" at Haiti and Nicaragua, and in numerous sites in the Pacific. This Air Wing had three squadrons of corsair fighter-bombers and four helicopters. Their planes would initially operate from the small carriers, *Sicily* and *Badoeng Strait.* This Brigade was scheduled to land in a week at Pusan, South Korea.

If it was still there.

Because they belonged to the Navy, the Marine Corps had escaped the ridiculous rulings of the Army's Doolittle Board. In 1950, a Marine Officer was still the old school Officer. They were expected to Lead, and they led from the front.

The USMC- NCO's were still the old school non-commissioned officers similar to the ones of Rome. They were tough, knew their job and did not allow any slack.

When they gave an order the enlisted ranks performed.

Another positive factor was that the Marines were still a volunteer force. Anyone who wore the globe and anchor wanted to serve, and the Corps always trained for war. Because of the small size of the Marine Corps only the best and most motivated Officers and NCO's were kept on or promoted. The final factor that made the USMC so lethal was that all of their senior and mid-grade officers and all of the NCOs had served in combat in WWII.

Those leaders knew their jobs and knew how to fight.

The second Marine regiment to be organized was the cobbled together 1st Regiment, Commanded by the legendary Chesty Puller. (He had fought almost everywhere.) The three infantry battalions of this reborn regiment were re-formed from smaller units that had remained in the states and it included some reservists.

The last infantry unit of the Division to be reconstituted was the 7th Regiment from Camp Lejeune, North Carolina. It was led by Col. Homer Litzenberg another old hand and former "China Marine". Litzenberg had landed at Casablanca during Operation Torch, the invasion of N. Africa, he returned to the Pacific fighting at Kwajalein in the Marshall Islands, then Saipan and Tinian in the Marianas.

His 7th Marines were mostly comprised of reservists and men rounded up from the seven seas. *One Battalion assigned to them had actually been reassigned from the Sixth fleet which was sailing in the Mediterranean!* Those men and units were re-assembled and re-organized, but had little time to train together before shipping out from California.

They would discover en-route that their next port of call was to be the Invasion at Inchon, South Korea!

MacArthur had actually conceived of this idea when he observed the rapid advance of the communists that first week. Knowing that the enemy would be overextended as they pushed everywhere down the peninsula, he enhanced his basic invasion concept and that was when he asked for the four U.S. Army Divisions.

As stated above after hearing from Commandant Cates, MacArthur had asked the JCS for the operational Marine Brigade. That brigade was in their standby mode, and all of their supplies and equipment was already loaded aboard their own amphibious ships. Sailing together to Korea on July 14 were their attack transports, cargo ships, dock landing ships, and LST's, (Landing Ship Tank).

MacArthur actually had to send in a second written request for the entire 1st Marine Div before it too was finally approved. Knowing that he would have his amphibious assault force Mac now began assembling the pieces he would need to complete his invasion plan. But before any other magic could happen he had to insure that his forces fighting under Gen. Walker could hold on at Pusan. Without that diversion his plan was futile.

In addition to attacking the NKPA, the Navy was able to move men and material around the perimeter, such as the emergency landing of the 1st Cavalry Div. at Pohang in July. By the end of August their logistical units and capabilities were improving and had moved 77,000 tons of ammunition into Korea. Their supply ship catastrophe took a month to straighten out, and those few warships still on duty in the Pacific were all being rushed to sea and sent westward.

Complete control of the Air and Seas allowed the Pusan Perimeter to survive.

As additional Navy and USAF aircraft came on station they relentlessly attacked any NKPA units that tried to move in daylight. (The same treatment the Werhmacht and Japanese had received in WWII.)

AF General Emmett O'Donnell the head of Bomber Command was getting started on their plans to "burn five major NK cities to the ground". There were "18 strategic targets in the country, and he wanted them destroyed quickly".

Truman vetoed the idea because it was politically unacceptable for a "Police Action" to destroy a nation, but also because no one believed there were 18 worthwhile strategic targets in all of North Korea.

The major targets were tactical, and they were attacking into the Pusan Perimeter.

In Europe the 9th AAF had been instrumental in helping to defeat the German Armies in France. Their close air support had been vital as Patton's 3d Army raced around. But when that war ended the new Air Force leaders were only interested in bombers, and that meant strategic bombing. Their fine work in France was forgotten and no attempts to integrate air-army missions were ever made by the Air Force or Navy.

As the weeks went by the USAF again played their imprudent power games. Gen. George Stratemeyer USAF went to MacArthur and demanded that they have total control of all air operations in Korea, and that included any Navy or Marine aircraft!

(At the Key West Conference in 1948 the JCS had given interdiction of land targets to the Air Force. In their minds that meant "they were in charge of anything that flew.")

MacArthur refused his inane demands.

One downside to the increasingly effective tactical aerial assaults from FEAF and the Navy fliers was that the NKPA units became masters at camouflage and night attacks. Gradually FEAF began to improve its operations and their interdiction of the NKPA supplies and units were slowing the communist attacks. The *Inmun Gun* did not require the ponderous amount of supplies the way more modern armies did, but they still needed some logistical support.

Movement of enemy supplies across the expanse of Russia meant more than a 2000 mile train ride on the inefficient Soviet rails into Manchuria. At most they could send 17,000 tons per day. Then it had to be trucked to the Yalu River, brought hundreds of miles through North Korea and down to the South to the front lines. Even though the logistic effort was done manually at times, and their supply line was being disrupted, they could still fight effectively.

The tough NKPA soldiers could fight and advance by foot on 3 rice balls a day.

It was no problem for them to scurry up and over the hilly terrain like an army of ants. The road bound and heavily equipped Americans would be spent before they had climbed the first hill. This communist ability to fight and re-supply themselves using manpower alone was one of the most astonishing enemy accomplishments in the Korean War, and the one common feat of arms accomplished by all of the Asian armies.

It was also one factor that was totally discounted by all of their opponents.

(It is a terrible shame that the U.S. leaders forgot about this ability in the next war.)

To add new problems to the communist cause Gen. MacArthur had suggested using some of the Nationalist forces from Taiwan, or possibly allowing the Nationalists to invade China. (Former Sec-Def Johnson also proposed some operations of that sort in an earlier meeting with Truman.) After some discussions it was decided to send a survey team to Taiwan to analyze the possibilities.

MacArthur had just returned to the Dai Ichi (his HQ) from a visit to Korea and took the news as authorization for himself to go, instead of someone from the JCS.

The imperious general arrived in Taiwan like a head of state. *Time* magazine, a big proponent of the general insured him plenty of publicity.

Truman was upset by this potential power grab by MacArthur and admonished him for the staged event. Mac replied that he understood what his limitations were, *"and recognized Truman's determination to protect the communist mainland"*!

On August 2 Russia's Jacob Malik returned to the U.N. to take his place on the Security Council just as the Russians rotated into the chairmanship. From that position the Russians hoped to weaken the United Nations effort.

In Beijing the Revolutionary Military Council was meeting to discuss their potential invasion of Taiwan. General Peng Dehuai delivered a report that stated their forces were still incapable of mounting the invasion due to shipping and aircraft shortfalls.

Being unable to invade Formosa, the next question they moved onto was Korea. It was felt that it would take the CCF four months to move a sizable army into Korea. Mao was quite unhappy with both negative scenarios. Their council then discussed what they could do to help solve the problems the NKPA was having in the south. Most felt that they were suffering too many casualties.

The next NKPA attack was scheduled for August 5 and was to try to reach Pusan from the southern area around Masan.

Due to the increasing demands for combat manpower Pres. Truman was forced to call up the Reserves. Most of those troops had been vets from WWII and had stayed in the reserves to get some extra money. None were counting on going back into a war.

They too were not prepared mentally or physically.

Truman also called into service four National Guard divisions, hundreds of smaller units and thousands of individuals. The Pentagon renewed conscription to try to fill out the units. Another manpower program that was instituted used impressed Koreans to add bodies to the understrength U.S. units. Called *Katusa's*, (Korean Augmentation to U.S. Army), these impressed civilians had almost no training and no desire to fight.

(The troops hated the program as the majority of those Koreans were almost useless in combat. None spoke English, few had any skills with mechanical things, and they had no discipline. Their main value was in labor. They could work and climb hills all day, and using their Korean A-frame rig could carry incredible loads on their backs.)

After the initial battles the ROK units that had been based in the northern and western part of their country had been destroyed. Those in the central and eastern sectors had fought and retreated down the peninsula until joining with Walker's forces to form the Pusan Perimeter. During those difficult weeks the ROK units had bled the *Inmun Gun* as they too traded space for time.

By the time of the organization of the Pusan Perimeter the NKPA had suffered losses as high as 40%. Because they also suffered from manpower shortages, the communists impressed any South Korean they wanted and forced them to fight with them. Any who refused were shot.

After sailing across the Pacific the 5th Marines landed at Pusan on Aug 2. They were perfectly assigned along the southern sector of the perimeter. (At that point Gen. Walker had more men and tanks than did the NKPA.)

Once off the ships the Marines organized quickly and began attacking into the nearby NKPA units within a day. Because of the planning for the next NKPA attack (mentioned above), both forces were heading into the same area, around *Masan*.

Gen. Walker's battle plan was for the Marine and Army units in the south to re-capture the southern end of the Naktong River area and then fight northward.

His thought was that those southern attacks would force the enemy to stop assaulting the Allied perimeter further north, and relocate their units southward. Those NKPA columns would be subjected to air attacks and hopefully destroyed. Being freed from being attacked would allow Walker's other units to cross the *Naktong River* and strike at the NKPA too. In that way Walker hoped to make them react to our attacks and then beat them back using mobility and firepower.

The patented Marine attacks in the southern area worked out fine as they defeated the enemy in fight after fight. The NKPA commanders in the southern sector were surprised at the effectiveness of these different Americans.

After driving the communists back 22 miles, Walker was forced to stop the 5th Marines. Strong NKPA units were still breaking through the Pusan perimeter in other sectors.

Communist commanders never worried about casualties so they never stopped their northern attacks the way western armies might have. With his northern units being pushed back by the enemy Gen. Walker needed a Fire Brigade. It was formed from the 5th Marines.

Walker's orders to them simply stated that they had to stop the NKPA penetrations and retake any lost ground. On August 15th the 5th Marines left their southern attack, moved east and then north 100 miles to attack the recently created NKPA bulge in the Pusan perimeter. This first rushed battle occurred at a dusty place called *Miryang.*

The NKPA had gotten an entire Division across the *Naktong River* and more were coming using an old Russian tactic, they built the needed bridge **below the water at night**. Being unseen it was not attacked from the air, and NPKA infantry, heavy equipment and cannons had came across at night in large numbers. They pushed through the weakened U.S. units in that sector and threatened a major breakthrough.

(One flaw that continued to hurt American army units was the large number of support troops in each division. On paper there were thousands of soldiers assigned to each division, but most were service and support troops. In the line units where the fighting was actually occurring the numbers were always low.)

In two days of heavy fighting against the 5th Marines the NKPA 4th Division was decimated. *They retreated back across the river and left all of their heavy equipment behind.* With the battle won all of the lost ground was reclaimed.

There the Marines found abandoned U.S. defenses, tanks, guns, mortars, artillery and supply depots. They realized the army unit's had not been overrun, they had left their positions. (A major irritant that added to the Marine distrust of the Army commanders was that one Marine Brigade had recaptured an area that had been held by an entire Army Division.)

While the battles above were being fought another one occurred in the seam between the 1st Cav Div and the ROK units more to the north. The NKPA 8th and 12th divisions had broken through, and could eventually threaten the airfield at Yonil on the east coast. USAF Gen. Earle Partridge (on his own) ordered the unnecessary and panicked withdrawal of the 5th Air force planes and personnel back to Kyushu, Japan.

MacArthur was not consulted or warned.

(Back in June MacArthur had wrongly told the FEAF commanders Stratemeyer and Partridge that "they could run their own show". So they did.)

Due to the "proximity" of the Inmun Gun the senior FEAF officers decided to abandon the ground troops and leave their forward airbases inside the Pusan perimeter.

Their retreat back to Japan would cause long delays in their air support because of the greater flight distances involved in getting to the battles. Again that reduced the patrol time the planes could spend over the battlefield as they used up their fuel getting there.

Instead of having planes stacked up waiting to be called in, the troops had to wait for the air force planes to show up. That threatened the ground troops survival.

(This same illicit mentality existed in WWII with the previously described landings at Normandy and Operation Cobra. Gen. MacArthur was the overall commander and he should have ordered the Air Corps units to stay put, just as Ike should have ordered them to operate as needed during Normandy and Operation Cobra. There can only be one overall commander, and he is in charge. Everyone else works for him and does as ordered.)

With the threatening NKPA attacks in the north our recently enhanced naval units were able to return to Pohang and evacuate over 7,000 South Koreans, most of who were ROK soldiers. And all the while the ROK coastal patrol craft continued engaging communist ships that were still trying to slip in behind the perimeter to land commandos. To assist that allied effort the gunships of the U.S. Navy worked along both coasts shooting up anything that presented itself. And with allied control of the seas our commando teams were landed successfully behind the enemy lines. Tunnels, rail lines, bridges and roads were all taken out in the overall effort to slow the NKPA attacks. (Had the Russians interceded with their submarines, Korea would have been a very different war.)

For six long weeks the Pusan Perimeter held from one desperate fight after another. As the NKPA became weakened by their continued losses, positions that they had taken were being reclaimed by the 8th Army units. Time after time a unit would move up and find executed Americans lying in shallow graves. Some had even been castrated while others had had their tongues cut out. All were found with their hands tied behind them. And just as had happened in the battle of the Bulge in 1944, the GI's grew angry.

They began to fight harder and smarter. (Field Marshall Rommel had written that he had never seen such inept troops as the Americans in their first battle. And he had never seen any who learned more quickly once the chips were down.)

The veteran reporters in country also included Edward R. Murrow, the voice of the Blitz in WWII. They watched with disgust the continued poor tactics by the senior army commanders and the unnecessary losses to our units and Korean civilians.

Many felt the war was a wasted effort, and Murrow even felt we were causing more harm than good in trying to keep an anti-communist in power.

(His feelings would be echoed in Vietnam.)

When the British Army contingent arrived they too were quite unhappy with the American Army commands. Staff work was not being done, the senior officers seldom went into the field, and it seemed as if the only thing anyone cared about was good press relations.

In late August the Army's 2nd Division arrived from the states with over 500 tanks. Their presence greatly bolstered the defenses as the newer Pershing tanks were more than a match for the Russian built T-34s. All felt the Pusan Perimeter could now hold out indefinitely.

With his secret plan drawing near MacArthur directed the Air Force to conduct more ground support missions than strategic bombing. As had happened in WWII they voiced their objections but reluctantly complied when MacArthur ordered them too. Still the NKPA kept attacking.

Europe

But Korea was not the only troubled nation. In Germany Cold War tensions were again increasing. The Western leaders realized they needed a strong Germany to keep Europe free, but instead of deterring a war it was possible that German rearmament might incite one. The debates on this disrupting policy continued as the War in Korea started. German newspapers headlined the Asian crisis as the test run for Central Europe.

The Soviets had been unable to stop the creation of the West German State, but there were serious reservations on if they would allow it to re-arm and join NATO. In fact many felt that that one factor might prompt a Soviet attack. Fears of a Russian attack were so strong in Germany that stocks of cyanide capsules were increased so the Parliamentarians' could end themselves rather than fall into the Russian hands. Chancellor Adenauer ordered two hundred pistols for his office.

Polls in Germany showed that over half of the population felt that if the Russians attacked, the Western Powers would abandon the new Federal Republic.

East Germany's Stalin like clone was named Walter Ulbricht. He declared that Korea proved that "puppet governments" like Adenaur's would not last long.

Kim il Sung has shown the world the best way to reunify Germany!

He also declared that the Americans have deceived themselves if they think that Germans have less national consciousness than the Koreans. If this was propaganda for propaganda sake it was highly inflammatory as the Allied forces went on alert.

Had any conflict started in Europe in all likelihood it would have gone atomic quickly since the Russians had the bomb.

Stalin however did not have a plan for any such European attack. He alone knew how weak the countries behind the Iron Curtain actually were. Instead he relied on intimidation, subversion and political machinations to try to subjugate Germany. (On March 10, 1952 Stalin even offered to accept a unified but neutral Germany in an attempt to keep Germany unarmed and out of NATO. His offer was refused and his death would end any hope for a communist reunification of Germany.)

Korea

By the end of August 1950 the U.N. forces had increased to almost 180,000 troops, and this included many units from the other member nations of the U.N.

The *Inmun Gun* was down to less than 75,000 troops and as stated before many of those were impressed S. Koreans who were told fight with them or die in place. Intelligence coming in from Russia confirmed that the U.N. was getting stronger.

The North Koreans must attack and overrun the Pusan Perimeter soon.

On August 31 NKPA attacks resumed all along the front. Again a large bulge formed near Miryang and again the 5th Marines were sent in. After days of savage fighting the Marines and some Army units drove the NKPA troops back out. The NKPA had gone to the well once to often. They were exhausted and had suffered terrible losses. In some areas flies feasting on their dead could blot out the sun.

The NKPA could always penetrate the perimeter, but they could not exploit their success. U.S. artillery and air power would quickly come in on the communist assault and prevent any large scale enemy breakthrough just like in WWII.

In less than one month of fighting the Marine Brigade had taken 900 casualties, and gave the NKPA over 10,000. Not a single Marine had been taken prisoner and they had not lost a single fight. Marine Air had flown over 1000 close support missions and all of them were guided by Tactical Air Control parties deployed at the front with the infantry. Marine Air sends a pilot to serve with the infantry as the tactical air officer.

Knowing how to speak to the other fliers enables the TAC officer to guide the flights into the fight with near perfection.

(No one was talking about eliminating the Marine Corps now.)

During those first weeks the Marines were in Korea, USAF Chief of Staff Hoyt Vandenberg again tried to strip the Marines of their Air Wing and place it under FEAF control. MacArthur again turned him away.

And suddenly the Marine heavy equipment began to head back to Pusan. Not long after the 5th Marines were also headed back aboard ship. No one knew where they were going, but for certain it was not home.

Gen. Walker was livid and loudly complained that he could not be held accountable to hold the Pusan Perimeter with the loss of that unit.

MacArthur still did not tell him!

Gen. Walker had been assigned to Japan in 1948 through the JCS, (Joint Chiefs of Staff). He did not worship MacArthur the way so many others did and was considered an "outsider". The combat proven Walker despised Ned Almond who had been a lower ranking staff officer for most of his career.

(Almond's only war command had been in the terrible 92 Division in Italy in 1944. That unit was a segregated black unit with white officers. Almond was promoted to general officer and placed in command solely because he was from Virginia, and "knew how to handle blacks"! His abysmal record with the 92 (showed that thought wrong,) but was "excused" by the Army Hierarchy because he commanded an all-black unit. He never should have been promoted further.)

At a meeting with MacArthur in early September Truman advisor Averill Harriman made a point to warn the general not to interfere in political situations, such as happened in Taiwan. At the same time a JCS inspection was being conducted by Gen. Matt Ridgeway, Gen. Lauris Norstad and Frank Pace Sec of the Army.

After observing the Pusan Perimeter, Ridgeway came away concerned with Walker's leadership, lack of force, and acceptance of a mediocre staff and support commanders. Since the secret *Operation Chromite* was set to go off no command changes were enacted, although they were "suggested".

(The changes should have been made.)

Operation Chromite *was the code name for MacArthur's daring behind the lines amphibious invasion at the port city of Inchon, far behind the enemy.*

The JCS had felt his plan was reckless and exposed the units to the threat of being cutoff.

But MacArthur had used this attack method repeatedly in his drive back to the Philippines. And as his army had invaded by sea and advanced along New Guinea, so had the Marines who stormed island after island in the Southern and then Central Pacific.

Their complimentary missions overwhelmed the Japanese defenses.

Incredibly the Marines who would be the first ones landing at Inchon were not invited to the amphibious planning sessions with MacArthur and the JCS representatives!

It was an Army show. USMC Generals Oliver Smith and Shepherd had to fight with Almond constantly over the plan in closed door sessions. To maintain his power and control over everything, Almond did not want them to speak directly to MacArthur.

The Marines wanted the landings moved 20 miles to the south for better beach access. Almond downplayed their concerns about the difficulties of the operation, but then he had never been in one. Loyal to his boss, their astute recommendations were not implemented, if they had even been passed on. Most of the senior army commanders had not been exposed to those perfected amphibious assaults, they had served in various staff positions in Europe. To them the Pacific theatre with its invasions was as alien as Mars and about as useful. (The ETO had had only 5 major amphibious invasions, N. Africa, Sicily, Italy, Normandy and Southern France. In the Pacific there had been over 30.)

Inchon was a port city on the west coast of Korea that was accessible only through a dangerous narrow channel. It had a horrendous tidal swing, (20-30 feet) that would leave ships stranded on the mud flats for hours. (The Navy & USMC knew of those problems. One of their reasons for moving the invasion southward.)

Inchon was just west of Seoul, deep behind NKPA lines.

When the JCS argued against this plan their reasoning was that they wanted to use the Chromite forces to build up the Pusan forces. With those reinforcements and overwhelming strength the UN forces could then push the communists away from the Pusan Perimeter and drive north.

MacArthur however refused to follow that old and stale, bang your head against the wall tactic as wasteful in American lives and in time. It would simply result in a protracted and bloody campaign as our forces tried to push the enemy back.

He let the JCS rant on, but would not be denied.

When he finally spoke to the assembled leaders he stated that the unsuitability of Inchon is what made it the perfect place for the invasion. Surprise was what was desired, and closing off the enemy's supply lines would stop the NKPA attacks against the Perimeter. With Seoul being retaken from the sea, the 8th Army would breakout from the perimeter *and destroy the NKPA units as they tried to flee north.*

Any units who do get northward would run into the Chromite amphibious forces attacking in from the West.

Gentlemen, we shall land at Inchon and I will crush them!

Mac's wistful amphibious move was not only fighting the entire JCS, but the supply system too. He needed to obtain the specialized amphibious ships, personnel and equipment required for the operation. *Impossible as it is to believe, all of the U.S. Navy's specialized amphibious shipping and those finely trained crews were gone.*

Lost in the rush to de-mobilize, thousands of those vessels had been abandoned. Ships actually had to be requisitioned from the Japanese.

(At the House Armed Services Committee in Oct. 49 Gen. Bradley had stated that there would never be another amphibious assault in the world. Rockets and atomic weapons ruled warfare. Hence the cutbacks to the Marines and Navy could proceed.)

Fortunately Japan was for Korea as Great Britain had been for Normandy. Both nations were indispensible as the staging areas for the war effort. Without either, the battles could not have been fought. All of the shipping, supply points, repair facilities, airfields and hospitals were located in Japan's islands.

And Japan's industrial base began to recover as they worked to help the U.N. effort succeed. Japan needed the UN to hold, or they would be next.

The Inchon invasion force would be called X Corps, and consisted of the restored "1st Marine Division", the Army's semi-reconstituted 7th Division which used Katusa's and the barely serviceable 3d division. Around 70,000 troops were involved in the invasion and most of the units had been formed from scratch. (Gen. David Barr of the 7th Div was another senior Army commander who never had a field command in WWII.)

Aerial preparation for the amphibious assault would come from naval air units from the British and American carriers. There were now four on station, and they repeatedly sent their planes up and blasted the Inchon area for days on end. Since this was to be a navy mission, the air force was not invited.

The USAF would operate around the Pusan Perimeter to make up for the repositioning of the navy and marine fliers. (If the FEAF fliers had flown in from Japan at most they could make one mission near Inchon.) Another reason Adm. Rip Struble did not want the air force to operate at Inchon was because their air control teams were still not as reliable as the Navy and Marine fliers. There could be no errors as had happened earlier.

Recon teams had already gone in and analyzed the terrain, tides, enemy positions and minefields. Although not many were found, mines could have been decisive if the NKPA had had more time to sow them. The initial invasion plan had wanted the Marines to land first and then the rest of X Corps. All units would then drive on Seoul.

Chromite planners had to fight against every known handicap and logistic difficulty, but the first phase of the assault began on schedule.

Five days of preparatory bombardment had been given all around the landing area. Planes used napalm to burn off all of the vegetation on the island of Wolmi-do which sat in the middle of the Inchon channel exposing the enemy gun positions. The Navy even sent four destroyers inside the channel to pound the island and entice the enemy gunners to fire back. Any who did were killed.

Finally a storm landing was executed properly to save the lives of the Marines.

More than likely it was because MacArthur was in command and forced the Navy Commanders to operate his way, aggressively. Even with all of this early activity the NKPA commanders did not react and reinforce the Inchon area.

As stated before, on September 12 the 3d Battalion of the 5th Marines had left their battles on the perimeter and re-boarded their ships at Pusan. Three days later on September 15 they were landed on the small island of Wolmi-do in the middle of Inchon's harbor. Like the textbook operations of WWII, the Marines took out the 400 NKPA troops, while suffering just 17 wounded.

Then the tide went out and the Navy went back out to sea. While the tide was out the long range guns of the fleet put a ring of steel around the 3d Battalion, and Navy and Marine planes attacked anything that moved in the area. MacArthur was quite pleased that surprise had been achieved and the enemy caught completely off guard. (Just as he had said they would.)

Mac sent a cable to the JCS, "The Navy and Marines have never shone more brightly".

(David Lawrence of the NY Herald Tribune had printed a story in July about a possible amphibious assault in Korea. Fortunately for the troops the Russians missed it.

Prior amphibious planning had already been done for Inchon in 1945, and again in early 1950. That probably alleviated some of the numerous planning problems at Inchon.)

The tide slowly returned, and by 1730 hrs the first landing craft of the main invasion force hit the tall, rocky seawalls at Inchon. Forced to use scaling ladders to climb the wall, the USMC fire-team assaults were restricted and reduced.

A better defended shoreline like the defenses at *Tarawa, Peleliu or Omaha* would have resulted in heavy casualties. But the surprise was complete and the preparatory bombings had defeated most of the enemy defenses. Marine units stormed ashore taking light casualties. Fighting all night the Marines encircled the city by 0130 hrs on the 16th.

The next units sent ashore were the ROK Marines whose mission was to finish up the fighting inside the city of Inchon itself. That would free up the U.S. Marines so they could push inland to finish the encirclement and setup any needed defenses in the event of a counter-attack. The cost of the invasion was just 22 killed, 174 wounded.

(For the Marines, only the landings at *Guadalcanal* and *Okinawa* had been less costly.)

Once again MacArthur had worked his amphibious magic.

Gen. Ned Almond had been handpicked by MacArthur to command X Corps, and like so many Army officers he resented that the Marines were in the spotlight.

He actually tried to replace the 5th Marines with the 32nd Infantry as the first unit to go ashore. Gen. Oliver Smith USMC who commanded the 1st Mar Div was dumbfounded on just how Almond expected an unschooled and diluted unit to storm this potentially hardened target and win. Smith refused to go along with the idea and Almond had to back down. (This was the first of many obvious failures in his thinking and illustrated why the Marines did not trust him. Almond was a die cast MacArthur man, and blindly did whatever his boss said.)

The Marine Corps commanders were quite angry over "this unexpected and convenient command arrangement". Almond had very little command or battlefield experience, and he had no amphibious experience at all. There were three senior battle-tested and trained USMC Generals available in the Pacific, but MacArthur had made his loyal subordinate his pick. (Almond was still MacArthur's Chief of Staff, and this new command was payback for being loyal to the boss.)

Back in the Pentagon the JCS were also most unhappy over this clever arrangement. It was within their purview to pick the commander of X Corps, and there were **veteran commanders** available. The JCS could have and should have overruled MacArthur and made Almond the other guy's deputy commander. *But like so many other poor decisions by those senior officers, they sat on the sidelines and took no control over the war.*

To create diversions to help *Chromite* succeed air and naval attacks had occurred at all of the other potential invasion areas. The ports on the East Coast were much better sites to land at than Inchon, and for that reason they were more heavily defended.

However the coastal plains around them were small and the topography quickly changed to ragged hills and then mountains. So militarily it was not a good place to land since little could be accomplished after the landings. (Similar to Sicily and Italy.)

All along the East Coast the enemy had placed hundreds of sea-mines in the approach areas. As the aggressive navy ships went closer to shore they began setting off the mines. By the last week in September four ships had been severely damaged or sunk and the navy wisely moved their ships further out to sea. Many felt that the reduced pace of their operations in the eastern side would not matter for the war had already been won at Inchon. *But MacArthur had victory disease.*

Back at Inchon the invading Marines had to keep moving inland to seize their next objective. Their air control teams had landed early on and were decisive in directing close-in air support and naval gunfire. Again the coordinated attacks routed the defenders and by the 18th the Marines had recaptured Kimpo Airfield just outside of Seoul.

(Naval gunfire had stopped two NKPA armored counterattacks, just like Sicily and Italy.)

Within a day Marine Air Wing units landed at Kimpo and began flying close air-support missions just miles behind the front lines. (Unlike FEAF) This was one of the foundations of Marine Corps success, the combined arms team.

By having dedicated air support on call and on station the marines were assured of being able to overcome most obstacles. Any enemy counter-attacks would be spotted, attacked and harassed long before they reached the troops.

Excellent staff work by Smith's people had recognized that they would have to cross the broad Han River. They made sure to include portable bailey bridges and floating bridge sections in their list of supplies. And that forethought allowed them to keep moving forward, never giving the NKPA a chance to recover.

Almond then decided to rush the Army's weak 7th Div ashore so that they could get into the fight and garner some headlines. Their movements were slow and tangled as none of their commanders knew how to organize from ship to shore. It took them two days to get ashore.

Marine Major General Oliver Smith commander of the 1st Mar Div had fought at *Bougainville, Peleliu and Okinawa*. He did not like nor trust Almond, and they butted heads constantly. By the 20th his Marines were on the outskirts of Seoul in the industrial city of Yongdong-po. A brilliant night penetration by Capt Barrow's Able company took the dominant terrain and killed another 300 enemy troops. (macwar112)

That unexpected move enabled supporting attacks the next morning in the inner city of Yongdungp'o by the 1st Marines. *Almond then decided to send half of the 7th Division southward in a foolish publicity stunt to link up with the 8th Army.* This linkup would look good for the press as the breakout from Pusan had begun. (MacArthur however was unhappy with the lack of progress by 8th Army.)

However Gen. Smith and the Marines had needed and wanted the army's 7th Div to attack into the southern part of the city to free up the 7th Marines. Then Smith could send the 7th into a blocking position east of the city to cut off the NKPA escape. That would also allow the 7th Marines to attack into the communist rear from the east while everyone else would hit them from the west.

But that wise move was not done due to the differences between the services and in this disparate command arrangement. As a result the NKPA escapees from Yongdong-Po took up additional positions in Seoul resulting in a much more difficult urban fight than it had to be. (This was the same type of uncalled for command failure as the ones that allowed the Germans to escape from Sicily and Falaise.)

For the first few days after the invasion the NKPA commanders had believed the Inchon landings were a feint, to draw forces away from the perimeter. (Just as Hitler believed with Normandy). The communist commanders did not tell their troops attacking the Pusan Perimeter anything. They simply sent whatever units they had in the Inchon area to try to stop the invaders. But with the Allies having complete control over the air and sea that plan was impossible. The U.S. forces were ashore to stay and the strength of their attack showed that this was no feint.

Once the U.S. combat units were ashore the service and engineer troops landed with their equipment to rebuild, repair and rearrange Inchon's harbor for Allied use. Again they performed brilliantly despite the shoestring style operation.

A few days after the landings at Inchon the U.N. began dropping leaflets around the Pusan Perimeter. It was time to let the troops of the *Inmun Gun* know the truth.

When the word got around the effect was devastating.
MacArthur's prediction that a disaster would be caused by severing the enemy's supply line was again correct.

With the happy shock of the secret landings at Inchon, Walker and his staff issued new orders, Attack and pursue. Units were to strike out from where they were to destroy the enemy and move north to link up with X Corps. Beginning on the 16th the 8th Army units attempted to penetrate the Naktong River but were held back by the NKPA.

By the 19th the NKPA resistance began to collapse and by September 22 the 8th Army was miles past the Naktong River. *In an effort to escape many of the enemy troops tossed away their weapons, changed their clothes and became "refugees".*

A week later they became guerilla fighters and saboteurs.

(The pattern would be renewed in Vietnam and Iraq).

Units of the 8th Army were ecstatic at finally being on the offensive. At times they were advancing thirty miles at a clip. And as the 8th Army units advanced into NKPA controlled areas they began uncovering shades of the holocaust.

At Taejon 500 captured ROK soldiers had just been executed. In a nearby mission schoolyard over 5000 civilians had been recently shot and buried in a shallow grave.

Dozens of sites like this would be found as the communist indoctrination program was in full swing. Also found were numerous execution sites of captured GIs.

By September 22 an intense street to street fight for Seoul was raging.

Not since the fighting in Garapan on Saipan had the Marines seen such extreme urban fighting. The communists were desperately trying to keep the roads open to free as many of their trapped troops as possible. The NKPA even added their 9th Div to reinforce the 18th in trying to hold the city. Ammo shortages began to appear until the Marines found a warehouse stocked with captured U.S. munitions.

Late on the 25th Gen. Almond radioed Gen. Smith and told him to attack into the city again, that the NKPA were withdrawing. Smith and his staff knew this news to be untrue from the battlefield reports from his commanders. He asked for more information about the NKPA positions but Almond's staff refused to give any and repeated the attack order. (No such attack order was directed to the nearby Army's 32 Infantry Regiment.)

The result was a savage night battle in the darkened city which included enemy tanks. The fight lasted until dawn, and losses were heavy to the attacking Marines.

This only reinforced Marine beliefs that Almond was unfit for this type of command. *But the real reason for the X Corps attack order was that MacArthur wanted to reinstate Pres. Rhee on the 3d month anniversary of the invasion. Another of those symbolic dates to the oriental psyche.*

(The entire fight for Seoul could have been avoided if the units stayed out of the city and simply cut them off, but Mac wanted the city taken for this ceremony.)

Not to be deterred by the unfortunate heavy street fighting, Almond sent out a pronouncement that Seoul had been liberated. The grandiose proclamation occurred exactly three months to the day of the communist invasion. No mention was ever made of the five remaining days of intense street fighting, nor the additional week required in mopping up the last of the communist holdouts who were barricaded all over the city.

(The reporters who worked with the troops knew the truth but kept a lid on the story.)

On September 29th in a lavish ceremony *Gen. MacArthur returned President Rhee to power in the shattered Government House.* The 3d battalion 5th Marines were nearby on guard, but kept out of sight. Only spruced up U.S. Army troops were allowed to be seen and photographed. After the ceremony Mac presented Almond with his third decoration since the invasion!??

This "Police Action" had so far caused the U.S. to suffer almost 27,000 casualties.

Diplomatic problems began to appear as fast as the collapse of the Inmun Gun. MacArthur was announcing to the war reporters that the war would soon be over and that *he expected* that Pres. Rhee would preside over a unified Korea. In Washington President Truman was quickly cornered on if that announcement meant that the U.N. forces would cross the 38th parallel. Truman responded that that was a decision for the U.N. (In secret MacArthur had been told to pursue and destroy the NKPA.)

In the Communist press venues only allusions had appeared about the setback in Korea. But behind closed doors big decisions were being pondered.

On September 25th during the fight for Seoul, the Indian Ambassador to China, K. Panikkar had dinner with the Red Chinese Army Chief of Staff Gen Yen-jung. During the meal the General stated that MacArthur's forces would not be tolerated near China's common border. "We know what we are in for, but at all costs this "American aggression" has to be stopped. They can bomb us all they want, but they cannot defeat us on land"! Panikkar warned his host that the devastation of a new war could set China back a generation. Gen Yen-jung calmly replied, "We have calculated all of that".

Ambassador Panikkar immediately reported this information to the U.S. State Dept. but Acheson blew it off as nervousness by Panikkar.

Back in Washington the JCS should have known that MacArthur had big plans and they should have forced their input to become accepted. But in the heady triumph of the hour they only sent congratulations. George Marshall who had replaced the "mortified" Louis Johnson as Sec. of Defense, sent congratulations and an eyes only message giving MacArthur permission to cross the 38th. There was to be no announcement, just act like it was a military necessity.

(Which it was, pursuit of the enemy.)

MacArthur was pleased for he was getting his chance to attack the communists on their own ground. *With more glory dancing in his head MacArthur had already envisioned a second amphibious landing on the east coast, while Walker's 8th Army moved up the western side of North Korea.??* (Was MacArthur warned about the sea-mines?)

On Sept. 26th he directed his staff to come up with such a plan to finish off North Korea. No one on Mac's staff would think of suggesting something to the contrary, and so this seriously flawed plan was developed and enacted.

It would prove as disastrous as it was militarily ridiculous.

And it would deny Korea a chance at reunification.

Within the Diplomatic circles talks continued to discuss the problem of any Allied advance north. One group of Paul Nitze, Charles Bohlen and George Kennan warned that Russia and China would not permit our advance to go unchallenged.

Others like Dean Acheson, Dean Rusk and Averill Harriman felt there was no way too stop. "Psychologically it was almost impossible not to go on and finish the job".

Some in the press were also demanding the Reds be crushed.

The National Security Council had already produced a paper on Korean reunification titled NSC-81. The work recommended reunification by election, hoping to keep the Communists at bay legally. (Truman had approved the report on September 11, just before the invasion at Inchon began.)

But once again Pres. Truman on his own had formally shifted U.S. policy from preserving South Korea into reunification of the nation. To do this required destroying the NKPA, and he approved this aggressive action without any discourse from the Congress our military, our allies or the United Nations!

President Rhee was not helping the situation for he urged his commanders to ignore the Americans and move north. "We will not allow ourselves to stop".

And through it all Gen. MacArthur was holding additional press conferences and telling the world what had to be done instead of the *world leaders telling him what was to be done.*

The United Nations sent an updated memorandum, 81/1, on September 27th.

It authorized U.N. operations into N. Korea, but only if at the time of such operations there had been no entry of China or Russia, nor an announcement of such entry.

(The State Dept. had received such notification from the Indian Ambassador Panikkar.)

UN 81/1 also stated there was to be no Air or Naval actions across the Yalu River. Undeterred by the political rules MacArthur's next phase planning continued.

Americans have always accepted that there are checks and balances in the world.
But Americans forget that in the Real World, such checks have never been achieved with votes or papers with scrolling words.
They are achieved with force.
And in "modern times" it is achieved from the barrel of a gun.
Americans don't admire this style of resolution for it defeats their "moral purpose".
But they have never failed to resort to guns when other means fail.
America had never played the major role like this on the world stage before and would soon learn that there are many types of checks. It was inevitable that with the turning of the tide the U.S. would want to punish the North Koreans for their lawlessness and destructive ideology. It was also hoped that all of Korea could now be reunited under the Government of the *Taehan Minkuk*.
But in reality the communists had not broken any law, for in the continuing tragedy of mankind there is no international law.
The Communist World had tried to probe a weakness in the "other world" and had been strongly checked. They had not been checkmated. Now the Communists looked upon America's quest for justice as a probe of their world.
And that would not be tolerated. (19)

On October 1st, MacArthur called for the surrender of all North Korean forces and presented his incredibly flawed battle plan. Kim Il Sung made no reply.

Neither did the JCS.

On October 4th, Chinese premier Chou En-lai summoned the Indian Ambassador to a midnight conference. In plain terms Chou stated that if U.S. troops crossed the 38th parallel, China would enter the war. Again this information was forwarded to U.S. officials. *And again the news was treated as a communist bluff.*

At the front MacArthur's irrational plan for finishing off N. Korea was finally being enacted. **He had directed that the all of X Corps, which had just been completely landed with all of their equipment**

and units, was to be turned around and reassembled aboard their ships! The Navy would then transport them around Korea to the East coast and land them at the port city of Wonsan. X Corps would then advance northward on that side of Korea up to the Yalu River. 8th Army would remain in the Western sector and advance up their side of North Korea also going on to the Yalu.

At that point MacArthur felt the war would be over.

Seeing this unwise plan all of the other commands rightfully objected.

The Navy felt it imprudent and wasteful to re-embark these same units they had just dropped off and ferry them to the east coast. It would take weeks to accomplish.

The Air Force which was just returning to Korea was rightfully afraid of losing their supply lines as those difficult transfers would foul up the harbors at Inchon and Pusan.

General Walker correctly wanted to keep X Corps as part of his command. *They were his freshest troops with the exception of the 5th Marines, and he fittingly wanted them to continue attacking northward in the pursuit of the retreating enemy.*

They were also the northern most allied unit fighting in Korea.

It was a no-brainer to have them continue hammering the NKPA and moving north on towards Pyongyang, North Korea's capitol.

Gen. Walker's last and again correct objection was that North Korea was physically separated into two halves. The Taebaek Mountains constituted a complete separation between the western and eastern sides of the Korean peninsula. (Like our Rocky Mtns.)

The two separate armies would be unable to support one another and with X Corps again operating separately there would also be no unity of command.

Walker appropriately suggested that some of the 8th Army units currently operating in central and eastern Korea should simply move overland to the East coast areas that MacArthur wanted taken with this "needless amphibious landing".

In that way the Marines could continue attacking northward, and those other units would reach the east coast satisfying everyone.

The navy would land the latter's supplies at Wonsan or any other port those units wanted.

And the timeline of the overland movement would be far less than what was required in re-embarking X Corps, sailing around the peninsula and then landing them again!

Gen. Walker's correct objections and thoughts would have simplified the overall operation and more importantly allowed X Corps to continue the militarily vital concept of pursuit of the enemy. As usual MacArthur blew off all of the objections despite the fact that all of them were militarily sound. His ridiculous plan would go forward. Naturally he had ulterior motives.

With X Corps continuing to be a separate command his loyal subordinate Gen. Almond was guaranteed to get his third star. And with the Marines operating on the far reaches of the eastern side of Korea they would get no more press.

(It wouldn't look good for the Army to have the Marines liberate Seoul and Pyongyang.) *In promoting and executing this unreasonable plan Gen. MacArthur would lose any chance of defeating the communists and reuniting Korea.*

But he did lose thousands of lives and prolong the war.

Again the JCS did not ensure that they had a voice in the direction of the war. They did not like this new plan, but said nothing. In effect their lack of control and supervision allowed this vital United Nations action against communism to become *MacArthur's War.*

They "issued a weak directive" restraining U.N. ground forces from operating north of the line established from Chongju on the west coast, to Hungnam on the East coast. This line constituted all of the major cities of the North except one and ran across the narrow waist of N. Korea. There was no road or east-west crossing at that spot, but it did create the smallest front to defend, 120 miles across should Russia or China join in the fight. (As the Chinese had warned they would.)

The ROK units however had no restrictions on their movements.

The Joint Chief of Staff which included many of the nation's senior military minds including Chairman Omar Bradley did not argue or intercede to stop MacArthur's imprudent realignment.

They offered no alternatives either, and share half of the blame for the debacle that was soon to come.

A full week had passed since MacArthur had presented his plan and it was actually accomplished. *During that unwarranted pause in the fighting the remnants of the Inmun Gun had escaped from the UN forces and safely retreated back towards the Yalu River.* Like all good communists they had accepted this temporary defeat.

It was Communist Doctrine to always exploit success, but it was folly to reinforce failure.

They would wait for better conditions and simply try again.

By the 7th of October all of the Marine units had left their combat operations and headed back to the port of Inchon. The rest of X Corps was trying to do the same.

The exhausted units of the 8th Army who had been fighting non-stop since July had replaced them on the line. At noon on Oct 7th the U.S. 8th Army finally reached the border. *ROK units had already crossed it days before.*

Conveniently ignored by Almond and MacArthur were the reports from the *ROK Divisions already operating on the Eastern side of Korea.*
They had been on the northern part of the Pusan Perimeter and were already across the border in force. Resistance was light and they were advancing.

Their 1st Div was operating north of 8th Army and the ROK 6th Div had moved up to Chunchon. Their 3d and Capitol Divisions were already nearing Wonsan on the East Coast, where X Corps was planned to land in a week or so!

Thus there was no reason to have relocated X Corps.

And as the FEAF Commanders suspected the supply lines in Inchon became entangled. Gen. Walker had to order another halt in the U.N. advance to straighten things out. Days of inactivity followed and for weeks after the mess continued to affect 8th Army's supply lines.

It took five full days of port time just to reload most of X Corps equipment and USMC personnel. Then the Marines had to make the 850 sea-mile-u-turn around the Korean peninsula. *Things at Inchon were so fouled up that the 7th Division had to return to Pusan by rail and find ships to take them up the East Coast to Wonsan!*

(Almond was incensed that things were fouled up and took out his anger on the 7th Div commanders.)

The Navy was completely against this unneeded amphibious move. They were supplying the ROK units and knew how far they had moved up the East Coast. X Corps should have just gone overland since MacArthur insisted they go there.

Despite his self-imposed setbacks MacArthur was quite pleased with the overall events. Since the invasion at Inchon over 60,000 NKPA prisoners had been captured with most going to POW camps down by Pusan. They were becoming a huge burden to house, clothe, feed and guard. (About half were impressed S. Koreans.)

On October 10th ROK units had entered the eastern city of Wonsan finding little resistance. Some of their patrols had even reached the next city 50 miles to the north called Hamhung. With that information MacArthur decided to send some of X Corps further north which created more delays as units and equipment had to be switched around again.

But a serious problem was getting worse.

The sea-mines that had been found in September had only been the start of the enemy effort. Our Navy was uncovering sea-mines all over the Eastern Coast. More of their ships had been damaged and sunk, and it looked like the mine-sweeping effort could take weeks! The tidal swings on the West Coast at Inchon had exposed many of the enemy sea-mines to observation and quick destruction, when the low tides arrived. But that was not the case on the East Coast.

The waters there were deep and murky making spotting and sweeping hard and dangerous.

On October 11, Gen. Almond and his staff finally ordered the seaborne operation for X Corps to commence. While he and his staff were dining on a splendid table the Navy support units continued to try to sweep the thousands of sea-mines that had been set. The Russians had done a fine job of filling the waters with chemical, pressure activation, and electronic mines. These were the same types of sea-mines that were supposed to have been installed at Inchon during the week of Sept 18th.

(They were found near the city still packed in their crates.)

MacArthur hurriedly cobbled together a scratch force of "minesweepers", and even impounded nine ships from the Japanese. Over twenty square miles of water had to be swept and cleared to provide access to the needed harbors. Three of those ships were sunk with heavy casualties when they activated or struck a mine.

Because of the mining the transport fleet was forced to sail up and down the east coast of Korea for days on end. The Marines sarcastically nicknamed MacArthur's and Almond's incessant naval U-Turns, Operation Yo-Yo.

Most of the 7th Division would be redirected to the small coastal town of Iwon in far off NE Korea while the Marines remained cramped and seasick aboard their Navy landing ships. Admiral Doyle harshly criticized Gen. Almond and this idiotic debacle. This "move" *had already used up two full weeks of shipping time and accomplished nothing!* He also reminded Almond of the U.N. restrictions on using U.N. forces near the USSR or Manchurian borders.

Back in the Pentagon the JCS privately fumed at the loss of pursuit that MacArthur's new plan had allowed. But none of them had moved to correct things.

As the days progressed the 8th Army slowly continued up the western side of Korea while the ROK units were unrelenting in their advances in the central and eastern sectors. Untrained in coordinated large unit advances the ROK units left thousands of NKPA troops alive and active in the hills around them. Nightly skirmishes were constant.

And as Walker's units continued to move north more communist atrocities were being uncovered. The 21st regiment found a cave filled with massacred and burned South Korean civilians who had been shipped to the north to be secretly murdered.

Few Americans could comprehend what kind of enemy they were fighting.

Communist foreign policy is one based on expansion and aggressiveness.

Their ideology was more than a tool, it was their taskmaster. As shown in *Fatal Flaws Book 1*, they attempted conquests as soon as they took power in 1919.

Unless this Leninist ideology could be diluted or diverted there would never be a true peace between Communism and the West.

Liberals in the West were, (and still are), unable or unwilling to comprehend this driving reality of Communist dogma. And that was why they continued to seek peace using words.

Back on October 1 Stalin had been in the Crimea recovering from heart trouble. In his hand was a dispatch from Kim Il Sung stating that not only had the Americans retaken Seoul, they were poised to take over all of N. Korea. His forces were spent and broken. "We desperately need military support from Russia. If for some political reason this cannot be provided then we need your help organizing volunteer units from China".

Stalin was unwilling to be drawn into a direct war with America, but he desired to keep the Americans tied down in the Far East. Russia was still reeling from their ordeals of WWII and with the discontinuance of American aid the Soviet economy was dysfunctional. (The West did not know of this.)

Russia's "client states in Eastern Europe" were at best unreliable allies and their economies and nations also remained in ruins.

Stalin knew what the West did not, that Russia could not afford to fight them at that time. But he could bleed them.
And so Stalin dictated a message to Mao and Zhou En-lai claiming that at present Russia could only send arms. He requested that China move five or six Divisions into North Korea to force the aggressors out. He signed the note with his Chinese alias, Pheng Xi to hide the true voice.

Mao answered that a few divisions would not suffice. "If they committed to fight in Korea it would be in force. The U.S. may declare war upon us, and in that case Russia would have to assist as per their mutual assistance pact". (Wisely, Mao did not trust Stalin.)

Mao called in General Peng Dehuai, and on Oct 4th the decision was made to send in a large Chinese Army to fight the Americans.

Stalin replied to Mao's cable and reassured him that the U.S. does not wish a large war and if faced with such a prospect they would give in to China and her allies.

Such an accommodation could possibly include the U.S. abandonment of Formosa and a separate peace with Japanese reactionaries.

Speaking with his usual manipulative lies Stalin then added,

"The U.S. cannot allow itself to be drawn into a large scale war. The other capitalist states constitute no serious military force. Let us face WWIII now before Japan is rearmed and the West has a beachhead in Korea".

(Stalin's calculating view was ironically identical to MacArthur's in that a Western loss in Korea would be fatal to the entire region.)

Without intimating to Stalin that he had already decided to attack, Mao was happy to hear Stalin respond of their joint fight and sent Zhou to Russia to work out the arms requirements for nine Chinese Divisions. The communists had won the war in China by using weapons scrounged from the Japanese, gifts from Russia and arms captured from the Nationalists. This time they wanted up to date equipment and air support.

Stalin gave excuses and promises. He wanted adventure, but only on the cheap. The Russian Premier would send hundreds of thousands of tons of supplies, ammo, weapons, food and fuel. He also sent aviation units and thousands more of advisors and specialists in artillery and tank units. They would fight the capitalists, but only as volunteers. Stalin would wait until the last before committing Red Army units directly against the West. After Zhou returned to China, Stalin told Nikita Khrushchev, "If Kim falls so what. The Americans can be our neighbors."

On Oct 8, the Chinese army based in Manchuria was renamed, "The Chinese Peoples Volunteers", and they began to move south. They hoped to drive out the Americans before the harsh cold of winter. Ironically just the day before the U.N. had voted on a resolution to try to reunify the country of Chosun.

It was a wish that would never occur, but it could have.

Concerned with the verbal threats coming from China the JCS met and prepared a draft for Gen. MacArthur. **"In the event of the open or covert deployment of major Chinese-communist forces, you can continue your actions as long as in your judgment you have**

a reasonable chance of success. You must obtain authorization from Washington before any military action can be taken against China." (21)

The statement was approved by Pres. Truman, but in reality it was too vague and left too many loopholes to have any effect on someone like MacArthur. It was forwarded to Tokyo, and Truman decided he had to meet with Mac to discuss the war. Neither one knew that the resurgent armies of Communist China were already organizing their moves across the Yalu River.

(MacArthur was always imperious, and felt he was far and away smarter than all others. He had not been held responsible for his terrible failures in Dec/41. Truman had written in his diary on June 17, 1945 that FDR should have ordered Wainwright home and left MacArthur to be the martyr.)

On October 12, 1950 Pres. Truman left Washington DC to meet MacArthur at Wake Island. Mac had claimed to be too busy to fly all the way to DC, so Pres. Truman had to travel halfway around the world to speak to America's Caesar.

That same day Stalin cabled Kim and told him to seek sanctuary in Manchuria or Russia with as much of his army as he could save. Live to fight another day.

On the 13th, Mao cabled Stalin and announced China's plan, with or without his help. Stalin was pleased that the Chinese were fighting as "volunteers". He then cabled Kim to stay and fight, but gave few particulars. On the 14th he sent another message that China would help him and to have good luck. Events in Korea were going to change again.

The prior weeks of lost pursuit due to MacArthur's plan had given the NKPA enough time to reorganize and resupply to continue their fight. The NKPA had been in total disarray after Seoul fell. They had lost tens of thousands of their troops who were captured all over the South. However, none of the senior NKPA commanders were captured. Like the German escape from France in 1944, those leaders were able to re-organize and resurrect their forces. Kim's NKPA was regrouping near the Yalu River in western Korea. Chinese units joined them.

More intelligence warnings were passed onto MacArthur's staff regarding possible Chinese intervention and again all were dismissed. Chinese army units were even observed by USAF aircraft as they were moving into the common border areas.

As a cover story the Chinese broadcast messages that they were sending forces to protect the Suiho Hydroelectric plant in N. Korea. (The huge plant supplied the electric power for most of Manchuria but was declared off limits by Truman.)

Gen. Charles Willoughby's intelligence briefings in Tokyo acknowledged that there were large Chinese armies in Manchuria which could easily cross the Yalu River into Korea. His updates downplayed that possibility. *Even at that late date Gen. MacArthur and his staff were still located in Tokyo and trying to run the war from there.* And helping the enemy to plan their moves was the publicity hungry MacArthur and the western press. Always anxious to get out a story, they had forgotten the WWII motto, "loose lips sink ships". Newspapers routinely carried stories of unit locations, movements and personnel, all for the simple enjoyment of enemy intelligence services. This was a mistake that would occur again and again in the guise of "press corps rights".

On Oct 15 Truman and MacArthur met up at Wake Island. MacArthur did not salute, he shook hands with the President as if they were equals. They discussed Korea, Taiwan and China for about 90 minutes. Present at the meeting were Gen. Bradley and Averill Harriman. Notes were taken but never made public.

Conveniently Sec. of Def. Marshall did not attend the conference. Out of all of America's senior leaders from WWII, only Marshall was of the same stature. If anyone would have been able to control and talk to MacArthur as an equal, it would have been Marshall. (The two did not like each other.)

Truman came prepared with a large staff and up to date briefings. *The NSC had warned him as early as September that it was doubtful that the Russians or Chinese would tolerate any allied units near Manchuria. They also succinctly warned that Stalin would use the Chinese to fight any battles.*

MacArthur boasted that his units were rapidly advancing along both flanks and he expected X corps to be in Pyongyang shortly.?

(Apparently even MacArthur had forgotten where X corps was, and he never mentioned that most of this force was still bobbing around in their transports or stuck at Pusan.)

Gen. Bradley if he knew never corrected him. Like almost all of the senior officers in the military, Bradley was timid around MacArthur. MacArthur conceitedly expected the fighting to be over by Thanksgiving and most of the troops back home by Christmas. Scheduled reinforcements could be curtailed.

(Fortunately the extra troops still arrived in Korea.)

When asked about the POW situation Mac was again mistaken in his belief that all were *Koreans first.* Little did he realize that the communists were already dividing each POW camp into communist cadres and units and enemy units. (Stay behind organizers had given themselves up and were secretly preparing the POW camps for bloody revolt.)

As a final question on Korea Pres. Truman asked if there was any danger of Chinese or Russian interference. MacArthur arrogantly replied, "Had either one intervened in the first two months their actions would have been decisive, but not at this time. We are no longer fearful of their intervention.

The Chinese have at most 300,000 troops in Manchuria.
Of those not more than 100-125,000 are along the Yalu River.

They would have the greatest difficulty getting across and supplying 50,000 troops.

With no air force they would be destroyed."

Even as MacArthur spoke thousands of CCF troops were crossing the Yalu River daily. They were disciplined, moving only at night and experts at camouflage.

General Peng was at Andong directing the infiltration.

He moved on to Pakchon in Korea on the 18th and ordered his troops to appear to be refugees. Their movements were never spotted by the high flying air-recon planes.

(Twice Gen. Willoughby was given information from naval sources that the Chinese would come in. Both times he blew them off.)

The last topic to come up was of Indochina and the forthcoming disaster there. MacArthur wondered why the best of the French could not win against the poorly supplied communists. (The first ten American advisors had just arrived in Vietnam.)

Truman replied, "You can't do anything with the damned French."

On October 8, 1950, 3,500 French troops were trapped in their fortress at Cao Bang. Less than 1,000 escaped. *In their recent victories, (with China's help), the Vietminh had picked up tons of abandoned French equipment.* Included in the haul were 8,000 rifles, over 1,000 machine guns and 450 vehicles. Northern Vietnam was falling to the communists, and French Commander Marcel Carpentier drew up plans to retreat to the 18th parallel.

(Admiral Radford had warned the JCS and the Administration years before, "You can't make headway against the communists without the support of the people".)

There was a lot of talking at the meeting, but no real communication.

MacArthur left dismayed that Truman seemed to be willing to settle for a negotiated peace, while he was still determined to re-take all of Korea.

On Oct 20, Pyongyang fell to the 8th Army.
It was the only Communist capitol to fall to the armies of the West.

Unlike Seoul, the communists made sure all of the fighting was done outside of the city. When the North Koreans finally retreated the city fell without a shot.

No sense in destroying their homes.
Besides they knew they would be back.

Church bells tolled in the city for the first time in five years. Patrolling troops found more mass graves and wells stuffed with political prisoners who the Reds had murdered just before they had left. Units from the 1st Cavalry found an additional 66 murdered GI's in a railway tunnel. Seven others were found to have been starved to death. Twenty three others were just barely alive. Those ninety six were all that were found of the 370 captured GIs who had been shipped north from Seoul as the Marines drew near. (And if the Marines had been able to bypass and cutoff Seoul the POWs might have been freed.)

Intelligence teams recovered hundreds of documents showing that Russia had indeed been behind the invasion. One entire NKPA Division had been sent to Russia for its training. Also revealed was the already known fact that Russian pilots were flying most of the air missions!

But all of that information was deemed classified by the secretive Truman Administration.

On October 22 Red China invaded Tibet.

Protests had been growing over the annexation from two years earlier. To shut down the protests large communist invasion forces easily overran the peaceful nation. The Dali Lama escaped into exile inside India.

Almost half a million Tibetan innocents died that year.

Once again a peaceful nation was overrun by the aggressive armies from a communist nation. At the U.N. the Tibetans asked for assistance, but no help was available.
The few military resources the U.N. directed were committed to Korea.

India's Prime Minister Nehru decided to remain neutral over this "incident", despite the fact they shared a common border. He was not a fan of the West, but was afraid to incite the Chinese. His neutrality however did not deter the communists.

In August 1951 he was forced to warn the encroaching Chinese that India would fight for her northern provinces.

On Oct 25, 1950 the Marines finally started going ashore. Their entire Division would not completely land until October 31. ROK units had far outpaced X Corps arrival during the past three weeks!

(Even the Bob Hope tour had landed before the X Corps forces.)

ROK troops operating in the area had cleared some one thousand anti-tank mines from the beaches over the past ten days. (That was where the enemy expected a landing.)

Although our Navy and FEAF planes had attacked the enemy in Wonsan, the port itself was surprisingly in fine shape.

For the first few days the Marines patrolled, worked their weakened bodies and organized for the road ahead. Almond had been given orders to strike out past the coastal areas and go deep into the mountains of North Korea and up to the Yalu River.

He was determined to comply, but he and his staff totally understated and underestimated the severity of the coming winter. Most of the X Corps troops had no winter clothing, and the higher in elevation they went the worse the frigid conditions became.

(Almond had a large trailer unit with hot shower, refrigerator and flush toilet. Fresh food was flown in to him daily. The Spartan Marines had nothing of the kind and their commanders ate what the men ate.)

MacArthur's orders to drive to the Yalu finally prompted the JCS to react. But their weakly worded message did not stop the movements northward.

Paul Nitze and others on the State Dept. Planning staff did not agree with MacArthur's plan or that he should have had permission to go north of the 38th parallel.

Bypassed NKPA units continued to attack anyone within reach and always at night. The Marines had grown soft after the two plus wasted weeks aboard ship and their discipline suffered. Each morning their casualties were ferried out by Marine helicopters.

(At this time in the war only the Marines had figured how to use those strange craft.)

Gen. Almond had been "given command" of all operations in NE Korea by MacArthur. This now included the ROK I Corps, the 1st Marine Division, and the U.S. Army's 7th and 3d Divisions. Those units had just begun their movements northward when word got out that the 8th Army had run into Chinese troops.

It should not have been a surprise, there had been many warnings.

On Oct. 25 a patrol from the ROK 1st Div operating in N. Central Korea with 8th Army captured a soldier wearing a strange quilted uniform. One side was white and the other was mustard brown. When he was interrogated he replied that he was from China, one of *tens of thousands* in the hills near Unsan. Gen. Paik commander of the ROK 1st Div became alarmed, the ROK 6th Div was operating alone near the Yalu River.

Gen. Frank Milburn was a Corps Commander who was present at the interrogation of that captured soldier. Milburn went through Gen. Walker's staff in 8th Army, and quickly radioed the same information back to MacArthur's staff in Tokyo.

Willoughby and staff dismissed the report as "unconfirmed"!

Far north of the 38th parallel Col. Michaelis's regimental units were patrolling previously bypassed hidden hills and valleys. They began uncovering ammo dumps.

The ammo discovered was not the type used by the NKPA.

Local villagers who were questioned about those caches reported that the ammo was being stockpiled for the coming Chinese army.

(A tactic the North Vietnamese would also successfully use.)

Astonishingly this information was also ignored by MacArthur's staff. **What should have really raised the alarm bells was how those supplies got so far south from the Yalu River with no one seeing anything.**

Gen. Walker's 8th Army HQ had moved up with the advance of his units and was based in Pyongyang. His forces were spread out like a fan across the western sector from the coast to the Taeback Mountains in central Korea. He was growing worried. On the 26th the ROK 6th Division which was operating on 8th Army's right flank was suddenly attacked and driven back by the Chinese Communist Forces, CCF. The ROK's lost hundreds of men in the heavy night attack. As the ROK troops retreated the right flank of the nearby 1st Cav Div was opened to attack.

Almond's X Corps was on the other side of those same mountains and were stretched out all over the North-central and NE coastal areas. As stated before, those two forces had no contact with each other because of the imposing mountains in between.

(MacArthur's HQ should have been relocated to Pusan or Seoul, but he and his staff were still based in comfort in Tokyo.)

The Chinese Forth Field Army was commanded by Gen. Lin Biao and consisted of the 38th, 39th, 40th, and 42d Armies plus three artillery divisions and an anti-aircraft regiment. Most of those forces were moving into the eastern half of N. Korea. At the same time Gen. Peng's CCF troops had continued to slip southward on the western side of the Taeback mountains virtually undetected. At that time their total force was over 260,000 men. Many more would follow.

Their few vehicles moved only at night with no headlights, guided by troops holding torches. At first the units had used the concrete road atop the dam at the Suiho power plant. Construction was begun on wooden bridge roadways that were placed just below the water. Like the ones built at the Naktong River, these were almost invisible. Supply trucks rolled over them at wheel-top depth while the troops sloshed across the icy waterway. Before dawn sweeper teams would come out with branches and shovels to eliminate any signs of the passing units.

FEAF pilots overflew the Yalu River area daily and still reported no visible activity. But this wily enemy moved around the Korean lands totally on foot and only at night. And the U.S. planes were flying too high to see any human tracks in those empty wastelands. Gen. Willoughby continually brushed away any "unconfirmed reports" of Chinese troops from his daily information. *One ridiculous statement from his office dated on Oct 28 even tried to claim that the CCF units had no experience in combat operations.*

The communists had been fighting the Nationalists for 20 years, and the Japanese for eight years. They were the hardiest infantry troops the world had ever seen.

Lt. Col John Chiles was assigned to the G-3 staff at X Corps. He observed how Willoughby constantly altered intelligence reports and outright lied about the Chinese presence. Chiles later stated that Willoughby should have gone to jail.) (22)

On the same day as the above report from Willoughby the (28th), a patrol from the ROK 26th regiment captured sixteen fully equipped CCF soldiers at Sudong, south of the Chosin Reservoir in North Central Korea. *This battle was noteworthy for enemy use of tanks and mortars. Not something you would expect from a broken unit.*

Gen. Almond flew up to see for himself and interviewed all of them. The prisoners calmly reported their Division number and their commander in Manchuria, Lin Biao. When Almond asked them how far south they were to march all answered Pusan. When asked why their answer was to kill the enemy, Americans and South Koreans.

It was also learned that half of this group was a complete mortar squad with their mortar. They were from the 370 Regiment, 124th Division, 42 Field Army and admitted they were supported by tanks! They had crossed the Yalu on the night of the 16th using pack horses and mules. (The allies had done the same in Italy throughout the war because of the terrain.) *Almond passed this information on to MacArthur who again did not change his assessment.* Loyal terrier that he was Almond voiced no objections, and arrogantly referred to the captives as "Chinese laundrymen".

Gen. Willoughby was sent to view the POW's and reported that they were just "volunteers." On Oct. 31 the daily intelligence briefing acknowledged that ten Chinese prisoners had been picked up well below the Yalu, and that the ROK II Corps had suffered severe reverses in their operations in NW Korea. They were withdrawing.

No mention was made of the CCF POW interrogation by Almond.
To cover himself, Willoughby's report mentioned that Chinese forces may be in Korea.

(One of the most important intelligence signs that went ignored was a report by a Korean agent who stated that all of the road signs NE Korea had been changed from Korean to Chinese!)

Then American radio teams began hearing a lot of enemy voice traffic and all of it was in Chinese. On November 1 the 1st Cav Div was hammered by the sudden and intense attacks from the CCF 39th Army. Later a patrol from the US 24th Div found hundreds of Chinese setting up near them. That same day a communiqué from Beijing admitted that the Chinese were proud to help their brothers in Korea. By aiding Korea, we are protecting our homes.

The JCS and MacArthur knew of the statement!

In the Marine sector the nightly commanders meetings centered on Chinese entrance into the war. All of them knew that the enemy their patrols were running across were Chinese in spite of what the Army Brass spewed out. Questions ranged on combat queries, like how tough were their troops, what kind of tactics did they use, etc.

The 7th Marines had just moved north from Hamhung to Sudong to relieve the ROK 26th regiment. Those South Koreans had been engaged in many fights in the nearby hills and now it was the Marines turn. As stated earlier, the CO of the 7th was the cantankerous Colonel Homer Litzenburg, and he warned his unit commanders to expect a fight. "Since this would be Americas first battle with the CCF it was vital that the Marines win." (Like many Marines of that time, Litzenburg had served in China and understood how important perceptions and meanings were to the Oriental psyche.) Outnumbered and with little useful intelligence from MacArthur or Almond's HQ the marines moved into the sharp hills and ridges mentally prepared for a battle.

They did not have long to wait.

The Chinese had sent their 20th, 26th, and 27th Armies to the eastern side of Korea.

With their service personnel included the CCF in eastern Korea numbered over 170,000 men with Sung Shih-lun in command. He was a 23 year veteran commander, and had survived the Long March back in Oct. 1934-Oct. 1935. By November the reconstituted NKPA was back up to over 60,000 troops.

Over in the western zone the fierce fighting in the Unsan area with the CCF 39th Army had caused Gen. Walker to order a general retreat back to the Chongchon River. By November 6 the 8th Army had left the dangerous CCF enemy far behind, but at the cost of lost ground and the total abandonment of many vehicles and guns.

What had appeared to be imminent victory had vanished overnight.

Walker notified MacArthur of those initial lost battles, but again no defensive actions or preparations were taken by Walker, MacArthur or the JCS.

From their initial battle reports Mao summarized what the CCF forces could expect as the communist attacks grew. "The South Koreans fought incompetently, and the Americans were overtly dependent on firepower. Their men are lazy and weak.

They fear close combat, their rifle fire is poor and they live in their trucks.

Americans fail to dig in, and prefer the open areas rather than the hills.

We can eliminate all of these enemy units."

(As always their intelligence was first rate.)

When the 8th Army retreated from their battles in the west the Marines were not kept informed. They had continued to move northward. At dusk on November 2 burning flares and bugles announced the CCF attacks of their 124 Division against the 7th Marines. The confused two day battle lasted until dawn of the second day with Chinese and marines intermingled and in heavy combat. That morning **Communist tanks** sat among the marine fighting holes. And as the morning sun rose the patented marine combined arms attacks tipped the scales. Marine corsairs prowled the area and on call artillery pounded any enemy concentrations. Slowly the 124th pulled back.

Marine intelligence teams inspected the CCF dead and found them to be in good shape, ready to fight and each carried five days of cooked rice. Their weapons were not NKPA issue nor was their clothing. Almond flew up in his observation plane and observed the fields of dead Chinese. He spoke with Col. Litzenburg, but seemed puzzled over the battles. He made no notes and there were no entries in his command diary of the battle! *No one on Almond's staff should have hidden the truth of the fighting now, not with the hundreds of CCF dead lying around the Marine positions.*

By Nov 6 the 7th Marines had driven the enemy away from the only roadway in that sector killing over 1500 CCF troops. After their five day fight the 7th Marines were able to advance to the next town of Chinhung-ni. The battered CCF 124th Division retreated and contact with them had stopped by November 7. By the 8th the 7th Marines were based at the Funchilin Pass high up on the northern plateau. It was bitterly cold and the arctic winds were constant. Their elusive enemy had now vanished. (The 124th was mauled and rendered out of action.)

Marine tactics and discipline showed how to fight the CCF night attacks. Hang tough and hold your position. At daybreak air attacks and artillery would melt the CCF mass attacks to impotency.

At this same time Puller's 1st Marine Regiment was still fighting west of Wonsan far to the rear. They were not relieved until November 15 by the 3d Infantry.

Fifty more CCF soldiers had been captured in the recent fighting. The Marines insisted they were Chinese troops, and Almond actually concurred. But Willoughby yelled that it was a Marine lie and that the captives were just volunteers.

Had word of these large battles gotten back to Washington?

If so the JCS should have ended the advancing attacks and directed that the units dig in to hold what the U.N. had already freed or move back to better and safer positions.

That was what they had directed MacArthur to do weeks before.

But even at this date the JCS still did not ensure that they knew what was going on by having anyone over there.

It was all left in MacArthur's hands and he certainly was not going to report to the JCS. Somehow Mac's staff did keep the fighting quiet, and to his ignominy he never changed the objectives despite this clear and present danger.

Gen. Smith USMC was disturbed when they finally heard the news from western Korea. The fact that 8th Army had fallen back meant that for days there were no units on the X Corps left flank and they were never told. The inept Almond however cared not, and he ordered the Marines to continue their advance northward alone. During the past days the 7th Marines began fighting with the CCF 126 Division. *(Almond had sent the 65th regiment from the 3d Infantry westward to find Walker's units. They too were seriously overextended and alone, similar to the rest of X Corps.)*

Smith wrote a letter to the Marine Corps Commandant explaining the serious deficiencies in Almond and his staff. He relayed on how Almond was dispersing the units to the max sending them all over NE Korea on a 300 mile front! Because of the isolated terrain our patrolling and operations are limited. To protect the troops Smith insured that any patrol going out was covered by artillery fire.

As stated earlier, the U.S. 7th Div had landed two of its regiments at Iwon over to the east. That move was completed by Oct 29th. Then fatally ill winds had destroyed the landing beaches forcing Col. Maclean's 31st Regimental Combat Team to be shifted south back to Hungnam. They were then ordered to join up with the 1st Marine Div in its overland move north towards the Chosin Reservoir area. They would be joined with Lt. Col Don Faith and the 1st Battalion 32 Infantry Regiment.

Maclean had just replaced the first commander of the 31st who had been relieved by Almond. (Neither Maclean nor Faith had had a combat command during WWII.)

Like all of the Army Officers in X Corps, they had to do what Almond ordered despite the obvious absurdity. *It was a cruel and fatal twist of fate, as 170,000 Chinese were in the mountains waiting for them.*

Back in Tokyo MacArthur was finally growing alarmed.

A few days ago he had sent half of the B-29 heavy bombers home because the war was almost over. With the reports of the serious fighting on both sides of the mountains it was clear that their new enemy was in Korea in force. He ordered the remaining B-29s to strike the North Korean side of the Yalu to try to breakup any enemy concentrations.

FEAF commander Gen. Stratemeyer radioed back to the AF Chief of Staff Gen. Vandenberg. "This order from MacArthur was too close to the border, and he wanted the JCS to approve it". Hurried discussions were held in Washington.

Those seniors in the JCS could sense the panic in MacArthur's reversal of mood and decided to send the question to Truman. It was election day in America and Truman was upset with the news. Truman fumed, "Gen. MacArthur encouraged this by violating the JCS mandates, and now he wants to be bailed out".

Within hours Mac had his answer, No bombing near the border.
(The British also needed to be consulted since their colony in Hong Kong could have been threatened in a larger war with China.)

MacArthur quickly replied back in a new cable to the JCS,

"The limitations placed upon this command may well result in a calamity of major proportions. I cannot accept the responsibility of this unless the President is presented with my request. *Men and material are coming across in large amounts over the Yalu River bridges all across Manchuria. Those communist forces threaten the ultimate destruction of our forces. The only way to stop this is to destroy all crossings and all installations in the northern area supporting the enemy advance.*
Every hour this decision is postponed is paid for in the blood of our forces!"

Gen. Bradley read this latest message to Truman who reluctantly agreed to the bombing of the North Korean side of the Yalu River only.

But the real disgrace is that after Pres. Truman, his cabinet and the entire JCS had discussed those alarming messages,

NO ACTION WAS TAKEN BY ANYONE IN WASHINGTON TO PROTECT OUR FORCES.

With thoughts of, "A calamity of major proportions" being sent from the Commander of the war zone, Our Leaders did not tell MacArthur to call off his advance, and prepare defensive positions to protect his units. (This included George Marshall!)

They actually said nothing!

This was a blunder of alarming magnitude that would cost over 40,000 American and thousands of allied lives and prolong a war that had already been won.

Many people over the years blamed only MacArthur for the failures in Korea, but several of the major culprits were sitting right there in Washington D.C.

On Nov 8th FEAF began bombing the bridges and towns near the Yalu. As expected all targets were quickly destroyed. MacArthur and his staff were pleased, but he continued to push for outright war against communist China.

"We must win now, or face a permanent defensive line in Korea".

(That was and is true.)

No one in Washington reacted to his continuous calls for war with China.

(Another note of sad irony, the above mentioned Yalu River bridges were no longer of any strategic value. *Winter had arrived in the high plateau and the sub-zero winds had caused the Yalu River to freeze over completely. That enabled the CCF to cross whenever and wherever they wanted.*)

MacArthur was dead on in a few of his calls. He had wanted to destroy the hydroelectric dams in N. Korea that supplied the electrical power for Manchuria. It was senseless to leave them running, but Truman had refused for political reasons. *Red China was the new strategic problem in Asia.*

They had recently seized Tibet, were currently fighting with India and were actively aiding the communists in Indochina, Burma and Malaya. It was time to strike back.

(Perhaps because Truman was the one who had Lost China, he was reluctant to act.)

The lonely Marines of the 1st Division continued their cautious advance deeper into the wilderness where the Chinese had disappeared. By Nov 9th their advance units had passed the village of Koto-ri. Two days later they reached Hagaru-ri where the broken and constricted roadway had snaked its way up to the Chosin Reservoir.

Engineering units were hard pressed to improve the roadway but did so on orders from Gen. Smith.

Close to the actual reservoir logging roads branched off forming a Y near the village of Hagaru-ri. Initially the marines patrolled on the southern and eastern sides of the reservoir. Their mysterious enemy had completely vanished into the cold wastelands and remained invisible. As the days went by more of the division began arriving and their patrols fanned out to cover more ground. Around the 20th the unfortunate US Army's 1st Batt 32 Inf arrived at Hagaru-ri. They were directed over to the eastern sector of the reservoir to replace the 5th Marine units which were being re-deployed for their next advance over to the northwest of the reservoir.

Col. Murray 5th Marines had a meeting with Lt. Col Faith and warned him to dig in and not to push alone any further than they already were. Gen. Smith and Gen. Hank Hodes the Asst. Commander in the 7th Div repeated the warning when 1-32 was later joined by the understrength 31st RCT and Col. Maclean.

Because of the foolish redeployment of X Corps after Seoul, neither unit had seen much combat with the communists. Coupled with the inexperience of their commanders and men, the next weeks would result in a massacre of the units.

(An additional Army battalion was supposed to have joined the 7th Division's 31st Regiment, but they never moved past Chingha-ni.)

Dozens of miles to their east the other regiments of the 7th Division began fighting with NKPA and CCF units. Despite the combat the two regiments reached the Yalu river by November 17. So did the ROK units to their east.

With this latest repositioning of the units completed the 7th Marines slowly began to move westward followed by the 5th Marines. By this point Gen. Smith and his three regimental commanders, Litzenberg, Murray and Puller totally distrusted Almond and any information coming from the Army staffs. (Almond constantly complained that the Marines were "timid and slow". He yelled often to get moving and push on.)

Sensing a catastrophe was brewing Gen. Smith left Puller's 1st Marines at Koto-ri guarding their rear and to become his rescue force. After the work on the roadway was done Smith had his engineers finish a small runway at Koto-ri and then start another one at Hagaru-ri. He also insisted that supply depots be built up at each combat base.

Almond yelled and cursed the Marine efforts as a waste of time and asked Gen. Smith what those useless airfields were to be used for. Smith answered for my casualties.

Almond stared back blankly, he truly was clueless.

As a long term staff officer with limited command or combat experience he never should have been given a command of this magnitude. He was incapable of sizing up the battlefield and understanding the vast problems and dangers. Similar to Hitler's fixation with lines on maps in Russia, Almond constantly attempted to *push* the Marines on to the Yalu River as if that would accomplish something. (Unlike crossing the Rhine, getting to the Yalu meant absolutely nothing as the enemy was all around them.)

Gen. Smith's extensive combat experience warned him that this single file advance deep into the forbidding mountains during a frigid winter was suicide. He actually delayed his unit's movements as much as possible. On some days the advance would be a mile or less, and that made Almond even more angry.

Gen. Smith's useless airfields would save the 1st Marine Division.

As suddenly as they had appeared all of the Chinese troops had completely vanished from Korea. Air patrols crisscrossed the northern areas and saw what they had for weeks, nothing. Only deep aggressive foot patrolling into the forbidding terrain would have found those Chinese. They hid in caves, huts, mine shafts and in forests.

Light and noise discipline were exacting. Anyone who broke the rules was shot.

In Washington hard diplomatic discussions were ongoing. Since Nov 10 the State Dept. had been meeting with the Allies to discuss Korea.

Most of them, especially the British were totally against operating so far north! They saw no reason why the U.N. forces were provoking the communists and potentially causing WWIII.

The British knew that only a shorter front could be held against the unlimited manpower of this enemy. There was no way those few allied divisions could hold the line across the entire long northern width of Korea. (At the border with Manchuria and Russia N. Korea fans out almost 600 miles.) On Nov 21 the NSC met with Truman to review the discussions and MacArthur's memos.

During their respite the 8th Army was resupplied and reinforcements replaced their losses. They planned to re-start their move north to the Yalu River.

To their east the Marines had almost finished their airfield at Hagaru-ri and setup good firing positions for their artillery regiment, the 11th Marines which had finally joined them. A Division CP and supply point was created at Hagaru with great effort, and Gen. Smith moved his forward HQ into

Hagaru because he knew that was the key feature in the coming battle. Almond continued to beret Smith for his "lack of aggressiveness".

The US Army's 3d Division was ashore and emplaced protecting the western approaches to Hamhung. It had been planned that one of its regiments would move north to Chingha-ni and Koto-ri and allow the 1st Marine regiment to relocate to Hagaru-ri.

But Almond and his staff did not allow that to occur and that forced Col. Puller to breakup his regiment. One battalion had to stay at Chingha-ni and another had to protect Koto-ri. Thus his regiment only had one battalion that was free to fight.

(Thankfully a few other units made their way into Koto-ri just before the CCF struck.)

The bitter cold was present everyday and causing hundreds of frostbite cases and constant mechanical problems. Winter gear was being rushed in but the U.S. equipment was not designed for this type of cold, down to a brutal 25 below at night.

Weapons would not fire, ammo would misfire and all manner of equipment was failing.

By the 21st Gen. Barr's 7th Division minus the 31st RCT and 1-32 had fought off the enemy units in their sector and advanced up to the Yalu River. They could observe the CCF sentries patrolling a few hundred yards away.

To their east Gen. Kim's ROK I Corps units had also reached the Yalu. MacArthur was quite pleased that his promise to end the war by Christmas was coming true.

But on Nov. 23 villagers warned the Americans that thousands of Chinese were on their way to attack. Barr who had also served in China during WWII knew that no terrain was too tough for the CCF. He immediately passed on the warnings to Almond.

(No report was passed on to the Marines or the 31st RCT.)

On Nov 24th MacArthur sent another of his grandstanding communiqué's, stating that the large U.N. pincer movement was almost completed. The past weeks of bombing have greatly curtailed enemy attempts at resupply and reinforcement. We are approaching the decisive moment. It was obvious to see the overall reliance that Mac had on air power. How typically American to rely on machines for ultimate success.

Hiding deep in the mountains the Chinese knew almost everything they needed to know about the Americans and ROK's as the western media continued to print positions and timetables, as did MacArthur's communiqués. The communist commanders knew a head to head fight would play to the Americans strengths, their machines and cannons.

No the CCF would attack and fix the Americans in place, and then pass around behind them. Cutoff, the Americans would collapse.
It was the same tactics the *Inmun Gun* had used so successfully in June and July.

The basic CCF soldier was rested, fed and sturdy. They were of peasant stock, used to hardship, cold and hunger. They resembled the legions of old, and would soon inflict a great reversal on a modern army.

Generals Walker and Smith had delayed their advances as long as possible. Their units had to renew their movements north. (Marine Gen. Smith had sent a message to the Commandant days before that the U.S. should defend along the coast and leave the frostbite to the Chinese. It was folly to be up in those mountains during the winter.)

His 7th and 5th Marines had cautiously fought and moved NW away from the reservoir to the far off village of Yudam-ni. Their route was extremely constricted and torturous, a perfect place to be ambushed and cutoff. At a narrow point along the roadway called Toktong Pass the Marines left an under strength rifle company to guard the route. A few miles away they did the same at a hill called 1491. Intelligent decision making by combat tested leaders. Reluctantly Smith ordered his Marines on.
On the eastern side of the reservoir the Army units were doing the same. But they had far fewer men.

Unaware of the events in Korea, Mac was about to be interviewed by LIFE magazine. Owner Henry Luce was a proponent of MacArthur, and wanted his views to be given mass circulation. The issue this interview was about was scheduled to be on newsstands Dec 4th. But by the time the issue came out, the world had already changed.

Gen. Walker warned his advancing forces to move slowly and as soon as you smell Chinese chow come back. Unknown to him there were over 180,000 Chinese about to strike 8th Army. The North Koreans had steadily rebuilt their forces and now numbered over 100,000. As stated before the communist forces were split to allow simultaneous attacks on both U.N. Armies. After losing to the Marines the weeks before, the 42 PLA Army, (People Liberation Army) was repositioned to the west to strike 8th Army. New CCF formations moved around X Corps, the PLA 27th, 20th and 26th Armies. Over 170,000 communist troops were to strike X Corps, but they had to wait until the 27th before they could attack.
(More units were in reserve.)

(After the Reservoir battles had ended, many of the Marine commanders speculated that the initial fighting against the CCF 124th Division near Sudong and the 126th along the road to Hagaru was meant to slow X Corps movements north. This delay was needed to enable the CCF to emplace the rest of their Ninth Army Group and set their trap at the Chosin Reservoir.)

On the night of Nov 25th the U.S. 2nd Division was struck and their 9th regiment hammered. The extreme cold had reduced radio effectiveness and vital battlefield information was not relayed back to the commanders as it should have been.

The next night their 23d regiment was beaten up.

But as bad as the attacks had been on the Americans, to their right the ROK II Corps had collapsed. The CCF and NKPA forces made a point to destroy the "Puppet troops". The newly arrived Turkish Brigade of 5000 men was sent over to help the ROK's, but found themselves alone and quickly cutoff. The Turks tough fighters as they were did not fall back. They attacked **into** the CCF hordes with bayonets, dying alone in the hills.

Early on Nov 28th the Chinese attacked the U.S. 24th, 25th and 2nd divisions in daylight. The wait was over, it was a new War.

By noon on the 28th Walker radioed that his forces were retreating, and the Chinese were attacking. 8th Army had been hurt by these larger battles.

Gen. Almond was not informed of the debacle to his west until told by Tokyo the next day. Even then Almond and his staff delayed informing the Marines!

And so the Marines continued to move onward deeper into the trap.

To Gen. Walker's everlasting ignominy, he knew that bad things were possible. But during the previous pause no defensive arrangements, contingency plans or prepared positions were contemplated nor laid out.

Thus when his units fell back from the intense communist attacks there were no strong-points, havens or battle plan to be found. Units quickly fell apart and each failure led to other units being overrun. And all of those failures were his.

In the darkness on the high plateau the Marines prepared to move on to the next village of Mupyong-ni. A portion of the 11th Marines had moved with them to provide artillery support. As had been the case since Wonsan, Col Litzenberg's 7th Marines were to advance first followed by the 5th Marines. (Battalion 1/7 was at the front of the advance and breakout the entire time.)

Then a prisoner was picked up by a patrol and he reveled that the CCF 58th, 59th and 60th Divisions were lying in wait. Four other CCF Divisions were on the eastern side of the Reservoir and were set to assault the 31st Regiment and the other units further to the east. (The rest of the 7th Div and ROK I Corps.)

It was clear to Col. Litzenberg that as soon as the Army's 31st RCT was wiped out the CCF would descend on Hagaru-ri trapping everyone.

Unknown to the Marine Commanders, a recon platoon had been sent northward from the 31st RCT a few hours earlier. They were never seen or heard from again.

No report of their loss was made to Gen. Smith and so a vital warning sign was missed. Lt. Col. Faith's battalion was also separated from McLean's RCT by a mile gap.

To their south a separate armored unit was a mile or so nearer to *Hagaru-ri*. No plan had been made to link those units together for mutual protection.

A few hours later the 31st RCT Intelligence officer was warned by Korean civilians that the Chinese were coming to take back the reservoir. That warning too was not passed back to the USMC HQ at Hagaru-ri. (USMC Captain Ed Stamford was in charge of the air liaison team assigned to the Army units on that side of the reservoir. He was surprised at the Army commanders lackadaisical attitude to the foreboding information.)

Early that morning the CCF around the reservoir struck. With the temperature at -20 weapons failed to function and quickly the 5th and 7th Marine regiments were surrounded and under heavy attacks. Well trained and conditioned CCF units had been able to advance almost unseen in the swirling snow, and in many places the fighting was hand to hand. The advance was suspended as the marines counterattacked to recapture the nearby hills.

Hagaru-ri was not attacked initially, and the information flow between the commands was sparse because of the hills and weather. But Smith did learn of the fighting. At first light Gen. Smith had his operations chief Col. Bowser make a helicopter recon from Hamhung north to Hagaru. *They found nine CCF roadblocks along the roadway behind them, and enemy troops moving out in the open.*

Lt. Col. Winecoff then continued the flight up to Yudam-ni to consult with Col. Litzenberg. Flying over the roadway area the over-flight crew observed that Chinese troops were everywhere. From the strategy talks held between the two command posts Gen. Smith decided to plan a withdrawal from the reservoir regardless of what Almond said.

As the 8th Army's retreat began to fall apart, command mistakes and lapses compounded the tactical problems and turned them into a disaster.

The 2nd Div had to move back through a narrow valley in order to retreat but no one took command and control of their only escape. As a result CCF units sat on the high ground and savaged the entire Division as they tried to move past.

Late in the afternoon on the 28th MacArthur finally faced reality and he ordered all units to pull back. He then radioed the bad news to a stunned

Pentagon. Naturally this setback was someone else's fault as Mac described the assault on the order of a Pearl Harbor.

At the Pentagon Gen. Matt Ridgeway and the Army staff began immediate planning for a possible evacuation. In Japan Admiral Turner Joy saw the reports and quietly began to assemble ships for withdrawing X Corps. Generals Walker and Almond were ordered to meet with MacArthur back in Tokyo.

At a meeting of the NSC the President was there with all of the principals. Robert Lovett commented that the report from MacArthur was a CYA posterity paper. Acheson commented that if we abandon the South now we will be remembered as the greatest appeasers of all time. Vice President Alban Barkley was bitter as he commented on MacArthur's boastful assertions of having the boys home for Christmas.

Truman and Marshall felt it best to leave Mac alone. It was more important from Marshall's point of view to not get into a head to head fight with the Chinese.

(What is hard to understand is that we were already in a head to head fight with the Chinese despite all of Marshall and Truman's maneuverings. Why did they not forcibly react to the Chinese assault and bomb everything on the other side of the Yalu River? Every airfield, supply dump and troop concentration in Manchuria should have been destroyed.)

The next day Truman went to the Congress to ask for another $16 billion for defense. Korea was convincing all that the Communists could crush the West militarily.

More budget increases would be made.

In Tokyo Gen. Walker claimed that he could hold a defensive line across the narrow waist of Korea and it included the N. Korean capital. Almond foolishly stated that they could continue with the attack. He was confident that he could hold onto the coastal plain around Wonsan and Hungnam. With air and naval superiority there was little that the Chinese or NKPA could do to force them out.

Walker was told to hold only if he could, but was not to allow himself to be flanked and trapped. Almond was told to withdraw his forces back to the coastal cities.

(As stated above, without waiting for orders Gen. Smith had already directed the 5th & 7th Marines to begin to breakout from Yudam-ni and for the 1st Marines to re-open the road north of Koto-ri.)

By the 29th the 8th Army was in a headlong retreat while the Marines and the 31st RCT were surrounded and incapable of escaping. The 31st was not organized for this fight as they had expected to move out again in the morning. Prior to the initial attack there was no sign of the CCF and that was why they had sent out the recon unit. Faith's 1-32 was the northern most unit and was about to move northward when the unseen enemy fell upon them. In short order 1-32 was fighting for their life as the CCF 80th Div worked their way around the battalion cutting them off from the 31st RCT. With their adjoining attacks on the 31st also succeeding, the CCF then began attacking Hagaru-ri too.

Far to their east the rest of Gen. Barr's 7th Div was operating near Hyesanjin on the Yalu River, and the ROK units to their east had also made it up to the border.

Resistance had been light, but now they too were under strong attacks. Thus far those stretched out units had escaped from being cutoff and were slowly moving back towards the coast.

During that last week the Chinese had brought three new armies into X Corps sector. The Marine and Army units would be fighting 16 CCF Divisions in their quest for survival. Hindering the troops was the malfunctioning of the old M-2 carbines, BAR's, 4.2 inch mortars, batteries, machine guns and every thing you can think off that constant below zero temperatures affect. Fights that could have been easily won were turning into long affairs and casualties piled up.

The CCF 79th and 89th Divisions joined the attacks around Yudam-ni, while the 59th moved down towards Toktong Pass. (The Chinese had actually expected to annihilate both regiments that first night.) Despite the constant combat and losses the marine lines held while the CCF lost thousands of their soldiers. Outposts had wisely been left at hill 1419 and at Toktong Pass. They too had held on that first night despite being completely outnumbered. By the second morning the CCF 60th Div was also moving southward to cut the roadway and overrun the outpost on hill 1419. Toktong Pass had to hold out or everyone would be trapped.

At Yudam-ni the Marines counterattacked on the 29th and regained the hills overlooking the town. That protected their rear area from direct enemy fire and allowed their commanders time to plan and execute their escape. From their high perch they could watch the fighting on the eastern side of the reservoir.

Daylight air-drops supplied the defenders with ammo and medicines, while the Chinese forces waited for their ally, the dark of night. During the daylight Marine and Navy fliers kept a constant patrol over the trapped units and attacked anything that was asked. Col. Litzenberg was senior officer, and he and Col. Murray carefully planned and contracted their perimeter to allow for their egress. Everything that could be taken with them was, including their dead.

Air support from the Marine air-wing and Navy, and artillery fire from the 11th Marines based in *Hagaru* was coordinated and delivered as needed from the forward operating fire control teams. Despite the attacks by the CCF at Hagaru, one battery of artillery actually stayed exposed outside of the north side of the perimeter to insure that they could support Fox Company at Toktong Pass. Whenever a tank or cannon was knocked out the crewmen became infantrymen. (In the Marines everyone is trained to become a rifleman.) Fortunately for all the CCF 58th Div units were not strong enough in any one sector to breech the Hagaru perimeter, though they came close a few times. Their 80th was still fighting with the 31st on the eastern side of the frozen Chosin Reservoir.

As more news of the fighting got out the leaders in the West actually began to think that WWIII had started. Gen. Bedell Smith, Ike's former chief of staff was the "new" Director at the CIA. He reported that only diplomacy could save X Corps.

(I wonder if Admiral Hillenkoeter was retired because he had been right about Korea?) Late on the 29th the JCS had asked MacArthur about his plans to setup a defensive line across the narrow waist of Korea. Mac dismissed their suggestion outright, and his reply to them was according to Bradley, insulting.

Sec-Def Marshall also wanted the U.N. to hold at the waist and abandon far off NE Korea. But MacArthur refused any of their suggestions and continued his self-serving press releases blaming everyone in the world for his failures. On December 3 Gen. Ridgeway asked Vandenberg why do you people in the JCS send suggestions to MacArthur? Order him to hold the line in Korea! Vandenberg replied, "What good would it do, he would not obey them. What can we do?" Ridgeway exploded, you can relieve him can't you?

Vandenberg meekly walked away.

Back at *Yudam-ni* a vehicle convoy was finally organized and began moving back to *Hagaru*. The wounded had been placed inside the vehicles, while the dead were strapped onto the vehicles. To save the trapped defenders on hill 1419 Lt. Col Davis led his 1/7 into an uphill attack to drive of the CCF. With that accomplished cautiously the Marine column moved back towards Toktong Pass. Marine units fought off CCF attacks and ambushes all along the way. At the Pass Capt Barber's Fox Company was still holding out, but over half of his men were casualties including him.

(Despite the freezing cold and rock hard ground Capt. Barber had forced his men to dig fighting holes as soon as they arrived. Just after midnight that first night the CCF attacks against them started.

Fox Company survived and successfully fought off continuous Chinese attacks for three straight days because of his orders.)

To ensure that the Pass would be open when the convoy arrived Battalion 1/7 led by Lt Col. Ray Davis climbed and crawled the 10 miles from hill 1419 through a raging snow storm. They silently and slowly moved past the freezing Chinese units for 24 hours. Only once were they forced to fight off a Chinese attack, but the brutal cold was constant.

By dawn on Dec 3d, Davis's men had arrived and took control of the Pass which was covered with hundreds of dead Chinese. After five straight days of close in fighting most of Fox Company's men were casualties. But they had held the vital Pass.

(The Chinese dead were stacked up to make battlements by the Fox Co. men.)

As soon as the vehicle column from Yudam-ni passed safely Davis's men formed the rear guard. Every time a CCF hill position or roadblock (seven) was encountered a unit was organized and sent to occupy or destroy it. Patrols constantly moved along the nearby high ground to prevent any CCF attacks from forming above them.

(That was how the CCF was able to savage the 2nd Div from 8th Army.)

East across the Reservoir from Yudam-ni was the final location of Col. Maclean's 31st RCT and 1-32. All alone in the wooded hills the CCF attacked them the same night as the Marines at Yudam-ni. At first the unit held its ground and kept the Chinese at bay.

Unable to join their forces, their lines were finally penetrated which forced them into small pockets. Those army troops attempted to hold out assisted by Marine Air, artillery and Navy jets. (Due to losses Capt. Stafford USMC ended up in charge of one sector.) Gen. Almond flew in to the CP by helicopter after the first day and lectured the commanders Faith and Maclean to attack and regain the high ground. He then handed out silver stars and flew off. He never returned.

After leaving the 31st RCT& 1-32 CP, Almond went east to see Gen. Barr. When their meeting ended Barr reported in to Gen. Smith at Hagaru to try to arrange a rescue of the trapped 31st RCT& 1-32. Watching the intense combat all around them Gen. Barr realized it was impossible to help his trapped units with the forces present. He radioed his stranded units to fight their way the six miles back into Hagaru-ri.

Barr then flew out and remained with his other regiments which were further east. (No attempt was made to get a seasoned commander into the 31st perimeter.

Gen. Hodes was available, but it seems the 31st had been written off. The small armored unit made it back to Hagaru on its own.)

Once the 31st tried to withdraw towards Hagaru the CCF was able to fragment the column and units, and chaos ensued when both of the commanders were killed.

This under strength regiment would be massacred despite the attempts by Navy and Marine aircraft to assist. The CCF even attacked the trucks full of wounded and killed them all. Only 385 able bodied men escaped across the frozen reservoir to Hagaru-ri.

Only 385 men out of 3300!
(I wonder if that missing Battalion would have been the strength they needed to survive?)

But their demise was not in vain, for they had kept the CCF attackers from the 80th Div occupied for four vital days. And in that time Hagaru was reinforced with a makeshift battalion from Koto-ri and better organized for defense. Those few survivors from the 31st were re-equipped with weapons from marine stocks and they then joined the other 490 Army troops inside the perimeter to form a composite army battalion.

(Col. Ollie Beall USMC made numerous trips out onto the frozen reservoir with jeeps to recover dozens of wounded who had crawled away from the battle. He actually made it to the massacre site of the 31st and witnessed some of the terrible events.)

Hagaru-ri would not be considered a safe, safe haven. Since the night of the 28th, the CCF had been attacking there too. Lt Col. Ridge's 3d battalion of the 1st Marines (from Puller's regiment) had been sent in initially to become the defenses for this entire town. Artillery and service troops were also ordered into the overstretched defensive line.

After the second night the Chinese took the commanding east hill and held on through numerous marine counterattacks. By the third day Chinese troops from the 58th Div were joined with units from the 76th and the now freed up 80th Division. They attacked everywhere along the Hagaru perimeter eventually finding a few breaks. Again the fighting lasted all night and even the medical clearing station was riddled with machine gun fire. At that point even holding onto Hagaru-ri was in doubt. Those few defenders in Hagaru were cutoff as the CCF had completely cut the road south to *Koto-ri*.

Koto-ri was also attacked that first night, but the CCF were too few to force a breakthrough and had to be content with keeping the base cut off and isolated. Fortunately the supply depot that Smith ordered kept them fed and full of ammo.

As stated above, to assist in saving the severely threatened Marine HQ in Hagaru-ri, Col Puller sent a 900 man relief force from his limited forces at Koto-ri. This combination unit of Britain's Royal Marines, U.S.

Army troops and U.S. Marines battled for hours to make the eleven mile trip past the numerous roadblocks and ambushes that the CCF had setup. Only 1 in 3 men made it to *Hagaru-ri*, but 17 tanks and dozens of supply laden trucks did get in. They were instrumental in saving the day as their men and firepower from the tanks were added to the defensive perimeter. *The CCF never got through the Hagaru lines again.*

Koto-ri remained under continuous attack, but the time they had been there had been put to good use as Col. Puller established a solid defense. When Smith asked Puller how they were doing Puller replied fine, we have enemy contact on all sides.

During their next meeting a day later Almond ordered Gen. Barr that the 7th Division was to stop their screening withdrawal, (like the Marines were doing), and to "quickly move back". Barr had to comply, and the result was a panicky flight with lost equipment and abandoned men. This unintelligent and unwise order also imperiled the escape of the ROK I Corps which was positioned even further to the east and fighting as fiercely as the marine and army troops. (The CCF and NKPA wanted to exterminate them.)

Once the 7th rushed for the coast the ROK's had no allied unit on their exposed western flank. That enabled more communist attackers to close in on them.

Suddenly cutoff from the roads by the advancing enemy the bulk of those ROK units finally escaped overland and then used the port of *Songjin* in far off eastern Korea.

They too had to abandon most of their equipment.

A report by a U.S. liaison officer assigned to the 26th *ROK regiment stated that the retreat so ordered by Almond had resulted in large amounts of abandoned equipment, rations and ammo. He also reported that several groups of 7*th *Div stragglers had been left behind at Pukchong and Pungsan.*

Many of those troops were wounded and incapable of self-evacuating.

They were never seen again.

As the days went by at the reinforced Hagaru-ri forward base additional USMC counterattacks were made upon the East Hill finally driving the communists off and allowing the work to complete the airstrip to continue. Smith's "unnecessary buildup" of all types of supplies enabled the units to hang on through the days of non-stop fighting. Ammo was plentiful and used by the ton.

And after a fourteen mile-four-day fighting withdrawal by the 5th *and 7*^{h} *Marines, the last Marine marched into Hagaru-ri on Dec 4*th. The 5th and 7th Marines had brought out all of their equipment, their dead and over 1,900 wounded!

(Col. Bowser and Gen. Smith were amazed as those Marines came in marching and singing. "We knew then we had it made".)

Four factors enabled this Legion to survive.

(1) The Marines went up into the hills to fight and eject the Chinese. This prevented the enemy from maintaining control of the roadway below.

(2) The Marine Air Wing flew support missions almost non-stop. Marine air was trained to fly to help the infantry. Their attacks are called close air support and that is just what was delivered.

(3) Chinese Gen Sung Shih-lun had marched his men for 14 days. Then they attacked and fought for 7 days more, until they were bled white, froze to death or became exhausted.

It was too much to ask even for the tough CCF troops.

(4) The final factor that helped the Marines was that the Chinese had underrated them.

They thought that three CCF Divisions could defeat two Marine Regiments. They were wrong.

The Chinese had made a terrible strategic mistake in their battle-plan. Initially the CCF 80th Div went after the 31st RCT, while others were sent to cut and hold the road to Hagaru-ri and Koto-ri. Three Divisions also went after the 7th Div and the ROK units, while four Divisions had tried to crush the Marines at Yudam-ni and block the roadway behind them.

Had the CCF attacked at one key spot with more units initially instead of attacking everywhere at once, no one would have survived. (Concentration of force.)

Col. Litzenberg and Murray were both surprised that the CCF did not overwhelm the Hagaru area first. That was the key choke point.

If they had fallen no one would have escaped.

Late on Dec 4th Gen. Almond flew into Hagaru-ri and told Gen. Smith to fall back quickly and abandon all equipment for the sake of speed. Gen. Smith replied that the Division would withdraw as rapidly as evacuation and movement of the wounded permitted. He also told Almond that this equipment was needed to help in his fight to get out. "We will bring the bulk of it out"!

Air Force General William Tunner who had been the Commander of the air operations over the Himalayas in WWII and of the Berlin Airlift in 1949, had also shown up to work out the details of the "Aerial Dunkirk" that FEAF was planning. Smith thanked him and sent him on his way.
(Smith told Almond that if they wanted too they could have held onto Hagaru.)

Reporters who were there commented on the retreat that the Marines were making. Gen. Smith quickly admonished them for using the word retreat.

"We are not retreating, we are attacking in a different direction!"

With the contraction of the battle area around the reservoir the CCF could now regroup and send all of its units against the combat base at Hagaru-ri. Smith and his staff understood the battlefield situation and planned to move out before the CCF could complete their moves. The men of the 5th and 7th Regiments were given two days of rest while Smith and his staff prepared and planned. They had to make a tactical attack southward to defeat the numerous CCF roadblocks and units fortifying the hills that overlooked that single roadway, and organize their withdrawal.

Major Gen. Harris who commanded all of the Marine Air Wing units had arrived in Hagaru-ri to work out the air-cover plan personally. Marine units would fly overhead continuously while the Navy planes would work over the sides of the roadway.

The Air Force units would intercept everything further out.

(With the fast paced and unwarranted retreat by 8th Army some of their assigned FEAF units were freed up to help X Corps.)

Almond became incensed that the planning for the Marine escape was being done without any of his input. (Thankfully) Upon his return to his HQ in Hamhung, he berated the Air Force and Marine aviation commanders for keeping him out of the loop.

As overall commander he insisted that "he was the one to have total Operational control" of all assets! *(At the end of the NE Korean campaign, No allied unit was allowed to have a "private air force again"!!)*

The Hagaru-ri medical staff had been treating and evacuating the large numbers of wounded from the 5th & 7th Marines. Smith's "useless airfield" worked out fine as over 3,000 casualties would be flown out using small supply planes and Marine helicopters. And with each aircraft that landed replacements and supplies were brought in.

Those flights were done under extreme weather conditions on a poorly built runway and dodging enemy fire going in and coming out. Brave pilots all.

The CCF 58th Division had continued their attacks at Hagaru-ri, while the 59th stayed along the roadway. The 60th had moved further south and controlled the vital choke point at Funchilin Pass while the 69th controlled the area south of Koto-ri to prevent any overland reinforcements from getting through to them. The beat up CCF 79th and 89th divisions had finally regrouped and moved south from Yudam-ni, while the 80th having finished off the 31st RCT joined the fight at Hagaru-ri. Their 90th was still in reserve.

Even though the Marines had escaped from Yudam-ni the CCF was still able and determined to destroy them. The narrow and craggy terrain allowed for constant attacks and chokepoints to stall any escape.

On December 5th more CCF units arrived. The 76th and 77th CCF Divisions reinforced the 59th along the roadway between Hagaru and Koto-ri. The 78th and 88th divisions were also drawing near as their attacks against the U.S. 7th Div had failed to trap them and they had escaped.

(Maggie Higgins and Keyes Beach who had covered the war from the beginning were present at a 5th Marines briefing. Col. Ray Murray told his commanders, "We are getting out of here, and we are going out like Marines. We are sticking together, taking out our wounded, our dead, and our equipment.)

Back in the America talk was turning towards using the Atomic Bomb in Korea. In light of the impending military disaster many felt that the American people would demand its use to save U.S. personnel. Planning for atomic war was actually begun in July 1950, and the parts and planes were flown to Guam in August.

However we no longer had a monopoly.

In December 1950 many worried that the Soviets would retaliate by sneaking a bomb into an American port on a merchant ship. (The same fear we have had with the Islamic terrorists.)
The extensive espionage effort by the Russians which had kept Stalin and his scientists up to date in the Manhattan Project had paid off. It was believed the Soviets had two dozen atomic bombs. They were also ahead of the U.S. in work on the Thermo-nuclear bomb.

In two signed statements to the FBI on May 22 and July 10, 1950 Atomic spy Harry Gold provided intelligence as to where the Russian atomic program was and how it got there. *Joining him in the ranks of traitors and spies were the previously mentioned pre-war German* **Klaus Fuchs***, who was also arrested and interrogated in Britain. In the U.S.* **David Greenglass, Harry Gold, Morton Sobell** *and the* **Rosenbergs** *were picked up.* **Seven additional arrests** *would follow, which added to the earlier claims that communist spies were pervasive within the halls of government.*

In Britain there was outrage that there was any mention of atomic weapons. To them they should only be used as a last resort against Russia. Our allies and the U.N. were completely against using atomic weapons, and our desire to have allies meant that their input had to be respected. The Truman Administration was gridlocked.

By December 3 most of 8th Army had withdrawn to an unstable front just north of Pyongyang. In violation of standard military tactics the 8th Army made no effort to keep in contact with the CCF forces. That allows you to know where the enemy is and in what shape they are in. *The panicked withdrawal was not controlled or contained by its leaders and vital supply and ammunition dumps that had been built up with much cost and effort were being put to the torch.*

(Many of the most forward supply dumps fell intact into the hands of the CCF as the units were forced back. But the wholesale destruction of the rearward dumps could have been prevented by proper defensive arrangements.)

At this point the dispirited Walker no longer felt he could hold at the narrow waist of Korea. MacArthur **who still had not returned to Korea** to see for himself what the hell was happening was unsure if we could even hold at Seoul.

MacArthur radioed to a shocked Pentagon that we were facing the entire Chinese nation.

On Dec 4th the 8th Army again took to flight even though there were no enemy units around. The next stop was to the Imjin River in an "attempt to hold".

The CCF had no motor transport, they walked everywhere. With their panicked movement south the 8th Army forces drove so fast they had actually outrun the enemy. Reporters were lost for days wandering around looking for the "front lines" that no one had setup. Even the reporters complained of the decision to continue to retreat south below the narrow waist. This was a disaster that did not have to be.

And still the Joint Chiefs of Staff did nothing.

(Gen. Ridgeway argued with the rest of the JCS to order MacArthur to correct the disaster. If he refused or could not then the JCS should relieve him.)

The 8th Army had for all intensive purposes deserted the front.

British Gen. Basil Coad wrote scornfully "Of a 132 mile retreat for no obvious military reason. *British Gen. Mansergh sent a secret evaluation back to London complaining of the lack of Leadership, morale and any will to fight back.*

Despite the hard lessons learned the yanks will not get out of their vehicles. They are over-supplied with welfare stores that would be comical if not such a terrible handicap. The American infantry is poorly trained, discipline is weak, and their security a joke." (And all of that was the result of the cutbacks and the Doolittle Board.)

At a JCS meeting Admiral Sherman the Chief of Naval Operations wanted to order MacArthur to hold at the narrow waist, but Bradley felt it "inadvisable" to do so.

The JCS did nothing more than send Army Chief of Staff Lawton Collins back to Korea to get a first hand look. (Truman wrote in his memoirs he wanted to fire MacArthur then and there.)

On Dec. 5 Gen. Collins met with Walker to convince him to hold a line north of Seoul. But the despondent Walker was incapable of doing anything. *(Walker should have been relieved then and there and Collins put in charge.)*

Collins met with MacArthur the next day in Tokyo. (Mac still had not set foot in Korea.)

MacArthur's opinion was that all was lost unless he was given reinforcements from the states and Taiwan, and China itself was attacked. It was clear to Collins that MacArthur had no grasp of the situation and his staff was filled with incompetent loyalists.

Collins felt and reported back to the JCS that we could hold on.

On his last trip to Hagaru-ri Almond was angry that the Marines were not rushing to escape. He even complained about the American dead being loaded aboard the trucks. Gen. Smith had had enough of him and yelled out that the marines revere their dead and will not leave them in this desolate village.

Almond flew out and never showed his face again.

On Dec 6th the 1st Marine Division began its move south towards Koto-ri. The 11th Marines started the move by firing continuously into suspected and known enemy positions. Nine heavily defended enemy roadblocks reinforced with mine fields and blown bridges awaited the Marines. Their commanders had planned and prepared for these obstructions, and the young marines were ready for the fight.

Battalions took the ridgelines 700 yards out from the roadway ensuring that the Chinese units waiting in the hills could cause little direct damage to the convoy.

Tanks and infantry (1/7 & 2/7) were in the column lead and would destroy each of the roadblocks as they came upon them. Marine *Corsair* fighter-bombers swooped in to rocket, strafe and bomb where needed. They also reported in on any enemy movements they spotted.

As soon as the column began to move south from Hagaru-ri, Col. Puller sent units north from Koto-ri to engage the Chinese forces lying in wait. This unexpected Marine attack surprised the CCF and cost them hundreds of additional casualties and lost positions.

The long vehicle column slowly continued on its way south towards Koto-ri. Each CCF attack and strongpoint was defeated killing hundreds. Close on the heels of the troops were thousands of refugees anxious to escape the communists. Security was difficult for CCF infiltrators were hidden among the civilians. All had to be ferreted out and shot.

It would take **38 torturous hours** to move the eleven miles south into Koto-ri. Ten thousand troops, thousands of refugees and 1000 vehicles made the exhausting trip. They swelled Koto-ri to the bursting point. Again the wounded numbering over 600 were flown out while another difficult problem was being addressed.

South of Koto-ri the bridge over a deep chasm had been destroyed by the Chinese. There was no way for vehicles to get around this massive gorge.

Marine engineers led by Lt. Col. Partridge had to come up with a plan. Temporary timbers called Treadway sections were successfully air dropped by parachutes to the engineers, a great success for the Air Force. (First time it was ever tried)

The span was reconstructed under enemy fire allowing the vehicle traffic to resume.

There were only inches of clearance to spare.

With the USMC 1st Division's three Regiments reunited there was no chance that the CCF could stop the withdrawal. A well seasoned former marine and war photographer named David Duncan asked a young and frozen marine a question.

"If I could give you anything you wanted, what would it be.

The young lad was digging into a frozen can to try to free a bean.

He looked up and replied "just gimme tomorrow".

As stated before Col. Puller had left one Battalion guarding the southern most village of Chinhung-ni. North of that town lay the Funchilin Pass, another narrow part of the roadway. Hill 1081 sat over the Pass and the CCF were dug in with heavy weapons. Capt Barrow's Able Company scaled a sheer cliff at night during a blizzard and overran the Chinese company that had been covering the Pass. The CCF unit had sited its weapons perfectly, ensuring complete control of this vital chokepoint. Able's surprise attack caught the CCF unprepared and drove them from the hill. Three times the CCF counterattacked to eject the Marines from Able Company. All failed.

Thanks to that attack, on Dec 8th the convoy again moved out with CCF units continuing to attack the column. On Dec 9th units from the Army's 3d Div made contact with the Marines south of Chinhung-ni. Welcomed help was provided from Army anti-aircraft batteries which fired nonstop into the never ending CCF ranks. Again hundreds were killed in the senseless attacks. The Marine column continued on.

From that point the CCF did not impede the convoy any further.

After more than two weeks of solid combat seven of the Chinese Divisions were destroyed and another five badly beaten. Even the hardy CCF soldiers suffered terribly from the ghastly cold as hundreds froze to death and thousands more were injured from severe frostbite. USMC patrols would find frozen lumps lying and sitting in the snow on the ridges. After dusting the lumps off the marines discovered the frozen enemy.

Many were still alive but actually frozen to the ground!

The Army's 3rd Div which had been protecting the Hamhung-Wonsan area had originally been fighting the North Korean stay behind forces who were constantly trying to cut the roads. In early December they too began dueling with the Chinese who were trying to sever the roadway to the reservoir. Their 7th regiment was fighting the 69th CCF Div near Sachang-ni, when the CCF 126th Div began to close in from the west. (With 8th Army's' retreat the 126th was again redirected to help in the east.)

With those additional enemy units attacking, the ROK 15th Regiment and the ROK Marine regiment were cutoff near Majon-ni. The 3d division's last unit, the 65th Regiment had been moved north from Wonsan to Hamhung. As stated earlier, Almond sent them westward to link up with 8th Army. Almost cutoff themselves, they had a difficult fight getting back to the main defensive area. They held the line so that all the other units could escape.

Gen. Almond's interference in the planning of their withdrawal threatened to cost those troops heavy losses. During those imperiled times the X Corps staff became totally bewildered and incapable of dealing with so many threats.

Orders were issued and hours later abolished, each time creating chaos and delays. In three days, the 65th received three different sets of orders.

On Dec 2nd, their 7th battalion was finally chased out of Sachang-ni under Chinese guns. (At this same time the Marines had just "escaped" from Yudam-ni.)

The 7th regrouped at Huksu-ri and spent a cold and miserable night awaiting the inevitable CCF assault. Their commander wanted to remain on this high ground and felt that they could hold with air support. Morning came and Almond ordered the 7th to continue withdrawing eastward.

By Dec 4th numerous large enemy units began moving towards Majon-ni.

If that area fell to the CCF, the ROK Marines would be cutoff from their escape. Almond's incessant demands for rapid withdrawals had once again resulted in vital ground being given up, hundreds of abandoned vehicles and needed equipment being lost. The units of X Corps were saved in spite of the total inanity of their commander.

The air umbrella that had worked so hard to save the day over X Corps was finally being challenged by communist MIG jet fighters. Hundreds of Russian pilots flew those jets as the Koreans and Chinese were not yet trained. Their orders were to stay over communist areas in case they were shot down, but the U.S. pilots could see their faces and hear them speaking. There was no question as to who they were, and a few dead Russian pilots had been recovered back in September at Inchon.

The Truman Administration decided not to reveal their identities as Russians for fear of sparking trouble at home.

The communists were also setting up elaborate flak traps as more anti-aircraft guns were moved into the area and placed in operation each day. (This was a perfect display of CCF ingenuity in moving the heavy equipment and ammo around the mountainous terrain unseen and by hand!)

In the west the 8th Army's retreat continued on unabated and unprovoked. If a road connected to Japan everyone would have ended up in Tokyo. *Gen. MacArthur had yet to make an appearance and his command failures allowed this inexcusable condition to continue.*

With control of the seas and air X Corps could easily have held onto the entire eastern coastal area to continue the fight and to have a bargaining chip against the communists. And with control of that important area the enemy would be tempted to attack and offer plenty of targets for naval shelling and the bombers.

(Eighth Army should have stayed along the narrow waist of N. Korea and held onto Pyongyang for the same reasons.)

As the uncontrolled 8th Army units continued fleeing south of the 38th parallel it no longer made sense for X Corps to remain north of it.
Plans were made for a full evacuation from N. Korea. (Almond still wanted to attack.??)

On Dec 12th the Marines finally strode into Hungnam. "One observer remarked, Look at those bastards. Look at those magnificent bastards."
Major Gen. Oliver Smith stood proud as his command had accomplished the impossible.

Baker Company 1st Battalion 7th Marines landed at Inchon with 225 officers and men. They led the attacks from Wonsan to Yudam-ni, and the fighting withdrawal back to Hungnam. Only 27 survived.

(Army Historian S.L.A. Marshall called the exploits of the 1st Mar Div, "perhaps the most brilliant divisional feat of arms in the nation's history.") **(24)**

During the battles and Breakout from the CCF trap, the 1st Marine Division had suffered over 5000 battle casualties and thousands of cases of frostbite.

(Unbelievably MacArthur's office actually complained about the large number of frostbite cases from the USMC.) The Army units of X Corps also suffered thousands of casualties in the initial battles, though numerous men had feigned injuries and flew out with the wounded at Hagaru. ROK losses were unknown.

Among the CCF attackers, 12 Divisions had attempted to destroy X Corps. At least 9 of them went after the 1st Mar Div and the 31st RCT, and paid the price.

When our troops finally moved south of Chin Hung-ni on December 10 the CCF was no longer willing or able to pursue. It was unsure of the exact numbers of casualties the enemy had suffered, but guesses at 75,000 were probably close. **None of those twelve CCF Divisions were combat capable until March of 1951.**

During those last days aerial recon observed long lines of enemy forces moving towards X Corps positions along every road and path. It was possible they were planning a massed attack to crush X Corps. Yet another command failure was in not repeatedly striking those formations with daily B-29 bombing missions.

Another unreported facet of the Chosin Reservoir battle was the fact that the Marines had successfully fought and tied up all of those CCF Divisions. Had the Marines blindly listened to Almond's orders and plunged deeper into the trap, or had Gen. Smith not been such a great battlefield commander, the 1st Mar Div might well have been annihilated in those frozen wastelands just like the Army's 31st RCT.

If that had happened all of the CCF units involved in that battle would have been freed up to assault into the coastal cities and the main roadway.

As stated above there were only a few units operating south of the Marines, and they too were engaged in serious fighting with NKPA and CCF forces.

With the reinforcement of 2-6 additional CCF divisions, more than likely much of the Army's 3d Div, the remaining ROK units and the staff and support units operating in those coastal cities would also have been destroyed.

Who can say what effect that would have had on the war or the world. (If all or most of X Corps had been annihilated would the United States have stayed in the war? The only way to have stopped that from happening would have been using atomic bombs. What would Russia or our allies have done then?)

During those past weeks dozens of well trained communist spies roamed in and around the X Corps units and coastal cities. They attempted to poison wells, tap communications lines and provided up to date information to the NKPA and CCF units. Many were caught, though as always they ruthlessly murdered anyone who even tried to help X Corps. Near Hamhung 500 civilians had been clubbed to death and thrown into a mine shaft.

Lack of shipping and loading personnel slowed the evacuation. But by using a carefully enacted contraction of the final coastal perimeter all of X Corps was evacuated safely. Along with the troops there were over 100,000 Korean refugees who desperately wanted to get away from the Communists. All who could fit in the ships available were transported by the Navy to Pusan. *Unfortunately many thousands of refugees were left behind due to the shortage of Navy shipping.* (Thousands of tons of supplies were also blown up unnecessarily.)

As the sealift began the Marines went out first, then the ROK units. They were followed by Army units and then civilians. In all 105,000 troops, 17,500 vehicles, and 350 thousand tons of supplies were evacuated from Hungnam.

At Wonsan another 3,800 troops, 7,000 civilians, 1100 vehicles and 10,000 tons of cargo were removed. Not bad for a navy that was no longer needed.

(All of the civilians and supplies should have been evacuated.

After the beating they had taken the CCF was not forcing the U.N. military out of the area. They were not attacking, just probing the lines. And in actuality they could not have done much even if they tried with the Navy's gunships and carriers offshore. Defensive units should have stayed put and ships should have been sent back to pick up everyone and everything left behind.)

After their arrival in the Pusan area the Marines recuperated and absorbed replacements. None were aware that the world had thought them lost. (Those who fought at the reservoir would forever be known as the Chosin Few)

With all of the bad military news from Korea the American media became almost hysterical in its claims of defeat and calamity.

(Just like the hysterics the media used in Vietnam and Iraq.)

But in looking over the casualty lists from the last two weeks of fighting, the Allies had lost not even half of the men they lost in one week of combat in the Battle of the Bulge! All of the Allied forces who had escaped the initial battles were saved.

The United Nations forces had been beaten and suffered a setback, but all was not lost.

But the cries of the weak willed persisted and no one spoke out to correct them. (Just like Vietnam and Iraq.)

Time Magazine in two separate articles claimed that the flower of U.S. might was doomed and we were dragging down thousands of our allied soldiers. The loss of Korea would mean the loss of all of Asia to Communism.

Their article of Dec 18th even claimed that Truman's policy of containment was dead.

There only remained a policy of retaliation by the West to damage Communist power at its source. But that would have meant WWIII.
(And how long did those shrills think the casualty lists would have been after that occurred?)

As the news stories appeared at home the daily updates on the war by the new media aids of teletype and coverage by television allowed scare tactics and editorials to hit the streets before a realistic appraisal of the conditions could be made. This uncontrollable factor in the war became the norm as media saturation began. Bad news was learned quickly and repeated often. Morale at home was being affected.

(In the electronic age of today, it is a hundred times worse.)

America had plenty of beans and bullets to handle the Chinese addition to the war, but manpower was a different story. Truman had already called up the reserves and he next called the militias of Minnesota and Mississippi into service. Thousands more citizen-soldiers were inducted each month. But even then the bugles were never blown and the drums did not beat as these new warriors were rushed into service.

Pres. Truman did not want to engage in an extensive war with the communists in Asia. **The Soviets had 175 Divisions assembled in East Europe alone.**

The collective thought at that time was that only the U.S. nuclear deterrent had prevented those Soviet armies from overrunning Western Europe. The West and especially America had voluntarily disarmed after WWII, not Russia. The communists were militarily strong and menacing and Stalin knew that the West was politically weak.

After much discussion the leaders in Washington agreed on a policy. *We had to keep fighting and hope for the best. The "Conflict" in Korea had escalated but not fatally. Gen. MacArthur was given orders to punish the Chinese, but only those in Korea.*

In China Chairman Mao was convinced that the Americans could be pushed into the sea. He ordered Marshall Peng Dehuai to continue the pursuit and finish the enemy. Peng was a soldiers commander, and he tried to convince Mao to let his exhausted and starving troops rest and recover. While the Americans in the 8th Army had driven away, his forces had walked through the heavy snows and bitter cold.

Half of their force had been lost and Peng hoped to wait for the spring thaws before resuming their attacks. *Mao refused to wait, insisting they attack.* (Peng would later be critical of Mao's Cultural Revolution, he was imprisoned and tortured, later dying as a non-person.)

The collapse of 8th Army was finally stopped well below the 38th parallel.

All of the hallowed gains from Seoul and points north were **re-occupied** by the Communists. *Almost all of it was taken without a shot being fired.*

The panicked destruction of supplies, bridges, railheads, locomotives and hundreds of vehicles absolutely stunned the British Commanders and many considered it criminal.

(For days FEAF planes searched out and destroyed over six thousand vehicles and a thousand tanks and weapon carriers! Imagine the cost.)

General Walker had been killed in a road accident on Dec 23, (Just like his old boss Patton.). He was replaced by Gen. Matt Ridgeway the former leader of the famed 82d Airborne, and later commander of the Airborne Corps at the Battle of the Bulge and in Germany. (Gen. James Van Fleet was the other choice.)

A tough fighter, Ridgeway was just what the 8th Army needed to get back on its feet. He toured the units and the terrain learning details about both.

X Corps was finally and correctly made a part of the 8th Army. In a face to face meeting with Gen. Smith USMC, Smith made sure to tell Ridgeway that the Marines wanted no part of X Corps or Almond. Ridgeway was greatly impressed with Smith and the Marines and assured Smith he would comply. They were sent into *central Korea* and away from Almond, but they lost command of their air wing.

(If the Marines had stayed near the coast the air-wing would have been operating from their carriers and would have stayed a Corps asset.)

Some in the Army and all of the Air Force brass were actually angry that the Marines had their own air units. (All had seen how effective they had been.)

Now if the Marines needed close air support they had to go through the "Brass Heavy and unschooled Joint Operations Center". Overnight the combined arms team concept that made the Marines such a threat to the enemy was eliminated.

Response time for air support went from 15 minutes to 80 or more!

President Truman later awarded the 1st Marine Division a Presidential Unit Citation for their incredible escape from the massive Chinese trap. Not bad for the "Navy's Police Force". (He must have been choking on the award.)

In early 1952 Truman signed Public Law 416, which defined the Marine Corps as a separate service to be kept at a minimum strength of three divisions and three Air Wings. Their mission was amphibious operations and as a quick strike force.

A few months later Gen. Oliver Smith USMC was rotated out and replaced.

Unbelievably he was ignored by the nation's senior officers, and never even taught or lectured at the military Command Schools.

He was given command of USMC forces in the Atlantic and retired in 1955 to obscurity, gardening in the boots he wore at the Chosin Reservoir until the day he died.

(No monument to his incredible leadership has ever been made, even in the USMC exhibit on the Chosin Reservoir battle!)

In Washington and London the world leaders were coming to the realization that they may have to stabilize the war at the 38th parallel and pursue a settlement. Gen. MacArthur was still dead set against this and complained publicly.

(Even though MacArthur had been wrong about the Chinese intervention, done nothing to control the battlefield, and allowed a needless retreat, he was still in command.)

At the front Gen. Ridgeway actually had to stop trucks that were still running southward. He berated all of the 8th Army commanders to get control of their troops and get them up in the hills and off of the roads. "We are going to attack and kill these reds.
Learn the terrain and use it to your advantage".

But before he could retrain his units events again changed.

<u>The CCF had regrouped from their long walk south,</u> and were ordered to try to drive the allies out of *Chosun*. Around 5 PM on Dec 31st, the Chinese bugles blared.

Ridgeway had hoped to have an orderly withdrawal to make the Chinese bleed for every yard. But once again the ROK units were attacked first and again they broke and fled. Seoul was abandoned as the retreat continued.

With the abandonment of Seoul 32,000 troops had to be removed by the navy along with 132,000 civilians. Some supplies were packed up, but again most were destroyed as was the port at Inchon that we had just rebuilt! Ridgeway confronted Pres. Rhee complaining of the poor quality and lack of leadership among the ROK Units.
Ridgeway actually wanted all supplies to the ROK's stopped as most of our material ended up on the black market or taken by the enemy.

Rhee promised that the South Koreans would fight again.

Moving south on the improved roads the 8th Army again left the reds far behind. Days later the CCF moved south all the way to Osan, where Task force Smith had first fought the NKPA back in July! Discussions were had on how to evacuate the Army from the peninsula when the communist logistical weakness again showed itself and the CCF advance stopped. They had suffered another 38,000 casualties, but as the West would finally realize casualties meant nothing to the Communists.

(It would be another disgrace that our supposed leaders did not heed this lesson in Vietnam.)

Public opinion had turned sharply away from this "war", and most of the citizens wanted to abandon Korea and bring the troops home. even the troops were harshly complaining about Korea and their commanders in letters home.

In just six weeks the 8th Army had fallen back 275 miles!

One sergeant wrote, "Since Dec. 8th, I have seen no enemy, fired no shots, and the company has not had a single casualty.
I am ashamed and disgusted."

Sensing a possible American defeat Stalin had been sending more and more supplies and weapons to the Chinese. Russian pilots were flying the newest Mig-15 fighters from air bases in Manchuria. They were still ordered to engage American planes over communist held territory in case they were shot down. Reports about this again went on to Washington, but the Administrations of Truman and later Eisenhower decided not to release the information.

(Paul Nitze who headed the planning department at State prepared a secret document on the subject. It was felt that if the American Public knew that Russian pilots and advisors were fighting our troops calls for war upon Russia would ring out. It was better to deceive the public.)

And Mao still insisted that Gen. Peng was to continue to chase the Americans out of Korea. Peng knew that this would be a mistake as his forces were following in the same footsteps of the *Inmun Gun*. They were under continuous air attacks and their supply lines were over-extended. But Mao felt that the time was ripe for a total victory.

(Intelligence from the Russians claimed that the Americans were preparing to exit from Korea.) Marshall Peng who unlike many of the U.S. commanders went forward to see for himself what was going on, knew the information was untrue.

In January Peng ordered a general pause for his Armies.

After making some needed *Command changes* and getting in some training, Gen. Ridgeway finally got his units moving north. Because of MacArthur's continual doom and gloom reports Generals Collins and Vandenberg had returned to Korea in late January. They found things completely turned around. There was no need to consider evacuation, for Ridgeway wanted to attack.

Gen. Ridgeway had replaced five Divisional Commanders within a week. He was so aggressive in dismissing the incompetent's that the Army Personnel Office complained that they did not have enough open positions for them!!

Next to go were the Colonels who revealed that they were of no use on a battlefield. Some could not identify any landmarks in their sector.

In short order the Army General Staff was afraid that the Congress might start looking into the large numbers of dismissals. To put a good face on things the Army stated that those valued officers were moving on to training commands.

(Here is a thought, fire them because they were not good enough to remain on duty.)

Ridgeway also eliminated the segregated units. The Army would be desegregated (like Gen. Smith USMC had done) despite complaints from the southern Democrats. Under Ridgeway it was all for one and one for all. Recon units were organized and then sent out. They found a "soft front" abutting the "front lines". (The CCF always performed a tactical withdrawal whenever it needed to regroup.)

Operation Wolfhound was the first offensive operation for 8th Army since *the great bug-out*. It was limited in scope, advancing just over a dozen miles. That was soon followed by operations *Thunderbolt, Roundup, Ripper and Killer*. Those attacks were all small, well planned and coordinated. The Chinese were consistently pushed back.

(Aggressive as always, Ridgeway flew over the front to see where the Chinese were. At all times they were invisible and only ground action would find them.)

Suwon was retaken, and by late February units neared the Han River.

By having the U.N. units advance shoulder to shoulder the normal communist guerrillas and stay-behinds were quickly rounded up and eliminated. CCF attempts to penetrate between the units was also stopped. Success breeds success and soon the troops learned that the CCF were not ten feet tall. Units learned to stand fast and defend when attacked at night. This bought time and the dawn brought in the air support.

Caught out in the open hills and fields the CCF troops would be attacked and devastated. Advancing U.S. troops now found abandoned CCF equipment and men.

Ridgeway's incredible turn-around of that broken Army reinforced the growing feelings that MacArthur was finished as a war leader.

(Col. Harold Johnson was a regimental commander in Korea. He stated that in December 1950 the U.S. Army was a disgrace, yet nothing was done to fix it from the bottom up. Col. David Hackworth who was a sergeant and later a lieutenant in Korea echoed the sentiments in his fine book, *About Face*.)

This incredible shift in momentum was felt and seen on the battlefield.

It was also felt in the political arena. A cease-fire proposal from the communists was suddenly submitted in the United Nations. The U.S. agreed in principal on the need for one, but the Communists foolishly turned it down cold as long as any *American aggressor forces* remained in Korea. In early February the U.N. labeled the Chinese as the aggressors. (MacArthur began to reappear in Korea to grandstand and for photo ops.)

On the battlefield the gloom of the winter retreats was being replaced by a confident U.S. Army. All along the front the CCF was slowly being pushed back.

Seoul was recaptured, (the city was destroyed), and the U.N. units re-crossed the 38th parallel. In the spring of 1951, a tough battleground known as the Iron Triangle became the focus of the fight. (This area where my father fought was in central Korea and was formed from the towns of Ch'orwon-Kumwha-P'yonggang.) It was valued for its geography, and both sides wanted it. Again Ridgeway's planning and can-do attitude defeated the communist forces who tried to hold on.

Those spring battles of 1951 resulted in the U.N. forces moving north across the 38th parallel to stay. Losses to the Chinese units were again staggering as their human wave assaults no longer induced panicked retreats. The U.N. forces killed them by the thousands. And then the battle-lines became static as the Communists used their favorite tactic. *When losing on the battlefield, gain at the peace table.*

"Peace Talks" were held and there was a pause in the fighting which enabled the CCF to regroup for their next offensive. No pause should have been allowed unless the Military approved of the pause and actual concrete negotiations were being conducted. At the first sign of a scam the envoys should have left and the Allied attacks renewed. But this pause was made as a Political decision only, and was totally wrong.

(This was the same mistake Truman made in China in 46 and 47, and Johnson would make in Vietnam.)

Concerns soon grew of a large Chinese force that was assembling in Shantung province and in Manchuria. It was obvious that the CCF was not ending its fight for Korea. As shown before, atomic bombs and their component parts had already been secretly shipped out, and bomb loading pits were being readied at airfields on Okinawa.

On April 6, Gen. Bradley brought a JCS recommendation to Pres. Truman which would allow the commander to initiate a nuclear strike if the larger Chinese units prepared to attack. Truman pondered the idea, but preferred to use the bombs outside of Korea. It was hoped that a news "leak" would get the message out that things could get a lot worse and that concrete peace talks should proceed.

Truman thought he saw an opportunity to end the war and wanted to discuss his ideas at the U.N. Gen. MacArthur was infuriated and again said so publicly. He was then fired by Truman. MacArthur's feelings for war were typical of Americans of his "school". *War was to be entered upon with great sadness, but also with great ferocity.*

"When fighting wars of high moral purpose, there can be no substitute for total victory. Anything less is a betrayal of the purpose and the men who died fighting for it." (25)

The Japanese people were devastated by the news of Mac's firing, and in the U.S. many wanted Truman fired. But in the big picture Truman was correct.

The government is the voice of the people, not its generals.

MacArthur's statements needed to be presented within the halls of government first, not to the media. That should be a requirement and a law governing all our wars. *The Military Commanders must be allowed to speak frankly to the Congress before, during and after any conflict. Maybe then a useless politico would think twice before acting.*

But in the same light Pres. Truman never went to the Congress to get a Declaration of War. He committed our troops to this Korean War with **no voice** from the Military as to **if** we should fight, **how** the fight would be waged, and **what** were the objectives. How do you engage in a war when you have no idea what you are fighting for? (It would happen again with another Democrat all too soon.)

With MacArthur gone Gen. Ridgeway became the Commander of all Far East Forces and Gen. James Van Fleet took over in Korea. Van Fleet had fought in WWI, led the 8th Inf Regiment at Omaha Beach, fought through France and across the Rhine. As stated before, Truman picked him to head the advisory mission in Greece which defeated the communists. He was another tough resourceful commander.

America- More Spies

In New York, Judge Irving Kaufman was passing sentence on atomic spies Julius and Ethel Rosenberg.

"A murderer kills only his victim. Your conduct has put the Atomic bomb in the hands of the Russians years before our best scientist predicted they could achieve it. You have imperiled millions of innocents by your betrayal. In my opinion you have caused the Communist aggression in Korea, and may have altered the course of history to the detriment of your own country. Evidence of your treachery is all around us every day. You are sentenced to death."

Julius had worked on the Manhattan project and had passed dozens of in depth reports to the Soviet agents in the U.S. He was caught just as the ring that included Claus Fuchs, Harry Gold and David Greenglass was picked up and confessed all. (Nephew and Russian spy David Greenglass identified them after he was caught.)

One sad aspect to the executions of the Rosenberg's was that they were the smallest part of the ring. *None of the major spies were executed, and most served ten years or less in prison!* (Morton Sobell another small fry, was given 30 years.)

And contrary to the stated liberal lies and deceptions, Julius Rosenberg was a communist spy, while his wife helped at times. The Rosenberg's NKVD code name(s) were "Antenna and Liberal".

One other interesting note that was never publicized by the liberal media was that upon the arrests of the Rosenberg's, two of their inner circle of friends took flight.

Engineer **Joel Barr** abruptly fled from his Paris apartment taking nothing, and **Alfred Sarant** suddenly left his wife and small child and disappeared.

Both "turned up in Leningrad and lived their lives in luxury.

They worked on radar-directed anti-aircraft firing systems for the Soviets.

Their work was built, tested and then used in a place called Vietnam!

Hundreds of our citizens were killed, wounded and captured because of their work. *Yet in 1992 the traitor Barr returned to the U.S. when the collapse of his treasonous home the Soviet Union meant he no longer had any money or protection.*

Swine that he was, he returned to America to collect his Social Security and to live out his days in peace. He was a registered Democrat and voted in our elections!

Investigating FBI agent R. Royal testified that Barr had recruited 18 of his classmates to spy on this country. Barr died in 1998, and unto his death was still being protected by the liberal establishment.
(He should have been arrested and imprisoned as soon as he set foot on our soil!)

Throughout the years the Soviets were able to use the naive liberals to stage protests all over the western world. Those "enlightened liberals" of that day complained loudly over the fate of the Rosenberg's and other spies who were caught, caring not for the hundreds of thousands of innocents who suffered from their treachery. They still feel the same today.

In Khrushchev's memoirs he wrote that the espionage work by the Rosenberg's was vital to the Soviet military effort.
The Rosenberg's were also named in the secret Venona project.

Many months later Robert Oppenheimer the lead physicist of the Manhattan Project lost his security clearance. Evidence had come in that he was one of those who passed information to the Rosenberg's, and it was he who had brought Claus Fuchs into the Manhattan Project!

(During that same time line Dashiell Hammett who wrote the *Maltese Falcon and the Sam Spade stories* was jailed for six months. Dashiell was another member of the CPUSA. At the hearings he refused to identify the contributors to the Civil Rights Congress, a communist front organization.)

Lost to history was yet another story. A young boy in NYC was collecting his paper route dues when he noticed a strange nickel. He showed his father who took it to the local police who were able to open the coin and reveal a hidden micro-dot. The FBI was brought in and after four years of investigations one Emil Golden, aka Col. Adel Rudolph of the KGB was finally arrested.

Indochina

With the fall of China arms and fighters flowed across the border into northern Indochina. During February 1950 North Vietnamese Gen. Giap successfully sent his upgraded forces against the now vulnerable French border garrisons at Lao Khe, then at Cao Bang, and finally Dong Khe. French forces tried to retreat from the camp at Cao Bang and were steadily attacked along with a relief force as they moved along the roadway. (This would be a common and successful technique of the Vietnamese communists.)

By the time those units had safely arrived at the Red River Delta zone, over 6,000 French troops had been lost. Most felt that with those losses the French effort was doomed. Still the imperious French refused to quit, and sent in a new commander Gen. Jean de Lattre de Tassigny. He setup a fortified line along the Red River Delta to protect the people from the encroaching communists.

Sensing victory the *Viet Minh* next moved against Hanoi. But Gen. Giap had overestimated the French losses, and found that not only had the French regrouped, they had massed their firepower. By January 1951 Giap's forces attacked towards the population centers. When they moved into an open area the French firepower hit them. Losses to the communists were heavy, a common outcome whenever any of their units tried large scale open area attacks. Tassigny was also using planes to drop napalm on the Vietminh. Never having seen war like this, the communists began to lose. Chagrinned by their casualties, the communists retreated and quietly rebuilt.

With the war in Korea raging, the insurgent wars in Indochina, Malaya, Indonesia and Greece, and potential Russian action in the Balkans, the Western world came to the view that a full scale communist uprising was being orchestrated. Though afterwards it was found to not be so, the U.S. began supplying large stores of weapons and ammo to the French to aid them in that part of the anti-communist struggle.

It was then that Pres. Truman decided to recognize the inept rule of Bo Dai in spite of the dissent from the State Dept. Many of them felt that the "Emperor" was a wasted effort and we would do ourselves a favor by not tying ourselves to a battered kite. But Truman made that call and that was national policy. (35)

Tassigny was stricken with cancer and Gen. Salan replaced him. The French had 900 fortified positions in Indochina manned by 84,000 men. Heavy fighting in North Vietnam continued on for two more years with each side winning and losing battles in the jungles. Ambush of the road-bound convoys was the preferred engagement by the Vietminh. One such area was Route 4, or as the French troops dubbed it, *il Rue sans Joie*. The Street Without Joy. (Bernard Fall)

During that time losses to the French Officer Corps was outstripping their supply. Since 1946 the French had lost over 60,000 men. *They realized they could take an area from the Vietminh, but they could not hold onto it.* Every night the communist fighters would return to snipe and ambush anything within reach. Gen Navarre replaced Salan but could not change that reality. Aided by Red China the communists could fight forever. One of his most fateful decisions was to create a forward base in the open plain around distant Dien Bien Phu.

By this point France could not meet its NATO obligations plus fight in Korea, Africa and Indochina. John Ohley a senior DoD official alerted Dean Acheson that it may be better for all if we just ended our support of the French in Indochina to concentrate on more important goals.

Possibly the loss of China was what had hardened Truman and his Administration into staying with Bo Dai and the French. An Embassy was opened in Saigon and veteran Donald Heath became the first Ambassador. Even with our official recognition and hundreds of millions in aid given, the French refused to allow any U.S. supervision in the field, in planning sessions or in intelligence. They insisted on complete control of everything in the country, even the finances. (Bo Dai was just a figurehead.)

Back in Korea the U.S. was no longer fighting a holy war.

Our State Dept was afraid to call a truce and leave for fear of the Political repercussions. Our Military was scrapping the bottom of its manpower barrel and just wanted to end the war "with honor". The night that Truman fired MacArthur, he finally gave a radio address to America explaining his course of action.

Pres. Truman stated that the free nations have united their strength for "collective security" in an effort to prevent a third world war.
That it may come would be up to the leaders of the Communist world.

Truman's words had an element of wishful thinking in that "the collective security" was actually just a catch phrase.

The United States and the United States alone now protected the Far Frontier.

No one else had the will, the capability or the power.

Our "Allies" committed a thousand or two of troops, but could not come close to the forces or finances needed for this fight against Communism.

Neither North Korea nor Red China would ever be punished for their transgressions in the Korean War. The Communist evil that threatened all would continue to exist and even to expand and prosper.

"The peace the people of the world sought would not be moral, but pragmatic. And the door would be held against the invaders and many more thousands would die doing so, Not for victory, but for time." (26)

Many who wrote of the war in 1950-51 could not understand what had happened. We had the "bomb" and pushbutton warfare. Those "educated gentlemen" could not fathom why the battle had not gone completely in our favor. They were also dismayed to find that man was still an important part of war, and that men continued to die in mud, filth, fury and pain.

But as time and the fighting went on Americans were rediscovering a bitter truth, a lesson that they had been told would no longer occur.

You may fly over a land, and you may bomb it and vaporize it and wipe it clean.

But if you desire to defend the land or protect it for civilization's use you can do so in only one way, on the ground itself.

And in the same violent way the Roman Legions did, by putting your sons into the mud.

Any kind of war short of a jihad was, is, and will always be unpopular with the people. Wars such as those must be fought with *Legions*, and America did not want such units. They did not want to serve in them nor did they wish to allow them to be what they must. Liberals of the modern world feel they have no use or need of these *Legions*.

Thus *Legions* have no ideological or spiritual home in the "modern liberal society".

Paradoxically those "enlightened citizens" foolishly fear their *Legions* more than what may soon threaten them. But that is because they have lived in peace and comfort for so long they have forgotten the fundamental rule of the land;

"That there are tigers in this world". (27)
And they are always watching.

Prior to 1939 the U.S. Army was kept small but it was professional.

Those centurions devoted their time to their craft caring little for what went on in society.

When so ordered they went to war, leading the citizen soldiers who did the fighting.

But they did it the Army way.

In 1861 millions served in the Blue or Grey, but they were commanded by graduates from West Point. In 1917, four million answered the trumpet's call.

They may not have liked it but they operated and fought as they were told, and then they went home. The Army stayed the same.

The magnificent rise of the U.S. Army to the challenges of WWII was difficult, but it prevailed. And in this society there is no danger of the military dominating the nation. Our Constitution gave all of the power to the Congress.

The real danger was that the Congress led by naive liberals wanted and enforced liberal ideals onto the Army. Once WWII ended the battle-hardened U.S. Army was disbanded and then it was emasculated.

The Doolitle Board of 1945-46 met and listened to less than 100 complaints!!

(Why an Army Air Force officer was in charge of this vital function is a mystery to me.)

This Board made a flurry of recommendations which modified the Army's caste system and almost eliminated discipline. It was "desired" to have a more "humane and liberal" Army, one that mirrored the soft American society.

But if you want an Army that is worth a damn, by its very nature it must be hard and illiberal. Society's purpose is to live and thrive.

The military's is to stand ready, and if need be to die. (28)

It was not until the summer and winter of 1950 that the foolishness and stupidity of the Doolittle Board was revealed. But it wasn't the "enlightened citizen", the Congress, nor the members of the Doolittle Board that had to pay the price.

It was thousands upon thousands of young Americans who had been told to hold the line. Without hard Army training and rigid discipline, orders were ignored or disobeyed. Weapons and tactics failed, and the Army's units collapsed and fell apart.

Many thousands were killed, wounded and abandoned as the soldiers who could leave, fled. Many thousands of our young soldiers would be captured and many of them were murderously executed. Those who were badly wounded were left to die on the side of the road. Those who could march were forced to endure sunup to sundown marches northward. They existed on a cup of boiled goop each day.

More would fall to the roadside or be shot for being slow.

Onward the survivors marched until they reached the communist prison camps far to the north. Once there half of the survivors would die and many hundreds would disappear in the unseen frigid and snowy wastelands.

Captives have always been a part of warfare, but while western civilization has treated prisoners humanely the majority of the world does not!

Part of the answer is chemistry and part is culture.

The Japanese marched the thousands of Allied prisoners to their POW camps because they had no transport system for them. And because they were Japanese, any who could not keep up were murdered. They fed those who survived the same gruel that they gave to all of their captives, when they fed them. But the British and Americans could not live on that meager diet and they died by the hundreds each day.

The Germans had a caste system for their POW's with the eastern Europeans getting the worst treatment. And the Russians treated all POW's terribly, but gave special treatment to the Germans. Most disappeared behind the Iron curtain and were never seen again. (Russia held onto 3,500,000 German POW's and used them as slave labor.)

The Western nations were naïve to the extreme in thinking that their Korean War POW's would be treated in accordance to western standards. Our Government and the Army knew how the Communists treated POW's, and combined with being in Asian camps, they also knew that any Allied prisoners were in for a harsh time.

But again our leaders were at fault for not preparing our soldiers for that eventuality. Thousands of young Americans paid for that failure.

With Gen. Ridgeway's stern hand the U.S. Army in Korea was reborn.

Teamwork was restored and discipline renewed. Communications were improved and the dawn always meant help would be close by. Our young soldiers learned to climb the hills, to dig in and hold fast when attacked. And they learned how to kill.

Hundreds of valorous acts were done and seen by those modern legionnaires, but few would be recognized. Medals among the enlisted ranks were always hard to come by. And medals depend more on who writes them up than what was actually done.

By April of 1951, the 8th Army had again proved Rommel's words, "that no one learns faster than the Americans". The Chinese however seemed not to learn at all.

Again and again their units attacked en-mass.

After each battle thousands of them were left lying on the snowy ground. And that young American kid that hung out at the malt shop was glad to see such sights.

By 1950 the famous British Navy was a shell of its former self.

France which had fielded a hundred divisions in a matter of days in 1940 could not field 25 by 1950. The smaller nations of Europe were even more reduced in military strength.

NATO, which had been formed to keep those countries out of Russian hands existed only because of America's wealth and our promise to come to their aide.

But now that America sounded the trumpet in Asia only a few battalions were sent by the fifteen allied nations. Britain was already fighting the Communists in Malaysia, while France was engaged against them in Indochina.

And both countries had many units tied up in their colonial empires in the vain attempt to "hold on". While the numbers of their troops were small the quality of those soldiers was impressive. From the bayonet wielding Turks, the knife swinging Thais and the redoubtable Regiments from England most earned the respect and admiration from the "Yanks".

(Thailand was under communist threats of their own. Infiltrators and weapons were being smuggled across their borders with Red China, Burma and Laos. Their King reacted quickly and harshly to insure their survival.)

At the end of April 1951 the Allies were up to half a million strong and miles beyond the 38th parallel. The rebuilt CCF and NKPA forces now numbered some 750,000! On the 22nd the CCF attacked in mass hoping to regain Seoul and destroy a large number of allied units. They were stopped by the courageous efforts of Britain's Gloucestershire Regiment and the U.S. 3d Division.

After eight days of bitter fighting the bloodied CCF again retreated.

Seoul was saved thanks to British hearts and bayonets, and the reawakened Americans.

But Gen. Ridgeway was not interested in real-estate, only in bleeding this enemy. His strategy when attacked was to have the units fall back in good order while artillery and air support pounded the massed enemy. Once the enemy assault had failed the allies would immediately counterattack.

The last major Chinese attack into S. Korea began on May 15-16th 1951. The communists sent 21 CCF and 9 NKPA divisions into the allied positions.

They made a 20 mile advance and then fell apart.

Ridgeway cabled the JCS describing the major defeat the communists had just suffered. Over 17,000 dead, 30,000 wounded and 10,000 captured plus tons of abandoned equipment. **Eighth Army could now advance at will.**

If the political desire was there the Allies could have continued deep into N. Korea. **But from Washington there was nothing.**

And so another terrible mistake was made giving the enemy time to recover.

As the demands for troops increased to drastic levels, The Judge Advocate General ruled that anyone who once "held" a commission, whether they had remained active or not, could now be recalled. Thousands of men who had served in WWII and left the Army as inactive reservists suddenly found themselves being used as fillers for the ravaged units that were fighting in Korea.

(The paid and trained reservists and Reserve units were kept at home in case a bigger war started someplace else.)

Over 40,000 of these impressed men were forced to leave families, jobs and careers to fight in this "Police Action". Many would never return.

Then the Army made another terrible decision, they reinstituted the hated replacement policy from WWII. Instead of units rotating out to absorb and train the new replacements, units stayed on the line forever. Replacements were simply dropped off.

Hundreds of thousands of Officers and enlisted men were sent to units as individual replacements. They arrived alone and friendless and had no communal ties to the units nor their Divisions. With no time to be taught the fine art of survival on a battlefield those new men were simply dumped into the fight. Many did not survive their first days.

Whenever the battle-seasoned guys accrued enough "combat points", they could rotate out and go home. In short order through attrition, wounds and death, a seasoned combat unit could be staffed mostly with unschooled replacements.

To make the manpower pool even smaller there was also a draft or recall exemption for college students, for anyone who joined the ROTC programs, or if you were a new parent. It was not long before trainees coming into the Army had classification scores below the level deemed unfit. That these men could fight well when trained was proved when captured CCF documents rated the American units the best.

But an unfair burden fell upon the nations poorest citizens.

(This same unintelligent replacement system and rules determining who would serve, or would be made to serve would be emplaced again in the next war. It would have the same result on the units, and again be unfair to the poor and undereducated.)

With an uneasy equilibrium established on the battlefield Secretary-General Lie of the U.N. told the United Nations General Assembly that as of June 1, 1951 a ceasefire was in effect. (The opposing trenches were north of the original boundaries.)

The main purpose of the war was to repel the armed aggression from N. Korea, and in this we have succeeded.

Peace feelers went out and eventually Radio Peking agreed to "suspend military activities and hold peace negotiations". The first location of the talks was at Kaesong.

Gen Ridgeway however was wary of stopping all military operations until a peace treaty was actually signed. Otherwise the CCF would simply use the time off to again rebuild their forces and their defenses. (Same as China in 46/47.)

Washington reluctantly agreed and Ridgeway's reply to the Chinese stated that the agreement on armistice terms must precede cessation of hostilities. But the U.N. ceasefire went into effect anyway.

The Chinese were angry they did not get everything they wanted, but so was President Rhee. He still clung to the imprudent hope of reunifying his country.

The thought of having a million Chinese soldiers on his peninsula was a disgrace and he would try many tricks to stop the peace.

Peace talks were not started until July 10th, and the location was found to be unsound. Kaesong had been captured by the communists and was an armed camp.

U.N. negotiators were treated as criminals as they were paraded past lines of armed enemy troops. Admiral Turner Joy had opened the proceedings with a speech of goodwill and hope, and had placed a small UN flag on the conference table. After lunch, the NKPA representative Gen. Nam IL had a large N. Korean banner placed on the table.

The Chinese sat on high upholstered chairs, while the U.N. representatives had to sit on small wooden seats. At first only communist reporters were allowed in Kaesong.

It took until July 26th just to establish an agenda for the talks.

At the meetings the Communists continued to insist that all of the Allied military forces had to leave the country and that the original boundary be reinstated.

(That boundary proposal was the same proposal Truman had suggested in January 51, but at that point the CCF was winning and the Chinese had refused.)

Fortunately the Allies saw through the lies and refused to withdraw their forces off of the peninsula nor to hand back all of the gains made two months earlier.

UN forces had created a defense in depth at the front. They had no such defense along the 38th parallel. Had they moved back it was possible that the communists would revoke the treaty and then successfully attack them in the open.

Most had hoped an agreement could be reached within a few weeks. But petty problems like the ones mentioned above are an important test to the oriental need to "Save Face". Those negotiations with the Communists would take twenty four months to complete! The pace of the talks was so exasperating that Ridgeway cabled the JCS on Aug 6th; *"To sit down with these men and deal with them as representatives of an enlightened and civilized people is to deride ones own dignity and to invite the disaster their treachery will inevitably bring upon us!"* (29)

Ridgeway wanted the delegates to employ such language and methods as these treacherous savages cannot fail to understand and respect! (Ridgeway had served in China with George Marshall in the 1920s and was well aware of how they worked.)

Josef Stalin had once stated, "A diplomats words must have no relation to actions, otherwise what kind of diplomacy is it? Words are one thing, actions another. Good words are a concealment for bad deeds, and sincere diplomacy is no more possible than dry water or iron wood.

The JCS wrongly refused Ridgeway's suggestion and the talks dragged on. After weeks of continued communist verbal assaults the peace talks were finally suspended. In short order the fighting resumed.

But the Communists had achieved what they had really wanted, a long reprieve to rebuild.

Unable to force the Allies out with words or deeds the communists had decided on a strategy of fighting a war of endurance. During the past weeks the CCF had secretly established a defense in depth that could only be breeched with extreme losses to the attackers. Bitter and costly battles soon raged for control of hilltops and roads leading to them. By the fall of 1951 orders were sent down to limit attacks and losses.

Trench systems resembling Verdun were dug out and fortified. The U.N. Command continued to employ small adjustment type attacks, a hill here or a line straightening over here. Enemy casualties were still staggering as they died for every inch of ground. But with the new directives the war as a whole was turning into a stalemate.

Our Navy continued to operate at will sweeping the sea-mines, shelling enemy positions, supply lines and landing commandos behind the lines. Then one issue began to draw attention, the costs.

Producing and shipping a simple 5 inch naval shell across the Pacific so you could use it against the enemy was costing the taxpayers $200 dollars! *"Adm. John Gingrich realized that we were hurting ourselves more than this enemy."*(30)

And to the consternation of the naval ships working near the shorelines, at dusk they could hear the communists scrambling about. They would leave their caves and hiding places and begin relaying rail lines and moving equipment, canon and supplies. Occasionally a shell would hit some enemy munitions or fuel, and the explosion was gratifying. But within an hour the trains and trucks would be on the move. Before the dawn's first light they would undo the process and hide, safe from the allied efforts. (And the same thing was done in Vietnam.)

The U.N. Command realized that it was foolish to return the demarcation line to the indefensible 38th parallel. If a ceasefire was to occur, it would have to be at the point the lines were at. To make the point stick additional savage hill fights were fought on heavily defended enemy hills. Heartbreak Ridge would become infamous as one of the bloodiest battles in Korea. When it ended over 30,000 NKPA troops were gone.

Had we wanted too our forces could have continued back to the Yalu River.

Peace talks "suddenly resumed" on Oct 25th in Panmunjom.

After their recent heavy losses in men and territory, the communists finally agreed to use the existing front lines as the final demarcation line. But they insisted the line had to be fixed on that date!

Gen. Ridgeway again objected to the obvious stalling tactics these "new talks" were making. He stated that with our present attacks we can continue to gain ground and that Kaesong would have been recaptured had the first "phony" peace talks not stopped us.

But the Western politicians did not want victory, they wanted the war ended.

And they foolishly issued orders to stay in place.

Again that was exactly what the Communists wanted.

Their desire was to trick the U.N. into fixing the armistice line before any of the remaining problems were resolved.

That would relieve the Communist powers of any further military pressures as the final boundary lines were set.

Then this communist enemy could talk and stall for as long as they wanted without fear of battlefield reprisals. And that is just what they did.

During the long months of the static war the communist positions were harassed by accurate American air and artillery fire, so they moved completely underground. Their fortifications and fieldworks were built with unstinted labor, and almost always were better than ours. They became experts at camouflage, night fighting and became adept at ambushing the American patrols whose noise discipline was usually lacking.

The communists could attack and take an objective, but could rarely hold onto it come the sunrise. But that was acceptable as long as they killed Americans.

Except for the small area around Kaesong, the demarcation line ran 6-12 miles north of the 38th parallel. On Nov 17th the U.N. Command agreed to accept the Communist position on the cease-fire line, but only if the armistice was signed within 30 days.

Talks then bogged down over repairs to N. Korean airfields and prisoner exchanges.

The communists insisted that all communist prisoners had to be returned, while Pres. Truman and a few among the allies felt that anyone who chose to stay behind should be allowed to do so. (A clear and painful lesson from the Cossack debacle in 1945. While those in the U.S. Military wanted to send the commies back to bring our POWs home.)

This one issue so infuriated the communists that for nineteen more months it would stop the peace. Truman became so frustrated with the lack of progress that he wanted to warn Stalin of his plan to blockade all of China's coast. Any interference with our ships would result in the destruction of said port or city. But fears by his top advisors that Russia might overrun Europe if events came to a head in Asia stopped the idea.

Truman to his credit stood fast on the prisoner issue.
"We will not buy an armistice by turning over human beings for slaughter or slavery.

But he failed to fight for this promise by hammering the Communists on the battlefield. Massive bombing missions should have been employed daily to bleed them.

Instead the poor troops on the trenchline paid the price every day the truce was delayed.

Lists of POW's were finally exchanged on Dec 18th, 1951. The Allies were shocked that the Chinese claimed they only had 11,500 of their soldiers as POW's. Of those only 3198 were Americans.

The U.N. command had listed over 11,500 Americans as POW's and 88,000 ROK troops, plus hundreds from the other nations. **The communists only listed the ones who were still alive.** (During their years of captivity the disciplined Turks lost none of their men!)

The U.N. POW camps held 95,000 North Koreans, 21,000 CCF and 16,000 former ROK troops who had been impressed into the North Korean army. By the time the armistice was nearing completion and repatriation of the prisoners was being discussed only 50% of the enemy would return to the communist side.

It was one of the biggest propaganda coups against communism ever recorded.

To admit that such an outrage existed was a loss of face that could not be allowed. Communist stay behind agents and provocateurs that had been "captured" were ordered to organize riots in the POW camps. Hundreds of prisoners were murdered by these hard core communists in an effort to intimidate the ones who wanted to stay in the West and to enrage the world press. Again their trick worked as the western press releases gave great headlines to the communist cause. But those same minds never complained about the murders by the other side.

Since the U.N. POW camps were inspected by the Red Cross and other aid groups, media attention was constant. No such inspections or Red Cross workers were allowed in or near the communist camps! And that was why so many of the U.N. POW's were unaccounted for. Every day the peace talks dragged on an additional 25-30 American prisoners were dying in the camps. Many of those that were returned would be incapacitated for life. But the media never brought any of those *inconvenient truths* to the world's attention. (They had been killed using various means, and their unmarked graves would never be found.)

The communists refused to believe that their people would not voluntarily return and they again stopped any further negotiations until their demands that all of their troops be returned was accepted by the U.N. *The tragic irony of the prisoner impasse was that more men would die in the continued fighting than were being held as POW's.*

By the end of the thirty day reprieve the enemy was no closer to signing than they had been before. Their trick had again worked and their trenchlines were re-supplied and reinforced. Fighting in those desolate hills continued as did the killing. As the weeks went by whispers began to be heard among the mess tents and private gatherings that MacArthur had been right about these Communists from the start.

On April 28th 1952 the U.N. decided to allow the reconstruction of NKPA airfields if the communists would agree to no forced repatriation of POW's.

(This was a ridiculous quid pro quo, as we were restoring their military capability.)

Yet they still refused to agree to a peace.

During that spring the U.N. troops operating in the western areas began succumbing to a strange and deadly form of hemorrhagic fever.
The malady caused the victims to bleed from their skin and eyes!

In today's times the world recognizes this disease as **Ebola**.

Had the communists unleashed germ warfare upon the West in an effort to force the U.N. to send all of their POWs back? A hospital ship was setup to study the infections, but the information was and still remains classified!

Frustrated with the stalled negotiations the North Korean hydroelectric dams and plants that were sited along the Yalu River were finally considered fair game by the Allied high command. Continuous heavy bombing in that region knocked out most of the power plants, and at last it convinced the communists to re-think their plan.

Talks were resumed and progress was being made.

(The same problems would be repeated for Vietnam)

Just over the Manchurian border brand new and effective Russian MIG 15 fighter jets sat ready and unmolested on the runways. *Truman still refused to allow any U.S. flights into Chinese airspace.* The result of this "Political" safety area allowed continued attacks by the enemy aircraft on the U.N. aircraft, and a safe haven for all of the supplies and men entering North Korea. *(That same irrational "Political" boundary mentality would exist in the next war and result in the same un-manageable conflict.)*

To try to force the U.N. out, another series of devastating hill fights began. Old Baldy, Pork Chop Hill and others became scenes of intense fighting as thousands of CCF troops surged and overran them. U.N. counterattacks restored the positions, but resulted in high casualties. Unhappy with the stagnant situation numerous voices began to say it was time to use the atomic weapons.

By Oct 8th 1952 the U.N. delegation had had enough of the lies, stalling, and flaming propaganda. With no further progress being made on the prisoner issue the U.N. delegation walked out. "We are willing to meet with you again at any time you are willing to accept our proposals. We have nothing more to say."

During 1952 President Truman's approval ratings had fallen to just to 30% and he wisely decided not to seek another term as president. (Truman had declared a national emergency and instituted wage and price controls as well as federal control of railways and steel mills that were threatening strikes.) In addition to those economic issues the American people were dissatisfied that we could not win in Korea and end the war, get an armistice and end the war, or simply get out and end the war.

More and more citizens wanted to simply win it, or get the hell out.

But the major problem in finding a solution was that our unschooled leaders failed to grasp the simple truth of all communists; **They negotiate only when it is in their best interests to do so, or if military pressure makes them.**

The imprudent decision to fix the final war boundary had placed the U.N. in a communist trap. We could not "attack" the enemy, because the decision on fixing the boundaries made it useless. Why attack an area that you had to give back.

(Similar to why Ike refused to fight for Berlin or Central Europe.)

Thus our forces were powerless to affect the battlefield, or the solution.

One way to have forced the communists to negotiate was for the Allies to revoke the boundary proposal and institute a massive and repetitive WWII "Cobra" type bombing operations. *But that was a Political decision that had to be made by Truman and our Allies and by that point they weakly refused.*

Through the halls of power as many ideas surfaced to end the war as voices that spoke them. Gen. Eisenhower left NATO and came home to run as the Republican presidential candidate. Gen. Ridgeway replaced him at NATO and Gen. Mark Clark took over in Japan. (Gen. Van Fleet was not promoted up to take that position.)

Clark actually resurrected some of MacArthur's plans to expand the war should any more delays be done by the communists.

The Republican campaign message claimed that they would end the war or end the evil that had spawned it struck the hearts of many. They preferred to fight communism, rather than try to "contain it" as the Democrats did. Many called to roll back the "Iron Curtain", even though the architects of containment knew it to be impossible. With Soviet veto power in the U.N., the world could not "Legally" do anything to the communists. The campaign went on and received extensive coverage on television.

While the fight for electoral power continued in America the communists used the time to continue the savage fighting for hills and outposts. Despite taking appalling casualties the CCF hoped that their actions and U.S. losses would swing the election to the weaker candidate and he would give up and force the U.S. to leave Korea.

But after Ike won the 1952 election in a landslide, his team hinted that it might be time for the Nationalists to invade China with U.S. help. *Aided by the CIA, more than 200 raids were conducted along Red China's coast in the first months of Ike's presidency.* More missions were to follow.

Ike's presidential win was the first for the Republicans since 1928. They also picked up enough seats in both houses to control the Congress. Not since 1930 had the Republicans run the entire government. They reinstated the HUAC hearings, and actually won some seats in the South. (Since the Civil War the South had been an impenetrable stronghold of the Democrats. Those Republican victories were the start of a national electoral realignment that is still observed today.)

Another first was that the large national workers union the AFL, (American Federation of Labor), broke with the normal tradition of political neutrality and endorsed the Democrat Adlai Stevenson. It was the start of a long term conflict of interest between the Democrats elected to the government and the unions who put them in power.

(Despite Eisenhower's landslide victory the media was mostly against him. *Newsweek conducted a poll of the top fifty political reporters and found they overwhelmingly supported the Democrat Stevenson.* This was a sad view into America, that the media was so out of touch with the American people.)

Back in Korea Maxwell Taylor rotated into command of 8th Army in Feb 1953 replacing Gen. James Van Fleet. Van Fleet had followed Gen Ridgeway's fine term with an equaling commanding presence. The U.N. forces had continued the fight into the North and held up to every horrendous assault by this fearsome enemy.

By all accounts Van Fleet should have been moved up in the Army's hierarchy.

But a strange psychology was occurring in the Eisenhower years.
All of the Army's best war-leaders were being phased out.

Gen. James Van Fleet was the first of those leaders who was skipped over for promotion and then retired. This bizarre antiphony would have dire consequences for the next war as the "managers" replaced warriors.

A few months later a revolutionary development again occurred in the deserts of the southwest. *A tactical nuclear artillery shell* had been developed and successfully tested. Now it would be possible to selectively take out any small battlefield objective with precision and kill all who manned it. (Like a hill outpost.)

The massed armies that the communists had relied upon for protection and attack were instantly made obsolete. And the communists had none of those weapons.

(In October 1952 Britain built their own atomic bomb, with our help.)

This 280mm Nuclear Canon was "secretly" shipped to the Far East along with its destructive ammo. At the same time a rumor drifted into communist ears that the U.S. would not accept this stalemate beyond the upcoming summer. Word was leaked out that plans had been made to use the Atomic-bomb and artillery shells to turn the communist occupied border area into an atomic hell.

(This was the one time that it was good to have Soviet spies everywhere. Word got back to Stalin from the bugging of the U.S. Embassy that the rumors were true, Eisenhower was going to use the atomic weapons that July.)

Up to that point the communists had enjoyed a great deal of satisfaction and prestige in fighting the West to a standstill. But if those rumors were true all of their gains could vanish quickly. And from the Elbe to the Yalu rivers economic ruin was again in store for the communists. Harvests had been light and famine was possible once more.

Even in the U.S. the senior commanders openly stated that it had been a terrible mistake to have stopped the advancing U.N. forces back in 1951. No one had wanted to return to the Yalu, but all of them felt that a firm boot should have been kept on the Communist necks until they had signed the complete armistice.

If the U.N. and Truman had approached the bargaining table with a hard eye instead of a sigh of relief, the war could have ended in 1951.

(Tragically those same mistakes would be made by the inept, uncaring and naïve Johnson administration in the next war and have the same result.)

Far away in Africa the never ending Russian plotting was causing uproar and violence. Armed with stores of communist weapons, groups like the Mau-Mau in British controlled Kenya took to the jungle to foment revolution. *Other countries facing insurrection included the Congo, S Africa, Algeria and Mozambique.*

In S. Africa the infiltration was so severe the S. Africans had even closed the Russian embassies to try to stop their agitations.

In Egypt Gamal Abdel Nasser a senior army officer helped organized a revolt. During July 1952 a bloodless coup was organized with King Farouk exiled and fleeing to Italy. Gen. Neguib took power, though he was ill suited to the role. Events in the Middle East were about to change dramatically as the *Islamic Fundamentalists* saw a chance for power. And Russia a chance to make new roads.

Stalin and the Soviet Politburo saw the world as a sea of floundering fish. All that was needed was to foment unrest and take advantage of the chaos.

But on March 5, 1953 Josef Stalin died in Russia.

Careful to have eliminated any potential rivals, Stalin's death created a dangerous and unavoidable power vacuum in the Russian monolith. For almost thirty years he had ruled Russia with an iron fist.

None of his successors could even come close. The result was a four way line of eager plotters.

And all the while the satellite states in Eastern Europe seethed with revolt. America had come up with a brilliant way to counter the communist stranglehold on their people. *Radio Free Europe* had been started allowing the millions trapped behind the Iron Curtain to hear unfiltered news and information from the West. The program was so successful that it began to erode Russian control. By the summer open defiance would spring up in E. Germany and later in Hungary.

In time those satellite revolts would be dealt with ruthlessly, but not yet. Not with the potential specter of detrimental battles in the Far East. Subtle pressure was place upon China that it was time to take a pause.

Stalin's number two man and temporary successor Georgi Malenkov, (one of the four), made a speech about the war and agreed that all conditions for peace are easily reached. In accord with the stated U.N. position Chou En-lai announced publicly on March 30th that China might accept the terms.

Sick and wounded POW's were exchanged on April 26th, but for the Allies the numbers were far lower than anyone thought. *Over 58% of U.S. POWs died in those camps or under Communist control.*

And dozens of POWs were secretly kidnapped by the Chinese and Russians. They were never seen again, becoming "disappeared" as MIAs. (Missing in action.) The Russians had done the same thing in WWII with some of our airmen shot down in their territory. *(The Pentagon knew this had happened before, and that it was happening in Korea. Not until the details were declassified in 1998 did the public learn of it.)*

All queries about those missing men were simply brushed aside by the communists; "That they had never seen them". Since political events had progressed towards peace no disclosures of atrocities would delay them.

(That same terrible reality would haunt Vietnam.)

May 1953 was spent in arguing about the last points for peace as the battles continued. The CCF tried one last propaganda ploy, they attacked all along the line.

Through June and into July their attacks increased in strength and duration. Losses were again heavy and even the press reports turned against the communists.

After more last minute fighting the armistice was signed on **Monday July 27, 1953.**

Three years of brutal war had ended.

The POW question had been settled as follows:

Within two months each side would repatriate all who desired to return without hindrance. A "commission" guarded by Indian troops would be setup within the DMZ to accept all POWs who refused to return. *Explanations, (propaganda and threats), from the home country could be made to those POWs for* **90 days.**

Then for 30 days a conference would try to settle the eventual disposition of those determined POWs. At the end of this time any unsettled POW would be released.

The Red Cross would assist in relocations.

During those final days Syngman Rhee still could not accept this peace. It left his nation and its people divided after suffering over one million killed in the South. His nation had been savagely invaded by an unrelenting and unrepentant enemy. He rightfully wanted justice, and he wanted the communists defeated.

(Many in the U.S. became bitter at this "old man", but they should have thought of how they would have reacted if the same thing had happened here.)

In a last ditch effort to wreck the peace, Rhee ordered the release of 27,000 anti-communist POWs from ROK run prison camps.

The Communists used the event for further propaganda, but they too desired peace.

The Korean DMZ runs like a jagged scar across the peninsula predating the Berlin Wall, the most recognizable symbol of the Cold War by eight years!

And the Korean DMZ survives and thrives today, even though the Berlin Wall, all of Communist Europe and Communist Russia have collapsed.

(As Pres. Ronald Reagan would later say, "They had fallen onto the ash heap of history".)

South Korea became a ward of the United States.

Her survival like the rest of the western-democratic world could not have been attained without the sacrifice, courage and generosity of America.

Though none of the pundits or liberals would ever say so,

The War in Korea was a Victory, for South Korea is still free.

And the Far Frontier had been held by our tattered Legions, if only for a little while.

President Eisenhower spoke of America's fight for freedom and her will to remain ready too that end. *"We have not won an armistice on a single battleground, nor peace for the world. The enduring legacy of Korea was that the American Military would never be unprepared again."*

The Cold War as evidenced by Korea had created the need for a permanent, large military force. And so the Military Industrial complex was born. At its peak millions of citizens were employed in defense, intelligence, R&D, arms production and basing vast forces at home and abroad. *And Korea had ended any chance of a disarmed coexistence from the West.*

More than four million casualties had occurred in this "Police Action", with 54,246 U.S. killed, (over 33,600 in combat). America also suffered over 200,000 wounded, and at times was suffering more than 1,000 casualties each week.

Korea's civilians suffered over 4 million casualties.

It is believed the communist invaders lost over 1.4 million killed.

The war had cost America $67 Billion, and the rebuilding and protection of the nation over $10 Billion more. *Adm. Rip Struble would state, Korea was a major war confined to a small area.* By the end of the war the world had become more hostile and more militarized. America's defense budget went from $14 Billion to $49 billion dollars per year. Russia was spending over $25 billion per year, (cheap labor.) And both nations had the weapons to destroy vast areas of the world.

Lessons from the short but brutal war were clear.

Had the U.S. forces not held at Pusan, America would have had to face two equally bad choices, General atomic war to stave off defeat, or a forced and panicked evacuation.

The total humiliation from the latter could have meant the surrender of Asia to the communist cancer and the erosion of any claim to world power.

If further losses to the communist mantra had occurred, it would have resulted in the recurrent decline of the West and its ideals. More than likely the West would have collapsed or an atomic war would have occurred somewhere else to try to prevent it.

After the war Adm. Turner Joy would state, "There is nothing inevitable about our survival. History is littered with the graves of civilizations that assumed all was well." (31)

"Any nation that does not prepare itself for war should as a people renounce all use of it as a national policy.

Any people who are not prepared to fight for their freedom should be morally prepared to accept surrender." (32)

Because The Korean War was not an end of an era or an enemy nation, historians and society have misjudged its significance. Korea became the Forgotten War.

However Korea was but one battle in the beginning of the Cold War.

It was a battle that had to be fought, And it had to be won.

The Communist powers were actually surprised that an invasion in the backwaters of the world would rapidly escalate into a major war involving over a dozen nations. The violent backlash from the West shocked them. **After their adventure in Korea, overt communist invasion of a territory would be avoided.**

Not until 1979 would the ruse be tried once more.

And again that was due to the weakened state that America had fallen into.

All of the coming conflicts of the Cold War would involve subversion and proxy forces. *The communists had been checked in Korea, but not checkmated.*

They would be back.

President Truman's foreign policy towards communism was based on George Keenan's idea (and France), of containment. His programs in Greece, Turkey and Italy had succeeded in keeping the reds at bay. The dollar cost was high, but not prohibitive.

But in the battles of the "Cold War" the cost of containment was exceedingly high, in souls as well as treasure. Most of our political leaders began to realize that this cost had to be born for to fail meant collapse of the West to communism.

However this same Government that was created by the people and for the people failed to communicate and explain the need for this containment to its people.

As the free world's only surviving power, the United States had to patrol the far corners of the world with ships and planes and tanks, and with her sons.

Writer Sidney Hook wrote in 1952 that only America stood in the way of world-wide communist domination. Those who were paying attention knew him to be correct.

Without post-WWII America there would have been no order or freedom anywhere on the globe. And Communism would have conquered all.

Less than a year after the Korean War ended the next domino would fall in N. Vietnam. The French had begged for our help by having B-29 bombers carpet bomb the area around the base. Talk was even started on using atomic weapons to stave off their defeat at Dien Bien Phu. But after much discussion Pres. Eisenhower refused any thought on using the bomb or of our getting involved.

In the America of 1954 we could not and would not commit more of our sons to this subsequent battle against communism.

TR Farenbach aptly wrote of this quandary in his outstanding memoir of the Korean War, **This Kind of War.** "In his words he poignantly stated that America would be forced to fight these wars of policy, because the world still seethes with revolt and dissatisfaction.

Until mankind has freed itself from tyranny, greed and ruthlessness, war will always be close at hand. (His book should be required reading in all High Schools and Colleges.)

Military force cannot possibly solve all of the world's problems. But without using such force all will eventually be lost.

However repugnant this premise is to the liberals of the world, it is also incredibly true.

And the man who will go to the fringe to fight these wars, who will face and endure incredible hardships and death is still what he has always been. He is the stuff from which Legions are made.

Aristotle once wrote that almost all things have been found out, but some have been forgotten. If the free nations want a certain kind of world, they will have to fight for it with courage, money, diplomacy and Legions.

For There are Tigers in this World" (33)
And They Are Always Watching.

One of the unstated fallouts from the Korean War was the discrediting of everything the senior Air Force leaders had been saying. Their large armada of bombers did not deter the war, nor did it have any effect on its outcome.

Embarrassingly the Air Force had called their Korean interdiction campaign *Operation Strangle*. Throughout the war they bombed everything they were asked, rail lines, dams, bridges, truck columns and enemy areas. *In the end they strangled nothing.*

Enemy supplies and troops continued reaching the front in increasing numbers. If something was wrecked the communists fixed it. If it could not be repaired they replaced it. If it was blocking their path they went around it.

They moved and worked at night using their best resource, their numbers. And no matter how many casualties they took they continued fighting.

North Korea never had a large industrial capability of its own, and most of it was destroyed that first year. But their weapons and supplies were not being produced by them. Unlike our previous wars and enemies, in the Korea War, China and the Soviet Union were the merchants of death.

In June 1950 Pres. Truman and the U.N. had declared that China, Manchuria and Russia were off limits to any allied attacks. Months and years of fighting later those inane rules remained in place. Thus the enemy merchants could stock their wares and reinforcements just over the border with no fear of loss. And every night the supplies and troops were loaded onto trains and trucks and moved south in a never ending stream.

The flyers from the Air Force flew thousands of missions to try to stop the supplies and reinforcements from getting through, but could not.

At the beginning of the war it was believed the North had just over 7,000 trucks. By the end of the war they had over 50,000!

It was determined that in 1951 the enemy would fire about 200,000 rounds of mortar and artillery shells each month. At the end of the war the U.N. troops faced over 350,000 enemy rounds per month! And the poor wretch existing in the trenches along those desolate hills had to pay the price for that failure. (LBJ would make the same foolish decision in Vietnam.)

Because of the Air Force's post WWII propaganda and Truman's cutbacks, America's military machine was caught short, unprepared and untrained when Korea exploded. It took months to overcome the numerous supply problems and dozens of thousands of casualties to teach the new Army troops how to fight.

After the war ended all had realized (but few would admit) that the Navy had been the service supreme. Without the Navy no one could have landed in Korea, and no one could have been supplied. And it was also observed that carrier air power was more adaptable and better suited to the wars waged in the far frontier. An air force needs a large and secure base to operate from. The navy brought theirs with them.

With their outstanding WWII operations the Navy and Marine fliers excelled at close in air support. To them the planes were a substitute for artillery fire, and could be personally directed to a known target. (As shown in *Fatal Flaws Book 1* the program was started by the Marines in the Banana Wars of the 1930s.)

However the bomber minded Air Force of 1950 had to relearn all of the vital lessons the 9th AAF had used in France in 1944. Their leaders in 1950 believed that planes were to be used as an adjunct for artillery. They seldom wanted to get near the actual fighting, preferring to remain thousands of yards away. But that type of support did not help the line doggie who was in dire need of help from an enemy 100-200 yards away.

And flying high above the ground those leaders failed to grasp that the artillery the ground troops wanted and needed may not have been setup to fire yet, the artillery could be too far away to fire on your target, or maybe the troops could not contact them to fire a mission. But having on call air support over your head was a blessing and a necessity. Just ask the Germans on how effective theirs was from 1939-1941, and how good our close in air support was in France in 1944.

During Gen. Ridgeway's retaking of Seoul in the spring of 51, numerous times his Army units needed close in air support, but the Air Force refused and /or was unable to perform as needed. Ridgeway then asked the Navy for help, and in a short time Marine and Navy fliers were on station willing and able to fly the missions.

Seoul was recaptured.

"One Army Officer sardonically summed up the Air Force and its ideas on close in air support; If you want it you can't get it. If you can get it, it can't find you. If it finally finds you they can't identify the target, If they can identify the target they can't hit it. If they finally hit it, it doesn't do any damn good. (34)

When the Korean War ended the Air Force brass went back to their bomber and jet aircraft mindset. They were unprepared when called to Vietnam.

After the fighting ended historian and Korean War veteran Faris Kirkland researched and wrote a detailed report on why the Army had done so poorly that first year. *In his research he found that the Army's transformation from a disciplined service, (Infantry stayed in Infantry, Armor remained in Armor, etc.) to a corporate mindset of team players had been a key part of the failures.* Our senior Army leaders believed in moving commanders around to allow them to become "broadened". Somehow they failed to realize that that meant they did not intimately know their job.

In the Marines their commanders stayed in their field of expertise. Each man was promoted only as he excelled. After WWII, to get a promotion in a combat unit the officer had to have commanded the unit below that in combat.

As a result of that policy all of the Marine Commanders from Major General Smith to Lt. Col Ray Davis down to the rank of Captain had extensive combat in their fields of expertise in the Pacific during WWII. There were no quite sectors for the Marines.

Every one of their operations involved an amphibious invasion against a heavily defended shore. (Except for the first and last one.) With the exception of *Tarawa*, those operations took a month or more of sustained combat. And the Marine commanders that survived the war all led from the front, honing their skills as battle leaders. During those busy war years only one USMC General was beached for combat failures, and that was in the disaster at Peleliu.

But in the Army, which was a far larger entity, they had thousands of senior and mid level officers who had never commanded a unit in combat during WWII. Still on active duty, they were being promoted in the post war years to Major, Colonel or General Officers. With no first hand command experience to draw from they made abysmal mistakes that cost multiple thousands of lives in Korea.

Of the Six original Army Generals assigned to Korea, Four had never had a combat command!

Of the Eighteen Colonels leading the Regiments, Fifteen had never had a combat command! (That was why Ridgeway started firing them as soon as he took over.)

And this poor listing continued down into the ranks of Lt. Colonels and Majors, ranks that did a lot of the vital executive officer and staff work. Even many of the replacement officers going to Korea had no combat experience.

As shown earlier, X Corps Commander Ned Almond though personally brave had limited combat experience when he was promoted to general. His Division the 92nd was rated as poor. His chief of Staff Gen. Clark Ruffner was yet another senior officer with no combat experience. Most of the officers on Almond's staff also had no combat time. It was learned that the Army was actually using Korea to give those missing a combat command on their resume a chance to get "their ticket punched".

An Army inquiry conducted in 1951 uncovered the same findings.

But the obvious changes to stop this lunacy were never implemented.

Thus the seeds were sown to continue the poor performance in the next war.

This Fatal Flaw was the result of Gen. Marshall's desire to produce war managers.

Good leaders were stifled and shoved aside as the "politicians" advanced.

More Spies

Before the prior HUAC (House Un-American Committee) hearings were held then Sec. of State James Byrnes had stated that there were 205 known security risks inside the State Department. Mr. Byrnes had been "replaced" with George Marshall in Jan 1947. As soon as Truman won the 1948 election Marshall was replaced by Dean Acheson. Acheson was a staunch defender of communist spy Alger Hiss.

As stated before, in 1950 Senator Joe McCarthy gave his famous speech in Wheeling West Virginia detailing that communists were still active in our government.

McCarthy was highlighting a growing worry that had been brought out years earlier by Sec. Byrnes and the 1948 HUAC hearings.

Sen. McCarthy was a driven critic of the Truman Administration, and that included George Marshall and Dean Acheson. Voicing his complaints he laid the blame for the fall of China onto a "conspiratorial administration". (Similar to Obama's actions and the appearance of Isis.) Initially the Senator claimed that he could name 57 suspected agents, and later expanded it to 200.

Thanks to decoded Venona cables and the opening of Soviet archives, it is now known that over 300 communist spies were active within our nation.

The liberals of the day were still upset over the HUAC hearings, and became more enraged over McCarthy's new efforts. And with the Republican retaking of the Congress in the 1952 election the HUAC hearings resumed.

(Liberals then and today still refer to that time as Red Baiting and smear tactics in a Republican episode of "paranoia". *Interestingly they were not upset over the fact that potential enemies were operating within their own country.)*

Though some of McCarthy's claims were found untrue and done with too much theatre, Sen. McCarthy's main benefit to America was that he tried to expose the propaganda and lies and make it a disgrace to be a communist. But it would cost him everything.

The reader must remember at that point in time the West was actively fighting communism in Malaya, Burma, Indonesia, Indochina and Korea.

All of Eastern Europe was trapped behind the Iron Curtain, and we had recently faced the Russian's down over Berlin. Greece, Turkey and all of Western Europe had only just been saved thanks to the U.S. aid from the Truman Doctrine and Marshall Plan.

China had been lost to communism in 1949 and Russia now had the Atomic bomb thanks to the recent unraveling of a major communist spy ring.

Communism was definitely our enemy.

During that precarious time frame the "enlightened ones" continued to believe that the facts were wrong. When the earlier mentioned *Whittaker Chambers* left the communists in 1938, he stated he was leaving the winning side to join the losing side.

Such was his disenchantment with communism.

His earlier reports to FDR's officials exposed the extensive network of communist infiltration inside America, but they were ignored by the Democratic President. That was one reason why the world was in the condition it was in.

"There were few parallels in history where the agents from an enemy had been able to exert such influence from within."

Sec. State Acheson's intense and at times illegal defense of Alger Hiss during his 1949 trial further hid the truth of the problem. From that point on Senator McCarthy decided he was going to expose the issue to the American people. He publicly named 10 people which included Ambassador Philip Jessup and Owen Lattimore.

(McCarthy's claims were seconded by former spies Louis Bundenz and Freda Utley.)

William Remington had been on Sen. McCarthy's list and worked in the Commerce Dept. when he was indicted. (He was a small fry compared with the people that Chambers had named in 1938, and again in 1948 under the HUAC commission.)

Judith Coplon was arrested trying to pass a counter-intelligence file to a KGB officer. Yet the liberals of the day claimed it was all false.

The Senator next named the following enemy agents; **T.A. Bisson, Mary Keeny, Cedric Belfrage, Solomon Adler, Franz Neumann, Leonard Mins and Gustavo Duran.**

McCarthy wanted them removed from their jobs and away from the government.

Capt Irvine Peress was investigated by Army Intel because he was a spy.

Annie Lee Moss was a black cleaning woman who had access to the Code Room in the Pentagon. She was a poster child for the liberal cause and they and their media friends hammered the Army when she was arrested.

But in actuality she was a communist and was listed in the CPUSA records!

Journalist **I.F. Stone** was a huge proponent of communist ideology back in the 1930s. He constantly fought McCarthy's efforts and was a guest speaker at the "best colleges." Stone was given accolades and called the "Conscience of Journalism".

He too was a paid Soviet agent who was shielded and embraced by the "elites".

It was claimed that McCarthy gave **Owen Lattimore's** name to the Senate Hearings, but in reality it was anti-McCarthy journalist Drew Pearson who did.

Lattimore was found to be a spy in a unanimous Senate Committee vote, yet Lattimore was offered a position at Harvard!

Incredibly Pres. Eisenhower had his Attorney General Herbert Brownell announce on national TV that Pres. Truman had knowingly kept an identified communist spy, (**Harry Dexter White**) on in the government. Truman had even promoted him to the International Monetary Fund to get away from the scrutiny.

(After the story broke Truman denied having ever heard of any reports on White.)

The media never pursued the story.

Then in Great Britain high ranking British Foreign Service officers **Donald Mclean** and **Guy Burgess** suddenly disappeared. *Panic set in at the highest levels of our governments when it was discovered both were Soviet agents.* They had had high level access to vital classified information. (More on them will follow.)

Sen. McCarthy was smeared and denigrated by the liberals and the media in the same way that Chambers had been after he had testified. For four years the one voice who wanted to know, "What had become of those earlier communists" was hounded until he left office. (When Joe McCarthy left the political scene in 1954 all of the investigations ended. He died a short while later.)

After the Venona cables were released in 1992, Sen. Joseph McCarthy was shown to be the true voice for transparency he tried to be.
Many of those he had named were in those files, and they were indeed traitors and spies for Russia.

But the liberals and the major media will never let you know that inconvenient truth. They are still hiding and aiding the past and present enemies to our country.

(Even though those files have been out over twenty years, recent history books and media shows still wrongly claim that Senator McCarthy was a liar and a fraud.)

Part IV

America's Turn To Lead

With the end of the Korean War on July 27, 1953 the leadership role of the United Nations was ending. Great Britain and France were concerned only with the maintenance of their former empires. By default America now had the major Western role in the affairs of the world. At this point the Eisenhower Administration was in office. Unschooled in that endeavor, the Yanks tried but could not keep the Communists at bay.

Egypt

Col. Gamal Nasser was an educated and charismatic leader who had been appalled by the naked British power plays in his nation before, during and after WWII. He attended the Royal Military Academy rising through the ranks of the Egyptian Army. Like so many disenchanted people in the Third World, he was a nationalist. As he advanced in rank he taught at Egypt's military schools and came in contact with hundreds of like minded men.

In 1948 he fought in and saw the Arab failures in their war with the Jewish fighters and their quest for independence. Those failures convinced him that the tainted Royal Family must be removed and the Army tasked with changing and saving Egypt. As shown earlier, a bloodless coup was organized by Nasser and others with the Royals taking refuge in Italy.

Coup leader Gen Mohammed Naguib took over, but was out of his element politically. Given dictatorial powers Naguib attempted to form a

Republic and he banished the Monarchy which had ruled since 1805. He also dissolved all political parties, but years of little progress followed.

Sensing opportunity Nasser finally took over the government in late 1954 by forcing Gen. Naguib to step down. Nasser promoted and enacted land reforms and other Socialist policies, but his eye was fixed on ending the colonial domination of Egypt. Nasser had promised the growing movement of the **Muslim Brotherhood** that he would work with them in governing. (Naguib had placed a member of the Brotherhood in his civilian cabinet to get their allegiance.)

This group was **an offshoot of the Islamic Fundamentalists,** *and as shown in Fatal Flaws Book 1, formed in the Islamic nations as a reaction to the colonial rule of France and England. They wanted the European occupiers out and a return to the 9th century ways with Islamic control of all aspects of their daily life.*

Initially Nasser expressed interest in economic and military aid from America. The Israel lobby and U.S. guilt to help Israel stopped any progress with Nasser.

After a short time in power Nasser sided with the Soviets and began getting increasing amounts of Russian aid. Other Arab nations followed Nasser's lead and the Soviets quickly became the "new colonizer" of the Middle East. One result of that situation was closer ties between Israel and the U.S.

With Nasser moving nearer to the godless Soviets he began to distance himself and his rule from the parameters desired by the *Muslim Brotherhood*. They began to fight his authority which resulted in increasing arrests and then to executions. As the months went by the *Muslim Brotherhood* would attract new followers who were as disenchanted with Nasser and his friends the Russians, as they had been with the Royal Family and their Western colonizers. *Their ranks grew to over 500,000 members* and some even began to turn towards America for help. And in the ironic world of diplomacy, Pres. Eisenhower directed the CIA to give them aid in an effort to destabilize Nasser and the Soviet ambitions.

Nasser never gave in to the overall Soviet ambitions, and his attitudes on nonalignment appeared to be similar to Yugoslavia's Tito and India's Nehru. Those leaders looked out for their own nations and power, and used both sides in the Cold War runoff. They were not going to be anyone's puppet. But in the world of the Cold War you were either with the West or against them. The first summit of the nonaligned nations met in Belgrade, Yugoslavia.

Nearby the Sudan became an independent nation as the British continued their exodus from the Third World.

And Pakistan which had separated from India became the first Islamic Republic.

Indochina

During April 1953 Ho's communist forces invaded northern Laos which widened the war and further disperse the French military effort.
    Laos had a feeble military because of the prior years of French rule so it was easy for the Viet Minh to cross the border and remain. This move also secured the local opium crop which the communists used for finance, and gave firm support to the emerging Laotian communist movement known as the *Pathet Lao.*
    Gen. Giap had shown that he and his staff were capable of coordinating the movements of division sized units through the dense jungles. Facing a new war the French commander hoped to use a remote village in northwest Vietnam adjacent to Laos as a secure base of operations. From there he wanted to stop the Vietminh.
    Gen. Navarre placed 12,000 men in a complex series of interlocking outposts at Dien Bien Phu, 220 miles from Hanoi. It was expected that using an old airstrip for resupply and friendly Laotian tribesmen would allow them to wear down the communists. *(He would tragically say, "Now we have light at the end of the tunnel.")*
But by Dec. 1953 the communist ambushes had decimated the Laotian forces.
    Because of the constant road ambushes the French had to reinforce and supply their garrisons by air. As they increased their activity they seemed oblivious to the threat that was growing around them. Wrongly they had located their units in a valley ringed with higher hills. One of the cardinal rules of military strategy was to always take the high ground. An American liaison officer asked a French officer what would happen if the Vietminh took the high ground and emplaced artillery. He was told the Vietminh have no artillery and would not know how to use it anyway!
    Using thousands of impressed laborers, (a common tactic in Asia), Giap had a dozen artillery pieces, (gifts from Red China) broken down and moved through the thick jungles and hills by hand. (Similar to the CCF tactics used in Korea in 1950-51.)
    Those few canon would give the Viet Minh the punch they would need to defeat those isolated French outposts. (Despite hundreds of flights the pilots could not shut down the communist movements. Trees were tied together to create secret tunnels into the battle.)

Their bright and improvised strategy worked as the communists shelled and attacked each strongpoint during a three month siege. French commanders were stunned to find themselves facing artillery instead of just light infantry. (They also made many other mistakes in planning to fight in this isolated spot.) Navarre had expected to fight two Vietminh divisions, he ended up facing four.

Those French outposts were mutually supporting and the loss of one would threaten the next. And because they were so far into the wilderness there would be no relief force other than their paratroops. They came in and fought bravely beating back every poor attack Giap sent. Had they been able to resupply the French might have won.

To keep his large army supplied Gen. Giap had his impressed laborers use bicycles re-fitted for transport. Their bicycles could hold 300-400 pounds of supplies, far more than human porters. And they did not need to eat.

With their logistical needs amended the Viet Minh attacked continuously

(This innovative concept was originally used by the Japanese at Singapore, and was one the Vietnamese would use often.)

With their expert use of camouflage Giap's forces hid their supply trails and paths from the prying eyes of the French aircraft. And their losses from attacking French planes went down as the porters also brought in antiaircraft weapons.

(Again gifts from China staffed with Chinese advisors.)

Hundreds of tons of bombs and aerial fire could not stop the 100,000 laborers who kept the supplies coming. Giap had initially used the Chinese advised frontal assaults, the type they had used in Korea. But the mounting Viet Minh casualties convinced him to switch to a siege type of battle and strangle the French.

Not long after the Viet Minh were able to shut down the airfield and that doomed the French forces.

Back in Washington D.C. Pres. Eisenhower and his staff pondered what to do in this latest setback against communism. *The National Security Council decided that the U.S. should assist the French forces with air strikes.* Adm. Arthur Radford was one of the most vocal proponents for getting involved, and discussions were also held on using a nuclear strike. *Operation Vulture was a planned carpet bombing of the Vietminh positions using B-29 bombers.* The French asked for twenty B-26 medium bombers, probably to prevent the disaster like Operation Cobra in 1944. Ike sent a few B-26s and some cargo planes to drop napalm on the Vietminh artillery, but it was not enough. France then asked for atomic bombs but Eisenhower said no.

On April 7th 1954 Pres. Eisenhower gave a speech that presented to the world the view of the *"Domino Theory"*, a concept that each fall of a free people to the communists makes it easier for the next one to fall. The press picked up on the phrase. (My view as you already know is that North Korea was the first Asian Domino.)

During late April Admiral Radford CNO and CIA's Allen Dulles meet with Churchill and Anthony Eden to solicit Britain's support to using an allied aerial campaign in Vietnam. Both refused to have Britain engaged in another major conflict.

(Possibly the poor showing of American Generals in Korea made them nervous.)

With the War in Korea ended the past July, Army Chief of Staff Gen. Matt Ridgeway was also against our involvement in Indochina. To him this was just a colonial war and we were supposed to be anti-colonial. With his combat proven judgment he succinctly warned that seven divisions of troops would be needed in that large jungle covered land even if we used atomic weapons.

And if China joined in the fight we would have to commit twelve divisions. Ridgeway felt that the heavy fighting in the dense jungles would be ruinous.

Indochina was the wrong place to fight a major war.

Prior to any final decision on Vietnam, Gen. Ridgeway sent a diverse cross-section of army specialists to Indochina to do a survey of what we would need if we had to fight there. Weeks later their answer was everything, and at great cost.

They also informed him that the population there was unlike the one in Korea. In Indochina the people could not be counted on as being friendly.

Ridgeway and those officers had realized that Indochina was a political problem more like the Philippines, than a military one as in Korea. But they could not convince Eisenhower to work towards that goal. And as time went by Ridgeway was also completely against Eisenhower's New Look military strategy, (nuclear). Wars have always been and will always be settled on the ground itself. *But just like Truman, Ike was cutting back on the Army that had just been resurrected from Korea, and arming with nuclear weapons.*

On the other side of the spectrum CNO Admiral Radford tried multiple times to convince Ike to help the French and to use atomic weapons. Radford was convinced that if the French lost to the Vietminh, America would be dragged into the area anyway. Under Radford's plan we had to take Hainan Island to use as a forward base, even though the island belonged to Red China. (No one could say what their reaction would be.)

Senator's John Kennedy and Lyndon Johnson ironically complained that any U.S. intervention in Indochina was futile and self-destructive. Congress, but especially the Democrats and Lyndon Johnson were totally against our getting involved or in being blamed for anything if we did. They simply wanted all of our people removed.

Without full Allied or Congressional support Pres. Eisenhower would not allow any air strikes, and he had already decided against using any Atomic weapons.

Eisenhower's refusal to get more involved were similar to Pres. Hoover's feelings vs Japan in 1931. The French were angered over this "betrayal". (By 1954 America had supplied over $3 billion dollars of aid to the French effort in Indochina.)

On May 7th, 1954 the French military forces at Dien Bien Phu finally surrendered to the communists. Over 9500 French troops began a captivity that few would survive. (Like Japan, the Vietminh marched the captives through he jungles with little water or food.) And with the other 8,000 troops lost in the recent fighting, much of the strength of the French colonial power in Vietnam was gone. But more importantly so was the will to fight on.

(Giap could not have relocated his force back to Hanoi, and if the French had the means they could have recaptured most of the Vietminh strongholds.)

During the seven years of fighting over 250,000 civilians had also been killed, while the Vietminh seemed to have lost around 200,000 troops. The French and their colonial forces lost over 75,000 men.

The French had been warned years earlier, "That you will kill ten of our men and we will kill one of yours. In the end it will be you who will tire of it."

Their inglorious end prompted their government to dig in their heels even deeper in N. Africa. And they would turn against the U.S. when we fought in Vietnam.

Gen. Matt Ridgeway probably had the most distinguished battle record and career of any of the senior U.S. commanders. *He felt his greatest achievement was in keeping America out of Indochina in 1954.*

He was staggered at what happened after Eisenhower left office.

During July 1954 France accepted a weak peace agreement reluctantly hammered out in Geneva. Similar to the Treaty at Versailles, this too guaranteed another war. Laos and Cambodia were granted their independence and Vietnam would be separated at the 17th parallel. (American aid went immediately to Laos.)

Ho Chi Minh and his Communists would rule in Northern Vietnam while the non communists took over in the South. Almost one million Vietnamese were relocated from the communist north into what was now South Vietnam. (Including over 6,000 die hard Vietminh organizers.) Only 80-90,000 people moved northward. Most of those people had been part of the Vietminh and they cagily buried their weapons before relocating. But not all of them went north.

As with the partition of Korea it was agreed that "Free elections" were to be held within two years. And as with Korea, no one could guarantee that any such elections would ever be free. *(Soviet Foreign Minister Vyacheslav Molotov had explained to a Western diplomat; "I like the idea of elections, and do not object to providing for them in a constitution. But there is one problem with elections, you don't know the results beforehand.")*

China's Foreign Minister Zhou En-lai was one of the Communist representatives in Geneva. *He insured that this particular compromise agreement would be reached.* Ho and the Russians had wanted the Vietnamese boundary to be at the 16th parallel, which was the surrender line of the Japanese forces in 1945. But the Chinese insisted and won the argument to have the boundary moved northward to the 17th parallel. Red China had lost over a million casualties against the United Nations in Korea, and they worried that America might use Indochina as a second way to threaten them. It was better to give the West a little and keep them at bay.

The peace that was gained in Geneva bought the Chinese years of time to recover from the Korean War and rebuild their military and defenses.

And with Indochina split into four small fragments, Zhou hoped to insure China's sovereignty in the region.

"For there Are Tigers in this World."

While at the peace conferences the wily Zhou also tried to establish contact with Sec. State John Dulles. Because of our recent brutal war with China in Korea, Dulles refused. (Pres. Eisenhower had recently authorized the CIA's first attempt to kill a foreign leader. Their target was Zhou En-lai.)

Many historians point to that episode as another missed chance for peace, but Zhou was furtively trying to reestablish ties to use America as a buffer against Russia. Trouble was brewing between them.

The reader need remember, China did not have to intercede in Korea, they wanted to. China's Communists used Korea as a way to get back at us for helping the Nationalists. With the war ended they sneakily hoped we would overlook their actions as they sought help in fending off the Russians.

They made another frail attempt in April 1955 by releasing 16 crewman from a B-29 that was downed in Korea in 1952. *If anything, the second event hardened U.S. policy because those men should have been released in 1953.*

(This was again proof that many of our MIA's from WWII and Korea were being held captive in secret by the communist states.)

When they left Indochina the French took with them millions of dollars of U.S. weapons and supplies. They left the fledgling South Vietnamese military with a hodgepodge of broken and unusable equipment and material.

There were few inspiring Vietnamese leaders to pick from as most had been murdered by the Vietminh or the French. Those who escaped death wisely went into exile. In June 1954 Emperor Bao Dai, (who had been appointed by the French occupation forces in 1947), appointed Ngo Dinh Diem as the Prime Minister of South Vietnam. It would be up to him that the West's hopes of stability and containment would be found.

Diem made his first political mistake by keeping the flag that Bo Dai had used during the French rule. He also kept the national anthem, the secret police and colonial police forces. Diem should have started with a clean political slate to show the people that he was an "alternative" to the "old rule of the French".

But Diem was not politically shrewd and he was not connected to these people.

Diem was a Catholic and had been living overseas in exile. In 1945 he had been captured by the Vietminh and met with Ho Chi Minh. They spoke for a while about Vietnamese independence, but Ho could not turn Diem to communism. Strangely Ho released him, though the Vietminh killed Diem's brother Koi and his son. (During the late 40s the Vietminh did try to kill Diem and that was why he had left Vietnam.)

"Even though we did not go into Indochina militarily in 1954, it was not the same thing as getting out of Indochina." (36)

Dulles ineptly claimed that we entered Indochina without the taint of colonialism.

But we just did it in our own naïve way, we sent our money and our advisors to try to turn S. Vietnam into a westernized democratic country. It was a small price to pay to try to keep the communists out. Congress was notified of Ike's and Dulles plan, but they were not happy. They thought we had stayed out of Indochina for good.

Meanwhile the Vietminh were looked upon as heroes for chasing out the French. And now the unknowing Americans were showing up. They had no clue what they were doing or what they were in for. The Communist Lao Dong Party of N. Vietnam was ruled by a small band of determined men who came from many walks of life. They felt that Diem and the South would quickly fail.

North Vietnam was being run by a man who had expelled the foreigners, while the South was being run by a man who was installed by the foreigners.

Amid all of the above turmoil Britain was still engaged in their multi-year fight against communist terrorists in Malaya. With the Nationalists driven out of China, Communist China was aggressively aiding their brethren in Malaya and Burma.

Nearby Indonesia was still suffering through its own communist uprising.

In the Philippines, America had committed much to aid the nation.

The Philippines Rehabilitation Act of 1946 had provided $520 million in direct aid and transferred over $100 million in surplus property and military equipment.

More help was committed each year, and as stated before the CIA was involved in ending the communist revolt in the Philippines. (The Filipino's donated large tracts of land to build Clarke AF base in northern Luzon and the large Naval Base at Subic Bay, home to the U.S. 7th Fleet.)

America

With the Korean War ended price controls also ended and a period of great prosperity began. America's GNP rose by 5%, while unemployment fell to less than 3%.

Food production rose and frozen foods became a common way to preserve it. Modern conveniences filled the lives of normal Americans, and it seemed that we had found the way to lead an easy and mostly carefree life.

In the nations of the West but especially in America, (R&D), research and development continued to improve the weapons that were being built. Missile technology was replacing canons, jet aircraft had replaced most of the propeller planes and helicopters were becoming key players in the military. Technology was now king and the humans were becoming pawns to keep the machines working.

In the Navy the battleships were being mothballed as aircraft carriers were the dominant naval weapon system. (The Marines yelled often as they loved the large guns.) Three 45,000 ton carriers came on line in 1954, and in late 1955 the first of many super-carriers, the 60,000 ton *Forrestal*

Class took to the waves. One benefit of the big carriers was that the larger flight decks were safer to be operating on. Techniques for carrier landings/takeoffs and firefighting also improved. Borrowing again from the British, these new flattops used steam catapults to launch the increasingly heavier jets into the sky.

The early Navy jets the F9F Panther and the F2H Banshee were superior to the YAK fighters used the first year of the war. But the Russian MIG-15 that was used in Korea was a different story. Only the UASF F-86 dominated the MIG-15. Wisely the testing for better jet fighters continued.

Although the propeller driven F4U Corsair was still a fine aircraft, the Douglas AD-1 Skyraider was indeed the best propeller driven aircraft in the world for day to day close in air support. It was not as fast as the Corsair, but had more and stronger armaments and was a lot tougher to bring down. But the USAF was not interested in keeping many of them around.

To protect the carriers numerous destroyers and escorts were needed for anti-air and the increasingly vital anti-submarine work. Following the successes of the escort carriers in WWII, the older carriers were also being reconfigured to anti-sub work.

When Russia overran eastern Germany in WWII they captured dozens of the most advanced German subs, type XXI and XXVI. Using that captured technology the Russians had by 1955 become a formidable submarine navy with over 200 boats.

If NATO was to protect Europe that growing menace would have to be beaten.

As the German and American subs of WWII had shown, submarines were a deadly menace to ships. With improvements in torpedoes and the recent submarine launched missiles the carnage on the seas promised to get worse.

Better sonar's were developed along with high frequency radios and radars. Ships became electronic monsters in the race for the best technology.

Atomic powered ships also began to be produced. Key benefits were less crew to house and feed, and no need to transport or load fuel oils to the war zone or on the ships. Atomic power meant sustained operations in whatever zone the ships went to.

For submarines atomic energy created a lethal strategic threat in their own right as the subs could remain submerged and hidden for months.

To help America's military services look ahead to procure the next generation of hardware and weapon systems, businesses and universities developed programs and invested in Research and Development. Gone was the day when a man could make his own bow and arrows. Now industry was needed to mass produce finely machined parts and turn them into weapons. To be ready for war, meant that you had to look far into the future to plan, design and build the latest machines of war. And as the education, science and experience of war making increased, a faster pace of innovation crept in.

The Navy used high-altitude balloons for testing the upper atmosphere, R&D pioneered new chemicals and chemical processes. They tested thermodynamic properties, used the bathyscaphe *Trieste* to explore the lowest depths of the seas, used data processors and computing machines to create high speed calculations, photographed the sun, developed better steels, and inaugurated a space surveillance system.

Transistors which had been developed by AT&T's Bell Labs in 1947 and patented in 1950 would revolutionize communications. They were joined with integrated circuits and became the basis for solid-state technology. Long range navigation, LORAN, was developed to aid sailing the seas. And all of those improvements were done in the name of military progress. There were many findings that benefitted the civilian world, but most of the R&D was to make war.

(Sadly these military updates did not prevent war, and our senior leaders still failed to grasp the nature of the enemy they faced.)

Eisenhower was in the White House, but regardless of what was seen and learned from Korea, the Army under his watch was still losing its leadership. (Ike's Sec-Def Charles Wilson was a former CEO of General Motors Corp.)

Ike had been Marshall's protégé`, and was following Marshall's program of developing team players, and turning the Army into a business of Organization men.

The true leaders and war-fighters were being replaced with yes-men and go along cogs. Disgusted with what they saw happening, *Generals Ridgeway, and Gavin (from the 82d Airborne) left the Army and wrote dissenting books.*

(Many others followed them out the door in protest.)

Competition among the Army's units was to be replaced with cooperation. Rotations among the commands and commanders created an impersonal atmosphere inside the units, and the Army as a whole. How do you build a team atmosphere when the coaches and players are moved about constantly.

And an Army staffed with young draftees at the lower ranks had many problems that needed to be dealt with using fire and discipline. But the Ridgeway's, Patton's and Allen's were no longer welcome as micro-managers became the norm. They were also political, and tended to watch out for others like them as they slowly weeded out the true leaders and thinkers.

Every six months all personnel were rated by a superior. Anything less than perfect ratings ended your career. Thus the raters had vast control over the subordinate, and the subordinate learned to kiss ass and play politics if he wanted any type of career.

Another ridiculous rule that was put in was if you had not advanced in a certain time frame, you were retired. (Not everyone wants to be a general.) If you reached age 55, no matter how good you were you were retired. Wouldn't it make sense to use the older fighters and leaders to run the training schools so the young troops would become better soldiers and leaders?

As the Army became a vast bureaucracy it became impossible to do something without getting permission from your superior and a host of "civilian experts". That factor stifled individuality and decision making which is so vital for young leaders to learn. And as the condition increased, *ticket-punching* became the standard.

Officers stayed in a unit only long enough to get their ticket punched, and then they moved on to their next temporary assignment.

Part of the problem stemmed from the Army not having a defined role.

Continuous scientific research and advances was producing a vast nuclear capability.

Any large war was expected to go nuclear, so what was the point of having an Army? Young 2nd Lt. Norman Schwarzkopf left West Point for his duty station at Ft. Campbell Kentucky with the 101st Airborne. He found the base staffed with alcoholics.

When Maxwell Taylor took over as Army Chief of Staff in June 1955 it appeared as if the Army was a minority party in the JCS.

Taylor did little to help a service that was fighting for its existence, and despite studies showing that the rotation and rating system of its personnel was poor it was never changed. None of the findings from the post Korean War studies were implemented either.

One bright spark in Taylor's term was his attempt to change the Army to fight the small wars that would and were popping up. (The zone the USMC normally occupied.) He established the "Special Warfare School" at Fort Bragg NC to prepare for counterinsurgencies and to give a more flexible response than just nuclear war.

Taylor's four year term had not benefited the Army as a whole, but it created the Army that was destined for Vietnam.

(Most of Taylor's thoughts on counter-insurgency were in response to the successful British SAS efforts in Malaya.)

Taiwan

Back in Asia Red China was again shelling the Nationalists who had escaped to Taiwan in 1949. They had also occupied the islands of Quemoy and Matsu in the straits of Taiwan. Both sides were routinely engaged in air battles over this disputed area and twice President Eisenhower had to send the 7th Fleet into the straits to stop a threatened Communist invasion of Formosa (Taiwan).

(Prior to sending the fleet Ike rightfully went to the Congress to tell them what was happening and what may happen. He was given a resolution by both houses to deploy U.S. Forces as he deemed necessary to protect Taiwan and the many islands they claimed and occupied.)

The small islands west of Formosa called the *Tachens* had also been occupied by the Nationalists when they were forced off of the mainland. On New Years Day 1955 the communists attacked again. Rather than fight for them, this time Eisenhower ordered the Navy to evacuate the islands and leave them to Red China. It took weeks of effort, but 27,000 Nationalists, tons of supplies and weapons and vehicles were relocated to Quemoy and Matsu.

Our 7th Fleet operated continually in the Formosa straits to ensure nothing further occurred. Most of the ships were on a war footing that luckily never came.

For many in the JCS and the Navy, the giveaway of the *Tachens* was a blatant and foolish retreat by the Administration. China had no navy that could fight us, thus the military leaders saw this episode as a retreat.

But by this point Red China had a 3 million man army with over 2,000 aircraft. North Korea's army had grown to 400,000 troops with tons of artillery and tanks. Russia's Far Eastern Army was 250,000 troops, over 1,700 jet fighters and over 800 bombers. If they wanted to start a new war we would have to use nuclear weapons.

And Russia had finally reacted and ruthlessly crushed the democratic revolts that sprang up in East Germany. Pres. Eisenhower again chose not to act during the Russian assaults out of fear of atomic war. Even though America had more bombs and bombers than our enemy, Eisenhower was stifled in his direct actions because any type of war with Russia would result in unconscionable losses.

Instead he turned to the CIA to perform back room solutions to the many foreign (communist inspired), problems. And that would start a dark road to trouble.

Oil

All through the 1940s America had produced 2/3 of the world's oil supplies. During 1945 America was producing almost 5 million barrels of oil a day, but our production was going down. (Such a travesty so much was wasted in the wars.)

Oil was also flowing from the Caribbean, Iraq, Iran and to a lesser extent Saudi Arabia. *At the same time the use of coal was decreasing each year as oil was more easily transported and used.*

Due to a harsh winter in 1948, the cities on our East Coast were so short of heating oil the Navy had to give them one million barrels from their supplies. And as the increasing world demand grew it began to cause disruptions as the supply could not catch up. *By 1950 it had been realized that 60 percent of the world's known oil reserves were in the Middle East.* Then Sec-Def. Forrestal had warned the State Dept. to make more effort in the region to "safeguard" the supplies the West was now dependent on. Deals were made with the sheiks to ensure the supply continued, but as the French and British control of the region waned nationalistic forces increased.

Hidden within those forces were the Islamic Fundamentalists.

But in the world of the 1950s, all attention was focused on the growing threat from worldwide communism. As shown in *Fatal Flaws Book 1*, the Ottoman Empire had unwisely joined the Kaiser in WWI. At the end of the war the Ottoman Empire was broken up. England and Winston Churchill had a major role in redrawing the maps of the Middle East. All of the ruler straight boundary lines were artificial, and based upon Britain and France's colonial needs. Iraq was particularly configured in a piecemeal fashion. By keeping the local populations at each others throats, it ensured that no ruler could organize a country wide revolt to push the Europeans out.

But the main result of that subterfuge and colonial mindset was the appearance of the Islamic Fundamentalists. They despised the interference into their lives and greatly desired a return of Islamic life. They could do little to the Europeans until WWII changed the world. During the prior decades their following grew in leaps, and by the 1950s that issue became a serious problem.

Iran and Britain had had oil treaties brokered with their Shah since 1919. As always Britain had the better part of the deal. As stated earlier, after WWII ended there was trouble in getting the Russian troops to leave the Islamic nation.

(The Russians and British sent in troops in 1941 to prevent the Shah from joining up with Hitler.) By the time they left in 1946 the Russians had setup a credible communist network behind represented by the Tudeh Party.

Mohammed Mossadegh had been a minor Iranian politician during his life but was elected to Parliament due to his stance against the colonial powers and their "oil deals". Britain controlled the Anglo-Iranian Oil Company, AIOC, and Mohammed wanted the young Shah to renegotiate the oil royalties Iran was to get and to increase their control of the nation's oil industry. At that time in the late 1940s Iran was only receiving 22 cents per barrel of crude, which was the same as the Saudi's were getting.

(Meanwhile Venezuela was receiving 80 cents per barrel from their oil.)

Mohammed tried but failed to get the Shah to act, and he then became the head of a special commission that tried to force the issue. Months of talks with the British produced nothing and Mohammed finally declared the former oil agreement void. Their commission broke off further talks with the British and their Labour Party.

To try to prevent a bad situation from getting worse U.S. Ambassador George McGhee flew to London to get the British to reconsider. Truman and Dean Acheson were even involved in trying to get the Brits to wakeup. Still they refused.

Then in March 1951 Prime Minister Ali Razmara was assassinated by an *Iranian Islamic extremist*. The nation was thrown into turmoil and Mossadegh was elected to be Prime Minister due to a coalition of *radical Muslim ayatollahs* and socialists. **Those extremists were dedicated to ending all ties to the West, and were becoming a growing faction in every nation in the Middle East.**

In Iran their party was called the *National Front Alliance*.

(King Abdullah of Jordan was the next one assassinated in July 51, and Ali Khan of Pakistan was murdered by a Muslim extremist in New Delhi in October.)

Within months Mossadegh's National Front Alliance (of which the Russian brokered communist Tudeh Party was a part) decided to nationalize the country's oil wells and refineries. The British were in an uproar, but Mossadegh's actions were approved in the International Court at The Hague in June of 1952.

Time magazine even voted Mossadegh Man of the Year for 1951!

(Acheson sardonically wrote of the British folly in his memoirs; "Never had so few lost so much so stupidly and so fast"!) (37)

The British were not happy to lose their great deal, and Churchill who had been voted back in as Prime Minister somehow persuaded the incoming Eisenhower Administration to "make changes" in Iran. Ike had placed John Foster Dulles in as Sec of State, and his brother Allen Dulles to run the CIA. John Dulles felt that Egypt was more important strategically than Iran, and he and Allen tragically gave their support to a plot to overthrow Mossadegh.

Operation Ajax was formed to get rid of a popular and democratically elected leader of a nation we were supposed to be friends with.
Numerous attempts were made to remove Mossadegh but he remained in power.

Finally on August 16, 1953 the young Shah intervened and had him removed. Riots quickly broke out which forced the Shah and his family to flee to Italy.

Heavy fighting erupted in the capitol between the Mossadegh followers and the (CIA/MI6) directed detractors. Iranian General Fazlollah Zahedi who was loyal to the Shah mobilized their tanks and troops breaking the rebellion and reinstating the Shah under U.S. protection. A renegotiated oil deal was also put in place. Mossadegh refused to engineer a counter-coup and he later died under house arrest.

(It was probable that a government run by Mossadegh's National Front Alliance may have been a danger to Western interests, both politically and strategically. But the coup was wrong as it sent a terrible message to everyone in the Middle East about democracy and freedoms offered by the West. CIA's role in the coup and its aftermath was kept hidden from the public for over 25 years! It would be remembered in 1979 and used as a reason for the turmoil.)

Unlike the other autocratic rulers in the region, the Shah would use a lot of the oil money in an attempt to modernize his ancient nation. Some of that additional money led to corruption, but that is how the world works. (Just look at America.)

Thanks to the Shah and his liberalized policies, *Iranian women went to school, healthcare for all was free and advances in health and safety were made to improve the lives of the people. Major westernized changes were being made to the traditional Islamic way of life in Iran.*

However the Islamic Fundamentalists vowed to continue their fight to rid Iran of this corrupting western influence. For the next decades they fomented revolution in every country that moved from their old way of life.
And they too morphed, into violent extremists.

(In Tunisia Habib Bourguiba made similar changes.
Kamel Ataturk of Turkey had been the first Islamic ruler to start this fundamental change to Islamic life back in the 1920s.)

Latin America and the CIA

"Someone once said that an emergency was something that needed several things to be done, and each of them needed to be done first." (38)
That seemed to be the new normal for the post WWII world.

Latin America had always been taken for granted by their large neighbor to the north. As long as tourism and trade flourished, and the local caudillos did not stray to far from accepted lines the gringos let things go. The host of problems in those impoverished lands was never considered high on the list of things to do because there was never an emergency requiring any action. (During WWII Argentina had been a solid supporter of Germany and Italy. Stalin even suggested that they be attacked.)

However the postwar expansion of Soviet Communism began to spread their poison into the region. To try to prevent any emergencies aid agreements and goodwill efforts began anew such as the missions Sec. Marshall made in 47-48.

Two nations that initially kept their distance from the U.S. aid were Argentina and Venezuela. Both had socialist regimes.

By the 1950s most of the regional navies of Latin America regularly had maneuvers with the U.S. Navy as a way to show the flag and warn away any conspiring Marxists. But in late 1953 the leftist regime of Jacob Arbenz of Guatemala was beginning to show signs of a potential emergency. Arbenz had recently nationalized the United Fruit Company's lands, a Boston based company. International law allows nations to nationalize their resources, they just need to compensate any claims.

Arbenz and Guatemala could never meet the sum needed as United Fruit was the largest employer in the country. In addition to that event numerous leftist revolutionaries had started accumulating in the country including Dr. Ernesto Che Guevara. (Guevara and Fidel Castro were picked up in a sweep and arrested.) Fears for the region and the vital Panama Canal convinced the Eisenhower Administration that this regime must not be allowed to hold on, not after what had happened in China, Korea and Vietnam.

Fresh from their "successful" effort in Iran, the CIA was brought in to overthrow the Guatemalan leftists. An airlift brought in 50 tons of small arms to neighboring Nicaragua and Honduras which were both ruled by strict anti-communists. Ike called for an emergency meeting of the OAS, and then instituted a naval blockade upon Guatemala. The Soviets responded by trying to ship supplies to the revolutionaries, but the freighter was seized by the U.S. Army when it stopped in Hamburg, Germany.

Then an exile force of anti-communists fighters was secretly inserted into Guatemala. Aligned with them was a Guatemalan Army group led by Col. Carlos Armas which was poised to act against Arbenz.

With the help from the CIA and Ike's approval for air support, the fighters were able to topple the regime with little resistance. The incident went off so quietly that few were aware of the U.S. involvement or the implications. (Though the NY Times did report on it.)

Eisenhower and the CIA had again flaunted international law respecting national boundaries and made sure the Big Stick was alive and well in Latin America.

Col. Armas installed the traditional military regime that was so popular in Latin America and returned all nationalized assets back to United Fruit.

Just four years later Col. Armas was assassinated by Gen. Miguel Fuentes, who conveniently allowed the CIA in to train the Cuban exiles for the upcoming Bay of Pigs operation/disaster.
(Arbenz went to live in Cuba in 1959 after Castro took over.)

Those "successful events" mentioned above plus the operations that worked in the Philippines and Greece created the impression that the CIA could achieve our political goals at will. But the **Fatal Flaw** in that winner take all way of thinking was that certain factors were unique to each country. What worked in one place may have no relevance in another.

The Greeks (and British troops) had fought and finally won a brutal civil war against communists trying to take over. They were greatly helped by U.S. Aid and Tito stopping Russian infiltration through his country. Prior to the attempted communist takeover, Greece had also enjoyed a long history of Democracy and freedom and their people refused to fold.

In the Philippines the communist group known as the Hukbalapaps had also been aggressively attempting to take over the vast island nation. Because of our long and mostly friendly relationship with the Philippines, and our vital bases in the Philippines, Truman used the CIA in stopping them. Agent Edward Lansdale knew the Philippines, and was picked to lead the CIA's effort to keep President Ramon Magasay in power.
(Magasay had fought against the Japanese in WWII, and had a good following.)

This operation became the linchpin of U.S. success as the large communist subversive force was finally defeated. Lansdale and Magasay did everything right from spreading economic aid and arms straight to the people, too treating the peasants as a vital part of their new nation. The fighting had been bloody and brutal at times, and it was kept out of the limelight, but then the end justifies the means.

By late 1952 the Huks had been beaten and a year later Magasay was elected as their first president. Staying true to who he was Magasay made land reforms, improved housing and was stopping the corruption that seemed to pervade every land the Spanish had once controlled. (As always though, the good man was killed in a plane crash in 1957. The Filipino's would suffer thirty years of corruption and despair for that loss.)

Lansdale was next ordered into Vietnam by Dulles and told to do what you did in the Philippines. **But Vietnam was not the Philippines, and Diem was not Magasay.**

And in the halls of power, the arrogant principals of secretive group 5412 never gave a thought to the fact they knew nothing about the country, the politics, the people, or the situation in Vietnam. *(Group 5412 was created by Eisenhower to shield him and the country from "those secret operations".)*

America

To assist U.S. intelligence efforts in thwarting the communist strategic plans the production of the *U-2* spy plan was begun. The U-2 would replace the current recon-jets, converted B-47 bombers. At that time the aerodynamics of aircraft was still limited so the spy planes could fly high and far but not fast. Those recon planes would be able to fly over a large area on each mission and take thousands of high quality pictures.
In that way our Intelligence services would have at least some idea of what was happening behind the *Iron Curtain that all of the Communist states hid behind.*

At a conference to limit arms in 1955 Ike, Khrushchev and Anthony Eden met to try to reduce the atomic threats to the world. (Khrushchev was of a more moderate mindset than Stalin. He actually returned Port Arthur to China, gave the Porkkala naval base back to Finland, removed Soviet troops from Austria and tried to improve relations with Tito.)

The U-2 would be our way of watching the Russians, but Khrushchev refused to allow the flights. And we refused his over-watch of us. We flew the missions anyway.

*Pres. Eisenhower was warned that those planes would soon be vulnerable to advances in Russian defenses, advances made with the work of those **two traitorous U.S. spies, Joel Barr and Alfred Sarant.*** But the need for up to date information overruled safety concerns.

When Ike took office in 1953 the Defense budget had grown to almost $50 billion per year. Eisenhower cut it back to $40 billion and kept it at that level until he left office. The Army suffered the biggest cuts, followed by the Navy. Similar to Truman, the Air Force budget grew by twenty percent to man the increased bomber forces and the new missile units being built. The Air Force was placed in charge of all land based strategic missiles, while the Army controlled the tactical ones with ranges below 200 miles.

In addition to those weapon systems, a line of Distant Early Warning, (DEW), radar stations were built across northern Canada and Alaska. (The fastest way for Russian bombers to get to us was over the Arctic.)

In spite of the budget cuts the U.S. Navy had begun to revitalize.

(With the War ended less money was spent on munitions, fleet and flight operations.) With roles spanning the globe the Navy became a key aspect to U.S. power.

Advances in shipbuilding, (65,000 ton carriers), propulsion, (nuclear power), missile and aircraft technology demanded newer ships. NATO became another pressing need as the 6th Fleet was officially formed to operate in the Mediterranean.

But a major problem began to surface. It was difficult to find men to fill the hundreds of military specialties that were now required. (Technology driven specialties' on board their ships, planes and equipment was growing rapidly. Gone were the days a high school dropout could enter the military and fit right in.)

Highly skilled officers and seamen would not reenlist due to low pay, constant deployments and low morale. America's economy of the 1950s was growing every year and jobs were plentiful. Unlike the devastated lands of Europe and Asia, America had not suffered physically from the war. A massive housing boom was occurring all over the nation, and consumer goods were in high demand.

Once the Marshall plan kicked into full gear huge orders had gone out for all types of goods. And as Europe recovered even more trade was created since the Europeans needed all sorts of products to restart their lives. Add in the military armament needs and there was much money to be made in the civilian world of the 1950s.

(Unlike the never ending media propaganda that JFK's three years were Camelot, the real Camelot was during the eight Eisenhower years. America enjoyed a long, unbroken time span of almost full employment, low inflation and no wars.)

As stated before Russia had almost 300 submarines, a dominating number if war broke out. As shown earlier the WWII Essex Class carriers were converted into anti-sub carriers using patrol planes and helicopters fitted with a deployable sonar and torpedoes. Mine warfare capabilities were upgraded as did the coastal patrol forces.

But the secret key to helping defeat the Russian subs came from a shore based sound surveillance systems, called **SOSUS**.

Giant strings of hydrophones were laid upon the sea floor along shipping channels and choke points. The first of the lines was called *Caesar,* and it was laid along the Atlantic and Gulf Coasts. *Colossus* was the second SOSUS line and it covered the vast Pacific coast, while *Barrier* stretched across the North Atlantic. *Bronco* covered the area around Japan and Russia, while newer lines covered China, the Mediterranean, the Indian Ocean and the Central Pacific!

The units were linked by fiber-optic cables and were buried in the sea floor. All of those systems were classified Top Secret, and again required skilled operators.

Russia may have been increasing their naval presence, but they were being watched by our military and intelligence services.

On May 18, 1954 a landmark Civil Rights decision was handed down by the U.S. Supreme Court, 9-0, which banned separate schools for blacks and whites.

The court cited many studies in reaching their decision and all of the justices were well aware of how idiotic segregation looked to the rest of the world. America was supposed to be the bastion of freedom, but part of its citizenry was being shut out.

Most of the schools in the northern and western part of America had already integrated their schools. Most had eliminated laws that allowed segregation.

(Not all of the integrated areas had the same levels of education though. Schools in Harlem were old and overcrowded, and staffed with inexperienced staff.)

Seventeen states did not believe in integration, and all were run by Democrats.

Despite the intent of the Court to end segregation in all public schools, numerous Southern States used legal tricks to try to prevent it. In Mississippi the outrage over the decision prompted voters to abolish public education if they were forced to integrate. In Clinton, Tennessee riots occurred to stop the *federally mandated integration of its schools which was set down by the Eisenhower Administration.*

The same problems had just happened in Kentucky.

In Virginia *Senator Harry F. Byrd* organized the Massive Resistance Movement that insisted they would close the schools rather than integrate them.

Texas Attorney General Ben Sheppard tried to design legal impediments to prevent their integration. In Arkansas the Governor called out the National Guard to prevent any integration. **Eisenhower sent in Federal Troops to enforce the new Civil Rights laws.**

(More court cases would follow right up to 1977!)

Rosa Parks, an African-American seamstress decided in December 1955 that she would not ride at the back of the public bus anymore. Her actions prompted a boycott of the buses in Montgomery, Alabama. Peaceful protests continued for over a year until the Supreme Court upheld the legality of her actions.

(Unlike the liberal propaganda, it was the Republicans who were the party that was pro integration and trying to help African Americans. That was why prior to the 1960's, most African-Americans voted Republican, and that included Dr. Martin Luther King!)

Asia

As stated before President Eisenhower was a firm proponent of the "Domino Theory". Non believers would claim that the Domino theory was invalid, but history clearly proved them wrong. (JFK, LBJ and all of their staffs were followers of that principal.) Following on Kennan's containment premise in Europe, an attempt by the Eisenhower Administration was theorized to create "a wall of containment" against any further communist expansion in Asia.

Unfortunately Pres. Eisenhower and his people failed to recognize the unique problems that S. Vietnam was suffering from. None of the nations of Indochina had had strong and effective civilian leadership in the past century. Having suffered under colonial slavery there were no solid bureaucrats or business people to make the government function.

Corruption was normal and rampant, and the Diem government was completely out of touch with the needs of the masses. Thus the people were indifferent to which political side they should support. Not understanding the depth of those issues, Ike failed to organize the U.S. advisory units with effective commanders and staff. (CIA's Lansdale was still there with his people.)

On September 8th 1954, The Manila Treaty was formally signed which established **SEATO**, the South East Asia Treaty Organization. Part of the wording in this agreement gave jurisdiction of Laos and Cambodia to South Vietnam. (A wishful attempt to try to keep them free.)

SEATO would operate in a similar fashion as the **NATO** treaty did in Europe, providing for a common defense and regional stability. The signatory nations included Britain, France, Australia, New Zealand, The Philippines, Thailand, Pakistan, South Vietnam and the United States. (Absent from the list were the freed but unsympathetic India, Ceylon, Burma and Indonesia.)

Unlike NATO, none of those nations were required to contribute forces to a permanent joint defense. That was a huge failure, in that the organization was incapable of taking any action as a group. That meant that the United States was singled out as in charge and taking any actions they desired. (A cohesive organization may have overruled some of the things that we did wrong.)

On a recent visit to America Diem had met with numerous U.S. Legislators including Senators Mansfield and Kennedy from Massachusetts. *(Senator Mike Mansfield told Ike there was simply no alternative to Diem.)*

Diem had been admonished before that he needed to make helpful reforms to get the people on his side, like Magasay had. But Diem was stubborn and refused to listen.

(This was a case when Eisenhower needed to be hard and straight to the point. If the U.S. was investing in S. Vietnam, Diem needed to make the changes that our advisors recommended.)

In November 1954 Pres. Eisenhower sent Gen. Joe Collins to S. Vietnam to get an appraisal of the aid needed by the South and to advise them. Ike had just committed a 650 man advisory mission into S. Vietnam, which meant we were invested into the country. Collins had been a solid General Officer on Guadalcanal and in France, and his input in Korea was spot on. All knew he would give a solid assessment.

Gen. Collins returned a month later and recommended we get out.

After observing and speaking with hundreds of workers, officials and other representatives, Collins did not feel that Diem could succeed in the fractioned country.

Collins reported correctly that Diem would only take advice from his family and had no following among the people in the South.

(Even the remaining French Advisory people became convinced that Diem would not work out.)

Ambassador Heath did not agree with Collins, saying underwriting Diem was a gamble, but not doing so was a sure loss. Col. Lansdale had the exact same opinion, but also claimed that he could make Diem a solid bet. Allen Dulles the Director at CIA wrongly convinced Ike to give his protégé

Edward Lansdale more time to "get things organized" and to continue to support Diem.

Gen. Collins was recalled in May 1955 and retired soon after.

He was replaced by a mediocre officer named Sam Williams.

During WWII Dwight Eisenhower had been a good war manager, but a poor commander. He had many failures during WWII, planning and battlefield judgment, personnel assignments and lack of forcefulness. His failures led to the needless casualties and prolonging of the war in Europe, which helped create the Cold War. (See *Fatal Flaws Book 1 1914-1945.*)

What was his reason for picking someone like Williams over Collins? Why not recall Gen. Van Fleet? This repeated failure was one of the reasons so many outstanding senior officers left the US Army under Eisenhower's watch.

In December of 1954 Ho Chi Minh signed an aid agreement with Red China. Later that year the first 160 Soviet Military advisors arrived in North Vietnam. They were sent to provide modern training in communications and staff work.

Hundreds of Vietminh leaders were sent to military specialty schools in Russia. Trained to perfection in the "Soviet School", they returned to N. Vietnam and took over command and training positions in their own forces. **North Vietnam's military would be trained as North Korea's had, to attack.**

During January 1955 the U.S. Military Assistance Advisory Group known as MAAG was officially formed in South Vietnam to train their soldiers and marines.

Diem then made another crucial political mistake in February by revoking the land reforms instituted years before by the local Vietminh. Those reforms had taken land away from the rich landlords and distributed it to the peasants by the Vietminh. Once again vast amounts of land were controlled by 2% of the owners causing hardships and deep resentment among the poor. It also proved to many in the agrarian nation that the communist system was the only one that helped the peasants.

The communist rebels still operating in South Vietnam were derisively called Viet Cong, VC. They quickly capitalized on the peasant unrest particularly in the unhappy and fertile Mekong Delta. During the remainder of 1955 Diem sent his troops to crush the remaining criminal or religious sects that were hostile to his rule. Caught up in those raids were many of the VC, most of whom were former Vietminh.

After this successful eradication campaign Diem rejected the Geneva accords of 1954, claiming that South Vietnam was the only "Legal State".

He dismissed any reunification with the communist north and won the election in S. Vietnam with 98% of the vote. On Oct 26, 1955 Ngo Diem declared himself President of the Republic of Vietnam. (After another unsuccessful coup attempt against the Catholic Diem the warring factions of South Vietnam finally formed a coalition government under him.) Ike sent a letter to Diem offering increased U.S. support and military aid.

Years later President Johnson would use that letter as part of his justification for sending U.S. combat units into Vietnam.

In the desire to bring stability to Indochina the Western powers all recognized the Diem government. The U.S. consulate in Hanoi was wrongly closed and the Senate ratified the SEATO treaty and all of its provisions. To stay on the offensive Diem promulgated Ordnance No 6, which allowed the internment of anyone thought to pose a threat to the South. He used this rule to round up more of the former Vietminh and by the end of 1956 his forces had actually destroyed 90% of the communist cells in the South.

The remaining communists and supporters scattered and began a low level insurgency to stay "under the radar". It appeared on the surface that Diem had won his war.

(This was similar to what the French had thought in the North in 1949.)

If effective and directed support for the local militias of the South been given at that time they might have finished off the remaining local communists.

Protection of the villages was vital, and if done might have dried up the native communist effort that supplied the Viet Cong.

CIA's Chief in Saigon was William Colby. He tried to convince the U.S. principals to follow those guidelines for helping the local militia.

Similar to Gen. Collins, he was ignored by those who thought they knew better.

None of our senior leaders in Washington, MAAG, or the following **MACV** Officers, (Military Assistance Command Vietnam) understood Vietnam or the stages of "communist revolutionary war". All hastily agreed with whatever Diem wanted, and what Diem wanted a "large army" to keep him in power.

They mistakenly viewed the new border at the 17th parallel in the same mindset as the 38th parallel in Korea, and vowed to create a military force that could prevent a Korean type communist invasion.

But what had failed and then worked in Korea had no chance in Vietnam.

Korea was a peninsula jutting into the China Sea. A strongly held DMZ could prevent an overland invasion, and effective air and coastal naval units could stop most seaborne enemy forces.

Vietnam was not a peninsula.
Vietnam is attached to the landmass of SE Asia with a long and porous border with Laos and Cambodia all along its length. It also has an extensive and permeable coastline. New communists and supplies could and did infiltrate virtually unimpeded.

And the country was covered with heavy double and triple canopy jungle. Perfect for hiding in and obscuring what you were doing.

And after having seen that the Russian-Korean invasion model did not work, the communists under Ho Chi Minh chose to follow the Chinese version of takeover.

They would start with subversion and then move on to local fighting.

They would follow and perfect the stages of revolutionary war.

(In his definitive book on strategy *The Art of War*, Chinese strategist Sun Tzu penned this line. Know your enemy and know yourself and you will never be defeated in battle. Unfortunately none of our leaders knew anything about Communists or Vietnam.)

MAAG advisors were creating S. Vietnamese Regiments in an attempt to bring them up to our standards. But that effort was unwise for those people were not Americans in thought or in history. They were Vietnamese. Instead of trying to recreate large U.S. Army type units they should have trained the forces in the South for small unit tactics and operations. Their diminutive frames were ill suited to the heavy U.S. equipment which also reduced their capabilities.

And similar to the Koreans, the subjugated Vietnamese had never had an Officer or NCO class of soldiers. Like S. Korea, the Vietnamese in the South needed years to develop the skills of leadership, staff work, coordination and logistics. Trying to organize them into large military units at that time was an extremely poor decision that would have disastrous consequences.

(This was one of replacement Ambassador Elbridge Dubrow's major complaints. Even CIA's Lansdale had recommended against trying to build large military units. Both recommended concentrating on a counterinsurgency military force.)

To help the South by hurting the North, CIA's Lansdale and Major Lucien Conein worked long and hard. One of their programs was lacing oil tanks in the North with acid, and concealing explosives in coal reserves. (Coal piles generate heat which can cook off the explosives.) Another tactic was forming secret commando squads who stayed behind to ambush and observe the Vietminh. Most of those teams accomplished little because of the closed nature of communist societies. And when the communists captured those team members they interrogated them to learn the techniques and tactics.

Europe and Russia

On May 5, 1955 West Germany was admitted into NATO. In response on May 14, 1955 the *Warsaw Pact* was created. All of the Communist nations in Europe and Albania formed a "defensive union" against the West. The Soviet Union was in charge and this pact legitimized their still having large forces in those countries. All of the member nations armed forces were modeled on the Russian military and used their standard weapons and tactics. (Not until 1958 was the process completed.)

On the 15th the Austrian State Treaty was signed allowing Austria to remain neutral and act as a buffer between East and West. Soviet troops were withdrawn from Austria, but it was clear to all that this applied only to Austria.

A major strength for the West was that all of the economies of Europe had recovered spectacularly. Infused from the Marshall Plan and other programs those war ravaged nations worked diligently to rebuild. And safe behind America's might, nations which had been extremely militaristic could maintain smaller forces.

All of their energy and capitol was spent on rebuilding.

One of the unstated economic advantages those nations would also benefit from was that they were rebuilding. Their old infrastructure and industries were being replaced with modern and updated systems. As a result those nations would enjoy a competitive advantage in the years to come. (Japan and S. Korea were also being rebuilt.)

In Russia the Soviets had finally united under Nikita Khrushchev. He did not want to provoke President Eisenhower at that time so no overt missions against the West were initiated. Like all cunning Bolsheviks, Khrushchev was playing for time to ensure his rule. It had been a Machiavellian fight against the other three leaders to become number one, and it may have been fortuitous for the world that Khrushchev finally won.

As shown earlier he began a policy of trying to correct the excesses from Stalin. Nikita openly admitted that Stalin and his loyal members were guilty of crimes against the people. He ordered the instant liberation of untold hundreds of thousands of political prisoners. Those who had died were rehabilitated posthumously and he was trying to reduce world tensions that had multiplied after Korea. The West did not pick up on his desire for a "more peaceful coexistence", though Poland and Hungary did, or so they thought.

On a fact finding trip to Russia in the summer of 1955 Paul Nitze attended the meeting of the Supreme Soviet. Over fifteen hundred delegates were there to listen to speeches from First Secretary Nikita Khrushchev and Premier Nikolai Bulganin.

While in the audience Nitze was informed that the Russian word / phrase called *Mir* was translated to mean the world and those who live on it. But in 1955 the Russians also used the word to mean "a condition in which socialism, the first stage to communism, had triumphed worldwide. Class tensions had been removed and the conditions for true peace would be found under the leadership and preeminence of Soviet Communism!" (39)

Nitze realized that the speeches given in Moscow were not made to relax tensions in the world, but to quietly continue the struggle for *Mir*. He also realized that there was a vast disparity between what Western ears heard, and what the Communist leaders said. *The Soviet phrase "peaceful coexistence" might sound like "live and let live" to a liberal western ear, but it was definitely not what the communists meant.*

That summer the Soviet delegation to the U.N. proposed that both Vietnams should be admitted for membership since both were separate countries. This ruse would give them another communist voice at the U.N., and the world would recognize N. Vietnam as a viable country.

Ho's stated purpose like Kim Il Sung of N. Korea, was the reunification of Vietnam under his communist rule. He was upset at this Russian action of announcing Vietnam was two nations. But in actuality he could not protest too much for the North was dependent upon Chinese and Russian support. (To simplify their supply line a railroad was completed in February which linked Hanoi to Beijing, Moscow and East Berlin.) **In 1956 the 17th parallel and the DMZ became the "international border" between the two Vietnams.**

America

During the early Eisenhower years Ike had stated that the U.S. would never be unprepared again for conflict. Though the military was recovering from the cutbacks and Korea, *his main theme was to deter war by the policy* of **MAD, Mutual Assured Destruction.** Pres. Eisenhower had decided that our forces would not engage in battle because any battle would probably involve nuclear weapons. Though that reasoning was possibly true of a direct conflict between Russia and America, it had no relevance to the battles in the developing world.

During his first term our nuclear forces consisted of intermediate range bombers and some larger long range bombers, the new B-52s. Those bombers were located on just a few bases and were thus vulnerable to destruction. That created a potential reason for an enemy to engage in a first strike, if it could be decisive.

(Also included in our strikes were nuclear armed F-86 Sabre jets. Gen. Chuck Yeager was a squadron commander in Europe, and all knew the missions were one way.)

Ike enlisted an ad-hoc committee of private citizens known as the *Gaither Committee* to examine and determine the requirements for and the feasibility of Civil Defense. Paul Nitze was a member of that group and like many who examined the data from the CIA and the military he realized that we were woefully unprepared should the Russians strike first.

One of the main issues was that our current Radar network was not strong enough to cover all of the potential approaches and give ample warning. Should the Russian bombers or their medium range atomic missiles get in they could destroy our bomber force on the ground. That in effect would checkmate us into surrender, or else we would face total destruction if a second Russian strike were launched. Because of that report a program was enacted to keep our strategic bombers on "pad alert" so that they could take off within fifteen minutes of a warning.

Also recommended was the need to build and maintain a second strike capability.

German V-2 rockets used in WWII had shown that a ballistic missile was a scientific reality. That knowledge had been the basis for the ICBM programs being tested in Russia and the U.S. The Gaither Report recommended we build up a larger ICBM force and shelter them in hardened facilities. By doing so the Russians would realize that they could not take out our strategic forces in a first strike.

The authors felt that that one factor would stop them from even trying.

By becoming stronger the chances for conflict with Russia would actually be reduced. They also recommended a large increase in our conventional forces. Eisenhower did not embrace all of the report's recommendations as he wanted to be seen as a man of peace. (CIA's Dulles was critical of the report.) But work on the hardened ICBMs commenced.

With the U.S. presidential elections approaching the Democrats re-nominated Adlai Stevenson and Sen. Kefauver as the V.P.. Senator Kefauver had been the chairman of the committee that exposed the rise of organized crime and corruption in America. (Senator John Kennedy who was being pushed along by his father and some party elders was edged off of the ticket at the last moment.)

Stevenson had been the Democrat's choice in 1952, but had lost to Eisenhower. Former President Truman was quite dismayed at the Democrat's choice believing Stevenson was too defeatist to win. (But with the ongoing peace and prosperity that America was enjoying no one would have defeated Ike.)

Pres. Eisenhower had had a heart attack in 1955, which left him hospitalized for a month. Vice President Nixon took over the day to day operations and no issues or problems had came up. When Ike recovered Nixon went back to his old office. The Democrats tried to use the illness in the campaign, but Eisenhower was re-nominated anyway. Many Republicans wanted Nixon to move over to a Cabinet position to open up the vice-presidents spot for someone else. Though Nixon and Ike were never friends, Eisenhower kept him on the ticket. They would win again by a large margin.

Middle East and N. Africa

Tensions continued to rise over the existence of Israel. Former French mandates in Syria and Lebanon had signed a mutual defense pact against Israel on Jan 13, 1956. And the militant Baa'thist Party was growing stronger in Syria and Iraq.

On March 4, King Hussein of Jordan dismissed British General Glubb from his Arab-Legion. The move followed more and more anti-Western moves as Arab Nationalism gained momentum.

The Arab Alliance of Saudi Arabia, Egypt and Syria was bitterly opposed to the 1955 British and American led *Baghdad Pact* of Iraq, Iran, Turkey and Pakistan.

This western inspired Baghdad Pact sought to form a defensive line to keep Russia at bay, maintain the peace and allow western influence in the region. (That Pact would form the basis of the 1959 creation of CENTO, the Central Treaty Organization.)

All during those years the *Arab Alliance* had turned to the Soviets for aid and arms. Ironically it was this British/American line that actually helped keep the nations of the Middle East free. But the antagonists in the *Arab Alliance* were too jaded to see that truth. With the coming exit of Britain and France from the region, the vital Suez Canal and Horn of Africa were accessible for communist infiltration and it quickly started.

When the British left the Sudan on Jan 1, 1956, they left a functioning government with adequate civil servants. But the Sudan was really two nations, the educated Muslim north and the rural Christian south. In short order a civil war broke out.

Naturally the Soviets used the conflict to aid their goals of conquest and they eagerly supplied arms. Access to the ports in the region would mean a large Soviet military presence astride the sea lanes where Europe bound oil tankers had to travel.

In 1955 two-thirds of the Suez ship traffic were oil tankers, and two-thirds of that oil was bound for Europe.

In Egypt the *Muslim Brotherhood* began fighting with the government of Abdel Nasser. The violent unrest resulted in mass arrests and even executions. Even so by 1956 the ranks of the Muslim Brotherhood had grown to almost 500,000 members! Their nationalistic and Islamic fundamentalist desires were at odds with Nasser and his growing reliance on the godless communists.

(In a typical case of political irony, the CIA was getting aid to the *Muslim Brotherhood* in an effort to thwart Nasser and any Soviet plans for the area.)

Pres. Nasser was actually following Iran's Mohammed Mossadegh's nationalistic ideology about ending all colonial treaties. He began exploring an aggressive foreign policy, and on April 21 Egypt signed a military pact with Yemen and Saudi Arabia.

Over on the western side of the continent after years of fighting, during March 1956 France reluctantly granted independence to Morocco and Tunisia. Algeria's civil war grew more violent as their rebels fought for independence from the hated French. The Socialist government of Premier Pierre Mende`s had reluctantly let go of Indochina, but they wanted to keep Algeria even though it seethed with revolt. Even liberal Interior Minister Francois Mitterrand rejected any negotiations with the Algerian rebels.

(One of the proposals leading Democrat Adalai Stevenson wanted to explore was for NATO to become less of a military solution in Europe and to become more engaged in the development of Africa. He felt that an aid package similar to the Marshall Plan would help those nations and reduce the military tensions.)

On June 13, 1956 the last of the British forces left the Suez Canal zone after a 72 year occupation. However British and French ship pilots still captained all of the ships through the canal itself. As shown in *Fatal Flaws Book 1*, Britain had "purchased the canal rights" from the Egyptians in the 1870's. They had kept the Egyptian monarchy in power and invested much as they realized the strategic importance of the Suez Canal. And the Suez Canal was also a big money maker for its European investors, the largest being the British Government.

Egypt, (which is really just a small strip of arable land along the Nile River and its delta), assumed total control of the vital waterway once the Europeans had left.

Pres. Nasser led a five day celebration of the end of the European imperialists. In private though he was still seething that the Europeans had not trained the Egyptians to run the Suez Canal on their own, and that the profits were still going elsewhere.

The oil producing states in the Gulf were getting 50% of the profits from their oil production yet Egypt was only getting about 25% of the profits from the Suez.

Upset at the economics and in retaliation for the U.S. and British withdrawal of 1.3 billion in aid, on July 26, 1956 Pres. Nasser suddenly nationalized the Suez Canal. (That aid was going to help Egypt build the Aswan Dam on the Nile River, *but was removed because Nasser was becoming too pro-Soviet.*)

Heated talks were held as Britain began mobilizing troops and enacted a trade embargo upon Egypt. Moscow then released a statement that it would send volunteers to help Egypt should the West attack. British Prime Minister Anthony Eden warned the Soviet leaders Nikolai Bulganin and Nikita Khrushchev that they must stop "fishing in those troubled waters". "I must be absolutely blunt about the oil, because we will fight for it!" *Eden told Eisenhower that Britain could not live without oil, and would not sit by and be strangled.* Nasser now had the power to restrict their access. (Britain could still have tankers deliver the oil, but it would have to sail around Africa.)

Pres. Eisenhower was against any type of action.

His position was that any violence by the West would only inflame the growing anti-Western attitude that was present in the Middle East. He counseled negotiations. (Not much has improved in 60 years.)

Ike felt the Suez Canal belonged to the world, similar to the Panama Canal. It was an open highway for the trade the world needed to function and he felt the British were behind the times. They still had empire in their heart but not the power to have one, nor the power to control the intense nationalism that was springing up around the globe.

By the end of August Britain agreed to allow French troops to be stationed on the island of Cypress in the eastern Mediterranean. Britain had also called up 50,000 reservists and sent additional air and naval forces into the area. Their extreme show of force was meant to convince

Nasser to negotiate his Suez position, but Nasser would not agree to the West's position to "internationalize" the canal.

Pres. Nasser was considering India's plan to have an advisory board of user nations run the canal. The worry of that idea was that nations hostile to the West could close off the canal on a whim for political reasons. As a co-sponsor of the Baghdad Pact, America had not made any friends among the Arab nations that had nationalistic ideals.

Nasser felt the U.S. was helping the colonial powers stay in power.

(U.S. policies had worked against most of the Arab desires, aiding Israel, Britain, Iran, France etc. But that was because the main threat to the world was the Soviet Union and the Communists. In order to protect America, it was vital to keep Europe intact even at the expense of the rest of the world.)

To protect America's interests the 6th Fleet was kept at sea and ready for action. Within those assets were three aircraft carriers, hundreds of aircraft, two heavy cruisers, over a dozen destroyers and an amphibious group ready to land a Marine Battalion. *CNO Adm. Arleigh Burke met with the president and counseled that he and the JCS felt it best to back the British and stop Nasser's belligerent action.*

(Britain wanted to topple Nasser and retake the Canal.)

Eisenhower again rejected the side for action, insisting diplomacy try its hand.

During those tense weeks Afghanistan admitted that it too was being supplied with Soviet military aid. As was becoming normal, the Russians looked to move in wherever the western powers vacated.

Then the negotiations broke down over the Suez Canal crisis.

War loomed as multiple Soviet supply ships bringing large stores of military equipment began docking in Egypt. Seeing what was coming Israeli Foreign Minister Golda Meir stated that again the U.N. has failed in its mission to prevent violence.

(Nasser refused any Jewish shipping from using the Suez Canal.)

To make the foreign policy stew even worse in Eastern Europe more revolts sprung up, this time in Poland and Hungary. The formally free people of those countries despised their communist masters and strove for liberation but for a second time the West did not help. One of the issues that inspired the Polish people was the insistence by the Soviets that large numbers of their units remain in each Warsaw Pact nation. All knew the West would not invade, so there was no reason for the hated Russian presence.

On June 28, 1956 in Poznan, Poland students and factory workers protested demanding bread and their freedom. They were warned that their strikes would not be tolerated. Later that day the Headquarters of the Secret police was stormed by angry citizens. Arms in the militia buildings were taken in preparation for combat.

Riots began and the local authorities brought in the army. Initially the Polish soldiers from the Poznan garrison refused to hurt their own people. Special security troops were brought in at sundown. Using tanks and artillery the communist authorities battled their poorly armed citizens. Polish newspapers gave credit to the people for their just demands, but Moscow saw things quite differently.

By October Khrushchev arrived in Warsaw with a retinue of top Soviet politicos and military officials. Interim Polish leader Wladyslaw Gomulka warned the Russians not to try to coerce them into submission, or there would be war.

Naively he still wanted "a Polish version of Socialism".

Tensions were high as both sides readied for open war.

Increased demonstrations wanting freedom flooded the capitol as the Soviet tanks stopped just sixty miles from Warsaw. At a meeting Khrushchev would accept this minor setback as long as the Poles stayed in the Warsaw Pact and allowed some Soviet forces to remain.

That night Gomulka stated to his nation that their party was taking its place at the head of the process of democratization. There must have been some back room threats for Gomulka soon lost his taste for liberalization and democratization. *Brutality and executions began in earnest and defectors reported the construction of over 73 forced labor camps which housed over 300,000 Polish prisoners.*

Days later anti-communist riots also broke out in Hungary.

Their press had followed the story in Poland, and their people too demanded freedoms. On October 23, 1956 the initial rally in Budapest of thousands of students began demanding the exit of the Soviet units, ending their participation in the Warsaw Pact and greater freedoms. The next day over 300,000 people filled the streets of Budapest in support of Poland and themselves! Soviet forces exited the country but quickly re-assembled on the borders.

By evening of the 24th the reinstated Premier Imre Nagy went to the Parliament building trying to get the large crowds to disperse. He knew the Russians would not tolerate a second uprising. Similar to Poland, the Hungarian Army units refused to fire on their own people. By late night a full blown uprising had occurred and in fact some of their troops even handed out weapons. Despite Nagy's wishes violence happened anyway as special security forces killed dozens around the city in small skirmishes.

The next day rebels were storming Police stations and government buildings, and Nagy released 5,000 political prisoners. At that point the Soviets ordered their tanks and infantry to go into the city and battle the protestors. (Erno Gero may have been the sinister Hungarian agent who kept Moscow appraised of events. Nagy had been appointed premier, and the story "leaking out was that he had asked for Moscow's assistance".)

Throughout the nation workers councils assumed the functions of government. Rebels and Hungarian soldiers stood together battling the Russian troops and tanks.

On the 25th Nagy was arrested as Russian tanks fired into crowds of civilians.

Gero escaped into a Soviet held area, and on the 27th Nagy was told to setup a "new government". At this point the Russians were having a difficult fight inside the city.

Instead Nagy abolished the secret police, the AVH, and asked for a ceasefire believing the Hungarians had won the day.

Janos Kadar an old school communist who had been caught up in Stalin's last purge (and been tortured), was brought in as First Secretary of the Hungarian Communist Party. Things seemed to quiet down and the government was functioning with representatives from all political parties. (This was just what had happened in 1945 before the Russians took over.) Soviet forces began exiting the cities, especially Budapest.

To prevent all out war with Russia on the 30th Hungarian military leaders left Budapest for "talks" with the Soviet officials who showed up.

They were never seen again.

On November 1, 1956 Soviet troops and tanks reentered Hungary in a secret deal worked out by Ka`dar and Russia's Yuri Andropov. The next day Hungarian Premier Nagy assailed the Russians and renounced Hungary's participation in the Warsaw Pact. All of the requirements were in place for a full scale war to erupt in Eastern Europe.

At dawn on the 4th the Russians struck hard capturing the capitol in an organized assault. Most of the protesters were students and younger adults who detested living the life of slavery under the communists. Soviet tank units entered the city and again fired into the crowds. Days of carnage followed.

Eighteen days went by when Nagy was taken out of the city under the protection of Yugoslavian officials. Nagy and his defense Minister Gen. Mal`eter were murdered in a field, after a quick trial was held.

The U.S., Britain and France protested in the U.N., but nothing was done.

By mid-November the Hungarian revolt had been crushed, but it cost the Russians over 7,000 dead. Clear evidence that the people wanted their freedom.

Over 20,000 Hungarians were killed outright, with another 30,000 wounded. Unknown thousands were taken away and "disappeared" into the Gulags.

In addition to the casualties some 200,000 Hungarians fled the nation escaping into neutral Austria. Those bright sparks never returned and emigrated into the West.

A new government was formed under the hard-liner Janos Ka`dar. When tensions renewed in December he declared martial law and arrested every protestor. Many more disappeared.

(It is quite possible that Khrushchev had to send the tanks into Hungary because he had not done so in Poland. If he wanted to stay in power he had to crush the opposition. As it was he was nearly tossed out by the Politburo in June, and only aggressive actions kept him in power. He then replaced Molotov and Malenkov on the Politburo with Zhukov the famous WWII general and Leonid Brezhnev.)

In 1958 the Rumanians were able to get the Russians to quietly leave their country. More than likely Khrushchev was confident that the Romanians knew not to stray.

The West and especially the United States did next to nothing during and after this atrocious event. Though they had campaigned to deal harshly with the communists, the Republicans were forced to face the truth that there was little direct action the West could do short of WWIII.

All during those dangerous days of fighting inside Eastern Europe Britain and France had concocted a bizarre scheme to get control of Egypt. Israel would preemptively invade into the Sinai and then ask for help from France and Britain to protect them from the Arab nations. That scheme would provide all of them with a pretext for the former colonizers to invade Egypt.

(How tangled the web of history is. Eight years earlier the Israelis were fighting the British to gain independence.)

The Israeli pre-emptive assault started in the early morning of October 29, 1956. Surprisingly the Egyptians were caught unprepared and the Israeli's advanced westward and southward across the Sinai Peninsula.

Pres. Eisenhower was outraged as all of the weeks of negotiations had been for nothing.

On the 31st French and British forces also attacked Egypt. Their bombers struck various Egyptian military targets, and on November 5 British paratroops were landed west of Port Said, while French paratroops landed just to the south. Their goal was to recapture the Suez Canal intact.

(Units from the 6th Fleet sailed into the harbors and rescued almost 2,000 U.N. workers, tourists and Americans working in the region.

By November 3 the Israeli's had taken the Gaza Strip and by the 5th they controlled most of the Sinai. Their forces also ended the Egyptian blockade on them by capturing the Sharm al-Sheikh at the southern tip of the Sinai. From Cairo Pres. Nasser claimed that Egypt would fight on, but they were losing quickly.

In England the war decision by Prime Minister Eden was condemned in the divided House of Commons. Britain which had ruled the waves for 300 years was tired of the never ending costs and problems of empires.

Eisenhower had just been condemning Russia's invasion of Hungary when the Suez fighting broke out. He felt that "he had to do the same to the French and British effort" even though they were fighting to keep the Suez Canal open to all nations.

(In the U.S. presidential election Eisenhower was reelected in another landslide.)

The United Nations also condemned the British-French effort.

On November 4, Sec. State John Foster Dulles took a ceasefire proposal to the United Nations. It passed 64-5, demanding that England, France and Israel stop the fighting.

Then the Soviets stated that they were going to send troops to fight with the Egyptians. In addition Khrushchev threatened to use a missile attack upon England and France.

Ike warned the Russians to stay out of the area and told them that any attack against the NATO allies would result in a U.S. nuclear attack against Russia.

He then imprudently worked non-stop to keep the Allies efforts restricted and to convince them to withdraw. To emphasize the point the U.S. orchestrated a run on the already unstable British pound. (Britain had recovered from the war but was still economically weak. The run on their currency also clearly showed that their empire was finished. They could no longer take action without America's blessing.)

A ceasefire was put in place on November 7, and the Anglo-French forces would withdraw by December 24, 1956. Both the British and the French were seriously angered over this ruthless behavior from their ally. Anthony Eden became ill and soon left office.

He was noted as *"the last Prime Minister to believe Britain was still a great power, and the first one to realize she was not."*

Pres. Eisenhower's peace-making efforts were in vain, for rather than gaining friendship from Nasser over the peace, Egypt became even more contemptuous towards the West. The only one who gained from the crisis was Nasser for standing up to the former colonizers. In anger he ordered the forced exodus of some 25,000 Egyptian Jews who had lived in the country for generations.

By the time the waterway was cleared of sunken ships in April of 1957, Egypt alone operated the canal and collected the tolls. Nasser would nationalize more British assets as he preached his Arab nationalism continuously. Syria also turned to Russia as their patron, and this latest fighting had greatly increased the hostility towards Israel.

Years later Eisenhower would regret putting the reigns on our Allies and saw his actions as the strategic failure it was. His intrusion was similar to Truman's flawed moves in China in 46/47. Had Nasser been toppled and a more accommodating ruler taken over, it may have been possible to prevent the future wars with Israel.

And if the Soviets had been successfully challenged during those months of crisis that may have altered the perception of the many rulers who had embraced them.

Instead it appeared as if Eisenhower and the West had been the ones to give in.

Adm. George Miller commander of the 6th Fleet called Ike's failure to act one of the great strategic blunders of the century.

When the U.N. voted 64-5 to stop the fighting in Egypt they also demanded that the Soviets stop the mass "deportations" that were still occurring in Hungary.

Most of those people had been sent to the Gulags deep in Siberia and would never be seen again. *No action was taken by the U.N. over the Soviet's war of occupation of Hungary, and it highlighted how impotent the world body actually was.*

(That was the perfect time for all of the non-communist nations to act against the Soviet Union, but no one in the West led that effort.)

Because of the war over the Suez Canal the Arab league stopped all oil deliveries to Europe. The U.S. offered emergency oil supplies to counter the embargo, but that was the beginning of the stranglehold that the third world's oil producers would use to fight the West.

Even though the Suez Canal War was ended quickly by a United Nations ceasefire the Canal Zone was heavily damaged during the fighting.

Israeli General Moshe Dayan's forces had captured 12,000 Egyptians and over 150 T-34 tanks while racing through the Sinai. (It was believed that 18,000 Egyptians were killed or wounded in the fighting there.)

Eisenhower had cabled Israeli Prime Minister David Ben Gurion urging quick compliance with the U.N. mandated troop withdrawals by all nations. However Ben Gurion renounced the prior 1949 border treaty between Egypt and Israel claiming that the treaty was broken by the war and thus ended. Israel remained in Gaza too.

During March 1957 the Israelis left Gaza to the United Nations. Within days strong Egyptian forces returned and chased the UN peacekeepers out. The Egyptians remained in control of the area that had been ceded to the Palestinians back in 1949. From there border raids continued.

All during those tense weeks Soviet supplied arms and agitators were turning the volatile region into tinder boxes as border tensions next arose between Syria and Jordan against Israel. Fears of a broader conflict were increasing and by the end of December 1956 Pres. Eisenhower asked Congress for authority to oppose any Soviet aggression in the Middle East. Even though Eisenhower had clearly won the election, Congress was nervous about Ike's request.

(In another measure of insane irony, Democratic Senate leader (LBJ), Lyndon Baines Johnson made sure that the bill that was passed prevented Eisenhower from using any troops without direct Congressional approval! Senator William Fulbright also denounced the measure as having too many opaque areas that had no time limits or constraints on who was using who or where or when. In less than a decade LBJ would commit us to a new war with the help of Senator Fulbright!)

At his January 1957 inaugural address Eisenhower stated that the U.S. would respond militarily to any crisis in the Middle East if a nation asked us to. This Eisenhower Doctrine began a period of structured American influence in the region formally protected by Great Britain and France. Poorly trained and as was common unprepared to become such an envoy, America would cause more problems to an area that harbored deep resentment to the Western world.

(Unlike the Caucuses which had been invaded by Russia, none of the nations in the Middle East actually turned communist. Those Islamic nations despised democracy and communism, because both took the power from the native Islamic rulers. They simply needed weapons and supplies and turned to the one source willing to give it.)

Political fallout from the Suez Crisis resulted in a serious division inside England and the toppling of Eden's government.

France on the other hand became united from the crisis. Possibly de Gaulle was able to convince their nation that again Eisenhower and America had turned against them.

From that point on France through de Gaulle was determined to act alone in advancing and protecting its interests. And France began a secret atomic program.

In April of 1957 pro-Nasser politicians in Jordan realized what the Eisenhower Doctrine could mean. After they won more electoral seats they demanded that the pro-western King Hussein end his ties to the colonizers. Jordan was another artificial country that had been created by the British after WWI. They had no national identity, and existed in a mostly barren desert. Hussein realized that the Arab Nationalists could eventually overthrow him so he asked for help from America claiming that communists were involved. The U.S. via the 6th Fleet responded in a big way bolstering his rule and providing him with $10 million in aid.

The Arab nationalists watched with dismay and a growing hatred.

At their Eighth National Congress in 1956, China's Chairman Mao Tse-tung decided that communist China needed to break from being so closely aligned with Russia. *Lack of support from Russia during and after the Korean War, Stalin's death, Khrushchev's attempts to make peace with the capitalists, and their weak showing in the Suez Crisis had convinced him that China needed to modernize and become independent.*

To accomplish that would require a major economic realignment. It would be called the *Great Leap Forward*, and it was a complete disaster.

In the Caribbean former student and leftist rebel leader Fidel Castro had returned to Cuba. Castro had been caught and imprisoned at the time of the CIA operation in Guatemala. Upon his release he, his brother Raul and Argentine Marxist Che Guevara returned and regrouped in the jungles of central Cuba. He and those leftist rebels would attack rural army outposts and capture arms and supplies. In that way they could continue their fight against the corrupt Fulgencio Batista and his inept regime.

As was common in that region Batista had taken over Cuba in a coup in early 1952 just prior to their national election. Pres. Truman and his Administration and then Eisenhower had been unconcerned over the incident because Batista was considered anti-communist. We had given Cuba their independence in 1946 with the intent that a democracy would flourish. Since the time of the coup Batista's regime was destroying the fledgling democracy that had been growing in Cuba. The rebels continued their fight against Batista and thanks to the corruption by 1957 it was becoming a sizable force.

Nicaraguan President Antonio Somoza Sr. was assassinated while visiting Panamanian President de la Guardia. Nicaragua's Congress elected Somoza's son Luis to serve out his father's term. The continual instability of that vital but overlooked region was getting worse. And the more time that went by the more inroads the communists were making. Yet little was being done by the Administration to address that problem.

Unlike his predecessor, Eisenhower did not embark on any large scale foreign aid packages (which had been proven to work), in the quest to stop communism.

South and Latin America were still in trouble economically and needed help. Despite the billions being spent to stop and fight communism overseas, Ike paid little attention to the trials close to home, (except when the CIA would assist in a coup.)

Brazil's visionary President Juscelino Kubitschek had proposed a plan for a joint U.S-Latin American economic endeavor. His Pan-American Operation was presented to the Administration, but went ignored because it "smelled like socialism". Eisenhower had missed a golden chance at bringing democracy to our neighbors, something that all of Latin America needed.

(To offset the future Castro revolution and any possible copycats, in 1961 John Kennedy would enact his "Alliance for Progress" program. It was a carbon copy of the program Kubitschek had proposed in 1955. When the civil projects of the program began to be financed, sarcastic signs thanking Fidel went up all over Latin America.)

Argentina's leftist ruler Juan Peron had been ousted in a coup in September 1955. His replacements were more pro-U.S. and conservative. During his destructive rule Peron had greatly damaged the country's economy, which had once been a showcase to the Latin world. In Peru, Columbia and Venezuela their conservative dictatorships were taken over by younger military officers. As was common in that region the rightist regimes we supported or backed would not do much to help their own citizens. So the people turned to the socialists for help, which naturally led to communist worries.

America and Russia

During his second term which started in January 1957 Pres. Eisenhower was still against using any U.S. troops in SE Asia. His presidency was focused on Europe and the nuclear deterrent based on the premise of,

"Mutual Assured Destruction, known as MAD". *His policies were aimed at preventing a direct Soviet attack, but did not address the communist inspired insurgencies that were occurring all over the globe, especially in our backyard.*

Unlike the easy time the communist spies had coming in, moving around and recruiting in America, it was extremely difficult to do so in the closed societies of communist states. Once the high flying U-2 spy planes went on line in late 1956 high definition photo-recon became available. And with those photos came many realizations about the increasing military strength in Russia.

To integrate our strategic defenses, NORAD was created, the North American Air Defense Command. America's missile capabilities had been put on hold to increase the numbers of B-52s being built. Then in October 1957 Russia launched Sputnik, a small satellite that could orbit the globe. That launch spread fear and panic in the highest levels of government for the Soviets seemed to be capable of striking us from space. Sputnik II was launched in November and showed that we were falling behind the communist efforts.

U.S. Intelligence and Russian specialists were stunned that Russia had accomplished such a difficult feat of engineering, underestimating Soviet capabilities again. And at that point the Russians were far advanced in computing systems too. Reluctantly Ike pushed forward with a U.S. space program. Eisenhower felt that too much governmental spending would hurt the economy that was still robust. (Unknowingly he had set the stage for JFK's later goal to reach the moon.)

At a 1957 conference at the Kremlin, China's Chairman Mao Tse-tung proclaimed that the Soviet Union was the head of world wide communism. *At that conference it had been decided that Russia would share its nuclear secrets with China which would double the West's security concerns.*

As good as the Russians were doing scientifically, they never released to the world the fact that in September 1957 Russia had suffered a cataclysmic nuclear disaster. The blast at Kyshtym (involving nuclear wastes) in the southern Ural Mountains destroyed almost 70 square miles! Tons of radioactive dust was swept up in the world's air currents poisoning millions with silent unseen radiation.

One of the biggest problems in the communist nations was a complete lack of safety concerns. Their only management concern was success at whatever project they were working on. Safety was never a consideration.

(Both the U.S. and Russia had quietly used thousands of their military members as atomic guinea pigs by exposing them to radiation and other dangers.)

As shown before, in late 1957 Khrushchev again narrowly averted a potential coup against him. To maintain the reigns of power all of the plotters and former Stalin confederates were expelled from the communist party. Gone were some senior party members which included Molotov, Malenkov, Gen. Zhukov and later Premier Bulganin. (The removal of so many senior members weakened the Politburo and allowed Khrushchev to hang on.)

Within a year of Sputnik our engineering and scientific capabilities caught up and the U.S. deployed the early model Atlas ICBMs. We also tested the Titan ICBMs, began development of the future Minuteman ICBMs, and deployed two nuclear submarines which carried the Polaris ICBMs. One of the many missile problems that had to be overcome for the Navy was that the large land based missiles used volatile liquid fuels. Not something anyone wanted on a navy ship. It took years to surmount that main issue, but solid fueled propellants were finally developed.

For the Navy, 70% of the earth was covered by oceans and it provided them with the perfect cover to hide a submarine in. That would allow us to hit any enemy at any time, but there were additional problems that had to be overcome. The Navy faced difficult navigation in a submerged sub, which made it very hard for targeting of the missiles. Both issues would take years to fix.

In addition to their warfare capabilities it was found that our submarines were excellent at snooping and eavesdropping on Russian radio transmissions and shore based activities. U.S. Subs routinely moved close to Russian shores to gather intelligence.

U.S. Subs in the vast Pacific used Japan as a way-station for their long deployments in those cramped boats, while those in the Atlantic used the NATO bases. Russia had no such help at that time and their crews suffered in those long duration missions.

As the research and development (R&D) of these technological issues continued the costs of the weapons and systems naturally went up. By 1959 the Polaris missile program took up 10% of the Navy's budget. At that time the Navy was at 28% of the military's total budget, the Air Force 48%, the Army was at 20% and the Coast Guard was bringing up the rear. As the threats to the West increased the costs of defense rapidly increased. (Arms Race) Because the 1950's were a time of prosperity those costs could be accepted. But the more the time went by, the less anyone could afford. That was one of the reasons Great Britain had fallen from power.

As a counter to the potential worldwide communist threat Eisenhower and Dulles would often invoke the right to wage atomic war if the situation called for it.

When China again became aggressive towards Taiwan in Sept. 58, Ike threatened atomic strikes. Khrushchev sent Ike a reply on the 20th warning him that Russia had those same weapons and would fire them if America used them on China.

A similar confrontation occurred between Syria and Turkey. As troops massed on the common border Russia threatened to attack into Turkey. Ike again warned the Russians that war would erupt if the Russians attacked our ally. Every day the leadership of the West looked at their crystal balls and saw the world as day and night. Nothing else mattered.

In reaction to the increasing threats of atomic war the U.S. Interstate Highway Act had been passed creating standardized four lane express highways linking vital cities and regions. Should bad things occur, it was hoped our Government could move forces and supplies anywhere relatively quickly. All of the roads and overpasses were uniform to insure that the movements could not be compromised by being off by an inch.

But what that highway act also did was to change the face of our country.

Numerous high speed freeways were built across the nation linking the cities to each other and the surrounding rural areas. This opened up tremendous possibilities for commuting and transportation. It did not take long for the citizens to realize that they did not have to stay tied to the overcrowded cities. They could live in the "suburbs", and own a private house. Areas like Long Island which had had some growth after WWII ended, suddenly became one huge suburb as people could leave the old city apartments behind.

One aspect to this exodus was the increasing movement of African-Americans and immigrants from Puerto Rico into the vacated urban areas, especially in the north. During the economic boom time of the 1950s there were plenty of unskilled jobs available for the newest immigrants, (Puerto Rico) and any unschooled populations that migrated into the cities. (Things would quickly change for the worse in the 1960s.)

Neighborhoods that had been predominately white were transforming, and many who did not like what they saw left too. No nation on earth had such a diverse population as America and for some living together with different nationalities was not a good thing. Coupled with the integration of the nation's schools many people decided to leave the cities completely.

Because America is a nation of immigrants our country was and is always changing. Some of those changes occurred in a logical social order, such as what happened with the Irish. They had been the first large scale immigrant group to land on these shores since 1800. They suffered discrimination and harassment throughout the first decades of their move. (No Irish need apply.) As time went by the Irish integrated into our society and during the first part of the 20th century the Irish-Americans were the dominate social group among the immigrants. Their rule could be seen most clearly in the venues of the movies, politics and sports. Almost all of the major names of that time had been from their homeland.

The next wave of immigration 1880-1920 came from the Mediterranean areas with Italians predominating. They too suffered from hostility and discrimination, but in many cases it was the Irish were who the enemy. And as had happened to the Irish, it took decades before the new immigrants began to mix in and become part of the national landscape. Starting in the late 30's, into the 40's and 50's, Italian names began to dominate the media sources. All of the big name singers and many of the sports figures were Italian-Americans. *This "changing of the guard" is a normal pattern in the ever changing America that had taken in millions of immigrants.*

And just as the Italians were reaching their zenith, in the 1950s the next group began to be noticed, African-Americans. Though they would not be considered as immigrants, the social restrictions keeping them from their rightful place in America were being removed, though quite slowly because of intransience from the Democrats. By the mid-60's many of the dominate names in entertainment and in sports belonged to African families, as they took their place in the social lineage of the nation.

As stated before, during Ike's years in office the Air Force received major funding for large bombers, missiles and bases to store and deliver the nuclear weapons.

They were also in charge of the development of rocket technology and used captured German engineers (like Werner Braun) with their expertise from the WWII V-2 program. Like the German V-2, America's land missiles were to be large and liquid fueled.

(Unbelievably the Air Force Brass also tried to insist that they had to have control of the Navy's missile boats since the USAF was the "service in charge of missiles".)

As the tensions between the West and Communism continued the planning and development of the next generation of surveillance aircraft also progressed.

Military planners knew the Soviets were improving their anti-air missiles and they hoped to build a fast high flying plane that was invulnerable. That aircraft in development would be the incredible SR-71. Probably the best jet aircraft ever built.

During the rest of the decade the military services slowly recovered and planned on fighting against the many communist enemies. The Army's next generation main battle tank was the M-48- *Patton*, an upgraded version of the M-26 *Pershing* which had gone into service in 1945. (The Russians on the other hand would develop and deploy *a new tank every 10 years.*) To replace the WWII era M-1 rifle the Army developed the M-14, a close cousin of the WWII German designed assault rifle. As always the Marine Corps which was at the end of the money and supply pipeline received the hand-me-downs from the Army.
(The Russians also copied that design and built the infamous AK-47, still in worldwide use today.)

The Navy looked to all nuclear powered ships as a way to extend their ships capabilities. Anti-air and anti-ship missiles were developed to replace the machine guns and canons of old. Using missiles and rockets meant the end of the gun turrets, heavy shells, hoists and powder magazines. And the newer missile technology also allowed for smaller, lighter ships, crewed with fewer personnel.

All of those advances and planning was centered on fighting the Soviets or China and their communist allies. Little was being done to fight the war in the shadows.

(Sadly no one thought to keep a few of the WWII Heavy Cruisers from the scrap-yards. Built for ship-ship battles and armed with 9- 8 inch cannons, they were perfect for coastal-shore bombardment. They would be missed all too soon.)

Vietnam

Back in Hanoi Ho and his communist followers still had major problems in their country. With the mass exodus of the non-communists and Catholics the majority of the trained civil servants and technicians had fled. Lansdale and Conein had insured that industrial sabotage was conducted as well as the stripping of as much important equipment as possible. Most of the rice supply for the North had come from the South and the stoppage of all trade with the "capitalists" was causing serious food shortages in N. Vietnam.

Then to make things even worse the North's communist rulers were enacting their own brand of social revolution to ensure that everyone understood that communism was the new law of the land. *Ho was motivated by his communist ideology and insisted that the peasants be classified into five classes, ranging from landlord to farm worker.* Their land reform campaign was predicated on that factor, but the idea was ludicrous as 98% of the peasants owned less than three acres of land.

Truong Chinh the Secretary General of the Party allowed the land reform campaign to get out of hand. *Teams were dispatched to liquidate any "landowners", and starting in 1955 they zealously filled their quotas. For every 2000 peasants, 20 were to be killed as "capitalist landlords"!*

Quite quickly fear motivated those trapped innocents and to avoid being in the group of twenty, neighbors trumped up charges against each other. (Which is what the communists wanted, to create fear, suspicions and breakup any social groups.)

Another group that was to be eliminated was anyone who had previously worked with or for the French. The last group of victims to be executed included anyone who was not overly enthusiastic over the communist takeover. Again neighbors turned on each other to avoid being the one picked.

Internal Terrorism was the base of power for the Vietnamese communists, the same as the Bolsheviks had first used in Russia in 1919.

When the "Peoples Agricultural Reform Tribunals" were finally ended estimates placed the death toll at 10-15,000 killed, and 50-100,000 imprisoned or deported. Even Ho was shocked and publicly apologized.

Gen. Giap also admitted that "we executed too many innocent people".

In 1956 Chinh was blamed for the butchery and dismissed from control.

All of the imprisoned survivors who were still alive were released. But the damage done to the people was not forgotten. Years of suspicion and apprehension coated the nation.

Then in November the 325th NVA Division was used to suppress a revolt against the forced land reform program. More than 1,000 additional peasants were killed with thousands more deported. (Those peasants had dared to complain to the Canadian members of the International Control Commission.)

By the end of 1956 any remaining threats to "Uncle Ho's" Communist run state had been eliminated. Now it was time to look south.

Starting in 1957, U.S. Army Special Forces members began training South Vietnamese commandos. The plan was to insert them into the North to destabilize the communists and report back on what was happening there. But the mission had little chance for success in the sealed off country.

When the Vietnamese populations were shifting sides back in 1955 Ho and his leaders shrewdly made sure to leave 8-10,000 military and civilian communist cadres hidden among the South. *Most of them were communist party members and all were told to remain hidden as farmers, teachers and government workers. They were to wage the silent "political" struggle, keep the movement alive, scout, learn, and integrate themselves into the South's military and civilian government.*

And in keeping with good communist training they did this expertly.

(The CIA did not try this tactic on a large scale in the North, hence the need for the additional but failed commando teams.)

Despite the progress Diem had made in eliminating his enemies thousands of those communist stay behinds had remained undetected. Their efforts kept the communists viable, and in many rural and obscure areas they soon were the real power since the Diem government was an absentee ruler. By the end of 1957 the surviving cadres of the Vietminh had re-organized in the South, and thirty seven company sized units (100+) were operating primarily in the Mekong Delta area.

U.S. Ambassador Elbridge Durbrow was correctly critical of Diem's corruption and nepotism. He repeatedly clashed with the U.S. military advisors, specifically MAAG Commander Gen. Sam Williams. (Williams had replaced Collins.)

His MAAG command was wrongly trying to recreate U.S. Army type units from the Vietnamese. Even into 1957 they still were not ready to staff and control those large types of units.

Only Durbrow and William Colby saw that the repressive policies of Diem were helping the communist efforts at recruitment. Diem needed to work with the people to win them over, and he needed to get rid of his brother and the inept commanders in his army. But like Chiang in China, Diem refused the advice from the westerners and plodded along taking down his nation.

To continue with his pro-Diem actions Lansdale undermined the Ambassador in his communiqués. After years of effort Lansdale had become a friend to Diem and had invested everything in trying to keep him in power. His drive was so one sided it colored his thinking and prevented him from seeing the truth.

To the west the defeat of the communists in Malaya was finally achieved. Malaya became independent from British rule on August 31, 1957.

Britain's SAS commandos had shown how to defeat that communist insurgency. Use small units, stay in and learn the area, and separate the people from the enemy.

But no one in MAAG or the Administration was paying any attention.
(Malaya joined N. Borneo and other territories forming Malaysia in 1963.)

Middle East

On Oct. 13, 1957 Egyptian troops landed in Syria to assist them in their border dispute with Turkey (which was in NATO and aligned with the West.)

In early Feb 1958 Egypt and Syria signed a mutual aid treaty, and by mid month Jordan and Iraq did the same. *Then in May 58 Pres. Nasser signed a treaty with Russia.*

Egypt would support Russian policies if Russia agreed to help free all of the countries in Africa and Asia. Nasser was being naïve in the extreme, for no country that had "been freed" by Russia was ever free.

In reaction the U.S. and Britain sent planes and troops to reinforce Jordan's security. Lebanese officials in Beirut also asked for U.S. help in stopping the flow of arms from the Arab pact nations to rebels in their country.

As stated earlier for security reasons Israel had refused to leave the Gaza Strip or the Sharm el Sheikh area as the U.N. had insisted. Ben Gurion stated that if Egypt would sign a non-aggression pact with Israel, they would exit from Gaza. Nasser naturally refused.

On 1st March 1956 Israel reluctantly pulled out of those areas with assurances from the U.N. that their peacekeepers would patrol and stop the terror attacks. Not long after Nasser changed things by again denying Israel the use of the Suez Canal and using his troops so Egypt could retake Gaza from the U.N. peacekeepers. Saudi Arabia followed Nasser's actions by denying Israel the use of the Gulf of Aqaba in the Red Sea.

In mid-March the Anglo-Jordanian treaty of 1948 officially ended and Britain pulled out completely. Aid had been arranged for Jordan with the Eisenhower Doctrine as soon as Britain exited. In late April King Hussein of Jordan agreed to accept U.S. aid as the many attempts to end his rule by foreign nationals had convinced him to agree to the assistance and the new security rules. Purged in this pro-U.S. agreement were hundreds of pro-Egyptian and communist activists. *That purge enraged the Fundamentalists.*

(Hussein's cousin was King Faisal of Iraq, another pro-Western ruler.)

Lebanon had been granted their independence after WWII. Split between Maronite Christians and Sunni Muslims the small nation was an example of a bartered life. A Christian was president and another was foreign minister, while the Muslims ran the Parliament. With no military per se they existed as a neutralist nation that specialized in banking and commerce. Pres. Camille Chamoun had also backed the Eisenhower Doctrine, earning hatred from every Muslim in the region.

Egypt's Nasser used radio broadcasts to incite the local Sunni's who were pro-Nasser and also leftists. Syria funneled in weapons and additional leftist fighters which caused worries that again Russia was behind this latest tension.

In May 1957 Chamoun cabled Eisenhower that he may need America's help. Again, Ike temporized, not wanting to cause an uprising in the region.

Then on July 13 a bloody coup erupted in Iraq.

Pro western King Faisal, (who had fought with T. E. Lawrence in WWI), and his son were murdered. *To insure the message was clear the Islamic Fundamentalists also murdered the Prime Minister Nuri as-Said, and a street mob tore the body apart.*

Ten other Royal Family members were also butchered as the Fundamentalists aligned the new government of Gen. Abdul Kassem with the Arab League.

Lebanon's Chamoun was certain he was next and again asked for help. Knowing nothing about Levantine politics, Ike and Dulles wrongly refused to consult with the French as to what they thought was happening. In mid-August 1958 Ike sent in the 6th Fleet which flew aircraft over the nation as Marines stormed ashore.

(They landed on beaches filled with sunbathers.)

Navy ships were visible just off shore, and for the first time in two months Beirut had a quiet night with no gunfire. (Britain sent 3,000 troops to protect King Hussein in Jordan.) Throughout August 15,000 Marine and Army troops patrolled the area around Beirut as the Navy controlled the Eastern Mediterranean. It was a perfect example of the speed and power of a Navy Fleet in action, but this effort accomplished little lasting peace. After a short time the units went back aboard their ships. Though there was not much they could do, the Russians complained loud and long. Khrushchev again threatened atomic action, but was incapable of interceding.

Observing the U.S. response Syria sent delegations to Moscow to increase the ties between those countries. The Soviets had become the arms-supplier of choice to the hostile states, and on Sept. 9 U.S. planes were sent to Jordan to protect that country from possible Syrian aggression.

The Arab nations watched with growing alarm how the Eisenhower Doctrine was controlling their region, just as the British had before. Their benefactor Russia was seen as powerless to intervene should America choose to take over.

Nasser however was the real target of this show of force. Our military moves were made to intimidate him and stop his trouble making. Like the Syrians, he got the point and flew to Moscow looking for a commitment of Russian forces. All he got was a ticket home.

When the U.S. pulled out from Lebanon in late October peace had been restored, the elected officials were still alive and functioning and the nation was still intact. Gen. Fouad Chehab became the new Lebanese President.

Though peace was the desired outcome, Eisenhower still missed the point that every other leader had missed since 1919.

The Arab Nationalists and Fundamentalists did not want any interference in their lives from the West. The instability in the region was due to internal power struggles which involved religion and it's control on their lives. The Fundamentalists wanted a total commitment to Islam, and were motivated by a deep hatred for the Western colonial powers. Because the Soviet Union had become an implacable foe, the leaders in the West saw every hostile situation as a test between us and them, instead of seeing the truth between the lines.

On the other side of Africa, Algeria was becoming a cauldron of hate and death. Their war against the French colonialism was increasingly savage and by this point in time caused the collapse of the French Government. Charles de Gaulle was restored to power as the hard-liners insisted on holding on. But seeing the reality of events, de Gaulle tried to reach a settlement with the Islamic nationalists in Algeria. Their NLF, National Liberation Front refused his offers, they wanted France out.

America

Back in Washington it was decided that the major cities in the U.S. would have nuclear missiles emplaced to protect them in case of attack from Russia, (Sputnik).

The U.S. defensive missiles were designed to explode in the atmosphere hopefully destroying the incoming enemy weapons. (Good choice wasn't it?)

After years of effort Civil rights legislation finally passed in the House of Representatives. Pres. Eisenhower then told the Senate not to water down the legislation.

He preferred no bill to a weak and useless one, but on August 7 the Senate approved the lesser bill. Eisenhower like Truman had wanted to end the separate America that existed. But racist forces were still strong in the Congress, especially within the Southern Democrats.

(In 1955 Rosa Parks had refused to ride at the back of the bus as was law in the south. That led to the famous bus boycott in Montgomery, Alabama. That resulted in a Federal Injunction prohibiting any type of discrimination on public buses.

In September 1957 the next civil rights fight was the integration of public schools. Again a Federal Order by the Eisenhower Administration was used to force the issue.)

After the Civil War African-Americans led many units and were a big part of the US Army during the rest of the century and into the early 1900s. Most people are unaware of this fact, for when Teddy Roosevelt was charging San Juan Hill African-American led units were with him. But as shown in *Fatal Flaws Book 1*, Democratic President Woodrow Wilson had re-segregated the military in 1915. Wilson was a southerner and he still harbored deep racial feelings. His decision to return segregation resulted in all black units operating under white officers, and set back Black advancements by fifty years!

By the time of WWII the segregationists in the Navy had insured that most of the black seaman worked in the galleys or as stewards. Little room was available for promotions or in combat positions. The Army used the black servicemen only in their transportation and maintenance units. FDR forced the Army to create a fighter plane unit which was famously known as the Tuskegee Airmen. But FDR was unable to get the racial climate changed in the Army or Navy as a whole. Not until Sec. Navy Forrestal came aboard after WWII was he able to start changing things.

(One of the most prominent examples of African-American battlefield capabilities was noted at Pearl Harbor. Steward Dorie Miller was on the *West Virginia* during the attack. Besides trying to save his stricken Captain, he manned a machine gun and shot down two of the Japanese planes. He was awarded the Navy Cross for his unselfish actions during the battle, but was soon sent back to the galley. He died at Tarawa when his ship the *Liscombe Bay* was torpedoed.)

On August 16th 1957 the first black family was finally able to move, (under police protection), into the Long Island suburb called Levittown. *Their segregationist attitude was so strong in the Democratic Party that post war housing bills contained hidden rules to prevent African-Americans from moving into the new housing!*

Once they were established the new suburbs passed their own rules trying to prevent Black Americans from getting in.

On the 29th the first Civil Rights bill since reconstruction went to the White House for Pres. Eisenhower to sign. He did so, and then he enforced the measures in the bill!

Pres. Eisenhower sent troops to Little Rock, Arkansas in September to enforce the court ordered integration of the public schools. Many of the southern states were still fighting the changing times and racial tensions were high. At that time all of those states were controlled by Democrats.

(JFK and Al Gore Sr. refused to endorse the new Civil Rights legislation.

But you will never read or hear about any of that from the liberal establishment.)

The Democrats were the party of the Slavers in 1850. After they lost the Civil War democrats were the organizers of laws to prevent African-Americans from voting. They created the KKK as a local terrorist arm to terrorize and intimidate the black citizens. *The NRA, National rifle Association was organized to protect the rights of Blacks to keep and bear arms so they could defend themselves.* (It boggles the mind as to how and why African-Americans feel the Democrats are the party that cares about them.)

Despite the new laws little would change over the next few years.

Rev. Martin Luther King and other Civil Rights leaders began organizing protests to force the changes into being. (During the 1950s King and most Black Americans supported Eisenhower.) Ironically many former and current members of the CPUSA were active in the civil rights groups. Anti-communist FBI director J. Edgar Hoover used the FBI to investigate them in his never ending quest to eliminate communism in America.

In the mid-term elections of 1958 the Democrats again gained, and Alaska was admitted into the union to protect it from the Russians. Ike's total budget had now grown to $73 billion, with 64% going to defense and foreign aid. At the same time the national debt had grown to $280 billion!

The 1958 Fulbright Study, the result of a Senate Resolution from the Foreign Relations Committee, predicted that a major arms race would create serious hazards to all nations. It was expected that improvements in the missile systems would shrink the warning time we could expect and increase the temptation by Russia to use theirs. Accuracy would also increase, which added to the thoughts of striking first.

This in depth look at strategic problems and potential future problems was part of the reason America went into the *strategic triad solution.* By having our nuclear capabilities divided among the three platforms, bombers, land based missiles and submarine launched missiles, it would prevent the Soviets from being able to strike a quick knockout blow. They could never get all of them in one strike.

On the economic front passenger airlines began to use jet aircraft starting a huge trend in trans-oceanic travel. The drawback was the end of the great Ocean Liners. A similar fate would befall our railroads as Ike's interstate highway program allowed the masses to drive anywhere they wanted whenever they wanted.

A revolution had also occurred in electronics with the invention of integrated circuits. Because of that invention a satellite radio-relay station was placed into orbit which would enable rapid communications around the globe. After much testing, NASA, (National Air Space Administration) selected pilots for project Mercury, America's plan for manned space flights.

Latin America

In Cuba, the rebels led by Castro were steadily winning over the populace as they defeated the nationalist troops in fight after fight. President Batista suspended all constitutional rights as Cuba slowly broke up. Within weeks Batista announced he would not run for re-election as more uprisings occurred.

By late 1958 the CIA was warning that Castro was likely to form a communist government based on the people he had worked with and those who were helping him.

Pres. Eisenhower was told to back Batista as the lesser of two evils.

But again Ike refused to commit troops or get involved.

Vice President Nixon had aptly filled in for the ailing Eisenhower when he was ill, (heart attacks and a stroke), and in May 1958 he went on a tour of Latin and South America. His trip was meant to soften relations between our many nations after the fall of Gustavo Pinilla in Columbia and Marcos Jimenez of Venezuela. The upcoming meetings would be centered on the growing communist inspired uprisings in the region.

Nixon's first stop was to Buenos Aires to welcome incoming President Arturo Frondizi, a left of center candidate in the post Peron election. Nixon and company were surprised by some negative reaction to his visit. In La Paz Bolivia the sentiments grew worse. At Montevideo, Uruguay Nixon was able to verbally dress down angry mobs of communists and leftists. In Lima, Peru he held his own against a better organized mob, but the entourage was attacked with bricks and stones. This was the first time an American statesman had been attacked abroad.

In Quito, Ecuador the days activities were pleasant, but in Bogota and Caracas the protests turned violent. This was five months after Jimenez of Venezuela had been ousted in a coup and replaced with pro-western leadership. The mobs were organized and violent, and in numerous attacks Nixon, his wife and small staff were nearly killed by the aggressive leftists.

Over the decades American military and economic support had been vital to keeping many of those poorer lands viable. Truman had started a permanent aid process in 1950 with $34 million in aid. And each year after that our foreign aid increased in an effort to promote freedom and democracy and keep the communists at bay. But for Nixon and those with him all of that previous help meant nothing to the left wing groups that instigated the troubles that summer.

(In our time of 2017, it has been almost 70 years since Truman began providing foreign aid. Has the world benefitted, have we? Did we make any difference in the problems in the world? Or is it all just a lost cause. No nation or entity on this planet has ever been so generous to the rest of the world. Yet even today so many still hate the United States.)

Asia

Laos was a poor and landlocked country created from the 1954 Geneva Accords that had ended the first Vietnam War. Like the "other" French colony of Cambodia, both were granted and guaranteed their independence and neutrality from those peace accords. An International Control Commission was created with representatives from Poland, India and Canada, to oversee any violations.

The Polish representative was a communist, so he saw no violations occurring, the one from India was at best neutral, so he saw no violations and the Canadian was neutral.

With no military capability to protect and insure their access, the U.N. peace delegates were overseeing the treaty in the dark. North Vietnam began spreading their disease into Laos. That was and still is the primary lesson all must learn from making treaties with any Communist nation or leader. They always lied and obscured the truth.

(A perfect recent example of their deceit was the foolish anti-nuclear treaty that Bill Clinton "made" with N. Korea in 1993.)

Laos's northern border was shared with Red China and it's long eastern one abutted North and S. Vietnam. It was not long before the communist subversion began.

The weak government of Laos followed traditional and dynastic guidelines and had to work through the treaty framework that was imposed on them. Prince Souvanna Phouma was able to create a fragile coalition government that included groups/armies of each political following. As usual the communists were the strongest and best organized and quickly they began to take over.

Pres. Eisenhower had decided that we could not allow another country to fall so the anti-communist elements were "encouraged with CIA help" to vote Phouma out of office. By July 1958 a neutral government had been formed, but it too was soon challenged by the growing communist **Pathet Lao** forces which were directly backed by North Vietnam. Short of civil war Laos became partitioned with the communist forces controlling the vital border areas.

And that enabled N. Vietnam to begin and continue a large and covert infiltration into South Vietnam.

By the spring of 1958 N. Vietnam was finally able to feed its own population. With Russian and Chinese help their industrial base was returned to pre-WWII levels. Photos of the North showed the usual drab and colorless existence of communist life, but also showed that there was no barbed wire around any government facilities.

The people who had survived the transition had "accepted communism".

In the South every government building was protected by barbed wire.

Ho Chi Minh sent a personal envoy, Bui Tin to tour the South to see if the time was ripe for their revolution. Bui was to also assess the potential for secretive pathways that would go through Laos and Cambodia exiting throughout S. Vietnam.

Those pathways would be called the **Ho Chi Minh Trail,** and were absolutely vital if the North was to subjugate the South. Once in the South, Bui Tin was to inspect and rate the VC political and military capabilities.

Months later with his return to Hanoi Bui Tin reported that it was time to fight. *As the monsoons ended the first few hundred infiltrators were sent south through Laos on their way to S. Vietnam.*

The second Vietnam War was starting.

(Bui Tin became the editor of the NVA newspaper *Quan Doi Nhan Dan*.

After years of faithful service he was promoted to Colonel and fought in the final offensives during 1975. *It was he who took the surrender of South Vietnam.* Ironically years later he too became disenchanted with the Communist Party and left Vietnam to settle in France.)

Back in 1954 Ho Chi Minh had been adamant about saving the Vietminh resources and personnel during the partition. Their southern comrades had been discouraged from making any direct attacks and were to remain hidden. Recklessness would only provoke Diem into action.

With the positive report from Bui Tin, Ho determined the time was right to begin the insurrection. (In certain parts of the Mekong Delta the fighting had already begun. Diem's troops and policies had been hurting the VC and they were fighting for survival.) With Ho's blessing the VC, (former Vietminh) were to begin terrorizing the populations of S. Vietnam. They had to turn or else.

Any Government officials or workers were to be murdered at will. (Many times brutally as a warning to everyone else.)

North Vietnamese Foreign minister Pham Van Dong sent a letter to Diem recommending that delegations from the two countries meet to discuss reunification.

Naturally Diem dismissed the request. (Just like Korea.)

In December 1958 the CIA intercepted a directive from Hanoi. *This message was directed to their unit operating in S. Vietnam's Central Highlands.* **"Open up a new stage in the struggle, and use overt insurgency".**

For the VC it was time to start actively fighting with the ARVN.

A month later the CIA intercepted another message directing the opening of a new guerilla base in the Central Highlands and a second one in the Tay Ninh Province that abuts Cambodia. Increasing numbers of reinforcements from the North were setting up their supply and training centers. They did so expertly and secretly.

From 1959 to 1961 the death toll in the South in this low-level insurgency rose from 1,200 to over 4,000 per year. Predictably Diem responded with military rule and strict policing. He should have setup an organized economic and social/military pacification process to try to offset the indoctrination being done by the VC.

The result of that failure was that the rural villages were supervised by the ARVN in the daytime, and run by the Viet Cong at night.

During April of 1959 the North Vietnamese *Lao Dong Central Committee* formed Transportation Group 559 under Gen. Vo Bam

They were ordered to create a hidden overland route from N. Vietnam through neutral Laos and Cambodia that would allow them unrestricted access to S. Vietnam. By snaking their way through the dense jungles the network would be invisible to air observation. *This unit would become infamous as the builders and caretakers of the Truong Son Route, which would later be called the Ho Chi Minh Trail.*

Secrecy was vital to their mission so no obvious routes or existing roads could be used. Group 559 was to create new pathways through the jungles. They were assisted by the *Trinh sat*, North Vietnam's secret intelligence group.

Their initial efforts would terminate near Tchepone in Laos. Nearby was the terminus of Rt. 9 from S. Vietnam and Khe Sanh in the northern most province. *As time went by a multi-faceted supply and infiltration route was taking shape and used by the North Vietnamese to infiltrate and* **invade** *S. Vietnam.*

CIA Saigon Chief William Colby soon learned of the effort but was unable to get good intelligence about the Trail because of its location deep in the wilderness. Few dared go there, and those commandos who did fared poorly as the communists controlled the area with aggressive, roving patrols.

In May 1959 the 15th Plenum of the Central Committee of N. Vietnam decided to take absolute control of the insurgency in the South.
With N. Vietnam recovered from the first war their politburo felt confident it could act. Their decision was also made so they could complete the overthrow of the South **before** America could make any significant military improvements.

Large scale infiltration would begin with an additional 4,000 fighters sent south. (Many of those first troops were southerners who had moved North in 1954/55.)

Communist Group 759 was organized in June 1959 and tasked with seaborne operations and infiltration. The long and tortuous coastline of the South allowed for easy infiltration as larger sea-going vessels could transfer cargo and fighters into local fishing craft. From there the smaller craft would navigate inland unseen. Their efforts enabled the VC to rapidly distribute tons of supplies and hundreds of fighters all over the country.

Security and secrecy were the orders to both support groups.

It was vital to give the impression that the North was complying with the terms of the Geneva Agreement. The Vietminh needed to increase their forces and materials to wage this new war, but it had to be done unseen.

Secretary General Le Duan even traveled to the South to learn and observe. Le Duan had been a commander in the Mekong Delta against the French. He pushed for the war to begin as soon as possible. And when the Americans entered the fight he pushed to fight them too. France had turned against the war as soon as the costs rose, he felt America would do the same.

To offset this latest communist initiative Diem asked for patrol boats and advisors in their use. Gen. Williams was dubious that the effort would succeed without coastal patrol forces, but he sent in Diem's request. Ambassador Dubrow was more cynical, expecting the effort to fail. "During Prohibition America could not keep the bootleggers out, how could that effort succeed here?"

On July 8th the first two U.S. military advisors were killed in a raid on Bien Hoa air base. With the military problems increasing a larger contingent of Army Special Forces was sent into Laos in the hopes that the Laotians could stay in power to intercept and stop the infiltration along its common border with N. Vietnam.

It was known even back then that the North was using the neutral border area to infiltrate into the South. NVA Group 959 was formed and directed to control Laos.

In mid-August Khrushchev finally agreed to equip China with nuclear weapons. A few days later China unleashed its largest attack to date upon the Nationalists living on Quemoy Island in the S. China Sea. On Sept. 8, 1959 the communists sank a Taiwanese transport ship. Days later the Reds lost five Mig-17s jets and three torpedo boats in direct combat with Taiwan. On the 24th, ten more communist Mig-17 fighters were shot down. Pres. Eisenhower again ordered the 7th Fleet based at Subic Bay in the Philippines to sea to stop any Chinese invasion of Taiwan.

As stated earlier, at the Eighth National Congress of 1956 Chairman Mao decided that China needed to modernize, and to do that would require a major economic realignment. It was called the *Great Leap Forward*. His aim was to out-produce Britain in steel production. To do so would require a nationwide commitment, which foolishly included the country's farmers.

(In 1945 Russia produced just 12 million tons of steel. By 1958 they were producing almost 60 million tons per year. China was producing far less.)

On a whim bordering on lunacy Chairman Mao ordered farms to be tilled over and abandoned. Millions of former farmers, city dwellers and ordinary people were ordered to produce steel in their backyards. To ensure the effort was done steel quotas were placed in effect and had to be met. Anyone who did not produce was imprisoned.

Naturally those "impressed civilians" knew nothing on how to make steel. To avoid prison or death they simply gathered every piece of metal they could find regardless as to condition or type and melted them down. At first it seemed to the ignorant communist hierarchy that their order had worked.

During 1958 steel production went up 45%.

During 1959 and 1960 the gains were almost 30%.

But in reality most of the metal was worthless as it was simply recycled scrap that was melted down. By 1961 steel production had fallen below the levels of 1956, and what was worse a great famine had taken hold. Food production had decreased greatly during the past three years. With their population over 680 million the loss of foods produced a man-made disaster called mass starvation.

During 1961 China's population had dramatically fallen to 655 million. And living under a starvation diet caused their birth rate to radically decrease.

Even as the calamity progressed the communist hierarchy refused to admit that the *Great Leap Forward* had been a mistake.

Back in 1954 Mao had instituted *the Hundred Flowers Campaign*. At that time he had asked for input from the masses to assess the views from within communist China. The flow of critical letters was slow at first and then the complaints became a flood. *In short order the program was stopped and the "counter-revolutionaries", those who were foolish enough to have replied, were rounded up and arrested. Most went to prison or re-education camps.*

With that recent past in their memories no one would dare speak out against the *Great Leap Forward*. So the insanity continued.

By the end of 1961 the Great Leap Forward policy had to be abandoned and those farmers who had survived were quickly returned to farming. But it would be years before their farm production could catch up. Chairman Mao kept a low profile for a year until the many criticisms finally reached his ears. Then he ordered a terrible crackdown on "dissidents and intellectuals". The consequence of his murderous failures of the **Great Leap Forward** (58-62) would take a new name, the **Cultural Revolution.** It was a politically correct name for murdering more innocents.

Mao's homicidal inanities seemed to emulate Stalin's insane purges, but were way worse. By the time this next episode of political repression ended in 1966 another twenty million had died. **Chairman Mao's death count in that ten year period was well over 40 million dead, far surpassing Stalin and Hitler combined!**

(Yet many "enlightened liberals" in America feel that Mao was someone to look up to, including some in the Obama retinue. And many of them are teachers and professors.)

Increased fighting occurred in the Jarres Valley of Laos in May 1959. During July a second province was beset by fighting. By August the communists were advancing in all six provinces that were closest to S. Vietnam.

At the end of 1959 a CIA led revolt saw Phoumi Nosavan take over the government in the hopes of stopping the communists.

A second coup in August brought back Phouma, who then tried to form an alliance with the Pathet Lao. Phoumi's western backed forces took over the capital of Vientiane and his rule was naturally recognized by the Western nations.

Phouma's alliance group was recognized by Russia, China and India.

It was then the USSR decided to airlift supplies and weapons directly to the communist Pathet Lao forces in Laos. This was a unswerving Russian challenge to America and the West. Supplied with large amounts of Russian weapons the communists could take over the entire country. Phoumi's pro-western forces with help from the CIA and Thailand countered and were able to push the communists back into the area known as the Plain of Jars. But those latest victories would not last long.

Cuba

Cuba finally fell to the guerrilla forces of Fidel Castro and Che Guevara in late 1958. The U.S. recognized this new government on Jan 7, 1959.

On the 8th mass executions began inside the two main prisons, La Cabana and Santa Clara. "Courts" had been setup to sentence the guilty, and over 600 Batista supporters were murdered within five months.
(Communist enterprises always ensured that "courts" were held and the guilty "signed" confessions before being shot.)

The first order of business for the interim government of President Urrutia was to restore the citizen's constitutional rights that Batista had revoked. He also planned to honor all international agreements, rebuild Cuba's economy, refurbish its democracy and oppose dictatorships in Latin America. Fidel Castro was named the head of Cuba's military.

And then in February Castro also became the Premier.

At first the feeling was unsure if Castro was a nationalist who simply led a revolt over a corrupt and empty regime, or a Marxist. Liberal support from America was present and he impressed many with his visit to the U.S. in April. *American oil companies even loaned Castro $29 million dollars as Batista looted everything before he left.*

Vice President Nixon received Castro in Washington, (Eisenhower chose to go out of town to play golf.) Their meeting quickly turned sour. Both men had a serious dislike of the other as Castro denied that he was a communist and stated that none were present in Cuba. But soon after his visit those wanting democracy in the Cuban government began "leaving office". Castro relied heavily on his brother Raul and Guevara who was a staunch supporter of the Soviets and their ideology.

During May 1959 agricultural reforms were instituted, always a first step in the communist process. On May 18 Castro took control of all U.S. sugar assets. On May 23 he nationalized seven Cuban airlines.

By June his radical policies began to foment opposition.

On June 5 more Cuban ministers resigned in protest over Castro's land reform program. Then on the 25th over two million acres of land were seized from large or foreign land owners. Cuban Air Force leader Major Lanz also resigned complaining that Marxists were present and taking over their military. He escaped to the U.S.

On July 18, 1959 Castro ousted President Urrutia and took control of Cuba. In a speech months later Castro allowed the truth to come out.

"Cuba has never had an honest election or a truly free press, therefore Cuba has no right to expect them under me"! (40)

As Castro's Marxist ways increased so too did U.S. concern in having a communist state just 90 miles from Florida. A further worry was that other countries in the perpetually unstable Latin America would follow suit. Most were poor and ruled by dictatorships that cared little for the populace. And as Castro became more stridently anti-American tit-for-tat moves made it impossible to work out a solution.

Thousands of Cubans, mostly from the middle class and some who had supported the revolution looking for freedom from Battista were fleeing the communist run island. Most landed in Florida. This mass exodus of professionals and business people would cause great harm to the Cuban nation, and happened in every nation that turned communist. But that did not concern the Marxists, staying in power did.

Castro next closed all of the religious colleges and confiscated their properties. The Catholic Church was marginalized and all who continued their religious beliefs lost access to education and government occupations.

Political moderate Pazos, the last one in the government was forced out.

In late November Castro named his communist pal Che Guevara to be President of the National Bank of Cuba. Guevara was a known leftist and long time rebel from Argentina.

His control over Cuba's finances and land reform promised to destroy whatever was left of U.S.-Cuban relations. What remained of the Cuban economy was quickly destroyed by communist dogma and the flight of capital. By the time Kennedy became President, Cuba had become a complete communist state with close ties to the Soviet Union.

Throughout 1960 Ike and his Administration worked on a CIA plan to remove Castro.

Russia

France had finally developed their own atomic bomb.

To try to reduce tensions between the major powers Russia's Nikita Khrushchev was invited to come to America to see how we lived. Driving past rows of private homes, supermarkets, shopping, etc. he and his entourage thought it was a scam. Khrushchev was stunned when they went into a modern supermarket and saw all of the foods for sale. In their typical suspicious minds none of the communist envoys believed what they were seeing was real. They assumed everything had been staged as they had done.

Both national leaders agreed to some minor cultural exchanges and an expo of America was opened in Moscow a few months later. Millions of Russians went and saw "their enemy" up close for the first time. At the expo were American music, food, dancing, art, photo galleries and the normal American consumer goods. In a nation suffering from chronic shortages of everything, the Russian citizens were mesmerized. America was truly a rich and prosperous nation and the people lived lives of comfort. All of the flyers, books and brochures on display were taken by the touring crowds. The expo was a huge coup for our side as millions of Russians were exposed to our way of life and realized that the Soviet propaganda was a lie. (Coke was a big hit.)

(In private Khrushchev and Nixon argued heatedly about how all of this was just U.S. propaganda.)

A short while later Khrushchev suddenly revoked the promise of supplying China with nuclear weapons or technology. With the murderous Great Leap Forward policies fresh in his mind, Mao's aggressive moves near Taiwan, and Mao's earlier statement to Andre Gromyko that he would use nuclear weapons on Taiwan, must have convinced Khrushchev to change his mind.

(Perhaps this was an olive branch to America too.)

America completely missed the significance of this fallout between the two communist powers. The Great Leap policies had nearly collapsed China's economy, and after Khrushchev's negative decision China then stopped all trade with Russia.

During 1962 67,000 Chinese escaped into Soviet Kyrgyzstan in an effort to survive.

Vietnam

During January 1960 the city of Ban Tre was taken over by the insurgent communists in open combat with the Army of the Republic of Vietnam, (ARVN). Later that month the first large scale VC attack overran a Regimental HQ in the Tay Ninh Province near Cambodia. (Where a new base area had been setup.)
Again the communists captured large amounts of weapons and supplies.

The U.S. consul at Hue went to Kontum in the highlands for an inspection. He wanted to go out into the tribal areas along the border, but was told it was no longer possible. Enhanced by the weapons and supplies from group NVA Group 559, the VC were setting up a large base area in the deep jungles. They had forcibly ejected many tribal villages and all of the ARVN patrols had been chased away.

Another military coup was attempted against Diem but it too failed.

In the vital Mekong Delta Four VC companies were operating openly. The HQ of the ARVN 32 Regiment had been overrun, again with hundreds of weapons lost.

Meetings that April highlighted the sudden turnaround among the VC. Ambassador Durbrow informed Washington that it may be necessary to find an alternative to Diem. He had no following among the people and things were getting worse in the country.
Again Eisenhower could not decide a course of action.

A collection of business leaders known as the Caravelle Group attempted to lobby against Diem and his corrupt government. They called for sweeping political and military reorganization of the nation, and it did not include Diem.

Tragically the Administration ignored the effort.

As the problems up in the Central Highlands worsened the decline was seen not just as a failure of the ARVN and MAAG, but a result of the victorious communist effort in Laos. Weapons and fighters were infiltrating into S. Vietnam at will and all knew it had to be stopped. **Intelligence from French sources still in Hanoi reported on the large communist effort being made in Laos.**

Durbrow and Williams agreed with the French findings, but also felt Diem needed to make diplomatic efforts with Cambodia and Laos to find some common ground to make a stand against the communists. And they correctly felt that Diem needed to get more of his troops into the fight. As it was most were not fighting the enemy.

In addition to the guerrilla fighters and supplies being sent down the trail, "agitation-propaganda teams" were also entering the South in large numbers. Their missions were the same everywhere they went, terrorize and convert the people.

During 1959 the Diem government had listed over 500 assassinations by the communists. During 1960 it tripled, and by 1961 there were over 5,000!

At that pace no one would survive the communist effort.

Pres. Eisenhower finally directed the Pentagon to develop a counterinsurgency plan for Vietnam. (Was he listening to Ambassador Dubrow, the British or just realizing that the prior work by MAAG had failed?) Despite his directive, the conventional minded service chiefs in the Army, Navy and Air Force had no clue on what to do. Army Special Forces teams were training the ARVN and fighting in Laos, but only the Marines had won against large insurgencies. *Only the USMC had done that type of operation during the Banana Wars in Latin America during the 20s-30s.* (Book 1)

Wrongly the Special Forces program started by Gen. Taylor was not being accepted by the Army's senior generals as anything useful. Most disliked any type of special unit, and the principals in the Pentagon never bothered to look at or learn from the examples of what had occurred in Malaya, Philippine's, Cuba, Algeria or Indochina as the new directions of war.

In March of 1960 Ho Chi Minh and the Politburo next created the *NLF, (National Liberation Front)*. Its purpose was to bring together all of the forces needed to defeat Diem. *Wisely the communist NLF which was run from Hanoi decided that the rebels fighting in the South need not be communists to fight.*

They welcomed all enemies of Diem.

(The remnants of the Cao Dai, Hoa Hoa and Binh Xuyen were all welcomed.)

Ho and his principals knew that to recruit the other rebels in the South the nature of the NLF organizers had to be kept secret. And by doing so it gave Hanoi plausible deniability that they were breaking the 1954 Geneva agreement. By September 1960 the North was fully committed to their war effort in the South.

So effective was their hidden program, that European and American liberals and intellectuals thought they were supporting a civil war for freedom, but were actually helping the communists under Ho.

Cuba

On February 21, 1960 Castro placed all Cuban industries under direct government control. That June Castro seized the Texaco refinery at Santiago. Pres. Eisenhower decided that Castro had to go.

Back in March 1960 the CIA proposed a plan of action, the U.S. would train and equip Cuban refugees and paramilitary commandos to enact covert operations inside Cuba and to aid any resistance forces living there. Most of the supporters of Cuba's former ruler Batista had fled to the U.S., the rest were executed or imprisoned. They demanded repeatedly for the U.S. to oust Castro. About 400 of those "operators" were to be placed inside Cuba to assist the "anti-Castro forces springing up".
It was hoped that they could use subversive tactics against the communists.

However Communist doctrine was centered on rapid and effective counter-insurgency programs. The communists knew that the people would revolt against them as soon as they realized what was happening. (Seizure of assets, loss of freedoms, unwarranted arrests, executions and/or imprisonments etc.)

By their very nature the communists instantly shut down any chance for a counter-revolution knowing that some of the masses may try to emulate what they had done.

Thus the CIA commandos-plan would find few within Cuba to recruit or to even trust. And Castro was in a solid political position as the latest "Cuban Military Courts" had convicted an additional one hundred and four people as foes of the government. **The communist police state was and is very good at finding dissenters and of making examples of them. Protests within the country stopped.**

On August 8, 1960 Castro seized all remaining American owned assets worth hundreds of millions of dollars. On August 18, 1960 Eisenhower approved the initial CIA plan and the required funding, but insisted that no U.S. personnel were to be used in the combat units.

Over the last year of communist rule large weapons shipments had been arriving in Cuba from Czechoslovakia. The advanced nature and impressive array of weapons was a "gift" from the Warsaw Pact to ensure that the communists in Cuba could hold onto power.

By the fall of 1960 the last remaining opposition leaders, William Morgan and Humberto Marin were arrested. *Morgan had been a high ranking anti-Batista rebel leader fighting in the Sierra. Because of his leadership potential he was callously executed a few months later.*

In Africa eleven new states were formed from former European colonies, Dahomey was followed by Niger, the Upper Volta, the Ivory Coast, Republic of Chad, the Central African Republic, The Republic of the Congo, and the Republic of Gabon. Earlier that year the former Belgium Congo, Somalia and Madagascar also became independent. *However civil war loomed in the Congo because of Marxist separatists and possible direct Soviet intervention.* United Nations troops were sent in to restore order, and the CIA became involved. Belgium troops stayed until 1964, but as soon as their troops left the strife resumed.

Neighboring Angola was also in turmoil as Civil war loomed.

The Middle East nations of Iraq, Iran, Kuwait and Saudi Arabia united to form *OPEC*, the Organization of Oil Producing States. Together those nations hoped their union would generate economic and political power. (They were correct.)

America

Back in America more racial protests sprang up as blacks rightfully protested segregationist policies. The complaints began in Greensboro, North Carolina and spread to a half dozen larger southern cities. The Senate finally approved the 23d amendment banning any type of poll tax. (An illegal tax levied on blacks who wanted to vote.)

In May President Eisenhower signed the Civil Rights Act of 1960.

(One completely overlooked and ignored Civil Rights case was finally settled in May 1959. Japanese-Americans who had illegally lost their citizenship in WWII were finally reinstated. However they did not receive any compensation for their illegal imprisonment nor for their loss of homes, possessions or businesses!)

The 1960 Presidential election was up for grabs. Vice-President Richard Nixon was running against Democratic Senator John Kennedy from Massachusetts.

John had had an undistinguished six years in the House, and eight years in the Senate. He was among the lowest in role calls and initiated few bills of note. But Kennedy was from an aristocratic and wealthy clan. They traveled widely and lived in luxury at Hyannis Port and Palm Beach. They were part of the "in" crowd and had a large following among the elites. He was the complete opposite from Eisenhower and Nixon.

John was also a schmoozer, one of those people who can go anywhere and charm the crowd. And he looked good on television, so vital in the video driven age where style was way more important than substance. (It is far worse today.)

His strength and his weakness was his belief in America and his unwavering hatred for communism. He rightfully accepted that America was the bulwark of the free world. But his campaign was full of rhetoric and dangerous ideas, even blaming Nixon for Cuba.
(Adalai Stevenson complained that Kennedy and his team "were the damndest bunch of boy commandos running around you ever saw.)

As stated earlier Joe Kennedy the senator's father had been a bootlegger during prohibition. He had made a fortune in those years and used the illegal proceeds on Wall Street in the scandal filled years of the late 20s. More riches followed and with his fortune assured the senior Kennedy became an ardent "New Dealer" supporting the Democrats and FDR in the 1932 elections. As payback for his years of service Joe Kennedy even pressured FDR to make him Ambassador to England from 1937-40.

His efforts there were mostly concerned with his fortune, and his political leanings were actually pro-German. (Requests were actively made to get him removed.)

Upon his return to the U.S. he stayed active in Democratic politics and after the war pushed son John's career along. The 1952 Senate race saw John defeat Henry Cabot Lodge. In 1960 Joe used his old "contacts to help to win the presidential election for his son." Mob boss Sam Giancana from Chicago had his people "get out the vote" in that vital Democratic stronghold. *(The father had told John, "Buy every vote you need to win, but I'll be damned if I'm going to pay for a landslide!")*

JFK "won Illinois" by just 9,000 votes, which gave him the electoral votes of the state and the election. This closest of presidential races was won by the Democrats because of this "timely help". JFK won by less than 120,000 votes nationwide. *Reports quickly came in that fraud had occurred in Chicago, but Nixon decided not to investigate, "for the good of the country".*

(He should have, because the next three years that JFK was in office become three of the most dangerous in our history.)

Kennedy was portrayed by the media as a virtuous fresh face. He was however not. While traveling in Ireland in 1947 John was stricken with a severe case of Addison's disease. He was given last rites, and Pamela Churchill was told that her young American friend had less than a year to live. For the rest of his life John lied about his health. From 47-49 he routinely went for secret treatments and his father stashed covert supplies of cortisone all over the country in case John had an attack.

By 1948 John followed his father's routine of living a secret life. In public he was saintly and proper, while in secret he was ill, hooked on pain medications and adulterous to the extreme. JFK was a liberal Democrat and close to the liberal-intellectual wing of the party. They were influential beyond their numbers because they were allies with those same minded power brokers in the media. He realized early on that he had to keep them happy.

John trusted few outsiders and picked his brother Robert to be the Attorney General. That move would cover him legally from any unexpected problems or investigations. During his years as President John Kennedy ordered the greatest number of wiretaps without warrants in our history!

In one case the Kennedy's tapped a phone of a reporter who was writing a book about Marilyn Monroe. Both Kennedy's had had affairs with her and they wanted to know what he was checking on. (Some have speculated Monroe was actually murdered to get her diary which had entries about the Kennedys.)

Another "unreported" but highly charged case involved wiretaps and bugging the hotel rooms of Dr. Martin Luther King, the civil rights activist. But secrets were not JFK's alone.

Lyndon Johnson of Texas had been picked as his running mate in 1960 because he was a senior Senator from the South who "knew how to get things done". Johnson had scammed a Silver Star during an over-flight in the South Pacific in 1943. He used this "decoration for bravery" to inflate his resume for the post-war elections.

And Lyndon Johnson rigged his election to the Senate in 1948.

Running in an extremely tight race in his home state of Texas LBJ used a helicopter to fly everywhere twenty hours a day. Still his effort was falling short and George Parr the political boss of South Texas stuffed the ballot boxes with as many illegal Mexican votes as he could. LBJ won the Senate seat by 87 votes, and then fought off all of the challenger's legal actions.

As a first class scam artist and politico, Lyndon Johnson rose quickly in the political world of the Senate eventually becoming the majority leader. He was placed on the ticket "to support the easterners", first would be JFK. (It was planned that after eight years Robert would follow.) As the incoming Vice-President LBJ was not happy serving as the legislative gopher to this part-time Senator who was nothing more than a rich playboy.

Pres. Eisenhower had placed Richard Bissell in charge of the CIA's "Cuba Plan". (Bissell had formally been in charge of the U-2 program.) By the end of 1960 Ike was convinced that nothing short of a severe shock could dislodge Castro. On December 8, 1960 the final CIA plan for Cuba was presented to Eisenhower. It called for an amphibious landing in Cuba.

Initially 60-80 commandos would secretly enter and prepare the landing area. Then air strikes from Nicaragua would destroy nearby Cuban military targets, followed by landing an amphibious force of 600-750 commandos. *While the air strikes continued, it was **hoped** that the raiders would hold onto a section of Cuba and attract dissidents.*

They would be re-supplied as the fighting continued, and after a few weeks the U.S. would recognize the "new rebel government" and send in a pacification force.

Our Military leaders were not thrilled with the venture but Ike was interested simply because there was no other option if Castro was to ousted.

In October Castro had two more Americans shot as "Cuban Invaders", and in mid-November Ike had to send the Navy into the southern Caribbean after communist insurgents provoked uprisings in Guatemala and Nicaragua. Castro had to go.

Eisenhower's time in office ran out, and this mission like so many other problems was left to John Kennedy and his incoming administration.

Kennedy began staffing his Administration with the plan of reforming the defense establishment. He wanted a counter strategy to Eisenhower's main deterrent policy based on MAD. Robert Lovett who was the final Sec-Def. for Truman became Kennedy's main advisor in picking his cabinet. He was joined by Dean Acheson, Clark Clifford and Paul Nitze. Lovett was an old school Democrat and had served long within the government. He advised that the next Sec-Def had to be an analytical-statistician who could look through the overlap and empire building. He recommended Robert McNamara who had served in WWII as a numbers cruncher in the supply and maintenance sector.

When McNamara left the Army he and others like him worked at Ford Motor Co. JFK asked him to become the new Sec-Defense and the demanding McNamara insisted he had to have a free hand in organizing the DoD and in picking all subordinates.

Not understanding who he was dealing with Kennedy agreed.

Originally JFK wanted Adlai Stevenson for Sec-State, but Stevenson did not want to be a part of that administration's arrogance or aggressiveness. Former Sec. of State Dean Acheson (the defender of spy Alger Hiss), Lovett and Nitze then recommended the well rounded and long serving Dean Rusk for the spot.

Unlike McNamara, Rusk was unprepossessing and introspective, perfect for JFK because he wanted to be his own Sec State. (Rusk was one of the principals assigned to SWINK when they partitioned Korea in 1945.)

To get away from the "usual crowd of politicos" JFK wanted academics to staff his Administration and McGeorge Bundy, (another eastern elitist), became his National Security Advisor. His deputy was Walt Rostow a critical thinker who coined a term, (though quite untrue), that they were the "company commanders of WWII."
They were replacing the old guard of Eisenhower and company with their youth and toughness. They were "hard nosed realists". Again the compliant media ate it up.

(Of all of those in his administration, only JFK had been in combat.)

The large organization that Eisenhower had collected at the NSC, (National Security Council) would be trimmed back by Kennedy. This move diminished the voice of the Joint Chiefs of Staff, (JCS) as Kennedy sought to reevaluate and control all aspects of U.S. Foreign and Military objectives.

After he left the Army in 1960 Maxwell Taylor wrote a bitter critique of Eisenhower's defensive policies, *The Uncertain Trumpet.*
(Two of his staff officers John Cushman and William Depuy wrote most of it.)

John Kennedy liked the book personally and it also gave him ammunition to use during the campaign. Kennedy picked Taylor as his military advisor. Although he was made during the years of George Marshall and his influence, Taylor was the opposite of Marshall. Taylor was political and ambitious. Under Eisenhower, Taylor felt like a sideshow. Working with JFK, Taylor was becoming a big player.

Vietnam

By the end of 1960 North Vietnam's infiltrated communist fighting force in South Vietnam had increased from 2,000 to well over 10,000. More were coming down the trail each month greatly increasing the communist fighting strength when added to the local VC contingents. And as the resurgent enemy continued their winning guerilla activities they captured even more weapons from the ARVN units and bases.

Gen. Ed Lansdale was sent back to Vietnam in Jan 1961 for an evaluation. He was stunned at how bad things had gotten and reported on the situation to JFK and Dean Rusk soon after. Lansdale returned again in May 1961 and recommended more pacification and psychological warfare to defeat the VC. *He also pressed for a "separate force" to attack into Laos at Tchepone which was rapidly being built up as a communist supply area.* (Even air drops had been used to bring in supplies.)

Ambassador Durbrow had written up a report for the CIP, Counter-Insurgency-Plan, recommending additional money to increase Diem's army by 20,000 troops.

(This was in response to Ike's request months ago.) *Durbrow also insisted the aid be linked to streamlining Diem's civil and military organizations to make them function.* Kennedy was not aware of how Diem detested American interference in his rule, or that he did not like or trust Durbrow. JFK was also thinking that Durbrow should be replaced with the James Bondish figure of Lansdale. (And Lansdale was lobbying for the post.)

When the JCS and Eisenhower had discussed U.S. options in Vietnam in 1954 Gen. Ridgeway and the USMC Commandant Lem Sheppard were against any direct action in Vietnam. Ike concurred not wanting to get mired down again in Asia.

But in 1955 Ike acted peculiarly when he recalled Gen. Collins and sent Lt. Gen. Sam Williams to be in charge of the advisory effort. *Williams had been relieved in France in WWII, and was not of the correct mindset to the problems in Vietnam or in dealing with communists.* (Here was the perfect place to have assigned Gen. Van Fleet with his experience and abilities. But he had been retired.)

It was Williams who wrongly began building up the S. Vietnamese forces into U.S. Army clones. (That was all he knew.) He naively dismissed the Viet Cong capabilities and prepared for a Korean type of invasion. Though he correctly advised Diem to be engaged in pacification efforts to win the hearts and minds of his people, he failed to follow through with any successful efforts from MAAG.

The suspicious Diem would not permit any U.S. personnel to go into the field with his units out of fear they would become Americanized and a potential threat. Because of those issues the advisory personnel could not ascertain how the ARVN were actually doing out in the field.

(*There again was a situation in which Ike should have met with Diem and insisted on our supervision.* We were footing the bill and needed to be sure on the results.)

In spite of the increasing infiltration from the North in late 1958 Williams disbanded the six light infantry divisions he had formed because he felt they could not stop the North Vietnamese forces. As the insurgency increased through the next year Diem finally began a program of counterinsurgency operations in the countryside.

That program was exactly what was needed, and just what Dubrow and Lansdale had brought up in 1956. Yet in 1960 Williams denounced the program as hasty and ill-conceived.

Williams gave little overall support to the effort and fought often with the demanding Ambassador Elbridge Durbrow who was critical of Diem and his "government". Durbrow rightly wanted and demanded results. He also insisted that the U.S. mission to S. Vietnam should be run from his office to maintain unity of effort.

In official reports Durbrow routinely questioned Williams capabilities, judgment and ability to get along with anyone.

The ineffective Williams was finally replaced in September 1960 with Lt. Gen. Lionel McGarr. But McGarr was "unusual" in that he would barricade himself inside his Saigon home for days at a time. And this general was even less of a people person than his predecessor. *The result of these tragic failures by Eisenhower were years of lost and wasted effort.* (There was little media coverage of the area so few knew how bad things really were.)

In Laos Communist Pathet Lao forces were rapidly taking over the northern and eastern sections of the country with help from the NVA units operating with them.

Ike warned Kennedy when he took over that Laos was the key to Indo-China. Losing Laos would doom all of those nations, Thailand, S. Vietnam and Cambodia. But in his five years Eisenhower never came up with a plan of action.

As his term ended Ike suggested to Kennedy that he may have to use U.S. troops there if he wanted to keep the communists out. That strategy was not desired by the new president either, as Kennedy had been vocally against us getting involved back in 1954. *JFK had the perfect chance to give up SE Asia and get out when he took office since we were not yet overly committed.*

During January 1961 Russia's Nikita Khrushchev declared that the USSR would back all "Wars of National Liberation" wherever they occurred on the globe.

Many of the post WWII anti-colonial uprisings had developed into guerrilla wars against the "Western imperialists". Russia and China were supporting those efforts, and those communist inspired uprisings were especially anti-American.

Khrushchev also spoke enthusiastically about Cuba's revolution and of how that had opened up all of Latin America to change. The Russians had never stated such a direct challenge to the West before and many in the U.S. government became concerned. JFK was about to be sworn in and it was felt that this was a direct challenge to the young President.

Just as JFK was taking office neutrality seemed to be over in Laos.

As Ike had warned when he initiated SEATO, North Vietnam was controlling the shots in Laos for their own agenda. Kennedy and his team had to find a way to deal with it.

In the interim the CIA had recruited the native Hmong and Meo tribes to aid the West in this growing war in the jungles. Those indigenous tribal people were good fighters and at home in the dense jungles. And if they were killed no one would know.

To counteract the growing U.S.-CIA effort the North Vietnamese Army, (NVA) sent in their 925 Battalion to fight with the communist Pathet Lao troops. And Soviet aircraft continued to fly in a steady stream of weapons and supplies.

It was absolutely vital to N. Vietnam's master plan that Laos become communist.

The new administration was divided over what to do. *Most of the civilians recommended military action, while the military wanted to avoid fighting in those dense jungles.* By March 1961 the fighting in the Plain of Jars was going to the communists as Phoumi's semi-trained forces were retreating.

Pres. Kennedy then authorized *Operation Mill Pond*, a seventeen step process of escalation. The first step was to provide advisors and some service units into Laos. Sec-Def McNamara sent a USMC helicopter unit to work with the CIA and Special Forces personnel already in country. *Many of the SF commanders wanted the effort to include isolating southern Laos with more forces to stop the NVA infiltration.*
Options were discussed including using U.S. troops.

(At one point a reinforced Marine Brigade was sent to the western Pacific and kept on hold until a decision could be reached.)

Pres. Kennedy was thinking of committing troops but the JCS was actually against it. The Chairman of the JCS, Army Gen. Lemnitzer warned Kennedy that if we went into Laos we would need at least 60,000 troops and should expect to fight a major war which probably included N. Vietnam and China. Sec-State Dean Rusk asked the general if he thought we could get the 101st Airborne Division into Laos.

Lemnitzer replied, "Getting them in would be easy. It's getting them out that I'm worried about."

On March 23, 1961 JFK issued statements at a press conference warning of the communist efforts in Laos. A Naval Task Force had been sent into the area to advise the communists of our intentions. A week later Gen. Paul Harkins and his staff were in the Philippines preparing his US Army units to enter into Laos by force upon getting orders.

Then a serious distraction occurred in Cuba.

Bay of Pigs

As stated earlier at the end of the Eisenhower presidency the CIA and Pentagon had finally prepared the requirements for an *overt assault* against Cuba. Their updated plan was to use almost 2,000 Cuban volunteers to secure a base area in Cuba and assist an internal revolt against the communists. The Navy would be involved in making the sea-borne landings and U.S. air support was to be used as needed.

(General Lansdale was against the invasion and warned Paul Nitze it would fail.
Senator Fulbright also warned JFK not to allow the mission.)

Bissel at CIA wanted to use a *graduated scale of operations.* (A foolish notion that would color the thinking of most of the war plans for the next few years.)

The idea was to slowly turn up the force level to compel an opponent to realize that they could not prevail against us. But that premise went against all military logic.

This Cuban operation would be undertaken to assist a "provisional government" that was requesting our help.

The original invasion site would need an existing landing strip for the air supply part of the operation. Because of that logistic need only a few sites were possible. One other absolute requirement in this dubious scheme was that a popular uprising had to occur to get things started and to maintain the fight. Without it the planners knew the effort was doomed.

Pres. Kennedy and his new team had been briefed on this plan for Cuba. The operation had momentum but extremely poor intelligence of the target. Once again the closed society of a communist country presented many obstacles for intelligence gathering. And Bissell like MacArthur in late 1950 refused to see the intelligence there was. All of it was bad.

JFK soon found himself in a political jam. If he failed to act against the communists in Laos and Cuba he would be perceived as weak. During the campaign Kennedy had repeatedly stated that he was for the freedom fighters of Cuba in order to mollify conservatives and get their votes. Now they demanded action.

All during the campaign JFK had been briefed and updated by "friends" in the CIA, so he knew what was happening and what was being planned. He had used this inside information to blast Nixon all during the campaign.

V.P. Nixon knew what was being secretly planned, but had to keep quiet on the subject. (Kennedy was actually afraid that Ike would help Nixon win the election by invading Cuba before the election. But unlike most of the Democrats, Eisenhower would never have gambled on the lives of the soldiers for politics.)

Once the election was over the CIA "advised Kennedy that delay of the Cuban Project" could be fatal to its success. In actuality the Cuban Exile Unit that was scheduled to land in Cuba had low morale and the rainy season was slowing its training. "Helpful leaks" about those "Guatemala training camps" also insured that political pressure was maintained on the new administration to force the mission to go off.

(In Guatemala their President actually began publicly complaining about the camps and wanted them closed down by the end of April.)

During that same time frame Castro's forces had received the following from Russia, 125 tanks, 160,000 rifles and 7200 machine guns plus munitions and supplies to beef up their defenses. Word had gotten out over this "secret Cuban mission". Dulles at CIA warned Kennedy that time was running out, he had to act.

(It is inconceivable today that these "intelligent minds" actually thought that a few thousand semi-trained fighters could defeat those kinds of forces and arms.)

The original invasion plan wanted to land those forces at the town of Trinadad. It was a good distance from Castro's main force, it was close to the Escambray Mountains and it was felt that the local population was still somewhat Anti-Castro. U.S. Military commanders felt that to have any chance of success the force would need a minimum of 5,000 troops plus continuous air cover.

(Gen. Grey of the JCS felt that only U.S. troops would have any chance of success.)

JFK then decided he did not want any overt U.S. participation during this operation and insisted on changes to that effect. It was impossible to make those changes work, and at that point the operation should have been canceled.

Retiring Assist Deputy at State, Thomas Mann wrote a scathing report about the impossibility of having a popular uprising in present day Cuba. He stated that there were three equally bad alternatives to the plan, abandonment of the rebels after they were ashore, getting them into the mountains to act as a guerrilla force, or having to use U.S. troops. He felt each of those scenarios would end up hurting America's credibility and prestige.

His report was dated at mid-February 1961 and was given to the new President along with Bissell's report which claimed we could succeed.
(This would be a nagging problem within JFK's team, consistent diametrically opposite viewpoints.)

Pres. Kennedy knew the political risks of going ahead and insisted on *plausible deniability* to shroud the operation. But nothing could shroud U.S. activity if this operation went in. *CIA's Dulles wanted the operation to be large and noisy to bring about a revolt or at least alert the Cuban citizens we were there and possibly instigate massive defections.* Dulles felt that if the Cuban people saw that we were committed to trying to eliminate the communists the people would rebel and help fight.

More meetings followed and on March 11, 1961 McGeorge Bundy drafted NSAM-31 stating that the President would authorize U.S. support to get patriotic Cubans back to Cuba.

Castro was well aware of what had happened to Pres. Arbenz in Guatemala in 1954. Castro's communist comrade Che Guevara had been there, and they were taking solid precautions against any type of U.S. led coup. It would be too bad for any Cubans that got in the way. Cuba had a militia of over 200,000+, and a Revolutionary Army of 32,000 that were being trained by the Russians. As always the Communists were extremely efficient in controlling the citizens. The latest U.S. intelligence estimates mirrored the report from Thomas Mann;

No foreseen revolt was in the works, nor even possible at this time.

On April 1, the Cuban operation was renamed *Bumpy Road.*

JFK was still trying to ensure deniability and insisted on more last minute operations changes to Bissell who agreed to all of them. *Bissell's staff however was exasperated as those latest reductions in support guaranteed failure.*

On April 4 a final meeting was held and among the principals who was present only Senator Fulbright argued against it. Leaks from Guatemala had continued and destroyed any hope for secrecy or deniability.

On April 12 stories about the planned operation appeared in the NY Times which incensed Kennedy. In a public announcement he stated that there would be no U.S. intervention in Cuba. He also falsely claimed that the exiles understood that rule.

But in reality they were not aware that this was the new plan for the battle. They had expected our help from the sea and air.

On the 15th preliminary B-26 bomber attacks on Cuban airfields accomplished little actual damage but caused a fury at the United Nations. U.S. Ambassador Adlai Stevenson was livid as he had not been briefed about the Cuban operation and a U.N. debate on Cuba was set for just two days off.

Sunday the 16th, Dulles's deputy Gen. Cabell who was also not fully briefed about all of the recent changes asked Sec of State Rusk if the 2nd set of air raids should even go off. With the vocal fallout from the U.N., it was decided not to allow the second raid. When this military support change was revealed, calls for cancelling the mission came from Bundy and Rusk. Bissell reported that it was too late for that.

Rusk spoke to JFK and briefed him.

During that time the JCS were not informed of any of those events nor asked for input. Forty air sorties had been planned, but so far only eight had been flown.

On the 17th two battalions of 1,400 exiles landed safely in Cuba but were then beset by Cuban planes and strong behind the beach defenses. *Over 20,000 Cuban troops were close by waiting for the rebels to land.*

One supply ship became stuck on an unknown reef while another was sunk by Cuban planes that bombed it. Communications with Washington were lost.

On the 18th National Security Advisor Bundy reported to JFK that things were bad and getting worse. Bundy also concluded that our planes had to knock out the Cuban air and defensive units or all was lost.

Khrushchev denounced the invasion and warned the U.S. to stop the conflagration from spreading. "A small war can produce a chain reaction in all parts of the world"! He also added that Russia would render all support possible to the Cuban people. Almost all of our Allies condemned the foolish effort. (Payback for the Suez.)

That same day the CIA and the JCS asked Kennedy to reverse his position and allow U.S. air and naval actions to help the exiles. Admiral Burke on hearing of the pending disaster had placed two battalions of Marines onto ships heading for Cuba.

That night at a Congressional reception renewed requests for action went to JFK. He refused all of them.

Admiral Burke aggressively recommended that naval air power had to step in.

Kennedy stammered that he did not want America involved in this.

Admiral Burke exploded, "Hell Mr. President we are involved!

Adm. Burke lamented later that JFK had "chickened out" when the going got rough.

(Eisenhower had also refused to listen when Adm. Burke and VP Nixon warned him to take quick action upon the leftist Castro back in 1959.)

By the morning all intelligence pointed to a debacle as no uprising or guerrilla activity was noticed or heard. The forces that went ashore were fighting a lost battle and they were fighting alone. By the next day some ill conceived air support was finally tried, but it was too little too late and the exiles began to surrender. In the end 1189 were captured, with 140 killed. (The exiles did fight well, causing over 3500 casualties.)

As soon as the attacks had started communist leader Castro had over 10,000 Cuban dissidents rounded up and arrested. Many would never be seen again.

Because of the tight Cuban Communist security efforts no previous contacts had been made with anyone in Cuba prior to the landings. Thus no organized support from the Cuban people was waiting for the rebels to land. It was doubtful if any organized resistance would ever have been possible with communists efficient and lethal security forces.

Kennedy knew of the risks of this plan and he rolled the dice with half measures. He had gambled and lost because he feared the political costs of not acting.

The CIA and Military had assumed that rather than face a defeat the President would change his mind and use U.S. forces to help the attack succeed. He had assumed that they had understood his no meant no.

The Bay of Pigs disaster had a lasting effect on JFK and his decision making. He was somehow convinced that the CIA and JCS had misled him.?

At the CIA Dulles and Bissell were removed.

Strangely the public rallied to the President, and his ratings went up 10 points.? After the Bay of Pigs disaster JFK had the Dept. of Defense install in the White House Situation Room the latest communications technology. In that way the White House could closely monitor all military activity.

Such was Kennedy's nervousness of our military.

(Maxwell Taylor led the investigation into the Cuba Project. His commission claimed that the CIA was beyond their scope in trying to run the operation. From that point on all such projects would be run by the military, and that included the CIA activity in Laos and Vietnam.)

JFK concluded that to defeat the communist monolith new methods would be needed in the third world where all of the subversive activity was occurring.

In a speech on April 27 he stated that what was required was a proper understanding in the methods these ruthless communists used to undermine nations; infiltration instead of invasion, subversion instead of elections, intimidation instead of free choice, and the use of guerrilla forces at night instead of armies by day.

He hoped that the Bay of Pigs would provide lessons from which we could profit in preparing for this struggle.

Despite his failings Kennedy clearly understood the enemy of communism and how it had morphed to take advantage of any weakness in any destabilized country.

His major mistake was in hiring and trusting the ones he did. Even Robert Kennedy the president's brother and Attorney General was convinced of the righteousness of their Cuban effort.

In an April 19 memo, RFK told his brother that they dared not retract from the endeavor. **The weapons that Cuba possessed were not just for Castro, but to foment subversion throughout the Latin Americas.**

"Our long range objectives on Cuba are directly related to our survival, more than what is happening in Laos or the Congo." (As stated earlier, Communist subversion efforts were underway in Africa too. China was the power behind the conflict in the Congo.)

"If we don't want Russia to set up missile bases in Cuba we had better decide now what we are wiling to do to stop it"!

Robert's revelation was dead on, but JFK had already ruled out invading. Thus the only options available for the U.S. were coexisting and trying to contain Castro's subversions or just leaving everything to chance.

The second thought was obviously not possible, and in order to affect the first scenario the U.S. would have to convince the other nations of the hemisphere to take this risk seriously. But with the leftist expansions into Latin America that plan was also weak.

Robert Kennedy also suggested faking an attack on the U.S. base at Guantanamo to get some action from the Organization of American States- OAS.

This thought would be reviewed a few times over in the next few months. RFK went into a few tirades at some of their meetings, demanding some sort of action to show the Russians that we were not paper tigers.

Walt Rostow remarked that perhaps it isn't that important if Cuba has defensive arms. Our missiles in Turkey are a serious threat to Russia but they have not stirred over it.

National Security Council, NSC, discussions continued over the next months. **One possible scenario they discussed was that the Russians could use Cuba as an offensive missile base.** It was also felt that the major problem of Cuba would not be Castro exporting communism, but of copycat followers who were fed up with the status quo. Then more countries could turn.

Laos

While he and his team was still reeling from the Bay of Pigs, JFK was again beset with problems in Laos. Kennedy sent Under Sec-Def Roswell Gilpatric to Vietnam to study the worsening situation. Many in the Administration again recommend action, but how could anyone justify anti-communist military intervention in a nation 6000 miles away, when he had refused to do so in a country just 90 miles away.

In actuality the decision had already been made as JFK's confidence in those who had prompted action had fallen. (Kennedy however was the one who had ordered the multiple changes to the operation.)

The White House fell into a deep gloom, and on April 20, 1961 JFK approved a recommendation that the U.S. Special Forces advisors be added into the Military Assistance and Advisory Group, *MAAG* for short. In that way the advisors could operate in full uniform as a "warning to Moscow".

Initially it seemed to the Administration that the measure may have prompted a reaction in the Kremlin for they suddenly agreed to the need for a cease-fire. But once again the communists were just scamming the naïve Americans. The enticing possibility of negotiations slowed the U.S. led advisory and support activity, while the Pathet Lao forces intensified their efforts. Phoumi's forces quickly fell apart and calls again went to Washington for military intervention. Once more hurried meetings were held. *On April 26 permission for the use of B-26 medium bombers for air support was given.* (Step two of Operation Mill Pond.)

Those planes were flown and operated by the CIA.

The logistical nightmares of trying to get a lot of military units into Laos and to supply them had convinced many in the Pentagon that a large scale military involvement was not possible. Laos shared an extensive common border with Red China and N. Vietnam. Thus the communists could easily get arms and men into the fight while we could not. And then there was the specter of renewed war with China.

Kennedy called in Congressional Leaders the next day to discuss the issue. Admiral Burke briefed them. He covered all of the pro's and con's and ended with a warning that any battle in Laos would be extremely difficult and long. It could also bring in the Chinese.

Adm. Burke warned them that if we do nothing we will lose SE Asia.

And if we fight there it will be a long war and we may need nuclear weapons.

He recommended that a large force be deployed to Laos and S. Vietnam.

(The same reasoning he had used with Ike back in 1954.)

Army Chief of Staff Gen. George Decker and USMC Commandant David Shoup responded by saying that the small airfields in Laos could only handle 1,000 troops a day. It was not possible to get enough of a ground force into Laos and keep them supplied safely. They were against the mission.

Congressional leaders replied "That there was complete unanimity and strong views that even though it was recognized that our position in the remainder of South East Asia may well be affected, we should not introduce U.S. forces into Laos".

It was obvious to all that the Laotians were not in the fight as deeply as they could have. The communists were advancing steadily and the importation of U.S. arms and some ground forces would not bring freedom into an indifferent and weak country.

Should the war expand we could also face new attacks in Korea, Okinawa and even Japan. (The communists could always threaten you somewhere.)

JFK then told all that no decision had yet been made.

At the Pentagon the JCS issued a general advisory to all commands. In the Pacific, commanders were told to prepare for air strikes into China and N. Vietnam. On the following day the meeting with the JCS was the worst Walt Rostow had ever seen. *Rostow was a senior advisor to the President and a leader in the calls to fight in SE Asia. He was upset with the splits among the JCS and felt that that was holding Kennedy back.* Confusion reigned over what to do about Laos, and whether the U.S. should make any stand in SE Asia.

Erskin Bowles and Gen. Curtiss LeMay USAF wanted to fight the communists in Laos. If it included the Chinese forces fine, hit them before they acquired their own nukes. At some point we will have to confront them anyway. But landlocked Laos was a terrible place to fight. Militarily Vietnam was the best choice.

Our Navy could easily access the nation along its long coastline. Our ships could sit off-shore and attack with planes and canons, and we could supply the ground troops over the beaches. Additional meetings accomplished little as each of the adherent groups found fault with every other position. Kennedy was unsure on what to do. He also became upset because there was no consensus.

But getting differing advice from different people is part of the process of having meetings to decide the issues. It was normal and reasonable.
This was a dangerous move that was being contemplated by our government and each service saw the situation differently based on their battlefield needs and experience.

(Gen. Lemnitzer had warned JFK about this months earlier.)

A "ceasefire" in Laos was finally arranged and on May 2 it went into effect. Hanoi broadcast the order to the Pathet Lao, revealing who was actually running things.

By this point North Vietnam's Group 559 had infiltrated over 10,000 cadres into Laos. McGeorge Bundy had actually predicted that a ceasefire would be arranged.

He had an awareness of the SE Asian area and knew that the monsoons were due for early May. Movement in the flooded jungles would be almost impossible. Bargain for a "pause", and keep the West at bay.

(So much for negotiations with the communists, but then no one ever learns that lesson.)

Spies

During 1961 another round of highly placed Russian spies were caught.

A Polish spy had defected and warned his interrogators about a British Chief Petty Officer who worked at a submarine base. His name was Harry Hauten and he and his girlfriend had been passing secrets since 1952! Hauten's handler was KGB Col. Malady, a sleeper agent who based in Canada. Malady used front companies to mask his travel to England picking up the stolen intelligence. Weeks later Malady was also arrested.

The previously mentioned Cohen's had gone back to spying after a short time hiding in Russia. Unknown to them their fingerprints had been found years before by the FBI when the last batch of spies had been caught. They had been observed meeting with Malady, which meant they too could be spies. Both were arrested, and their fingerprints sealed their fate. Then in April another British agent named George Blake was picked up when it was learned that he was a double agent.

All were quickly convicted and sentenced to 20 years.

But in 1964 Malady was returned to Russia in a swap. Months later Blake somehow "escaped and made his way to Russia". In 1969 the Cohen's were also swapped and returned to Russia. Back in their communist homeland the formerly successful spies passed on their knowledge of the West to the next round of communist agents. All lived well compared to most in the Soviet Union.

(Those spies had worked long and hard for the Soviet Union believing in their political cause. But as the years went by all of them became disenchanted with communism. Living in Russia full time they saw the truth of what communism was first hand. All died alone and unhappy when they realized they had wasted lives to keep a corrupt regime in power.)

On May 10, 1961 Air France Flight 406 from Africa to Paris was blown up by a bomb secretly placed in the luggage. This was the first direct attack by Islamists against the West and 78 were killed. This incident went unnoticed by most of the Western world, but portended a violent outbreak that was soon to come. Terrorist attacks had occurred many times in the Middle East and in nations undergoing violent communist uprisings, like Vietnam.

But never before had an attack been directed against innocents on an aircraft.

America

In the Pentagon Sec. McNamara and his team of "whiz kids" had come into office and attacked the traditional military establishment and bureaucracy. They demanded information in volumes and wanted it within days.

By 1961 the Pentagon had become a huge infrastructure of its own and coupled with the inter-service infighting became a tortoise like bureaucracy. (Gen. Ridgeway the savior in Korea became the second commander of NATO, and then went on to become the Army Chief of Staff. In 1955 he had angrily retired in protest because of Eisenhower's continual reliance on MAD, Ike's Administration policies and the "Pentagon bureaucracy".) In their zeal to reform McNamara and his "whiz kids" lost sight of reality and actually believed themselves superior to the learned military men.

Adding to the unhappiness at the Pentagon was the appointment of Maxwell Taylor as the White House Military Representative instead of an active duty member.

(Kennedy did not want someone from the JCS so he found someone outside of the Pentagon. Unfortunately he just added another layer of bureaucracy with Maxwell, with yet another agenda.)

McNamara continually battled the Pentagon over cutting costs and duplication of weapon systems. He wanted a single fighter to serve the Navy and Air Force without realizing that their physical requirements were totally different. Then he wanted to end the USAF bomber command and add 300,000 troops to the Army. (Why?)

The JCS complained often that these new civilians would cut programs ignoring any military advice about them. Then they would simply tell the services what they could have for the year. In short order JFK's attempts to streamline the decision making and curb the bureaucracy were actually creating an entirely new one within his "inner circle".

Pres. Kennedy was enamored of the Special Forces concept.

He liked their flexibility and capabilities that were lacking from normal military commands. (In the Solomon Islands in WWII he had dropped off Marine Raiders who were running Recon missions. There he met Lt. Krulak.)

He increased five fold the SF budgets and directed each service to provide units. (SEALS, Army Special Forces etc.)

JFK's *New Frontier* foreign policy nameplate was predicated on American Globalism, and these Special Forces were to be his instrument. *Kennedy used his belief that America had the capacity and the right to intervene in foreign lands to stop the spread of communism.*

His years were the most unabashedly militant of our century, and an arms race of unprecedented proportion continued with an increase of $17 billion dollars.

(John Galbraith the exasperated U.S. Ambassador to India asked Kennedy which God decides what country is strategically important?)

It would be tragically ironic that the rich playboy and media darling in the White House was more militaristic than the five star general he had replaced.

For the upcoming Vienna Summit meeting Ambassador Averill Harriman wanted to have JFK pin Khrushchev down and stick to the agreements reached over Laos. Though the immediate crisis there had eased with the ceasefire, evidence had come in that the Pathet Lao and N. Vietnamese continued to operate quietly.

In Vietnam a large battle had occurred north of Saigon and the ARVN won the fight. U.S. Secretary of State Dean Rusk reported at a press conference that over 12,000 Viet Cong were now fighting in the south and that "all possible U.S. help will be given". JFK created a task force to work out the details.

On May 5th 1961 Pres. Kennedy stated that the use of U.S. troops in Vietnam was being considered. *Secretly an additional 400 Special Forces and 100 other advisors were sent to Vietnam.* Kennedy also ordered clandestine commando strikes against the North as more and more U.S. aid and weapons were shipped to the South.

To enhance the firepower against the communists, U.S. fighter and bomber squadrons were being sent over too. *Operation Farm Gate* pilots, (CIA), were allowed to fly the combat missions if a S. Vietnamese national was aboard the plane. In that way the Administration could claim the flight was a "Training Mission".

In Central S. Vietnam, Army Special Forces teams began organizing the Civilian Irregular Defense Group, CIDG, composed of the native mountain people who were called Montagnards. (Similar to the Meo tribes in Laos.) The idea was to train and equip those local forces to help in the fight against the communist infiltration that was occurring in their backyard. Those native fighters were hardy and knew the local terrain. When well trained and led they too were a match for the VC.

(This was exactly the program Diem should have instituted back in 1956 when the communists were weaker, but Diem refused in fear they would rise up against him.)

Europe

With the rebuilding of Europe completed the fortunes of those countries had also recovered. The NATO Council made up of member nations decided to reduce their military commitment. Those countries felt that the economic costs required to try to match the Warsaw Pact forces was too high, so why bother. (By this point the Warsaw Pact had reorganized and often war-gamed for conflict into Europe.)

Those Nations also figured that should an attack occur the U.S. would respond with tactical nuclear weapons so having a front line force was meaningless. But their viewpoint was just the opposite of what JFK wanted and pushed for.

If war came he did not want any use of nuclear weapons.

Kennedy did not realize that a profound change in relations had occurred since NATO's inception. Back then the countries of Europe feared an imminent Russian invasion and takeover. When S. Korea was invaded all of the nations saw it as a prelude to their own future. They eagerly rearmed and were grateful to Truman for committing the U.S. to NATO to save them. But in 1961 Stalin was gone and the dreaded Russian invasion had not occurred. Safe behind the "A-bombs" they wanted a renewed military commitment from America. The feeling was to let America fight for us. And with Britain and France having joined the nuclear club, it added to their thoughts of why bother with expensive conventional forces.

Kennedy's 1960 election team learned from allies inside our government that Russian nuclear missiles were difficult to build and they did not have the capacity for mass production like America did. The infamous missile gap that JFK had pitched as one of his campaign slogans to win the election was found to be totally false. His campaign rhetoric had painted a picture of the U.S. military in dire straits. The media never checked into the storyline, and insured it was disseminated. V.P. Nixon's campaign could not correct the stories as the information was considered Top Secret. (U-2 and SR-71 flights had provided the proof that Russia was far behind us, but Nixon could not say so publicly.)

Now that they were in office the new Administration learned that our atomic systems were being designed to survive a first strike because they were emplaced in deep underground silos and quietly being carried on submarines.

When incoming Sec-Def McNamara learned of our atomic secrets and procedures, he was stunned to learn that we could hit **2500 targets**, *some repeatedly to ensure destruction!*

Another learned "secret" was that regardless of the size of the conflict every communist country was to be hit with nuclear weapons!

Kennedy was aghast at the thought of any war going nuclear. He correctly insisted on more non-nuclear options, and a conventional buildup be started so we would have the ability to do so. During the past eight years of Eisenhower's reign MAD had worked to prevent any direct conflict between the West and Russia.

But during his eight years in office communism was still spreading by aggressive insurgent efforts. And for those issues Ike had no answers.

Our Allies were against any new way of thinking and took Kennedy's statements on the subject as proof that the U.S. would not stand up when needed.

In today's world it is almost impossible to convince the younger generations what we went through during the cold war, and how dangerous the world truly was.

And the worst of the trials was still to come.

In June JFK met up with Charles de Gaulle in Paris, while on his way to Vienna and his summit meeting with the Russians. The appearance of success in Laos convinced Kennedy that he had to stay strong in SE Asia and that would mean sending a larger US military presence. **De Gaulle tried to reason and warn him that it would not be tenable politically or militarily to fight there.**

Kennedy refused the advice, believing that his counter-insurgency plan would stop the North Vietnamese.

JFK had heard about Che Guevara's manual, *On Guerrilla Warfare*, and ordered it translated and distributed to the Special Warfare School and the Foreign Service Offices. He also directed those groups to read Sun-tzu's treatise on warfare. Unfortunately JFK only had the SF people read about counter-insurgency. The senior officers in the military knew nothing about it and understood even less.

Vienna

In early June 1961 Khrushchev and JFK met in Vienna for the previously listed summit. It was hoped that relations between the superpowers could be improved.

(As stated earlier, Eisenhower's similar trip to Paris had ended when Khrushchev walked out of the meetings with the shooting down of a U-2 spy plane over Sverdlovsk, Russia on May 1, 1960. Khrushchev did not think much of Ike as every time he asked him a question Eisenhower had to turn to Dulles for the answer.)

Pres. Kennedy's overall goal was to curtail atmospheric testing of nuclear weapons due to the radiation fallout. Previous discussions since 1958 had gone nowhere because the Russians refused any on site inspections.

Khrushchev however wanted the problem of Berlin to be worked out before any other issue would be discussed. And because of the poor U.S. showing in Cuba Khrushchev felt he could win the debates and the treaties.

Like all good Soviets, Khrushchev laughed at the idea of American so called Kremlinologists. "They do not understand the Politburo. They think that since they are from an educated country that we are too. They have no idea that we are dominated by unimaginative and unattractive scoundrels!" (41)

Though they may have been both of the above, those senior Soviets had also survived the revolution, the Stalin purges and WWII. They were tough and seasoned realists who understood geopolitics and power. And they were not intimidated by the weak willed leaders of the West.

Their first face to face meeting occurred on June 3, 1961 and turned into an ideological debate which Kennedy lost as he tried to reason with the Russian Premier.

(Reason has no place at any sit down with the communist mindset.)

Khrushchev lured the young president into an ideological debate that stretched into hours. The Russian leader was a skilled dialectician, honed from a hard life inside the Bolshevik political world. And Khrushchev was riding an impressive tide. Not only were their technological abilities improving, so was the Soviet economy. In 1945 Russia produced just 12 million tons of steel. By 1960 they were up to 65 million tons per year!

Electrical production had gone up 20 fold, vehicles by a factor of eight, and their overall industrial output was increasing 10% per year.

With Stalin gone everything was doing better, even in Eastern Europe.

Khrushchev now demanded that their political objectives be realized.

After observing the poor U.S. operation at the Bay of Pigs, Kennedy's reluctance to use military force there, and the failure of the U.S. effort in Laos, it convinced Khrushchev that he could intimidate the young president at the meetings. *Ironically Laos was the only thing they agreed on, in that neither country wanted a war there.*

One of JFK's favorite warnings was that a *miscalculation* could occur and escalate a problem. To Khrushchev's crooked mind that only showed more weakness, since Russians never miscalculate! He ranted on about finalizing the situation in Europe including the recognition of the post-war Polish and Czech borders, and that the problematic situation in Berlin had to be ended.

Russia wanted to turn over total control of Berlin to E. Germany.

The city was deep inside the E. German communist zone and to the Soviets there was no reason for it to still be divided among the former allies. They also felt the move would close off the city and stop the hundreds of E. Germans who were escaping each week to the western side. (Once those civilians had crossed over to West Berlin they were free to fly out and escape. Though many spies used that factor too.)

The West's position had been and still was to refuse any thought of leaving West Berlin. It was a prize won in the war. However the growing unseen danger was that the E. Germans could attempt to take over the entire city on their own.

(Again this was another Failure by FDR and Truman in not insisting on a land bridge into Berlin from our occupation zones.)

Kennedy warned the Russian Premier that the U.S. would fight for Berlin.

Khrushchev decided that instead of negotiating any further he would demand concessions on Berlin. The Russian space program had recently had a successful manned mission which implied that we were way behind them in everything. Using their advances in space as a threat he tried to force JFK to make a deal.

The State Dept did not anticipate this bellicose strategy and JFK was caught unprepared. There was no progress on anything else, including Kennedy's testing ban.

By the end of August Russia resumed their nuclear testing.

By mid-June Maxwell Taylor was among those recommending strong action against Cuba. He too felt that there was no living with Castro in the long term, and Cuba was getting more Russian arms weekly. It would be easy for them to export those weapons throughout the region causing even worse problems.

Navy commanders wanted to blockade Cuba while the Air Force felt that bombing them would cause Castro's collapse. Others wanted Castro assassinated.

Initial thoughts on the latter scenario had actually been started in August 1960 when the Eisenhower Administration had contacted members of organized crime including Sam Giancana of Chicago. The Mob like many big American Corporations had lost millions with the fall of Cuba. It was naively hoped that the mob could get a Cuban stay behind partisan to act. The efforts had not progressed far before Ike left office.

By the fall of 1961 even JFK had thoughts on that potential operation.

In the Pacific the fragile peace in Laos was slipping away due to the non-stop communist infiltration. The two world leaders had reached a "limited agreement on the sovereignty of the country", but in keeping with their master plan, Russia continued sending aid and refused to stop their brethren from acting.

That fall Averill Harriman met with Georgi Pushkin in Rome where the two diplomats discussed Laos. Pushkin promised that Russia would help enforce peace in Laos, and that convinced Kennedy to sign the Geneva Accords in 1962.

Naturally the Russians did not live up to the agreement.

Berlin

Berlin was an anomaly as it was still divided into four separate occupation zones deep within communist controlled territory. The American, British and French sectors had coalesced into West Berlin, with open and unrestricted access.

The communists were deeply threatened by this fact as hundreds of disaffected East German residents were crossing into W. Berlin and then freedom every week.

Khrushchev had demanded that the West leave Berlin back in 1958 when it appeared the Soviets were taking the world military lead. (Sputnik and their missile programs were ahead of the U.S. at that time.) Eisenhower however stood firm on the issue and with the forces of NATO as the bulwark the situation remained unchanged.

The Russians then sought a treaty which would recognize the separate state of East Germany. With that treaty in place East Germany would then be in charge of the situation, and Khrushchev felt that they could slowly cutoff access to and take control of Berlin. Thus far the West had refused to grant any such treaty despite the saber rattling from Russia. And the more they threatened the peace the more the communists weakened their own position. Increasing numbers of E. German citizens were leaving as the West dug in their heels further.

Since 1949 the population of East Germany, (GDR, German Democratic Republic), had fallen by 2 million mostly trained and educated people. They had seen that communism offered nothing but slavery and pain.

As with every country that had fallen to the communists the citizens who could voted with their feet and escaped. If the situation was allowed to go on it was possible the GDR would completely collapse.

The collectivization of the farms in East Germany was enacted in 1960. As had happened everywhere it was done, collectivization caused food shortages which added to the misery of life under the communists. No matter which country turned communist all enacted farm collectivization and all had dire food shortages and famines.

In February 1961 over 13,500 people had escaped to the West.

During March 16,000 had left.

JFK feared that of all of the hot spots in the world Berlin was the one that could lead to a nuclear war. The U.S. had shed much blood to defeat the Germans in WWII but then found ourselves trying to save Germany from the Russian menace.

During 1948 the West used the massive airlift to defeat Stalin's attempt to shut down Berlin. One of the reasons the Russians did not shoot down those U.S. supply planes was because Gen. Curtis LeMay had recently organized and equipped the Strategic Air Command. The larger jet powered USAF bombers could and would carry nuclear weapons into the communist heartland and the Russians knew it.

Thus no aggressive military actions were taken as only we had the bomb. But by 1961 both sides had nukes and Berlin had become a Capitalist Oasis in a communist desert. It was also indefensible using conventional military means.

Like all of the rulers of countries split apart by the communists Chancellor Adenauer stuck to his beliefs that West Germany must be reunited with the East.

And similar to Truman and Eisenhower in Korea, Kennedy felt that that attitude was too rigid for this nuclear armed environment. Any attempt to reunify would lead to war.

Back in 1958 when the problem had re-gained world attention Dean Acheson had interpreted Khrushchev's demands on Berlin as a war warning and wanted Eisenhower to begin a military buildup. Ike resisted the impulsive move because of where it could lead. Given time Khrushchev backed down from his saber rattling and tried to trick the West into a negotiated fix.

Now in 1961 the same problem had reemerged on Kennedy's desk and Khrushchev felt he was close to getting his way with this weak president. Acheson again insisted that the U.S. must show firm resolve over Berlin and he wanted a call-up of the reserves, increased troop strength in Europe and strategic aircraft moved to Europe. "If the U.S. was not prepared to go to war, then it had better not pretend that it was." Some at the State Dept. warned that our Allies were anxious over the ideas being passed around. Acheson's reply, "If our allies have serious inhibitions against action, we had better find out now!" (42) He wanted a U.S. Armored Division to be sent to Berlin as a show of will. In that way the Russians would clearly understand the implications.

In late June those work shop plans were passed onto Kennedy.

The basic premise was that negotiations were pointless unless the U.S. was prepared to demonstrate to Khrushchev that we would not tolerate any changes in Berlin. Acheson felt no communist action would be taken until after the elections in Germany, set for Sept 17. By that time his recommended U.S. military preparations should have been completed.

At a televised press conference on June 28, JFK *explained the problems of Berlin to the American people.* The polls taken that night were in favor of U.S. action to save Berlin. (This one event shows how important it is to explain the problems and actions to the people. It should actually be a law forcing the politicians to speak before being able to act.) Acheson also desired a national emergency declaration similar to Truman's action over Korea. His thoughts were echoed by Gen. Maxwell Taylor the president's military advisor. "It was illogical to wait until we were challenged to start a buildup."

Kennedy was finally swayed, and on July 25 issued a serious warning that the U.S. would not be driven out of Berlin gradually or by force. He derided the Soviet approach of what is mine is mine, what is yours is negotiable. JFK also promised to seek a peaceful solution if one could be found. His declaration of a national emergency was unexpected and alarmed the world's liberals. But polls still showed an 85% approval of those actions in the U.S.. In Europe Britain wanted talks, France was opposed to any talks, and Germany did not know what they wanted.

Russia was also caught by surprise from the hard line taken by Kennedy. The Americans had not retreated after the Vienna conference and the crisis atmosphere that was created was actually making things in

Berlin worse. Russia was spending a fortune trying to keep East Germany's economy afloat, but no one in the West knew that.

West Germans would actually cross over to buy up the subsidized communist goods and then head back home taking more of the GDR residents with them. By July over 1,000 people were leaving communist E. Germany each day!

E. German leader Ulbricht warned the Russians that if Berlin was not closed down collapse of the country was inevitable. Khrushchev was then informed by his Intelligence sources that the U.S. was developing new military responses to the expected showdown over Berlin. The final straw was Kennedy's broadcast of July 25.

Khrushchev decided to agree with Ulbricht's request for a wall closing off the communist section of the city. It had to be done quietly and quickly, before the West could react.

Just after midnight on Aug 13, 1961 the E. German police stopped all subways before they could enter West Berlin. Obstacles and barbed wire fences quickly sprang up on the roads. Construction of the actual wall started on Aug 19.

Now the West had been caught completely by surprise.

(Col Oleg Penkovsky of the Soviet General staff had been a spy for the West. Even his office did not know of those events.)

Worries quickly sprang up concerning a possible insurrection in the GDR. The U.S. had been unable and unwilling to help the citizens during the uprisings in the GDR in 1953, Poland or Hungary in 1956. All were ruthlessly crushed by the Soviets with thousands being killed and unknown thousands disappeared into the gulags. If a new revolt sprang up in the GDR what would or could the U.S. do?

Warnings went out to U.S. personnel not to exacerbate the problem. Kennedy had long worried about this possibility and stated privately that there was nothing we could really do. (The same problem Ike had faced during the 50's)

It was their country and nuclear war would result from any U.S. action. He was not alone in this feeling as most of the world leaders also saw the position as untouchable unless the world wanted another war.

During the 1952 Presidential campaign the Republicans had talked long and loud about rolling back the iron-curtain. The hopes of the captive people in E. Europe may well have been aroused by those early political discussions, and ultimately led to their destruction. JFK insisted that care must be used not to allow that miscalculation again. It took time but word soon got out that over five communist divisions were stationed around

Berlin. Any attempt to force entry against those odds would result in a bloodbath inside Berlin.

As the tense days went by alarmists began predicting secondary moves by the communists. The West had done nothing about Berlin so far, why should they stop?

Pres. Kennedy wrote a letter to Khrushchev that Vice-President Johnson was to personally deliver to Berlin. (The idea actually came from columnist Marguerite Higgins, the tough woman reporter who had been in WWII, post-war Europe and Korea.)

Lyndon Johnson refused to go, fearing for his safety.

Gen. Clay the first commander in Berlin was sent along to stiffen the messenger, and as a warning to the Russians. Timed to go with the Johnson / Gen. Clay trip was a Berlin bound military road convoy of 1,600 U.S. troops, led by Col. Johns and Captain Hackworth. (Read their books!) The Russians did not stop the convoy though they did delay it at intervals. Communist recon aircraft constantly swooped low over the vehicles which also invited shooting incidents. Fortunately the U.S. troops were well disciplined.

TASS the communist news agency reported that Russia was resuming open air nuclear testing. Their bomb would be a massive 50 megatons, and it went off on Sept 1. Three more Russian tests followed and JFK announced that we too would resume atomic testing. Khrushchev was again posturing, trying to intimidate the threatened people and nations with the size of the Russian weapons. In actuality they were hiding their low numbers. (Khrushchev had once warned the British that he could obliterate all of their islands with just six of their nuclear bombs.)

During that tense summer and fall the U.S. had had a number of successful Corona Satellite flights that had taken great pictures of the Russian ICBMs.

Coupled with reports from Col. Penkovsky that Russian missiles and subs were having operational problems, it greatly reduced the Russian nuclear missile estimates and the danger.

France's de Gaulle and Germany's Adenauer had common ground to complain over the U.S. domination in NATO and the nuclear shield. What they really wanted were their own nuclear forces and a stronger independent Europe. With the reconstruction from the Marshall Plan and a steady economic recovery that was into its second decade de Gaulle saw a chance to restore their glorious past and get out from under the superpowers thumbs.

Adenauer agreed, as West Germany was starting their period of *Wirtschaftswunder,* their economic miracle. Rebuilt from the war's devastation, their modernized infrastructure, factories, transportation networks were turning into a massive commercial success. Germany contained a well educated, productive workforce swollen with emigrants from behind the Iron Curtain. They possessed great stores of natural resources and were unburdened with most defensive requirements as America was their guardian. Like Japan, large companies and banks grew and prospered. Only in the political arena were those restored nations falling short.

Khrushchev was becoming alarmed at the increasing tension and used back-channels to let it be known that he would meet for another summit.

As time went by the Berlin Wall actually performed as expected and reduced the tensions and strain on E. Germany. The situation stabilized and the crisis seemed ended.

And then in late October, 1961 the military forces in Berlin went face to face at checkpoint Charlie. The communists in Berlin felt that the West was preparing an attack against the wall. (Which would have been ridiculous.)

Tank and infantry units took up firing positions on each side as tensions became unbearable. Luckily Russian officers were in command and able to keep the communist units (Russian and E German), in check. The world was one shot from war as the two world leaders continued their back-channel diplomacy.

In the U.S., most in the Administration now realized that the nuclear option that Ike had used as his leverage against Russia was out of date. The Allies had to have strong conventional forces in theater to check the communists. Because of the recent crisis in Berlin our leaders wanted the NATO countries to provide 32 active, combat ready divisions to be on duty with another eight in reserve. The U.S. already had five of our divisions in Europe and had promised another one by the end of 1961.

Our Allies delayed for they were unhappy with the costs of keeping these large forces on permanent guard. Their populations and governments were content to have the U.S. provide and absorb all of the costs to keep the communists out. Political pressure had to be applied and maintained on Europe to force them to provide for their own defense. Kennedy authorized an increase in the Army from 11 to 16 Divisions.

Pres. Kennedy correctly identified other potential challenges over Berlin that would have to be met *conventionally*; interference with civilian air traffic, closing the roads and rails, GDR police problems with West Berliners and a possible E. German revolt. A second airlift might work, but other than that the NATO countries had nothing but nukes. Changes had to be made to offer a more *flexible response.*

Sec.-Def McNamara and Paul Nitze went to see Gen. Norstad at his NATO HQ to discuss the conventional military options. They found that there were none.

All of the war-plans envisioned a rapid and detailed use of atomic weapons.

In fact, 85% of their targets were on the SIOP list. (Single Integrated Operational Plan). After touring the various commands and seeing the battlefield reality the pair realized that there was not much we could actually do. NATO was too weak to fight the Warsaw Pact forces using conventional weapons.

With the increasing nuclear threat JFK wanted a heightened Civil Defense program to protect U.S. civilians. Casualties in event of a nuclear war ran into the appalling guess of 100 million. Throughout America training and bomb shelters became common place within the stronger buildings. When I was in the 1st grade, we were taught to react to flashing lights and certain bells to hide and cover-up under our desks and in the hallways. We practiced this for years. It was hoped that millions could be saved if an atomic war did breakout.

*Kennedy also directed the military to plan a scenario on **if we** could launch an offensive 1st strike to destroy as many Russian missiles as possible.*

U.S. strikes would use bombers as well as missiles and the initial attacks would be directed at communist military targets only. This plan was designed with the thought that if we struck first and struck well it would reduce U.S. casualties by <u>preventing</u> and or reducing a Russian attack. **Those meetings were so secret that no one was allowed to even say what the discussions were about.**

Gen. Lauris Norstad the U.S. commander in NATO objected to those theoretical sessions claiming it was ridiculous to think in *terms of gradual response and step by step battles*! Norstad warned them that once a war started in Europe no one would control anything. Most of his complaints were directed at the uneducated and annoying Sec. of Defense McNamara who seemed to think he was setting up a business deal instead of debating a potential nuclear war. *Gen. Norstad was soon retired.*

Tensions in Europe eased a small amount in early November when Khrushchev announced he was delaying the December deadline for the East German peace treaty.

However the harassment around Berlin continued. Talks with the NATO members continued over trying to build up larger conventional forces.

Then the French Defense Minister admitted that France had nuclear weapons and would use them on their own. That information caused huge problems in NATO since no one would have control or know when or if France would use the weapons.

It also caused problems for Russia for those same reasons.

Asia

*In reaction to the rising infiltration of troops from N. Vietnam JFK increased the U.S. troop/advisor levels to **over 3,000.*** He then issued statements that the U.S. would remain in S. Vietnam until the Viet Cong were beaten.

The first peace march was held in Washington, mostly comprised of college students. They demanded an end to atomic testing and the cancelation of the Civil Defense Program.

On October 16, 1961 S. Vietnam's President Diem publicly announced that his country was at war with the communist insurgents.

He sent an urgent letter to Pres. Kennedy asking for more funding.

JFK sent Taylor and Walt Rostow to make an assessment.

Because of LBJ's earlier trip to Vietnam back in April, Diem had realized that he was in a great position. Johnson had told him he was America's guy in Vietnam and Diem could get whatever he wanted to fight the communists.

Upon his return LBJ reported back that Diem had some good qualities, but was remote from the citizens and surrounded by a lot of bad people. Vietnam could be saved "if we moved quickly and wisely"

(As with Berlin, the self-absorbed Johnson had refused to go to Saigon back in April fearing for his life. JFK had to coax him, and even sent along his youngest sister Jean and her husband as "hostages" to convince Johnson to do his job! As a joke JFK told Johnson that if he died they would arrange the biggest sendoff Texas ever had.)

Taylor and Rostow were the administration hawks. Rostow correctly recommended that SEATO collect and send 25,000 troops to operate near Laos as a way to stop the North's use of the country.

A JCS report called for 129,000 U.S. troops to monitor the entire length of S. Vietnam's border with Laos and the DMZ. They felt that was the best way to try to stop the infiltration from the North.

U.S. authorities cited evidence that the NVA 304 & 324 Divisions were operating in the area around Tchepone, Laos. Their 325th Div. was on the DMZ.

Multiple independent NVA battalions were sited along the Bolovens Plateau and lower Laos. Photo-recon flights had spotted and confirmed unit positions and that communist flights were coming into Tchepone often.

The National Intelligence Estimate felt that as of the fall of 1961, only 10-20% of the VC and communist cadres fighting in the south were northerners. They felt the main fight was with the southerners and all effort should be directed to them.

In response the JCS recommended we send 20,000 men initially to the Central Highlands, and increase it to 40,000 to help finish off the VC. If the Northerners or the Chinese came in then 200,000 troops would be needed.

While in Korea in 1953 Taylor had irrationally told Erskin Bowles that America should never again fight a land war in Asia. Taylor ignored what Generals Ridgeway and Van Fleet had accomplished in 1951 before the inept politicians interceded, but his statements got him noticed by the State Dept doves. Yet here he was in late 1961 recommending to Kennedy we commit large numbers of U.S. troops into Indochina.

He arrogantly felt N. Vietnam was vulnerable to conventional bombing and that their logistic capabilities were strained. He felt the same was true for China, and with their great starvation ongoing (word was getting out), they would not be militarily aggressive. Taylor compared S. Vietnam to Korea and on how our army learned to adapt to the terrain and climate. (Taylor was supposed to be an intellectual, and JFK's expert on counter-insurgency. But here he was comparing Vietnam to Korea instead of to the French-Indochina War, Malaya or the Huk rebellion in the Philippines.)

America's Special Forces program had produced the exact warriors JFK had wanted. In October the entire White House press corps had been taken to Fort Bragg, NC to view these physical and intellectual specimens in action.

Their performance was perfect and impressed all but one.
Francis Lara had been a French correspondent in Indochina from 1949-54. He told his American colleagues that this all looks impressive, but it did not work when we tried it in Vietnam.

Soon after Diem sent in another request for more aircraft and advisors, but also asked if Chiang could send him a division of their troops. Replacement Ambassador Nolting recommended serious and prompt attention be given to those requests.

When Nolting realized that JFK was sending an increase in our troops he became upset. He too wanted a civilian fix to the political problems.

From the discussions generated when Taylor and Rostow returned from Vietnam, *in mid-November JFK increased our advisory force to 6,000, and promised to have 16,000 "advisors" in country within two years.* Also included in the aid package were more planes and arms. He did not give into the vast numbers the National Intelligence Estimate / JCS had sought or the proposals from Diem and Nolting. He preferred to stay "moderate and cautious". That created the media illusion that he had held the line. But in reality Kennedy did not see that our efforts thus far had failed. Increasing them could only make things worse.

George Ball at State Dept. was a lone voice against sending even advisors.

He had been involved in Indochina with the French and had seen the same false optimism and arrogance from their leadership. *He warned Bundy and McNamara that we were following the French mistakes with our own.* And Ball echoed the sentiments used by Kennedy and LBJ in 1954 when he and many others were against helping the French. But both of the Administration principals believed in their abilities, and they downplayed his reservations.

By the end of 1961 despite all of the work and fighting, the infiltration from the North and the addition of new converts had actually *increased* the VC communist fighters to over 16,000 with another 6,000 weapons captured.

In all probability Pres. Kennedy did not want a war in Vietnam personally, but he was about to get us into one. He was convinced that after his poor meeting in Vienna, the tensions in Berlin, his failures in Cuba and the continued communist subversions in Indochina, Africa and Latin America he had to take a stand against the Russians somewhere. *Kennedy even told James Reston of the NY Times that Khrushchev had felt that he, JFK, was in over his head.*

"The Russian beat the hell out of me at the Vienna meeting, so I've got a terrible problem. We have to make our power credible, and Vietnam will be the place". And so in November 1961 President John Kennedy had secretly decided that the U.S. would have to intervene militarily in Vietnam.

That was why he increased the number of Army Divisions. And that was why he was raising the advisory numbers to such a high level so quickly. He wanted the infrastructure in place before the next round of problems began.

Once JFK started his Vietnam buildup Khrushchev told U.S. Ambassador Llewellyn Thompson that Kennedy was making a major mistake in Vietnam.

The U.S. has stumbled into a bog and would be there for a long time.

William Jorden was a well traveled and learned former journalist that Sec State Rusk brought in. He had accompanied Taylor and Rostow to Vietnam in October and compiled a separate "White Paper" on the situation. *As one of the early experts on the area, it was hoped his paper would have some weight on any Vietnam debates.*

Rusk was pleased with the final report which was released on Dec. 8, 1961. Jorden's work highlighted in detail the intensive N. Vietnamese effort to conquer the South. For some reason the report sank into oblivion.

To help out the British sent in a survey team to Vietnam.

They recommended a classic counter-insurgency program that was aimed at winning over the population. It would be modeled close to the one they had successfully used in Malaya, to separate the insurgents from the people.

But the unknowing Gen. McGarr in MAAG objected to it because "it would take too long and undercut the offensive spirit." During his brief tour little had been accomplished, and that too greatly aided the communist efforts.

McGarr was replaced with Gen. Paul Harkins in early February 1962. *JFK was building up our presence in Vietnam and MAAG was converted into MACV, Military Assistance Command Vietnam.*

(One cannot help but wonder just what were the motivations and who had been responsible for retaining those inferior general officers (Williams and McGarr) in the Army. Why were they given such a vital command? It is a certainty that Eisenhower knew of or was involved in their assignment. And Harkins was no better.)

Africa-Middle East

During December 1961 more fighting broke out in the Congo.

By this time the Marxist rebels controlled most of the country while the breakaway province of Katanga was trying to stay free. United Nations Secretary General Dag Hammarskjold went to the Congo to prevent the secession of the Katanga Province and prevent a civil war. He too died in a suspicious plane crash.

Because of his efforts the U.N. sent in their peacekeepers, (a first), and brokered a treaty to reunite the country. Many of the conservative leaders in the U.S. were upset at that outcome, as the reunification forced the Katangese people into the Marxist state.

(JFK and his administration had actually worked to affect that outcome.)

Nearby the country of Tanganyika was the latest to proclaim their independence from British rule.

De Gaulle finally accepted that France's past was past, and agreed on Algerian independence. Their war had claimed thousands of lives in a futile quest to stop Algerian nationalism. Kennedy was glad for the change, but was placing America inside a similar cauldron.

In the Middle East Syria revolted against its political union with Egypt.

Nasser had merged the two countries with his 1957 United Arab Republic entity. His dream had been to create a united Arab world. (Similar to what is happening now.)

But after four years of trials the conservative lawyer Mahmoun al-Kuzbari was able to create a new civilian government in Syria. Their nation was able to re-establish their independence and for a time that reduced the tensions there.

Then in February 1962 another coup occurred and a new regime took over Syria. That new regime was again seeking aid from Russia and border raids with Israel began anew. In late March yet another coup by the military took back control over Syria.

Behind the complex scenes the Baa'thists were becoming the dominate political group. *In June the Iraqi Kurds asked the U.N. to acknowledge their right to autonomy.*

Their rightful query was ignored by the only political entity that could have gotten involved. Kurdish freedom is still a serious problem today.

As shown in *Fatal Flaws Book 1*, Iraq was artificially formed by Winston Churchill and the British after WWI. Despite having been warned by the Foreign Service Officers not to try it, Churchill and his staff at the Colonial Office did just that.

In fact, most of the boundaries that formed the nations of the Middle East came from those few weeks of foolhardiness. *It was those failures and the harsh colonial mindset that led to the formation of the Muslim Brotherhood and their unending and understandable anger and hatred of the West.*

Iraq was also under the sway of the Baath Party.

Cuba

Cuba still occupied much time and effort in the administration.

The cutting of trade ties to Cuba had definitely hurt the regime, but it also forced them to rely completely on the Soviet Bloc. Those nations imported Cuban sugar, and sent back weapons. Three varieties of aircraft were brought in, MIG 15, 17 and 19. Dozens of Russian made tanks, artillery, SAMs, coastal missile units, patrol boats and electronic equipment were also sent in and organized to repel the Americans.

On November 30, 1961 a new Cuba planning group had been organized.

Robert Kennedy and Douglas Dillion were added to Gen. Taylor's planning group, now called the Special Group Augmented, SGA. (RFK was so enamored of Taylor, that he named one of his children after him. He also became close to Gen. Krulak and Director McCone who had replaced Dulles at CIA.)

They were tasked to oversee operation Mongoose, the overthrow of Castro.

The SGA brought in agent Lansdale and directed him to "make things happen." But Lansdale was not schooled in creating insurgency, his specialty was in countering one. And even if he did try to create one McCone alone among those principals felt that it would be brutally crushed like the 1956 uprising in Hungary. Any sabotage efforts attempted in Cuba were instantly linked to the U.S. and resulted in increased security. Every move that this secret group created or attempted was instantly checked by the communists. By April 1962 only limited intelligence gathering could be obtained from inside Cuba, though the U.S. base at Guantanamo still conducted some military exercises and picked up some intelligence. Castro's communists completely controlled the country.

Castro repeatedly demanded that the treaty that allowed Guantanamo be ended and the land returned to Cuba. His forces threatened action and the base was garrisoned by 1,000 Marines as well as the Navy and service units already there.

(I think that before Obama leaves office, he will unilaterally give the base back to Cuba as a way to "close it".)

Richard Helms who had replaced Bissell at CIA tried once more to have the gangsters get to Castro, his brother and Che Guevara. All told fourteen attempts were made to kill Castro. *Although those efforts accomplished nothing, one of JFK's mistresses was found to also be involved with Giancana the Chicago crime boss.*

(Kennedy was a serial adulterer, a secret that was kept quiet thanks to friends in the media, politics and other venues. This episode had it been revealed could have caused numerous political problems and probably finished JFK's career.)

By the summer of 1962 there was no confidence that Cuba could be turned away from communism without direct U.S. involvement. And dozens of Russian ships were docking each month bringing in additional arms and supplies. Containment and undermining were the only non-military options. But unknown to the U.S. policy makers, big changes were planned for Cuba.

Vietnam

Beginning in early 1962 the earlier approved *Operation Ranch Hand* had started operations in Vietnam. The program was directed to and planned for deforestation of large tracts of dense jungle using a chemical, (agent orange), that would kill all vegetation in its spray area. It was enacted in the hopes of eliminating the communists well camouflaged hiding spots and food sources. This elusive enemy was still growing stronger even though the U.S. led advisory effort had increased dramatically.

On March 20, 1962 a large airdrop by the communists (using Russian planes), was picked up near the ARVN radar station at Pleiku in the Central Highlands.

All along the border near Kontum and Pleiku were major nexus of the Ho Chi Minh trail. From that central point numerous branches fanned off into Thailand, Cambodia and the lower reaches of S. Vietnam. This communist air drop was one of many over the past weeks, but this one was the largest. A B-26 from the *Farm Gate* program was scrambled to intercept the flight but was unable to engage the Soviet supply planes. Upon investigation by ARVN Rangers dozens of supply packs were found hanging in the trees. The next night an even larger operation was picked up, warning of a large enemy action.

Discussions on the overt Soviet supply effort resulted in JFK agreeing to the shooting down of the aircraft! However he insisted it could not happen near Saigon or over Cambodia. And the media was not to be told a thing.

Late on March 22nd three USAF F-102s left Clark Air Base in the Philippines for a night landing at Tan Son Nhut airbase in S. Vietnam. They were on the secret mission to shoot down all of the Soviet supply aircraft that were being flown by Chinese and N. Korean pilots.

The Administration directed Gen. Harkins who commanded the military at MACV and Ambassador Nolting to keep things "quiet and to set up cover stories" in case the reporters started asking questions!

Once again a president was using American forces on his own volition, and keeping it a secret from the Congress and the people.

(Frederick Nolting had replaced Durbrow in late 1961 because the truthful and argumentative Durbrow was at odds with Diem, the leaders at

MAAG/MACV and JFK's new aggressive policies. Nolting knew nothing about Asia, and his last post had been in NATO. He followed the party line until he too was sacked.)

Two weeks after the communist air drops large VC units attacked all along the coast from Da Nang to Qui Non. Two SF men were killed and two were taken prisoner.

A relief force was sent out too late to help, and NBC reporter Rheinstein was present and shot film of the incident. Harkins and his staff were upset that the film went out and were "trying to clean it up." (Again, the Administration was looking for damage control instead of explaining what was going on.)

The search for the two captives continued until April 17th when the rescue force was ambushed by the VC. News of that attack also leaked out and soon the story hit the papers. Kennedy was forced to answer questions about Vietnam.

But the lies from the Administration and MACV in Saigon were becoming more and more numerous, and the reporters picked up on them. It was the beginning of a loss of trust that would affect the entire war effort.

(For some reason seasoned diplomat Averill Harriman warned the president that publicity and leaks to the press were the top two items he had to address.)

And then another incident occurred which would set the tone of our destruction. Gen. Harkins' Intelligence Chief Col. Winterbottom USAF and two others heard about and went to observe the ARVN in "action" against a platoon of VC.

What the officers observed was the ARVN troops refusing to charge the enemy position and the ARVN commander blindly calling in an airstrike of napalm. Hours later there was a search of the area, it revealed no enemy dead or equipment found.

Upon his return to MACV Col. Winterbottom wrote a report that listed 36 dead VC! The other officers were horrified over this blatant lie, but this fabrication was in keeping with Harkins directives to post continuous reports of optimistic gains!!

At the same time the Administration was also reporting on how good things were in SE Asia. **McNamara even told the Congress that the end of the war was in sight!**

In his office Vice Pres. Lyndon Johnson was reading classified reports on how bad things really were over there. His military aide USAF Col. Howard Burris updated him that "the U.S. advisory program in SVN has not reversed the level or intensity of the Viet Cong operations. *Previous small teams of communist enemies have grown to company sized units."*

(Burris was getting memos from the JCS, Taylor's office and the CIA.) **Yet JFK and his Administration kept the lie going.**

Gains in Laos by the communist Pathet Lao forces clearly showed that the country was almost gone. *Kennedy then sent 4,000 troops to Thailand in an effort to protect them from the communists and to assist the Laotians.* The year long "peace" was unmistakably broken by the Pathet Lao forces, and Kennedy was dismayed that the communists and Khrushchev did not keep their word.

With Taylor having a larger voice in the Administration and JFK's desire to get involved in Vietnam, the JCS slowly began to adjust to the fact that the Army may have to fight there. Taylor had in fact sent a memo to Kennedy in November 1961 that we had to send troops to Vietnam and that bombing North Vietnam may need to be done.

However the Joint Chiefs had their own ideas over this potential fight.

Gen. George Decker the Chief of Staff in the Army warned the President in April 1961 that we could not win a conventional war in South East Asia.

"If we do go in, we must go in to win and that meant bombing Hanoi, China and possibly using nuclear weapons". *Kennedy was not happy with that assessment and Decker like Lemnitzer and Norstad would be replaced because they disagreed with the president and his administrators. The conniving Taylor would recommend yet another protégé, Gen. Earl Wheeler to replace Decker. Again Kennedy wrongly agreed to the change.*

JFK began changing the mission of the advisory team in Vietnam. He wanted them to use the Special Forces teams to fight and think outside the box. Theirs was a new way of operating and could have yielded the results the president wanted.

But again at the insistence of Gen. Taylor, Gen. Paul Harkins who had been Patton's chief of staff in Sicily had been formally placed in charge of the new command of MACV in Feb 1962. *Taylor had lobbied JFK hard to get his friend Harkins this post even though Harkins knew nothing about infantry operations or counterinsurgency.*

And Harkins was another WWII senior officer who had not had a combat command!

He had been good at logistics and in public relations, but was not considered a clever man. This foolish pick would be one of the most devastating occurrences' of Taylor's enhanced position. *Similar to MacArthur, Taylor picked loyalists to staff the important command positions that came up. And like MacArthur in 1950, the effect would be destructive to the interests of America and the world.*

As the President directed U.S. personnel in MACV were expanding from 3,200 to 11,300 by the end of 1962. Months later they would hit 16,000 in S. Vietnam alone. Almost 5,000 more were in Thailand and Laos. Tasked with missions from military training to civil works, the advisors faced multiple challenges in this foreign land. Harkins however was not an effective war leader and did only what was asked. His time in Vietnam seemed to echo the three monkeys, see no evil, hear no evil and speak no evil.

North Vietnamese troop movements down the Trail had finally reached the Tay Ninh Province west of Saigon! That sector was adjacent to the "Parrot's Beak" area of Cambodia. This location was far from their border, and reflected the capabilities of the NVA. It is the hard to fathom their difficult and successful work in creating the Ho Chi Minh Trail.

NLF leaders in that sector directed many of their NVA troops to begin creation of a base area in Cambodia to be used for training and sanctuary. Their new compound was to train 200-300 soldiers in each cycle on weapons, tactics and operations. And ominously the number of enemy radio stations operating in the South had increased from eleven to twenty nine in a year!

When Lt. Col John Paul Vann was assigned as the advisor to the ARVN 7th Division on March 23, 1962 the area swarmed with over 15,000 native insurgents and invaders from the north. That was three times the level from 1959.

Constant infiltration and conversions were steadily increasing the communist forces fighting this shadowy subversive war. And the ones Vann fought against were well trained, not the pajama clad guerilla fighter most thought of.

Unlike Harkins, Vann had served in combat in the Korean War and his keen eye spotted the telltale signs that this area was not under government control despite what Harkins and his sanitizing staff reported. *The Viet Cong were controlling the initiative and organizing to fight when and where they wanted.*

Sweeps by ARVN units through the countryside were like a ship passing through the sea. The ship could plow through the water, but the sea simply flowed back around it. (And when we took over in 65 it was still the same pattern.)

The people of the South were ambivalent about who ruled for no one ever treats the poor with any concern. Most of the citizens were neutral or assisted the VC in small ways. *Because of the extensive terrorism used by the VC few openly supported Diem.* All they wanted was to be left in peace, from the communists and the government.

Over two million souls lived in this southern area and 85% toiled the soil. They were the most at risk for conversion for they had the most to gain from the communist propaganda. To make a difference out there the S. Vietnamese government had to help these people. *But all of the senior command positions in the ARVN were given out because of loyalty to Diem, not because of capability.* Lt. Col Vann had to cajole, convince and bribe in order to try to motivate his S.V. counterpart Col. Cao.

Despite having spent over 1.5 billion dollars in U.S. aid and equipment since 1955, most of the ARVN soldiers were poor marksmen and had little proficiency in small unit tactics. Their ranks were initially formed by the French, but since 1955 they had been under U.S. standards. *All of the time spent under Generals Williams and McGarr had accomplished nothing for the ARVN.*

Vann observed a key failure of the ARVN and the semi-trained regional forces, they were afraid of the night. When forced to patrol at night most of those units would fake the mission or compromise it by making "accidental noises". Lt. Col. Vann could see that the ARVN were terrified of the VC. This he hoped to change with his leadership and by planning smart battles.

At that time the VC tried to avoid causing U.S. casualties to prevent any excuse for American retaliation. And any U.S. personnel who were wounded or killed were not entitled to any military awards. *Pres. Kennedy hoped to keep this fight low-key to avoid having to explain to the public that America was again at war.*

As stated above, Pres. Kennedy expressly did not want details of the U.S. operations to find there way into the media and he became angry when they did.

His demeanor encouraged those in his Administration to work hard to keep the war a secret. But with the increased presence of Americans in country and with the growing reliance on air attacks, it was inevitable that American deaths and civilian casualties would occur. Gilpatric wanted the obstructionist head of the JCS Gen. Lyman Lemnitzer to establish cover stories in advance of all operations.

Kennedy was increasingly upset that the reporters in Vietnam were able to find the stories and report truthfully. *The news reports were embarrassing and contradicted the party line that JFK and McNamara were spinning.* But the more the administration tried to hide the truth the more it hurt the overall effort in Vietnam.

(The Kennedy years were protected by the progressive and well educated reporters who worked for the "enlightened news organizations". Instead of performing as objective reporters those people liked the Kennedys and insured they had good press relations. After his death all of the books and reports about him mirrored the myths and self-serving versions of the truth.)

Pres. Kennedy wanted an expanded Army capability to help in finding the "flexible response" the U.S. would need in fighting these "limited wars."

Everyone in the administration had observed how the communist guerrillas could buildup, gain support and finally overthrow what had appeared to be a semi-strong government in Cuba. **He instructed the Army that they were to use South Vietnam as a laboratory, to develop the techniques of counter-insurgency.**

Just as JFK had taken office Soviet Premier Khrushchev had publicly stated that the USSR would avoid a nuclear war, but would support all popular uprisings and "wars of liberation" using guerrilla tactics. Most of the U.S. leaders assailed those tactics as wars of subversion and covert aggression. But for the communists the system worked out fine. Had it not been for the Truman Doctrine and the Marshall Plan most of Europe would have fallen along with Greece, Iran and probably Turkey.

Thus the war in South Vietnam was more than a laboratory.

It would be a test of whether the free world or the communist world would prevail.

China

America's leaders paid little attention to the hostility that had appeared between China and Russia. To most, communism was communism whatever flag it flew. And to the West it was the Sino-Soviet block that controlled this communist world.

But unknown to the West, Khrushchev had cutoff all aid to China in 1960 and withdrawn thousands of Russian technicians who had been working in there. Like the split with Yugoslavia in 1948, and Albania in 1961, not everyone followed Russia's lead.

Mao had always distrusted Stalin but had also recognized his leadership in their world. He did not think much of Khrushchev for he did not use the much trumpeted Russian technological and military strengths against the capitalists. And to the hard-liners in China, Khrushchev's perceived failures in Berlin and Cuba were also viewed with suspicion. By 1962 China and Russia had become two separate enemies.
(Both were determined to thwart any American effort wherever they could.)

The Democrats were especially connected to the Sino-Soviet theory since it was they who had been in power when "China was lost". Since then Communist China had become a major provider of material support and inspiration for the other communist movements seeking gains in Asia. In the U.S. many had forlornly hoped that our former ally China would come around, but with their determined and unprovoked effort against us in Korea it was clear that our friendship was past.

Enough Nationalists had escaped and gone across the sea to Taiwan (Formosa), that the U.S. refused to recognize Red China. This allowed the Nationalists to stay on the U.N. Security Council throughout the 50s. When JFK took over in January 1961 the political tide was turning and it seemed that Red China could get accepted into the U.N. in place of Nationalist China. Kennedy hoped to get concessions from the communists in exchange for a seat at the table.

By 1961 Red China was in desperate economic shape, (Great Leap Forward), and the U.S. offered some food aid to try to get things started. But China declared themselves implacable foes to America and her "imperialism". They saw no reason to modify their behavior. (Red China was still involved in the border disputes with India.)

Then in 1962 the Nationalists thought there was a chance to reverse their fortunes. They knew that Russia had isolated Red China in the communist world, and with their economic disaster and mass starvation the aging Chiang felt it time to try to take over. Similar to the failed Bay of Pigs plan, Chiang dreamed that if his small amphibious landings were successful, a popular uprising would begin.

U.S. Intel had noted the dire economic and social circumstances on the mainland, but also recognized that communist control was intact and absolute. Sec. Rusk warned JFK that Chiang's plans were nonsense and could not succeed.

To head Chiang off, the Administration stated publicly that it would not back an assault by Taiwan against Red China.

U.S. Intel briefings showed that the communists were alerted to the danger and moving multiple divisions into the anticipated landing areas. Their action could be for defense, or perhaps another attempt by the Reds to invade the off-shore islands that the Nationalists had taken in the escape in 1949. Yet another crisis had formed.

Any effort to invade by Chiang could be delayed or stonewalled by us, but an attack by Red China could not be affected by words. The U.S. would have to respond with military force. At a June 27 press conference Kennedy stated our basic position on the area and warned that if Red China took aggressive action against the offshore islands, "The U.S. would take action to defend Formosa."

Tense days followed, but by July 5 photo-recon had come in that showed no further increase in communist Chinese military activity. The warning had worked.

Once again it validated the common sense plan that to stay out of a war you have to be prepared to fight one.

Gen. Larius Norstad was retired because he had opposed JFK's views on Europe and his thoughts on graduated response. He was replaced at NATO with the other "obstructionist" Gen. Lemnitzer who had been the Chairman of the JCS.

Gen. Lemnitzer had gone to Vietnam in 1961 and again with McNamara in May 1962. McNamara was in the country for just two days!

Incredibly McNamara came away stating that every quantitative analysis showed we were winning. Hundreds of studies were done by dozens of civilian research groups.

Yet all missed the key points of the war.

Gen Lemnitzer on the other hand was still against fighting in Laos and was convinced that any war in SE Asia would require over 140,000 troops. He also believed that we should plan on using tactical nuclear weapons, as he did not think the American people would tolerate a long slow paced guerrilla war.

And he did not think we were winning in Vietnam.

Because of his "negative attitude", Kennedy realized that promoting Lemnitzer into NATO would get him out of Washington and conveniently open up his spot for an ally as the President could pick his replacement. *JFK broke completely the normal JCS rotation for command and installed his military advisor retired Gen. Maxwell Taylor as the new chairman in 1962!*

(JFK and McNamara forced two other senior officers to retire to complete their takeover of the senior military command.)

In making all of this political intrigue JFK was politicizing the JCS and creating a military panel that he felt would think the way he wanted. Kennedy was again completely wrong.

Having yes-men installed in important positions gave him a common line of thought but not a creative or effective one. And with the President's ear Taylor as head of the JCS now had the power to hand out assignments to his protégés.

That would prove to be one of the worst aspects of JFK's years.

He had a terrible grasp of the people he picked for senior positions.

The three worst were Taylor, McNamara and Lyndon Johnson.

(Even the abrasive De Gaulle understood that vital point.

It was important to have difficult and contentious debates. There was no worse policy than to exclude people who are hard to work with. If you wrongly do that, you will have subordinates that have leanings instead of opinions. You need people who can stand up to the test of great events.)

Back in Vietnam Lt. Col. Vann and his colleagues in the military had watched the post WWII world become transformed into night and day. Those men had resolved themselves to keeping the night at bay.

(Notable speaker and author Col. David Hackworth ret. had like Vann requested a transfer into Vietnam as an advisor. Hackworth had done two tours in Korea and felt he could help the beleaguered ARVN become soldiers. *The bureaucrats in the Army refused his transfer because he had too much combat experience!)*

Vann began going out on night ambush missions and recon patrols to see for himself how the ARVN were doing and to show everyone that the "boss" was out there.

He knew from experience that to survive an ambush you had to push forward into it to break it up. If a unit stayed put they would be continuously exposed to the enemy's fire. The hard part was training your forces to assault into an ambush.

Unlike most of the Americans, Vann actually liked the ARVN soldiers. They were stoic when wounded, could work all day and had a cheerfulness about them. If well led he knew they could win.

The mission that he could see required creating a solid military force that could protect the villagers from the VC, thus creating the security any functioning society needs to thrive. Without that solid foundation, nothing we could do would last.

Vann's weapon of choice was the new Armalite rifle, the AR 15. It was light, had a rapid rate of fire and used a small high velocity round.

The first versions were well made, but the ones given to the U.S. combat units from 1965-67 used cheaper parts and poor powder that would cause jamming and malfunctions. Those rifles would be called the M-16, and the soldiers and Marines hated them. *(The Army had changed the type of powder in the rounds despite the objections from the manufacturer. Jamming was constant and many a GI and marine died with a cleaning rod in his hands.)*

Lt. Col. Vann was able to collect a staff of equally motivated younger officers and NCO's and his Intelligenec chief was named Jim Drummond. It takes time to sift through all of the radio chatter, battlefield debris and verbal reports to build up an Intelligence profile. But slowly his staff began to unravel the clues as to where and how the VC trained and operated.

(As hard as it is to believe MACV was just starting the same Intel program. No dedicated intelligence profile had been conducted under MAAG!!)

In making a profile, a pattern of enemy movements was developed such as when they entered a village the common peasant traffic was reduced. To a trained eye the VC safe houses stood out from the villagers homes, and roads through VC controlled countryside would have ditches dug across them to prevent vehicle traffic. (Before the use of helicopters and observation planes this would have gone unnoticed until someone crashed into it.)

A program had just started in which all radio traffic in Vietnam was being recorded and analyzed by over 400 ASA technicians. In that way specific radio communication could be pinpointed to specific units. Soon after the Intel people could actually "fix" the location of the radio itself, and even identify the user.

By June Vann and his staff were using planned and systematic attacks on the VC. They used helicopter assaults to bring in the ARVN attackers, and then a blocking force behind the VC to trap them. Vann also used the U.S. made M-113 APC, (armored personnel carrier), to speed across more open areas and crash into the assault.

The APC's had a .50 cal heavy machine gun that could savage most fieldworks and defenses, and the vehicle could crush or slam through most obstacles and men.

They also held a squad of soldiers in relative safety until dropping them off at the fight.

At that time the VC did not have anti-armor weapons.

Those well planned battles killed and captured many VC, who in turn would yield more intelligence about the area. (The same situation as the later Phoenix Program.)

Also captured were hundreds of weapons including many that had been taken or sold from the regional forces and base areas. (Corrupt ARVN would sell weapons and supplies to the enemy.) Vann's stock rose at MACV, but he needed to turn the timid Cao into a tiger and crush the VC in this sector.

(Vann said Cao was actually a mere kitten who could swagger but would not fight.)

Near the Cambodian border Vann and his staff caught a VC battalion in their patented trap. Just as the ARVN units were about to slam the door shut Col. Cao cancelled the rest of the mission.(??) All the U.S. advisors could do was to coach the ARVN commanders, which Vann tried, but Cao would hear no more.

Dozens of vital senior enemy commanders escaped into Cambodia.

Found at the battle scene were communist training manuals and other intelligence that showed this camp was actually a communist training school on how to shoot down the U.S. helicopters. Because of Cao most of those vital enemy instructors had also escaped into Cambodia. Back in Saigon, Diem and Cao played the story as if it were a great victory.

But Vann's after action report was accurate and scathing in his assessment of Cao and other commanders. The ARVN had an "institutional unwillingness" to close with and fight the highly motivated VC. (This was the same problem Vann and other U.S. commanders saw in many of the Korean troops that first year, there were few good officers.)

Vann complained to Gen. Harkins that the poor commanders in the ARVN were kept on, while the good leaders get dismissed if their units take casualties.

Petty jealousies were the norm, and unless this condition was rectified and the entire ARVN retrained, no acceptable combat capability could be achieved. Vann put a lot on the line with this report, but Harkins simply filed it away.

In Vann's first four months over 4,000 VC had been killed or captured in his sector, the same number as had occurred in the rest of South Vietnam! Because this was a war without "front lines", the only way to measure success against the VC was in the "body count". Over time the liars and schemers realized that to have success they needed good "numbers". (The lie Winterbottom had done months before.) This scam was repeated up the chain and inflated the "success" that was claimed. And this lie was done throughout the war as those seeking promotions fabricated "the body count to get ahead.

Vann would not play that numbers game, but then he did not have to.

Occasionally a dignitary would drop by for a chat and Vann would try to convince them that all was not well in S. Vietnam. But Gen. Harkins and his staff would pour the drinks over dinner and smooth things out. Anything needed was done to keep the lie going.

The Dept. of Defense sent a team of Intel people over to formulate an order of battle profile from the offices at MACV. It took weeks of hard work checking, double-checking and investigating all of the intelligence available. By mid-April they had found a figure they were confident in. **There were over 40,000 VC operating in SVN.**

Harkin's Intel chief Col. Winterbottom became upset demanding the team "massage the numbers" because McNamara would never accept them. (And MACV would get into hot water.)

Harkins concurred, and the two officers cooked the books to insure the true state of SVN was kept quite. **The enemy numbers were reduced down to 20,000.**

Col. Cao continued to reduce the night patrols and Vann's training programs. Then Vann's Intel staff realized that even with all of their many small victories the VC troop numbers were still going up. (Just as the DoD team had found.)

Unlike the staff at MACV, Vann's staff did not change the numbers.

Col. Porter who was Vann's CO wanted to eliminate the local militias since they appeared to be the source of most of the lost weapons and ammo. (Those were the supplies Vann and his men kept finding in their attacks.) As time went on the VC firepower was becoming the equal of the ARVN causing more casualties and making it even harder to get them to fight.

It had been decided by MAAG and then MACV that the South Vietnamese had to have an Air Force, and it was called the VNAF. Because of the lack of pilots and candidates the planes were usually piloted by an American with a Vietnamese riding with him. In this way the Kennedy Administration could call it a "training mission", in case it was shot down.

But using aircraft to attack the hidden enemy in Vietnam was foolish because at the height and speeds the planes flew at it was impossible to tell who was who.

Vann continually complained that the U.S./ARVN air attacks and artillery fire were causing more casualties to the civilians than to the enemy. And that resulted in increased conversions to the communist side. Vann correctly saw the war as a political war which meant you had to use discrimination in your attacks. (Like Malaya.) For him the best weapon to use was a knife. The next best was a rifle. The worst thing to use was an airplane and second worst was artillery.

But Harkins and his USAF counterparts could point to their graphs and charts and claim success. And that was based on McNamara's new way of "running the military, using statistics".

In 1961 there were only 400 USAF personnel in country.

In 1962 after Kennedy's buildup began there were more than 2,000. More flights out meant more ordnance dropped, and increased numbers of dead VC, whoever they were from that high up.

(Remember reader, Statistics don't lie, but liars sure know how to use them.)

Vann and Col. Porter would use helicopter over-flights to try to convince Harkins that things were not going well. But Harkins was not a Patton for he never would go out into the field. It became impossible to persuade him to the reality of the war, and as time went by he no longer cared to hear from Vann or Porter at all.

Soon they would rotate out and those two problems would be gone.

Diem and his upper ranks of the South Vietnamese were indifferent to the plight of the peasants. The majority of the peasants were non-Catholics and for the most part invisible to Diem and his family. This caste system was one component of why Diem could not connect to the people of S. Vietnam. His imperious manner caused him to believe himself above these peasant people, not with them. And the peasants did not connect to him either.

That segregation was even worse for the Montagnards. In Vietnam they were known as the mountain people, rough, uncivilized and looked down upon.

It was the Special Forces soldiers who took them in, trained them and turned them into outstanding militia forces. By mid-62 over 100,000 Montagnards were living in well protected villages. Their militias teamed up with SF soldiers to patrol keeping the communists away. Their outstanding work in the Central Highlands was an example of their capabilities, and of successful counterinsurgency.

Even Ngo Dinh Nhu (Diems brother and security chief), came away impressed with the work done by the SF teams. Enemy units took losses and learned they did not own those areas. (Soon after ARVN SF teams teamed up with ours to learn their trade.)

But the one group that should have looked upon the Special Forces counter-insurgency work and realized the positive implications were at MACV.

But they never went into the hinterlands to see for themselves.

Communist propaganda ministers and enforcers would enter villages when the government forces were gone. They would tell the villagers what they wanted to hear, and a percentage would convert after each session. The communists paid for their food and helped in the fields to show the peasants solidarity.

Diem's government officials never did that.

As time went by the VC and their converts were slowly taking over.

When a tribal chief or pro-government leader spoke out against the communists they and their families would be publicly tortured and murdered.

Just in case the peasants missed the point.

Another one of those "bright ideas" that didn't work was the strategic hamlet program. In Malaya the British had used the hamlets to isolate the incoming communists. It took years of effort but it did work because the villagers wanted the security and accepted the hamlets. Diem was a catholic and believed that if they moved the Vietnamese villagers into barbed wire hamlets they too could keep the VC out.

But Vietnam was not Malaya. The Vietnamese have a curious religion that is a mix of Buddhism, ancestor worship and animism. They worshipped their ancestral homes and graves, and despised the government for forcing them out. *Even the cowardly Cao had warned Diem that the Strategic Hamlet program could not work in Vietnam.*

In forcing the Vietnamese villagers into those hamlets required that they also had to walk miles to get to their fields. What everyone forgot, missed or ignored was that once the villagers left the hamlet to work the fields the VC would still be out there with them. None of the ARVN troops were.

The program quickly bred corruption and a black market creating even more strikes against Diem and his government. Over time the population that was forced from their homes by the heavy handed government turned to their only hope, the communists.

Diem and his ruling family realized early on that the Americans could be verbally bullied, and if you lied to them they seldom checked on what you said.

They stated whatever some U.S. official wanted to hear and went through the motions of creating a stable country. During those years Diem and his family eagerly accepted the massive amounts of U.S. aid that landed on his doorstep.

And like Chiang in China, much of that aid was "lost".

After seven years of extensive and expensive effort nothing in the South was improving.

Diem had not served under French Rule, so he was not "tainted" as a collaborator. He was an ardent anti-communist and a Christian which appealed too many in the West. But by singling out the minority Catholics for power against the majority of the Vietnamese people, America was acting just like the French.

(The hated French had instituted their foreign religious beliefs into the country. Then they converted many Vietnamese to it and used those "Catholics" to assist their rule.)

In his earlier superficial meetings in America in 1952, Diem had impressed Senators Mike Mansfield and John Kennedy. (Mansfield became Senate Majority Leader when LBJ became Vice President.) With all of the other problems filling the world in the early 50s, (including the just ended war in Korea), it had been hoped that Diem was to be "our man in Vietnam". But even after having been exposed to French and American Democracy, Diem did not believe in representative government.

Diem looked to dynastic rule as his goal.

Gen. Ed Lansdale was sent back to Vietnam to check on his protégé`. As stated earlier the U.S. did not want a colonial empire, but only America could supply what was needed to try to check the worldwide communist advances.

The post war hope was that using native rulers would resonate with the local people and the U.S. would only have to provide aid to prop up the regimes.

It was not a perfect system, but it was the only one that could be found in the power vacuums that were created from WWII and the First Indo-China war.

(Once again the problem was one of having an anti-communist ruler despite his faults, versus allowing another nation to turn communist. The reader must also remember that none of these former colonies had any recent history of self-rule, leadership nor democracy. All of those nations would have to start out as new entities ruled by autocratic leaders. Some were good, most were not.)

After their defeat at Dien Bien Phu the French forces were broken.

The U.S. had to get involved to give the South any chance at freedom.

Lansdale and his assistant Lou Concin worked tirelessly during the 50's to setup the Diem regime. They had organized stay behind teams to operate in N. Vietnam and had been the driving force in relocating the 900,000 non-communists out of the North. They also made sure that counterfeit money was left behind to try to ruin the North's currency. Their rumors and plots distracted and delayed the communists and their efforts.

But all of the agents and senior policy makers working in the region and the Eisenhower Administration knew that the communists would eventually make a move south. That was one of the reasons the rush to pick Diem was made.

The many problems the communists in the North caused themselves, and those made by Lansdale's maneuverings had bought seven years of time.

But Diem, Williams, McGarr and then Harkins had wasted the effort.

One factor that trumps all others is time.
And you can never make up for wasting it.

Secretary of Defense McNamara personified the arrogant corporate boss of the late 1950-1960's America. His imperious manner made him feel incapable of being wrong. *In one month in 1961 he made 692 major decisions!*

Not once did he doubt his calls nor did he ever look back to see if his plan was actually working. He regarded that aspect of his nature as a virtue.

His specialty was in statistics and management orthodoxy.

McNamara and his whiz kids did good work in cutting costs and organizing the logistical side of things saving the nation millions. But he and they knew nothing of how anything in the military actually worked. All that mattered were the numbers.

Incredibly after just a few months in power McNamara and his staff actually felt that they had a firm grasp on military strategy, tactics and management. He overrode advice from everyone creating a real concern in the Pentagon. Many of his younger staff were too young to remember WWII, and some even to young for Korea. They knew next to nothing about anything and became the poster children for the generation gap. As time went on the military bureaucracy they were re-creating was becoming a huge, paralyzed mess. There were so many assistants to assistants that the Pentagon became a city. And that vital issue McNamara did not address.

His first actual visit to Vietnam was in May of 1962 with Gen. Lemnitzer. McNamara had been making hundreds of vital decisions on policy and National Security during those first 15 months in power. And dozens upon dozens of them were about a country and situation he had never even seen!

As stated earlier, after his *two day whirlwind tour* he gave a press conference that everywhere he went he could see progress and hope.
He returned to Washington to brief the President that all was well.

(This arrogance and imprudence underscored the great weakness of John Kennedy and almost everyone in his Administration. Though they may have been well educated, where as Harry Truman was not, there is a great difference between intelligence and wisdom.)

Pressure from the Administration finally forced the Laotians to form a coalition government. On June 23, 1962 Souvanna Phouma became the Prime Minister with General Phoumi and Prince Souphanouvong acting as deputy Prime Ministers.

All three had to agree on any action. They declared a ceasefire, rejected SEATO, and declared Laos neutral. All other nationalities were told to leave.

The Geneva Declaration was presented at a conference in Geneva on July 6 and the agreements signed by all nations involved. Pres. Kennedy directed all of our efforts stop and all personnel to leave Laos and Thailand.

Around a thousand U.S. and Filipino technicians departed through the ICC checkpoint. Only 40 out of over 10,000 NVA troops did!

As always the communists delayed and obstructed at every turn.

And the ICC, (International Control Commission) was unarmed and incapable of forcing the issue.

The Rand Corporation had just completed a study highlighting the Pathet Lao and NVA forces in lower Laos. Their study warned that the communists controlled the entire Annamite Chain of mountains all along the common border. To stop this enemy infiltration would require extensive defense at the border and would be heavily challenged.

The United States made no issue nor created a casus belli of this known deception. Acceptance of those overwhelming NVA forces from group 959 was the price JFK paid to "neutralize Laos". But the price the president was willing to pay would imperil all of Indochina as the NVA continued to move forces south through Laos and Cambodia along the Ho Chi Minh Trail.

At MACV intelligence teams quickly saw the impact on SVN. But again Harkins worked to suppress the reports. Harkins irrationally told Diem that the SF camps at Aloui and in the Ashau Valley would stop the NVA infiltration from Laos. But that was impossible with their low numbers and firepower.

No one in the Administration would admit that what they had done was wrong.

On July 23, 1962 Harkins met McNamara in Honolulu.

His reports always stated progress on all fronts even though this was just three days after the battle where Col Cao had allowed over 100 senior VC to escape into Cambodia. Vann had included an up to date report on his sector and that battle, but Harkins was able to play it off.

The strategic hamlet program was progressing at full steam and generated tons of data and statistics. McNamara was impressed, but the data meant nothing.

The peasants hated the program and it was rife with corruption.

Harkins ended the briefing with this, "There is no doubt that we are on the winning side!"

One disturbing facet on the faked intelligence from Harkins and his staff was the existence of the monthly battle maps that showed the site and size of the enemy force.

It was clear for all who wanted to see the increased communist effort plotted on those maps. It was also evident that MACV was lying about who was winning.

(Special Forces camps had been opened all over I & II Corps in northern and central Vietnam. Everywhere they went they found heavy enemy forces.)

A report from the Embassy in June highlighted that the VC were winning the battles and the support of the people.

On 9/11/62 at a MACV luncheon with the Chairman of the JCS Gen. Maxwell Taylor, Lt. Col. Vann again hoped to highlight the myriad problems that he and his team were witnessing first hand. Once more Harkins overrode all of Vann's key points.

When Taylor returned to Washington he too reported on what "his man" Harkins had presented, that things were going well. Once more the evidence was right in front of them that things were not what they seemed.

And then Cuba again became the focus.

Cuba

Air clashes had occurred around Cuba for weeks.
A recent U-2 photo-recon overflight had caused a hostile reaction, but it was vital for the Administration to gather the information about the arms buildup on the island.

And if violating Cuban airspace was needed so be it.
(Robert Kennedy stated, "Let's sustain the overflights and the hell with international issues".) (43)

On October 1, 1962 Gen. Taylor his colleagues in the Pentagon were given a secret briefing on Cuba. It was possible that ballistic missiles were being setup.
With the exception of CIA's McCone, most of the Administration dismissed the report.

The mid-term elections were at hand and JFK wanted Cuba to stay off of the front page.

Since January of 62 polls had consistently showed that Americans wanted something done about Cuba. Their potential threat to us was growing and the everyday citizens wanted some sort of action taken. The last thing the Democrats needed was more bad news from Cuba.

On the other side of the equation, the Bay of Pigs disaster, the U.S. trade embargo and the many small acts of sabotage had convinced Khrushchev that he had to act to save Cuba from us. Kennedy's failure to act during the Bay of Pigs and their meeting in Vienna convinced the Russian leader that JFK was also weak and could be intimidated.

Back on April 12, 1962 the Soviet Presidium approved sending 180 SA-2 anti-aircraft missiles to Cuba to stop any potential U.S. air attack. At that time Russia had just 20 ICBM's while America had dozens.

To counter this potential strategic threat Khrushchev decided to send medium range nuclear missiles to Cuba. He was certain that his plan would complicate any potential U.S. first strike attack on Russia. The Soviet staff in Cuba warned him that Castro would not agree to foreign military bases in his country without a declared military alliance.

But by May 24 after many private sessions Castro had been talked into accepting the missiles as a guarantee of his safety from any potential American invasion.

(Castro was not aware of just how strategically weak the Russians really were.)

The Soviet – Cuban missile base plan envisioned 60 medium range missiles housed in 40 launchers. They would be protected by 45,000 Russian troops with 250 armored vehicles. Also included were 42 Russian fighter jets and a submarine base for eleven Russian submarines. **Seven of those would also carry nuclear missiles.**

Senior Soviet Military staffs stated that deception could be achieved in their setup operations and the weapons in place before the U.S. elections in November 1962.(??)

During July 1962 Raul Castro had gone to Moscow for more meetings over the weapons shipments. A short time later the SA-2 anti-aircraft missile batteries began showing up in Cuba. Those modern missiles threatened even the high flying U-2 spy planes, but more importantly their presence implied that there was something special that needed defending.

It was confirmed in late August by photo-recon that the SAM sites were being setup and that thousands of Russians were being stationed in Cuba. To the conservative McCone at the CIA that meant that Russian nuclear missiles must be there. His thoughts were predicated on how we were protecting our medium range weapons that were currently based in Italy and Turkey.

His view of this potential calamity was his alone as no one else in the administration felt that the Russians would be so bold.

Previous staff meetings on Cuba had discussed just this possibility and were always strained as to the course of action it would require. Numerous work groups had been held to try to decide what world-wide affect all of this and our actions could have.

(One interesting study, NSAM-181 dealt with taking our missiles out of Turkey as a trade-off.)

On October 1 the previously mentioned intelligence briefing was held.

A day later Senator Keating of New York "cited reports" that Soviet technicians and antiaircraft missiles were entering Cuba. **The Administration denied it.**

The President knew politically there was no way Russian missiles could be allowed to remain in Cuba. Constant complaints had been directed at him and his Administration as "being soft on communism." JFK's reaction to the criticisms was to limit those intelligence briefings to his "most trusted advisors". *He was terrified of "leaks".*

Continued intelligence efforts soon reported that a large scale Russian military presence was taking shape on the island. Soviet Ambassador Anatoly Dobrynin was called in and warned of U.S. concerns. He stated that Khrushchev had told him that nothing would be done to unsettle America's internal politics before the election.

(Was this an attempt to buy off the Democrats so they could hold onto the reigns of power? Or a hint that nothing bad would happen until after the election?)

Days later JFK publicly stated, "If at any time the Communist buildup in Cuba were to endanger our security in any way or if Cuba should try to export its aggressive purposes by force, or become an offensive military base for the Soviet Union, then this country will do whatever must be done to protect our security and that of our allies." *A second message was back-channeled to Khrushchev asking if he desired better relations with the U.S.*

On October 6, Khrushchev's reply came back stating that only defensive weapons were being supplied and that no action would be taken until after the election. *Khrushchev then upped the ante by sending 80 nuclear armed cruise type missiles, six Luna rocket launchers which had two short range missiles each and carried small tactical nuclear warheads, nuclear bombs for the Il-28 bombers which were now also being sent and nuclear depth charges!* (The existence of the Luna rockets was not made public for thirty years!)

Work on the SS-4 medium missile sites was speeded up. *The Soviets realized that we knew what they were doing and were rushing the construction in the hope that everything could be emplaced before America could act.*

Khrushchev had wanted to send the medium range missiles in secretly by plane but the Russian military convinced him to send them by ship. Their camouflage efforts were poorly done, and the missiles were spotted and photographed.

Intel analysts continued to doubt themselves by claiming that Russia would not be risking so much on such a foolish move. But satellite photos and U-2 flights continued to bring back the damaging proof. Reports from the few observers still in Cuba also stated that large areas were being cleared of all civilians and military convoys carrying large, long cylinders had been spotted in mid-September.

On October 10 intelligence reports confirmed 15 active SA-2 SAM sites, large numbers of Soviet troops, sightings of SS-4 missiles and peculiar activity in the Pinar del Rio Province. Anxiety levels jumped and the JCS was tasked to discuss options.

Two options were presented; an air strike to eliminate the missiles, or an air strike followed by an invasion. The Navy would be tasked to blockade Cuba to isolate them for the coming war.

On October 11 McNamara and Paul Nitze joined the JCS in a briefing. Discussed were the various sources that highlighted the increased (since July) Soviet shipping heading towards Cuba. *In the briefing was information from the French Embassy in Cuba describing missiles being trucked around Cuba in the dead of night.*

McCone then showed JFK photos of Russian bombers sitting in crates on a newly built airfield. *Kennedy's main concern centered on the photos not getting to the media for they could cause him and the Democrats a crisis prior to the election!*

The Administration continued to publicly deny all reports that Cuba was being turned into a missile base. National Security Advisor Bundy even went on television and refuted the claims made by Senator Keating who had learned of the photos and spoke of them. (Obama did the same over Benghazi.)

McNamara then directed the JCS to plan on invading the island and overthrowing the hated Castro. The JCS requested additional U-2 overflights so they could have up to date intelligence on the numerous enemy units, but JFK refused them.

He was afraid of the potential political costs with the election so close.

Sec-State Rusk warned that the U.N. and neighboring nations would object to any military action taken by us. By Oct 14th Kennedy had relented on the U-2 overflights and the latest photos clearly showed the construction of missile sites, plus the Il 28 bombers in crates on San Julian airfield.

After dinner on the 15th Sec. Rusk told Nitze that the photos from a U-2 proved that nuclear missiles were in Cuba.

On October 16 public reports surfaced that additional missiles had arrived in Cuba. Kennedy was told of the latest findings on the morning of the 16th, and yelled, "He can't do that to me!" (44)

JFK had to walk a political tightrope as the missiles he and his Administration had said were not there suddenly were seen and now he had to act. The JCS asked for mobilizing the reserves, around 150,000 troops. Most of the naval units had already gone to sea and were ready for war. At the same time the USAF began sending dozens of fighters and bombers plus loads of ammunition into the southern U.S.

Word of this military activity began to get out.

With the intelligence concerning Cuba coming in regularly a crisis group had been established, the *EXCOM.* (Executive Committee of the National Security Council).

Present was Robert Kennedy, Dean Rusk, McNamara, Nitze, Sec. of Treasury Douglas Dillon, McGeorge Bundy, George Ball, a few other advisors and Gen. Taylor.

The JCS was excluded from those discussions.
They were updated only when Taylor returned from the White House.

Over the next 13 days JFK and this group of civilians would argue and discuss the future of the world.

In their first meeting a firm political objective was established, to eliminate the bases. One of the many facets of this problem (to Kennedy) was the question of whether the Soviets were orchestrating all of this and preparing a new offensive against Berlin for after the election. Berlin preyed on the President's mind and may have actually added a constraint to his actions. (In May a small fight had broken out over an attempted escape.)

Kennedy warned the JCS that if we attacked Cuba the Russians would move on Berlin. And naturally our allies would blame us for any conflict. JFK also worried that politically he and the Democrats would be viewed as soft on communism just before the election. (I never realized that anyone or group could be so self-centered to be worried about their standing during a global crisis such as this.)

For over a hundred and fifty years the Monroe Doctrine had tried to keep the Americas free from the European power struggles. WWII had brought sea battles and losses to the region, but now it appeared that the ultimate challenge was at hand.

(Polls routinely showed most Americans were with Kennedy over Berlin but against him on his failed Cuba policy.)

Castro had actually wanted the Russians to publicly announce that they were going to build the bases. In that way there would be no surprise to the U.S. leaders and a hurried and potentially dangerous reaction instituted. If Khrushchev had done that, Kennedy's political problems would have been far worse. Instead of reacting to this "surprise danger" and thus having the nation behind them, the Administration would have had to face a potential problem that was being done openly.

During the discussions on the 17th it was felt by some that this aggressive move was designed to get us to give in on Berlin and the German question. Some felt this action could also be a reaction to the Russian split with China, in which the Chinese accused Russia of giving up the revolution.

Tommy Thompson brought up the question of a tit for tat move over our placing Jupiter missiles in Turkey. (Months ago.)

On October 18 JFK met with Russian Foreign Minister Andre Gromyko who displayed no reaction to the president's words. President Kennedy read his dispatches and warnings but did not show the Russian any proof of what we knew. (Perhaps he should have.)

One thing that JFK did get across was the reason for our concerns and the basis for the deal that ultimately solved the crisis. *Gromyko's swift report to Moscow outlined how JFK had stated on five occasions that no invasion of Cuba would occur and that he was willing to give assurances.*

With this obvious weakness clearly visible on the President's part, Gromyko felt that the overall situation was completely satisfactory for Russia. He stated that U.S. plans to invade Cuba have been shelved because of Russia's courage.

The intent of his message was for Russia to continue with the buildup.

Then to make the foreign disaster stew even worse, Red China was again fighting with India over their common border. This was actually perfect timing for China with America and the West preoccupied with a potential nuclear war over Cuba.

"There are Tigers in the World,"
and They are always Watching. (45)

The Russians became distressed as they did not want any further tensions in the world that might provoke a nuclear response. And they had their own designs for India. For them the Chinese were just complicating everything.

In India the border battles were increasing as they were fighting on two fronts over an old demarcation line that had been setup by the British.

Normally the presence of nuclear missiles near our shores would have been the perfect pretext for invading. Those Cuban based Russian medium range missiles had the reach to destroy most of the Strategic Air Command bases and cities in America. Added to the Cuban threat were over 500 medium and intermediate range Russian missiles spread throughout eastern Russia. Those missiles could reach all of Europe's Capitols and NATO bases and defeat our forward most strategic capabilities. It was again possible to be checkmated quickly as at that time there was no early warning radars that could detect those missiles.

With all of the other problem areas in the world it was felt by many of the principals that if we invaded we would then be committed to Cuba for a long time, as had happened in Korea. Should that occur it could hinder any other world-wide efforts we might need to make. (That same line of thinking was used on most of the crisis that occurred, including those with Truman.) Preparations for a potential invasion of Cuba were continuing despite the deadlocked discussions at EXCOM. Almost 90,000 troops were moving to Florida, hundreds of aircraft had arrived plus over 150 ships.

U.S. estimates as to Russian troop levels had started at 8,000, and on Oct 22 were raised to 10,000. Two days later it was raised to 22,000.?? *In actuality there were already 41,000 Soviet combat and support troops on the island!*

(Even in Cuba just 90 miles from our shores our "intelligence guesses" at enemy troop strengths were dead wrong.)

Photo analysts had spotted and logged the operational Mig-21 fighters, the Il 28 bombers, the increase to 144 SA-2 missiles, and the Luna rockets. What had not yet been seen were the nuclear warheads or the bunkers housing them. Battlefield estimates came in for around 18,000 U.S. casualties if we invaded, more if the nukes were armed. But again this was just a guess for no one had any idea what the invasion would precipitate.

With the increasing threat from Cuba the Navy sent nine Polaris Missile boats to the N. Atlantic to surround northern Russia. Each boat carried 16 missiles that could go 1,000 miles. If war came it would be devastating.

As the war planning continued surgical air strikes directed solely at the missile sites became the most promising plan. Follow up questions concerned how the strikes should be conducted, surprise attacks vs forewarned. Gen. Taylor warned Robert Kennedy that we could never achieve a 100% take-out of their nuclear missiles. That meant a possible nuclear strike against the U.S. would follow.

(Strange how when Taylor gave that warning Pres. Kennedy and company accepted it, but when Gen. Norstad at NATO had given the same counsel he was retired.)

After the past days of meetings the JCS wanted to bomb the sites and then invade.

A year earlier Kennedy and his politicos had been able to deflect the criticism of the Bay of Pigs failure onto the JCS and CIA. The Military Chiefs were growing incensed that at this critical juncture they were again being ignored. Neither Taylor nor McNamara seemed to care about any input from them.

Sec. Rusk asked if we should bother worrying about the missiles at all for the Russians knew that any attack on us from any source would mean destruction upon Russia. McNamara and Dillon wanted to hit Cuba with just one large airstrike before their missiles became operational. Bundy who also wanted to hit the missiles remarked that the punishment fits the crime. They were warned not to do this publicly, now we would have to strike. The President was bombarded with more questions than answers for no one knew how the Soviets would react to anything we did.

(A recent Soviet defector had warned, in a report called the Ironbark Papers, that due to the great differences in naval strength, any war with the U.S. was to be countered with the heavy use of tactical nuclear weapons upon our ships and submarines.)

By the 18th, four levels of air attack had been worked out. The favored was using a small air strike that could go in unannounced to hit the missiles. If the Russians were forewarned of our position then a larger strike would be needed because of expected losses. Other scenarios used multiple small or large strikes. The JCS still wanted a comprehensive airstrike to take out everything, and then invade Cuba. But the Kennedys again began to reflect on Europe.

The Europeans had lived under the communist guns for years and might view the U.S. reaction as "hysterical."

Slowly the idea of a naval blockade was changed from helping the war effort to preventing a war. Politically it was viable and a blockade meant that no irrevocable acts were committed to start the shooting. By the afternoon of the 18th the blockade idea was the one in the fore. CIA's McCone mentioned that it had to be a total blockade otherwise we would still be stuck with Castro and the communists. Taylor worried that while we waited for the blockade to succeed the missiles that were present would become operational. Then we might have to invade to ensure that all of them were gone.

On Friday Oct 19th, the JCS were convinced that war was coming and that it would be better to hit them hard immediately. USAF Gen Curtiss LeMay told JFK that we were approaching the threat level of Munich in 1938. We had to act now.

The rest of the JCS agreed, calling his inaction a greater threat.
Kennedy was beside himself.

Rusk then came up with a legal trick by calling the blockade a quarantine. This would allow an "escalation" up to blockade if required. It also sounded less threatening and gave the Russians some room to maneuver. JFK readily agreed.

This "quarantine" however could not stop planes or subs from coming into Cuba, nor the use of the weapons that were present. (Navy photo-recon planes buzzed across Cuba numerous times bringing back detailed photos of equipment, units and even personnel.)

This quarantine was not a solution, just a way to buy more time.

On the 20th the planning for it was completed and given to the White House. Monday October 22, final briefings for the air strikes still showed at best a 90% take out of the Russian missiles. Since this option could not guarantee success JFK decided that we should implement the blockade.

That evening Pres. Kennedy gave a speech that had been crafted with great care. He informed the American people that sites for Russian missiles had been discovered in Cuba. Steps would be taken to get them removed.

First a strict quarantine of all offensive weapons being shipped to Cuba would be implemented.

Second continued close surveillance would be conducted and the armed forces were to prepare for any eventualities.

Third, any missile fired from Cuba was to be considered an attack from the Soviet Union and would be met with a full retaliatory attack upon them. (MAD)

JFK called upon Khrushchev to work with the U.S. to pull the world back from the abyss of destruction. Any further Soviet threats would be met with determination.

Particular emphasis was placed on Berlin. Americans were also warned that it could not be foreseen where this crisis would lead or what cost or casualties could be incurred.

His speech had achieved political surprise.

(Again thanks to administration deceit and helpful people in the media who were told to hold off on the story due to "national security".)

Harold Macmillan the British P.M. sent a letter expressing sympathy for our problem and a warning that Khrushchev might try to trade Cuba for Berlin. This must not be allowed as it will endanger NATO's unity. The initial Soviet response to the speech was muted and railed against the blockade with the usual communist warnings. Khrushchev however spoke privately to U.S. businessman William Knox and admitted the presence of the missiles.

He also told him that if any Soviet ships were sunk his submarines would retaliate.

(The Russian subs were instructed to use nuclear torpedoes.)

At 930 PM Robert Kennedy met in secret with Soviet Ambassador Dobrynin. (He was told that as of that time all Russian ships were continuing on to Cuba.) Their clandestine meetings would decide the crisis.

By 1000 am on the 24th the quarantine was in effect.

It took a while for the Navy to actually identify the ships that could carry offensive weapons and two were scheduled to hit the "blockade line" around noon the next day.

A Russian sub was escorting the ships and it was tension of the highest order.

The U.S. Navy was trailing the noisy Russian subs and upon the start of the shooting had orders to sink all of the Russian ships. One eighth of our bomber force was airborne at all times, ready to fly to Russia to drop their nuclear bombs.

At 1025 am on the 24th McCone had news that 16 ships approaching the quarantine line had turned back. It turned out that the Russians decided they did not want any of their equipment to be seized, especially the nukes. Their cargo ship Poltava was carrying SS-5 IRB missiles. They had a longer range of 2200 miles which would cover most of the U.S. and Canada!

By the morning of the 25th it was confirmed that 14 ships had turned back, but 5 tankers and 3 cargo ships had continued on. The first tanker that hit the line had been challenged and had claimed to be carrying petroleum. It was allowed through, which was significant for it showed that the U.S. was displaying an equivocal attitude towards enforcement.

The first ship boarded was a Lebanese registered ship the *Marcula*.

It had been loaded in Riga, Latvia, and was stopped, inspected and allowed to proceed.

On the 27th the tanker *Groznyy* was carrying a cargo of ammonia.
The Navy wanted to stop this ship and commanders had rounds loaded in their canons warning the ship to stop.

Again heated arguments took place in EXCOM over what cargo to stop and what type of "command" was needed. The "administration doves" won this call and the Navy was told to let this Russian ship through. Ship commanders followed orders, but then "cleared their guns" by firing the rounds! The shots landed close enough to the *Groznyy* to alarm the captain. He radioed Moscow and then reversed course.
(Firing the guns was a unwise mistake that could have started the war.)

All during those tense days the work on the missile sites had continued.

EXCOM was in a quandary over how to deal with that aspect of the Cuban problem. McNamara wanted to use low-level surveillance as a way to make the Russians react "without using force". Low level flights would also get better pictures, but the big gamble would be if a plane was shot down. Those flights were announced to the world and it was stated that they would go in unarmed. At 1040 am the first recon flights were approved and flown without incident.

McNamara and Kennedy were leaning towards adding petroleum to the embargo list. Cuba was totally dependent on those imports and its economy would crash within six months. Air strike proponents still pitched their case as the SS-4 medium range ballistic missiles, (MRBM), were now considered operational. Warhead storage sites had been identified for those 1100 mile range weapons. It would take 6-8 hours to arm the missiles once the launch order was given.

McCone and his analysts noted that the missile batteries were not easily moved and thus could be taken out in one strike. But the same nagging question continued to come up, what if some of the missiles were missed and then fired at us?

(And this dear reader is why it is so vital to have a missile defense system in place. It does no good to hit back when you have just lost a state or three! Obama closed our MDS- Missile Defense Program just after taking office. Why)?

At the U.N. General Assembly Ambassador Stevenson spoke on the 25th about the crisis and embarrassed his Soviet counterpart Zorin by showing the world the photos of the missiles. Stevenson sent *EXCOM* questions for the next day's deliberations and hit on one special topic.
What would be the Administrations attitude if, (as he predicted), the Russians asked for guarantees of safety for Cuba and the dismantling of our missiles in Turkey? Rusk reiterated that under the prior Rio Treaty, Cuba was safe from any unprovoked invasion. That second question of his proposal was quite different.

Turkey was instrumental in helping the West contain Russia by helping to prevent their takeover and infiltration of Iran since 1945. They were the bulwark of NATO's defense of the eastern Mediterranean and their troops had fought valiantly in Korea during the first all out war between the West and Communism.

In 1959 Pres. Eisenhower had agreed to give Turkey 15 Jupiter medium range nuclear missiles under a dual key arrangement.
(That meant that both countries were needed to fire the missiles.)

Those missiles had just been given over in a ceremony, and Turkey attached considerable importance to this agreement.

Days earlier Stevenson had given his assessment that we should abandon the Guantanamo Naval Base, (which we had used since 1936), and exchange our Jupiter missiles in Turkey with those in Cuba before we did anything rash.

Bundy had also raised the possibility of a quid pro quo for the missile bases.

After a while McNamara, JFK and Ball also supported the idea, and they even added in the Italian based missiles to the offer if need be.

Not long after this very idea was being discussed in political and diplomatic circles as a way out. (*Nitze however disagreed with them. The West was not infiltrating and attempting to takeover the world, the communists were.*)

Columnist Walter Lippmann had mentioned that exact scenario in an article in the NY Times on the 23. His article showed how *we had boxed the Russians in* with our forward deployed medium range missiles. His next column proposed a publicly viewed trade off, and he was not contradicted by the White House.

On the 26th British PM Macmillan privately offered to JFK the dismantling of the THOR missiles based in England if that would help alleviate the tension.

The Under Secretary for politico-military affairs Raymond Garth argued against all of those thoughts claiming that we had the upper hand and Khrushchev knew it.

With this battle area in our back yard the Russian and Cuban forces would have been crushed fairly quickly. "It would be a remarkable thing if they disrupt our base and alliance structure due to our political weakness."

Then a surprise letter from Khrushchev arrived and he privately agreed to remove the Russian missiles if the U.S. publicly declared Cuba safe from any invasion.

The initial reaction from *EXCOM* was that this offer was too good to be true. Could it be that the Russians seemed to have staged all of this only to ensure Cuba's safety?

And then a second message was broadcast from Moscow demanding the removal of the U.S. missiles in Turkey. *EXCOM* was taken aback and wondered what had happened to increase their demands. (Perhaps an agent was close enough to the meetings and discussions and was able to get word out, or someone in Moscow had read the NY Times?)

Khrushchev and the Russian commanders had initially been afraid of U.S. air attacks upon Cuba. Then they worried that the naval blockade would get out of control. (Our ships harassed all of the Russian submarines forcing three of them to the surface.)

All it would take was one shot from a young seaman, like the clearing of the canons, to start the war. Thus far no military episodes had occurred showing that the White House was still in control. (In Russia there was always a fear of the Generals.)

The initial U.S. attempts to "negotiate" had also showed an aversion to war.

And with the Times article mentioning the possible missile base exchange and no recanting from the White House, Khrushchev saw his opportunity to win the day.

Instead of a deal that would have been a draw, the Russians could now come out on top.

Khrushchev's sudden introduction of our Jupiter missiles based in Turkey into the equation created confusion and tension at *EXCOM*. (Why, many of the principals had stated before that they would agree to this if it came up.)

Suddenly all of the senior leaders were against the exchange. The Hawks in *EXCOM* gained traction in claiming all of it had been a ruse to weaken the U.S. global position.

A statement from the Turkish Government denied any chance at this tradeoff, and Gen. Lemnitzer at NATO warned that Turkey could not be treated the same as Cuba. More proposals came up such as only responding to Khrushchev's written letter and ignoring the Moscow radio message. Also suggested was tightening the blockade or using an air strike. Tensions and tempers flared anew.

Meanwhile Castro had grown wary of the constant U.S. low level recon flights and had secretly issued firing orders to his forces. He was convinced that the overflights were gathering the latest information needed to make an attack against him.

Around 10 am on the 27th the Cubans used a SAM to shoot down a U-2. The initial U.S. response to an attack of this type had already been pre-planned. We would destroy the offending site only.
But just before Gen LeMay could order the strike he was told to stand down until the President issued the order.

Talk at *EXCOM* somehow went from the earlier approved tit-for-tat strike, to a 500 sortie attack, to daily strikes, to an invasion? And then the discussions returned to if we hit Cuba, Russian bombers could then strike Turkey or even Berlin.

(The propaganda and myths from the Democrats and liberals showed that JFK and his administration were handling the crisis, but in reality the administration was in complete turmoil.)

In the U.S. everything was at full boil.
SAC B-52s were at their forward most attack stations over the Arctic waiting for the attack order. Nine Polaris missile subs were hiding under the ice, and Minuteman missiles were being readied for launch.

After a short period of time McNamara led the discussion to accepting the trade off. The Jupiter missiles were considered obsolete, (which probably explains why we gave them to Turkey.). New missile carrying subs would soon be operating in the Mediterranean Sea replacing the Jupiter's anyway. We could afford to lose those missiles, though no thought was given to the effect on NATO or Turkey.

(At that point the President was greatly concerned that the military would "get away from him" and provoke a war. McNamara shared his suspicions.)

Kennedy had a letter prepared to answer the first Russian request.

But for unknown reasons Kennedy's proposal did not include any language demanding that Cuba not act against the U.S. or any other Latin American state.

(A poor level of global statesmanship is a common problem in U.S. foreign policy.)

The letter was sent to Moscow and published for all to read.

RFK was again secretly sent to see Dobrynin in a back channel meeting to explain the mood in the discussions. He warned the Russian diplomat that matters would soon come to a head. Robert was also told to mention that the missiles in Turkey would be removed, **but only off the record**. He told Dobrynin that time was running out. If the Cubans continue to fire at our planes we will shoot back.

Their missile bases had to go and they had to go now.

He warned Dobrynin that if they were not removed by you then we would do so. If there were any retaliatory strikes by you Americans and Russians would die.

No public statement would ever mention the removal of the Jupiter missiles, but RFK again promised that in four or five months they would be removed.

(The U.S. election was only days away, and if the missiles were still there the Democrats would surely lose at the polls.)

The leaders in NATO and Turkey were told that "any offer to remove the Jupiter's should come from them". *(This aspect of the proposal was needed to save face for JFK.)* Our Ambassador in Turkey Raymond Hare reported back that the Turks would be outraged **over our removing the missiles.**

(The British were told to hold back on any offer regarding the THOR missiles until the last minute.)

Khrushchev read the report from Dobrynin and also the one from Castro desiring that Russia **use the nukes in Cuba now in a first strike** to prevent the Americans from doing so. *In actuality the tension* *from the Cubans shooting down the U-2 had worried the Russian Premier that more mistakes would occur.*

U.S. hesitation in counter-attacking actually impressed him, but he knew that it was just a matter of time before the shooting began. Russian intelligence collected from within America also warned that the calls for invasion within the U.S. would be unavoidable if the matter wasn't settled quickly.

While Khrushchev deliberated on that latest intelligence a message was received that Pres. Kennedy was to give a speech at 5pm Moscow time. *It was assumed in Russia that it would be a U.S. Declaration of War.*

To head it off Khrushchev had a broadcast made from Moscow ordering the removal of the missile weapons and sites. A cable was also sent to Washington. To the unknowing it appeared as if we had won.

One of the by-products of the *naval quarantine* was the image that it had worked.

The Administration's gradual response of "mounting pressures" was given a depiction that this was a viable strategy. In actuality events were closing in on making air attacks as the MRBM sites were being completed. One or two more days of the standoff would have triggered a war. Khrushchev to his credit read the tea leaves correctly and accepted the "deal" that was made. *It was Khrushchev's decision that stopped the war.*

Another flawed facet in the fallout from this dangerous episode was that to JFK the military minds could only think of attacking. Kennedy wanted to warn his successor that just because they are military men, their opinions on military matters weren't worth a damn.

To placate the JCS and keep them quiet about the *Secret missile Deal*, JFK invited them to the White House for thanks and praise. While there USAF Gen. Curtiss LeMay remarked that this was the greatest defeat in our history. Chief of Naval Operations, (CNO), Adm. George Anderson stated, "We have been had."

Pres. Kennedy was stunned over their hostile candor, and according to McNamara was unable to reply. Relations between JFK and the JCS were at an all time low.

(Adm. Anderson fought with McNamara over many issues, and he too would soon be forced out. He became the Ambassador to Portugal to keep him quiet.)

Dean Acheson who had been brought in as a special advisor to the White House retorted that "JFK's half-hearted actions worked from just plain dumb luck".

McNamara advanced from being a bean counter to a "strategic planner". His lack of experience and judgment was about to reach a critical level.

During those tense days he was constantly incensed over Adm. Anderson's calm demeanor, and other trivial matters. One such occurrence involved ordering the CNO to write up Soviet submarine surfacing and identification procedures. The paperwork was unnecessary and unneeded as the Russian subs surfaced only when they had to. (There was no way to ask them to surface.)

Negotiations over Cuba continued quietly until Nov 20 when the White House declared the crisis was over. During that "quiet" time the U.S. troop buildup **had wisely continued** as the Soviets tried to re-negotiate what they felt they could gain or hold on to. In the follow on "negotiations" the Russian bombers also had to be removed as they were considered offensive weapons. *In reaction to those issues, Khrushchev then wanted to pin JFK down on paper over the Jupiter missiles deal. Proof was needed by him to show the Politburo that "America had backed down" to his demands.*

At a following meeting Ambassador Dobrynin handed a letter from Khrushchev to RFK demanding public disclosure. RFK looked over the letter, handed it back and refused to make the deal public or on public record. Everyone in the Administration knew that if the nation found out about the "deal" over the Jupiter missile removal it would be politically embarrassing, and cause irreparable damage to Kennedy.

So secret was the "deal", that even Turkey was not told of it.

All of the principals were sworn to secrecy so that JFK could be perceived as having steely resolve. (And the Democrats did well in the mid-term elections.) McNamara would eventually "tell" his opposite number in Turkey that the missiles were being removed because of the "threat they were to Turkey".

"If we had attacked their missiles in Cuba, Russia would have attacked you. They still might, so in Turkey's interests, the missiles had to go by April". Similar moves were also made in Italy, to hide the direct link to Turkey and the Secret Deal.

The Russians who were always on the sneak did not pull out all of their troops as Khrushchev had stated in his Oct 26 letter. Kennedy tried to let the matter rest by claiming that only 17,000 Russian troops had remained in Cuba for training and security.
In actuality over 30,000 Russians had remained in Cuba.
Their nuclear capable bombers the Il 28s also remained in Cuba.
Russia "transferred ownership" to the Cubans, which meant they now belonged to them. Not until late December were they finally crated up.

Castro refused to allow any U.N. inspectors on his island, and Senator Keating would claim that many of the Russian offensive weapons had been hidden in caves as intelligence agents were reporting that weapons were still being seen. As time went by most American people wanted a full blockade on Cuba and complete removal of all of the Russian troops. But with the election won the Administration allowed the matter to fade away. *(One can only speculate on the public reaction if America had learned the whole truth about the "Missiles of October".)*

Like Stalin's mistaken judgment over the invasion in Korea, Khrushchev made a grave error in his estimation of America's reaction over Cuba. By trying to secretly change the balance of power he set the stage for the crisis that followed. (If the Russian military had done what Khrushchev wanted, and flown the missiles in they might not have been noticed until they were operational.) In the strategic nuclear realm of late 1962 Russia only had 44 ICBMs, 97 submarine launched missiles, the few missiles in Cuba and 200 or so medium bombers with which to attack us. They faced 156 ICBMs and 144 sub launched Polaris missiles plus hundreds of land based bombers from SAC. Only a madman would seek nuclear war on those terms.

In all probability war was not what Khrushchev was after.

Keeping Communist Cuba safe was the great strategic benefit for the Soviets.

Cuba was the first nation to turn Communist without any Russian involvement.

It was hoped their success could be repeated many times in Latin America. And Cuba gave the Soviets an advance bases right in our backyard.

(Conventionally speaking the Russian effort had no chance of success so far from home against our Navy and Air Force. After seeing and being intimidated by those hundreds of gray Navy hulls the Russians wisely backed off. So inferior was the Russian surface navy that the Russian sub captains had been told that as soon as the shooting started they were to use nuclear weapons on our ships.)

Fidel Castro became convinced and incensed that his country had been put at risk just so the Soviets could remove a threat to themselves. (Jupiter missiles)

He had recklessly ordered his troops to fire at any planes flying within range. Those orders could well have started the nuclear war the world rightly feared.

By the end of the crisis over 150,000 additional Cubans fled the communist island by boat. Yet another example of which society is desired by the masses. Most of those refugees came to America and their continued calls for action against Castro would resonate from this group and hard line Hawks.

RFK wanted to keep plotting against Castro, often asking what the U.S. could do to bring on a coup. And all the while U.S. submarines continued to drop off commandos and agitators while bringing out prominent Cubans and agents.

To placate the Cuban refugees JFK spoke to 40,000 of them at the Orange Bowl in Miami. He claimed it was the desire of the U.S. to overthrow Castro.

But his empty words could not hide the truth from those who could actually think for themselves. He had his chance in 1961 and failed.

By this point there was nothing more America could do without a nuclear war.

(His speech was the hallmark of these new Democrats. They said a lot but did nothing.)

After the Missiles of October the crux of the matter was trying to separate Castro from the Soviet Bloc. But a communist ruler was not about to trade sides, especially with a country that wanted him dead. Despite the obvious chance to try to make up, (serious strains had developed between Cuba and Russia), Castro the murderer and thief was hated in the U.S. And Castro the communist still desired fomenting revolutions in the region to hurt America's interests. Trying to make nice at that time was impossible.

(After their trials, the Cuban rebels captured at the Bay of Pigs were imprisoned. Castro desired to trade those men for 500 bulldozers. After months of talking all of the "survivors" were released for 53 million dollars in U.S. foods and pharmaceuticals.)

Over the following months raids were still being staged in Cuba and two attacks occurred on Soviet ships. Loud protests came from Moscow and it was naturally assumed that the U.S. was behind the attacks. The President denied our involvement, but wanted the raids to hit Cuban targets only. He could not understand why the "secret agents" could not operate from within Cuba and get at the real target, Castro.

CIA's McCone had to inform him that if anyone stayed ashore for any length of time they would quickly get caught by the communist security forces.

One indirect result of this dramatic heating of the Cold War was that any attempts to reform the political world had to be done with extreme caution. (As Cuba had shown.) That meant the U.S. **had to stick by** some unsavory regimes like the one in Vietnam and those in S. America. Britain was asked by the Administration not to grant independence to British Guiana for fear that the radical Marxist group Cheddi Jagen would sweep to power. The U.S. and other nations had been taken in by Castro who had posed as a reformer. He revealed his true nature only after taking over. The last thing the Administration wanted was another Communist takeover in our hemisphere, especially if it happened on Kennedy's watch.

Venezuela was ruled by Romulo Betancourt, a liberal anti-communist who had been elected in 1959 much to the chagrin of the leftists. His government was semi-democratic and the next regime the Administration was worried over. Their armed forces were weak, there was a radical student population who were turning Marxist, and it had oil. During the missile crisis Venezuela had stood by the U.S. instead of its Latin neighbor. Cuba had quick sea access to Venezuela's long coastline and Castro could cause much trouble there. A good deal of covert support was done to help Betancourt stay in power.

In actuality the World and the Cuban people got the short side of the Secret Deal. Castro was able to stay in power, safe from attack. His people have suffered and endured over 50 years of strict communist rule. Within a few years he would export Cuban troops to help in the continued Marxist revolutionary fighting that plagued the nations that made up "The Third World". Well trained Cuban proxy forces enabled the Russians and Chinese to remain in the background, supplying weapons and advisors. It was the Cubans who did the actual fighting against the West in places like Angola, Mozambique and Central America.

And overlooked because of the Cuban Crisis was a war in Yemen.
After the Imam of Yemen died in September, 1962 Egypt's Nasser saw an opportunity to expand his Arab Socialism to new ground on the Arabian Peninsula. He organized a coup to topple the Imam's successor. The Saudi's reacted quickly and moved their few troops onto the common border to support the Yemeni Royal Family.

Nasser sent in some of his troops and the fighting started.

As shown many times, the region was strategically vital and Britain and the U.S. quickly became involved. Ellsworth Bunker was the State Dept. Senior negotiator who tried to end the fighting. *It took years for the battles to end, and then Yemen quietly slipped back into obscurity. But the damages to the country were never repaired and appalling poverty took over. And that laid the seeds for further conflict as Islamic Extremists became active and organized.* Decades of trouble followed.

India

In Southern Asia the small border battles between China and India were also growing larger. Not long after China was invading and the Indian troops were in full retreat. Another crisis loomed, and on November 19,

1962 India's P.M. Jawaharlal Nehru asked the U.S. and Britain for more aid. China's communist troops had easily advanced into India's northern provinces. (Again this was the fallout for losing China to the communists and the fall of Great Britain from power.)

Paul Nitze was called in and it was decided that the State Dept and military needed to be sent over to appraise the situation. The team consisted of Nitze, Averill Harriman, Gen. Paul DeWitt Adams and Roger Hilsman. Adams would be the commander of the strike team if U.S. military forces were needed.

Just twenty four hours later the Chinese declared a unilateral ceasefire and claimed they would withdraw their forces back to the positions of Nov 15th. *Their catch was that India had to agree to the armistice, and would not attempt to reestablish their outposts in the Ladakh area of Kashmir.*

That area enclosed the most direct and easiest route to link the stolen nation of Tibet to the Chinese province of Sinkiang.
(China had to control that area to ensure they could hold onto Tibet.)

Still en-route, the U.S. team analyzed the crisis and decided that China's ambitions were limited to that border area. Otherwise they would have continued on. They also felt that India could loose the land without suffering any long term danger. Upon landing in India they met with Ambassador John K. Galbraith and the distraught Indian Prime Minister Nehru. He was still unsure on what to do.

After making overflights of the region it became apparent to all that the Chinese could advance at will if they so desired. *Nitze's team realized and reported that to provide long term security against China would require that India and Pakistan stop fighting each other and prepare a joint defense.* That would be a difficult sell with the deep and bloody hostilities between the two religious groups.
(The aid the Administration approved and sent was deceptively re-routed and used to continue the fighting between India and Pakistan.)

One often overlooked issue is and will always be that Muslims do not get along with any other religious group. (Middle East, India-Pakistan, Indonesia, Philippines, Africa, Europe, U.S.) In spite of the danger to themselves from China, the Pakistanis were unsympathetic to India's fight. They even hoped that China's attacks might convince the Indians to concede the disputed territory of Kashmir over to Pakistan.

The Communist Chinese moves were well calculated and designed to force the Indian Government to accept their prior proposals and "agree to the peace".

Otherwise the Chinese forces would return to take more.

Their military move was successful and their "diplomacy" gained Indian approval. It ensured China's control of Tibet as they worked to suppress the ancient and honorable culture. *(Again the Communists had gained from a direct assault upon a free people.)*

Vietnam

Senator Mike Mansfield was sent to Vietnam by JFK in December 1962. After his survey was completed Mansfield returned home and presented a brutally frank assessment. (As he and all should have.) *Mansfield told Kennedy that we had spent over $2 Billion in the past seven years and had nothing to show for it. Instead of improving, the problems were actually getting worse.*

It was their country and Mansfield stated that they must fight to preserve it. To ignore that reality will be immensely costly to us in treasure and lives. Kennedy became upset but continued with his hard line messages that we would stay in Vietnam and win. On the inside he began to doubt.

On December 28, 1962 Lt. Col. Vann and the 7th ARVN Div received an order to seize a radio transmitter that had been operating near a village called Tan Thoi. Usually the presence of the radio meant high ranking targets, so Vann and his staff planned for a large multi-pronged attack.

The political hold the VC had enjoyed in this area was actually falling as Vann and his staff's work was demonstrating to the people that the VC might just lose.

Gen. Harkins and his staff felt contempt for the simple VC guerrilla, but then they were safe in the plush HQ in Saigon. But this operation would be very different.

At dawn on January 2, 1963 units of the ARVN 7th Div boarded helicopters as part of Vann's well planned assault. Miles away the 261st Main Force VC Battalion had been training hard for just this eventuality. Today they planned to stay and fight.

As shown earlier, some of the communist stay behind cadres had infiltrated into the ARVN commands and would learn of attacks and commando raids as they were being planned. Many times their warnings would successfully go out enabling the VC/NVA to be ready for the ARVN attempts. Of the twenty two commando teams airdropped into North Vietnam, only five were not intercepted. The reason for this incredible luck was never exposed, and was another failure in the U.S-ARVN war effort. (It mirrored the bad luck Germany and Japan had had in WWII, since neither country believed their radio codes had been cracked.)

Vann's carefully thought out battle plan called for the helicopter forces to come in from the north and land first. Two battalions of Civil Guard's infantry would attack from the south in separate columns, and finally a company of ten APC's, (Armored Personnel Carriers), plus troops would attack from the west. Artillery fire was to be available and on call. Everything looked like a solid victory would be had.

However with the warnings from their hidden spies and the local signs of an impending ARVN attack; (ammo dumps being readied, over-flights from planes and helicopters, and registration rounds fired by the artillery), the local VC commander perfectly prepared his defenses, (exact spot!), and organized for the ARVN attack.

Those senior communist leaders had over 20 years of combat experience and were confident that they could learn how to defeat the American machines and tactics. Their motivated fighters were tough and good soldiers. They dug deep fighting holes and tunnels and set them into the tree lines to make them invisible. They also set numerous mines and traps around the expected battle area to increase the ARVN casualties. (Nothing slows an infantry attack like walking into a minefield.) The ancient Vietnamese tree lines that marked the rice-fields were like the hedgerows of Normandy, dense and centuries old. They had been turned into fortified bunkers.

At the last minute Gen. Harkins did not give Vann's planned battle the priority on helicopter or artillery resources. He had another "mission" going on in war zone C.

(That mission was actually a bust as the forewarned VC had prudently left the area just before the mission started.) Half of Vann's helicopter units and his artillery had been reassigned to the other attack. **Vann was not informed of this beforehand.**

This change in his helicopter support reduced the initial landing force to a smaller one than planned and that greatly reduced their firepower. It also required additional helicopter lifts to bring the rest of the troops in.

But the extra flights coming in would not have the element of surprise that Vann had counted on. And without their expected on call artillery support the dropped off light infantry would be helpless against any heavy resistance.

To make things even worse an unforeseen fog covered the battle area and that also delayed the condensed helicopter landings. That resulted in the Civil Guards infantry units arriving and finding the enemy first at the village of Bac. This unexpected and early fight at Bac lost any surprise and shock value of the helicopter assault.

(Again, intelligence is key.)

The well equipped VC battalion expertly ambushed the first Civil Guard unit and killed the commander and his exec. No capable leader stepped up and the entire battalion was trapped behind rice paddy dike walls. The local ARVN commander refused to commit the second battalion into the fight nor did he call for any artillery fire.

Vann was flying above in his spotter plane but was not told of this first disaster in his pre-planned battle. Then the ARVN major in command of the operation decided to land the helicopters *behind* the first group of VC, instead of using Vann's planned site. That caused the helicopter troops to actually be landed between the two enemy forces. One after another the helicopters were shot down or damaged and the onboard troops took many casualties. These VC had crew served weapons, mortars and machine guns, and they knew how to use them. At that point the ARVN commanders were mentally incapable of reacting to the battle and most stayed still and did nothing.

Vann was overhead screaming into the radios to get them to move and attack but they refused. Because of the heavy fighting audible on the radios the planned assault of the APC company was delayed by their commander. Then he abruptly refused to attack at all. The trapped ARVN forces suffered enemy fire all day.

And to complete the disaster Gen. Cao refused to drop his available paratroops to cordon off the battle-site, or to use flares during the night to spot the escaping VC. Almost all of the enemy escaped.

This battle resulted in five destroyed helicopters, eighty dead ARVN and three dead U.S. advisors. Vann was livid over the defeat and he decided that Harkins had to be made to recognize the ARVN failures and that Saigon had to change their policies.

If Harkins would not listen, Vann was prepared to go over his head!

At that time the U.S. had over 14,000 "advisors" in country. There were few reporters in Vietnam, so media coverage was still limited. But Vann was close to David Halberstam of the NY Times and had taught him what to look for as if he was a soldier on a mission. In return Vann knew that Halberstam's dispatches to the NY Times would get read. At that time the NY Times was the most prestigious newspaper in the world. *(Even though our government was keeping much from the public eye as possible, and manipulating what was left at every chance, JFK and others were still concerned with what the Times did publish.)*

Gen. Robert York was in country with a special section to test weapons and tactics for the US Army. He could go anywhere at anytime to see and to learn but could not take over command. To avoid the fluff he often went without Harkins or anyone on his staff. York even took off his generals stars so he could slip in and out unnoticed.

For three and a half years he had been assigned to watch and learn from the British effort in Malaya. Despite having a 20-1 advantage in police and troops, it still took the British **12 years** to defeat those communist insurgents.

Most of the communists were of Chinese origin and hated by the local Malay people. It was easier to know who was who, versus Vietnam where everyone looked the same. Malaya had at most 10,000 communist troops and supporters.

The number operating currently in Vietnam was about five times that.

From his solid experience Gen. York knew that our effort in Vietnam was imperiled. Though he always reported back on his observations, there was no follow up or investigations into anything he had observed or learned!

One day after the disastrous battle at Ap Bac Gen. York was there observing the results. (With no pursuers the victorious VC units had easily escaped during the night.)

Walking the same battle site were reporters Neil Sheehan and Peter Arnett. Suddenly artillery fire started landing all around them.

Gen Cao was *staging a battle* so he could report a victory to Diem.

Upon his return to MACV Gen. York wrote a scathing report about the battle to Harkins.

Gen. Harkins was approached later that day by Arnett and David Halberstam and asked about the ARVN defeat and the near miss they had just gone through. Incredulously Harkins told them the battle was obviously not yet over.

This core of young reporters was not fooled by the completely out of touch Harkins, and using contacts from Vann and his team they reported on the reality of the battle at Ap Bac. Their reports went out on the AP wire service and almost got Vann fired. (The staff at MACV knew that those detailed reports could only have come from Vann.)

Halberstam was one of the first of his generation that did not conform to the wishes of those in charge. He asked pointed questions and saw through the fluff. He was not welcomed by the establishment in Vietnam or Washington.

Prior to Ap Bac the fighting in Vietnam had gone mostly unnoticed.

But after the battle numerous negative reports and stories went out, and the public became aware that things were not all that good in Vietnam. With all of the other Foreign Policy disasters that had happened to JFK recently in Laos, Cuba, Berlin, Yemen, India and the Congo, the last thing he needed was for Vietnam to hit the front pages. But that is just what happened.

JFK and Sec of Defense McNamara demanded an explanation. Gen. Harkins was embarrassed and enraged that so much "information had gotten revealed". It was obvious to him who the source was.

Diem simply wanted to use Vann as the convenient scapegoat, but Harkins was afraid that if Vann went down a bigger scandal could follow. (One that would include him.)

It was better to ease him out quietly upon his rotation.

Vann's command team produced an impressive, well documented account of the battle. Col. Porter who was Vann's boss sent in his report that backed up Vann's. In addition he sent along all of the prior warnings that the other U.S. advisors in his command had forwarded. And like Vann's, there were no positive comments in any of the reports.

(Gen. York forwarded his "after the battle views" and was also critical of the ARVN.)

But the inept (or dishonest) Harkins still thought and stated that everything went fine. It was the VC who had left the battlefield. Content to stay in his starched uniform this career staff officer was simply unqualified to command MACV. *AP photographer Horst Faas had wanted Harkins to go out in the field in battle gear for some stock shots. Harkins replied, "I'm not that king of general".*

General Yarborough who headed the Special Forces School at Fort Bragg or Gen. York should have been the ones placed in command of this complicated assignment. But the old-boys club was hard at work and Maxwell Taylor was in charge of it.

As stated before, Harkins was a friend of Gen. Taylor. He had lobbied JFK hard to get Harkins the MACV command despite the fact Pres. Kennedy had wanted a younger more up to date commander.

Gen. Harkins capacity for self-delusion was astonishing, and for that reason America was about to fall into a morass. His main strength was his ability to go along so you can get along. He had been sitting behind a desk becoming mentally lazy and arrogant over what had been done in Europe. But Europe in no way resembled Vietnam.

And the vital lessons of the Korean War had not been learned by him nor so many other Senior Career Officers, including Taylor. Few of them had fought or served there.

(Taylor was "given command" in Korea the last few months of the war, accomplishing little and learning less. Harkins had been brought in to be his Chief of Staff.)

The brutal lessons that the French had suffered through in the first Indochina war had not been absorbed by any of our Senior Leaders either.
They simply wrote off the war because the French were the ones "who lost it".

If anyone had bothered to read *"Street Without Joy", Bernard Falls masterpiece book on the French failures, or TR Farenbach's outstanding book on Korea, "This Kind of War"*, maybe things could have turned out differently.

The communists however would always learned from a bad performance. They would routinely have self-criticism classes, for they were there to succeed. The U.S. Army does not even have a "failure, mistake or a correction report".

All U.S. Officers were rated by their superior every six months. Anything less than perfect evaluations would end that person's career instead of helping them to learn. This foolish procedure had been instituted in the 50's in the effort to create "managers". It also created a phenomenon called "Ticket Punching".

All officers also had to rotate through various assignments. It was vital to keep the paper trail clean. You got your "ticket punched" and moved up or onto the next assignment. (*"About Face"* by Hackworth. Another great read.) Thus Harkins could never admit to a failure, let alone the many setbacks that had occurred. If he had he would never get his "next star".

To assist him in maintaining this lie and get their "ticket punched," his staff used graphs and statistics to show paper advances. Numbers of enemy killed, shells fired, aircraft sorties flown, villages relocated and men, money and material expended in the MACV effort were all well documented on their reports. The U.S. was spending over $300 million per year in Vietnam and his team knew how to make a paper impression.

In his report to Gen. Taylor, Harkins claimed that the Strategic Hamlet Program had successfully moved 2800 villages. During 1963 his "Operation Explosion" would be ready to *attack and attrite the VC*! And so the lie continued.

As stated above by Jan 1963, despite Harkin's and Ambassador Nolting's efforts word had finally gotten out that all was not well in Vietnam. Increasing enemy attacks were also striking the annoying and disruptive SF camps that had been setup along the long border from Khe Sanh southward. JFK sent out a group of Senior Officers to get the "real" story. *Harkins slyly took the group to areas were there was almost no fighting.*

There were no trips to the SF border camps or in the dangerous Central Highlands. And only one day was spent in the embattled Delta area.

No stops were made near Vann or Col. Porter.

Gen. York was present at one stop, but he was not approached for his input.

On the last day of the visit an aide to the Senior General saw a copy of Vann's report on Ap Bac. Vann was questioned about his report and he gave it to them straight.

The "Senior Team" decided that the view from this advisor was unduly harsh because he wanted the ARVN to fight like Americans.

And so the "Senior Team's" report mirrored Harkin's assessments, all was well.

Unless those Seniors stayed out in the field and sat in the mud there was no way they could learn the reality of Vietnam. (One of those visitors was Gen. Brute Krulak, a pioneer in Marine Corps tactics during WWII. If anyone should have seen through the fluff he should have. But he too flew from stop to stop and saw what they were supposed to see. To his shame he allowed himself to be blinded. When he awoke it was too late to alter the disaster he had helped create.)

The detailed work that the young reporters had done in the field was at times under fire. It should have been viewed and analyzed by MACV, the Pentagon and the Administration. But instead they arrogantly brushed it off as unjust reporting or out right lies. Most of those reporters wrote books about their early 1960's time in Vietnam and all warned of the impending debacle with their reporting.

(*The Making of a Quagmire* - Halberstam 1965.)

And Halberstam was actually on his second tour in Vietnam having been in country since September 61. *Prior to Vietnam he had covered the fighting against the communists in the Belgium Congo. For fourteen months he stayed in Africa observing and reporting on the chaos and conflict until they were granted independence.*

Because of his years long reporting and observing communist insurgencies he knew what he was talking about, more so than many of the senior army officers.

Even so many U.S. Military leaders could not understand why these young-turk reporters were not going along the way their predecessors had done in WWII and Korea.

Once again, WWII was a different war and we were fighting for survival.

The few episodes of negative coverage involved "our working with Vichy in N. Africa to make the invasion and occupation easier", and the early complaints about FDR's handling of the war during 1942.

In Korea the U.S. and the free world Allies were not fighting for "immediate survival", but to stop the communists from conquering a free nation.

Those generals in charge that first year made many obvious and major mistakes. They were noted and written about by a few reporters who were combat wise in their own right from fighting or covering the battles of WWII.

But little was done by the Army about any of those problems they highlighted.

Few of the poor leaders were sacked until Gen. Ridgeway showed up.

And even after the war ended the JCS never bothered to learn and adjust their services to reflect the many lessons from Korea. (Some changes were made in training and weapons.) *One result of their failures was a complete lack of understanding on what we were up against in Vietnam or on how to deal with subversive communists.* And similar to Truman and Korea, during those vital years the meetings and decisions concerning Vietnam by the U.S. leadership were done in secret. They did not communicate what they were doing or wanted to do to the Congress or the military.

In Vietnam the number of skeptics among those reporters slowly began to increase because of *what they had seen themselves in the jungles and fields.*

Before the Vietnam War was called a War, and long before most of those Senior Officers had flown in, those reporters were in country and living in the mud. They often saw, worked with and spoke with the lower ranks. And what they were saying was completely at odds with what Harkins, his polished staff, or Ambassador Nolting said. *And the repetitive discrepancies between those two groups are what led to the wholesale refusal of the later-war reporters to believe anything from MACV.*

(The daily briefings at HQ would come to be called the 5 o'clock follies.)

French reporter Francois Sully had witnessed the first Indochina war in person. The errors the French military and political leaders had made gave him a clear perspective on our operations. And what he observed convinced him that we too were failing. He reported on what he saw and was often in trouble with the authorities.

"In one talk with Nolting the Ambassador asked him why he always saw the hole in the doughnut? Sully replied, because there is a hole in the doughnut."

Diem finally had Sully expelled in September 1962.

Harkins and Nolting wanted the same to be done to those other pains, or maybe their editors would simply recall them. Meanwhile Lt. Col. Vann hoped that those reporters would finally get the real story out and wake America's leaders to what was happening.

It was obvious to Vann that the military channels were not listening.

Diem had told the visiting Sir Robert Thompson the architect of the British victory in Malaya, that only the U.S. press could lose the war. Their negative reporting was undercutting the country's morale and the effectiveness of the anti-communist programs. (Thompson had been an advocate for S. Vietnam's strategic hamlet program because it had worked for him in Malaya. But it was wrong in Vietnam.)

Diem was partially correct about the media. The U.S. press was against any harsh civil actions or policies by his government. Anything done in the South they did not like they highlighted. They forgot that Vietnam was not America, and that the communists were the enemy inflicting hundreds of casualties each month to innocent civilians. And they had been doing so since their inception in 1919.

At home the Pentagon had realized that the helicopter was becoming a vital weapon in the war effort in Vietnam. McNamara directed the Army to speed up a program to create an airmobile unit. Testing was begun in early 1963 and General Harry Kinnard another Taylor man was picked to command the unit. (Again the USAF was against the Army having an air-unit.) Training and helicopter procurement was difficult due to the constant need for replacements in Vietnam. Despite the myriad problems the work progressed.

After their successful battle at Ap Bac communist infiltration from the North was increased to 1300 men per month. *Starting in 1963 North Vietnamese Army, (NVA), troops were being sent.* Heavy weapons, the kind used so successfully in the AP Bac battle were also being sent down in large numbers. As shown before, the normal human porter and bicycle–mule that had carried Vietminh ammo and supplies since 1950 was being supplanted by using ocean going trawlers of unit 759. But as the numbers of patrol boats increased the interception of those supplies went up. (By 1966 it had stopped.)

Harkins staff would review the monthly status reports from each Advisor. They complained that the last few from Vann were showing **"too much red"** on their map overlays. Despite all of the fine work Vann and his team had done over the past months their intel work showed that the communists were still gaining ground.

Vann and his staff sent in the truthful reports to MACV and never tried to make them "look good". *Those reports would be sent back to Vann with orders for them "to be fixed". Vann and his staff would never alter them, so the people in Harkins HQ would create their own.* After Ap Bac the monthly report from Vann was going to be a bombshell. The VC were becoming so confident that they were routinely operating in the daytime.

On Feb 8, 1963 the latest report went from Vann to Col. Porter as required and a second one went directly to Harkins. The report stated that Col. Dam, (who had replaced the promoted Cao), was keeping his forces away from the areas that we know have platoon or greater strength of Viet Cong. Vann wanted to prepare a master list of these targets and have Gen. Harkins order that they be attacked.

Harkins was infuriated by the report and sent his Intelligence chief, Col. Winterbottom USAF, with a few others to go over all of Vann's material. If anything was out of order Vann was to be fired. (How curious to have an Air Force officer in charge of intelligence for an insurgent ground war. Even civilian visitors wondered at the choice.)

Col. Porter was rotating after more than a year in country.

He insured that his final report would also be alarming. Porter questioned all of his advisors at length on their areas and problems. He also reported that *the Strategic Hamlet Program was an abject failure.*

In keeping with Army "protocol" he (wrongly) made just one copy of his report. It too was sanitized by Harkins.

Unlike every other Senior Advisor who rotated home from Vietnam Col. Daniel Porter was not called into the Pentagon to give a briefing on his tour.

Like all bureaucrats, Harkins was very good at manipulating the system.

(Porter's honesty cost him his promotion to general and he was "retired". The same happened to Colonel Fred Ladd and Wilbur Wilson, West Pointers who also made waves with Harkins.)

One alarming item that now caused Harkins serious trouble was that Winterbottom's investigation had reported that Vann and his people were correct!

"The only thing wrong with what Vann and his people wrote is that all of it is true". (One of Lt. Col. Vann's most disturbing statistic in his year long tour was that out of the 1,400+ S. Vietnamese killed in his sector, only 50 were ARVN killed in action.)

Harkin's had all of that troubling information sanitized, and the Great Lie of Vietnam went on unchecked. Since Harkins had ordered the investigation the reports generated could be changed and the "Commander accepted the responsibility".

But this wasn't a case of losing some backpacks or supplies.

Gen. Harkins actions were creating and maintaining a fabrication of the truth that President Kennedy and his principals needed to make policy.

He compromised all of the prior years of work and all that would follow.

And hundreds of thousands would die and be wounded in the coming war.

Because of the Vietnam War America would be ripped apart and our military would almost be destroyed. The United States would fall from grace and from its position as world leader. Two more countries would fall to the curse on humanity and new wars would erupt causing even more needless death and destruction.

When the truth came out Harkins and everyone else involved should have been court-martialed and imprisoned.

In March 1963 Syria went through their 8th revolt since 1945. The new regime was inclined to rejoin the United Arab Republic. Jordan however was still opposed to the union.

Riots in Iran were prompted by *strict Islamic religious leaders* and meant to topple the decade of rule by the Shah. Iran's Shah had pro-western views and Iran was the most westernized country of the Moslem world. (Turkey was second.) Mobs of rioting Fundamentalist Shiite youth causing extensive damage as they violently protested in their quest to reverse his rule. Three women were savagely massacred by the mob because they were unveiled!

One of those arrested was the Ayatollah Khomeini, a Muslim fanatic who authored the extremist views. Like so many thousands of Islamic Fundamentalists, Khomeini was insistent that all of the nations of Islam revert back to the 9th century.

And like the communist charlatans who sought to take over the world, Khomeini was unyielding in his beliefs and efforts. Whatever needed to be done was done in the name of Islam. He would be back.

On April 1, 1963 Lt. Col. Vann rotated out from Vietnam and went home. At that time he was scheduled to attend the military's Industrial College for a year, the topmost rung of the military schools and an almost guaranteed promotion to full Colonel.

Neil Sheehan accompanied him on the flight back to the U.S.

On the 10th JFK authorized covert Headquarters 333 to open up in Udorn Thailand. The nondescript building was the HQ for all of our secret operations in Thailand and Laos. Kennedy was setting up the pieces for his Indochina war.

Upon his return from leave Lt. Col. Vann reported in to the Pentagon to the Directorate of Special Warfare on May 24. When he went to the Officer in charge to schedule to be debriefed on his tour in Nam, **he was told that "at Saigon's Request" he was not going to be interviewed.**

His final report was so critical of Harkins and MACV that it had been flagged and pigeonholed as had Col. Porter's report. (Vann had expected as much as Col. Porter and even Col. Kelleher from Harkins own staff had been given the same treatment.) *So Vann decided to brief people on his own.*

Neil Sheehan returned to Vietnam just as the Ngo Dinhs set off the Buddhist crisis. Diem and his family had passed a ridiculous ruling that flags of the Buddha could not be flown to celebrate his birthday. On May 8, 1963 at a demonstration in Hue (the former Imperial capital) turned bloody with nine civilians killed including children.

Instead of meeting and mollifying the head monks the Nhus decided to crush the Buddhists like they had done to the criminal Cao Dai and Hoa Hoa sects years earlier.

On June 11, a seventy three year old monk immolated himself in the middle of a busy Saigon intersection. *The media had been forewarned that something was going to happen and a photo of the event became page one all over the world.*

The Buddhist protests grew in size and intensity garnering much negative press. *JFK and his Administration were embarrassed and chagrined to watch on TV and in the printed media so much discontent in a land he had been told was improving.*

The demonstrations and reprisals lasted for weeks.

This was one of those times when JFK should have done what he did best, gone on television and explained to the world what was happening and why the West had to be more understanding.

Vietnam was not America or Europe. It was a fledgling nation that was being assaulted by communist insurgents. That some of their policies were not up to our standards was and is irrelevant for the country was still developing. For the people of the Western world to dismiss them and their attempts at democracy would be a huge failure and would cause the country to collapse and fall by default to the communists. The world needed patience.

But JFK did not react that way for his re-election campaign was beginning.

Instead talk was begun about "replacing Diem".

For John Vann his Pentagon assignment was boring and Vann had plenty of time to track down other advisors and put together a comprehensive report that would expose the failures and lies at MACV. By late June several hundred officers including many Generals had gotten the Vann talk. One of them was U.S.A.F. General Ed Lansdale, (CIA). He listened to Vann and agreed with his findings, but could not successfully intervene. Lansdale was out of favor and Taylor too slick.

(As shown earlier, because of the intense humiliation from the Bay of Pigs disaster JFK had directed Lansdale to come up with a way to rid Cuba of Fidel Castro. The Kennedys were not concerned with propriety. After the Cuban Missile Crisis the pressure to perform was intensified, but Lansdale was unable to execute a solution and his rising star had fallen. He was exiled into the bureaucracy.)

Vann finally met up with Maj. Gen. H. Johnson, the Army's Assistant Chief of Operations. After a long and successful talk he sent Vann to see Gen. Barksdale Hamlett, the Vice Chief of Staff. After also being convinced Hamlett went to see Taylor.

Taylor dismissed the claims from Vann but Hamlett set up a briefing for the JCS on July 8, 1963 anyway. One of those who would be present was Gen. Krulak.

Krulak had just returned from another "inspection trip" and had written a 129 page report claiming that the shooting part of the war was moving to a climax.

The boys would be coming home right on schedule.

(Col Kelleher, Harkin's former Chief of Staff had been replaced by a Gen. Stilwell. That officer questioned nothing Harkins told him and actively worked to suppress dissent within the command. Gen. Krulak used much of Stilwell's staff work as his own to write the report.)

In his report were the latest updates on Hanoi's use of Laos and Cambodia to assist in their infiltration of the South. With Harkin's staff work on display this "new report" would refute everything Vann had stated or would state by claiming that the Viet Cong were becoming an endangered species. And according to the report, the Strategic Hamlet program was behind all of this success! The Great Lie was still strong.

The Pentagon grapevine alerted General Krulak that Vann was going to speak. Before the July 8 meeting Krulak's staff began requesting copies of Vann's report. Vann's colleagues warned him to put off Krulak's requests for as long as possible.

Just one hour before Vann was to give his briefing, Generals Taylor and Krulak succeeded in stopping the briefing.
Apparently they could not stand to be contradicted by a Lt Colonel.

Both had open access to the President, and both would be under attack from his report.

Gen. Earl Wheeler had headed the recent JCS mission to Vietnam. He had also allowed himself to be "shown the war" instead of conducting the investigation he was supposed to do. Incredibly even Gen. Wheeler had no combat command experience. *He too owed his position to Gen. Taylor. To the shame and detriment of our nation those "men of influence" were able to silence the one critic who had the tactical knowledge to defeat this enemy.*

(Why Taylor had such influence is hard to understand. He made only three combat jumps during the war unlike Gen. Ridgeway and many others, and missed the Battle of the Bulge completely. The 101 Airborne fought fine without him. If anyone deserved to be working for the White House it should have been someone like Gen. Ridgeway who had saved the war in Korea and then commanded NATO.)

One overlooked section of Krulak's report came from the U.S. Intelligence people. *It contained extremely vital information that was missed by all of those experts. "The passage referred to the sudden growth of VC heavy weapons units."*

Radio intercepts picked up from the now numerous enemy commands stated that those heavy weapons units were to **"be kept secret"** until the proper time arrives. (Just what did those senior officers think that information and passage meant?)

Vann was upset about this latest bureaucratic scam and wrote to his students the reporters in Vietnam. He told them not to let up. "Go for broke and use all of your ammo now that the people were really watching" Like so many fine officers, Vann retired from the Army in disgust.
(Which suited Taylor and Harkins just fine.)

One of JFK's major failures was the inability to keep Laos free and neutral. With the communist Pathet Lao and NVA controlling the eastern side of the country the NVA were free to use the area to infiltrate into S. Vietnam. The CIA tried hard to help the Laotian's, even using Thai volunteers. *But the rulers of North Vietnam simply increased their military commitment, eventually using four Divisions of troops!*

This too was never explained properly to the American people.
On the battlefield the VC efforts were becoming continuous and effective.

In the Kien Hoa Province a July 63 battle resulted in eleven helicopters being shot up. An advisor with the unit reported that the enemy pinned down and out gunned the ARVN immediately *despite the numerous attacks by planes and helicopter gunships.*

As always the VC broke off the fight during the night and escaped.

At Tchepone the communists were flying in multiple aircraft each day. Their buildup in Laos was reaching a breakthrough level. And just as had happened to the French, the MACV commanders and the Nhu's refused to accept or believe the information that was coming in.

On August 15, 1963 a Halberstam story about VC gains in the Delta made the front page of the NY Times. He wrote that a year earlier the VC units were no larger than 250 men. Now they could field units of 600-1000!

They have increased the smuggling of communist made weapons to supplement the captured U.S. weapons. They use radios and conducted fast, hard hitting warfare.

JFK was incredulous and demanded to know if the story was valid. *But by using the same faces and names to investigate, he was again given false information.*

(In his second book on Vietnam, *The Best and the Brightest*, Halberstam exposes and highlights the ruinous propaganda of JFK and his Administration.)

"An administration which flaunted its intellectual and academic credentials, made years of the most critical decisions with virtually no input from anyone with any expertise on Indochina. And they did not factor in any part of the French experience in their war there!" "A large part of their problem stemmed from the arrogance of all of those elites from the Atlantic. It was as if those men in power did not need to know about such a distant and less worthy part of the world. They knew it all" (46)

On August 20 more attacks were made against the S. Vietnamese Buddhist monks and the next day numerous Vietnamese officials resigned. Additional riots followed as did the alarming news stories. Many in power would continue to complain that the young reporters were undermining the regime in Saigon the same way reports had hurt Chiang Kai-shek by calling attention to the corruption and incompetence in his regime.

The *NY Times* was not happy with this latest controversy. They had given reporter H. Matthews's early stories on Castro a sympathetic tone and look how that had turned out. Now they were being accused of trying to pave the way for a Vietnamese – Castro.

In late August the Nuh's staged a series of mass arrests. The U.S. Embassy and the CIA station gave reports of the arrests in one political direction while Halberstam's reports stated the events completely opposite. At first the *Times* wanted to put the State Department's version on page 1 and Halberstam's story inside the paper. But his patron Scotty Reston who was running the Washington Bureau convinced the editors not to second guess the man in the field.

To their credit the Times put both stories on page 1, side by side.
(Let the reader decide which story is the truth. This is the same premise that FOX News alone tries to do.)

Three days later the events in the country forced the State Dept to admit that their official version had been wrong.

At a meeting of the National Security Council on Aug 31, 1963 Far Eastern expert Paul Kattenburg spoke up saying that Diem could not win against the communists.

He was the first senior civilian in the administration who recommended that the U.S. withdraw from Vietnam now, or we would be forced out within six months.

McNamara, Taylor, Rusk and others vehemently opposed his viewpoint and he was soon removed from the council and transferred to a lesser job.

Again Pres. Kennedy did not realize that this blatant move to eliminate dissent was sabotaging our efforts. So many dissenters had been replaced no one else wanted to speak out. **Months later Kattenburg would state that the war was lost long ago. If the U.S. went into Vietnam now it would require 500,000 troops and five to ten years of blood and commitment.** (How right he was.)

More and more racial demonstrations were being held in the U.S.

Some of the southern states still refused to abide by the civil rights laws passed by Eisenhower. RFK met with Alabama Governor Wallace to convince him to comply.

He refused, and in May 1963 large protests and arrests resulted in Federal troops being used to keep the peace. In Mississippi over 600 children were arrested, and Civil Rights activists were murdered. Even into September Gov. Wallace still defied the federal laws.

In England former senior diplomat/agent Kim Philby was finally named as the 3d man in the infamous spy ring that had included Guy Burgess and Donald Maclean. To protect the latter two spies the Soviets insured that Burgess and Maclean escaped back in 1951 when the evidence against them was getting strong. With the other two gone, Philby naturally became suspect number one. He was questioned on and off until 1955 and was wrongly cleared of being an enemy spy.

Philby was next posted to Beirut, but his luck finally ran out in 1963. Another British agent in Lebanon obtained concrete evidence of Philby's guilt. Knowing he would face life behind bars or possibly a death sentence, Philby hid on a Soviet freighter and escaped to Moscow. Instead of a hero's welcome, the treacherous dog was treated as a low level KGB agent because even the Soviets did not trust him.

Philby was one of a villainous group known as the Cambridge five which had included Burgess, Maclean, Anthony Blunt and John Cairncross. As shown earlier Philby was the spy who had contacted Moscow about the damaging testimony Elisabeth Bentley had given. Because of that warning and other Intel they quickly shut down the entire spy ring and no damaging arrests were made. During his career he had ruthlessly betrayed dozens of British and allied agents leading to their capture and deaths.

But his most important mission of treason had been in 1949. Albania was starving and in disarray. The people had had enough of the communists and Stalin. Home grown insurgents became active and they reached out to the West for help. *Philby who was still based in Washington in 1949 was given control of the operation. He planned the pro-freedom insurgent attacks and insured supplies reached the them.*

Philby then tipped off the Soviets, who ambushed the insurgents killing and capturing all of them. As a result of his treachery, Albania would remain communist and their people suffered another 40 years of tyranny!

Vietnam

The White House had announced in late July that Henry Cabot Lodge would replace Nolting as the Ambassador in Vietnam by late August. "More policy moves would follow". The politician in John Kennedy sent Lodge in as they prepared to remove Diem.

Lodge had been the Republican senator from Massachusetts that JFK had beaten, He had also been Richard Nixon's running mate in 1960. By having a major Republican in on the coup, Kennedy hoped to defer the conservative complaints on Vietnam.

(Why Lodge took the appointment is a mystery. Surely he could see that it was just a blatant political move by the scheming Democrats as the election neared. William Perry would accept the same type of appointment from Bill Clinton after Somalia in 94.)

Throughout the fall of 1963 the numbers of Viet Cong fighters and sympathizers continued to increase due to NVA reinforcements, propaganda, communist terrorism, the Buddhist crisis, casualties to civilians and the rampant corruption that was undermining everything that was being done.

Over 1500 additional fighters and support personnel were infiltrating in from the North each month. Defeat was around the corner.

Like Paul Kattenburg, Ambassador Lodge was well seasoned and had traveled widely through Vietnam. He was soon aware of just how bad things really were and began arguing with Harkins. (If he realized the issues within weeks of arriving you would have thought everyone should have too.)

One of Lodge's assistants was David G. Nes. He too consistently warned that ARVN were losing and would soon disintegrate. Within weeks Nes also began arguing with MACV about the accuracy of their reports. (After JFK was murdered the realists in the Administration were quietly moved aside or forced out, Nes included.)

At MACV the military briefings run by Harkins had painted a picture that those young reporters were completely wrong about Vietnam. But Lodge found it hard to believe that *all of the reporters* felt the same way. Once in his new post he questioned Sheehan, Halberstam and Browne about the regime and the many problems. Lodge had arrived during the Buddhist crisis, in which the regime brutally put down a Buddhist revolt. That effort was the last straw for most as they felt the regime's time in power had to end. All of the reporters agreed that the Ngo Dinhs had to go if there was to be any chance against the VC. Lodge felt the same way as the reporters, and when the Pentagon papers were released illegally his secret cables would show this.

Soon after he had arrived Lodge cabled JFK and said that "there was no way to win under a Diem government". Lodge began to insinuate that maybe it was time for the Ngo Dinhs to be replaced. Word quickly got back to Diem.

Lodge put former Lansdale partner Lou Conein to work to court three possible generals as replacements. Conein had worked with all of them back in 1955, when all were colonels. They trusted him and meetings were held but at that time there was no support among the S. Vietnamese for a coup. Pres. Kennedy was updated at a meeting with Nolting and later by Harriman and Roger Hilsman.

Averill Harriman who was under secretary of state for political affairs, and Roger Hilsman who was in the Far Eastern affairs section were also actively trying to persuade JFK to replace Diem. Hilsman had briefed the president that of the 20,000 "VC" reported killed in 1961, no one knew how many were just civilians caught in the crossfire or bombings.

The JCS and former Ambassador Nolting were against removing Diem for there was no replacement to be found at that critical juncture. Gen. Harkins was also against any coup, he did not want any unknowns

to disrupt the war effort. (*He knew nothing about the war he was supposed to be leading, but was dead right about the coup.*)
It was the wrong thing to do militarily or politically.

On his side were Taylor, McCone and McNamara.

Lodge made sure not to confront Harkins over any issues. Instead he undercut him by using the CIA cable system to bypass him. Lodge also sent JFK cables that told the truth about the war, just the way Vann had wanted to do a year ago.

The ARVN generals knew and had admitted that they were losing the war. They were now eager to overthrow Diem.

(It is not clear if their motives were nationalistic or inspired by greed. They were not helping to win, but were anxious for a chance to be number one.)

On September 19 Lodge sent a "President only cable" that reported the view of Gen. Minh; The VC were gaining everywhere, the prisons were full and the population under VC control is larger than the one under the S. Vietnamese government.

Kennedy was uncertain what to do. He feared the communist expansion but had no understanding of the political and social revolution in Vietnam. He sent Gen. Krulak and Joseph Mendenhall from the Dept. of State back to Vietnam for yet another assessment. Upon their return days later they had diametrically opposed reports.

Krulak as always stated we were winning, while Mendenhall stated we would lose soon. JFK was stunned when the NSC briefing ended.

"You two did visit the same country didn't you?!"

Krulak replied that Mendenhall had visited the cities, while he went to the countryside where the "war was". In actuality the war was being fought everywhere, but Krulak was ignorant of that reality since he saw only what he wanted.

At the meeting was Rufus Phillips also from State. He backed up Mendenhall's side of the story because he had talked with many of the ARVN Commanders one on one. (Similar to what Gen. York had done when he was roaming around.) Phillips told JFK that there was a crisis of confidence in the South and he knew of only one man who might be able to help, Lansdale. He also flat out told the president that we were losing and things were in a tragic state.

Phillips then produced a report from an Army major at Long An who was an advisor. The report so contradicted Krulak that JFK was speechless.
Averill Harriman yelled at Krulak calling him a damn fool.
(The Army Major was ruined for giving the report to Phillips.)

This was a classic case of our military being turned into a separate bureaucracy intent only on its institutional needs, its priorities, egos, vanities and careerism by those in authority. As one of the original whistleblowers, he should have been treated with praise and those who went after him should have been imprisoned. (And Kennedy should have insured that officer was not harmed by the military bureaucracy.)

More acrimonious debate followed over four days.

Roger Hilsman had also commissioned an earlier report that ended up highly critical of MACV. McNamara, Krulak and the JCS were angered that the State Dept. dared to challenge the DoD, yet here they were again on opposite sides of the issue.

Those in the hot seat then followed the same pattern of attack and defense they used against Phillips. The President's advisors were hopelessly split over what course to take, and so was he.

JFK told a friend that his government was coming apart.

In an interview with David Brinkley, JFK stated that the U.S. had to stay the course in Vietnam to prevent another communist takeover. He reiterated his belief in the domino principal and that Red China was the key to the problems in Asia. That was why **25,000** Americans were in SE Asia, to help in the struggle.

Two weeks later Gen. Taylor and Sec. McNamara were sent to Vietnam.

They were to discuss all of the issues including a coup. McNamara spent a week traveling all over but any time he asked questions Harkins and Taylor were nearby ensuring the advisors gave the correct answers.

At a meeting with Diem, his staff and Vice President Tho, the Americans admonished the Diem government for their repressions and social unrest. *Tho eventually tired of their umbrage, and chastised them for the VC advances. Tho stated that the disastrous strategic hamlet program was what had caused the increased conversion to the VC.* Taylor became upset that this pet program and general were under fire, but Tho parried all of his responses.

"There are only 20-30 secure hamlets in the entire country, the rest are captive audiences for the VC".

Vice President Tho's statements and accusations were deceitfully deleted from the reports filed by Taylor and McNamara. None of his ruler straight criticisms made it to Pres. Kennedy's eyes or ears.

The pair and staff returned to Washington at the end of September and still professed that "the military campaign was making great progress.

Victory would come by 1965". To maintain their Lie, they reluctantly recommended and JFK endorsed a proposal that 1000 advisors could come home in December 1963." (47)

(This move was also made with an eye on the reelection campaign.)

Despite their report the President gained no peace of mind as the CIA was still reporting on the same dire outlook as Lodge had weeks before. *JFK again spoke to Senator Mike Mansfield and told him that we could not leave Vietnam until 1965, after I'm re-elected.*
Arthur Schlesinger tried to explain away the remark by reminding people that the Republicans won in 52 because Truman "lost China". (48)

(According to the book *JFK and Vietnam*, JFK asked Sen. Mike Mansfield to do an appraisal of S. Vietnam. As stated earlier Mansfield reported back that we should give up and get out. At first Kennedy was angry, but over time he may have seen the reality.

He told Mansfield at a later meeting that he could not get out of Vietnam politically until after he was reelected.)

Updates from South Vietnam indicated that the ARVN Generals were unanimous that they could not win with Diem. **On October 5, the unsure Kennedy wrongly decided to allow the coup.** He had wanted a guarantee that the coup would be successful, but Lodge cabled back that they could give no such guarantee. *JFK also insisted on no direct U.S. participation and that any actions must be secure and fully deniable!* Robert Kennedy was unsure on if we should do it, while Rusk warned if we can't win with him there is no longer a choice. LBJ was completely against the coup.

Taylor was upset over this whole affair. Since August all of this was being done behind Harkin's back. Harkins even tried to stop the effort. He met with Col. Khuong who wanted his support, but instead Harkins refused and warned Diem about the plot.

(The Nhu's planned for the coup, but were outfoxed by a traitor.)

All incoming reports from Lodge and the CIA were completely at odds with those from MACV. At best the situation in Vietnam was back to the beginning of the year.
Lodge warned that the struggle in the country was Political and Military, and they were intertwined.

On Oct 22 NY Times publisher Arthur Sulzberger saw JFK at the White House. Kennedy wanted Halberstam transferred. His reporting was causing major <u>political trouble</u> for the White House. (It always hurts when the truth gets out.)

JFK need not have worried for Halberstam was soon to leave as he too was rotating out. (Vann had actually sent letters out defending the reporters in Vietnam, but only Newsweek had the courage to publish them.)

The coup plotting continued and on November 1, the National police HQ was taken over. Three hours later Diem called Lodge and asked what the position of the United States was. Lodge dodged the question and repeated that safe passage had been offered to Diem and his brother Nhu. Lodge was basically telling Diem that his time was over and the offer was genuine.

Instead the brothers escaped into the Chinese district of Cholon while the Palace was taken over. His trusted guards died not knowing Diem was already in hiding.

Gen. Minh was the principal architect of the coup and would be taking over the Government of S. Vietnam.

The next morning the Nhu brothers were found, bound and shot.

Minh did not trust them to stay away.

The youngest Nhu brother had sought refuge in the U.S. consulate in Hue. He was tricked into getting on a plane for a flight to safety when in reality he was taken to Saigon and also shot. Madame Nhu was in the U.S. at the time and she joined her brother the Archbishop in Rome.

Lodge was not unhappy with the ending though the Kennedy's were not as pleased. *This event became the most sordid episode in U.S. Foreign Policy and was a huge mistake. The infighting among the generals would grow and grant 15 months of political chaos to the VC. And once again a Democratic President had turned on an ally with catastrophic consequences.*

(The White House records of the meetings after the coup were never de-classified and are now lost!)

It was true that Diem was not in the same league as an American politician, but we were not fighting communists in America. Like Chiang in China, Diem's efforts were based on his cultural background and were quite similar to John Kennedy.

Diem's most trusted officials were his family.

It takes decades to turn a country that had never known Democracy into a cohesive nation with the rule of law. (Just look at America's beginning.) Vietnam was like dozens of nations ruled by autocratic rulers, harsh and at times upended. But things would not improve with the Nhu's gone.

It was Pres. Eisenhower and his State Dept. failed to get Diem on the right track. All of our aid should have had strings attached to make him fix what was broken. Kennedy had inherited Diem and his Fatal Flaws. **But JFK was completely wrong for not standing up to the media and the complaining liberals and explaining the situation. Diem** was far from perfect, but the world needed to know it was the communists that were causing Diem to rule so harshly.

(Former V.P. Nixon was in Pakistan on a worldwide trip. At a reception with Pakistani Pres. Ayub Khan the Pakistani ruler told Nixon that everyone in Asia was unhappy with the U.S. complicity in the Diem coup. "It was dangerous to be a friend of America. It pays to remain neutral, and sometimes it helps to be an enemy.") (49)

Within a week of the coup reports coming into the Ambassador's office displayed outright honesty. All of their information was terrible, staggering the staff.

Even those who had been somewhat pessimistic of the MACV fluff could not fathom how bad things really were.

And then the VC launched major attacks all across the Delta and in the rubber plantations north of Saigon. Numerous S. Vietnamese outposts were assaulted and overrun at will. Roads were under constant ambush and snipers were always present.

The communists claimed that the attacks had been planned earlier and were not affected by the coup, but they certainly reacted quickly and always in the right locations.

The extent of those latest battles actually revealed that all of Gen. Harkins (and Taylor and McNamara) previous claims of success were all lies. If MACV operations had been performing as stated those numerous strong attacks could never had happened.

But the slick Harkins and MACV took advantage of the coup and conveniently blamed the Diem government for the military collapse. (It is always expedient to blame the dead.) Areas that had been constantly listed as "under Government control" suddenly could not be entered without a battalion of troops. Hundreds of Strategic Hamlets that were listed on those stupid charts ceased to exist. With the fall of so many outposts, another 10,000 weapons and tons of ammunition fell into enemy hands.

By mid-November the situation in the south was looking grim. **Kennedy became somber and shaken by this point, realizing that his policies in Vietnam had completely failed.**

JFK's approved increases at MACV had expanded our advisors in S. Vietnam to over 16,000. He had authorized our advisors to engage in combat, to fly combat missions and conduct covert raids in the North. He had stated many times that America was unequivocally committed to preserve South Vietnam. And his initial drawdown of 1,000 troops was done bureaucratically, by delaying their replacements.

On November 20, 1963 in a meeting at Honolulu, Krulak wanted to institute additional clandestine warfare in the north by dropping in teams of commandos. He vainly and imprudently hoped that increasing the raids would relieve the pressure in the South. CIA station chief Colby had started that very program in 1959 with little success. And the insertion of the earlier McNamara-Krulak teams had all failed as the communist stay behind spies had learned of the time and locations of the planned raids before they even left S. Vietnam! All of those teams had been captured or killed, costing the ARVN many of their most promising personnel.

In desperation McNamara agreed with Krulak, while Colby who was now head of the Far East Division at CIA disagreed. With prior team losses of greater than 95%, Colby knew the effort was worthless. McNamara insisted that they had to continue despite any losses. (This bureaucrat was typically unconcerned with the lives that would be lost.) None of the principals could grasp that these commando style operations had been compromised. No one has that much success at intercepting those types of teams.

But McNamara was also doing JFK's bidding for he too was behind Krulak's scheme. All of them desperately hoped that with the military running larger units over the border some success might be achieved. **At the present pace Vietnam would probably fall before the 1964 election, and that would cause Kennedy to lose.**

(Ironically one thing was achieved with those additional commando teams, the incident at Tonkin Gulf that Lyndon Johnson would use as a pretext for war.)

Two days after the Honolulu conference JFK was shot and murdered in Dallas.

Four days later Lyndon Baines Johnson, (LBJ), the new President signed a top secret national Security Memorandum NSAM-273 accepting the recommendations at Honolulu and continuing the U.S. war effort. But the paper Johnson signed was different than the original draft.

LBJ was escalating the covert war in the South because he did not want to lose it, not with the 1964 election looming. But he also had to be careful not to draw too much attention to it lest he be voted out. *With Kennedy gone, Johnson was finally getting his chance at the White House.*

There were many inconsistencies in the saga of JFK's murder. The event was supposedly investigated by the Warren Commission, but dozens of eye witnesses were never interviewed. And many of those who were interviewed gave statements that directed the fatal shots to the grassy knoll. One witness helped place the president into a decorative wooden coffin in Dallas. Because "officials" insisted he had to be autopsied in Washington, the coffin with JFK was placed on the plane and flown to D.C. But film of the coffin coming off of the plane in Washington was a plain metal one.

What happened to the decorative wooden one? One of the naval corpsmen who had worked on the president in Dallas had wrapped him up when he was placed in the wooden coffin. He was present when the body was placed on the autopsy table and saw that the wrapping was different. When they unwrapped the body he saw that the wounds were different. Conspiracies grew quickly and have not ended.

As shown above, just before his death JFK had signed off to reduce the numbers of advisors but it is not clear if he would have pulled out completely. And the one person who had the most to gain from Kennedy's death was now in power. At a White House reception just before Christmas 1964 Lyndon Johnson told the assembled military leaders,
"Just get me elected and then you can have your war." (50)

Now that he was in charge Johnson was fearful that Vietnam would be lost before the election. Then the Republicans would smear and destroy him as they had Truman for losing China. *All of the U.S. actions undertaken during that time were declared Top Secret, and kept from the eyes and ears of the American people.*

Johnson kept everyone in place during the rest of that term.
"McNamara gave LBJ a self-serving excuse for the failure to perceive the erosion in South Vietnam". In a report on Dec 21, 1963 after another whirlwind "two day trip", he stated that the *Nhu's and lackeys like Gen. Cao* were to blame for the deteriorating situation in the countryside that had occurred *since July!*

"Because of our dependence on distorted Vietnamese reporting, the Viet Cong successes were unforeseen."

McNamara was careful to include some truth, by referencing to an October analysis from The State Dept Bureau of Intelligence and Research.

But no effort was made by any high ranking officials to look back further than July 1963! If they had the "Bright Shining Lie" and its architects would have been exposed.
And that would have wrecked the careers of McNamara, Taylor and Krulak, who were as guilty as Harkins. Thus far over 120 Americans had died in that troubled land.

Many more would follow. (51)

David Halberstam and his negative reporting about Vietnam were vindicated by a Pulitzer Prize in Dec 1963. He continued to write articles and bring up Vann's ideas and succinct warnings. His 1965 book, *The Making of a Quagmire* tells a sad tale. Vann was quoted often and told how the senior officers lied repeatedly. He was shown to be the one true David, for resigning in protest to Goliath's lies and corruption.

On January 22, 1964 the Joint Chiefs sent McNamara a referendum on Vietnam and SE Asia. The documents they sent referenced the NSAM 273 from November 26, 1963. But the report Johnson's signed called NSAM 273 was exactly the opposite position of what the JCS advised. *It had been altered.*

This report from the JCS warned again that the U.S. must be more aggressive in its operations in Vietnam which included mining the ports of N. Vietnam. Victory could only happen if we fought on our terms, not the enemy's.

McNamara did not forward it.

On the 24th MACV established a special operations group that would have control over the upcoming DE SOTO patrols. Using U.S. destroyers, the naval force would run missions in the Gulf of Tonkin for sabotage, recon, photographic missions and electronic surveillance of the North. The ships were authorized to get as close as four miles to North Vietnam.

South, Vietnam's Generals were good at plotting coups but could not govern. At 4 am on Jan. 26th Gen. Minh was himself overthrown in a coup. Gen. Khanh and forces loyal to him reacted to rumors that Minh was about to enter an agreement with the communists. Khanh took over, but he was no better.

LBJ was unhappy with this latest change in rulers but wrote to Gen. Khanh that it was vital for him to fight the war aggressively. Ambassador Lodge visited the new leader and pushed LBJ's message.

This latest coup proved that McCone and the others were right to have been against the Diem plot. There was no one else. Divisions within the LBJ Administration began to grow as many could see that Vietnam was falling apart. McNamara was optimistic in public but privately told Johnson that if things don't turn around soon the South would only last a few more months. *(Quite a change of view considering he had told JFK in late September that we were winning.)*

To try to "help the effort" in Vietnam Harkins was "promoted out" and his deputy Gen. William Westmoreland placed in charge. *(Westmoreland was yet another pick by Taylor. He had guided and helped Westy throughout his career.*

Gen. Harkins was not relieved or sent home in disgrace. He was not officially blamed at all. He was simply undercut, ignored and insulted in the press.

His deputy Gen. Westmoreland attended all of the latest conferences and planning sessions. In late January 1964 Harkins rotated out, went to the White House and was decorated". His legacy was destruction and despair.

After the Diem coup Lodge and Harkins would not work together so the American effort was further undercut. With Harkins gone Lodge had hoped to work with Westmoreland and offered him an office in the Embassy so they could plan together. Westy refused, because of the coup.

As time went by Ambassador Lodge was becoming increasingly frustrated with the evident collapse of S. Vietnam. He recommended bombing the North as a way to buy time. More and more red areas covered the maps of the South.

Plots and attempts at plots controlled the government of the South and its actions. And all the while the communists gained more ground and converts.

The imprudent coup against Diem had actually handed the South to the communists on a silver platter. Statements from Hanoi after the war detailed how happy they were that Diem was gone. With their only potential rival removed from office, the communists rushed their efforts to take advantage of the power vacuum.

Ho and his people were increasingly upset that the mounting desertions from the ARVN did not result in large gains for the local VC. They felt it should have.

But almost all of the disgruntled civilians, soldiers and former governmental people stayed away from the communists.
Chairman Mao suggested the Vietminh should slow their efforts.
"A long road tests a horse's strength, a long march tests his heart." (52)

On March 10, 1964 David Nes wrote a memo detailing how all communist efforts needed safe supply zones, such as China had provided to N. Korea, and the Balkan communists gave to their attempts in Greece. In SE Asia the enemy's use Laos and Cambodia as sanctuary, and was the main reason for their successes.

If we did not end that sanctuary the war effort was doomed. His report was not well received by the Johnson team.

By the spring of 1964 the Central Highlands also fell to the communists.

MACV personnel had been silently increased to almost 20,000. LBJ had kept all of JFK's team relying on them to make things in Vietnam work. Had he known that those people were the ones who created this debacle, or was he beholden to them? Or was he so preoccupied with his election that he did not care about Vietnam?

LBJ would lie and spin his extremely short WWII public relations time in a visible effort to gain from it. He did not like the military as a whole and disliked most of the senior officers. In one week he fired three military advisors and often berated the JCS stating that he would not follow any of their advice.

During that time McNamara and Taylor "went back to Vietnam on another fact finding mission". All knew the NVA were coming in through Laos but they had no "proof of how it all worked". McNamara insisted the ARVN troops search west from Khe Sanh as far as Tchepone in Laos. SOG (Special Observation Group), commanders responded that only their people could pull off those tough recon missions. But at that time they were not allowed to do so.

No new military information was brought back to LBJ since McNamara and Taylor's staffs had drafted "their report" before they had even left the States. With the collusion from those two the JCS would have no say in the future course of America's role in Vietnam, only the civilians would. *McNamara actually felt that prior military experience was irrelevant in Vietnam.*

And Taylor tried to make himself king among the JCS by recommending the elimination of the JCS. He continued to staff every position possible with loyal subordinates, and as stated above worked closely with McNamara to close out any JCS input into the military voice in Vietnam. Gen. Krulak would get his 3d star and became commander of the Fleet Marine Force based in Hawaii. There he would see first hand the disaster he had allowed.

At MACV Gen. William Westmoreland had been an artilleryman in N. Africa and in Sicily during WWII. In Korea near the end of the war he transferred into an airborne unit but saw little of the war because there was no real use for airborne troops in the static trenchline fighting. *The current war in Vietnam was an Infantryman's war and needed someone who truly understood infantry operations down to the squad level.*
Westmoreland was not that person.

Gen. Westmoreland was one of those who looked good, but seldom was good. He was the exact opposite from the Terry Allen's or the George Patton's.

And despite the "New Army" requirement that all commanders were supposed to become educated, Westmoreland had only attended two Army Schools. The Airborne School at Fort Benning in 1952, and an Army cook and baker school in Hawaii!
(He also attended a 13 week Harvard course on business management in 1954.)

Westy never attended the Army War College nor its Command and General Staff College. Yet he was the one picked for this most vital assignment by, Maxwell Taylor.

(Gen. Harold Johnson the Asst. Army Chief of Staff was upset at Taylor's pick. Attempts were made to intervene with the Sec. of the Army but it had already become a done deal.)

By this time McNamara had successfully pushed his premise of *graduated response onto our operations in Vietnam.* Having never served in the frontline of a conflict he sought to "control the war with what he thought was the successful strategy used in the Cuban missile crisis" and relying on quantitative analysis. Once again the observation reappears of how one bad decision was used to justify more bad decisions. The naval blockade appeared to have worked in Cuba because Khrushchev stopped the missile shipments and no shots were fired.

Had it not been for the secret deal that Kennedy made, JFK would have been required to try to eject the Russians by force of arms, surrender, or do nothing and lose the elections for the Democrats.

McNamara conceitedly felt that Vietnam was just like Cuba, and he intended to use the same policy. He believed that; *"The use of force was not to impose one's will on the enemy, but to communicate with them". Gradually increasing the pressure would convey America's resolve and convince the adversary to change their course of action.*

Almost all of the "whiz kids" that McNamara had brought into the Pentagon followed the same ridiculous line of reasoning. *Cyrus Vance* was one of those who worked behind the scenes controlling the war effort during those years.

"We believed in graduated response and felt that if the restrained application of force were applied in S. Vietnam, one could expect a positive result". **(53)**

(Vance would become Sec of State in the disastrous Carter Administration.

His prior failures and mindset would continue during Carter's years and bring more problems to America and the world.)

LBJ embraced their policy since it gave the appearance that we and especially he were the moderates in the war. The presidential election was close at hand and Johnson was determined that he would keep his chance to be number one.

The JCS was still being ignored by the Administration even though the senior generals were warning that the U.S. had to take a hard line in Vietnam or not go at all. At their meetings Taylor insisted on the military working within the premise of graduated response. *To ensure that his version was the one heard by the White House, he would downplay any misgivings from the JCS. He also eliminated all back-channel communications between the military and the White House.*

Thus the only opinions that would be heard were his and McNamara's!

Gen. LeMay USAF was completely against that line of thought, and had the command and operational experience to back it up. *LeMay succinctly warned that the current poor policies being followed would result in direct American involvement over an indefinite period of time. And accomplish nothing.*

JFK, LBJ, McNamara and Taylor disliked the USAF Chief of Staff because of his outspokenness and they tried to ignore his ideas as often as they were made. While he was Chairman, Taylor would listen to the general's statements but never present them. Now that he was in power, *Lyndon Johnson was afraid that a Gen. LeMay retired would begin speaking out about the subterfuge and mistakes by the Democratic Administrations.* (The same fear about George Patton.)

LeMay had the resume, experience and following that the media would listen to him. To keep him quite, LBJ reappointed LeMay for another year as USAF Chief of Staff. *In that way he could be legally silenced until after the election!*

Gen. David Shoup Commandant USMC was absolutely against any U.S. war effort in SE Asia. He had gone to Vietnam in 1962 to learn for himself what was going on. Again this senior officer had plenty of command and battlefield experience to develop his negative decision. He also based his anti-involvement feelings on the derisive effects the "limited scope" of the Korean War had caused.

(If you are going to fight, fight to win.)

Even though the U.N., (especially America), had won the Korean War, it was not perceived as a victory because N. Korea still existed. As a result of that "half truth", none of the lessons from the war had been learned by any of our political or military leaders. *Military schools were not even teaching classes about the war, instead just concentrating on fighting the Russians in Europe!* In Korea unwise political decisions had overruled sound military ones.

Shoup felt the same stupid thing would happen in Vietnam.

Gen. Wallace Greene soon rotated in replacing Shoup at the helm of the USMC. Greene also had a lot of combat on his resume and demanded that we either pull out completely or stay there to win. *He had his staff prepare a 24 point plan for the USMC part of the war, to secure all of coastal Vietnam.* Most of the population lived within 15 miles of the coast and operating near the coast would be the USMC forte. They were not designed or equipped to do anything else.

Again the conniving Taylor never forwarded this well researched proposal.

This time he held it up because it "only concerned Marine Operations".

(Instead of being deceitful and petty Taylor should have had all of the service chiefs enact similar war plans in a coordinated effort. They knew their services best and knew their limitations and strong points. But he did not. Why?)

Johnson created the "Sullivan Committee to explore and pursue" his slowly escalating war against N. Vietnam. *He worked hard to forestall all efforts by the military for a larger buildup until after the election was over.* His self-serving scheming further weakened the South and allowed the communists more time to grow stronger.

In no time the Joint Chiefs of Staff were so tired of the Administration's runaround that they war-gamed LBJ's and McNamara's graduated response program on their own. **Their month long workup was eerily prophetic as every move the U.S actually enacted, the communists made the exact moves the JCS staff had predicted!**

As stated above to shut down any attempts by the JCS to communicate directly with the president McNamara also severed all lines of communication between the Pentagon and the White House.

The military chiefs could only speak through McNamara, and he ensured that none of their ideas or demands were ever heard.

In May 1964 the JCS met without either of the micro-managers being present. *They produced a statement that expressed their concern over the lack of military definition for Vietnam, lack of objectives in Vietnam and confusion over how to achieve any objectives there.*

They were also against using the military to "send messages or signals" to the communist North. (Their intent was for this serious message to be read at the next Honolulu Conference.)

Relying on photo-recon missions the JCS developed an updated bombing plan for use against the North. They had pinpointed 94 primary targets, suppression of anti-aircraft batteries, missions to rescue downed pilots, and other tactical issues.

Aircraft carriers would be stationed in the Gulf of Tonkin and launch the raids repetitively.

On June 1 Taylor had the document withdrawn because he had not been there to oversee it! The JCS resubmitted the paper while the principals were meeting in Honolulu to "discuss the war". Gen. Greene used well placed officers to ensure the duplicitous Taylor would read the document as written.

But Taylor again refused to submit their paper because he opposed their viewpoint. Thus their outstanding work was kept hidden.

One of the most distressing aspects to Vietnam was that no one in either Democratic Administration ever asked the American people if we should become engaged in a war in Vietnam.

Following the lead of Truman in Korea, both JFK and LBJ simply made the decision to send troops into those countries.

Only after multiple thousands of the troops had been committed and placed in combat did Truman, Kennedy or LBJ look for approval.

In the Congo the multi-year communist rebellion had been gaining ground. Working with the CIA, George Godley oversaw the U.S. led counter strikes that finally stopped the Chinese backed rebels. That war was one of the places David Halberstam had covered. He knew what a communist insurrection looked and felt like, and that was why he and so many others knew what Harkins had been doing in Vietnam was wrong.

The peace that was obtained would be short lived.

Maxwell Taylor became the new Ambassador to S. Vietnam. Working from Saigon Taylor was to oversee all civilian and military matters.
He then handpicked his successor to head the JCS, Gen. Earl Wheeler.

Wheeler was wrongly promoted above many other senior generals, and his selection again went against the previous protocol for picking the head of the JCS which was supposed to be a rotation among all of the military services.

Wheeler was the third successive army officer to head the Joint Chiefs. (As hard as it is to believe Wheeler too had almost no combat experience as he had been a staff officer throughout WWII.)

Ambassador Taylor arrived in Saigon on July 7, 1964. Within a week he realized that things were far worse than he had thought and immediately sent in a request for two thousand more advisors. Days later the figure was increased to 4,200.

He hoped that within a year the 24,000+ U.S. personnel could make a twofold increase in the number of places they worked.

Taylor was another one of those micro-managers who insisted on total control. Over the past two years he had controlled almost everything going on in Vietnam. But once he was assigned there he was finding he controlled nothing in S. Vietnam.

Nothing worked.

U-2 flights were mapping the entire region. **They had also picked up the construction along the Ho Chi Minh Trail as roads were**

now being built using heavy machinery! And anti-aircraft guns were spotted. As a result of that buildup McNamara and Taylor wanted the SF teams to scout "illegally" into Laos. But the Ambassador in Laos William Sullivan did not want any SOG teams operating in his "neutral" nation.

Limited by those rules the SF teams had to secretly walk into Laos to make their recon, a difficult mission at best. By the summer 1964 thousands of NVA troops were moving down the trail each month and over 30,000 were employed in construction, security and logistics of the trail.

Gen. Westmoreland then asked for another increase in the helicopter units being sent. The lack of good roads in the South and the constant VC attacks on the roads made it a necessity to hop around in the helicopters. (Remote areas could be accessed in an hour by air vs a week long overland journey subjected to mines, snipers and ambush.)

LBJ insisted that all of this bad information about South Vietnam and the need for more troops had to remain secret. He did not want any public disclosure of the problems or troop increases with the election just four months away. In all of the speeches and talks during the final months of the campaign the Democrats led by LBJ worked nonstop to deflect any criticisms away from him. Misrepresentation of the facts was a common tactic. (Sound familiar.) Gen. Wheeler accidentally mentioned the needed increase in advisors on July 15, and the media ran with the story. The Administration became enraged as they had to work hard to cover up the issue. But they did.

And that was the greatest failure by the Joint Chiefs of Staff.

They should have gone to the media/ Congress and given detailed accounts of Vietnam.

The American people had the need and the right to know what was going on, for again the Democrats were running a war in secret. And again it was not their sons and daughters who had to pay the price.

With the increasing tensions with America, Mao Zedong told N. Vietnamese Army Chief Gen. Van Tien Dung that their two countries must fight the imperialists together. Soon after Zhou En-Lai and staff traveled to Hanoi to speak with their communist brethren from Laos and Vietnam. China was committing to supplying both countries with large scale military aid.

William Colby's assertions that Krulak's commando schemes would not work was proved correct. The Studies and Observation Group, (SOG), had overseen the training of the personnel and implementation of the latest commando teams.

Every team was caught within two days of parachuting over the border.

Some were destroyed, and some were turned to transmit communist messages.

Their naval counterparts also accomplished little in their shore raiding parties. Despite their lack of accomplishments or success McNamara insisted that the attempts continue.

As alluded to earlier, the only thing those raids did accomplish was to incite the North to increase their security by augmenting their PT boat fleet operations.

As the shore raids continued they provoked the North Vietnamese to attack any ships that were operating north of the 17th parallel.

On August 2, 1964 North Vietnamese PT boats made runs at a U.S. destroyer in daylight in the Gulf of Tonkin. Their action was in retaliation for an ARVN-U.S. raid on the islands and bases of N. Vietnam the day before. Three communist PT boats charged at the USN Destroyer *Maddox* in the early afternoon. The *Maddox* left the area at high speed but was pursued by the PT boats. Shots were fired hitting two of the enemy boats. The N. Vietnamese boats hit the *Maddox* with one machine gun bullet, but missed with two torpedoes. LBJ "refused to counterattack", to be seen as the man for peace.

In the background however he directed McNamara to be prepared to strike the North should they attack the navy destroyers again.

At a breakfast with Democratic leaders LBJ pressed them to provide a resolution allowing him to strike if another attack occurred.
The party faithful readily agreed.

In the early hours on the 4th a second enemy attack was reported but was never confirmed! The U.S. destroyers had been patrolling in the Gulf over a dozen miles out at sea. No battle damage or actual sighting was confirmed of any enemy PT boat, torpedo or wreckage. And flying above the destroyers had been eight planes from the aircraft carrier the *USS Ticonderoga*. They too saw no enemy ships, or wakes.

Admiral Sharp CINPAC, (Commander in Chief Pacific) was informed that the issue was questionable and he relayed the information to Washington.

(NSA intercepts were also sketchy over the incident. Most showed that the North Vietnamese boats were at sea trying to salvage the ones shot up on August 2.)

Despite the many negative updates from the scene the President announced to key Democratic members of Congress that the destroyers had definitely been attacked! He also told them that this time we would retaliate and expected a resolution of support from the Congress. (This was all part of the plan that his team had laid out.)

Just before midnight LBJ appeared on television to report on the "repeated acts of violence against our armed forces". We will respond to their attacks with alert defenses, and a positive reply.
Our reprisals will be "limited in scale".

(Johnson had already ordered the U.S. Navy to send planes to destroy the enemy PT bases and oil storage at Hon Gai and Quang Khe. It was reported that 25 patrol boats had been destroyed at a cost of four of our carrier planes.)

LBJ used those *Tonkin Gulf battle reports* to get the Senate to give him an advance declaration of war without actually giving one. LBJ had been a member of the Senate since 1948 and was a power broker and a player in that world. Many owed him.

The Democratic controlled Congress gave him everything he wanted with the resolution that his staff helped write.
"Johnson would later quip, The new resolution was like grandma's night shirt, it covered everything!" (54)

(Senator Fulbright was told by Johnson to make sure the resolution passed as fast as possible with the largest vote as possible. Fulbright worked on the doubters like McGovern, Nelson and Cooper to ensure unanimity.)

In the short Congressional hearings that were held on the Gulf of Tonkin Rusk and McNamara actively deceived the Senate committee about the clandestine raids we sent to North Vietnam.
And LBJ wanted it that way.
It was better if they could avoid a long public debate on Vietnam and any policies.
Gen. Wheeler was there too and he never volunteered the truth about the raids.

Walt Rostow had convinced Johnson months earlier that he would need this resolution to prevent Vietnam from becoming a partisan topic in the upcoming election. Nearly every senior Administration official agreed that they needed this **Congressional Prop** to underpin their efforts for a larger U.S. presence in Vietnam.

While they plotted all of this Bundy insisted they should wait until after the Civil Rights Bill had cleared the Senate. With that done the Democrats would feel virtuous which would help to get rapid approval. He also wanted a substantial majority in the Congress to vote yes to alleviate a lot of unwanted scrutiny. To help their plot the Administration would make a major promotional effort. To gird for any disagreeable queries, the officials practiced fielding the tough questions during planning sessions.)

On August 7, the Senate passed the Gulf of Tonkin Resolution, 88-2.
On the 8ᵗʰ the House also voted it in, 416-0.
As can be seen by the dates and timelines there was limited discussion or investigation of the attacks. The two dissenting Senators were Morse and Gruening. They stated that the measure was unconstitutional.

(Some who approved of the measure did say that they feared our troops would be committed to a war but they voted for it anyway.)

Senator Wayne Morse had heard from a source at the Pentagon that the destroyers had been closer to shore than listed, and were on intelligence gathering while the secret raids were going in. **He also heard that the second "attack" could not be verified.** *The next day Morse begged Sen. Fulbright to hold real hearings on the situation and alter the resolution. It was too open ended for someone like LBJ.*

Fulbright refused claiming there was no time with this emergency.

Morse was incredulous, What emergency?

We need to have real discussions on Vietnam and Morse decided he was going to bring in Generals Ridgeway, Schoup, Gavin and Collins to testify.

Fulbright refused to hold any hearings!

The Tonkin Gulf Resolution gave the President as Commander in Chief the authority to use all measures necessary to repel any armed attack against U.S. forces.

But foolishly it also stated that he was allowed to prevent *further aggression.*

It basically gave LBJ *carte blanch* to act in Vietnam.

Statements quickly erupted from Beijing and warned that America was opening up the gates to war. Zhou and China's military leaders asked Hanoi what they needed and convened a major meeting. China went on alert and sent fighters, MiG-15 & 17s near their border and onto Hainan Island. New airfields were constructed in southern China housing MiG-19s.

Ambassador Taylor was becoming more and more vocal about hitting the North hard. (The same message the JCS had tried to voice since 1963, the message he had stopped.) Increased fighting and the political maneuverings by the ARVN senior officers was throwing the country into complete chaos. His new found sympathy for Gen Khanh and the serious trials in the south placed him in direct conflict with Sec. Rusk.

Taylor suggested that the U.S. begin a bombing campaign for January 1965, right after the election was over and LBJ sworn in!

Bundy agreed with Taylor's assessment. The JCS was informed of those discussions days after they had occurred.

They stuck to their original war aims of destroying Hanoi's ability to aid the communist insurrection. As always the members argued among themselves as to which service could best help the South.
Gen. LeMay wanted to bomb the hell out of the North, while Gen. Greene insisted the Marine coastal enclave strategy would solve the problems.
There was also talk of allowing cross border raids to strike the ever growing Ho Chi Minh Trail.

Before arriving in Washington for more conferences Taylor forwarded a memo that advised the U.S. must accept that there is perpetual political instability in Vietnam and that there was no "George Washington to be found. (Taylor threatened the ARVN senior officers, but they were typically unafraid of any repercussions. "The Americans feared the communists more than they did. If we fall short they will come in to stop them.")

To try to convince our civilian leadership of the problems in Vietnam the JCS ran a second war game called **SIGMA II.** Their brain storming was to try to predict the political and military questions should the U.S. fight a ground war in Vietnam.

SIGMA II predicted the Vietnam War's outcome before we started fighting,
The Graduated Response policy would lead to a disaster.

Again the results were ignored by those in power.

The conferences accomplished nothing other than to follow the present course.

Walt Rostow was a counselor for policy planning at State and assured Sec. Rusk that the North was vulnerable to bombing. (Another study stated they were not.)

He also believed they could be coerced into changing their plan after feeling the effects of graduated response. *The academics were plotting and analyzing the situation as if they were at a boardroom meeting. They arrogantly assumed the communists would act and react as we would.*

Using Canadian Diplomat J. Seaborn a message was sent that the U.S. was running out of patience and preparing to bomb them. N. Vietnamese Foreign Minister Pham van Dong was approached with the same warning for a second time on August 10th, (after the Tonkin resolution passed). Again he was totally un-intimidated.

He stated that the North was committed to their purpose and expected a successful conclusion. The communists were prepared to sacrifice for their total war, especially one that they were so close to winning.

Seaborn of the (ICC) repeatedly brought backchannel messages to Pham Van Dong from Johnson promising economic aid if the North stopped the insurgency. *Pham warned that if a war began with America it would spread to all of SE Asia.* To counter the expected American air power the North asked for sophisticated anti-aircraft weapons and SAM's from Khrushchev. The Russian Premier supplied them on the condition the North Vietnamese consider negotiations.

During October 1964 Leonid Brezhnev suddenly replaced the deposed Khrushchev as the Russian Premier. (Even Prada the Russian communist paper denounced the former Premier for his schemes and immature and hasty conclusions.) Brezhnev increased the arms shipments to North Vietnam and was expected to try to improve relations with China.

And then on the 16th of October the Chinese explode their first atomic bomb. Mao had decided in 1958 that China had to have the atomic bomb to defend themselves since Russia was not to be trusted.

In Moscow the Politburo was very unhappy with this dangerous development. *(In fact, they pondered using an atomic strike on China's arsenal to destroy it!)*

As 1964 was coming to a close more plotting and protests erupted in South Vietnam. Gen. Westmoreland reported that the political deterioration of the South was reaching a critical level. Unless the situation was stabilized nothing we would do would forestall their collapse.
During that same time frame the aggressive VC began actively attacking American targets killing and wounding dozens.

Part of the buildup after the Gulf of Tonkin incident had Sec-Def McNamara send a B-57 bomber unit to S. Vietnam. Admiral Sharp tried to warn him not to do so because of the ease of Viet Cong raids upon the airfields. Naturally McNamara refused to heed the advice, and on November 1, 1964 a VC raid on Bien Hoa airfield north of Saigon destroyed six of the large and expensive bombers. In addition the VC destroyed twenty other aircraft, killed five and wounded seventy two US servicemen. This was the first time the communists had directly targeted a large unit of U.S. personnel and equipment. It was another sign of their growing confidence and capabilities.

Taylor, Westmoreland and the JCS demanded retaliatory military attacks be made against the North. But with the election just two days away LBJ refused. (The attack galvanized the Administration hawks into pushing for our involvement, including air strikes into lower Laos.)

The 1964 Presidential campaign had been in full swing the past months with hawkish Republican Barry Goldwater going against "moderate" Lyndon Johnson.

Goldwater insisted that the answer to Vietnam was to bomb them into submission. "It was better for the communists to die than even one U.S. service-member, and we have already lost enough of them!" Goldwater told and spoke the truth, the exact opposite of what Johnson and the Democrats were doing. (Just like Trump in 2016.)

LBJ and the liberal media portrayed Goldwater as an out of control nut and war-monger. The media was especially brutal in their assessment and coverage of him, coming close to how they had sanctimoniously ruined Sen. McCarthy a decade earlier.

To ensure he was seen as the moderate Johnson had stopped the air attacks and Desoto patrols against North Vietnam.

Following the "re-election strategies" used by Wilson in 1916 and FDR in 1940, Johnson repeatedly pledged not to send America's sons into a foreign war.

In the last days before the election LBJ's team repeatedly showed a TV ad of a little girl playing in a peaceful field. Claiming that Goldwater the Republican candidate was a right-wing maniac, the screen suddenly showed a mushroom cloud in the background and then the little girl was gone. With no time to refute the misleading ad, the election was a big win for LBJ and the Democrats.

Funny thing though, a few months after he won claiming he was the candidate for peace, America's son and daughters were again at war.

Bill Moyers had been tasked with controlling the media messaging and polling the public to find out if inaction in Vietnam would hurt LBJ. It did not as the Democrats again misled the voters. *Johnson and the Democrats had deceptively kept the war out of the minds of the voters and they picked up large majorities in the House and Senate.* (A lot of the vote was sympathy votes for JFK.)

With near total control of our government, LBJ the politician could institute his destructive Great Society plan upon the nation with little discourse and guaranteed approval.

(Never have so many been deceived by so few.)

With the election locked up Johnson also created a working group to study and produce an intensive look at Vietnam. The group would report to the Administration as a way to shield LBJ from any negativity, as he planned on using U.S. troops.

However many CIA analysts began expressing doubts about using our troops in a ground effort. Because of the virtual collapse of the South the CIA concluded that the VC could now fight on even if North Vietnam backed out. **Vietnam was a lost cause.**

George Ball had been on the Nitze team that investigated the bombing of Germany in WWII. *He stated that all of the allied bombing effort in Germany over five years had done little to weaken them. He seriously doubted any effort against North Vietnam would sway them either.* Even after viewing those reports LBJ was committed to war.

By December 1964 the VC could successfully ambush ARVN armored columns. On the 9th, fourteen M-113 APCs were destroyed by communist recoilless rifles firing 57 and 75 mm shells! Also shot down were two Huey helicopters and an L-19 spotter plane.
Killed in the battle were over 100 ARVN Rangers and 5 more Americans.

All over the country the hapless ARVN units were being repeatedly lured into ambushes and crushed. Only the intervention of U.S ground forces could stop the complete collapse of the South. But that was no guarantee of a victory either.

(Vann had warned of this end and had also stated that it would be the worst alternative. If the ARVN has trouble telling friend from foe, how would the U.S. citizen soldier fare?)

That month another deadly VC attack struck a hotel in Saigon, then a VC battalion overran an ARVN CP south of Da Nang, and a VC regiment struck the ARVN base at Binh Gia near the DMZ. The fighting there lasted over a day and included the enemy hitting the ARVN relief force.

By the end of the year 1964 U.S. MACV personnel topped 23,000.

Another 149 Americans had died in S. Vietnam, with 19 MIAs. And nothing good had come from our effort.

The strength of the Viet Cong had more than doubled to **over 100,000 troops**.

Total NVA forces on the trail and in the South were **over 40,000 and growing steadily.**

Their mission was to finish off the ARVN and complete the takeover. *They expected to complete their victory by the spring of 1965.*

Sensing victory the leaders in the North were no longer just sending small units down the Ho Chi Minh Trail. In December the lead regiment of the 325th Division arrived in the Central Highlands. The other two were on their way down completing a force of over ten thousand fighters. (This was the second round of the intensive NVA reinforcement that Bui

Tin had advocated on his previously mentioned trip into the south back in late 1962.)

To coordinate this large effort, the Viet Cong forces of S. Vietnam would be officially known as the People's Revolutionary Army. They would now be commanded by the Communist Headquarters in the South called COSVN. (Communist operations S. Vietnam.)
Their instructions and orders would come from Hanoi!

Gen. Tran Do was the overall commander at that time and his small HQ was moved often to escape detection. Their initial location was in Tay Ninh province, adjacent to Cambodia.

To support the incoming reinforcements, the Ho Chi Minh trail was being modernized to accept vehicles. Using Russian and Chinese equipment and labor battalions, the NVA built numerous underground bunkers, hospitals, supply depots, fuel storage areas and workshops. Their intensive effort would be defended by hundreds of antiaircraft guns and companies of patrolling troops.

To try to stop the constant infiltration through Laos Johnson had approved of a secret bombing campaign called **Operation Barrel Roll** *back in June 1964.*

Those bombing raids were directed to hit NVA and Pathet Lao forces attacking in the Plain of Jars area. Naively it was felt that the bombings would cause the communists to shift troops from South Vietnam to the Laotian war to make up their losses.

In December Johnson supplanted the effort to go after the Trail itself. Missions were called "armed recon", to give the impression they were just scouts.

To keep the bombing a complete secret from the American people the Ambassador in Vientiane was in charge of all air assets and targeting lists. All missions were run from his office.

(There were no reporters there.)

For nine years the U.S. bombed Laos, ending the mission in April 1973. It did not work, just as it failed in WWII and Korea.

During Ambassador Taylor's visit to Washington in November he had pointed out how bad things were in the South and advocated escalation. **However Johnson refused to be detracted from enacting his Great Society programs. Once the new Congress was in session, he planned on forcing through 150 bills in the first 150 days of his new term!**

The egotistic Johnson greatly desired a lasting legacy and outdoing his former idol FDR and his "New Deal, Truman's "Square Deal" or Kennedy's "New Frontier".

And to ensure his plans lived on he had to be reelected in 1968.

A full-scale war would stop him cold.

Since Vietnam would only cause him unwanted problems everyone in his Administration was told by him that "for Vietnam, they were to keep the lid on". **The Congress and the public were to be deceived.**

Senator Richard Russell of Georgia warned LBJ it was time to leave Vietnam. Polls showed the public was unhappy with his handling of Vietnam and with the problems there in general. McGeorge Bundy explained LBJ's Vietnam game-plan as such; *To get agreements at the lowest level of intensity he could, on a course that would meet the current needs in Vietnam and not derail his legislative itinerary.*
To ensure this was accomplished his administration lied repeatedly about all aspects of the war.

In January 1965 General U. Thant the Secretary General in the United Nations arranged with great effort to get a meeting between N. Vietnam and the U.S.

Ho Chi Minh agreed to meet in Burma, but LBJ refused to be a part of the Rangoon Initiative. Thant then tried to arrange a meeting in Geneva.

Again Johnson refused.

Thant then took the unprecedented step of going on TV to make public Johnson's refusals to negotiate.

More political intrigues began pushing S. Vietnam into chaos.

The military officers had removed the limited civilian government and another serious bombing had occurred. Taylor could not understand LBJ's motives for not responding to these latest attacks. And LBJ felt that Taylor had failed in his duties to prevent then from happening. By late January Buddhist demonstrations again filled the streets and the U.S. media was actively reporting on the many problems in Vietnam.

Johnson and McNamara continued to hide the truth from the public even though the discussions about using U.S. troops had already been sealed. McNamara even restricted media access to naval units in the Pacific to prevent any leaks.

Pres. Johnson decided that we needed to provoke another attack by the communists as justification for retaliatory strikes and sending in the troops.

To that end McNamara directed Gen. Wheeler to notify the Pacific Command to resume the destroyer patrols in the Gulf of Tonkin. Before the ships began moving Wheeler ordered the reprisal forces be ready to strike. They need not have worried.

On February 7, a well trained **NVA demolition teams** attacked the U.S. airbase at Pleiku in the Central Highlands. Eight more servicemen were killed and over 100 seriously wounded. Another twenty aircraft were damaged or destroyed.

Few of the enemy were killed, but one that was had a detailed map of the base and airfield. Like all of the previous attacks enemy intelligence was outstanding and their attacks planned to perfection.

(Which showed the enemy had easy access to the targets and / or a spy or two inside. *Even today Vietnam celebrates Feb. 7 as the day the North "joined in the fight".*)

McGeorge Bundy was in country on a survey and cabled the president it was time to bomb the north. Johnson then ordered *limited carrier air strikes* called Operation *Flaming Dart I* to be conducted on the North. Targets were the military barracks and port facilities near the DMZ. (Russian Minister Alexi Kosygin and staff were in Hanoi to work out the details of Russian supplies and advisors. They were angry that Johnson dared to bomb the North while they were there.)

Plans for *Operation Rolling Thunder*, the limited (graduated response), bombing of N. Vietnam also progressed. Dissenters at the meeting were Sen. Mansfield and Vice President Hubert Humphrey. *Due to this disagreement Humphrey was banished from any Vietnam discussions for a year by LBJ!* (Humphrey was repeatedly abused by the overbearing Johnson and should have resigned in protest then and there. Johnson was another womanizer, and his secretarial pool was nicknamed his harem. He also used the women in a Texas whore house for his escapes.)

Two days later a second VC attack at Qui Nhon killed 23 more Americans. *Flaming Dart II* was sent in again attacking only along the DMZ and the nearby Trail. Those missions had no effect on the communists.

Days later shipments of SAM missiles arrived from Russia. Bundy warned Johnson he needed to inform the American people on how bad things were in Vietnam and how long this effort would be. But as before LBJ ignored the advice and continued to hide the truth.

At a Senate Foreign Relations Committee hearing George Keenan told the group that Vietnam would not be a threat to our interests and we should not fight there. James Reston at the NY Times began denouncing the duplicity from the Administration. But having won the election and armed with the Tonkin resolution LBJ was free to do as he pleased.

As stated earlier Gen. Westmoreland had been given Command of MACV, (Military Assistance Command Vietnam) in June 1964 at the urging of Taylor.

Once he was in charge at MACV Westmoreland found that he could only command the Army Units, not the Navy, Air Force or CIA.???

This disjointed command arrangement coupled with the complete failure by the Administration in establishing any political or military objectives, and being forced to fight a large "limited war" crippled the overall American effort.

U.S. forces could not go into Laos or Cambodia to disrupt the Ho Ch Minh Trail system even though it was already well known what the communists were doing.

(Only small SF SOG teams could go in for recon, and then air attacks could go in.)

And to make things even worse for the war effort, MACV could not send any ground forces into N. Vietnam to threaten them directly. **Those unreasonable and unwarranted political handicaps instilled by LBJ reduced the available military options. That resulted in the perverse condition that virtually all of the fighting would have to be done in South Vietnam killing and wounding innocent non-communists.**

Gen. LeMay's term as Chief of Staff was ending in the USAF.

Ever conniving, LBJ had already chosen his replacement ten months before. Gen. John McConnell had passed LBJ's loyalty test by stating that he would follow the president's orders even if they went against all military logic!

Like Wheeler, McConnell irresponsibly thought that his job was to be loyal to the politicians, instead of the troops and nation.

To form a consensus within the JCS Wheeler worked hard to suppress the increasing dissent among the other senior officers. They must follow the Administration's war plans despite the fact that Sigma II had proved. Most of them knew that Graduated Response and the administration's political handicaps would not work.

And all the while McNamara continued to ignore, suppress or pre-selected the advice he was getting from the JCS. His actions further clouded whatever judgment LBJ used to arrive at his wrongful decisions. By the end of Feb 1965 over half of S. Vietnam was under communist control.

Hanoi directed the VC commanders to step up their attacks to try to crush the ARVN before America intervened. Isolated outposts and roadways became constant targets.

Even near Saigon the communists were defeating ARVN units.

Casualties rose sharply, and in one week in late February 36 Americans were killed with 196 wounded. During that same week the ARVN lost over 1500 men!

Morale fell apart.

With no choice Johnson decided to bomb the north. Thus far nothing that had been done had worked. Bombing was easy, quick and relatively painless.

LBJ's and McNamara's graduated bombing campaign of N. Vietnam did not actually begin until March 2, 1965. Political intrigue and poor weather slowed *Operation Rolling Thunder* to a crawl. However VC attacks against the U.S. airfields were constant.

The purpose of those bombing missions had been to reduce or stop enemy infiltration down the Ho Chi Minh trail by hitting roads, supply dumps and rail links that were near the DMZ. Additionally it was hoped that a show of U.S. air power would boost the failing morale in the South and persuade the communists that they could not expect to win. **The operation failed on all counts.** (Incredibly even Taylor had expected Graduated Response to work. And he deleted the CIA station reports which reported the bombings did not work.)

German military writer Carl von Clausewitz penned this decades earlier; *If the enemy is to be coerced into doing what you want, you must put him in a situation that is more unpleasant than the one they are in. The hardships of that new situation must not be transient, otherwise the enemy would simply wait for things to improve.*

By April a reluctant Gen. Wheeler reported to McNamara that the initial bombings had indeed failed. So tight were the restrictions as to where the planes could strike that the enemy moved supplies to those exact locations in order to protect them.

The civilians which included Pres. Johnson refused to hit the Red River Dikes that would have flooded the North's farmlands causing great hardships.

They also refused to hit Hanoi or Haiphong, the main urban areas and port. Thus the enemy could continue their present path with no fear of adversity.

Always adept at manual labor, the North kept repair supplies close by to quickly fix whatever had been bombed. They rebuilt the small bridges below the water to hide them from view, and made extensive use of the U.S. invention of pontoon bridges.

Those would be hidden during the day and then reconnected at night.

Gen. York had been promoted to Major General and been given command of the 82d Airborne Div. Knowing his unit could be going to Vietnam he tried to have John Vann reinstated to command one of his battalions. *The Army would not let him back in.* York tried again in the summer of 1964 and was again refused.

In Washington the Agency for International Development, AID, was trying to recruit people to serve in Vietnam. The White House had given AID principal responsibility for the civilian pacification program and they desperately needed someone with Vann's background. After LBJ won the election in November 64 Vann got an assignment, Regional Director in the Mekong Delta. Since Taylor had replaced Lodge as Ambassador in S. Vietnam he would look over the personnel assignments coming into the country and saw that Vann was on it. The last thing Taylor wanted was for the voice of truth to fall upon his doorstep so he rejected Vann's appointment.

Repeated requests for Vann's services finally forced Taylor to reconsider, and Vann came in as just a pacification officer in the Hau Nghia province west of Saigon.

In March 1965 Vann returned to a country on the brink of collapse.

He had been gone two years.

Gen. Westmoreland had asked for and two U.S. Marine Battalions landed at Da Nang on March 8, 1965. They were initially tasked to protect the U.S. airbase since the ARVN could not. With the marines guarding the base the ARVN units in the area would be "freed up to pursue the VC". *Johnson had stated the Marines were "there just to protect the airbases", but within weeks the marines were tasked with patrolling because the ARVN units were ineffective.*

That spring a regimental size VC unit became active in the southern Delta. *Their previously secret heavy weapons teams finally come out of hiding, along with complete engineer, communication and other specialty units.*

In eight years the original 2000+ Vietminh of 1957 had recovered and grown to a confident 156,000 by the spring of 1965. Their numbers continued to grow monthly despite taking combat losses.

When you included the NVA combat units coming down the Trail it increased the enemy strength countrywide to over 200,000! *Previously the North drafted men once or twice a year for a two year term of service. Hanoi changed it that spring to drafting at any time and service for the duration.* **They were not backing down.**

Despite LBJ's attempts at keeping our operations in Vietnam a secret antiwar demonstrations began to occur on college campuses and among liberal groups. Congressional opposition also increased. The State Dept. tried to quiet the antagonism with a report to highlight Hanoi's involvement, but so much information was considered "secret", that their report actually made things worse.

On April 1, LBJ held an impromptu press conference emphasizing his Great Society programs. Questions about Vietnam were brushed aside with references about following the actions of previous administrations, honoring the commitment to SEATO, and the Tonkin Gulf resolution.

Johnson deceptively stated that there was no division within the Government over Vietnam. He stressed that it was wrong for those who publicly opposed his policy and speculative journalists to complain while "our soldiers were dying in Vietnam". (The place he told the voters four months earlier that the U.S. kids would not go.)

In an off the record meeting with his staff LBJ was told that the graduated bombings of the North had been ineffective and that large U.S. ground forces were needed. **CIA's McCone argued that we were accomplishing nothing unless a decisive bombing campaign was instituted against the North including closing down their ports.** With the passage of his domestic plans completed, LBJ approved an increase in our forces. (McCone's days were numbered.)

Johnson next met with Democratic Senators Mike Mansfield and George McGovern. They warned him that his policy of expanding the U.S. military effort in Vietnam was a grave mistake. (But both had gone along with the No Discussion Tonkin Gulf Resolution.)

On April 7, Johnson gave a televised speech professing his seeking a peaceful solution to Vietnam. He again offered economic incentives to the North.

The nation and the antiwar activists were pleased that LBJ seemed to be on the side of peace, forgetting that Johnson had refused to meet with the North Vietnamese earlier. *But as shown above the scheming Johnson had already approved the deployment of two more Marine Battalions, an air squadron and twenty thousand logistical troops who were to support the possible arrival of three divisions of combat troops.*

It took Ho Chi Minh and the North's Politburo less than twenty four hours to reject Johnson's proposal. They saw it as a ruse for America to save face. They also knew that they were close to winning the insurrection.

In Saigon the U.S. Embassy was car-bombed resulting in dozens killed and hundreds injured. This had occurred despite repeated warnings to block off the streets around the building and to install safety glass. Neither Lodge nor Taylor had complied.

By mid April 1965 Gen. Westmoreland directly asked for more troops, up to 33,000. Because of the poor ARVN performance it was impossible to defend the bases by sitting in the bunkers awaiting an attack. The Marines guarding the airbases were "allowed" to go out to patrol around their assigned sectors and institute clearing operations to breakup enemy concentrations.

LBJ insisted that no publicity surround this change of mission. Even at this late date Johnson was still working to deceive the people and the Congress. *At a meeting in the White House the JCS was instructed to keep their criticisms from reaching the media and the public!* Again Taylor was against this plan.

The ARVN had the numbers and ability to win, but no motivation.

He feared the instant we started fighting the ARVN would stop fighting.

U.S. officials were long aware that larger units of North Vietnamese Forces, NVA, were secretly infiltrating into the South. Some came by boat, some directly across the DMZ, but most were using the growing network of pathways of the Ho Chi Minh Trail that snaked its way along the common border with Laos and Cambodia. American SOG teams had been observing and ambushing those hidden trails since 1964. They also knew that they were just a finger in a massive dike. *The only way to stop the flow was to invade and occupy those areas.*

But that would expand the war effort and would require an extensive explanation to the American people, and Johnson refused.

During the early spring of 65 VC attacks around Saigon had tapered off as they regrouped from previous fighting. They were reinforced by **four NVA regiments**. Intel had been effective in picking up the NVA units in transit and they had been bombed during their move along the trail. It made no difference, as the NVA units had come a long way to fight. They arrived into their sectors and prepared for battle.

At first the communists tried to avoid fighting the Marines, concentrating their attacks on the inept ARVN units that showed little heart for fighting. Losses to the South had increased to hundreds of troops per week and unless stopped would become unmanageable.

An attack on an ARVN Ranger unit in John Vann's new province highlighted the skill of the communists. Thirty five ARVN rangers were killed, eleven wounded and 16 captured. The VC unit that attacked them employed numerous machine guns to sweep across the ARVN unit pinning them in place. Since the ARVN soldiers were detested by the locals no warning was given of the pending VC attack. Vann could see that the S. Vietnamese Government had no control or support from its own citizens. Corruption was rampant and no effort was being made to unite the people to the common danger.

Then in May 1965 a new problem appeared close to home. The Dominican Republic was under increasing civil unrest as fighting was occurring. Three years earlier the long ruling and brutal dictator Rafael Trujillo had been assassinated when **Pres. Kennedy supported another coup which involved the CIA.**

Trujillo had taken over after the USMC operations ended in 1930. His rule was another harsh one full of intrigue. *The Kennedy Administration decided to end our "support to him", and similar to what was happening in S. Vietnam, his death had resulted in political chaos.* After an initial honeymoon the new government of Juan Bosch was seen as a strategic threat when he made clear his intentions to support Fidel Castro. Gen. Elias Wesin's forces overthrew Bosch in September 1963.

Repression, brutality and fighting continued as the unrest grew. (Just like in Vietnam.) By June 1965 LBJ feared a new communist nation would be on our doorstep.

Initially Johnson sent 14,000 Marines into the country, but the force soon grew to 20,000 Army troops and marines who tried to keep the peace and prevent a Castro want-to-be from coming to power. (Gen. York was sent there with the 82d Airborne.)

During May the conniving Johnson took advantage of this anti-communist issue to his advantage. *Despite complaints from many political adversaries over his actions, on May 4 Johnson sent in an appropriation package to the Congress for $700 million to support his anti-communist actions in the* **Dominican Republic and Vietnam!**

He then conspired to remind the legislators that over *400 of our men had died* in Vietnam and they must be supported.
Following "his advice" the Congress again overwhelmingly passed the bill which allowed our operations in Vietnam to continue.

This episode highlights another failure in our system of government. LBJ was able to join two separate appropriations into one bill.
If you wanted aid for one crisis, the other measure would also have to be sneakily passed.

This ludicrous procedure has been used for decades to add Pork Barrel and unwarranted measures into our laws. All spending bills need to be passed individually, in that way the scammers would not be able to cheat and deceive the public.

To highlight the anti-communist ideals so prevalent in that time, a year earlier Johnson had sent the CIA to Brazil to get rid of their incompetent and corrupt president Joao Goulart. Over the years Goulart had slowly maneuvered his way into power but he was shifting the country to the left ala Castro. Peasant organizations began causing unrest and Johnson followed his predecessor's practice and pushed for a coup. The Brazilian army took over and for the next twenty years Brazil existed under brutal dictatorships.

To further prop up his dubious goals, Johnson persuaded Arthur Goldberg to leave the Supreme Court and become Johnson's man in the U.N. Like so many, Goldberg was easily swayed by Johnson and faithfully supported LBJ's policies until 1968. Then he like so many others regretted his decisions and resigned. But it did not matter at that point for Johnson had gotten what he needed from all of them. Our nation and citizens would pay the terrible price.

In May 1965 the 173 Airborne Brigade became the first intact Army Unit to arrive in Vietnam. Unperturbed over the introduction of new troops, the enemy launched attacks all across the country similar to what would happen during TET 1968. Song Be a province capital was overrun just fifty miles from Saigon. Two battalions of ARVN troops were lost in the Central Highlands, then an ARVN HQ was destroyed and a Special Forces camp almost lost. By the middle of June the ARVN had lost its best mobile battalions.

Westmoreland was in a panic. To avert defeat he cabled LBJ that he had to have 180,000 troops by year end or Vietnam was lost. He warned Johnson that more men would be needed and we are in for a long war.

Intelligence photos confirmed that the Soviets were building anti-aircraft emplacements all around Hanoi and Haiphong. If any effective strikes against the enemy were on the table they had to go in soon. Johnson knew the stakes, face the defeat now or plunge the nation into a major war. *He chose the latter, but still did not tell America the truth.* By late June 1965 MACV had permission to expand U.S. troop patrols. And with the Tonkin Resolution in his hand Johnson could do so with no explanations.

After much pain and turmoil McNamara had approved the creation of the first airmobile Army unit. They had trained for over a year, and the 1st Air Cavalry Division arrived in Vietnam with its numerous helicopters. It took four aircraft carriers and a dozen transports to move this "heavy" unit to Vietnam. There were 16,000 men, 3,100 vehicles, 22,800 tons of supplies and 470 aircraft.

The 101st Airborne Div was the next unit to be sent over as the Administration began to unravel. The dissenters within began to step back, and Rusk was finally agreeing with McCone at CIA that our forces could not stop the communists. *George Ball wrote Johnson a strong memo that even if we inflicted heavy losses we still won't win.* It was too late, we were in the war in force.

In the Marine zones the marines were already following the book that they had written and used to pacify Latin America during the prior rebel insurrections in the 1920s and 30s. They would go into the villages and stay.

(Their operations were similar to the later counter-insurgency guidelines used by the British SAS teams in Malaya in the late 40s and 50s.)

The first objective for the Marines was the enemy forces operating in the area. They were killed or driven out. Then the marines occupied the exposed villages offering protection and the rebuilding of community services and social aid. Even after all of the above was accomplished, the Marines detailed a squad or platoon to remain and provide the village with security which kept the VC enemy away.

Their program was so successful that other nearby villages lost residents who wanted to live in the safe and cleared ones. By their nature those tactics and policies were slow and time consuming, tying up squads of marines in each village.
But they were effective at keeping the communists away from the citizens, and in keeping the citizens from turning into new communists.

This procedure was considered "too low key" to cope with the "possible communist invasion envisioned by MACV".

In late July Westmoreland imprudently ordered the Marines to create large base areas and go deep into the countryside looking for the elusive enemy. The Marine commanders resisted because they could see the progress they were making. But since Westmoreland and his staff were living in a large base near Saigon they could never realize what the Marines had accomplished in such a short time.

And MACV and Taylor constantly knocked down the CIA warnings and proposals to forget the normal military thinking and to use counter-insurgency programs.

Admiral Sharp had warned Commandant Greene to be wary of Taylor and Westmoreland. Both greatly disliked the Corps and would do everything possible to prevent them from getting any credit for their work.
(Their mindset is probably why the Marines were wrongly sent up north into I Corps. They would be far away from the media and any headlines.)

Sent out into the bush the marines stumbled into booby-traps and ambushes just as the French and ARVN troops had. In one operation a film crew filmed the marines burning down a VC controlled village called Cam Ne. Commentary on the film never mentioned that the area had been a VC strongpoint, and the film became a propaganda coup for the communists that could not be rectified.

(The news commentary downplayed the prior battle and the VC organization in the hamlet. This falsified and biased reporting would become a staple of the media from 1965 onward. It continues to this day.)

America

LBJ was enacting his massive social programs at home during this same time frame. His Great Society programs needed large amounts of money, and most of the legislation his party was passing was also semi-secret.

(Similar to the ruse the Democrats used for Obama care.)

Explanations to the public as to expected costs and terms of these handout-subsidy programs were kept to a minimum to ensure little discourse. That was the main reason Johnson insisted the legislation be passed quickly during his first months in office.

Minority party Republicans in the Congress complained often that many of the "Great Society programs" would only perpetuate the poverty and make permanent the subsidies. Johnson's programs did not offer a way out from poverty, they would perpetuate it. But because they were so few in numbers they were unable to stop the Democrats. (Fifty years later it is crystal clear that they were correct.)

A sociology professor at Harvard named Daniel Patrick Moynihan also warned of the destructive influence the Great Society programs would result in. He was harshly attacked by his fellow liberals and Democrats. (FDR had started a welfare program in the 1930s to provide for widows and the elderly. That was the program LBJ and the Democrats prostituted into the Great Society disaster.

In 1965 the breakup of the Black family structure had 22% of children being illegitimate. By 2012 the figure reached the disgraceful and nation-breaking figure of 74%!)

Another veiled change that was enacted by the Democrats was reneging on the Social Security Act from 1935. (When it was first enacted the SS program did not benefit everyone, mostly those well off. Over the years it was amended to included most of our citizens.) Originally any funds collected had to be deposited into the independent SS Retirement Program only. But LBJ and the Democrats saw the growing fund as a cash cow to secret into the U.S. Treasury's General Fund.

Thus transferred the money was spent to continue funding LBJ's agenda without having to try to pass additional spending bills that would call attention to their scams. IOU's were deposited into the SS fund.

By enacting this secret theft of Social Security, the Democrats could delay having to raise taxes to pay for the war in Vietnam and Johnson's domestic welfare programs.

Those scheming politicians began a dangerous concept that was copied by many others over the years, underfunding the future pensioners.
(In our time of 2015 their scamming and scheming has bankrupted many of those vital pension funds. As a result many of our municipalities are nearing insolvency too. And who will suffer for those lies, you will, the worker and taxpayer.)

Sweeping changes were also made to our Immigration Policy by the Democrats. This was another perfect example of a single ruling party passing anything it wanted even though the American people did not ask for any "changes". (Just like Obamacare.)

Gone were the requirements that an immigrant had to have job or skill, a sponsor or be educated. Health exams and background checks were no longer done. America had benefitted greatly from previous immigration because the nation was growing from sea to sea and needed millions of workers. Their influx fueled the industrialization of our land and changed the nation.

But there were no handouts in those decades, you worked. That was why we had those listed rules in place.

In post-WWII multiple thousands of educated Europeans emigrated here resulting in the brain drain phenomena from those countries. America was the hallmark of safety and security, and those masses of well schooled and learned men and women emigrated to our shores bringing their talents with them. Because of that America was greatly enhanced.

With those parameters removed by the Democrats, America would now be importing the poor and have not's. Limits on their immigration were removed and special grants were given to the poorer nations of the world. **America was importing the poor.** Many of them would not be a benefit to the nation, instead they would become a burden. Those changes were again quietly implemented and would become a savage blow to our nation's future and security. But that did not interest the Democrats at that time. **They saw a chance to "stack the voting deck" and ensure their electability by creating a large class of subsidized citizens who were dependent on them and their welfare programs. It was a win-win for the Democrats.**

All through 1965 race riots and demonstrations occurred across our country. Alabama was again the main stage until the deadly riots occurred in the Watts section of Los Angeles. Police brutality was a main charge leveled by black Americans. Despite the Civil Rights acts of the past decade the vial treatment of the minorities continued in some states and regions.

Vietnam

In the first months of 1965 U.S. aircraft were tracked flying near Chinese airspace as they bombed a few targets near Hanoi. China increased their defenses and prepared for large scale battles. Another incident occurred while Le Duan and Def. Minister Gen. Giap were in Beijing meeting to discuss armaments needs. On April 2, 1965 Zhou Enlai had the Pakistanis warn the Johnson Administration that a war between China and America would have no boundaries.

An agreement was completed in which Communist China agreed to supply 320,000 unarmed troops for construction, air-defense, engineering and railroad-transportation needs. That freed up that same number of Vietnamese troops who would now be committed to the fighting in the South.

As shown before, Chinese weapons and supplies had been delivered in large quantities to the North and that included a MiG-17 squadron which they deployed just after the Gulf of Tonkin incident. Service troops began arriving in June 1965. Besides working on construction and logistic projects, they also manned crew served anti-aircraft weapons right into 1975 when the NVA finally completed their conquest. (China would lose over 1,000 troops killed during the war and initially supplied 70% of the military material used by the VC and NVA. During and after 1968 the Russians supplied 80% of the material.)

Worldwide opinion was growing louder against the bombing in N. Vietnam. LBJ reacted to it, and a pause was initiated to "show good faith", but his effort failed miserably. (The JCS was not consulted or advised about the bombing pause.)

Soviet Foreign Minister Gromyko called the American pause an ultimatum. The N. Vietnamese simply ignored the effort. They had been lulled many times by the French and would not be tricked again. They also knew how close they were to victory as only the introduction of U.S. troops and firepower had prevented them from winning. With the release of their troops thanks to China, Hanoi was committed to reinforcing as fast as America could send in new units.

Under LBJ the civilians were running the war. It had been their planning that brought forth the ineffective *"Rolling Thunder"* bombing program, not the JCS. Johnson saw the war only as something that could hurt him politically. He sought advice from all of his sources and sent the troops in as the least damaging move to him politically.

On June 7, 1965 Westmoreland sent in a report detailing the presence of large NVA, (North Vietnamese Army) units operating in the South. To avert the coming military disaster he requested even more troops from the U.S., Australia and S. Korea.

LBJ was still trying to keep our ground warfare a secret until a PR official in the State Dept. accidently let it out.

Even after the June 8 slip up the White House still lied about the heavy fighting.

(George Reedy was Johnson's press secretary. He was crushed as his reputation became ruined covering up for the neurotic secrecy and outright lying from this White House. Similar to Truman's early effort, LBJ tried to hide the war until he had no choice but to come clean.)

Johnson had his staff prepare the needed legal justification for his war by referring to the Tonkin Gulf Resolution. When the JCS met with McNamara they were upset that the president had approved only half of Westmoreland's troop requests.

They also complained that no one in the Administration had done any planning on how our forces were to be used or what we were trying to accomplish.

There was no battle plan, master plan or even a hint of common sense.

On June 23 George Ball again recommended that we cut our losses and leave Vietnam. McNamara and Rusk still wanted a deeper involvement, so Johnson directed them to "write down their views." McNamara was afraid that Ball might win the argument, so he persuaded Ball to ask for troop reductions instead of a withdrawal.

After Ball prepared the report McNamara then argued that Ball's report was defeatist and a danger to our credibility. Rusk concurred, and Ball was made to look ill informed.

LBJ then directed his advisors to plan for a large war, but the JCS was again excluded. Bombing of the North would continue but Hanoi and Haiphong were off limits.

The key to "their war" would still be a limited one based graduated response.

Maxwell Taylor resigned as Ambassador to S. Vietnam and Lodge was quickly returned. (I wonder if Taylor realized what his scheming had brought to Vietnam.) Lodge had tried to get the best chroniclers of the first Indochina War to talk to our senior leaders back in 1963. Bernard Fall and Jean Larteguy tried to impress upon the US principals what they were in for. But none of them would listen. Why did Lodge return?

In a July 10 meeting McNamara told the JCS that the president had approved a 200,000 man force that would be in Vietnam by November 1, 1965. Their first priority was to get forces into Vietnam as fast as they could be absorbed. The Army and Marines would need to create new forces and possibly call up their reserves. Some of those units might have to remain on active duty.

The military was again directed that none of this information was to become public. Congress and the American people needed to be softened up and that was the reason for McNamara's next trip to Vietnam. To Commandant Greene the July 10 meeting and the news given was astonishing.

Again the JCS was not questioned or asked for any strategic input.

They were simply secretaries being directed to carry out the implausible war decisions that had already been made by the "civilians" in this dubious Administration. (Johnson would later refuse to activate the reserves.)

The Goodpaster Group that McNamara had earlier directed to map out and examine the war plans and goals was finding their task difficult. *High level civilians like McNamara and McNaughton defined the war effort as simply maintaining America's credibility and prestige. The U.S. could succeed by demonstrating to the VC that they could not win.*

To the Sec-Defense "A stalemate was a victory if we could get a favorable settlement".

But Gen. Andy Goodpaster did not take this idea seriously and his planning efforts were along the line of winning the war. His group planned for large forces and few political restrictions on the military. *They recommended the destruction of the enemy as the way to force a favorable settlement.* Since he worked for the civilians Goodpaster never confronted anyone over those vital differences. *But his planning group counted on a full air campaign against the North and ground operations into Laos to cut the Ho Chi Minh Trail.* **After seeing the** (militarily sound) **proposals McNamara never forwarded the study to the White House.**

South Vietnam had formed yet another new government with Nguyen Van Thieu as President and Nguyen Cao Ky as Premier. Ky was a brave and skilled pilot who had worked with the advisors and CIA for years. These two men were able to form a semi-functioning government.

On his latest trip to Vietnam, McNamara was upset that he could not get the "exact information" he wanted from MACV.

Gen. Westmoreland was upset and could not give any precise numbers of troop levels needed because there was no plan as to what we were doing there!

Westmoreland correctly warned McNamara that the enemy was too entrenched in their effort to be influenced by anything except the overwhelming application of force.
His statement was the complete opposite of McNamara's policy of graduated response.

Gen. Westmoreland had heard about McNamara's policies and was against the premise of "stalemate as a military objective". *As soon as he stabilized the disaster in the South he was going to ask for substantial additional forces to attack into Laos and North Vietnam.* Westmoreland expected an open ended commitment to win the war by overwhelming the communists. He too anticipated that a massive bombing campaign would be conducted to weaken the North. Those requirements were an integral part of his and any sensible war plan.

On July 20 McNamara returned from Vietnam and forwarded his prefabricated report to the president. *He stated that the objective of our military force was a demonstration to the enemy that they could not win. His proposal if enacted with continuing determination had a good chance of achieving a favorable outcome within a reasonable time frame.* (What a load of crap.)

Johnson approved the 200,000 man force to go to Vietnam and take over the ground war.

While McNamara was in Vietnam the Armed Services Committee met with and questioned the JCS. The Service Chiefs had the proper venue to alert the nation to what the administration was about to do, but they acted like scared children and did not answer the questions directly and honestly.

The Committee chairman even asked why North Vietnam's ports had not been mined and all of their oil storage taken out. The JCS deflected the question and did not mention that the military was not running the war, Johnson and his civilians were.

Because of their timidity they failed their services and the nation, and doomed thousands upon thousands of Americans and South Vietnamese.

LBJ knew full well that he was deceiving the Congress and the nation. He directed that all military actions were subordinate to his Great Society programs.

He also knew that the costs would hit eight billion dollars in fiscal year 1966, but dared not ask for more than $300 to 400 million more. Instead he had McNamara go to the Congress to try to get the votes to raise taxes to finance the war. McNamara returned empty handed.

At a meeting with the JCS on July 22 Johnson brought forth his many worries, especially his repeated warnings that if we strike too hard the Chinese would come in.

Commandant Greene warned the president that the way we were "operating", the war would take five years to win and require 500,000 troops. We must intensify Rolling Thunder and blockade all of their ports.

He also emphasized the effective USMC enclave strategy as the most effective use of our ground troops.

No discussion were held by those present as to how to use the extra troops being sent. (At that point the 101st Airborne and the 4th Inf Div were on their way, raising our total to 79,000.) Hearing nothing that they said, Johnson blankly told them that we will take a lot of criticism for what we will do. He expected all of them to support him.

During July the fighting had intensified in II Corps which contained the Central Highlands region. Large VC units overran a border town west of *Pleiku*, and then another one near *Kontum*. On July 7 they overran Dak To, but were unable to hold onto it. Then the SF Camp at Duc Co near the border was hit and surrounded. Patrols and battles ensued and for ten days as the camp was besieged.
Relief units were also ambushed and pinned down.

An ARVN unit advised by Capt. Norman Schwarzkopf was ordered to do a sweep of the area but unbelievably they were given no air or artillery support. Schwarzkopf refused the foolish mission pissing off a lot of incompetents back at MACV.

SF and ARVN recon teams knew the area was swarming with enemy especially near a mountain called *Chu Pong*. Days later a well prepared mission went off saving the SF camp at Duc Co. These enemy troops were no longer peasants in black pajamas firing blindly through the jungle and then running away. These were well trained infantry units pressing their attacks home. To save the area U. S. troops were needed and MACV sent in the 173d airborne to force the issue. (After the siege at Duc Co was broken Schwarzkopf met up with Westmoreland in the wrecked camp. *Stormin Norman* was born at Duc Co as he realized that MACV did not have a clue about what was going on.)

In August 1965 the Marines fought the first of their large battles near *Chu Lai* called *Operation Starlite*. Intel had confirmed that 1500 VC troops of the 1st VC regiment were at a base area called *Van Tuong*. Intel had expected them to attack soon so Lt. Gen. Lewis Walt decided to hit them first. Their multi-staged battle started well but the entrenched VC fighters put up a hard defense. Using naval gunfire to smash the VC emplacements the marines attacked from two sides as enemy survivors broke off from the battle to escape. (A successful tactic they would employ in every fight.)

Enemy losses were over 600 killed, Marine losses were 45 KIA.

This was their first major ground battle against the Vietnamese communists and the Marine commanders were startled at the battlefield stamina of this enemy.
They could see that this was not going to be a quick war.

As always MACV claimed this battle as a victory, first over the kill ratio but also that the enemy had "left the battlefield". (Just like Harkins at Ap Bac in 1962.)

What they failed to see was that the Marines left the area too a few days later. They were sent to another site to look for more of the enemy, and a short time later the communists drifted back and rebuilt. They observed, analyzed the battle and improved their defenses. The next time we fought there our losses would be worse.

(Lt. Philip Caputo penned a line in his book, *A Rumor of War*;
"When they had splashed ashore they carried their packs, rifles and a conviction that the Vietcong would be quickly beaten. As the struggle continued we kept our packs and rifles, our convictions we lost".) (55)

At the battle for Dak To the NVA used three regiments in their attempt to shut down the SF camp that was interfering with their movements along the Ho Chi Minh Trail. *Their efforts began in late June and continued right into November.*

Reinforcements from the 173d and then the 4th Inf were needed to hold off the determined enemy. *Casualties were heavy and the enemy left when they decided to.* After those battles ended Gen. Westmoreland began making the same mistakes the French had made in their war, *underestimating this enemy.*

In his first person experience chronicled in the book, *Street Without Joy*, Dr. Bernard Fall detailed the nine year French effort of trying to pin down those skilled communist fighters and of how they were never able to do so. He saw our efforts as a repeat of theirs. And he tried to warn all that the effort was doomed. (Dr. Fall was killed by a mine on his street while patrolling with the Marines in 1967.)

To "interdict the Trail" without actually doing so the Administration used *Operation Steel Tiger*. It was a new limited air campaign that targeted the northern Ho Chi Minh Trail and panhandle area of Laos. *Again the civilians in Washington picked the targets and sent the mission on to Saigon and Laos.* In this imprudent manner LBJ, McNamara and staff could "control the war". It also prevented any intelligence-directed quick strikes because all missions had to be approved in Washington.

(This non-functional operation was ended in mid-68 after TET had proved their irrational ideas did not work.)

Asia

India and Pakistan begin fighting again over the northern provinces of Punjab and Kashmir. A ceasefire was arranged on Sept 22, but on the 28th the fighting became worse. China was aligned with Pakistan (as a chance to steal more territory from India.), and again massed their troops on their border with India. A short time later the fighting with India was renewed. In all probability the Chinese had encouraged and helped this war to begin with. No matter what happened, the communists could gain.

To the southeast in Indonesia the rule of Pres. Sukarno had become dictatorial and repressive. His close alignment with the communists during the 1950s, (infiltrating in from Malaya), and the uncontrolled corruption within his government became too much too bear. As always the communists had sought power by infiltrating labor unions and other civic organizations. But after watching the subversion and invasion of S. Vietnam to their north, the Indonesian citizens reacted.

Starting in late 1965 and continuing into 1967 a brutal revolution swept the nation. Plotters in their military assisted by the CIA eventually toppled Sukarno.

And as had happened after WWII, the ever dangerous Chinese backed communist party was placed under arrest. As the civil violence grew worse *fighting broke out and by January 1966 almost 100,000 communists were reported killed!* During the next year an additional 100-200,000 more were killed. Indonesia had a large Muslim population and they harshly turned against the godless communists, leftists and ethnic Chinese.

This desperate hidden war against communism was almost unknown to the Western world and media who were fixated on Vietnam. **One factor that has been almost totally ignored by the liberal media and establishment was that the U.S. effort in Vietnam was what allowed the Indonesians time to observe and react to the communist threat in their nation.**

Had America stayed out of Vietnam the South would have fallen quickly and quietly. With no one was stopping their efforts the Communists would have been free to destabilize all of the nations in that part of the world. Even with our efforts they still tried to take over Indonesia.

General Suharto who led the revolution was elected president in 1968 and installed a shaky democracy. Suharto was another highly authoritarian ruler but he worked to better the lives in Indonesia. (Similar to the Shah of Iran.) Indonesia returned to the U.N. and restored links to the western world. After their civil war ended the people of Indonesia led a relatively quiet existence until 1976 when Jakarta decided to take over the former Dutch colony of Timor. The Timorians have waged a guerrilla war since.

Back in the Central Highlands of Vietnam the communist forces had been building up and attacking at will using the now extensive Ho Chi Minh Trail.

South Vietnamese leaders actually expected that they would have to abandon the entire northern region (called I Corps) and the area of the Central Highlands soon.

As stated before the U.S. Army's rapid response force the 173d Airborne Brigade had been sent to the highlands in April 65, followed soon after by the 4th Inf. Div.

Into the fall those troops were still engaged in some bitter and costly fights around *Dak To*. Near *An Khe* the 101st Division began their first big fights with main force VC units. In late July 1965 the 1st Cavalry Division, a complete helicopter-airmobile force had arrived in country. They were equipped with scout, attack, transport and logistical helicopters in their inventory.

Westmoreland had initially split the untested unit into three separate brigades to three different battle zones. After showing and impressing MACV with their new capabilities the unit was finally sent *intact* to the Central Highlands to head off the infiltration of large numbers of NVA troops.

Pres. Johnson had decided in late July not to ask for additional funds to activate the reserves or to extend any service members who were due to leave the service within six months. Congressional approval would have been required for those decisions and LBJ refused to chance any discourse. (He asked for more money in January 1966 only after the troops were committed!)

Because of this scheming the Army Units going to Vietnam suffered unexpected losses of their trained personnel. Members who were close to leaving the service could not be extended. That reduced the personnel in some cases by 25%.

Units lost dozens of valuable men who had years of service in infantry, and months of service as mechanical / flight crews.

They would have to be replaced by the new draftees who were coming out of Basic Training.

The Army Brass had also counted on using 100,000 trained reservists to get them started in Vietnam. They did not expect Johnson to not only refuse to extend the tours of those soon to leave, but to use their reserves. It is difficult to overstate how damaging those decisions were to the Army that went to Vietnam in 1965-67. Army Chief of Staff Walter Johnson came close to resigning over that terrible failure.

The NVA had sent their 325 Division to the Central Highlands near *Pleiku* under Gen. Chu Huy Man. Man was another tough long time communist and fighter.

His mission was to take the two adjacent provinces of Pleiku and Kontum from the weak ARVN forces and then strike east to split the country in two. Their initial attacks had been centered on the Special Forces camps sited along the borders with Laos and Cambodia. Those SF camps provided patrol bases and scouting/recon missions to keep abreast of what the NVA were up to. (Eliminating all of those SF border camps was a top NVA priority, and by mid-66 all of the border camps but two had been overrun.)

During mid-October 1965 the 33d NVA regiment went after the SF camp at *Plei Me* while the 32d waited in ambush for any relief force. Days of fighting intensified and soon the camp was surrounded. Multiple battles ensued and air support was vital in saving the camp. With the increased capabilities of the NVA units they inflicted damage to twenty aircraft while four were shot down. Five NVA were captured and admitted they were from the 3d batt-33d Regiment.

Because of the heavy NVA commitment at *Plei Me* the Air-Cav had been relocated to *Pleiku*. Troops from the 9th Cav began to pursue the enemy by flying around in their helicopters. Their aggressive tactics caught the enemy unprepared for their violent assaults and the Cav troopers won fight after fight. On Oct. 26 they found a few targets but on Nov. 1 they ran into an NVA field hospital between *Plei Mei* and the *Chu Pong mountain*. The NVA 2d Batt-33d Regiment fought fiercely for the complex loosing multiple dozens of men and tons of supplies. Forty two enemy were captured. Additional battles were fought in that sector with some occurring at night similar to the fights against the Japanese in WWII. **Scout pilot David Bray followed an obvious trail through the jungle and ended up going into Cambodia. He observed camp after camp of NVA units, sitting nice and cozy across this border.** His observer recorded NVA mortar, heavy weapon and company positions, but due to Johnson's "idiotic rules of engagement" the enemy hiding in Cambodia could not be touched!

On Nov 14, 1965 the 1st Battalion of the 7th Cavalry was airlifted into a clearing called LZ, (landing zone), X-Ray close to the *Chu Pong Mountain*. This battalion was another well led and trained unit, but those prior political decisions by LBJ would imperil their effort as they were short almost 150 infantrymen.

An NVA prisoner was captured by troops from the first helicopter lift and he revealed that the 33d NVA Regiment was based in the nearby *Chu Pong mountain*. They were expecting the Americans to come and wanted to fight them.

(As always the NVA were fighting on ground of their choosing.)

Within an hour a large scale battle began, the battle of the *Ia Drang*. Even though they had suffered heavy losses during *Plei Me* the 33d was quickly sent in.

The outnumbered Americans in the first and second lifts were just able to stave off annihilation due to the excellent work of their commanders, the nearby artillery units and the helicopter pilots who flew non-stop.

Lt. Col Harold Moore who commanded 1-7 recognized early on that he was in a precarious position. His units had unintentionally set down between two NVA Regiments. He perfectly positioned each of his incoming, (but reduced strength), units to hold off the massed charges of the NVA. Reinforcements from Moore's battalion and men from the 2nd Batt 5th Cav were continually landed the over next two days as the fighting intensified. At times it was hand to hand and enemy troops even died inside Col. Moore's constricted command post.

As reinforcements and ammo came in wounded troops were medevacked out.

Thousands of artillery shells were fired from nearby temporary firebases to create a ring of steel around Moore's troops. Air cover became a vital factor as planes were stacked up waiting for missions to be called in from Moore's CP.

The heavy losses the NVA suffered were ignored as the communist commanders persisted with their frontal and flanking assaults. They did not despair their losses for they were learning valuable lessons on how to fight the Americans and their machines.

Late on the 16th the NVA decided to break off the fight.

They had died by the hundreds because they came out in the open to attack the American positions.

If not for Moore's outstanding command instincts, the aerial attacks and the U.S. artillery the NVA might well have won the battle and massacred the helicopter dependent troopers. Helicopters were great for getting the troops and supplies around but by 1965 the communists had learned all about them and understood their weaknesses. They would eventually bring hundreds of heavy machine guns into the South and could when given the chance close off the airspace with their intense and accurate fire.

During this first part of the continuous battle the NVA had lost over 1,000 killed, at a cost of 79 U.S. soldiers lost and 121 wounded, a 40% casualty rate in the under-strength Cav-battalion. Despite the positive ratio this was a heavy loss rate for the U.S. troops to suffer and could not be tolerated for long.

Because of the casualty ratio Westmoreland again touted the battle as a great victory.

(One of the understated reasons that Moore's Battalion had held on despite nearly being overrun was that the units and men had trained and lived together for almost two years. The men were fighting for each other.)

A third unit, the 2nd Batt 7th Cav had come in overland to augment the exhausted men of battalions 1-7 and 2-5. On the following day the U.S. units began leaving the battle area and naturally the exhausted men of 1-7 went out first. Later that day the men of 2-5 were also airlifted out. Heavy B-52 bombers were coming in to hammer the suspected NVA jungle base area with hundreds of 750lb bombs. Those missions were called *Arc Light*, and all troops were directed to get out of the "kill box".

Battalion 2-7 was the last unit to leave the battlefield and it was directed to walk / patrol over to a landing zone called Albany a few miles away. As they moved to the northeast on foot they unknowingly entered into a well prepared large scale ambush.

(It is possible the NVA had waited for reinforcements to come into Albany and had been sitting there to ambush those troops. Instead they ambushed the ones trying to leave.)

Their patrol alignment was directed by their commander and was tactically unsound. He did not anticipate any action even though they were deep in "Indian country". His companies were marching out in single file and did not have units out on the sides to patrol / protect the column. And the commander did not pre-plot artillery fire so to be ready in case something did happen. Those mistakes allowed his entire battalion to be caught inside the well planned ambush and resulted in major problems as the close-in fighting lasted for over a day.

In keeping with the Fatally Flawed Army rotation system, the Battalion commander of 2-7 was in his first combat command and his first infantry command. He had been moved over from supply and logistics. Just before the ambush began, the Battalion Commander had all of his company commanders move up to the head of the column for a conference. For some it was a 550 yard hike. It was at that time the enemy struck.

With the complete surprise achieved by the NVA and the poor U.S. command and control a debacle resulted with an additional 151 U.S. troops killed and 124 wounded.

During the night NVA execution teams moved through the battlefield murdering the wounded. Many were bound and shot in the back of the head, similar to Korea

(Gen. George Patton felt it took ten years of troop experience for a young officer to fully learn his trade. He never would have gone along with the Marshall-Eisenhower plan to create well rounded war managers who bounced through assignments so routinely that they never even knew the names of their men. For those of us in the FDNY it took five years before the journeyman firefighter understood the job.)

Back in the base camp Battalion 2-5 was hastily re-embarked onto their helicopters and sent in to try to help. They were staggered at the scope of the disaster.

Dozens of troopers of 2-7 were killed before they even knew what was happening. About two hundred NVA were also killed.

In Saigon this 2nd part of the battle was virtually ignored by MACV.

(To protect that officer and his patron, the records on the second battle were disappeared.)

The press had been at the first battle site and had a good understanding of the first fight. (Reporter Joe Galloway actually ended up fighting with Col. Moore's CP staff.)

It was obvious to everyone that the second battle had been lost, and they reported it as such after interviewing survivors. MACV totally disagreed and threatened censorship.

It was the start of the loss of credibility by Westmoreland's MACV.

MACV declared the battles in the Ia Drang a victory as the NVA had "left the area" and escaped back into Cambodia. Gen. Kinnard the Commander of the Cav made repeated requests to chase after the NVA into Cambodia to convert their tactical success into a strategic victory. (The JCS agreed.)

His requests were always refused and Kinnard eventually became convinced that the political leadership in Washington had no desire to win the war.

To try to prevent the 33d & 32d Regiments from going back into Cambodia ARVN Airborne units were dropped around the area on Nov 17. Led by Col. Ngo Quang Truong and advised by Major Schwarzkopf the confident ARVN paratroopers battled the NVA close to the border. Another two hundred plus enemy were killed with additional prisoners picked up.

But by escaping into Cambodia the NVA were able to rebuild their units from the supply coming down the Trail.

John Vann investigated the battle of the Drang and came away convinced that the NVA had stayed in the fight in order to learn about this new unit and their tactics.

He was eventually proved right as the NVA commanders digested the battle and sent reports out to all of their commands. They were told not to get into head to head fights. *A French journalist in Hanoi was told that with the Americans now fighting our victory will be delayed. Americans do not like long inconclusive wars, and this one will be long.*

During the 33 days the Cav was in action they had killed over 1,500 NVA and wounded over 1,700 more. *As a result of the continuous battles with the Air-Cav, the 173, 4th Inf and the 101st, the NVA invasion into the Central Highlands was stopped!*

But with the heavy losses to our units it was decided that certain areas were just too dangerous to operate in. Chu Pong was one of those areas.

Because there was no defined strategy in Vietnam, Westmoreland continued using Harkin's flawed battle plan which was based on "attrition."

After the many recent battles Gen. Westmoreland became convinced that this attrition strategy was a viable one. But the major lessons to be learned from those battles were completely ignored in order to have them fit in with that strategy.

1. *Disregarded were the facts that the enemy chose when and where to fight, and they also determined when it was time to retire.*
2. Asian armies do not attrite because they do not fear casualties. Especially communists.
   The Russians took over 100,000 casualties just to take Berlin in 1945. During Korea they suffered almost a million casualties in that loss to the West.
3. In Vietnam the communists had been fighting for this cause for over 20 years. They were not going to give up without suffering extremely heavy
4. casualties.
5. Battlefield attrition only works if the enemy has a fixed number of troops.

Attrition worked during the Civil War when Gen. Grant kept the pressure on the South in the last year and they finally collapsed from the losses they could not replace. In WWI all of the original embattled nations were at the end of their manpower limits by 1918. The final victories by the allies were possible because of America's entry into the fighting and that Germany had run out of reserves.

In WWII attrition worked in the island battles against the Japanese because they could not land any reinforcements. The only exceptions were the 1942-43 fight for Guadalcanal and New Guinea. Both dragged out because the Japanese were able to land reinforcements.

Attrition helped against the Germans in Africa and Sicily because the Germans could not reinforce those commands, but attrition did not work on the Germans in Italy (peninsula), because they did reinforce. Attrition worked in France since by June 1944 the years of fighting a multi-front war had weakened the enemy and most of the Germans were desperately fighting off the Russians. That prevented them from sending reinforcements to France.

Attrition was helping against the N. Koreans in 1950 when they bled themselves white against the Pusan Perimeter. After MacArthur landed the Marines behind them at Inchon the communists had no reserve troops left to hold off the invasion.

The NKPA broke down and retreated.

But the addition of hundreds of thousands of Chinese troops changed the war. Since Truman had declared China and Manchuria off limits, the Chinese could and did send unlimited manpower to continue the war in Korea.

Gen. Ridgeway had shown how to defeat those communists in battle after battle, but being unable to stop their reinforcements meant years of constant war.

That simple truth showed that there was no chance attrition would be a viable strategy in Vietnam against another group of Asian communists on another unsecured battlefield. Vietnam could be and was infiltrated from all four sides. All of the Administration, Pentagon and MACV principals knew about the communist supply efforts. And all knew that NVA troops were continuously infiltrating into S. Vietnam.

With a population of over 14 million, the North could send 200,000 new fighters a year into the fight and keep it going for 10 years before they had a manpower problem. And that did not include the VC fighters being recruited in the south!

A good commander would have digested the battle reports from Korea, Malaya and the first Indo-China War. And a wise one would have sought the council of Generals Ridgeway and Van Fleet before making any battlefield decisions.

As shown earlier, secretly trying to keep track of the Ho Chi Minh Trail were the small SOG teams tasked with observing and reporting. Their extremely dangerous missions are all but unknown to most people, but their work was vital to keeping the intelligence up to date. *Shamefully many of their die hard missions were not believed by the starched officers sitting at MACV.* SOG troops often reported on vast truck parks, well constructed dirt roads and large supply points. Even tracked vehicles and elephants could be heard operating on the Trail or in the jungles. To hide their work, the NVA tied trees together at the top to create a dense green canopy.

To inflict the losses needed for attrition to work, the Trail had to be cut.

Since Johnson had refused that strategy the only alternative was the limited bombing of *Operation Steel Tiger*. On Dec. 10 a twenty four plane B-52 Arc Light mission went in.

Though the strike did some major damage, enemy control of the area prevented any follow up efforts or observation. (Air Force rules were also affecting the efficiency of the operations. As in Korea, the AF pilots were told to fly high and fast.)

With the heavy fighting during November 1965 the JCS finally went to see the president and demanded he institute changes to the war policies. They called for an end to gradual escalation, heavy bombing of the North and lobbied to attack into N. Vietnam itself. *LBJ was not happy the service chiefs had shown up, and he vehemently cursed them and their military wisdom.* **They were ordered out of the White House.**

(As a group they should have immediately resigned and went to the media and the Congress to warn the nation of what was coming.)

Compounding the failures listed above another horrendous mistake made by LBJ and McNamara was on insisting that **they** and their staffs pick the targets for the bombing campaign instead of allowing the field commanders or JCS to make those calls.

At the beginning of the bombing campaign N. Vietnam had minimal anti-air defenses. *But by the end of 1965 Russia and China had provided almost 5,000 AAA guns!*

And in April of 1965 air-recon flights began to spot the telltale signs of Russian SAM sites being built. (Surface to air missiles.) Those same types of photos had appeared in Cuba just three years before. Incredulously LBJ refused to allow attacks on the sites for fear of hitting any of the Russians who were working there.

LBJ insisted that the air attacks could only occur after the sites were finished!

By October 1965 over 50 SAM sites became operational in N. Vietnam and losses to U.S. planes and pilots increased dramatically. And as the weeks went by more SAM sites became operational. (Shortly after was when the JCS went to see LBJ and were thrown out.) And to make the air attacks over N. Vietnam even more dangerous Russian fighters were being flown by Russian and N. Korean pilots.

LBJ foolishly ruled that the enemy airfields were also off-limits because of Russian personnel being present. (Like Truman in Korea.)

The only way we could stop the enemy fighters was to engage them in dog-fights over N. Vietnam. But the U.S. jet fighters had been hobbled in dog-fighting capability because years ago the decision had been made by staff / bureaucrats to take out the plane's cannons since "only missiles would be used in modern aerial warfare".

The art of air-air combat was no longer even being taught in the training schools.

Once aerial combat reappeared our military had to rebuild the schools and curriculum (Top Gun etc,) to train the incoming pilots in skills the "managers" had thought would no longer be needed.

Back at MACV Gen. Westmoreland's next great mistake was in ending the productive Marine program called the enclave strategy and their pacification efforts.

As stated earlier using their CAPs, (Combined Action Platoons), the USMC had made good headway in pacifying their areas. Like the British SAS teams in Malaya, the Marine CAP units learned the local areas and who belonged in them. By staying in one area for a while they spotted "things and people that were out of place". Infiltrating VC would then be killed and driven off. Safe in their homes, the peasants ignored the communist propaganda and went on with their lives.

But Westmoreland was acting blindly just like Almond did in Korea, complaining of the "lack of aggressiveness" from the marine units. Like Almond in 1950 he directed them to go out into the wilderness and "hunt for the enemy". And the results would be the same as we took terrible casualties doing so.

(McNamara had toured the USMC areas and saw first hand how well their efforts worked when they stayed in the villages. He also saw how quickly the VC returned if the marines left an area to traipse around looking for more. Even so he did not intervene to stop the madness.)

Some of the Special Forces troops had operated in a CIA run program based on the Malaya model, to improve village defenses and security. Within months that program also posted a record of unbroken success.

It was then that former Ambassador Taylor (who supposedly understood and started a counterinsurgency program) stepped in and forced the CIA to turn over the program to MACV. Soon after the program failed because as William Colby stated,

"The MACV / Embassy commanders foolishly wanted the semi-trained militias to chase around the jungles in an offensive mode, instead of allowing them to stay safe behind their defenses and kill the approaching VC"!

Another implausible Fatal Flaw that the Army never admitted to was that all of the French battle reports from Vietnam during 1946-54 had been translated and sent to the U.S. Army Command School. **But they had never been checked out by any officer prior to our involvement in Vietnam or even during our war!** Thus no effort was made to dissect the French experience during their years of fighting. The result would be that we made the same mistakes in the 1960s that the French had made fifteen years earlier.

To further highlight the lack of command knowledge and progressive thinking in military education; *None of the Senior Army Commanders went to or ever saw the need to send as many officers as possible to the excellent British Jungle Warfare School in Malaysia. No one in the Army ever looked to the work the Marines had done in the Banana Wars of the 1920s & 30's when the Corps defeated those insurgencies.*

And MACV never made an effort to examine what the Marines had accomplished in just six months in Nam.

Strangely almost all of the senior Army commanders disagreed with the USMC tactics. Even Gen. Harry Kinnard who was the aggressive commander of the Air Cav was "disgusted with the Marines because they did not want to go out and fight".

As a result of that command psychosis every U.S. Army unit that arrived in Vietnam was simply sent out to the bush to troll for the enemy. Pacification was not to be done.

But the real prize was the civilians, and only the communists were dealing with them.

(After the war ended the surviving senior commanders stated that the USMC CAP program would have worked to defeat the insidious VC. Stopping the NVA would have required a different tactic and would have meant a longer commitment similar to Korea, but it would have been the wisest way to have started.)

Back in the U.S., anti-war protests sprang up in forty cities. Although they were small their numbers would grow rapidly. By Christmas 1965, there were over 185,000 U.S. troops in Vietnam. On Dec 25, 1965 LBJ suspended the bombing of the North to induce the communists to negotiate. They ignored him and the bombing resumed on Jan 31. (His thoughtless and weak offer convinced the communists that they had the upper hand and any further attempts at negotiation would have to be met on their terms.)

In the Congress many members were becoming aware that this small war pushed by LBJ and McNamara was not all that small. Casualties were high and costs were way above estimates. The guess for 1966 was $10 billion. Questions were being asked.

Our losses in 1965 hit 1,369 killed!

During 65/66 John Vann was analyzing and planning his moves for increased pacification. He lamented the lost years of waste and corruption from Saigon and realized that the South was lost even with our battlefield help if they did not change their vile ways. His boundless energy and passion for his efforts struck all who met him.

Ambassador Lodge, William Colby and other principals were soon amazed at how correct he was in his reasoning.

Like the Marine Corps, Vann only wanted the U.S. forces to secure the populations, roads, towns, and act as a garrison/reserve force. With the people safe behind our troops a stable and honest government could be created and made to govern for the people. That would defeat the VC insurgency allowing the ARVN units to beat back the NVA, with our help. He also knew that the South Vietnamese had to fight this battle themselves.

But like S. Korea in 1950, the people and military of S. Vietnam were inferior to the disciplined communist menace. That was why America's legions were being committed to this latest challenge. But unlike Korea there were no defined battle lines with great armies aligned on each side. This was a war where the battles were everywhere and nowhere. And the only thing worth fighting for was the people.

Vann and Gen. York actually wanted to duplicate the KATUSA program used in Korea. The idea of pairing ARVN troops with U.S. troops might help teach them how to be soldiers and leaders. Since none of the prior MACV programs had worked the thought was why not try that one. But Gen. Westmoreland did not desire any system like that.

Similar to many of the senior U. S. leaders, he wanted nothing to do with the Vietnamese. To him they were mostly worthless.

Besides, a constant pool of drafted young American soldiers was guaranteed to come to him every week. And no glory could be had by leading foreigners.

(Once Westmoreland took over he could see how poor the ARVN leadership really was. He also realized that a decade of effort had been wasted and he had to retrain the ARVN from scratch.)

With the arrival and engagement of more and more heavily armed U.S. units, more and more civilian casualties were occurring. (Just as Vann had said.)

One demoralizing event summed up our altruistic but poorly led war effort. Air attacks had destroyed a province capitol in an effort to kill the enemy. An Army officer told the assembled reporters, *"We had to destroy the town in order to save it"*. The reporters were stunned, and their dispatches reflected their negativity.

And as time went by those continual events were turning the South into a land of refugees.

On Jan 24, 1966 the 1st Air Cav Div began their next major operation, called *Masher*. During the multi-week battle hundreds of VC and NVA became casualties, but again no pacification was being accomplished. After the fighting ended the Cav units flew off to another area to try find more of the enemy. *A month later the empty battle area was reclaimed by the NVA*.

In March Gen. H. Johnson of the JCS commissioned a study to see if what the Army was doing was working. After reviewing reports from earlier advisors and staff the conclusion was reached that the war had to be won from the ground up.

That would require pacification. Thus far the VC were still relatively self-sustaining, getting their aid and fighters locally. Again Westmoreland totally dismissed the report, never mentioning it in his memoirs or in his official report on the war.

Into 1966 LBJ still remained evasive and vague in public about his strategy for Vietnam. He also realized that public opinion would play a vital role over our effort and he had to try to control what was seen and heard. Polls were already "getting soft on Vietnam", and the anti-war protestors becoming more vocal and noticed.

Sen. William Fulbright the chairman of the Senate Foreign Relations Committee decided to hold hearings into Vietnam. (By this point many of the legislators were also turning against the war.) Sec. State Rusk was one of those called in and his testimony was coated in spin doctoring and propaganda. (Sound familiar.) Those high level deceits were setting the stage for the citizens to loose faith in their government as thousands were dying each month.

After the hearings ended Johnson called in J. Edgar Hoover and ordered the FBI to investigate Sen. Fulbright. LBJ was outraged that one of his own party was turning on him. He told Hoover to find evidence that he must be a communist or one of their dupes. *Like FDR, Johnson used Hoover and the FBI to his own agenda.*

In April 1966 Johnson banned any Congressional trips to the beleaguered country! (That one act should have instantly caused a revolt in the Congress.) **LBJ then instituted an interagency committee to control all information. Congressional members and staff could receive briefings only by Administration officials which included the president, McNamara and Rusk.**

McNamara had again gone out to speak with Westmorland over manpower requests and it was agreed that another 100,000 would be asked for with long term plans for 400,000 troops. Allied nations of SEATO supplied more forces with S. Korea sending 48,000 tough, hard troops.

Disciplined and inured to hardships, the area between *Cam Rahn Bay* and *Qui Nhon* in II Corps remained under S. Korean control throughout their time in country. (Their Marine Brigade operated with the 1st Mar Div.)

Villages they pacified stayed pacified.

The ROKs were hard and ruthless against any communists they found. *And the area they operated in was one of the few where the VC were afraid to fight.*

Australia sent one regiment initially and then committed to a second.

They were given a single province to operate in, *Phuoc Tuy* on the SE coast and were able to control the communists despite their small force. One of the keys to their success was in using their Special Air Service (SAS), 5 man-recon teams. The Aussies were able to recon and control large areas of remote territory and their teams had the highest kill ratio of any Allied unit, over 500 enemy to none of their own.

The Australians had a great deal of counterinsurgency experience after their operations with the British in Malaya from 1952-1960, and operations during the civil war in Indonesia from 1960-1966. As they arrived and began their maneuvers the Aussies rightfully questioned the strategy and tactics used by MACV. Mirroring the many British commanders in Korea, the Aussies observed that many of the U.S. units operated poorly and their commanders seemed to have no idea what they were doing.

Major Hackworth of the 101st had met with and admired the Aussie system. He tried to get some cross training in with the knowledgeable Aussies but Westmoreland arrogantly refused. Regular U.S. Army Officers disliked any of those "special units" and their tactics. Like every type of bureaucratic dinosaur those people would only use what they understood even when their knowledge was shown to be completely outdated.

(That was why JFK had wanted a younger General to run MAAG, but instead he listened to Taylor and wrongly allowed Harkins to go.)

Gen. Krulak had been in Vietnam when the Marines fought their first big battle in August 65. He did not like what he saw. Then after the battles with the 173, 4th Inf and 101st Airborne in northern II Corps and the Air Cav in the Ia Drang in November he became convinced that Westmoreland's attrition strategy could not succeed.

Krulak wrote a paper to McNamara warning him that attrition would fail because that was the enemy's game. In the large battles we fought in 1965 America had lost over 300 of her sons and then left the hallowed ground to the enemy to go find more enemy to fight. *He also mentioned how Gen Giap had boasted that when the cost in casualties and francs was high enough the French would defeat themselves in Paris.*

It was probable that they are expecting the same outcome with us.

If the North had the estimated manpower pool of 2.5 million soldiers, we would have to take 10,000 deaths a year for 10 years just to whittle them down at the rate we are at now. Krulak recommended a strategy of pacification which was central to any victory. The people are the prize we must win. We must use our troops to protect the populated areas fighting only when it was necessary. Admiral Sharp and Marine Commandant Greene concurred with those findings but were unable to get McNamara, Westmoreland or the JCS to force the change in strategy.

(If it seems like you have read or heard this before, you have from Col Vann in 1962 and the Marine Commanders in the Pentagon and Vietnam when they started to pacify the villages in 1965. If the reader also remembers, Gen. Krulak was the one who had prevented Vann from giving that report on Vietnam to the JCS in 63!)

Krulak's report also stated that it was folly to try to interdict the supplies once they have made it onto the roads. The bombing and mining of the ports and railheads were required to stop the flow and win the war. (That is what the JCS had been saying since 64.) Naturally LBJ was against any of the advice and Gen. Krulak was sent back to Pearl Harbor to watch the horror he had helped create unfold.

Sec. of the Navy Paul Nitze visited in July 1966. He too was impressed with the USMC progress at *Da Nang, and Chu Lai*. The areas were more secure, the VC had been driven out and the civilian safety area provided by the Marines had grown from 25 to over 500 square miles. Nitze could see the areas being revitalized with schools, small businesses and roads. He was also impressed with the morale and work ethic of our troops and sailors. *But when he returned to Washington even he could not convince McNamara or LBJ that the Marines were on the right course.*

(He and Gen. Krulak had observed search and destroy operations where we shelled and bombed areas and villages. Both knew it was wrong and barbaric.)

Marine Commandant Walter Greene also went back to Vietnam on another inspection trip and to see Westmoreland. Greene and Westy met in private and they argued over the attrition strategy. As before Westmoreland refused to hear the truth or the logic. (If he had agreed with the Marine Generals and their strategy for pacification and security there would be no glory such as leading a great military machine to battlefield victory.) *Like MacArthur in Korea, Westmoreland saw only the reality he wanted and ignored the available intelligence and truth.*

In addition to the combat operations in Vietnam Gen. Westmoreland also directed an enormous construction program to accommodate his massive "Army". (Which he and his staff did quite well.)

Four new airbases were added to the three already built. The airbases had runways over 10,000 feet long plus miles of taxi-ways, aprons and ramps. On the bases were dozens of hangers, shops, offices, barracks and other buildings.

Four central supply / logistic centers were established with 26 permanent bases for these service personnel. Seventy five tactical airfields were added to the 19 already in use for helicopters and transport aircraft. Twenty eight hospitals with over 8,000 beds were built, plus a new two story HQ building that could hold 4,000 people!

The base at Long Binh covered 25 square miles and had 43,000 personnel assigned to it!

Six new deepwater ports were constructed which could accommodate 28 deep draft freighters. An entire pier complex was built on the East coast of the U.S. and towed across the Pacific to Cam Ranh Bay. Added to the nearby piers were warehouses, ammo storage bunkers, fuel storage, barracks and mess halls. The fuel storage alone could hold 3.1 million barrels of fuels.

To provide for the comfort of all of those service troops, permanent barracks and buildings were built. Theaters, bowling alleys PX's and service clubs were constructed. Ice cream and ice was provided along with flush toilets and full course meals.

Air conditioned housing and offices were the norm for the senior ranks which necessitated a massive electrical generating capacity. To help the military man these complexes, over 200,000 Vietnamese became "workers for the Green Machine".

The pacification efforts by Vann and the hundreds of other AID managers also added to the building boom. Camps and facilities were also needed for the hundreds of thousands of refugees the war and relocations had created. This extensive effort further alienated the populace as their independent way of life was being uprooted and irrevocably altered. America had invaded, and their ancient life would soon be gone.

And with all of this effort came an unprecedented feast of corruption.

Thieu and his wife made millions at the trough eventually acquiring control of their own bank. Graft which followed all aspects of the "American Invasion" further corrupted the populace and reducing any hope of maintaining their independence.

Political considerations in the South meant that four vital areas had to be protected first. They were *Saigon*, the *Mekong Delta* area, and coastal *Qui Nhon* and *Da Nang*. Each had to be secured and the existing VC and NVA forces pushed back.

It was hoped that with those areas cleared the large scale offensives could then be conducted. Thus the year of 1966 was tied up in all of the above endeavors.

Just the fact that those areas had to be secured by large numbers of U.S. and Allied troops illustrated how far along the communist control had progressed.

(At a follow on conference in Honolulu McNamara "predicted" that during 1967, 40-50% of the communist bases would be destroyed and 60% of the South reclaimed.?)

While MACV was preparing their support infrastructure the enemy was still **increasing** their force levels unabated and mostly untouched along the Ho Chi Minh Trail. SOG Team strikes, Arc Light and Steel Tiger missions were still occurring, but the buildup on the Trail had progressed so fast the enemy could easily replace their losses.

No active consideration had ever been made by LBJ to attack into N. Vietnam or Laos.

And with LBJ publicly stating that that would not happen, the communists were freed from that worry and could send as many units as possible into S. Vietnam.

Thus the NVA virtually matched all of our troop increases with their own.

The NVA knew that those SF-SOG camps were the home base of most of those annoying recon teams, and it was decided to eliminate the one in the *Ashau Valley*.

Their 95B Reg. was tasked with the assault. ARVN commanders refused to reinforce the camp forcing the SF command to bring a few of their troops. After days of battle it was clear the camp would have to be abandoned and only half of the defenders escaped.

Numerous aircraft were shot down, and only limited patrolling by recon troops from the 101st could enter the valley. And so another area was deemed too dangerous to enter.

Then in April 1966 the ARVN units in the I CTZ, the northern sector where the Marines were fighting ceased all operations due to collapse of morale and belief in their cause. The loss of so many ARVN combat units at once allowed the NVA to gain complete control of the entire A Shau Valley in the western zone of I CTZ.

They also crossed over the DMZ in large numbers, and frequent large battles were fought with the Marines though none were decisive. The same scene soon occurred all across the South as the U.S. Divisions were finding communist forces everywhere.

Sensing the time was right, in the summer of 1966 the NVA sent the 324B Division across the DMZ. Their purpose was to lure the Marine units northward into the hinterlands and away from the cities. Marine patrols out in front of *Operation Hastings* began fighting with the NVA advance parties. Recon and intel confirmed the presence of the entire NVA unit. Westmoreland ordered Gen. Walt to stop all of the "USMC pacification nonsense", and get everyone after the enemy. As ordered the Marines of the 3d Div went north and fought the first of their border battles near the DMZ.

The NVA stayed long enough to bait the trap and then they withdrew to safety back across the border.

By late 1966 the Marines began their <u>forced construction</u> of firebases deeper into the hills and jungles of northern and western I Corps. Bases such as Con Thien, Dong Ha, and Cam Lo signaled their increased presence along the DMZ and were noted by the NVA. The Marines also took over a Special Forces camp at a site the marines called Camp Carroll, displacing the Special Forces and their CIDG's further out to the west to the village of Lang Vei. (This new SF base was constructed and used as their forward area to patrol into Laos and the upper Ho Chi Minh Trail.)

Each of those marine firebases needed to be staffed and protected, and that requirement reduced the manpower available for patrolling. It also provided a group of nice easy targets for the growing number of NVA artillery units being based just across the untouchable DMZ. And the broken ground along the DMZ provided an ideal region for the NVA to run ambushes and quick hit battles. And as soon as they decided to leave, the

NVA would escape to safety across the Z. *Despite repeated requests from MACV to chase after those escaping enemy units LBJ would never allow it.*

The western part of this northern most province of S. Vietnam consisted of numerous foothills and then wild mountains where humans never went.

An army could actually be concealed within the dense green vegetation.

In mid-1966 the Red Chinese made an "arrangement" with Prince Norodom Sihanouk of Cambodia to allow them to ship hundreds of tons of weaponry and supplies to the Cambodian port of Sihanoukville.

This vital logistical program greatly simplified the NVA war effort in the southern areas of III and IV Corps as the materials and supplies no longer had to be carried all the way down the Ho Chi Minh Trail. (Our/ARVN coastal interdiction and patrolling was shutting down the enemy sea supplies.) In return for helping the Cambodian Army was given a kickback of some of the weapons, while Sihanouk and his generals took bribes.

One of Sihanouk's wives actually owned the trucking company used to move the weapons from the port to the NVA supply depots placed all along the eastern Cambodian border with South Vietnam!

But this treachery by the Cambodian leaders would come back to haunt them. The tragic shame of it was that they were not the ones who would pay the price.

On Sept 1, 1966 French President de Gaulle publicly condemned the U.S. led effort in S. Vietnam and called for the withdrawal of all of our forces. (One of the only reason we were in that predicament was because of French arrogance on reclaiming their former colonies.) To further his insult, he also ordered all U.S. troops and personnel out of France within 48 hours. Numerous battlements and base areas had been built up at great cost to the U.S. taxpayers since the start of NATO. All had to be cleared as much as possible within the time frame.

Sec. State Rusk acidly asked de Gaulle if that order included the 100,000 American dead who were buried in France's cemeteries!

(I met two of those Army troops when researching these books. Both told me how shameful it was to be ordered out of the country and of how they were angrily ordered to destroy anything we did not have time to take. Leave nothing for the French.)

On Sept 23, 1966 MACV reported that large areas of Vietnam were being de-forested with the chemical agent orange to uncover enemy base areas. Despite destroying hundreds of square miles of jungles and forests the enemy remained hard to find.

At the SEATO conference the Allied Nations pledged to continue their aid until N. Vietnam ceased its infiltration of forces into the South. Because of photos and video shot by SOG teams the lie that N. Vietnam repeatedly claimed of not having any troops in the South was proven false. *This intelligence was shown in a closed door session to convince the doubters in Congress and the State Dept. that this was an invasion of the South.*

During October the U.S. Navy was finally allowed to shell the coastal areas of the North to silence some of the enemy artillery batteries. Their work was reminiscent of the shore bombardments of WWII. But again the Navy was not firing the proper munitions nor at the correct angles. Like the Japanese, the NVA had placed their guns in well prepared and protected positions. High angle firing was needed to drop the shells down onto the fortifications and armor piercing munitions were required to penetrate into those same positions before exploding. As always the high-explosive munitions made a good show, but were not destroying enough of the fortifications to help the marines.

On November 12 a *NY Times* article complained that almost half of our aid to S. Vietnam was not reaching the final destinations due to corruption.

On the 17th a report from McNamara to LBJ stated that our increased troop levels have not reduced the enemy's strength. The report was rejected by Johnson.

(Around this time some of those in his administration began leaving.)

Operation Attleboro, run from September-November was a multi-phase US Army attack into enemy areas NW of Saigon. Tons of supplies were captured and over 1,000 enemy were killed. A solid win to be sure, but as always as soon as the shooting ended the U.S. forces moved away to a new sector to continue Westmoreland's attrition strategy. A short while later the enemy returned from their sanctuary in Cambodia to retake control of the vacated sector. *This was a new type of war, one without front lines.*

It was called area war, and consisted of moving around the country looking for the elusive enemy. It was a ludicrous waste of lives and effort. After this first full year of fighting the Americans the communists wisely avoided the large scale battles that they knew they could not win. Unlike the French, the Americans had unlimited resources and a huge air armada to hammer the communist units. It made no sense for them to stay in place and fight.

After each battle the enemy would steal away to regroup and recover.

They would examine the battle, critique their tactics and our operations and try again.

On Dec 13, 1966 Soviet leader Leonid Brezhnev made a point of drastically increasing the aid to N. Vietnam. This aid was also being sent from the Warsaw Pact countries, (communist version of NATO). Included in the list of supplies and weapons were more military specialists. Among the specialist ranks were Soviet radar operators, communications teams, anti-aircraft units, artillery units, infantry and armor forces!

Soviet personnel traveled in civilian clothing and were ordered not to speak to anyone about their tours in Vietnam. Flights from Russia stopped in Beijing and planes were exchanged in an effort to hide their identities. Supplies were sent via railroad through China and via ships to the port of Haiphong.

(After 1968 the relations between China and Russia were so bad that the flights were directed across Afghanistan, Pakistan, India and Burma. The planes landed in Karachi and Calcutta for fuel stops.)

Once the Soviet personnel arrived in Vietnam they wore NVA uniforms, but their height and face color gave them away when they were spotted by our troops or aircrews. To rectify part of this problem N. Korean pilots were used to fly the MiG fighters.

During the war over 15,000 Soviet servicemen fought as "military advisors". And as with Korea almost 1,000 Soviet pilots were flying against our pilots.

All of the work by Soviet personnel was coordinated by the Ambassador Extraordinary and Plenipotentiary of the Soviet Union to Vietnam, Ivan Scherbakov. He was in constant contact with the leadership of Vietnam, especially Ho Chi Minh. All needs were quickly forwarded to Moscow to ensure that their communist ally had the latest supplies and munitions.

Russian aircraft gifts started with the older MIG-15 and 17 designs, but were upgraded to the Mig-21 by 1969. The T-54 tank replaced the vintage T-34, and the AK-47 became the preferred weapon for their infantry simplifying the problems of supply.

The AK47 fired the 7.62 round, the same as our M-60 machine gun. And in their insightful and dangerous minds the Soviet mortar systems were 61mm and 82 mm designs. In this devious way the enemy mortar crews could fire our captured ammo, 60mm & 81mm, but we could not use theirs.

The Russians also used Vietnam as a place to test and train their weapons and tactics. For them, Vietnam was just one more fight in the overall struggle to destroy the West.

As shown above much of the U.S. led war effort was spent in preparing, building and protecting the huge base areas that our forces used. Ports had to be built and/or upgraded to enable the logistical system to supply the massive needs of the U.S. military. The supplies were then trucked and airlifted to the various commands. But this extensive supply system also required security forces to protect the roads and convoys.

It was estimated that *more than 60% of our troop totals* were engaged in those "logistical requirements" and not actually involved in fighting the communists in the fields and jungles.

Despite having a peak force of over 500,000 personnel in S. Vietnam, *the NVA and VC always outnumbered our troops in the field.*

At our peak there were only 80,000+ U.S. infantry troops out in the jungles countrywide. That meant that at almost every battle the enemy could mass their troops and fight when and where they wanted. And every time a major fight started the enemy was free to move into the vacated areas.

(This logistical burden was the same as the one that had hampered our effort in Korea, and had been complained about by the British Commanders. If one looks at the drastic conditions the Marines existed in at Guadalcanal and all of their following campaigns, a happy medium of logistical support was possible and desired. By tying up so much of our forces in support services, our infantry combat power was greatly diminished.)

America's military has relied on air support since WWII. A downside to that need was the logistical requirements involved in flight operations. In Vietnam the U.S. used jet aircraft for much of the air support, but jets required much more fuel and maintenance than the simpler piston engine fighter/bombers of yesteryear. After Korea the Air Force Commanders did not want to use those old reliable propeller planes, they wanted only sleek jet aircraft in their inventory. Once it became obvious that the jets were no good at close-in air support a propeller driven plane was reluctantly re-introduced. The Korean War vintage A-1 *Skyraider* carried 4-20mm canons and 8,000 lbs of bombs or missiles. Its slower speed enabled the weapons to be deployed with great accuracy compared to the fast moving jets. They became workhorses in Vietnam.(The A-10 Warthog replaced it and was just as desired for close in work. And yet even after seeing how effective it was in Kuwait, Iraq and Afghanistan, the USAF wants to eliminate all of those air units to keep only sleek fighter jets.)

As the White House directed air campaign called *Rolling Thunder* continued LBJ would invoke Korea into every effort by the JCS to strike harder. *Intel reports from the JCS and CIA repeatedly stressed that neither China nor Russia would join in the fighting as long as the U.S. troops stayed in the South.* (In fact the Vietnamese and Chinese were bitter enemies from

China's last invasion and occupation and that may have been why Ho and his Politburo only allowed unarmed Chinese support troops in.)

And with the onset of Mao's "Cultural Revolution" in October 1966 China was being ripped apart by their self-inflicted communist purges and atrocities. Millions of Chinese citizens were dying in these demented acts of "purifying" the revolution. Caught up in the purge were some of Mao's closest associates and many of their critical planners. China lost an entire generation of leadership, and their Army actually had to intercede to end it.

Russia was in just as bad a logistical position as we were if they had wanted to send troops to the region. The Russian Navy was small and not equipped to send or supply large forces by sea. Since they had not committed troops to the fight in Korea where they shared a common border, why would they commit troops to this war?

Russia's main interest was still in Europe and the Middle East, not a small country near China. Any communist fight against the West was worth supporting, but not in a large scale head-head battle against America.

North Vietnam had only one major port at Haiphong and it was completely filled with supply ships. *The JCS argued repeatedly that we could choose to blockade or attack that one area which would cut off most of the Russian and Warsaw Pact access and their massive supply effort.* **But LBJ still refused to listen.**

By the end of 1965 over 35,000 NVA troops had crossed into the south.

As 1966 came to a close the number would mushroom to over 150,000 troops. The first unit that entered in 1966 was the NVA 18B Regiment. A week later came the 24th. regiment. Fifteen more came down the Trail plus dozens of individual battalions and company units. Two divisions came right across the DMZ to fight the Marines.

Many more units were sitting across the borders waiting their turn to join in.

Rather than follow our efforts and flood the South with troops, the NVA kept theirs safe in sanctuaries across the DMZ, Cambodia and Laos. They would enter the South only when a fight was ordered.

The city of Tchepone was a town about 25 miles inside Laos and a major NVA hub on the Ho Chi Minh trail. *It too was declared off limits by LBJ.*

Photographs and numerous reports from SOG teams had noted and observed the buildup at Tchepone and the continued growth of the Trail network around it. Dirt roads had replaced the original jungle trails as NVA Transportation **Group 559** worked tirelessly improving and repairing their networks. (After every bombing mission the ants went right to work restoring a damaged road within days.)

Their efforts were later joined by the aforementioned Russian, Chinese and North Korean "advisors" who assisted in building actual roads, bridges and eventually fuel pipelines! Due to the distances and needs, **Group 470** was formed to oversee the trail extension and construction in Cambodia. At times the enemy was building almost 60 miles of roads a year!

China was sending over 6,000 tons of weapons, ammunition and supplies daily to N. Vietnam over their border. (Not including what they also landed in Cambodia.)

Even though they had to face the limited daily bombings of *Rolling Thunder* the enemy was getting the supplies they needed. And by 1970 the built up trails/roads were moving multiple thousands of tons of material and thousands of troops each month.

Because of Johnson's inane rules all that MACV was allowed to do to hurt the enemy was to send million dollar jets with expensive payloads to try to bomb a truck and cargo worth $10,000. (Hard to Fathom that this was the strategy from our President and his team.)

In the Central Highlands area and all along the Cambodian border U.S. units were fighting an enemy who would retreat across the common border as soon as a fight turned in our favor. Operation *Cedar Falls* was indicative of the problems. Large U.S. formations would move in to take objectives at great cost, but the enemy simply disappeared once they realized the extent of our effort. Some battles would be intense while other times an area would be empty as the enemy slipped away into vast tunnel complexes or ran across the border.

Gen. Larsen of the 101st had given a talk to reporters after they had decimated an NVA battalion at Bu Gia Mop. Dan Rather and camera had shown up after the fighting had ended, and in the film footage shot Gen. Larsen spoke on how the NVA would run back across the border to break contact and reach safety. The interview went on TV and caused a furor at home. But the liars in the White House and the Administration denied it was true, and Gen. Larsen was ordered to retract his statement.

His acid reply, "I stand corrected."

Here again was a chance for the senior generals to stand up and face down this corrupt Administration. Westmoreland should also have stood by Gen. Larsen's statements and informed the world the truth about SE Asia.

But Westmoreland was only looking to get his ticket punched for his next star and so he played his part in the charade and allowed this stupidity to continue.

As always once the fighting with the 101st had ended the U.S. units were pulled out to attack some other area in keeping with MACV's futile strategy. Within days the enemy would drift back in and take over the vacated sector. Then they would rebuild the destroyed defenses and improve them so that the next time our forces showed up the area would be harder to attack. As our troops humped through the harsh, torrid landscape the enemy sat in their sheltered defenses and waited for our troops to show up.

A classified CIA report on the war stated that for every dollar of damage we were doing to the enemy it was costing America $9.60.

(By late 67 Rolling Thunder had caused over $300 million in damages to the communists. But cost the U.S. taxpayers $900 million just in lost aircraft!)

When 1966 came to a close, another 6,053 Americans had died during the year. The ARVN in their reduced capacity had lost almost 12,000.

At home the mid-term elections had been concluded. Fallout from the Democrats Welfare / Social Programs, the growing war in Vietnam and helpful campaigning by former Vice President Richard Nixon resulted in the Republicans picking up 47 seats in the House and three in the Senate. They also picked up six governor spots. Though the Democrats still had majorities, the people were starting to show their discontent. And Nixon picked up a lot of political IOUs.

During February 1967 a twenty six Battalion attack called *Junction City* was directed into the enemy base area northwest of Saigon. Thousands more enemy soldiers were killed, but thousands of others escaped back into Cambodia. Not long after the units left the area to patrol a new location. The rebuilt enemy quietly returned.

Westmoreland finally complained to McNamara and his staff in March that unless the flow of NVA reinforcements was stopped, the war would go on indefinitely.

In the wild far northwest region of Vietnam lay the large, flat plateau called Khe Sanh. Since 1964 the Army had used the site as a launch base for Special Forces recon and raiding parties which had gone across the border into Laos and/or N. Vietnam.

(That was how we knew what the NVA were actually doing in those sanctuaries and on the Ho Chi Minh trail. SOG teams even tapped into NVA telephone lines running into Laos.)

The site was suited for a small airfield and firebase and Westmoreland had sent in the Seabees in Sept 1966. A firebase was constructed and finished in early 1967.

Gen. Walt CG 3d Mar Div was told to send in a battalion of Marines.

But even to an untrained eye the major drawback to Khe Sanh was that it was surrounded by higher hills. Hill 861 was northwest of the airstrip, and nearby were hills 881S & 881N. It was not long before the NVA took notice of the U.S. effort.

(I worked with a firefighter in Ladder 36 FDNY who had been a member of an army construction unit. Even though he was a corporal he was appalled that anyone in authority would place a base in the middle of those dominating hills. He was happy as can be to leave when their work was done.)

Units from NVA Div 325C quickly and silently moved in to take over and buildup defenses on the surrounding hills. And because of the heavy jungle in the area they were never seen or heard. Gen. Krulak returned to Nam to argue with Westmoreland about the foolishness of picking the Khe Sanh site for a combat base. At least another battalion would be needed to occupy the nearby hills tying up even more units and entail a large helicopter commitment to supply the fighters on those hills. *Both were assets the Marine Corps was in short supply of.*

(Despite having developed the use of helicopters their restrictive budgets caused USMC helicopter units to remain small. At that time the Corps was not blessed with unlimited helicopter assets like the Army, and was actually using their older and obsolete models from the 1950s. They flew extremely slow and had a poor weight capacity.)

Krulak argued that the enemy would have an easy time attacking the base due to the terrain and surrounding heavy jungle. Westmoreland argued back that the location would serve a greater purpose, especially if we attacked into Laos. As their talk progressed it became apparent to Krulak that Khe Sanh was being setup as bait. Westmoreland could not be swayed.

Not long after five more Marine battalions were operating up along the DMZ. In reality the Marines should not have been used the way Westmoreland and MACV did anyway. The Corps was designed as shock troops, not regular infantry and they did not have the logistic capacity for long term operations like the Army did.

The Marines should have been given operational control from the shoreline westward to Highway 1 only as commandant Greene had said. (About 10 miles.)

Then the Marines could be supplied when needed over the beach and protected using the Navy's ships as floating artillery. That was the way they were programmed, supplied and trained to operate. **And with fewer base areas to defend and supply the additional freed up marines could have pacified the entire coastal area of I Corps.**

(Because of their small numbers the USMC could only commit two of their three divisions into Vietnam. They also kept a BLT, Battalion Landing Team offshore as their emergency reserve. They too saw a lot of combat.)

The Army divisions especially the mechanized units should have been the ones to operate from the Highway westward into the interior. Then the Army could use their large helicopter forces to concentrate on the western zones and the borders.

(To highlight the thoughtlessness at MACV the Army had to create a Riverine Unit from scratch to operate on small boats in IV Corps and the Mekong Delta instead of letting the Marines do it.)

Around this same time Sec. McNamara naively directed the construction of a ground barrier across the length of the DMZ. His less than insightful thought was to "build a Korean type DMZ that would prevent the NVA from crossing over".

The project had no hope of stopping the NVA from crossing the Z, and there was no hope of being able to build it at that late date. As the engineers worked the NVA constantly shelled them to slow the construction. And the numerous planned strong points would have required three or more regiments to man and patrol around them. Confined to those sites the Marines would have been under constant artillery fire from the NVA.

During the increasing battles along the DMZ the Marines like most of the infantry units had to walk, (hump) everywhere carrying everything on their backs. Continual losses in the line units were hard to replace and companies that were supposed to have 220 Officers and men were fighting with 100 or less. Following MACV's directions the units spread out across the landscape patrolling in the intense heat or torrential rains looking for signs of the enemy. Booby-traps and mines were constantly set off, killing and injuring dozens each day.

When a battle was started it was usually initiated by the NVA who had been sitting in their bunkers waiting for the marines or army troops to walk past. After a while they would stop shooting and disappear. The ever present U.S. casualties would be air lifted out and then it was repeated the next day.

Gen. Westmoreland returned to the States in April to speak with Johnson. Though the enemy appeared to be suffering, Westy needed more troops.

LBJ was not thrilled with the request for 100,000 more men. Their talks brought forth more questions and concerns than true answers. LBJ had the general speak to the Congress to quite the critics, and to chastise the anti-war protestors. The PR effort failed.

The only bright spot in Vietnam concerned Robert Komer's increasingly successful efforts at pacification.

On April 24, 1967 a Marine recon team was ambushed on hill 861. Only one Marine survived. From April 28 to May 12, 1967 a series of tough battles occurred that were known as the Khe Sanh hill fights. The Marine units involved were not aware of the new and extensive enemy fortifications on those hills and walked into a killing field. *Two regiments from the 325C NVA Div had silently moved in and occupied the hills.* (This was the second full NVA division to have invaded across the DMZ.)

The Marines who climbed the tall ridges were unaware of the enemy traps or bunkers until their point units were ambushed luring additional teams into the fight. Then those units would be hit from silent, unseen bunkers along the edges.

Days of headlong assaults into the teeth of the defenses resulted in hundreds of casualties. The enemy fortifications withstood everything fired at them, and Hill 881S had ten times as many bunkers as 861. Even airstrikes failed to destroy them as high explosives were used instead of armor piercing munitions.

(The presence of such numbers of secretive and well built bunkers on Hill 861 should have instantly alerted the Marine Commanders to the dangers and the threats looming on 881S and 881N.)

Gen. Walt arrived when word of the disaster finally reached him.

He went forward with a squad of Marines to analyze the battlefield and defenses. Having fought at *Peleliu*, Walt clearly understood what they were up against.

He ordered the Marines down and had the AP munitions used. The hill became shrouded in dust as the massive Armor Piercing munitions did their job. Advancing units found hundreds of enemy soldiers dead from the bombings and assaults. As always the NVA retreated at a convenient time and silently took up positions on hill 881N. Once the fighting began there, Walt had that hill bombed.

Bad weather again closed in cloaking the area and Walt had the forward units withdraw for safety. That night the NVA infantry mass attacked through the storm trading their lives for as many Marines as they could. The tactic was eerily similar to what the Marines had faced in the Pacific against the Japanese.

After the two week battle had ended, 155 Marines had died with 425 wounded. (Almost an entire Battalion.)

And as always as soon as the battles ended the companies were needed elsewhere and only smaller units were left to guard those dangerous hills.

In Hanoi conferences were held over the American successes. Because of the heavy firepower the Americans used enemy losses were high and getting worse. Reports from the field also unveiled the increasing gains by the U.S. led pacification teams. *To defeat those efforts Defense Minister Giap proposed a countrywide offensive to be timed for their next TET Holiday.*

Giap wanted to strike the as yet untouched cities to provoke an uprising. To do so would require fixing the U.S. effort in the jungles.

In keeping with Giap's strategy to pull the U.S. forces away from the cities the NVA next attacked on the eastern side of the DMZ near the USMC base at Con Thien. That base was a vital chokepoint and defensive position against any NVA attack southward. *In May 1967 4200 rounds of artillery landed on the base.*

Everything that the Soviets had given the NVA was fired; 85mm, 100mm, 122mm, 130mm guns, 120mm mortars, 122mm Katyusha rockets and by July 152mm guns.

The U.S. responded with artillery, Navy 5 & 6 inch shells and bombs but failed to shut down the enemy fire because HE munitions could not breech the emplacements. The NVA would hide their guns in pits, tunnels and caves and wait until our fire ended. Hills were hollowed out from the rear so the guns could fire through small openings that were perfectly sited on a particular target. They would fire just 1-3 rounds from each gun and then shut down. Phony gun positions were also set up to attract U.S. counter-battery fire, and charges were set off to simulate muzzle flashes.

Anything that could be done to confuse the U.S. response was.

(Half of the USMC casualties in the war were from shell and mortar fire. And most of it was fired from the other side of the DMZ where Johnson said we could not go.)

Operation Buffalo was directed to scout the area north of the Con Thien combat base. Lying in wait was the NVA 324B Division. On July 2 two companies from the 1st Batt 9th Mar Regiment were ambushed by those superior NVA units and heavy losses were incurred. For days the Marines were involved in savage fighting in the semi-open ground north of the combat base. Units from five USMC battalions became involved in trying to hold off what had become determined enemy attacks to overrun Con Thien.

Four NVA divisions were eventually sent into the fight, over 35,000 troops. They were supported by several battalions of artillery.

When the initial part of the battle ended on July 14, the Marine units had suffered hundreds of additional casualties. But the enemy was not done.

During September follow on NVA attacks had troops in the wire trying to overrun the Con Thien combat base. B-52 strikes, tactical air strikes and even naval shelling finally broke the siege at the Con Thien. Though enemy losses were high, so were the additional casualties to the marines. As always Westmoreland called the battle a crushing defeat for the NVA. (And another Marine Battalion became casualties.)

From 1967 on more than 52% of the U.S. deaths occurred in I Corps which consisted of just 5 of the 44 Vietnamese provinces. During the war 14,691 Marines died, three times the losses in Korea, but less than the 24,511 lost in WWII.
In just the northern 10 provinces, 77% of our battle deaths occurred as our forces fought off the NVA invaders.

Middle East

The bitterness in the Middle East had grown worse since the fighting in 1956. Israel shot down numerous Syrian MIG-fighters during the spring of 1967. They also clashed with Jordan and suffered the ever present border raids and terror attacks. At the end of May 1967 Egyptian President Nasser ordered the U.N. peace keeping troops out of the Sinai. (The UN complied which made it easier for the war to occur.)

Nasser then warned the Israelis that they would be destroyed if they persisted in "attacking" her neighbors. Nasser closed the Gulf to Israeli shipping and on May 30 he was able to conclude a military alliance with Jordan. The move was a surprise since pro-West Jordan had been at odds with the other Arab nations. This created a dire threat to the Israelis, enemies on three sides.

Pres. Nasser then proclaimed that the goal of the United Arab Republic was the destruction of Israel. He claimed the nations of Egypt, Syria, Kuwait, Iraq and Algeria are ready for war. Egypt had over 100,000 troops, 1000 tanks and dozens of Russian built jets in the Sinai. Even the PLO, (Palestine Liberation Organization), a terrorist network was preparing new attacks against Israel. *(Fatah was the guerilla faction founded by Yassir Arafat, nephew to the Gran Mufti, which eventually became the PLO, Palestinian Liberation Organization.)*

Israeli Prime Minister David Ben-Gurion had gone to Paris to speak with de Gaulle in 1963. No notes of the meetings were made but France sent large, updated armaments to Israel and began assisting them in building nuclear weapons!

(Their atomic work took years to develop, but the CIA knew about it.) As this new threat of war became imminent the leaders in Israel decided on a bold plan to save themselves. They would attack first in what would be called the **Six Day War**.

Their well trained and equipped Israeli Air Force launched dozens of French built Mirage fighter-bombers after dawn in a series of surprise pre-emptive attacks all across Egypt. Within three hours on the morning of June 6, 1967 their unimpeded airstrikes resulted in over 300 Egyptian planes being destroyed, most were on the ground. Next to be hit were the airfields in Syria, Jordan and Iraq. By the end of that first day over 450 Arab planes were lost and Israel controlled the skies over the Middle East. On the ground the Syrians relied upon their border bunkers to keep the Israeli's at bay. But after the second day of fighting the Israeli Army was taking control of the Golan Heights. They also forced their way back into the Sinai.

The King of Jordan had been asked by the Israeli's to stay out of the conflict since they were not initially attacking. But when Jordanian artillery began shelling Israel eight brigades of paratroopers surged into the West Bank of Jerusalem.

By the 3d day the Israeli's had regained the Western Wall in old Jerusalem, a sacred site that had been lost to the Jordanian's during the war of Independence in 1948.

On the southern side of the battle area the three Israeli tank formations swiftly penetrated the Egyptian defenses in the eastern Sinai Peninsula. After six days of heavy fighting the Israeli tanks had reached the east bank of the Suez Canal. The Egyptians had emplaced a 100,000 man army in the Sinai equipped with the latest Russian weapons. Yet within that week over 15,000 Egyptians had been killed and most of their equipment lost.

In less than one week the political and geographic landscape of the Middle East was altered. Israel now had breathing room to keep her enemies at bay as Egypt would have to cross 150 miles of the open Sinai desert to get to them. And with the taking of West Jerusalem and the West Bank of the Jordan River, most of Israel was out of range of Jordanian artillery.

The dominating mass of the Golan Heights was also in Israel's control as they forced the Syrians back and out of range. Had they wanted to the Israeli's could have attacked into Damascus. In fact now it was the Arab Capitals that were within range of Israeli weapons. The performance of the Israeli Defense Force was so brilliant that they began to think of themselves as invincible. Their victory disease, (belief that you can't loose) would soon hurt them as much of their success was due to Arab failures.

The UN Security Council passed Resolution 242, and all hoped it would provide a lasting peace. Their goal required that Israel's boundaries

would be recognized as a nation and in exchange they would withdraw from "occupied territories".
But none of her neighbors would agree to the former requirement.

At a meeting in Khartoum, Israel agreed to pull back from the new territories.

But the Arab nations gave them the three No's. No negotiations, No peace and No Israel.

Thus the problems and hatred remained and throughout the next few years the combatants continued to exchange fire, at times heavily.

Back in 1948 Israel gave citizenship to any Palestinians who wished to stay. Many left. And as the hostilities in the Arab world continued more and more Jews left the Arab nations and moved into Israel. Their numbers grew until they were higher than the number of Palestinians who had actually left in 1948.

As the populations in the countries of the Middle East continued to grow there was no corresponding increase in their economies. Millions of unemployed and unhappy people lived in those autocratic societies with no chance to affect their destinies.

Islamic Fundamentalism became attractive to those who had little, and their ranks swelled rapidly. Their extremist views grew worse.

One little known aspect of the war was that the Israeli's had deliberately attacked a U.S. Navy communication ship that had been operating in the Eastern Mediterranean. The U.S. ship the *Liberty* had been collecting all types of intelligence and was communicating with the U.S. Sixth fleet. It was clearly marked and unarmed but, the Israeli's objected to their mission and viciously attacked the ship killing and wounding over two dozen sailors. (During the Israeli air attacks in Egypt numerous Americans had been caught in harms way.)

To protect our ship the Navy and Air Force scrambled fighter planes but they were called back on LBJ's orders. Pres. Johnson did and said nothing about the deliberate attacks. (I spoke with a USAF crew member who was based in Libya. He backed the claim that our planes had been recalled because he had loaded them with munitions.)

With the Six-Day war ended Soviet leader Leonid Brezhnev fell short in his first venture into world politics. Russia's Mid-East client states had been trounced and their Russian equipment quickly destroyed or captured. All the communists could do was to severe diplomatic ties with Israel. They promised the Arab states better weapons for their next war.

America

In the U.S. the summer of 1967 more race riots occurred in our cities as Newark and Detroit suffered terrible damages in the latest outbreaks of racial problems.
Over 60 people died and troops had to be used to stop the violence.

Detroit had been the most integrated city in America with an active African American population. However once the violence started the Police lost control and over 4,000 arrests were made.

The riots in Detroit caused irreparable harm to the integrated city as businesses relocated away taking with them thousands of lower and middle class jobs.

And without those entry level jobs there was no way to escape from poverty. Detroit lost millions in tax revenue which caused them to run deficits. To counter that financial pitfall the city began to cut services, (Fire, Police, Sanitation). That resulted in more crime and tax loss as arson began razing the city block by block.

Other cities that were also hit with 1967 riots were New York, Toledo and Grand Rapids. Young militant black leaders were calling for armed rebellion to end "white oppression". "We stand on the eve of a black revolution." Despite the many new laws passed to help with poverty and discrimination, America's cities were becoming war zones. (And the racial problems were affecting the military.) Once an area is subjected to the violence and arson of a bad riot there is little chance for social or economic recovery.

Most people do not realize this, but insurers Do Not Cover Losses from Civil Disorder or War. Businesses that are struck by looting or arson lose all of their assets which many times are over one million dollars. They are incapable and many times unwilling to try to return to that community to start again.

Homeowners are also not covered for those losses and even those not directly affected will leave due to fear. This was especially so in Detroit, Newark and New York.

(I had lived through and worked at many riots in NYC. The most infamous was the Bushwick, Brooklyn riot in 1977. Others were the riots in Tompkins Square in lower Manhattan, the riots in Washington Heights Manhattan in the 80s and 90s, and the Crown Heights riots in Brooklyn in the 90s. Bushwick never recovered from their unnecessary riots during the Blackout of 1977. Of the other areas Tompkins Square came back because of the value of the land.

(Another harsh example of the fallout from wonton civil destruction was the Rodney King riots in LA in the early 90s. Hundreds of businesses were torched, costing thousands of jobs and millions in tax losses.)

In October 1967 the body of Che Guevara and six other communist rebels were put on display in Bolivia. Guevara and four Cubans were leading a guerrilla band when government troops overran them. For two years the Marxist rebel had been fomenting trouble in Argentina, Brazil, Columbia, Venezuela and Peru. His loss hurt Castro's efforts at exporting his revolution to the Americas, but did not stop it.

Vietnam

Another terrible failure in Vietnam was again directed by the "Military Bureaucracy". Gen. H. Johnson and others still looked at the war as an educational exercise and officers were rotated out after only six months in command. Just as the new guy was learning how to fight or perform his job he was sent to another assignment. To the military bureaucracy it was better to spread the commands to the maximum number of officers, and to "prevent burnout". The result however was that "ticket-punching" was in full swing and the early rotations compromised the units because all levels of leaders moved around so often.
(The NVA/VC did not rotate their people out, and in WWII neither did we.)
None of those rotations helped the military effort, or the individual officers develop and learn what wartime leadership really was. When Gen. Walt was rotated out his knowledge of how to beat the enemy bunker complexes went with him.
And this loss of knowledge was being enacted in every unit all over Vietnam.

American enlisted personnel had to serve 12 month tours for the Army and 13 months for the Marines. (MACV instituted the idea for morale purposes, similar to the failed rotation program used in Korea.)
The learning curve took about four months to pickup if you made it that long. But when the men hit around 9-10 months they began looking for details in the rear to ghost out the rest of their tour. Thus the U.S. infantry units were always losing experienced personnel and replacing them with new, unskilled draftees.

After basic training most of the new draftee-troops went to AIT, advanced infantry training to learn how to use different weapons, some went to specialty schools.

But almost all of their training was geared to fighting the Russians in Europe. Virtually nothing was done to prepare these young soldiers for jungle fighting, fighting a guerilla war or learning anything useful on Vietnam.

Once the replacements arrived in Vietnam there was almost no time to train them anything about the combat there. They were simply dumped into a unit that was usually out in the field. Most had limited indoctrination and no training with their new unit. It was criminal.

Meanwhile the enemy was in the fight to the end and they learned how to fight us. The communists never lost experienced fighters unless they were wounded or died.

A war in which we were a part of for nine years should have yielded highly skilled military machines. But instead everyone who went to Nam had to relearn the lessons of his predecessors from scratch.

The U.S. military did not gain 9 years of war fighting experience.
It basically fought the war 9 separate times.

In Washington the JCS and Admiral Sharp the U.S. commander in the Pacific were continuing their requests to increase the air war campaign against N. Vietnam.

Once the commitment to war had been made no restrictions should have been forced on the military other than preventing operations inside China. All of the operational decisions should have been left to the military commanders.

But the civilian oversight of the Military that had begun with Truman and increased under Kennedy was a full time occupation under LBJ. Everything being done was under the eye of micro-managers, the majority of whom had never heard a shot fired in anger. Many were too young to even remember Korea.

McNamara returned to Washington from a conference with the Senior Military Commanders in July 1967. All of them still wanted to mine the ports and increase the bombing in the north to include destroying Hanoi and Haiphong. Again, this was totally the opposite of what McNamara and LBJ wanted.

As before McNamara reported to LBJ only what he wanted done, and left the military leaders voiceless.

(John Vann and his boss Robert Komer continued their work on leading the pacification programs. Vann finally spoke directly to McNamara. Their discussions centered on how bad things actually were and why.)

After hearing numerous complaints from the military Senator Stennis began holding hearings into the conduct of the war and announced that witnesses would be **subpoenaed**. (That would force them to appear and testify.)

To try to circumvent the hearings the ever notorious LBJ approved a few more targets in the hopes of buying off his critics. Once again the military leaders stated to the Administration their battlefield aims and needs to win the war, while the civilian managers tried to hide their backchannel activities.

The sub-committee released its findings complaining that the civilians were overruling military decisions and that the Johnson administration was beset by policy splits. (Dissent within the Administration was increasing.) Soon after LBJ gave approvals for more targets in the North, but by now the task was exponentially more difficult. Air losses grew worse.

Ambassador Lodge had become increasingly unhappy with the attrition strategy. *Gen Patton had told him that every war was different than the one before and it was vital that the next generals heed that simple adage.* Lodge repeatedly voiced his feelings and opinions and it eventually cost him his job.

Ellsworth Bunker had overseen the peace talks in Yemen from their war, and the pacification effort in the Dominican Republic in 65. In May 1967 he became the new Ambassador to S. Vietnam. Bunker was unaware of the problems in Vietnam so his instinct was to trust the judgment of MACV and the Administration. (Which was why he was sent.)

David Halberstam also returned to Vietnam in the fall of 67.

At dinner with the Ambassador, Halberstam saw the same mindless false optimism that he had had to endure back in 62/63.

Graduated Response and the *Rolling Thunder bombing* campaign in the diluted form they were did not stop the North's invasion or their overall war-plans. As much equipment and supplies was flowing south as ever and the Ho Chi Minh Trail was still being expanded.

In some places gravel was now used to create semi-permanent roads.

After the war retired NVA General Vo Bam wrote in his memoirs that the Americans knew where to hit the Trail, they just hit it the wrong way. Their aircraft would come and go, sometimes they struck well, other times they missed.

But we were always able to fix the roads.

He stated that the longest time his sector in Laos was shut down was two days.

(In addition to the SOG teams, SEALS and Marine Force Recon also patrolled the Trail. The CIA even used *unmanned drones*, U-2s and SR-71s for aerial recon. But until ground units overran the Trail it would remain open.)

For over two years the combined Allied air forces had tried to shut off the German war production. They failed.

For two years they tried to stop supplies from getting through to the German Army in Italy. They failed.

In Korea the recently created U.S. Air Force insisted that nothing would get through their air armada flying over N. Korea. Yet 380,000 Chinese soldiers with all of their supplies and weapons were able to sneak into N. Korea and fall upon the Allies in Nov 1950. And to make the insult worse, they were able to stay supplied and reinforced for an additional two and a half years.

Air power was not the do all capability that the Air Force Brass and some of the war managers claimed it was. A determined enemy can and will continue to fight on until they are stopped by troops on the ground. Unless overwhelming air attacks are made to cripple an enemy, air power has to be used in conjunction with all of the other military options to affect the desired result.

The reader must also remember that in Korea, Pres. Truman restricted some of the targets and areas that could be bombed. Eventually he changed his mind and areas that should have been hit early on finally were.

But he never allowed air strikes against the enemy airfields, troop concentrations or supply depots in Manchuria.

And we had to fight the Chinese anyway.

(Instead of bombing them in Manchuria, our legions and my Father were shooting at them in close quarters in the Korean hills.)

Once the Chinese came into Korea and started fighting Truman should have added all of those targets to the hit list.
If he wanted to limit the war then just hit the targets in Manchuria.

In the 1960s, the same inane claims of not wanting to bring in the Chinese were repeatedly made in Vietnam by LBJ and echoed by McNamara. They severely undercut the air campaign by refusing to allow the bombing the way the military commanders needed in 65, 66 or even into early 1967. *By the time LBJ did increase the targeting it was too late.*

The North Vietnamese defenses were built up to Russian standards with Russian equipment and personnel. Losses to our aircraft and aircrews were increasing monthly.

It is vital that the Military have a voice in how or if a war is to be waged.

In WWII there was no presidential or civilian interference, just the will to win the war.

In Korea, Truman was initially keeping the "Police Action" to a low publicity level and refused to allow any actions that might cause trouble with Russia or the recently lost communist China.

Despite his accommodating actions Russia provided most of the weapons and supplies, while Red China infiltrated a massive army and fought for 2 ½ years.

When the Allies were finally pushing the Chinese and NKPA enemy back in the spring of 1951 they were ordered to halt by the civilians seeking peace despite the military's objections. *And that decision resulted in two more years of war.*

With LBJ's Vietnam War restrictions in place the communist North had unimpeded access into the South. The East Bloc countries and Russia could and did send hundreds of ships into N. Vietnam's ports with no handicaps. China supplied more material aid from road and rail and sent their ships into Cambodia.

All of those communist supply targets were off limits.

Thus our Soldiers and Marines were fighting a never ending war. But the Military leaders were forbidden to talk to the press or to give their honest assessments. (The same restrictions were placed upon all of us in the FDNY, to prevent the truth about operations from coming out.)

The civilian managers and LBJ were able to kill and maim thousands upon thousands of America's sons and daughters and get away with it.

(During the Gulf War in 1991, President Bush and his administration listened to the battlefield requirements that Generals Colin Powell, Norman Schwarzkopf and his team had to have and let them plan and prosecute the war. It was a resounding success.)

A young statistician named Thomas Thayer had spent the past two years analyzing the war while working for the Pentagon's Advanced Research Agency.

His interviews included Col. Hal Moore who had led the Cav in the battles at the Drang and then Bon Son. Like the Marine Commanders, Col. Moore was also convinced that what we were doing was just what the enemy wanted us to do.

"The communists were leading us around by the nose"!

By pulling our units into the jungles and away from the population the NVA were taking the Americans out of the important battle, for hearts and minds.

Col. Hackworth who had fought with the 101st also tried to convince Chief of Staff Gen. Harold Johnson that we were doing it all wrong. But none of our senior Generals understood anything about the war. At MACV the huge staff looked like soldiers but lived a life of luxury in air conditioned buildings. Few ever went out to the field to observe or to learn.

Dr. Bernard Fall's book ***Street Without Joy*** was the bible for Vietnam. But he became persona non-grata at MACV and the White House because he so vehemently disagreed with what we were doing.

Even Israel's Moshe Dayan who went to Vietnam and out on patrols was shocked at how poor we were doing.

Thayer's analysis and statistics showed that the attrition strategy was a failure.

A study of 56 battles in 1966 showed that the enemy initiated the action 85% of the time. They decided when to stand and fight, and they had the element of surprise in 80% of the battles. Thus the communists were able to control their losses by deciding when and if to fight, and when to break-off and hide.

His report also stated that the current battlefield conditions in Vietnam do not allow for us to attrite the enemy at any sort of fatal pace.

In fact, because Gen. Westmoreland insisted that our forces had to go out and find the enemy, they were actually grinding us down. *It is the enemy who controls this war.*

The battles that were examined in the research made no long term military sense for as soon as the shooting ended the area was abandoned and the units sent out to patrol some other site. **His report and presentation were exasperating, but still no changes were made in strategy or tactics.**

(It would have cost us less monetarily if we had paid the communists not to fight.)

Pres. Johnson had thought that the war would cost roughly $2 Billion dollars a year. That may have been true in 1965, but by 1967 the war was costing $8 Billion.

McNamara planned the budget for the next year and it came to $11-17 Billion! At that point it was taking up over 3% of the GDP and was definitely going to go up. Faced with those numbers Johnson proposed a 10% surcharge on individual and corporate taxes. Congress tried to delay the tax but it had to be done. Inflation was beginning to spiral upward and it would soon cripple our economy.

Working for Sec-Def, Alain Enthoven created a report on political issues facing our nation. In his paper he explained that in the fight for Vietnam the main issue was *nationalism, not communism.* Ho Chi Minh and his forces had been fighting for their freedom for over twenty years. No amount of fighting by us would stop that effort.

If we wanted the South to remain free, they had to have an equally strong emotion for that end. And we had to make it happen soon. If we stay on this course the Vietminh are winning.

As shown earlier in the spring of 67 Gen Westmoreland had requested still more troops, for a total of 550,000. (His optimum level was actually 678,000.) After those studies were done McNamara reported back to LBJ that all we could hope for was an unfavorable peace and that we should gradually disengage from Vietnam. The bombing should be limited to near the border areas and pacification efforts increased.

In June the disgruntled McNamara had commissioned the Pentagon Papers, the top secret inquiry into U.S. involvement in Vietnam from its origins to 1967.

LBJ was never going to approve all of Westy's manpower requests anyway, for to do that would have meant mobilizing the Reserves and the end of his Great Society programs. He sent McNamara back to see Westmoreland and increased his forces by just 55,000. (This was the July trip when Vann was able to talk to him.)

Johnson then had a special meeting to discuss McNamara's negative findings. Most of the Administration and special counselors dismissed his ideas, as had LBJ. From that time on McNamara was being phased out.

And to cause him further anguish now that he had awakened, McNamara began to listen and learn (Vann), of the hardships the peasant population was being subjected to, the dislocations from the strategic hamlet program, to bombings and shellfire.

He also realized that the Pacification program run by the Marines in 65 and early 66 had prevented most of the wonton destruction in their area since they were protecting the villages. But once Westmoreland sent the Marines into the wild, the destruction began in earnest.
This war that McNamara helped create was killing the South.

Around this time NVA Gen. Giap explained in an article in the *Military Peoples Daily* on how and why the leaders in Hanoi had enticed the American units to the periphery of South Vietnam. (The Politburo had discussed this potential offensive in late 65, and again in May 67. By July the basic plan and objectives had been drawn out.)

Giap's article was presented under the heading, *"Big Victory, Gigantic Task"*, and was meant as a primer to the NVA and VC troops fighting in the South. Their sacrifice was about to come to a head, and Radio Hanoi even broadcast the entire text!

The CIA translated and distributed the complete article to the various commands. Westmoreland paid as little heed to this report as he had to Gen. Krulak or Paul Nitze.

(The same way MacArthur and his staff had ignored all of the Intel warning of the coming Chinese offensive.)

At one follow on briefing in Saigon Gen. Westmoreland claimed that we had bled the enemy to the point were *they can only operate at the periphery*. A reporter challenged him stating, "The enemy has pulled us out to the borders and is bleeding us"! Westmoreland exclaimed that we had not been pulled out to the borders, we are beating them back.

When his Intelligence chief Gen. Joseph McChristian warned Westmoreland that he was underestimating the enemy troops in the South by a couple of hundred thousand, Westmoreland had him replaced.

When the CIA's specialist on the Viet Cong, Samuel Adams sought to raise the alarm bells, he too was muffled. His research showed a total enemy force of some six hundred thousand communist troops in and around the country!

This was the same type of deceitful authority that Gen. Willoughby had used in Korea in 1950, and Harkins used to continue faking progress during his time in MACV. And this illustrates why all aspects of military operations and briefings about operations must be on paper, signed and logged in. Maybe in this way the dishonest or foolish commander might not be so careless with the lives of others.

By October of 1967 the number of Americans who wanted out of Vietnam had doubled to 30%. A large protest in Washington was underscoring the nation's mood. Besides his Cabinet, LBJ often employed a group of wise-men to advise him.

Dean Acheson was one of them, and their suggestion to LBJ was that the Administration should mount a Public Relations campaign to offset the growing anti-war movement. Key to the PR effort would be Gen. Westmoreland.

A tall poster boy type soldier, Westmoreland was well tasked to give speeches and appearances. (In April he had addressed a joint session of Congress and left then applauding.) During November he was brought home and appeared with Ambassador Bunker on the Sunday talk show circuit. At a speech for the National Press Club he presented the argument that we were nearing the point for our victory phase. He claimed that losses to the enemy are higher than they can replace. Within two years or less Phase IV should have advanced far enough along to begin withdrawals. (Eerily similar predictions had been given by MacArthur just before the

Chinese assault in 1950 and by Harkins and McNamara in Vietnam in 1963.)

While the PR was going on in Washington the second battle of Dak To was being fought in the Central Highlands. During the first battle the U.S. troops bested the NVA, but took unacceptable casualties. This time the NVA had lured the Americans into a terrible sector they had specially prepared. U.S. casualties were higher than before, and their terrible sacrifice accomplished nothing.

One of the companies of the 173d captured an enemy document, a directive for the B-3 front operating in the Highlands. *In describing the coming winter offensive Gen. Hoang van Thai wanted to annihilate an American unit to cause the "collapse of the ARVN puppet troops".* This revelation was also missed by MACV.

During 1967, 9,378 more Americans had died.

John Vann had gone on leave to the U.S. on Nov 14, 1967. He was so discouraged that he was finding his work a burden. Now that he was in charge of a large part of the pacification effort he was chagrined that the leaders in the South could not stop their corrupt ways. Arriving in Washington Vann met with Walt Rostow at his new office in the basement of the White House. Rostow was upbeat after all of the recent speeches and promises of victory. But Vann's words about Vietnam were completely at odds with what Rostow had just heard these past weeks.

"Didn't Vann agree that the worst of the war would be over in six months"?

Vann sarcastically replied, "Oh hell no Mr. Rostow I'm sure we can hold out longer than that". Rostow was displeased, but also alarmed. (56)

Vann returned to Bien Hoa on Jan 7, 1968 and ran into a nervous Gen. Fred Weyand at his Command Post near Saigon. *The crux of Westy's soon to be enacted grand plan was that the VC and NVA were no longer capable of mounting any attacks.*

Large U.S. led attacks were scheduled to begin soon in the border provinces. Those assaults would require most of the U.S. ground combat forces. (Under Westmoreland's mindset the central provinces of III Corps were scheduled to be turned completely over to ARVN control.)

Gen. Fred Weyand CG of the 25th Inf Div argued often with Westmoreland's futile tactics. Weyand did not share Westy's view of the war and had picked Vann to be the senior advisor in his sector because he agreed with Vann and his ideas.

(Westmoreland did not want Vann to get the post because "Vann was a troublemaker".)

Unlike many of the Army commanders Weyand was actively supporting pacification. Vann and Gen. Weyand shared the same views and respected each others work. Weyand would get upset when MACV ordered his troops into the hinterlands looking for enemy troops. Every time they left a pacified village the VC would move back in and they would have to fight for it all over again.

Even though the 700 man enemy battalions we had faced in 1966 had been knocked down to around 400-500 troops, they were still a formidable foe.

And each of those enemy units had been marched into Cambodia to be trained and equipped with the newest weapons being shipped from China and Russia. Though their numbers were less, their punch was much enhanced as all of the enemy were now equipped with AK-47 assault rifles and RPGs.

When Weyand and his Intel staff added in the numbers of the local VC to the battlefield estimates of NVA they too realized that an additional two divisions of communist fighters were sitting on their doorstep.
(This mirrored the reports from Gen. McChristian from two months earlier.)

And while our forces were moving out towards the borders, the enemy was clearly moving inland towards the cities. Marine and Army recon teams had been saying the same thing in I & II Corps for months. Dropped off deep into the wilderness the small recon teams had been sent out to watch and observe. If they had not been discovered and pulled out they would finish the patrol and report their findings to their Intelligence officers. Their reports were supposed to find their way to the Div. & Corps Commands, eventually ending up at MACV.

All of the enemy units they observed were moving towards the coast and the cities. Despite the dozens of weekly reports from SOG, USMC Recon and Army LRP teams all of their efforts were ignored by the higher ups.

Gen. Weyand went to Saigon to speak with Westmoreland's deputy, Gen. Creighton Abrams. Abrams had been one of Patton's best unit leaders. He listened and digested the information. He and Weyand then spoke to Westy and warned him that the communists were going to attack. Westmoreland would not be swayed by the evidence, but Weyand was able to get him to *delay* the border battles.

Using this postponement Gen. Weyand was able to reposition his forces and keep them on alert. His actions would save the day.

Gen. Westmoreland actually had an ulterior motive for allowing Weyand some latitude, for it appeared to him that the communists were "taking the bait at Khe Sanh".

By the end of 1967 recon teams were reporting enemy buildup all over the mountainous region around the combat base. Khe Sanh and the hill outposts were reinforced with the entire 26th Regiment, the 1st Batt 9th Mar Regiment and an ARVN Ranger Battalion.

(Col. David Lownds was on his first tour in Nam, but had fought in the Pacific, Korea and the Dominican Republic in 65. He was unhappy with "Khe Sanh's defenses".)

A few treacherous miles outside the wire at Khe Sanh was the Lang Vei Special Forces FOB, (forward operating base) with another 300+ men. They were dug in deep inside fortified bunkers, but were completely isolated and miles from help.

Not blessed with heavy timbers like the Army, the marines in the area waited in their sandbagged bunkers and fighting positions.
Intelligence had revealed that the isolated base was almost surrounded.

Radio detection teams operating on Hill 881S had followed the movements of NVA Divisions 304, 308 & 320 as they moved down the Trail and crossed into the South just a few miles away. Gen. Giap and his staff had silently moved four infantry divisions and two regiments of artillery into the dense jungle ridges of NW S. Vietnam.
Over 40,000 NVA were in their attack positions around the airfield / base.

Total NVA movement down the trail from September was over 50,000 men, and truck traffic increased to almost 5,000 trips per month! Their heavy reinforcements and logistic efforts warned of a pending attack.

Gen. Robert Cushman had succeeded Gen. Walt in command of the 3d Mar Div. He and his commanders had reluctantly followed Westmoreland's orders to ship their Marine battalions north. While Westmoreland was anxious that the battle he had wanted was coming, he was also nervous to see if Krulak had been correct in his warnings from their meeting in Chu Lai in the fall of 66.

(Gen. Krulak was still in Hawaii having been turned down for further promotion by LBJ. His rancor over the attrition strategy had clearly angered those in power.)

Patrols began finding NVA company and battalion sized bivouacs, all recently used. Air and troop placed sensors were setup around the area to pick up the noise of enemy movements. During early January 1968 the fight for Khe Sanh began with attacks at the USMC hill outposts. Hill 881N had been secretly re-occupied by the NVA and attempts to get them off failed. And Marine patrols sent out from the combat base were being attacked constantly as the NVA slowly closed the ring around Khe Sanh.

(Gen. Giap would later state that they never had plans to overwhelm the base, just to pull the Americans from the cities. It is hard to believe they sent 40,000 troops and all of that artillery into a terrible fight like Khe Sanh just as a feint.)

Westmoreland then ordered the entire 1st Cav Div to relocate from the Central Coast to northern I Corps. They would be his ace in the hole, an entire division that could go anywhere to prevent a Dien Bien Phu type disaster. They moved north by Brigades.

Pres. Johnson was so nervous about the action at Khe Sanh he made the JCS sign statements that the base could be held. (He had reason to be politically fearful, for if the reader remembers he was one of those who opposed U.S. intervention to save the French in 1954.)

In actuality there was not much of a chance for the NVA to replicate their victory over the French. This battle area was only 40 miles from the coast, not in an inaccessible valley in far off NW Vietnam. We had an air armada to call upon, hundreds of artillery pieces, plenty of reinforcements that could be sent in, and the history of that earlier battle to learn from. Pre-plotted artillery barrages were fired at selected times and points to breakup any potential enemy offensives. Air bombing ran from fixed wing to rotary to massive B-52 strikes. Bombs and artillery were constantly falling around the base and in the nearby jungles.

For days Gen. Tran Qui Hai used his NVA artillery and rockets to pound the hill outposts and the base itself. On the night of Jan 21, 1968 a major NVA attack against Khe Sanh began with a rain of mortars, artillery and rockets, much of which was fired from Laos. Hundreds of 122mm rockets were also fired from hill 881N, as the airfield base and forward positions were bombarded. The largest of the base ammo dumps was struck in the opening phase, adding to the misery with its own explosions.

Khe Sanh village was then attacked and had to be abandoned as the combat base was now surrounded. The hill outposts held on that first night as the siege of Khe Sanh began and would last 77 days. *(Incredulously once the events began at Khe Sanh MACV officers clamored for information on Dien Bien Phu. Lectures and reports were held on the battle until Westmoreland stopped them. The accounts were so grim they were demoralizing.)*

In conjunction with the attacks at Khe Sanh strong NVA units operating out of the Tchepone area attacked deeper into Laos. And they used Russian made tanks.

Within days the last of the Royal Lao Army in that section of the country was defeated. Survivors surged into Lang Vei SF camp and village. Then it was quiet for two days.

Korea

N. Korea was still engaged in their constant border raids against the south. During 1966 there had been 50 raids. In 1967 the fighting greatly increased to over 550 attacks. Similar to the battles in Laos, the communists saw a chance to test the waters with America preoccupied far to the south.

On January 21, NKPA commandos used the cover of another raid and penetrated to within one mile of the Presidential Palace in Seoul. They were eventually discovered and after a bloody fight defeated. Twenty eight of the team lay dead.

(Because of that never ending threat over thirty thousand U.S. personnel were still in S. Korea ready for war.)

Then on Jan 23, 1968 the North Koreans sent their coastal naval forces to overpower a U.S. intelligence ship, the Pueblo which was sailing alone off the coast.

Unbelievably word of the NK boarding party was somehow sent to Washington D.C., but not to the commanders in the Pacific or Korea.

Sec. Navy Paul Nitze contacted CINCPAC in Hawaii and found we had no air or naval forces near the ship! Two hours after the ship was taken the 5th Air Force in Okinawa sent fighters out. They arrived an hour and a half later, too late to intercede.

The Defense Dept. stated that the ship was stationed 25 miles off the coast in international waters. The Communists naturally claimed the ship had intruded into their waters and been engaged in "hostile activities". Their claim was as always preposterous, as the ship's only armaments were two machine guns.

What the ship did have on board and what our communist enemies greatly desired were the communication and intelligence equipment. This ship had the latest naval communications gear that our submarines used.

An infamous new spy named John Walker had betrayed our country. Walker worked in naval communications and was having financial problems. He simply walked into the Soviet Embassy in Washington and offered to sell them important naval information. One of the first things he sold was the latest in communications intelligence. The same new type that was on the *Pueblo*. Walker alerted his Soviet handlers of the *Pueblo's* equipment list and sailing dates. *The North Korean border raids were actually a clever ruse to assist the communists in covering the theft of the ship.*

Proof that the communists wanted the ship and its gear was revealed by the fact the ship was boarded and captured instead of being attacked and sunk.

The ship was taken to the port of Wonsan and stripped!

The crew was arrested and tortured during their 11 month internment.

A year later at a hearing the *Pueblo's* Captain admitted signing a confession under duress. The Navy wanted to court martial him for failing to destroy the sensitive equipment, but the Navy itself was at fault for allowing such a valuable a ship to operate alone near a brutal enemy.

The timing of the attack on the *Pueblo* purposefully coincided with the serious battles occurring in Vietnam. Our Pacific naval units were so stretched in Nam that we would be unable to respond promptly to anything in Korea. (Though the USAF had dozens of jets in Korea and could have attacked the North Korean ships if there had been coordination among the military services and commands.)

What is noteworthy, was that after being attacked by an enemy nation and having a naval ship taken, impounded and its crew imprisoned LBJ did nothing.

And that amply illustrates why the communists would not negotiate on anything. There was no reason for them to.

Vietnam

As stated before all along the length of Vietnam U.S. forces had been chasing and battling the enemy in the far off regions. As 1967 came to a close Intel units began picking up information that seemed to imply a large enemy offensive was in the works.

On Jan 30, 1968 the first attacks of the infamous *TET Offensive* began. TET was a special holiday in the Vietnamese calendar, and in prior years the war would stop for the week long festivities.

But this year Gen. Giap under orders from Ho Chi Minh had developed plans for a country wide offensive. The communists would break the truce they had pledged to observe and shift the war from the rural and outlying areas into more than one hundred cities and towns.

All of the local VC units would strike the neighboring bases and cities while NVA units would strike special targets and outlying bases. Ho had felt the time was ripe for a complete takeover, though Giap was not. (Since he was ill, Ho and his followers wanted to see it done before he died.)

U.S. Intel gatherers had been using the eye in the sky system since Vann had been assigned back in 62. *Their radio detection equipment and analysis had been able to show and convince Gen. Weyand and Vann that three NVA divisions were now located in an arc just north of Saigon. Weyand sent out warnings, and hurriedly had base defenses improved and units in place for the upcoming holiday attacks.* He was not able to convince MACV of what was coming, and all of their senior officers had left for the night. (Vann was so certain of the threat he sent un-coded messages out to his people warning of the pending attacks.)

President Theiu and his senior commanders sat back and enjoyed the holiday, knowing that over 500,000 Americans were there to keep them safe. They refused to issue any alerts or restrictions to their forces.

Using the cover of the festival multiple thousands of communist fighters had infiltrated into the towns and cities over the past weeks. Porters and advance teams had entered the cities weeks earlier bringing with them the needed weapons and ammunition. Safe houses, supply and rally points were also designated and pre-arranged.

All the enemy had to do was wait for the signal.

A mix-up in enemy communications caused the local VC units to attack *Ban Me Thuot, Kontum and Pleiku* on the night of Jan 30th. Those isolated attacks were quickly and decisively crushed, but more importantly they served notice that something big was coming. Still MACV was caught short.

In the early hours of the 31st, the main attacks struck throughout S. Vietnam. The ferocity and coordination of the strikes overwhelmed some of the undermanned ARVN units but none of the American ones. The communists even broke into the U.S. Embassy compound and the Imperial Palace, but accomplished nothing substantial militarily. A well planned multi-pronged assault had also been planned for Saigon, but the alerted U.S. forces defeated all of them except an attack in the Cholon district.

Gen. Weyand had wisely placed helicopter gunships on pad alert, and as soon as the explosions started air support became available. Units of the 199 Lt Brigade, the 9th Infantry Div and the 25th Inf. Div. were immediately sent to counterattack enemy units in *Cu Chi, Bien Hoa and Saigon*.
The communists even sent a division of men to attack our big base at *Bien Hoa*, north of *Saigon*. Each attack was stopped.

Some neighborhoods inside *Saigon* suffered terrible street fighting for days as in Cholon, but the Capitol itself was completely under government control by February 15. By that date almost all of the other cities and towns had been cleared too.

Had it not been for Weyand and Vann, it was probable that Saigon and a few other cities would have ended up like the Imperial Capitol of Hue, devastated.

Because of their insights untold thousands of innocents were saved from the communist butchers. Every place the communists penetrated they murdered as many government officials, doctors, schoolteachers and missionaries as they had time to find.

In the ancient Capital of *Hue* in I Corps the secreted communist fighters became entrenched within the inner city. With their excellent Intel and the VC infrastructure to move around and setup strong-points, the enemy was able to capture the city and hold on to it for weeks. And that enabled their execution squads to move around the city at will eliminating everyone who had made onto their hit lists. **The "communist liberation" of Hue became a murderous reign of terror.**

Westmoreland had been so fixated on *Khe Sanh* that few free troops or marines were available to counterattack at Hue during the first days of the TET offensive. The Cav Div. was nearby and available, but Westy kept them on standby for *Khe Sanh*.

After the situation became clear their 1st Brigade was used to stop the enemy near *Quang Tri*. *The aggressive airmobile troopers stunned the enemy units which were used to fighting the helicopter poor Marines who walked everywhere.*
Days later the Cav 3d Brigade was sent south to help stop the slaughter in Hue.

As a result of the gridlock on our forces and the excellent advance work done by the communists the beautiful city of Hue would be heavily damaged in the month long fight. Die-hard NVA had to be cleared street to street and house to house. Casualties were heavy on both sides. Not since the battles for Seoul would there be such damage to an urban center and so many deaths among the innocents. Many of the civilian prisoners stolen from Hue ended up on the Ho Chi MinhTrail where they could be disappeared deep in the jungles.

With the nationwide attacks fighting was also renewed at *Khe Sanh*. Gen. Westmoreland decided that this was it, and he turned loose the pre-planned strategic bombing missions called *Niagara*. Every three hours six B-52's were sent into the region to obliterate a mile long box with 162 tons of bombs. Flights of fighter-bombers were stacked above the battle zone waiting for their turn to attack as directed. Artillery based at the Rockpile and Camp Carroll added to the carnage.

News reports showed the battle as it was occurring with nightly TV films. America was seeing the war as it was happening and it shook the nation's morale. (As a youngster I remember watching the war footage every night. My father who had fought in Korea was sick at the type of war we were fighting.)

For the North, TET was a terrible military and political defeat. Giap's communist fighters lost over 50,000 troops, with most of the local VC units and infrastructure being virtually wiped out. *One senior figure who did survive lamented that they had lost "our best people."* An intensive propaganda effort had gone into the preparations for the TET Offensive in order to get the VC motivated for the dangerous battles to come. Many of them were known to be one way fights. (U.S. Embassy, Saigon Radio station.) But none of the VC expected the Americans or ARVN to react as well or as quickly as they did. And none thought the civilians in the South would reject them.

(Perhaps the destruction of the Viet Cong was what was really desired by Hanoi. After TET almost all of the fighters in the Viet Cong units were replacements from the NVA. As time went by the southern communists actually despised the northerners.)

To the astonishment of the enemy, the people of South Vietnam did not rise up to join in "the revolt". Nor did the ARVN units turn sides as had been promised in the propaganda sessions. The citizens of South Vietnam remained on the side of freedom, as the ARVN units fought against their communist counterparts toe to toe and defeated them.

Gen. Westmoreland had finally gotten what he had desired, large, intense battles where the enemy was easy to get to. But his prior strategy and speeches had set the stage for the same kind of public relations disaster as MacArthur had suffered in Korea in 1950. Back then America instantly turned away from the war as had the reporters who witnessed the needless military failures.

At home in 1968 our media portrayed the well planned (communist) battles of TET not as numerous victories for us, even though the VC and NVA were defeated everywhere, but as proof that Vietnam was un-winnable and that the military and LBJ had lied about it. Almost overnight public opinion turned against Johnson and the war.

Sympathizers within the media and academia actually promoted the side of the enemy and were instrumental in aiding the communist cause at home.

Nothing like this had occurred during WWII despite the many early defeats at sea or later at the Battle of the Bulge. Why it was tolerated in 1968 is further proof of the disintegration of the Democratic Party and the radicalization of the liberals.

It did not matter that almost all of South Vietnam had been stabilized within two weeks, or that the communists had failed in every one of their objectives. (Except Hue)

The pictures of the intense urban fighting in Saigon and Hue had caused an uproar due to the savagery. One infamous shot showed a Saigon Police Chief executing a VC fighter with a shot to the head. What was never explained to the public was that the executed VC had just murdered another man's family. Other disturbing pictures showed the dead VC at the embassy, and dead civilians and soldiers lying in the streets. *This was the face of war brought to you live.*

It was the same face as seen at Tarawa, Normandy or Seoul, but this time the reporting had became biased by an almost turncoat media and they convinced many that the cause was lost.

One main point that was missed or conveniently ignored by the media was the fact that the communists had attacked those hundred or so sites. That was the real reason for the terrible destruction and loss of life in South Vietnam.

The communists had planned the battle of Hue for five months. They meticulously scouted out the city planning which targets would be hit immediately and what could wait for the next days. They also compiled an extensive list of undesirables. (All foreign nationals were to be arrested and held captive, except for any French citizens who would be safe.?)

Dozens of VC assassins were merciless as they moved through the city. They murdered hundreds of civilians and governmental workers. Those they did not murder were "arrested", and as shown above many were taken into the jungles. Another 5,000 civilians had been rounded up in the city during the time the enemy had control. They were taken out of the city and murdered as the communists performed their time honored tradition of eliminating anyone who was a potential threat to their rule. Many of those innocents had been buried alive. *(Also ignored by the media were the mass graves uncovered as Hue was liberated.)*

In keeping with communist dogma NVA Gen. Tran Do a senior general who had planned many of the TET attacks callously dismissed the post-attack claims and photos of the atrocities. But the people of the South had not missed this message for they knew what fate had in store if the communists took over. (SVN intelligence teams slipped into the destroyed city as the fighting went on. They were hunting for communist collaborators. All who were identified were killed.)

Those reporting *"oversights"* by our media had been ongoing for years.

Political murders and terrorism were a constant and normal tactics of the communists as they strove to quietly take over the peasant villages and towns that were out of sight. Anyone who protested their rule or who worked for the government was executed along with their families in front of the village. Just in case someone missed the point.

It was a simple solution for those ruthless enough to enact it.

Just after midnight on February 6 the Special Forces camp at Lang Vei along the Laotian border in NW I Corps was overrun by an NVA assault force led by **11 tanks.** Why this camp had not been reinforced or abandoned earlier is hard to understand. The NVA had already cutoff the Marine regiment at nearby Khe Sanh, what did the MACV superiors think, that Lang Vei would not be assaulted?

The Marine commander at Khe Sanh wisely refused to send out a relief force that first night. This enemy had a long history of ambushing such forces and the Marines had nothing on the base to fight NVA tanks anyway. Also any relief force would have to have come from the defenders of the Khe Sanh combat base itself which could weaken the defenses there. (Perhaps that was what the enemy wanted, to use Lang Vei as bait.)

By morning a rescue mission arrived by helicopter and recovered less than half of the camp's garrison. Five of the enemy tanks had been destroyed by the tough Special Forces contingent using the disposable bazooka type weapon called LAW.

The SOG troops had asked MACV many times for anti-armor mines and weapons as they could hear the NVA armored vehicles moving around the jungles at night. Again the desk riders at MACV did not believe the claims from those in the field that the NVA had tanks.

This attack also signaled just how powerful and deceptive the enemy had become. They were able to secretly move tanks through the dense jungles of N. Vietnam, Laos and S. Vietnam to make the assault on this camp. *This battle was clear evidence that this was an invasion by the communists in the North, and was a portent of what was to come.*

A post-battle study of TET showed that the communists had taken a big gamble and lost heavily.
It was new ball game. With adequate reinforcements MACV could have attacked into the communist hideouts in Cambodia and Laos destroying them and possibly ending the war. (Ironically one of the other proposals was for those extra troops to protect the people and the coastal areas.)

Gen. Wheeler decided to try to force LBJ's hand and mobilize the nation's reservists. A request for more troops had come in from Westmoreland and the JCS would tell the president he had to activate the reserves to do so. But Johnson saw through the ploy and he still refused.

More meetings were held but the dejected LBJ decided not to send any more troops. *Media coverage in America had been decidedly negative going so far as to call the battlefield victories the worst defeat in American arms*. Commanders in the field were stunned by the reporting. Here they were staring at piles of enemy dead, yet the reporters insisted we had lost.

On Feb. 23 the Marines on Khe Sanh endured their heaviest bombardment to date. Six days later they fought off a determined NVA attack that reached the base perimeter wire. All through March they hung on through constant shelling and rocket attacks. Unable to frontally assault the base the NVA began digging protective trench-lines. They had almost reached the barbed wire on the edge of the base when losses began to slow them. And as the monsoon weather began to clear around Khe Sanh air attacks on the enemy became more frequent and better directed.

Westmoreland then ordered the 1st Cav Div to implement their pre-planned linkup with Marines. *Operation Pegasus* began on April 1 and was a marvelous display of capability and ingenuity. Brave troopers reinforced with Marines, ARVN Rangers and Airborne troops "island-hopped" along Route 9 setting up battalion sized fire-bases as they went. The already reduced strength NVA forces in the area were outclassed and battered by tactical air attacks and the quick acting Air-Cav units. Cavalry and Marine platoons patrolled out from their bases supported by their ever present helicopters.

Unit after unit of NVA troops was shot up and driven off. After a few days the NVA holding the roadway of Route 9, (from Dong Ha and Con Thien), were thoroughly beaten and forced back. Security of the local area allowed for road repairs and mine-sweeping to begin. That enabled the vehicle convoys to move forward and by April 6 the linkup of the two commands was completed.

With their supplies and casualties replaced the Marines then re-took all of the surrounding hill positions by Easter Sunday. As always the NVA had successfully fled the Khe Sanh battle area, but they left over 10,000 of their comrades. Losses hidden within the dense jungles could not even be guessed at. No one will ever know the exact toll the NVA endured, but it was extreme.

This last battle of the TET offensive was another military victory for the U.S. *But it was yet another empty one as the Khe Sanh base was abandoned in July.*

(After the war ended NVA survivors lamented the carnage their units had suffered. Many had lost 90% of their personnel. *Even Gen. Giap was endangered when a B-52 bombing mission bombed near his forward HQ.)*

As the NVA withdrew from Khe Sanh they repositioned some of their forces to the western areas near the A Shau valley to support an offensive there. Starting in late January the NVA had repeatedly attacked and in mid-March they finally overran a USAF radar station that was atop a sharp peak called Lima 85. That site had been used to radar direct aircraft into N. Vietnam and Laos.

The small USAF garrison on the peak was continuously bombarded with artillery and mortars which caused casualties, destroyed their defenses and prevented any reinforcements. Lima 85 was finally wiped out in a frontal infantry attack.

There was also one last SF base along the border with Laos, called Kham Duc. The base had been vital for running SOG teams into Laos and the NVA wanted it out.

As the 1st Cav troops were advancing towards Khe Sanh in April, two of the relocated NVA divisions were closing a ring around that mountainous SF stronghold.

Intel learned of the enemy effort and the base was reinforced.

After they succeeded getting Route 9 re-opened Cav units flew over and helped recaptured the SF camp at Lang Vei. With that done they then attacked into the A Shau valley to assist at Kham Duc. But by May 10 two NVA regiments were attacking the SF base constantly. After two days of non-stop fighting and almost continuous artillery bombardments Gen. Westmoreland decided to abandon the SF base.

Unlike Khe Sanh, this intense battle received almost no press coverage. The bravery by all involved was incredible as the survivors struggled to escape. Over 1500 troops were removed as the NVA took control of all of north-western SVN. (The weather in the A Shau valley was always poor which hampered air support. Because of that the Cav was unable to remain.)

Gen. Giap and his staff had done an excellent job of planning the battles and the propaganda effort for TET. They had wanted to topple the regime in Saigon and cause a general uprising. Though they did not achieve any of their goals, the unanticipated political fallout in America forced Johnson to stop the bombings. From that point the U.S. was negotiating for peace from a point of weakness.

One person in Vietnam became increasingly confident as the fallout from TET became clearer. **John Vann finally felt that victory was actually possible.**
In his III Corps provinces over 20,000 VC had been killed in the many battles.

The hidden enemy that had been so evasive and effective was beaten, and now was the time to attack and finish the fight.

Over the years the non-stop fighting meant that many of the replacement soldiers for the VC units had to come from the NVA. (Initially they too had been southerners.)

But all through the war the VC leaders had been southerners.

Now most of those leaders had been sacrificed in the vain attempt to win before America could. There were few VC replacements available from local sources to replace the heavy losses during TET. Thus incoming NVA troops and officers had to be used to staff the VC units that were being rebuilt. (Though many would not or could not be rebuilt.)

Those northerners were as alien to the southern peasants as we were. Vann urged all of his advisors and teams to get out in the field day and night and secure their areas. We still had time to win.

(Communist losses from TET were so heavy they did not mount another major attack until the spring of 1972!)

But just as victory was finally possible the inept U.S. political leaders had fallen to the wayside and only wanted to get out. TET had shocked the nation, exposed the lies by the Administration and crushed any desire to continue.

Growing anti-war cries and complaints from returning veterans resonated across the country. As the anti-war rallies grew so too did the political challenges to LBJ.

Senator Eugene McCarthy of Minnesota became a front runner in this anti-war call to unseat him in the 1968 election. Joining the movement was Robert Kennedy using his new pulpit in NY. (To stay in the spotlight RFK had "moved" to New York and won election to an empty Senate seat.)

To separate himself from the growing skeptics in his administration LBJ had decided to secretly promote the now disillusioned McNamara to the World Bank.

Having his negative thoughts around the campaign could cause major problems in his bid for reelection. Long time Democrat Clark Clifford took over as Sec.-Defense in March 1968.

LBJ's popularity had been steadily eroding since his win in 64. After TET his political preeminence was falling fast and even the elites within the party were leaving his side. Though they had not been demonstrating it in public, their loss of confidence was a fatal blow. Johnson's Administration was paralyzed over their growing split on Vietnam. To try to contain the "political damage" Johnson had his staff and Administration get out and try to spin the story. "Thump the theme" in newspapers and on television to show the communist effort had failed.

But with the intensely negative press from the TET offensive and primary losses to potential opponents among the Democratic presidential candidates, LBJ decided that he would not run for another term as president. He gave a speech about not using a minute of his time campaigning while our boys were fighting in Vietnam, but in reality all he was trying to do was to help the Democrats win the next election. They hoped a fresh candidate would not have the stain of the war as an issue against them.

LBJ completely stopped the intensely hated, (by the anti-war activists), bombing of North Vietnam on Oct 31, 1968 as a way to help placate the liberal wing of the party. This was just before the election. (When it came to cheap politics no one was better at it than Johnson.)

But all of his scheming could not hide the fact that the disaster that Vietnam became was due to him. Johnson had refused to get a Declaration of War from the Congress so he could try to hide the fact that we were at war. He feared that any negativity that arose from the public war hearings could have imperiled his main goal of "The Great Society" programs that he was sneaking onto the nation.

Throughout his five years in office LBJ never presented a clear objective on Vietnam to the military or the State Dept. The broad policy aims of NSAM 288 dated 17 March 1965; "To preserve S. Vietnam as an independent and free non communist state." was a good starting point, but Johnson never moved on with any true goals.

How were we to save the South?
What was to be done to shape this end and what were the contingency plans?

No one knew what we were actually fighting for, and Johnson never explained anything to the American people. Again this was done to prevent discourse and unravel his true aims.

Johnson refused to listen to the military advice about the bombing campaign.

The JCS knew and wanted to hit N. Vietnam hard in the beginning before they could react and build up their defenses. Had LBJ allowed the military to take out all of the bridges, railroads, ports, piers, Red River dikes and other infrastructure, the North would not have been able to wage the war they did. That could have allowed the U.S. a chance to achieve a Korean War-type victory by stabilizing and building up the South.

The majority of supplies shipped directly to N. Vietnam came through the port of Haiphong. Recon photos in 1965 clearly showed dozens of ships waiting to be unloaded at the untouched docks and piers. Warehouses were filled with war supplies and their nearby transport infrastructure was in constant use.

Repeatedly the JCS and MACV asked for permission to destroy these vital facilities and close off the communist war effort. When LBJ finally caved in on some of the requests the anti-aircraft defenses had been aggressively upgraded and were extremely effective. The costs to our aircrews were very high because of his irresponsibility. The fits and starts and incremental air assaults directed by Johnson and his administration were unproductive, unwarranted and extremely costly.

If a nation is going to fight a war the effort must be by its very nature extremely violent and destructive. To engage in this effort in any other form is iniquitous to those who are sent to fight it.

A similar Oriental parable simply states, A tiger uses all of its strength to kill a rabbit.

LBJ refused to call up the reserves which would have increased the trained manpower to the war effort. *Instead he drafted our untrained citizens and sent them to fight in a counter-insurgency type of conflict. It was criminal.*

By its nature that type of war requires your best trained troops, not the least trained.

He also refused to end the draft exemptions that placed the burden of the fighting on the poor. (The same people his Great Society was supposed to help.)

He refused any thoughts to cutting the Ho Chi Minh trail in Cambodia or Laos even though in 1963 it was well known how the NVA were bringing troops and supplies into the South. Cutting the trail would have weakened the enemy units in the south and forced them to withdraw or fight for their supply lines. Either way the change in the fighting would have saved some of the South and bought more time for the ARVN.

In a meeting held in June 1965 LBJ was told by Gen. Wheeler and witnessed by Clark Clifford that winning this war would require 750,000 troops. Johnson blew his top yelling no one is using that figure.

Clifford asked Gen Wheeler if we win how long will we have to remain in Vietnam?

Wheeler answered we would have to keep a major force there for 20+ years.

That was the same time frame as was occurring in Germany, Japan and Korea, but that was the price that had to be borne to maintain the far frontier.

Lyndon Johnson refused to consider the issue further, for he had already decided **Not to win.**

Gen. Westmoreland would only be given the resources required to not lose!

In his book on Vietnam, *Strategy for Defeat,* Admiral Sharp amply illustrates the Johnson Administration and their failures. *One of his most important recommendations was how the JCS must be allowed to report directly to the Congress, bypassing the presidential political appointee of Sec of Defense.*

Their strategic views were routinely dismissed by McNamara and Taylor and never presented to the nation's leaders.
If they had been made public LBJ would have had a hard time dismissing them.

From the fallout of TET, LBJ and his administration were defeated morally and mentally. He let Westmoreland stay on until mid-June until he too was "promoted out". Quietly Gen. Creighton Abrams replaced Westmoreland at MACV. The command change had not been anticipated so Abrams continued with the current MACV policies.
But after having seen the problems first hand since May 67, Abrams was going to make changes in our operations.

Johnson still wanted to negotiate a withdrawal of all U.S. and NVA forces, but the <u>communists only wanted us to leave.</u> They were prepared for years of useless discussions and negotiations, sensing that things were only going to get better as the U.S. press and anti-war demonstrators drove us out.

While the battles of the spring mini TET were winding down the Presidential campaign was heating up. Eugene McCarthy had done well in the initial primaries, and as stated earlier, Robert Kennedy announced that he too was running. Like his brother he was a fine orator and convinced the crowds that he was the best of the anti-war candidates. *(He was one of the ones pushing for action back when JFK was in office.)*

Johnson's Vice-President Hubert Humphrey was another one of those dedicated New Deal Democrats, though not an inspiring one. The campaign promised to get bitter and divided as time went on.

On the Republican side former V.P. Richard Nixon who had lost to JFK and his father in 1960 was the front runner. *One can only wonder at what the world situation would have looked like had Nixon won the election in 1960, had JFK not been murdered, or if Goldwater had won in 1964.*

Some of the anti-war protests were now turning violent as thousands took to the streets daily to demand an end to the fighting. Over 50,000 marched on the Pentagon trying to provoke a confrontation.

Race relations in America were still poor and the inner cities began to resemble war zones. The drug culture that was becoming an accepted "cool" way of life was turning a large percentage of our youth into soulless zombies and bodies at the morgue.

(Those of us in the FDNY were still dealing with drugs, junkies and the ancillary crimes and social problems during my time frame of 1980-2003.)

This curse that organized crime brought into the nation and profited from was causing a synergistic crime wave of incredible proportions as "junkies" robbed and stole to get that next "high". Their street crimes added to the turmoil inside the cities and were exacerbating the "white flight" as middle class white families ran to the safer suburbs.

(Once again this aspect of human nature showed how those who have a choice in how to live their lives will do so once a certain threshold of detrimental factors is reached.)

Businesses also began to leave the cities as crime and the higher taxes needed to fund the Great Society programs forced them out. Those escaping or closing small companies took with them the lower paying jobs that had been a step up the ladder for the young, poorer and least educated workers of our society. And that loss further inflamed the economic and social tensions among the poor as those small economic venues began to disappear.

Most of the Great Society programs were hidden behind Democratic controlled committees and appropriation bills. Their true costs were "concealed" to promote their passage. Only years later would the true costs and issues "suddenly appear.

(The same way the Democrats passed Obamacare.) Those programs would alter the American social and political landscape in ways that most probably never realized, and none of the changes were positive.

The welfare acts gave tax money to the poor to help them get by, but destroyed their desire to work and move up. *No mandatory jobs training or educational programs were planned for or ever instituted to educate or teach our poorer citizens a trade or vocation.* In actuality, those in power never wanted the poor to move up.

If they became prosperous and independent they might not vote for row D, democrat.

If they stayed completely dependent on the government handouts they surely would.

And that would mean the Democrats would always win at the polls.

(Even China's Chairman Mao knew of that fact. One of his parables was; Give a man a fish and he can eat today. Teach him how to fish and he can eat everyday. For the Democrats, giving the fish was the way to ensure compliance.)

Conniving Sen. Ted Kennedy helped push major changes to our immigration policies that would also benefit the Democrats. Prior to the new laws an immigrant had to be educated, have a vocation or a sponsor before you could emigrate to the U.S. In that way the newcomers would not cause America any social problems as the immigrant worked and joined in our society. *But the changes the Democrats pushed for eliminated all of those requirements, and instead they recruited the world's poor. This created a permanent influx of needy people, people who would become beholden to the Democrats for social programs and eventual citizenship.*

Those changes cost billions of dollars to effect, but most of the costs were dropped into the laps of the States. Since the cities were the natural collection point for immigrants and the poor, their budgets would be the first to be broken. And the costs incurred in those first years were a pittance to what the nation is spending today.

On April 4, 1968 Dr Martin Luther King the black leader who had been leading peaceful protests about race-relations across the nation for years was assassinated.

The country exploded into race riots all across the map. Troops had to be called out to impose order. With his death many black leaders became militant and the Black Panthers and other violent groups began appearing across the country.

That same month saw protesters storm, take over and trash the Columbia University Campus in NYC. The protesters were against the college building a new gymnasium in Harlem because it was racist.? They were also against the war.

No criminal, civil or educational penalties were instituted on the guilty despite the expensive and extensive damages done to the campus. Because of that failure the school was "held hostage" by this episode in all of their future endeavors. Within years this fine university would become a bastion of left-wing radicalism and thought.

(All of the protesters who had caused physical damages should have been arrested, convicted, and held financially accountable for the damages. They also should have been expelled. As citizens we have a right to voice our protests but that does not include destroying public or private property.)

This arrogant and destructive scene would be repeated at many more of the nation's colleges and universities over the next few years. (Watching as a young lad it was hard to fathom why they acted that way, and harder still to comprehend why the Colleges and Universities tolerated it.)

On June 8 Robert Kennedy was shot and killed at a rally in Los Angeles. Like his brother a lone gunman was blamed and arrested. A young Palestinian refugee named Sirhan Sirhan was tried, convicted and imprisoned. (Recent forensic investigations have shown that there was a second shooter at the RFK scene. And years of investigations have shown there probably was in JFK's shooting too.)

That August at the Democratic Party convention in Chicago anti-war protestors gathered outside in large groups. They were rightfully upset at the party for the war, and hoped to influence the delegates to pick a candidate who wanted out of Vietnam.

Inside the building the Party was trying to pick a leader to get them out of their quagmire, when outside the building violent rioting broke out followed by mass arrests and street fighting. TV screens across the country showed a nation ripping itself apart night after night.

Hubert Humphrey was eventually chosen as the Democratic candidate, while Richard Nixon became the Republican one. Through the remainder of the year the fighting continued in our streets and in Vietnam, and all of it was on TV.

(As a young lad I watched the 60's play out and vividly remember watching the war and the violence on the nightly news.)

Lyndon Johnson and everyone who had been a part of his Administration were tainted by the war. Johnson had dreamed and lusted for glory as the greatest domestic president ever. He wisely did not go to the convention in Chicago in 68.

Nor did he attend the one in Miami in 1972.

Not even a photo of him was visible, such was the stain upon him. (Well deserved.)

Maxwell Taylor who had passed himself off as a new thinker had created the army that went to Vietnam. His political maneuverings destroyed the Army as a military force and created a skulking ruin of officers fixated on their careers. Poor officers who were politically adept were promoted while conscientious ones who refused to scam were removed from promotion boards and retired.

And because of the war our military and the servicemen and women were being blamed for that nightmare instead of the liars who had brought us there.

Robert McNamara went over to the World Bank and served for two years. He left government service enjoying a long retirement.

And their long list of failures went on and on.

Europe

In Europe tensions were mounting. Czech party leader Alexander Dubcek had been slowly instituting some democratic reforms into his country despite repeated warnings from other communist leaders not to. (Dubcek had fought the Nazi's as a resistance fighter and was done with the Soviet slavery.) On April 9 the Czech Communist Party announced a program to reduce party planning in the economy and instituting greater freedoms in industry and agriculture. Despite the clear warnings, hardliners and pro-Moscow communists were slowly being removed from their governmental positions.

Protesters in Czechoslovakia were soon demanding even more freedoms during that spring of 1968. They had not enjoyed such freedoms since the Communist coup in 1948. After weeks of "civil unrest" Soviet military forces moved into the border areas.

By the end of July 1968 the tension was building to unbearable levels and America was again powerless to help.

Russia's party boss Leonid Brezhnev met with Dubcek and Polish President Ludvik Svoboda on a luxury train near the border. Days of heated talks were held.

Brezhnev decried a "doctrine", warning that Russia could intervene in any Communist country whose policies deviated from their standards. **On August 20 over 300,000 Russian and Warsaw pact troops invaded Czechoslovakia.**

The Kremlin announced to an unhappy world that their troops had been "invited by their Czech comrades." True to form the Russians initially occupied the Czech governmental buildings and all offices of the "liberals" and journalists. In that way they hoped to shut down any credible voices of dissent. Dubcek and his colleagues were arrested and sent to Moscow.

The Czech military offered no resistance to the Soviet invasion, though by mistake the Russians forgot to shut down the radio and TV stations. Broadcasts went out for hours until machine guns dispersed the protective crowds. Prague then became the scene of deadly urban fighting as the Czech citizens used anything they could to destroy the Russian tanks.

By mid-October the fighting had finally ended and Dubcek had no choice but to acquiesce on his reforms. Hundreds had been killed and wounded as the Soviet led communist troops crushed the people's quest for freedom. The replacement regime of Gustav Husak was one of the most repressive regimes in the Communist bloc. All of the reformers were dismissed or demoted as the Soviets occupied the country.

Brezhnev like Khrushchev back in 1956 had crushed a potential satellite revolt. But this time there was severe fallout to the Soviet model. *Western liberals and intellectuals suddenly realized that after decades of turning a blind eye to all of the horrors, communism was not what it claimed to be.* In fact, communism was nothing but a scam.

For decades these elitists had covered up the numerous and apparent failures of communism in their blind belief that in time all would be fixed.

Czechoslovakia cured them of that notion.

In Italy their powerful communist party was so disgusted with the Russian actions they openly broke ties with the Soviets. France saw a rapid reduction in their communist party membership, and within a decade they had lost almost 70% of their members.

And that same feeling of dread and hatred grew throughout the Soviet sphere.

Unknowingly the brutal Soviet action in Czechoslovakia had set the stage for the end of communism in Europe.

As this war against Czech reform was occurring Russia was also sending large forces along China's northern and western frontiers. Tensions had been increasing there too and China expected to be invaded.

During May 1968 the first peace negotiations began with delegations meeting in Paris. Just like Korea and Harry Truman in 1951, the U.S. negotiators went into the conference euphoric and hoping for peace. That was not what the communists wanted.

They expected victory.

Our council stated that if we left Vietnam the NVA had to leave too.

The communists refused. They also demanded the Saigon government had to be realigned and admit VC representatives. We refused. Little was accomplished.

The location of the talks became a poor one when France was nearly paralyzed by multiple organized labor strikes. French leftists had used prior demands for higher wages as a front, closing factories, railroads and telephones. Streets in Paris were full of violent protestors and police. Similar to 1947, the mid-June clashes with police were occurring constantly, and President de Gaulle was outraged at the strikers warning that France was on the brink of Civil War. (This was an organized leftist plot.)

Not until October of 1968 did the communists finally trade with LBJ.

They gave unwritten and indefinite assurances of de-escalation along the DMZ and in Saigon for an end to all bombing of the North and admission to the peace talks of a delegation from their NLF, (National Liberation Front).

This agreement gave equal footing to the communists even though they were the invaders. Johnson foolishly agreed to their terms.

Gen. Creighton Abrams had been in Vietnam as Deputy Commander at MACV and knew full well the mistakes his predecessor had made. After their close call in Saigon from TET, Abrams was determined to route the enemy from their strongholds in III Corps. While continuing to fight the communists Abrams also instituted greater military support for the Pacification efforts. And ready or not, the ARVN units were sent back out into the field on combat operations.

CIA station Chief William Colby had like Vann also realized that the VC infrastructure had been decimated in TET. His office accelerated their pacification programs too and increased the arms and aid to the local defense forces in the villages.

With better arms and less VC moving around the villagers realized they could hold their own whenever communist cadre came calling. **In sync with that CIA aid was the implementation of a new policing- intelligence program called Phoenix.** Using all types of intelligence sources, multiple arrests and at times torture, Phoenix began uncovering the hundreds of the remaining VC.

During the violent year of 1968 and amid all of the nonsensical jabbering at the "peace conferences" another 14,589 Americans had died trying to keep S. Vietnam free.

As in Korea, the communists held out the carrot of negotiations.

And just like Korea their empty negotiations dragged on fitfully.

In tragic sadness they would go nowhere for four more years.

America

During the election campaign Richard Nixon ran a similar quiet campaign as Tom Dewey had in 1948. His large lead slowly evaporated but he was able to win the election by a small margin because of the split among the Democrats. Gov. George Wallace of Alabama had run on a third party, The American Independence Party. His platform centered on ending Johnson's Civil Rights platform as well as the hated Great Society Programs. Wallace garnered 9.5 million votes, which was 13.5 % of the total cast. He also took five southern states with their electoral votes.

Had Wallace not run it would have been interesting to see which side the angry southerners would have voted for.

Pres. Elect Richard Nixon promised to end the war and win a peace with honor. He did not have a concrete plan to end the war, just a blueprint. Nixon and his team needed to buy time to enact his promised outcome, and having won by a small margin meant that he had no mandate to do as he pleased. Thus his options were limited to what the citizens would tolerate. And at that time in America that was not going to be much.

Nixon had been made aware of Col Vann's theories and like others felt they were the only workable solution. (All of the "operators" from Special Forces also knew how to win the war, but the starched staff principals at MACV thought of them as animals. Even as good as Gen. Abrams was, he too hated the non-conventional people of Special Forces.)

Because of the beneficial leaks to JFK during the 1960 campaign Pres. Nixon was distrustful of the CIA and State Dept. He wanted and organized his administration to ensure as much secrecy as possible. And he wanted the White House to control the decision making.

Pres. Nixon did have one original and controversial idea that he was prepared to try, he would reach out to Russia and China and have them help to reign in the N. Vietnamese. Russia was straining over the endless supplies going to Vietnam, and China was still reeling over Mao's repeated failures. His idea would also take advantage of the growing tensions between the communist giants as clashes between them were occurring in Manchuria.

Nixon would offer them U.S. aid, technology and arms control to get their help in winning the peace. If that failed he was also prepared to use his "Madman Theory". Nixon was a still a well known anti-communist, and he hoped that word would get out that he would be capable of doing anything should the North continue to stall the peace. (Similar to how Ike was able to get the Korean Truce.)

Henry Kissinger directed his staff at National Security Agency to canvass all of the officials in Washington and Saigon to come up with ideas and appraisals of Vietnam. Like his predecessors the influx of reports was full of differing opinions. One of the ideas was for Nixon to go to the Congress and get a full Declaration of War. That would force the Congress to stand by the President as he tried to extricate us from Vietnam and buy some time for it to happen. Nixon however was afraid to go that route out of fear that he would not get such a vote from the Congress of 1969. They might force him to just give up and get out. Like most of the country Richard Nixon dearly wanted to get out of Vietnam. But after all we had done and sacrificed in Indochina he wanted a *Peace with Honor.*

To enable the U.S. to leave S. Vietnam viable and not just run away we had to rebuild the ARVN capabilities to defend their country. Sec of Defense Melvin Laird coined a term called *Vietnamization*, which became the program where our forces left an area and the re-trained and re-equipped ARVN took over. (Henry Kissinger who was the National Security Advisor complimented John Vann for this and other ideas.)

At the same time as Vietnamization, a vastly increased pacification program was also to be instituted. President Thieu helped both programs get started by mandating a nationwide mobilization for every male aged from 16-50. This doubled the size of the ARVN forces and they were outfitted with the improved M-16 rifle which greatly increased the ARVN firepower. (With every male under arms it also reduced those available for use by the VC.)

ARVN leadership and motivation were still lacking as was seen in the recent ARVN battles at Ben Het and Bu Prong in II Corps. But those in Washington hoped the effort would be aided since the NVA had lost over 50,000 troops and almost all of the regional VC at TET.

To facilitate his new strategy Gen. Abrams again had the 1st Air Cav Division repositioned. They left I Corps in the north and moved south into III Corps. Their new mission was to work with the 1st and 25th Infantry Divisions and ARVN units to beat up the NVA and VC (NVA) units in the area. Abram's long term plan was to destroy the enemy base areas and prevent any more attacks near Saigon.

As mentioned above those relocating moves were actually begun before our national election was held and their intensive effort was soon paying off. North of Saigon sat the infamous enemy redoubt known as War Zone D and Base Area 359. To the west were three more communist dominated areas that had always been difficult to penetrate.

Just to the west was Cambodia, and there were six NVA Base Areas there. All of the reinforcements and supplies the enemy received came from those areas.

As shown earlier, the communist war effort in that region was directed from a unit known as COSVN. (Central Office for South Vietnam.)

This command center was one of four that the Politburo of North Vietnam used.

SOG had searched for this one for years but the communists wisely moved it around. This time they would be up against the mobile Air-Cavalry instead of normal infantry.

Gen. Abram's plan began by hammering the enemy hideouts north and west of Saigon. Along the border with Cambodia ARVN and U.S. troops attacked any enemy trying to move back into S. Vietnam. Instead of the large multi-battalion attacks used earlier in the war all of the units involved in "interdicting the NVA" were broken down into smaller parts. Dozens upon dozens of platoon sized ambushes waited for and attacked into the enemy every chance they showed up. Flying above, around and behind everyone were the Air-Cav scout and attack helicopters.

They attacked anything they saw and called in artillery and ground troops as needed.

Against the U.S. and ARVN units were the 1st and 7th NVA Divisions and the VC 5th and 9th Divisions, rebuilt with NVA troops. Though they were mobile infantry units, they were totally dependent upon their pre-staged supplies stashed in secret caches.

Their former allies in the VC controlled villages were gone, lost during TET and the follow on pacification efforts. With no local support their losses mounted and their infiltration efforts from Cambodia slowed. During the following weeks the infantry combat was heavy as the enemy was determined to disrupt the effective pacification effort and to keep inflicting casualties on the Americans.

But they realized they were losing ground.

As 1969 continued along Intel efforts realized that the NVA were building up their forces and supplies in Cambodia for a quick invasion as soon as the U.S. forces left. (That was one of the reasons for the new operations instituted above.)

Since the communists were not engaging in productive talks at the peace conferences, it was time for America to create some real pain.

To assist the South in blocking the obvious enemy effort and to try to hurt the communists as much as possible, Pres. Nixon authorized the JCS and MACV to begin secret bombings of the communist bases and supply points in Cambodia. This decision had been reached in late Feb. 1969, but the actual operation was not implemented until March.

(The NVA routinely fired 122mm rockets into Saigon killing dozens of civilians. They had thought themselves safe in Cambodia.)

The military had long asked to attack those areas, but LBJ had always refused. Nixon and his team listened to the requests from Gen. Abrams and granted them as a way to buy time for the ARVN to transition during our withdrawal.

He knew what he was authorizing would be attacked by the media, the liberals and many in Congress. But it was the only way to disrupt the communist war plans, hurt them and get them to negotiate. *The Peace Talks were accomplishing nothing as per the communist playbook.*

(It would be almost a year before Pres. Nixon and his team realized what they were truly up against.)

It had been decided to utilize B-52 raids to disrupt the enemy buildup and kill as many NVA as possible. The first of those secret bombings occurred in late March 1969. B-52 Arc-light missions came over the border striking NVA base area 353 and setting off dozens of secondary explosions. There was no reaction from Hanoi, but then there couldn't be. They were still denying that any of their units were fighting in South Vietnam, let alone having base areas in neutral Cambodia.

With no positives in Paris, Pres. Nixon bombed them again in April.

This time they went after the suspected commanders at COSVN. SOG was directed to land a reaction force as soon as the bombing ended with the hope of finishing off any survivors. But the NVA monitored (with Russian help), the USAF warning alerts that directed all aircraft to avoid the sectors about to be bombed.

COSVN left before the attack and had ambush units close by. When the SOG teams landed they were caught in a desperate fight.
After losing dozens of these true warriors the rest were pulled out

Our Ambassador in Cambodia refused to allow tactical airstrikes into the country, only the high flying B-52s that could not be shot down. Reporters in Saigon picked up that B-52 missions had gone in, but there was no report as to where they went or what they accomplished. That got them agitated as Johnson had stopped the bombings.

Heavy NVA attacks then occurred on the Cav Firebases along the Cambodian border right into May 1969. Enemy losses continued to rise and COSVN realized they were up against a different mindset than before Nixon took over. The communists were slowly losing control of III Corps and nothing they tried worked.
More B-52 strikes went in and eventually the press learned where they went. They complained and protested.

Up in I Corps the Marines instituted Operation Dewey Canyon during the early spring. Division Commander Ray Davis, (Medal of Honor from the Chosin Reservoir), agreed with Abrams that a mobile defense was what was needed. He had closed down most of the Marine bases and used the freed up manpower in much the same way as Abrams was doing near Saigon.

His 9th Mar Regiment attacked an area adjacent to Laos to try to stop the NVA infiltration from coming in. **Three of their companies actually crossed over into Laos and ambushed NVA units moving down Route 922.** Their operation was small, and therefore its success and impact was limited. But it was indicative of what should have been done in 1965/66. Enemy losses continued though their overall plan had not changed. (With the loss of the SOG camps and Khe Sanh our recon efforts were reduced.)

Throughout Vietnam the war raged on with hundreds of U.S. casualties occurring every week. By this point most realized that we were not looking to win in Nam. Motivation and morale began to decline as the troops realized this was a wasted effort. Race and drug problems began to surface. But still those draftees performed.

(The best soldiers were the sons of the working and middle class where society's values had been taught and retained. Arthur Hadley would write; "In the line units in Vietnam it is the best of the middle class that we are losing".)

Far to the south in IV Corps the 9th Div was also doing well against the entrenched VC. Col. David Hackworth (formally of the 101st) had returned to Vietnam and turned a poor battalion of draftees into a VC killing machine. (They had decimated the VC 261 Battalion, the communist heroes from Ap Bac.) Hackworth was like John Paul Vann back in 62-63, using well planned hit and run tactics against the enemy instead of the prior MACV directed large units stumbling into enemy ambushes. The turnaround of 4th Battalion 39 Infantry was astounding, and showcased how good leadership could win. Unfortunately it came too late.

Pres. Nixon's secret bombing missions into Cambodia became public knowledge despite the attempt by those at MACV to try to keep it a secret. Again the press vilified the military for this political decision by the president. *Press indignation went into Cambodia and Prince Sihanouk was asked about the bombings on May 13. He replied that they had heard nothing of the action because there are No Cambodians in those areas, only NVA. The veil was off, as Sihanouk verified that N. Vietnamese Army units were in his country in force.* But the media did not care.

Now that it was out in the open the bombings grew in intensity and in numbers as all of the NVA sanctuaries and areas near them were being hit. Those missions continued all summer and began to pay real dividends. Still the media cared not.

At a summit conference on Midway Island Pres. Nixon and his staff met with Pres. Thieu and his staff to discuss the war. Nixon insisted that Vietnamization would progress and that U.S. troop reductions were coming. Thieu gave advice on what U.S. units could go first, but admitted that there was a sagging spirit in the South. *With the Americans leaving most feared for the future.*

Nixon wanted to negotiate hard with the communists but realized we had no leverage. All we could do was give them a deadline. **"After over half a year of sending peaceful signals to the North Vietnamese Nixon was ready to use military force on them to prevent a takeover in the South".** (57)

The president set November 1, 1969 as his deadline, and sent a letter of his intensions to Ho Chi Minh. Ho refused any concessions, and died soon after.

(Nixon's proposals for U.S. action to break the deadlocked peace talks are still classified, but it was planned to include heavy bombing of Hanoi and Haiphong. Called *Duck Hook*, it utilized Nixon's Madman Theory to destroy all of the North Vietnam's transport systems, mine Haiphong harbor and all waterways, and then invaded across the DMZ. Nixon met with and explained the proposals to Republican Congressional leaders at Camp David on September 24. All assembled knew the attacks would enrage the anti-war crowd, *but there was no way to force Hanoi to negotiate.*)

Asia

In April North Korea resumed their belligerent stance by shooting down an unarmed U.S. Recon aircraft. Nixon saw it as a test and refused to issue bellicose statements. Four days later he announced the Recon-flights would resume and that they would be protected by fighters. The media deluged the administration with questions, and again Nixon remained silent. Those reinforced recon flights resumed, and the N. Koreans kept their distance.

Then on December 11, 1969 Korean Airline Flight 45-11 was hijacked by N. Korean commandos. The aircraft was taken to N. Korea and the hostages were kept for 62 days. When they had learned what they wanted, the communists released 39 of the hostages. However the communists kept the aircraft, the flight crew and ten passengers. *They were "imprisoned as spies", and never seen again.*

Nearby the previously mentioned Russian/ Chinese border buildup was coming to a head. Russia had moved 44 divisions to the border areas anticipating a fight. During March 1969 China and Russia again went to blows over "border incursions". A disputed island in the middle of the frozen Ussuri River in eastern Manchuria was the latest flash point as shooting erupted between the communist powers.

China claimed that the Russians had been using the island to shell targets inside Manchuria, while the Russians claimed that Chinese units had killed 31 of their soldiers. As the fighting continued larger engagements broke out in other provinces. Their battles would continue into August 1969 and it convinced Mao Tse Tung that a rapprochement with America might be needed to offset the Russians.

Possibly it was time to end the war in Vietnam.

In Russia the same thought began to be heard. China was a potentially lethal opponent. Their massive peasant armies seemed immune to casualties, and even though their infant nuclear program was far behind, it could inflict fatal damage to the Soviet Union. *And the increasing fighting between them could well inspire other "client states" to cause problems.* Improving relations with the West, in the process known as *detente*, seemed like a good idea.

During August 1969 a SOG team was inserted into NE Cambodia to locate the NVA 66 Regiment. They were next on the list of B-52 strikes. What the team did find at great cost was a senior NVA Colonel who was killed in a firefight. This Chinese looking officer had a leather satchel which contained vital information.

After the daring escape by the SOG team it was learned that the captured papers contained the names of dozens of enemy agents inside S. Vietnam.

It was also learned that those agents had been the ones who had warned the North in the early 1960s that ARVN-CIA Commando teams were on their way.

That was why all of them had been picked up so quickly.

All of those communist spies were arrested and made to talk, unraveling more of the communist spy network that had done so much damage to S. Vietnam.

When Robert Komer finally left Vietnam he was replaced by William Colby. As stated before Colby had long served in country in the CIA and most recently as Komer's deputy. He had a fine grasp of the problems though he like so many others had been ignored by those in power. It was Komer, Colby and Vann who had persuaded Pres. Thieu to institute the new policing-intelligence program a few months before. This one would finally address and eradicate the secret enemy that was hidden among the populace and within the government. As stated before the program was called *Phoenix*.

During that same time democratic reforms were slowly being enacted within the villages of S. Vietnam. That allowed the residents to pick their own local leaders and decide their local issues including land reform. The freedoms they were given showed how life could be lived. They were thus emboldened to help the new Phoenix program succeed by exposing the communist agents who lived among them.

Operation Phoenix was fully enacted in late 1969 and was a major part of the accelerated pacification program. Using updated and relevant intelligence and help from the locals, communist sympathizers and VC cadres were found out and arrested or killed.

The heavy losses to the VC units during TET-68 had actually compromised their entire subversive effort. Few local VC fighters were available in the rural hamlets to shield this unspoken enemy, and the loss of the VC leaders weakened the VC communist effort. Without "the muscle and leaders" being present, the locals began to point out the VC members to the authorities. (Similar to exposing organized crime.)

Before he left Komer had set a quota for all of South Vietnam and wanted to pick up 3,000 VCI (Viet Cong Infrastructure) per month. All of the local Intel collected from police and the Provisional Pacification Teams would be pooled to ensure compliance and accuracy. Naturally the program started slowly, but as time and successes continued many of those VCI found themselves arrested or on the receiving end of assassination squads, payback for their years of terrorism.

(Technically no suspects were marked for death, as the dead can't give up any additional information, the key to the program's success. But many times the teams or the locals wanted revenge for past VC murders and brutality.)

Within months VCI suspects were being **openly denounced** by the locals in the villages, at checkpoints or captured on intelligence missions. In moving around the country directing his programs Vann found villages that had been listed as communist controlled were now "held" by a half dozen guerrillas. Teams would be sent in to investigate and the VCI would be exposed and arrested. *Success breeds success, and as word got out entire areas would suddenly become cleared.*

By early 1970 over 15,000 communist VC suspects had been removed. *Large sections of the IV Corps suddenly thrived with intact roads and bridges, TV antennas appeared on roofs and peaceful life began returning to a war ravaged land.*

Columnist Joe Alsop wrote that it was a celebration moving through "Vann Country", such were the visible changes. Even the notable Sir Robert Thompson who had been the British anti-communist leader in Malaya became impressed with Vann and the progress he saw. (President Nixon had used Thompson's expertise to help underwrite the Vietnamization policy.)

And all during those many months the communists continued their inane stalling tactics in Paris in the hope of winning the war. Dr. Kissinger even met in private with N. Vietnamese representative Xuan Tuy on Aug 4, 1969. Though this new channel was an important start, as usual nothing was being accomplished. Tuy repeated the same one sided demands that all U.S. and allied forces had to leave unilaterally and Thieu and his government disbanded. (That meeting convinced Nixon and Kissinger that no rapprochement was possible, and that the North would not negotiate.)

Islamic Terrorists

With the world focused on Vietnam and the war against the communists major Islamic terrorist attacks occurred in 1969 and 1970.
On February 18, 1969 four Palestinians attempted to hijack Israeli El Al passenger jet Flight 432 as it taxied for takeoff. Security forces stormed the aircraft but even so one civilian was killed and six were wounded.

On August 29, 1969 TWA Flight 840 from Rome to Tel Aviv was hijacked by Islamist gunmen. Israel's ambassador to the U.N. was supposed to have been on the flight.

Upon landing in Jordan the hijackers escaped. Despite the clear signs of danger from terrorists airline security was not addressed.

Israel announced that it would not give back the territories they seized during the 1967 Six-Day War. And during September Israeli tanks crossed the Suez Canal to attack Egyptian fortifications that had been shelling their outposts. Air clashes continued with another eleven Egyptian planes shot down. By Feb 1970 numerous ship sinking's and larger border battles were being fought.

On Feb. 21, 1970 Swiss Air Flight 330 was bombed by Islamists linked to the PLO. All 47 on board were killed.

On May 22, 1970 Palestinians slipping in from Lebanon fired automatic weapons and RPGs at a school bus near Avivam Israel. Twelve were killed and 25 wounded in the attack.

As the tensions increased in the Middle East Israeli planes shot down dozens of Arab jets during June. Air attacks against Israeli fortifications followed as the two sides continued their antithesis. *During August Israeli jets struck areas of southern Lebanon to try to stop the constant terrorist attacks along their northern frontier by the PLO.*

Then on Sept. 9, 1970 four Jetliners were hijacked by Palestinians and taken into Jordan. Three hundred ten hostages were taken to Amman on 9/11/1970. Most of the hostages were released, but 56 of Jewish descent were kept in jail. Three of the multi-million dollar aircraft were blown up by the Islamists, which resulted in King Hussein declaring martial law to reduce the unrest in his nation. (Pres. Nixon was going to order the Sixth Fleet into action, and USAF jets based in Turkey were on pad alert.)

This latest terrorist attack resulted in the formation of the Sky-Marshall program and the use of x-ray machines to screen passengers and luggage.

In Lebanon Arab agitators were conspiring with PLO Chief Arafat to attempt to bring down their pro-Western Government. Arafat wanted to use the country as a staging area to wage a guerrilla war against Israel. With Syrian help, PLO rebels made major gains in Lebanon which caused the Israeli leaders to warn that they would go to war should the Arabs take over Lebanon.

Jordan then became the scene of civil fighting as the PLO attempted to topple the rule of King Hussein and take over that nation. But the PLO lost their political fight in Jordan and King Hussein wisely exiled them from his nation. The down side to that episode was that more of the PLO terrorists moved into Lebanon. It would not be long before that beautiful country was destroyed.

Americas

Latin America returned to the front pages in two separate problems during September 1970. In Chile Salvador Allende Gossens, a Marxist was elected to the presidency by a small margin. Nixon viewed this episode in the worst light as had his predecessors. ITT (International Telephone and Telegraph) and the CIA spent over a million dollars in a covert plot to change the runoff election that was required in Chile. Nixon went so far to stop Allende that he authorized a coup if need be. The coup collapsed as one of the people to be used as leverage was accidently killed.

Allende took power but was undermined during his three years in office. A political neophyte, Allende allowed the left wing of his Socialist Party to ruin (as usual) their economy. During September 1973 he was overthrown in a bloody coup. Repression and terror followed as the military took control. (As usual)

Days after Allende won his election in Chile, Castro created a new crisis. Word had gotten around that the Soviets were building a base for their nuclear submarines near Cienfuegos. U-2 over-flights brought back pictures of new buildings, towers, antiaircraft positions and fields. Offshore the Soviet Navy kept a submarine tender, two barges to hold nuclear wastes, and at least one submarine within a days sail. Nixon was keeping things quiet to sort the situation out with diplomacy when the NY Times published an account of the problem.

(That furthered Nixon's suspicions of the media and "his enemies".)

The Soviets were warned that they had to abide by the 1962 agreement. Brezhnev insisted that no base was being built, but the work mirrored similar bases in the Soviet Union. Once again vigilance had caught an issue before it became a serious problem. (Had Brezhnev not backed down it is hard to guess as to where it would have led.)

Castro had other problems in Cuba. In the late 1960s he directed that Cuba must produce ten million tons of sugar per year. Cuba had never even come close when the U.S. agriculture companies were in Cuba. Not to be deterred, Castro used round the clock work by almost everyone on the island. (like China) The harvest fell far short of his dream and in the meantime food production had lapsed causing serious shortages. No matter where they ruled, the incapable communists cause dire problems.

Vietnam

As promised during the presidential campaign, Pres. Nixon was withdrawing troops from Vietnam as quickly as was militarily prudent. The first 100,000 Americans were out by the end of the year. *This unilateral withdrawal diffused the anti-war efforts, but caused great hardships for those still in SVN and those who were going there as replacements.* In effect the plug had been pulled, and we were not going to win. No one wanted to die for a lost cause, and morale plummeted. Seeing that we were leaving the communists delayed any negotiations, what was the point.

Sec-Def Melvin Laird insisted on implementing Vietnamization on schedule. Whether it worked would be up the Thieu Govt. in S. Vietnam. *Gen. Abrams and staff did not want to implement any more withdrawals because his interdiction strategy had been working.* He was ordered to plan for the draw-downs and get things moving.

His continual U.S-ARVN operations along the common border had greatly disrupted the NVA battle plan. In recent fighting over 3,000 NVA had been killed, but more importantly over 800 cached weapons had been uncovered in addition to 380+ tons of rice. That was enough food to have served 450,000 days of enemy troop rations.

And as the patrolling effort continued more of the enemy's secreted supply caches were being uncovered. Soon the communists were having trouble moving any new material into S. Vietnam.

Additional strong retaliatory communist attacks from Cambodia struck dozens of our firebases in August 1970. All were defeated causing still more losses to the North. Intelligence had picked up on some of the pending NVA attacks and B-52 missions were unleashed. Thousands more NVA troops became casualties in those bombings.

(As stated earlier on Sept 3, 1969 Ho Chi Minh died. He was replaced by a "collective committee", which was dedicated to unifying all of Vietnam under communism.)

John Vann met with President Nixon in Dec 1969 and they spoke of the progress being made and seen in Vietnam. *Vann felt that with improved heavy weapons capability and U.S. airpower the ARVN would be able to handle the NVA when they returned.*

Like many he knew that as soon as they had rebuilt their forces from the TET defeats the NVA would again attack in force.

Negotiations by the Nixon team with Russia resulted in the signing of a Nuclear non-proliferation treaty on Nov 24, 1969. This was followed with the beginning of the SALT talks in Helsinki between Russia and America. The SALT talks, (Strategic Arms Limitation Treaty), were seen as vital to reducing nuclear tensions worldwide. Conventional wisdom felt that the Soviets were far behind us in MIRV, (multiple independent reentry vehicle), capability. That capability enabled us to mount multiple warheads on each missile, thereby making each missile launch a catastrophic attack. (The Soviets launched Sputnik way ahead of us, why would they be behind us now?)

Because of that poor insight, the SALT negotiations actually benefitted the Soviets. When the agreement was finally reached each side had limits on the number of missiles, with the Soviets actually far ahead of America. Thus when they completed their MIRV program, they had many more warheads than the U.S. did.

(One positive note was that the Soviets had to stop their anti-ballistic missile program. Even though they had not made much headway, it was felt that if they did create a viable system they might be tempted to attack.)

On November 25 Pres. Nixon renounced Germ Warfare weapons and ordered the U.S. stocks destroyed. *Russia was supposed to do the same, but they deceitfully did not.* In December the "rabid anti-communist" Richard Nixon even allowed some easing of trade restrictions with Red China. Nixon was setting the table for his secret meetings.

During the late 60s into the early 70s the U.S. was spending $80 Billion a year on defense, while the Soviets were spending over $100 Billion per year. No one else could ever come close to those levels, and that was why both were called superpowers. Our largest expense was in SE Asia. One of the reasons for the high Soviet price tag was their non-stop construction of a large Blue-water Navy. Ever since the crisis in Cuba in 1962 the Soviets began building dozens of large missile carrying destroyers and cruisers. In addition helicopter carriers were being added to their fleets. And as their fleets grew the Soviets began sailing into waters they had not strayed before, the Mediterranean, Indian Ocean, South Atlantic and the Southern Pacific. New Soviet bases were being built in S. Yemen, Somalia and Egypt. This was a clear threat to the worlds oil supplies.

Twice that year the Democratic Senate shot down Nixon appointees to the Supreme Court. In both cases the choices were denied because they were not *politically acceptable to the left leaning Democrats in the Senate.* A dangerous standard was appearing, where politics were being used to decide the makeup of the court instead of capability.

The main strategy the Democrats began employing was their desire to use the courts to implement changes to our lives without passing laws.

Laws require discourse and have to go through the Congressional procedures. Judicial rulings only require a decision by conspiratorial jurists.

For them the Courts needed to be staffed with "acceptable appointees" who would then decide an issue with no input from the people.

(If politics are to be the keystone to staffing the Judicial Branch of our government, then all of those appointed judges must appear before the American people every two-six years and be voted on.)

During the heavy combat of 1969, 11,527 more Americans had died in the war.

As 1970 began in III Corps S. Vietnam Gen. Abrams units were actually driving the NVA out of the country. His hit and run and ambush strategy was working. During the recent fighting against the VC 5th Div another 500 enemy had been killed and they lost almost 450,000 rounds of ammo, 2600 large caliber shells, (rockets &mortars), and another 150 tons of rice.

COSVN decided to backhaul all of their remaining caches before the aggressive Americans and ARVN troops found them. With no more forward movement the tons of supplies shipped in from China and the Communist bloc had to remain in huge stockpiles inside Cambodia. As far as the NVA were concerned that was alright because they were immune from attack.

As shown earlier Cambodia's national integrity had been compromised by the communist N. Vietnamese forces in the early 60's. Prince Sihanouk had "tried to keep his country neutral", but recognized that his small military could not keep the communists at bay. He silently appeased and ignored their intrusion, and then made sure he profited greatly from his treaty with China and the growing NVA presence along his eastern borders.

And as the communist supply situation in the southern areas improved more and more NVA units were able to move down the trail and occupy Cambodia's eastern areas.

Sihanouk broke off relations with the U.S. in 1965 when it appeared to all that the communist North would soon win.

But during those initial "profitable peaceful years", thousands of native Cambodian communist rebels were being trained and supplied by the 75,000 man NVA force moving through and operating in Cambodia.

The Khmer Rouge was formed from native Cambodians, and like all good communists they began to make their presence known by slowly conquering outlying villages and advancing westward towards the capital of Phnom Penh.

After the heavy NVA losses from TET had been revealed the wily Sihanouk began turning back to America for support. He was waking up to the fact that Cambodia's northern and eastern provinces were "practically North Vietnamese territory" and that his rule and country were being threatened by the communists.

The Prince hoped his alliance with China would keep their common enemy the Vietnamese at bay, but Mao's insane Cultural Revolution had ripped China apart. They were not going to help him against the encroaching NVA.

Sihanouk tried to repair relations with America in 1968 but LBJ refused to get involved. Within a week of Nixon's inauguration the Prince requested U.S. help with his dangerous situation. Generals Wheeler and Abrams agreed that we had to get involved because Intelligence was reporting that some 40,000 NVA troops had moved into the border areas near Vietnam pending renewed assaults into the South. More were in the rear bases and moving down on the trail. *(Those issues were a large part of the reasoning as to why Pres. Nixon eventually ordered the secret bombing of the NVA base areas inside Cambodia during March-June 1969.)*

Sihanouk knew of and secretly approved of the bombing effort, and reported that no Cambodian civilians lived in those areas. (There were civilians there, but they were now communists.) The helpful bombings were not publicly announced for fear of putting Sihanouk in a political straitjacket and causing communist retaliation against him and his nation. As shown before, in April leaks to the *NY Times* made the bombings public. The Prince was asked about the bombings and publicly stated that Cambodia did not object. The anti-war activists became enraged.

Pres. Nixon was asked to come out on a visit to discuss the long term implications that Cambodia faced. *Soon after Prince Sihanouk ordered Hanoi to remove all of their forces from Cambodia, including any remaining Viet Cong.* Sihanouk appointed Lon Nol his Defense Minister to head the new right wing coalition government and to try to stop the communist rebellion that was growing.

It was too little too late.

From the many years of recon efforts the extensive NVA base areas inside the Cambodian border were referred to by number. Base Area 354 was the southern most and the closest to Tay Ninh and Saigon. Moving northward and east were areas 707, 353 and 352 which was the base area closest to An Loc. Further north were 350 and the last known one was 351. Each of those latter areas supported separate enemy units and each was so large they extended into both countries!

Base area 359 was located inside S. Vietnam in war zone D while 609 was to the north. With such a well established logistical support network it was easy to see why the communists were operating in a never ending cascade.

It was learned by the enemy that the U.S. 1st Inf Div was in the next round of troop withdrawals. That would cut 30% out of the U.S. presence in the border area and the communist commanders felt it was time to get aggressive. COSVN decided to try to extend new trail systems near Base 707 deeper into the South towards Tay Ninh.

On February 21, 1970 Henry Kissinger met in secret with North Vietnamese senior representatives Le Duc Tho and Xuan Thuy. They met in a private house near Paris to work on the peace treaty that would end the war. (The formal negotiations were ongoing but unaware of the secret meetings.) Using the usual communist philosophy Tho stalled and haggled over every minute detail that came up. While Kissinger had some leeway in the negotiations, Tho had to check in with the party leadership constantly. One of their ways of stalling.

It was around this time that the North Vietnamese directed the conquering of southern Laos. As stated earlier JFK had been unhappy when the communists had reneged on the Geneva Accords. All of the U.S. advisors had left, but only 40 out 6,000 NVA left. They continued their support of the Pathet Lao and actively helped in many operations. America however was forced to run a secret war to try to stem the tide.

Souvanna Phouma knew of and wanted our help, and did not object to the secret bombing of the Ho Chi Minh Trail in Laos during the 1960s. But by early 1970 Gen. Van Pao and his Meo tribesmen were overmatched by the NVA and Pathet Lao. When Kissinger brought up the recent NVA offensive in Laos he received another lecture from the communist hard liners. *"It was Vietnam's destiny to rule all of Indochina.*

When you were at your strongest you did not defeat us.

Now that you are leaving, the "puppets" in the South cannot win."

There was no way we could negotiate with the communists.

Kissinger reported back, and it took almost a month for Pres. Nixon to authorize additional B-52 strikes and to enlist the help of Thai troops to try to stop the communists in Laos. His band-aid approach worked for a while but Nixon received heaps of additional scorn from Congressional and media critics. Then the next problem hit.

Pres. Nixon had encouraged Cambodian anti-communist actions because it worked to tie up the NVA forces in that sector. **But in March 1970 open war finally broke out against the encroaching communist NVA who not only refused to leave Cambodia, but were attacking Cambodia's troops with their ally the Khmer Rouge!** It was a war the Cambodians could not win alone. But no one in the Administration expected that they would be alone.

Prince Sihanouk had gone to France for another vacation and was going to go to Moscow and then Peking to get their help in evicting the NVA.

On March 8 demonstrations in Phnom Penh began to protest against the NVA. The Cambodian people had learned of the secret trade deals with China and of the large NVA presence in their country. They were outraged. (Like all of the other people in that region, the native Khmer were ancient enemies with the Vietnamese.)

Later that month the Communist embassies were struck and besieged. More demonstrations followed and the Parliament passed a resolution to reaffirm their neutrality but also to defend their territory. All prior trade agreements were renounced and Sihanouk decided to go to Moscow for help. (SOG 244-46)

Lon Nol then ousted the missing Prince in a coup becoming the Prime Minister. Cheng Heng became their Chief of State. Nol asked Hanoi to remove all of the NVA and VC forces by the 15th and announced a 10,000 man expansion of their army. *He also sought the help of the United Nations hoping for Western troops similar to what had happened in Korea. But this was not the U.N. of 1950, and they refused to get involved.* Cambodia would have to face the communists by themselves.

(At that point the U.N. should have been disbanded or kicked out of the U.S.)

Undeterred by the change in leadership in Phnom Penh the North Vietnamese used the incidents to push up their plan to control all of Indochina. Gen. Tran Van Tra who commanded COSVN at that time sent two regiments of the 1st NVA Div towards Phnom Penh. Within two weeks the amount of territory they controlled doubled.

With the deterioration in his nation from the increased fighting Nol was forced to ask for active U.S. assistance. Pres. Nixon decided to send aerial aid since it would assist our overall goals in Indochina and make the quickest impact. But once the fighting began it became apparent that our bombing alone could not stem the communist tide. (Just like Vietnam.)

The well trained Khmer Rouge (with NVA help), steadily attacked westward into Cambodia. In short order the towns of Krek, Mimot, and Snoul fell to the NVA and Khmer troops. Two of Cambodia's seventeen provinces had fallen, and five more were on the brink. Sihanouk had deliberately kept the Cambodian military weak and ineffectual as a hedge against a coup. They could not keep the communists out. Now out of power, but hoping to get back in, Sihanouk decried that the capitalists had done all of this behind his back and he aligned himself with the Khmer Rouge.

To assist the Cambodians and themselves the ARVN launched a major ground attack into Cambodia's Kandal Province on March 27-28 1970.

They hoped to draw the NVA troops back towards them.

And advancing up to the border were the U.S. Cavalry units. Their advance firebases came under increasing attacks as the NVA fought the aggressive and encroaching U.S. troops.

At their secret meeting on April 4 Henry Kissinger was again chastised by Le Duc Tho. *He vowed to overthrow Lon Nol and install a regime acceptable to North Vietnam.*

Their new leaders will allow us the use of their territory for sanctuaries.

Kissinger tartly responded it is impressive that the Pathet Lao speak Vietnamese, and now so do the Khmer Rouge. But it was to no avail for Kissinger could see that Cambodia was doomed to suffer this invasion and we could do little to help.

Upon Kissinger's returning to the White House, Pres. Nixon learned of Hanoi's true aims and that nothing short of force could stop them. The CIA gave the Cambodians just weeks before they fell. There was no way Pres. Nixon could ask Congress to send troops to Cambodia to help them fight off the communists. *Nixon decided not to ask, a secret operation was being planned.*

As the Cav units moved up to the border in late March orders had gone out to plan an operation into the NVA base areas across the border. **A month later on April 30, 1970 U.S. armored and airborne forces crossed the border of Cambodia to join with the ARVN forces already there.** Their limited mission lacked clear intelligence, but was centered on striking the enemy base areas 352 & 353. Once those base defenses were crushed the forces would spread out trying to find the suspected NVA supply depots.

CIA Director Richard Helms told Pres. Nixon to strike hard for he would suffer the same domestic price no matter how much we did. The President thought about doing so, plus striking Haiphong in retaliation for the NVA attacks into Cambodia.
But at the last minute he wrongly decided not to.

President Nixon went on TV to explain to the nation that our forces went in to destroy the NVA sanctuaries and supply depots. The result of this action would safeguard our servicemen and shorten the war. Nixon wrongly mentioned we were after COSVN, the NVA command in the south. When it was not found the negative and hostile media claimed (erroneously) that the Cambodian Incursion was a total failure. *(Weeks earlier COSVN had (again) almost been hit by a B-52 strike. Their leaders and staff decided to move further into Cambodia to avoid any more attempts.)*

In Saigon and in Washington it was hoped that with the ARVN and U.S. actions the NVA would stop fighting the Cambodians and return to fight us. That would relieve the military pressure on the outmatched Cambodians and give them a chance to setup a defense. *This secret incursion caught the NVA by surprise and after losing the initial battles they wisely retreated rather than fight.*

In America the vocal anti-war protestors and the media screamed and demonstrated against this "expansion of the war". **Again the media was strangely silent on the fact that North Vietnam had silently invaded Cambodia years earlier, and was now attacking them, Laos and S. Vietnam at the same time.** In an effort to quiet the anti-war protests Nixon announced another round of troop withdrawals. But violent protests broke out at many colleges anyway, especially at Kent State University. *Days of wonton arson and destruction occurred on the campus and within the city by those "war protestors".*

The violence was so bad it caused the Mayor to declare a state of emergency and ask for the National Guard. On May 4 the protests culminated in the infamous shooting incident on the campus by the National Guard troops. Most of those hit by the fusillade were innocent students on the campus. (The firing should have been directed at the ones involved in the crimes of looting and arson, not kids walking around on campus.)

On May 14 the situation was repeated at Jackson State College in Mississippi. Police thought a sniper was firing at them and they fired into a crowd of students killing two and wounding 14. Because of its location and the mostly black student body this incident received little national press coverage.

(Liberal journalist James Fallow wrote a revealing passage that highlighted the drastic changes in our nation. In 1941 the graduating class at Harvard saw hundreds of their former students enter the military and serve in WWII. Thirty five never returned. Fallow's Harvard class of 1970 avoided the military like the plague. Service was something "other people" did, and few from Harvard went into the military. Because so few of those privileged elites (across the nation) joined the military services, the burden of Vietnam fell onto the underprivileged and the poor.)

Riots on college campuses were becoming a common nightmare.

In 1969 student radicals, liberals and black panthers took over the University at Berkley in California. Their aggressive efforts actually shut down the school. Ronald Reagan the former actor had become active in conservative causes, giving a fine speech at the 64 Republican Convention. In 1967 he won the election for California's Governor by over one million votes, a tough chore in the Democratic State.

Like many he was upset at the disruptive actions at Berkley. Reagan recognized that their hostile and intimidating tactics were the same as the communist led strikes he had faced down in Hollywood 20 years earlier. So Gov. Reagan called in the State Police and the National Guard to put a stop to the violent protestors. For seventeen days they stood watch across the state's campuses and trouble spots. Agitators were arrested and peace was restored. The protests stopped, and most of California's citizens were glad he had stood up to the agitators. Unfortunately he was alone among the nation's Governors. Most gave in to the student demands and demonstrations which only invited more troubles the next time an issue arose.

(In NYC a violent domestic terror group called the *weathermen* were putting bombs together in a safe house on 11th Street near 5th Ave. On March 6, 1970 they made a faulty circuit sparking an explosion which destroyed the brownstone killing three of them.)

The Democrats still controlled the Congress and reacted to the latest anti-war protests by revoking the Gulf of Tonkin Resolution which curtailed the Presidents power to commit our forces. Senators Mark Hatfield and George McGovern tried to pass an amendment to force Pres. Nixon to leave Vietnam by December 1970. It was revised to December 71, but was again defeated in the Senate.

With the heavy protests at home Pres. Nixon was forced to put restrictions on the Cambodian operation. U.S. forces could only go across the border about 15 miles, the operation would be ended within 60 days, and all Americans would be withdrawn from Cambodia by June 30. *Knowing of those restraints on our actions the NVA simply moved out of range and waited for our troops to leave.* Their lost supplies and weapons would be replaced.

The ARVN mechanized units and marines did not have any restrictions on their actions. They penetrated almost thirty miles across the border destroying anything they could.

On the plus side for MACV and the ARVN was the fact that many huge communist storage areas were uncovered. By using the Ho Chi Minh trail and the Cambodian port of Sihanoukville the NVA had secretly built up many substantial storehouse areas of weapons and supplies. One area was so large it was called the City.

It was one mile long and two miles deep, housing hundreds of structures with over 171 tons of ammo, 38 tons of food, and thousands of weapons. (Despite the claim that in communism all are equal, mess halls found in the City were listed as VIP/Officer, and enlisted.)

Another area housed a large motor pool with hundreds of vehicles. A third depot was called Rock Island East for the mountains of ammunition discovered. It contained 326 tons of ammo and weapons. A forth area was found a few miles further north and contained another 203 tons of ammo and supplies.

Base Area 609 was found in imposing terrain that all knew would be a bloody fight. It was bombed instead. Also found and destroyed were communist training centers, hospitals, office facilities, R&R facilities and class rooms. As the final days of the operation went on Base Areas 350, 351 & 707 were also entered and picked clean of thousands of tons of supplies and weapons.

Our Intelligence people were amazed that these massive supply depots were sitting there just across the border unknown to anyone. Fifty thousand ARVN troops and thirty thousand U.S. troops took part in the Cambodian Incursion. **They captured over 23,000 rifles, 2,500 crew served** weapons, 15 million rounds of ammo, 100,000 anti-aircraft rounds, dozens of tons of mortars, hand grenades and rockets, 435 vehicles and hundreds of tons of food and other supplies.

It was estimated that the captured equipment could have equipped 55 enemy infantry battalions, and 82 crew served weapons battalions!

(Also uncovered were thousands of 85mm artillery rounds, a gun not used south of I Corps, and tons of tank ammunition. Both types of ammo were clear signs of the coming NVA invasion.)

The liberal media never mentioned the massive weapons and supply caches found or what they meant. One cache that was found contained almost a million dollars of medical supplies from West Germany, Britain and American Quakers! As much of those supplies and munitions as possible were packed up and shipped to Saigon. Then those NVA supply crates were ironically flown to Lon Nol's Cambodian troops to help them in their fight against the communists.

This Cambodian Incursion stopped two enemy offensives slated for the end of the year. Because of the unrelenting operations by the U.S. and ARVN forces the fighting in III and IV Corps came to a virtual end! *One enemy officer wrote after the war that the Americans and ARVN did not realize how close they came to defeating those southern most units.*

But as staggering as those amounts of captured supplies and enemy casualties were, it would only buy two years of time for S. Vietnam since our part of the operation had to be ended by June 30. Had our forces been able to continue the mission much more could have been accomplished. Hysterics and hyperbole by the media and those few thousand anti-war activists were allowed to stop a very successful military operation, one that could have added years of time for Saigon to get stronger, or as the NVA officer said defeated them.

Because of those U.S. Senators serious fallout would eventually befall Lon Nol and his nation. The NVA forces that had moved westward had no reason to leave as U.S. domestic pressure and political rulings forced Pres. Nixon to scale back the operation. They continued attacking westward with the Khmer Rouge and would soon control a 125 mile stretch of the Mekong River. What slowed them down was the loss of their supplies.

The Cambodian Incursion bought Lon Nol and his country just six months to strengthen their defenses. It was not enough time. *It was possible that Cambodia might have been saved if we had been able to defeat the NVA in Cambodia.* But again that operation should have been instituted years before by the ones who had created and gotten us into this mess.

Knowing that we had to leave at the end of June the NVA quietly returned that last week to snipe and mortar our forces. Our casualties increased because our forces could not attack to drive the NVA off. By July 1, 1970 all 30,000 U.S. troops were out of Cambodia though the ARVN units remained on the other side of the border a while longer. We had lost 284 Americans in the raid, the ARVN lost 800.

The NVA lost over 10,000.

After the Cambodian Incursion ended a great quite settled over III Corps. The NVA in the area had had enough for now. Their total losses since Feb were over 16,000 killed. (Sadly ARVN Gen. Tri who led their part of the Incursion and Newsweek reporter Francois Sully the pain in the neck for Gen. Harkins, died in a needless ARVN helicopter malfunction and fire.)

Operation Freedom Dial allowed the use of U.S. tactical fighter-bombers in support of the Cambodian Army as it fought against the 100,000+ army of combined communist forces. *But on June 30, 1970 the Senate passed the Cooper-Church amendment that barred using U.S. funds to support operations in Cambodia.*

Negotiations with the White House delayed implementation, but this was a clear signal that the anti-war members in the Congress were against any further action in South East Asia. *On Dec 22, 1970 a similar bill was passed to isolate Laos.*

(Senator Frank Church had been one of those Democrats who jumped up to pass the Gulf of Tonkin Resolution in 1964. He soon realized he was wrong and fought with LBJ many times over the years earning Johnson's hatred. Now he was working against any effort to try to stop the communist takeover of Indochina.)

At home the anti-war riots and protests had died down but the colleges and universities seethed with dissent. A special commission was convened to analyze the situation and it reported that the nation was splitting apart. The war had to end.

But one factor that the protestors and the media did not comprehend was that you simply cannot pull 450,000 troops out of a war. A withdrawal from a war zone must be planned and enacted in a series of organized events or else you have a collapse like the despicable fall of the 8th Army in Korea in Dec-1950 or the collapse in France in 1940.

(An organized event was the 1st Mar Div fight from the Chosin Reservoir or the great escape at Dunkirk by the British and French.)

To protect your forces the movements have to be well planned.

As the months passed Pres. Nixon was keeping his promise and withdrawing our forces from Vietnam. But another issue that had to be addressed was the worldwide view that America was running away. It was possible that more wars could spring up if the communist world sensed we were collapsing militarily and politically.

The reason JFK decided to go into Vietnam was to stand up to the Communist's constant maneuverings and his belief that Khrushchev thought him weak.

Johnson was afraid to lose another nation to communism and be blamed like Truman was (rightfully so), over China. (That was one reason why Truman sent troops to Korea.)

Nixon knew we could not just leave South Vietnam.

In the secret talks in Paris the increasingly arrogant Tho insisted that the NVA would never withdraw from any territory they currently occupied in the South. Realizing that we had no leverage to get them to leave, Nixon agreed with Kissinger's assessment that we had to give in on that subject as we had in Korea.

As shown earlier, on November 4, 1970 Pres. Nixon explained to the nation the unwanted but necessary standstill-ceasefire idea. America had already removed 165,000 troops from Vietnam, and another 90,000 would be out by the spring. Vietnamization was proceeding as planned, and as our troops could be released they would come home.

He asked for the support of the vast silent majority of Americans so the war could be ended properly. That speech was one of his best as he explained,

"The more divided we are at home, the less likely the communists will negotiate. Let us also understand that North Vietnam cannot defeat or humiliate us, only Americans can do that." The public rallied to support him and the Congress backed off their demands for immediate withdrawal. During 1970 another 6,065 Americans were lost.

Europe and The Middle East

Poland was again the scene of brutal repression. In December 1970 workers in the city of Gdansk rebelled against government directed price increases on all foods. This was the worst outbreak of violence in the nation since the 1956 uprising. Wladyslaw Gomulka who was once a "liberal" was worried that his citizens would follow the Prague uprising and unrest from 1968. He ordered his soldiers and tanks to fire into the crowds, scores were killed. But after witnessing the butchery in Prague, (some of those attacking units were Polish), the mood of the Polish citizens turned angry and they threatened a nationwide protest and shutdown. To placate the masses the Polish Politburo ousted Gomulka and reversed the price hikes.

Edward Gierek became the First Secretary. He had worked in the coal mines in France and Belgium as a youth and remembered how the world was supposed to function. He began to relax the straitjacket of communist rule and tried modernizing his nation. *Soon after Gierek became the first Eastern European ruler to visit the U.S., and met with Pres. Nixon who approved loans to help him modernize.* A follow on treaty with West Germany increased their commercial ties with the West. (Food price strikes returned in 1976 and resulted in arrests, but no violence.)

Because of his harsh reaction to the protests in 1970 Gomulka became a non-person, the secret and common penalty to communists who are "out of favor".

His harsh actions had unknowingly sowed the seeds for the Polish Solidarity Movement that would emerge in a decade. And that brave movement would help bring the end of communism in Europe!

The SALT talks, Strategic Arms Limitations that had begun in 1969 were continuing slowly. Trade agreements had been enacted with the Russians allowing them to buy U.S. grains to makeup for their constant shortfalls. (Soviet work ethic was; they pretend to pay us so we pretend to work.) But even with this softening of relations with America the Soviets continued their expansion into the Middle East. Brezhnev had sent 15,000 troops to Egypt, installed advanced SAM-3 missile batteries, and had Soviet pilots fly combat missions all along Egypt's borders. A Soviet naval base was also established in Alexandria.

One result of this latest saber-rattling was the sale of U.S. made weapons especially jet aircraft to Israel. That effort was an attempt to maintain Israel's mastery of the air around the region. Egypt and Israel continued having air and artillery duels in their never ending conflict and terrorist attacks inside Israel were ongoing and deadly.

Nearby Jordan was also under increasing pressure and suffering their own attacks from guerilla fighters from the PFLP, Popular Front for the Liberation of Palestine. PFLP fighters had been using Jordan as a refuge but when the King started to crackdown on their activities they tried as shown before to oust him on June 9, 1970.

World wide terrorism continued to rear its savage head as the mostly Islamic terrorists continued murdering innocents at will.

In September PFLP guerrillas hijacked two jetliners flying them into Jordan. Then they attempted to hijack an Israeli jet but were stopped by their security forces. The next day they grabbed a British aircraft and forced it to land in Jordan.

In all the terrorists had 475 hostages. Threatening to kill them, the terrorists bargained those innocent lives for 450 Palestinians held in Israeli jails.

Jordan's King Hussein decided to end the PFLP presence in his nation and sent in his troops. Fighting began and Syria responded by sending in 300 of their tanks to support the Palestinian guerrillas. It appeared a full blown war was breaking out.

Pres. Nixon ordered the Sixth Fleet to prepare to respond to this crisis along with U.S. units stationed in Germany. Israel quickly called up their army. By August an uneasy ceasefire went into effect.

(Nixon was determined to support King Hussein, even if it meant a confrontation with Russia. With this threat to an ally Pres. Nixon was contemplating dropping paratroopers from the 82d Airborne into Amman and sending the Marines at sea into the country via helicopter assault.)

More Syrian tanks crossed into Jordan, and King Hussein informed the U.S. that Israeli jets would be welcomed. Luckily his U.S. trained air force was able to beat back the Syrian Armor. *Curiously General Hafez al-Assad the Syrian AF commander did not commit his aircraft to the battle.* If he had they might have bested the Jordanians, and who could say what would have been the fallout if King Hussein was toppled. (Or if we would have intervened.)

Instead, on September 24, 1970 the small war in Jordan was ended and the regime of Salah al-Jadid in Syria was suddenly overthrown. General Hafez al-Assad conveniently became the new ruler of Syria. It was a position he did not relinquish until his death in October, 2000. On the 28th Egypt's Nasser died from a heart attack.

He was replaced by Anwar Sadat.

The pieces for the next war were taking shape.

OPEC, the Organization of Oil Producing Countries decided they were going to reset the wholesale price of oil. Those countries consisted primarily of the lands of the Middle East and they saw the potential for using their oil as leverage on the world stage. The wholesale price change was announced to the major oil companies operating in Saudi Arabia, Kuwait, Iran, Iraq, Abu Dhabi and Qatar. Their price increase would generate an additional $10 billion dollars for those countries. Gasoline prices worldwide increased and this was just the start of a major economic problem for the West. Since oil was now a major part of modern life the price increase would resonate throughout the economies of the world as inflation took hold.

Cambodia and Vietnam

In early Jan 1971 Cambodian and ARVN forces tried to re-open Route 4 from their capitol Phnom Penh to the port of Kompong Som. The NVA and Khmer forces were too strong to allow any rebuilding of the road and bridges and all resupply to the city had to be done with boat convoys along the Mekong River.

By the end of the month the Khmer Rouge attacked Phnom Penh for the first time. By the end of 1971 over a third of Cambodia had fallen under communist domination! (Operation Freedom Dial continued on a smaller and quieter pace until August 1973 when President Nixon was forced by Congress to end all U.S. support in Indochina. Cambodia collapsed soon after.)

Following the (limited) success of the Cambodian operation Pres. Nixon was able to convince Pres. Thieu that the ARVN should attempt a similar move against the Ho Chi Minh trail at Tchepone in Laos. *Negotiations with the conniving North Vietnamese was making little progress and in a short while most of the U.S. forces would be gone. This might be the last chance to hurt the NVA and try to convince them to negotiate.*

Many in the State Dept. were against the action out of fear the NVA would react negatively and attack deeper into Laos as they had in Cambodia. But in reality they were already fighting in Laos and controlled a lot of the country. (As stated earlier the 1962 Laos Agreement was ignored by the North Vietnamese before the ink was dry.)

The North Vietnamese kept large and increasing numbers of troops in Laos, and by 1972 there were over 70,000 NVA troops based in Laos alone. This force guarded and operated the Laotian part of the Ho Chi Minh Trail, and when needed they fought the U.S. backed forces for control of the country. As time went on the south-eastern region of Laos became a huge forward base area #604, despite the repeated air attacks conducted by the U.S.

A large scale operation called **Lam Son 719** was planned and enacted. Firebases had to be organized and setup in advance of the actual invasion into Laos, and the U.S. sent in a mechanized unit with engineers to open up the area of Route 9 westward past Khe Sanh. Route 9 was the same road used by the Air Cav in 1968 when they went to help the Marines during the fight for Khe Sanh. But few ever traveled westward from Khe Sanh after 1969.

Word of this large operation was sent out by the communist spies before the final plans were done, but the ARVN units were still able to initiate the attack successfully on Feb 8. 1971. ARVN Gen. Xuan Lam planned to send an armored force westward into Tchepone and destroy whatever NVA supply depots and equipment they found.

Infantry, Airborne and Ranger units would seize the outlying ridges to protect the flanks of the attack. A total of just over 15,000 ARVN troops would be committed. (Division strength.)

For mobility Lam Son would use hundreds of U.S. helicopters to airlift in the ARVN troops and artillery into position. But no US troops would go into Laos. If the NVA fled the area the way they had in Cambodia, then the ARVN would continue the attack westward in the hopes of damaging the extensive Ho Chi Minh Trail.

Again the overall plan was to try to gain time by destroying NVA supplies and infrastructure. Massive NVA supply points and oil pipelines were known to be in the area, and the Laotian part of the Trail was now a hard surfaced multi-road network.

Operation Lam Son was successful for the first two weeks, but then angry NVA units began to counterattack. (SOG units attacked into the Ashau Valley to try to keep the NVA based there occupied.) *Unlike Cambodia, Hanoi directed that those areas had to be defended.* There was a larger number of NVA units in that area of Laos, much more than had been hiding in the eastern sections of Cambodia the year before. And because they had not been involved in any recent heavy fighting, (orders from Hanoi), most of them were at full strength. As time went by the attacking NVA forces greatly outnumbered the ARVN. (No U.S. ground units or advisors were allowed into the battle and that might also have motivated the NVA to stay and fight.)

As the ARVN slowly advanced into Laos some forward enemy base areas were found and destroyed, but not to the extent desired or needed.

A lack of intelligence about the area caused major problems when the ARVN force reached Aloui some 12 miles inside Laos. There was a dearth of up to date information on anything in that part of Laos and the western section of Route 9 had been abandoned for so long that it was basically impassible to anything except tracked vehicles. ARVN commanders and staff were still not capable of fixing the many problems they faced and their forward movement soon stopped.

As the ARVN units operated inside Laos they destroyed some enemy armor depots and supply areas. *Numerous fuel pipelines were uncovered and damaged, proof of the intensive communist logistical effort. (This was evidence that the next NVA assault would use armored vehicles.)* Facing increasing counterattacks the ARVN Marines were positioned outside of Tchepone and blunted the NVA frontal attacks. That allowed their armored units to fall back.

NVA counterattacks increased in strength as armor and artillery units were also being brought in. They also increased their infantry attacks as three divisions joined the fight. They began to strike into the periphery of the incursion. (Similar to what we had done to the Germans in the Battle of the Bulge in 1945.) The NVA human wave tactics reinforced with armored assaults began to breakup the firebase outpost network that protected the roadway and the ARVN mechanized forces. Dangerous helicopter missions were the norm as the U.S. pilots ferried ARVN units around and pulled other units out.

NVA Divisions 320, 304 and 308 struck into the northern side of the ARVN attack, while the NVA 2nd and 302 Div plus local VC Regiments struck into the southern side. All of the enemy forces had tanks, PT-76, T-54 & T-55s plus heavy artillery. After two weeks the NVA also began bringing in SAM missile units to reduce the effectiveness of U.S. air support. (Our air attacks repeatedly saved the day for the ARVN.)

Like Dien Bien Phu, those outlying firebases were mutually supporting and as each fell it forced the next firebase to endure heavier attacks. In short order the ARVN had to enact a rapid and eventually uncoordinated road and aerial retreat. Over 100 helicopters, dozens of vehicles and a thousand of their best troops were lost, (many were captured), to the fierce NVA attacks.

One of the negatives to the battle was that the ARVN lost many of their emerging leaders who perished trying to control the panicky troops. During the multi-week battle it was felt the communists had lost around 10,000 killed, in large part to our airpower. We lost about 200 men, most of them aircrews.

After the battle was ended the ARVN decided to pull back from the DMZ and the western areas of I Corps to consolidate their limited forces as best as they could. Their forces could not push the NVA out of the Ashau Valley, (nor could ours), and it was more important to protect the cities and coastal region in the north. In pulling back it gave the NVA a free ride to setup advance bases in the dense jungles of the region and prepare for their next invasion. But there were not enough units to hold the line everywhere.

On the plus side the ARVN had showed that they could plan and fight a large scale battle without U.S. ground troops. However they still had a way to go to fight the NVA toe to toe, and were also dependent upon American airpower.

Unfortunately that asset would also be leaving soon.

Detractors claimed the attack was a waste and a failure, (they claimed that everything was a failure), but the options available were few and getting smaller. *Pres. Nixon and his team knew that the best end to Vietnam that we could hope for was that our troops would leave and maybe S. Vietnam could survive.*

Trying to hurt the enemy to gain some time was all that could be done in 1971.

Unlike Johnson or Kennedy, Nixon had a better understanding about foreign affairs and was well traveled during his time as V.P. He was about to stun the world with his Foreign Policy initiatives. *(It was again tragically ironic that the "liberals" had created and dragged us into this quagmire, and the hawkish Nixon had to get us out.)*

After the war ended NVA Gen. Le Trong Tan who was the commander at Tchepone remarked that the American leaders failed to beat us because you fought wrong. Had you attacked at one point on the trail and held on to it we could not have fought the war the way we did. He felt that the time for us to have made that strike was during 1966-67, before the Trail in Laos was completed and the plans for TET began.

During Operation Lam Son the peace negotiations were still deadlocked, but the relationship between North Vietnam and China had fallen. Mao's Cultural Revolution had paralyzed the nation and they began cutting back on trade with North Vietnam. And the death of Ho ended the common ground and beliefs that he and Mao had shared. The final straw for China was that the North did not follow China's advice on the war. North Vietnam pursued their own strategy and fought the war the way they wanted. As China pulled back their logistic support they reduced their troops too. By mid-71 they had all left, so Russia stepped in to fill the void.

Pres. Nixon was aware that Brezhnev wanted better relations with America. Nixon decided to link Russia's needs with their actions in other parts of the world, like Vietnam. But Russia did not control Ho or the Viet Minh, just as they did not control Tito in Yugoslavia. It is also doubtful they would have stopped the North even if they could have. North Vietnam was bleeding and keeping the Americans busy, and all the while the Soviets were expanding their military forces and subversions across the globe.

One thing the Russians did not do was react to the Lam Son operation. They gave the North some lip service, but did not send any forces to the region. Russia desired a summit, and Nixon knew it.

America

At home Nixon was wrongly convinced by economist Milton Friedman to take America off of the gold standard. This allowed the value of the dollar to "float" as the marketplace demanded. (Our share of the world's gold supply had dropped to less than 20%.) This act also gave the Federal Reserve full discretion to intervene in the economy to "smooth out business cycles". *Since that time the unelected Federal Reserve has manipulated our economy by using the interest rates it sets.*

(In 1912 the Congress created the Federal Reserve to handle the nation's finances.

Prior to that the Congress had been so tasked.)

Pres. Nixon also established the EPA, Environmental Protection Agency to continue the work of reducing pollution and safeguarding our environment.

He declared a war on Cancer and set Federal Subsidies to aid in the research to beat cancer.

Another important social truth that the Liberals and the major media never gave credit to nor would they ever admit to, but under Pres. Nixon more affirmative action was enacted and more southern schools were desegregated than under any other Administration in history!

By this point America's cities were beginning to face financial collapse.

LBJ's Great Society programs had multiplied the costs of welfare and social programs exponentially. Without the revenue to pay for these programs the cities were spending and borrowing money in unsustainable amounts. In March California's Governor Ronald Reagan had urged that the state's welfare rolls be cut to save the budget. California's Democrats fought him hard and hoped he would not win his re-election.

Although everyone wants to help the poor, having them sit around and collect money was becoming ridiculous. Those in need must be supported until they could move off of welfare but the law gave no insistence that they had to! Birth control was not provided, even though the "pill" had been out and proven safe for years. Thus anyone on welfare was free to become pregnant with the taxpayers paying for the pre-natal, birthing and childhood costs in addition to the costs keeping the adults cared for.

And the laws the Democrats had passed stated that the more children in the household the more money the welfare recipient was given. That provided the incentive for unscrupulous participants to have more children. It was criminal.

Those adults could not provide for themselves, and now the taxpayers were handing them the resources to have additional children they still could not provide for.

The result was a large increase in the numbers of impoverished children. Many would grow up with social and psychological issues that would cause them to be dependent upon welfare. And so a second generation would be added to the system.

If the father was not present even more money was provided by the Democrats. *In effect the welfare laws were promoting fatherless households with multiple illegitimate children. This should never have been allowed for it guaranteed continued poverty for all involved.*

I believe that that is just what the Democrats wanted, a permanent supply of dependent poor who would always vote row D, (Democrat). That factor allowed the Democrats to elect and keep many useless and dangerous candidates in power, candidates who would not have gotten into and stayed in office without those extra voters. That detrimental issue changed our future having poor or crooked politicos in power passing additional conniving political measures. And those dependent citizens were free to continue voting for the very scammers that had cooked up this ponzi scheme.

Anyone who was/is on public assistance should have been given mandatory birth control. There is no justification for someone who is unable to support themselves to be allowed to continue having children that the taxpayers had to pay for.

In addition, jobs training, education and job placement should also have been mandatory. The Municipality providing the welfare assistance should be able to "place" the needy person into a job to get them back on their feet. And the individual who accepts the aid from the taxpayers has to return to work as soon as possible.

If they refuse to do so, the welfare benefits would end. (None of us mind helping those who need, but there is no justifiable reason to have three generations of people still collecting welfare and giving nothing back.)

To assist the jobs placement effort welfare money could have been used to help pay for the workers training and some of the payroll costs.

In that way employers would have an incentive to hire those "assisted workers".

And if the job was a minimal wage job the welfare benefits could continue being provided, but at a reduced rate. That would allow for a certain income level and still get the individual on the road to independence. e individual became self-sufficient they would be free to do whatever they liked the same as every other American citizen. (Having kids, moving, new car ect.)

And if the person had learned a viable trade or career, they would also have more mobility in finding the place they actually wanted to live.

But the Democrats did not and do not want that to happen. An economically independent citizen could not be "convinced" to vote for them.

And if the Democrats could corral the poor and dependent citizens within the urban areas, they could insure large, solid, sustainable voting blocks (Democratic strongholds), that would guarantee their re-elections.

During the Great Depression FDR used "class warfare", the haves vs the have-nots as a way to the presidency. Even though he was definitely a have, FDR became the champion of the have-nots. That enabled him to get into office and power, and to keep it as the depression went on. *None of his programs ended the Great Depression of the turmoil of those years, and in fact unemployment went back up in 1939.* He was reelected anyway. (His political advice is the bible so to speak for all of the Democrats who followed.)

Despite the many protests among the liberals in his state, Gov. Reagan was reelected to office. He had to work with the Democrats in the California Legislature who were opposed to any changes to their sacred cow welfare. *But through his efforts reforms were passed, and Gov. Reagan's labors saved the state over $2 Billion dollars.*

In Washington Pres. Nixon was forced to do the same.

The nation's founders had instituted a rule called Impoundment. Beginning with Thomas Jefferson, a president can Impound any monies that the Congress has appropriated which in the President's opinion could break the budget. Nixon used the power a few times in his effort to reduce the out of control spending being done by the Democrats in the Congress. He especially attacked the already discredited Great Society programs of LBJ. But Nixon's actions infuriated the Democrats and may have induced them to bring him down.

In 1974 the scheming Democrats who still controlled the Congress passed a law taking the Presidential Impoundment policy away. From that point on the Congress could spend as much as they could with no oversight!

And that is why the budget deficits have not stopped in 50 years!

Prior to the Great Society scams enacted by the Democrats 70% of African American households had a father and mother. By 2010 the number had fallen to 20%!

In 1964 90% of US homes had two parents, even among the poor. By 2012 over 50% of our children live in one parent households! Participation in the Welfare Scam guaranteed generations of followers. And the proportion of our population living in poverty has not gone down in 50 years.

After having been a solid professor at Harvard, Daniel Patrick Moynihan was picked by President Nixon to be one of his aides. *Moynihan had developed and organized a new Family Protection Plan, which was designed to keep families together as they worked through poverty. This change had it been enacted would have revolutionized the Welfare program by providing benefits not just to the unemployed, but also to those in low paying jobs. One major rule would be implemented, all participants were required to get a job.* Many in the media praised the ideas, but the Democrats assailed it. His plan was defeated by calculating Liberal Democrats for not being "bigger".

Vietnam

SEATO Allies Australia and New Zealand withdrew their forces during the year. On June 13, 1971 the NY Times began publication of the *Pentagon Papers*, the secret overview of Vietnam that McNamara had ordered two years earlier.

Daniel Ellsberg who had worked in the highest levels of the Government and been an ally of Lt. Col. Vann while assigned in Vietnam had been sneaking pages of the classified report out from his office. He had become totally against our military effort and wanted the history of our involvement revealed. (He gave the Times the report.)

Pres. Nixon became upset that the information was being released and could affect the peace negotiations. He did not stop the publication but became convinced that there was an antigovernment plot at work. Nixon directed some aides to look into that and get results. Those aides formed a group called the "plumbers".

In early August 1971 Nixon was forced due to "leaks" to reveal that the CIA was still conducting a secret war in Laos using the indigenous people known as the Hmong tribesmen. This war has been ongoing since JFK had been in office, but the anti-war Congress assailed the Nixon Administration over this news. This CIA led operation had been one of the most effective ones in SE Asia.

Their paramilitary units tied up several NVA divisions to protect the Ho Chi Minh Trail, and in keeping the Pathet Lao out of power.

But in 1969 the CIA tried to convert the Hmong-Meo tribesmen into regular military forces instead of the guerilla units they were. With this U.S. backed effort the Royal Lao forces were able to take back the Bolevens Plateau. But their endeavor was short-lived when the NVA again sent two divisions to support the Pathet Lao. The communists overran the 6,000 Hmong defenders and regained the entire Plain of Jars area. Heavy NVA artillery fire was used to chase the Hmong back into the mountains. Their fine worked had been compromised by those thoughtless directives killing hundreds of the tribesmen and ending their military presence.

And that secured the Trail for the rest of the war.

In S. Vietnam the communists were still losing ground as the Phoenix Program was reaping great rewards. **By the end of 1971 another 20,000 VCI were gone, and only 20% of the country was actually considered under communist control.**

This was an astonishing and complete political turnaround from two years prior when the program was instituted.

(Though that inconvenient truth was also ignored by the media.)

William Colby would state that by the end of 1971 almost 38,000 VCI had been picked up in the program. Twenty thousand had died, while 17,000 had "defected".

Each small victory via arrest revealed other VCI agents, and entire rings were quickly taken out.

Using propaganda and the leftist leaning media, the communists sought to discredit the Phoenix plan as comprised of atrocious assassination teams running rampant through the night killing innocents. *In reality, that was what the communists had been using and doing throughout the South since 1954.* (Maybe the communists did not like the U.S.-ARVN imitating some of their methods.)

During the war the communists had murdered / assassinated over 37,000 government officials! (That inconvenient truth was never reported on either.)

Their victims ranged from religious leaders to teachers, clerks, police and other civil servants. *Most of those innocents were murdered and butchered in front of their families and villages as a clear threat to those who watched.*

The communists also routinely shelled and rocketed the civilian areas just to cause additional casualties. Their purpose was to terrorize the peasants.

In the village of Dak Son two battalions of Viet Cong attacked using flamethrowers murdering hundreds of villagers.

Prominent German Journalist Siemon-Netto had accompanied an ARVN patrol in 1965. They went into a farming village that the Viet Cong had raided the night before.

Netto wrote; *"Dangling from the trees and poles were the village chief, his wife, and their twelve children. All of the males had been castrated with their organs stuffed into their mouths. The females had their breasts cut off."*

The VC had ordered that everyone in the village had to witness the tortures and executions. The communists started with the baby and went upward by age.

The statement was clearly understood, go along or face this end!
Netto recorded that the event was done with cold precision and became routine as we went from village to village!

That is how communists win the hearts and minds.

Early war reporters stated that they stopped filing those types of stories because it was so commonplace. The post-TET media no longer reported on the war effort, they critiqued it and demonized it. And they ignored the successes that were becoming evident.

On Dec. 28, 1970 the NVA/VC had purposely mortared and attacked the pacified village of Truong Lam in Binh Dinh province. An understrength platoon of the 173 Airborne and a platoon of ARVN troops had been given the mission of protecting the village. The NVA were upset that their previous attempts and tactics had failed during the year past, so the communists decided to just destroy the village.

Using mortars to keep everyone pinned down the enemy overwhelmed the inefficient ARVN troops, entered the village from that side and threw satchel charges into the peasant's homes. Anyone who attempted to flee was gunned down. The 173d troopers counterattacked killing many of the enemy and driving off the others, but the carnage had been done well. One third of the village was destroyed with multiple dozens of the peasants murdered and wounded as they slept. The next morning the disheartened and angry survivors fled into a refugee camp, and all of the hard work was lost.

Whatever propaganda the communists tried to claim about *Operation Phoenix*, the CIA and ARVN mission was dedicated to removing this enemy by arresting the suspects. As the populace realized that the Government agents were coming only for the communists they increasingly assisted the effort which further eroded the enemy's support base. The program's efforts were finally keeping the peasants safe, which is all they really wanted anyway.

After the war ended in 1975 the N. Vietnamese admitted that the Phoenix Program was the most successful anti-communist tactic used by the Allies.
It was also the one that they feared most.

(What a terrible travesty that these programs were not instituted at the beginning of the decade.)

Foreign Affairs

On the 1st of November 1971 Red China replaced Taiwan in the United Nations. The United States had resisted this move since the communists defeated the nationalist in 1949. But the times and politics had changed.

Pres. Nixon was instituting his stunning foreign policy changes by normalizing relations with China. Conservatives were stunned and Democrats snickered that it was just electioneering on Nixon's part.

U.S. Ambassador George H. Bush welcomed the Chinese saying that the issue was divisive, but events have changed with the times. The PRC, (Peoples Republic of China), should be accepted into the United Nations.

The Chinese representative then spoke of the mistaken U.S. and Japanese effort to maintain two China's. He also stated their desired purpose of "liberating Taiwan", and declared Chinese support for the Arab world to stop Israeli Zionism.

(Nothing like good friends, and their aims haven't changed.)

Besides being an anti-communist Nixon was also a realist. As stated before he knew that to end the war with a modicum of honor he would need to have Chinese and Russian help. That was why the U.S. suddenly allowed Red China into the U.N.

To further his goals, Pres. Nixon had his National Security advisor Kissinger go to China secretly and organized a clandestine summit meeting in Peking.

Nixon was also scheduled to meet with the Russians in Moscow, but never told them or anyone else of this enigmatic and upcoming visit to China. With the bad blood separating the two communist giants, Nixon wanted to use his visits to our enemies against each other.

Chairman Mao was no longer the revered figure he had been in 1950.

His insane purges and ideas, like the Cultural Revolution, had killed millions of his countryman. Defense Minister Gen. Lin Biao, the outstanding CCF leader in their civil war and in Korea was organizing a coup to remove the insane Mao in 1971.

The plot was discovered and Lin Biao was exiled. He "died when his plane crashed in Mongolia." (Gen. Peng Dehuai their other outstanding senior commander complained about Mao's programs and was removed from office in 1959. During the Cultural Revolution he was ruled mentally incompetent, tortured and jailed until his death in 1974.)

In Paris the Communist negotiation/stalling tactics were prolonging the war. As in Korea, it was obvious that only a stick and carrot arrangement could force this issue to completion. And Power Politics was clearly understood by this White House.

(As our forces withdrew the negotiating was becoming more one-sided. We had no trump cards to play and the communists knew that. They also held our POWs as hostages in the negotiations, knowing we would not abandon them.)

On Feb 21, 1972 President Nixon and his wife made his surprise visit to China. Upon landing in Peking he made a point of going to Chou En-Lai and warmly shaking hands. (Something Acheson refused in 1954.) After meeting with the ailing Mao, Nixon and Kissinger entered into substantive negotiations with Chou.

Their meetings were guarded to ensure no one could be hurt politically.

Chou told Nixon, "Your handshake came over the vastest ocean in the world, twenty five years of silence." *Mao was as well read as Chou, and told Nixon he had voted for him in the last election. He preferred rightists over America's leftists. Those on the right get things done the other side only talks about.* Both of the senior Chinese leaders were skilled negotiators and diplomats.

Like the Soviets, China's rulers and leaders studied America in detail. Chou spoke to Nixon stating that his career was marked by great victories and defeats. *The measure of a man is learned by his path in life.*

Those that walk a smooth road never develop inner strength.

(Both Chou and Mao had endured the Long March, and this comment was a great compliment.)

Their visit was so successful that Chou called for an early peace in Vietnam.

Pres. Nixon's trip and the toned down speeches in Beijing alarmed Hanoi that their ages old enemy was about to sell them out. (They still felt that China had betrayed them in 1954.) North Vietnam's leaders were convinced of the sellout when the Shanghai Communiqué was announced. Pres. Nixon proposed to reduce the U.S. military presence on the island of Taiwan "as the tensions in the area diminished". To the leaders in North Vietnam this was a clear indication of the fix, U.S. withdrawal from Taiwan and peace in Vietnam.

(Those Nationalists who had escaped from the mainland and the communists had established their own nation, a free and eventually prosperous nation. But in reality only America's might had kept the island nation free. I fear that one day a weakened U.S. will cave in to the communists and those poor people will also be taken over.)

There was additional fallout from this momentous trip. The Soviets saw this rapprochement as the formation of a potentially fatal anti-Soviet bloc! Always insecure, the Kremlin's leaders felt they would be boxed in with nuclear enemies on all sides. (Nixon had made a toast his last night in China, "Of a week that has changed the world." To the Soviets that meant bad news for them.)

Indochina

During early 1972 the continuing war in Laos saw 6,000 NVA troops overrun Sam Thong and drive 4,000 Thai defenders back to Long Tieng. This latest offensive insured that Laos was completely safe from any "imperialist" encroachment and guaranteed the eventual fall of the country. With their rear secured, the North Vietnamese began setting up the final pieces for victory.

Over the years North Vietnam had suffered severe losses from their failure in generating a "People's Revolution" in the South. They had based their efforts on the Maoist model of subversion, guerilla pressure and open battles. But at TET there was no uprising in the South.

Their additional losses from the Cambodian battles in 1970 and in Lam Son 719 in 1971 caused further disruptions to their efforts. But by this point most of the U.S. presence in Vietnam was gone. That convinced the N. Vietnamese it was time to make a massive conventional invasion of South Vietnam. It was felt that they should strike quickly before the ARVN could improve their performance, and the sellout from Nixon's secretive trip to China could take hold. **With the Americans gone N. Vietnam would take over the country with an armored invasion.**

Le Duan the first Secretary of the N. Vietnam's ruling Lao Dong party had gone to Moscow months before for secret talks about their offensive planned for that year. Brezhnev and company agreed with Le Duan and they encouraged the attack.

And lastly the Communists also knew that this was a U.S. Presidential election year. Their leaders felt that no sitting President would dare alienate public opinion by re-committing U.S. troops to save Vietnam.
The N. Vietnamese had thought of everything, or so they thought.

Soviet leaders had also been shocked by Nixon's trip to China and they wanted to put Nixon on the defensive during their upcoming talks. Brezhnev and the Russians hoped that a strong and unified communist Vietnam would show the world, (Nixon), that communism could not be stopped. They would also be indebted to Russia instead of the turncoat Chinese.

To help the NVA with their planned offensive massive amounts of aid was shipped to N. Vietnam from Russia during the following months. Included in the arms shipments were hundreds of T-34, T-54 and PT-76 tanks. Long range 130mm canons, mobile SAM systems and fleets of trucks were integrated into the overall invasion plan.

To the U.S. Intel people who learned of this re-supply effort it was clear that the NVA had no plans for peace. Long vehicle convoys were observed moving down the hard surfaced Ho Chi Minh Trail. And large NVA formations were building in eastern Laos and Cambodia, and all along the DMZ. *To protect their supply lines the NVA had placed dozens of SAM sites along the Trail.* (Once the offensive got going, a SAM site was even setup at Khe Sanh.)

Since the end of the bombing of N. Vietnam the enemy had begun relocating large numbers of anti-air assets southward. USAF gunships had been routinely flying along the trail shooting up the NVA convoys at will. (To replace their increasing losses, Hanoi was forced to ask the Russians and Chinese for 9,000 more trucks.) *Once those SAM batteries arrived and placed along the Trail the air attacks had to stop. Those USAF gunships were much slower than the jets and quickly succumbed to the enemy fire.*

Gen. Giap had published an article in December 1971 calling for dynamic attacks in the South. Pres. Nixon did not want to jeopardize his upcoming trip to China, but he did warn Brezhnev not to help or encourage the North Vietnamese.

Naturally they did not cooperate.

On March 30, 1972 a mechanized NVA invasion of S. Vietnam began. It was called the *Easter Offensive*, and the NVA were finally fighting the war Gen. Westmoreland had always wanted. But at this point there were almost no U.S. troops left in Vietnam. Only 65,000 troops remained and most of those were logistical and service units.

Giap directed a multi- pronged plan which invaded initially with 150,000 troops plus 1200 tanks, hundreds of armored vehicles and artillery.

Their first attack came across the thinly held DMZ, over 40,000 troops plus hundreds of T-54 tanks and heavy artillery crashed across the border.

A second communist attack came out of Laos, and then a third from the Ashau valley. Their goal was to take all of the northern provinces. Unable to cope with the massive armored force the ARVN border outposts were overrun. On April 2 Camp Carroll the strongest position in I Corps surrendered.

Invading NVA units then advanced towards Quang Tri City, shelling and firing rockets into the civilian population to cause as many casualties as possible.

Refugees filled the roads, reminiscent of the fall of France in 1940.

Thus far cloud cover had aided the NVA by concealing their movements and reducing the S. Vietnamese air attacks against them. ARVN armored forces moved up and dueled with the enemy stopping them at Dong Ha.

Then in the southern part of the country the second major phase of the invasion began as NVA forces struck from their base areas in Cambodia. *Those were the same NVA base areas the ARVN-U.S. forces had struck during the incursion two years earlier.* They took Loc Ninh and tried to enter An Loc. ARVN counterattacks and air attacks kept the communists out of An Loc, but the situation was grim. Pres. Thieu even committed units from the Saigon area to help An Loc. (That relocation was possible only because the VC units were no longer viable.)

In the north the surrounded ARVN 56th Regiment was captured at Khe Sanh. To their east the ARVN Marines held the line at Dong Ha inflicting serious losses.

Then the third major prong of this massive NVA offensive began.
It was a multi-divisional attack into the Central Highlands towards Kontum and Pleiku.

Again the NVA forces had been hiding in their secret bases inside Cambodia waiting to strike. One ARVN division shamefully fled the battle area, and in the Binh Dinh province the NVA captured three district capitols.

In Paris the Peace Talks collapsed as the communists saw no need.

President Nixon became outraged by this aggressive NVA invasion while the communist negotiators stalled at the peace table. He ordered massive bombing missions all over the region. *Operation Linebacker I* was being organized as the NVA attacks continued unabated. (There was little public outcry over this latest communist invasion as the media and anti-war crowd almost seemed happy.)

This new U.S. bombing operation had three objectives; to close the land routes from China, destroy the attacking NVA, their supplies and equipment, and interdict NVA supply lines to the South. *Pres. Nixon stated, "Those bastards have never been bombed like they are going to be bombed this time."* (58)

There was no way he could send in ground troops, but he was determined to teach the communists a lesson. B-52 heavy bombers would be used to strike into the North, and naval bombardments were to shell every enemy base and site within reach of their guns.

In I Corps the NVA were still trying to get into Quang Tri City but were stopped by ARVN Marine units holding at the Dong Ha Bridge. Tank battles continued with ARVN units using the American M-48 Patton tank against the Russian Pt-76 and T-54 models. In just one action over 26 NVA tanks were destroyed upsetting their timeline. A USMC advisor ran onto the bridge to repair and setoff the demolition charges that destroyed the span. That forced the NVA units to detour westward further delaying their attack. Eventually though they outflanked the ARVN defenders and in the following heavy combat the NVA destroyed the brave ARVN 3d Division.

By this point U.S. air attacks began striking at Tchepone destroying dozens of truck parks. On April 27 the communists falsely resumed the Paris Peace talks as their northern force closed the ring on Quang Tri City. (They hoped to trick Nixon into stopping our air attacks by returning to the peace table, but Nixon saw through their scam.) Hung up in the south, the NVA were still kept out of An Loc.

In Central Vietnam the NVA units took the outlying towns near Kontum, but were unable to enter the city itself. *John Paul Vann was still working in the country he loved, and was responsible for directing most of the major ARVN defensive moves and counter-attacks that kept the NVA at bay.*

And here it was evident that Gen. Giap made a fatal error, he had tried to do too many things at once. By splitting his force into three separate parts each was just a little too weak to accomplish their major goals. Blitzkrieg is dependent on surprise and shock value. The longer it takes to accomplish a mission the better prepared the enemy becomes to stop the next attack. And by this point the heavy and increasingly effective U.S. air attacks of *Operation Linebacker I* had begun inflicting severe losses to the concentrated NVA invasion forces. **Giap and the communists did not expect that Pres. Nixon would intervene. With his formations out in the open, air power could work their magic.**

On May 2 An Loc and Kontum were still being besieged by the NVA as the secret meetings between Kissinger and Le Duc Tho also resumed. Little was being accomplished, though the tradeoff for any peace was that all of our units would leave SVN within four months after the release of our POWs.

A large part of the negotiating problem in Paris was that our Congress continually orated legislation and complaints demanding we immediately withdraw from SVN. That foolish mindset was ruining any chance at real negotiation as the Communists knew what was happening in the U.S. Government and could simply wait until our Congress voted us out of SVN.

On May 8, 1972 President Nixon went on TV and broadcast his intentions. **He spoke to the nation about the aggressive and deceptive communist invasion.**
He had ordered the mining of the waters of North Vietnam and was resuming the bombings of North Vietnam itself.
Foreign ships were given three days to get out before the sea-mines self-activated.
Only five of the thirty five ships in the harbor were able to leave.
Polls showed over 60% of Americans supported the president's actions.
(Yet another unreported event was the order by the Soviets to intervene in Vietnam. Three Soviet Echo II submarines were sent into the waters around Vietnam. It is not clear if they were going to attack our aircraft carriers, but our submarines picked them up on sonar. Nixon warned the Soviets to pull them back or they would be sunk. **They left.***)*
After the U.S. aircraft mined Haiphong harbor they did the same to all of the North's rivers and other ports. All bridges and infrastructure were also targeted to stop the NVA supply system. These were the first bombings of northern N. Vietnam since 1968, and our planes were using "smart bombs" for the first time. The results were impressive as targets that could not be destroyed with 50 planes were now being taken out with five.
Heavy B-52 bombers were used to savage Hanoi and Haiphong for the first time in the war. Their massive barrages caused great consternation in Hanoi and among the anti-war protestors at home. (Somehow those fools thought what we were doing was so terrible, but what the NVA invaders were destroying in the South was acceptable.)
As the air attacks on the determined communists continued Nixon authorized more and more targets which were being picked by the military men not the bureaucrats' as Johnson had done. (Nixon was unhappy that the weather was hampering the USAF operations.)
One of the most difficult of those targets was the Hanoi thermal power plant located downtown. Again the "smart bombs" destroyed the target but not the neighborhood. American aircraft were using laser guided munitions with deadly accuracy as they degraded the North's military capability.

(This was also when Jane Fonda visited Hanoi and betrayed the confidence of the captive flyers. Two were beaten to death.)

By this point almost 1,000 aircraft had been moved into the theatre for the continued operations against the NVA forces and N. Vietnam itself. On May 23 Pres. Nixon removed most of the old restrictions on the bombing of North Vietnam.

At sea NVA patrol boats and MiG fighters attacked the U.S. ships operating off their shores. Numerous enemy ships and planes were lost along with their shore batteries and other coastal defenses in the heaviest sea action of the war. Our Navy was adding to the destruction of N. Vietnam by firing over 100,000 rounds of 5 and 6 inch shells.

(Here again was where the battleships and heavy cruisers would have made a huge difference. 16 & 8 inch shells vs the 5 & 6 inch shells that were used.)

A total of seven U.S. aircraft carriers had taken up positions along the coast of S. Vietnam sending off hundreds of air attacks every day. They were wrecking the NVA armored forces which had no choice but to retreat.

With the invasion tide finally turning from the non-stop air attacks the ARVN Marines aggressively counter-attacked towards Quang Tri. From May 25-30 desperate NVA forces tried frontal assaults to enter Kontum. They again failed and suffered heavy casualties. Helicopters were firing the new TOW missiles, (targeted-optically-wire guided), which were brutally effective on armored vehicles. Even B-52s were used to devastate known NVA concentrations in that area.

Into June the fighting continued, but sadly Col. John Vann was killed in a helicopter crash trying to organize yet another counter-attack. His tireless and valorous actions had saved the Central Highlands, and were the best example of what solid leadership is. (Radio Hanoi gleefully claimed credit for his death.)

John Vann was one of the first Americans who understood what we were up against, rebelled against the Army for its command foolishness, quit the Army because of the stupidity he saw, and returned as a civilian to try to make a difference.

Out of all of the people involved in Vietnam since 1954, his efforts did the most at trying to prevent the communist takeover. Yet few in America even know his name.

One arena that the Communists were actually doing well was in the air. Their large numbers of MiGs were actually wining many of the air-air fights against the U.S. fighters. (Our jets were heavier and less maneuverable than the smaller MiGs.) But the constant combat was taking a heavy toll on the Russian and N. Korean flyers.

By July 11 the siege of An Loc down in III Corps had also failed and the NVA were forced to retreat back into Cambodia. (Col James Hollingsworth was the senior U.S. advisor in that area. Like John Vann he became the ad-hoc commander for the ARVN III Corps directing the air strikes and counter-attacks with surgical precision.) **All over the South the ARVN troops were advancing and beating the NVA forces.** Quang Tri was re-entered and the destructive NVA troops chased out. And during those months the last American ground troops were pulled out of the South.

As a result of their battlefield defeat, the secret talks between Kissinger and Le Duc Tho suddenly resumed on July 19. As before little progress was being made, but the attitude of the arrogant North Vietnamese had changed considerably from May. Then they assumed victory was imminent.

When the NVA finally retreated and ended their invasion, they had lost over 110,000 troops and over half of their tanks, artillery and vehicles.

However due to the losses in the ARVN infantry units the NVA was able to remain in many of the outlying provinces they had conquered. Quang Tri City was not completely re-taken from the communists until Sept 16, 1972.

In the typical style of communist invasions the city was in ruins.
But that did not concern the communists, for their press corps is run by the party.

Operation Linebacker I officially ended on October 22.

It had been an illustrative victory in showing what skilled airpower could accomplish to an exposed enemy force that does not have the assets to prevent it.

For the loss of eighty-nine aircraft the U.S. had been able to destroy most of the bridges linking North Vietnam to China, bridges linking Haiphong and Hanoi to the war zone, war industries, supply targets, power plants and transportation networks.

The NVA invading armies had been mauled and all three retreated.

There were other long term consequences from the air attacks as it took months for Hanoi to begin to repair the massive damages inflicted upon them. One unseen byproduct of the aerial onslaught was the degradation of the North's air defenses. Special attacks targeting radars and missile batteries had been conducted during those past months and they were extremely effective because of the new munitions. Dozens of their anti-air units had been destroyed. And with the mining of their harbors no new units were coming in. During the final week the destruction of the North's air defenses had become a priority Most of their airfields and MiGs were targeted with sixty two more destroyed.

In Paris the peace talks seemed to be inching towards an agreement, and it was a better one than expected. The North would agree to a ceasefire in place.

Nixon agreed to reduce the numbers of air attacks, but he would not end them until the peace agreement was fixed.

To help the South, another 288 aircraft were transferred to them.

In America the only thing the turncoat Congress was concerned about were the complaints from N. Vietnam that their vital irrigation dykes had been attacked. Investigations by the State Dept., (ordered by the Congress), revealed that only twelve cases of damage could be found, and all were near other targets that had been hit.

Despite the NVA invasion of South Vietnam and our devastating bombing campaign President Nixon still went to Moscow for the May 20 summit meeting with First Secretary Leonid Brezhnev. *To the surprise and dismay of the Russians, Nixon was confident and not on the defensive.* Their discussions ranged from Vietnam to Arms control to trade.

The Russians seemed reluctant to agree on anything, apparent political fallout from Nixon's successful and secretive trip to China. *It was in Moscow that Nixon was finally able to get the Russians to agree on reducing nuclear arms.* SALT was the acronym for Strategic Arms Limitation Treaty, which would be a bilateral agreement freezing the number of ICBM's to what each nation had at the time of signing. A separate ABM treaty limited anti-ballistic missile sites to two per nation. (Research purposes.)

During July additional agreements were reached by negotiators on large grain purchases and cooperation in the sciences and technology fields. Jewish emigration was increased to 35,000 annually, and the framework for further long term arms control was also begun. And the signing of the Basic Principals of Mutual Relations paved the way for further summits and peaceful negotiations. It appeared that *détente*, which was the easing of tensions between the two superpowers was taking hold.

Even with the talks of arms control on the table our military designers were hard at work. New fighter jets were being designed and they would become famous as the F-15, F-16 and F-14. To replace the fifteen-twenty year old B-52 strategic bombers a new design was being tested and a prototype was finally completed. *Using a state of the art computer aided navigation system, the new B-1 would be able to fly fast and low to the ground.* In that way the bomber would be hard to pickup on radar and therefore difficult to stop. (As always Russian spies quickly learned of the programs and the implications. They began work on a jet fighter that could defeat the B-1, and in 1975 the MiG-31 was completed.)

June 17, 1972 was just another day in the U.S., but a minor break-in at an office in the Watergate Complex would cause unforeseen turmoil for America and the World. Five would-be burglars were caught in the offices of the Democratic National Committee. Found among their tools were cameras and surveillance equipment.

The five were arrested and processed, and the incident caught only a little attention. It would soon become a scandal as they worked for one of the Presidents aides.

Weeks of negotiations had droned on in Paris, until Oct 8. Then Le Duc Tho presented a simple solution to the peace. The U.S. would leave and take their POWs, and all of the political questions would be "resolved among the Vietnamese".

Kissinger was optimistic but his staff was nervous as once more no corresponding NVA withdrawal from captured areas was in the agreement. Pres. Nixon had again sent aide Col. Alexander Haig to Saigon to assure Pres. Thieu that we would stand by him if the communists reneged on the agreement.

Still there were anxious moments as the South Vietnamese President was unhappy with the pending agreement.

On October 26 North Vietnam unexpectedly released the text of a draft agreement that would end the war in the hope of forcing it to be accepted. On Nov 1 President Thieu condemned the pending peace agreement as a document of "surrender". (Similar to Pres Rhee's reaction in Korea in 1953.) And as had happened in 1953, political events in America dictated that the agreement would be acted upon anyway.

The U.S. Presidential election was held a few days later with the anti-war Democratic candidate George McGovern having taken a platform of unilateral cessation of the war. McGovern was a proponent of the Progressive Party of old and had incorporated some of their ideals in his platform. (It is interesting to note that even back then polls taken of the media showed that 82% of them supported McGovern.)

A Yale Law School grad named Bill Clinton worked for the McGovern campaign. What most do not know, *was that this "student" who went to and graduated from Law School was AWOL from his army unit*, (absent without leave), *as of October 10, 1969.* Because of that his prior enlistment with the Reserves had been revoked and he was subject to arrest under Public Law 90-40 (2) (a).

Clinton had used the Reserves as a way to avoid the draft and active service, and never had any intention of serving. As a draft dodger he never should have been accepted into a Law School, let alone graduate and be involved in any governmental legal proceedings. *(Incredulously after Nixon left office Clinton ran for Congress while still a federal fugitive, as were all of the draft dodgers. Most of the draft dodgers of the 60s supported action like his, but you the reader must realize, because Bill Clinton did not go to Vietnam, some other mother's son did!*

Despite all of the problems during the past four years the pending peace proposal that Pres. Nixon had obtained in Paris resulted in an election landslide for him.

It would have made more sense for the communists not to have released the proposal, but they felt that it would force Nixon's hand on other issues. Nixon and Agnew carried 49 states, including McGovern's home state of N. Dakota. His win of 520 electoral votes was the highest margin ever.

It took weeks of conversations, but Pres. Nixon and others finally convinced Pres. Thieu to agree to the peace proposals. Nixon gave the S. Vietnamese President his assurances that the U.S. would take "swift and severe retaliatory action" if North Vietnam violated this pending ceasefire.

Back in mid-1971 the CIA had discovered a main telephone trunk line that was 15 miles southwest of the city of Vinh, N. Vietnam. With the peace negotiations stalled at that time it was hoped that having some inside information might help at Paris. Their plot to actually place wiretaps on the line took another fifteen months to execute.

On Dec 6, 1972 a secret mission was successfully employed to place taps on the phone lines to Hanoi. By the time the plot was accomplished the peace treaty was almost finished. Most felt it had been a wasted effort.

Then for unexpected reasons the N. Vietnamese negotiators stopped the final peace talks. Everything was suddenly stonewalled, and on December 13 the peace talks abruptly collapsed. *Henry Kissinger was so upset by their scamming he publicly called the communists tawdry, filthy piles of dung.* He stated to Le Duc Tho that we were 99% in agreement, but will not be blackmailed into finishing it.

The next day Pres. Nixon warned the North to resume the negotiations or else. *They refused.*

Nixon did not make any public announcements of what was coming.

For days the media pressured him and his people to fill them in and state his parameters.

He refused them, getting the media even more upset.

On December 18, 1972 *Operation Linebacker II* **began.**

It was a thirteen day non-stop air assault. This bombing campaign existed for only one purpose, to force the leaders in Hanoi to stop playing their word games and return to the negotiations.

Linebacker II was a strategic bombing campaign that was similar to the ones used in WWII. To get the maximum impact from the raids B-52 heavy bombers would fly 742 missions against targets in Hanoi and Haiphong. An additional 640 fighter-bomber missions would also strike those cities. Other attacks went in to support those missions. (Because of poor weather many of the normal aircraft could not be used.)

For those raids the B-52s were given unrestricted access to the Hanoi/Haiphong areas. Each night up to 150 of the huge bombers would arrive proceeded by the supporting fighters and bombers. The North would throw up their usual defenses firing hundreds of SAM missiles and thousands of shells skyward. But the degradation inflicted on them in May had not been repaired. Without their radars the majority of their AAA fire completely missed our flights.

In desperation to compensate for the loss of their radars was the North simply fired hundreds of SAM's and shells skyward set to explode at the height they thought the B-52s were at. (This tactic worked twice and six of the large planes went down.) Enemy MiG fighter jets attempted an aerial defense but dozens more were shot down by the better pilots and planes of the U.S.

At home the public was mostly silent as the vast majority of our men and women had already come home. In the Congress the Democrats planned to make moves to end all operations in Vietnam as soon as the holiday recess ended.

It was the media that screamed the loudest.

Many of their commentators and bylines cursed the president and his "savage actions".

Their hysterics and propaganda had reached treasonous levels, and Nixon's approval rating dropped 14 points. *To try to stop the hysterics Malcolm Browne of the NY Times actually reported that the damages and casualties in the bombings were being grossly overstated by the liars and propagandists in our media.*

Liberal U.S. Jurist Telford Taylor was also in Hanoi. He too was convinced that the raids were not being done to kill civilians. (Gen. John Vogt was the head planning officer for both of the Linebacker Raids. He and his staff worked diligently to strike only essential targets, not civilians as in WWII.) *When the operation ended less than 2,000 civilian casualties had been caused by the well planned and directed air raids.*

It was never reported by the turncoat media but during N. Vietnam's 1972 Invasion of S. Vietnam over 100,000 innocent civilians were killed by the murderous NVA.

On December 26 dozens of air attacks concentrated on the North's antiaircraft sites destroying hundreds of their weapons. Later that night further low level attacks cratered NVA runways and MiG bases. Then the B-52s flew in and struck Hanoi.

Enemy defensive fire was decreasing each night from losses, and they also ran out of ammo and missiles. *Much of that reality was due to the fallout from the raids of Linebacker I and the mining of their harbors which prevented much of their resupply.*

On the 29th dozens of B-52s attacked in waves bombing Hanoi for 15 solid minutes. Destructive explosions resonated across the city destroying everything that was targeted. North Vietnam's communists were stunned. Those continuous and massive bombardments hammered the cities of North Vietnam causing widespread fear and panic. Rail yards were obliterated, barracks and buildings flattened, oil terminals and supply areas were ablaze, warehouses destroyed and the electricity was out.

By the time those raids ended on December 30, N. Vietnam was defenseless.

This was the intense commitment to the war effort that LBJ had refused to make. Night after night the bombs fell upon Hanoi not for a few minutes, but for hours.

Our POW's who were languishing in terrible prisons and had been suffering severe tortures for years gleefully saw the terror in the faces of the guards.

Many of them spoke later on the instant reaction in this brutal enemy. *After the forth night of this onslaught the enemy's will had been shattered.*

The communists realized that under this President total destruction of their country was possible.

This was victory in the making.

This was what war is and will always be, imposing an outcome on another nation that your leaders desired by violent means.

In just thirteen days President Nixon's bombing campaign caused more damage to the North than had happened in the proceeding eight years.

And the communists of N. Vietnam, well they returned to the Peace Talks.

While the final talks went on additional bombings went in striking transportation targets.

They did not stop until Jan. 15, 1972.

By then the war making potential of N. Vietnam had been stopped.
On January 27 the Peace Agreement was finally signed.

Before and during the final signing of the Peace Agreement the Administration was receiving almost real time intelligence from those tapped phone lines.

And Kissinger was greatly aided by that information during those last days of talking.

Pres. Thieu was still against the treaty but Pres. Nixon told him to sign it or we will sign alone.

Although it cannot be stated definitely that the peace was won over those 13 days, it is blatantly obvious that *Linebacker II* forced the North to reevaluate their position.

And this one operation showed just how naive and unintelligent LBJ and his Administration were in committing America to a part time war based on graduated response.

Had this JCS sanctioned bombing campaign which was first proposed in 1964 been enacted then, it is conceivable that we would not have had to fight a large scale war in Vietnam. And that is why the Military Leaders should have been able to force this issue onto the politicians by having public debates. If nothing else happened, at least the public discourse might have prevented the bloody stalemate of Vietnam.

Our President is the Commander in Chief of our military. But it is almost impossible for someone who has never heard a shot fired in anger to make intelligent decisions as the C in C. They just don't have any first hand knowledge of the weapons, capabilities or tactics needed for warfare. Nor do they have any idea what warfare is and the sacrifices by those who are in it. (Just look at how poorly draft dodging Bill Clinton did during his eight years, and the horrible decisions by the Obama regime in his years.)

But the reader must also realize that having served does not mean the person is an expert either. Harry Truman had served in the Army in WWI. He unilaterally disarmed and destroyed America's armed services after WWII.

That was one of the reasons the Cold War grew and turned hot.

After the communists won in China, they then invaded Korea in 1950. Only the sinking of the NKPA transport that first night and American air power kept the NKPA from conquering South Korea in June 1950. And what would have been the outcome??

Dwight Eisenhower was the Supreme Commander in Europe during WWII. During his war years he made multiple poor decisions that lengthened the war. In 1953 he threatened nuclear battles to end the war in

Korea, but had no understanding of the communist insurgencies that were occurring or how to stop them. By the time he proposed counter-insurgency programs it was too late to stop the North Vietnamese from their aggressive expansion into Laos and Cambodia without a war.

John Kennedy served in the Navy's PT boats in the Solomon Islands in WWII. But most of his military minded decisions (Laos, Bay of Pigs, Missiles in Cuba, Vietnam) were wrong. Part of his problem was the people he had placed in senior positions, and the fact that even in 1960 none of our leaders understood the communist mindset.

LBJ was in a Public Relations position during WWII. He fabricated a citation for his resume but was never in a dangerous place. His policies and directives over the war were totally wrong and ruinous. It was his deceptive policies that led to the tragedy of Vietnam.

Richard Nixon had also served in the Navy in WWII, and like JFK was stationed in the South Pacific. *He alone seemed to understand that to make the enemy agree to a peace, they had to be convinced that to delay meant ruin.* To persuade the Northern communists to sign the peace he let the military run the Linebacker missions. (That was the same line of reasoning that Truman had used when he dropped the A-bomb on Japan in 1945, and Eisenhower had used when he warned the Chinese to end the war in Korea or face atomic artillery in 1953.)

Unlike Johnson, Nixon did not let up until the communists gave up.

As stated before our major media sources had become liberalized and left leaning by 1965. Their coverage was completely against both of the *Linebacker* campaigns even though the first one had saved South Vietnam from a mechanized communist invasion. *Linbacker II* was implemented only because the enemy refused to honor the peace agreements that they had already agreed too.

Walter Cronkite the senior correspondent/spokesman for CBS had gone on National TV to claim that the TET Offensive proved we could not win in Vietnam.

His reports like most of the rest of the post TET media actively disheartened the nation. After *Linebacker II* began Cronkite's nightly coverage was so negative that Gov. Ronald Reagan remarked to Pres. Nixon that if this had been WWII, CBS would have been charged with treason!

The Paris Peace Agreement that was finally signed allowed for the withdrawal of U.S. forces, the return of prisoners, and a ceasefire based on current positions. President Thieu was still angry about the last component, but Nixon's promise to him and his threat had won the day.

Neither side was supposed to add to their armaments in the South.

Weapon supply stocks were to remain frozen in the effort to insure stability. Resupply of used stocks was allowed, and was to be reported to the ICCS, International Commission on Control and Supervision which had been established to monitor the peace. (The same impotent commission that oversaw every peace agreement.) **South Vietnam setup their control points for inspection, but the communists of North Vietnam refused to do so.** (Big surprise.)

The North also refused to engage with the election commission which was to supervise the open elections which were to be held.
Over 200,000 NVA troops occupied areas in northern and western South Vietnam, and another 100,000 were encamped just across the borders.

Days after the agreement was signed the communists also reneged on allowing inspectors into their occupied zones to keep track of violations.

They were already preparing for the next battle.

During the war almost 9,000 of our aircraft had been shot down.

Over 2,000 pilots and crew members had been killed, with another 1,000 missing.

Our POWs numbered almost 600.

On February 12, 1973 the first 100 of them was released.

Over the following weeks all were returned, and it was then learned of the brutal tortures and treatments our people had suffered through.

All of their years of sacrifice and torment were ignored by the major media and many of the citizens who sanctimoniously shut them and all of the returning veterans out.

America had suffered over 47,300 combat deaths, 11,000 non-battle deaths and 304,000 wounded during the war. The war had cost us $141 Billion dollars! Many myths were created about the war losses, but the actual facts showed among other topics that Black Americans suffered just 12.5% of the deaths.

It came out that 77% of those killed were volunteers, not draftees.

The Army lost a higher ratio of Officers in Vietnam than had been lost in WWII, while the Marines suffered more losses in Vietnam than in WWII.

Armored units actually had the highest casualty rates of all forces, losing 27% of their personnel.

But the biggest casualty was that the Army hierarchy learned nothing from the tragedy of Vietnam, just as in 1953 they learned nothing from Korea.

Liberals tried to portray those who served as losers and drugged out failures. Ninety seven percent of those veterans left the services with Honorable Discharges. Despite the vial treatment returning vets endured from the anti-war protestors, Eighty five percent of those who served made a successful transition into civilian life.

With U.S. involvement now ended, the incredible sacrifice in the second Vietnam War had only been able to generate an uneasy pause in the worldwide communist effort.

The stalemate that became the peace meant that for a time South Vietnam was free.

And the Far Frontier had been held, if only for a little while.

The North's disrupted supply situation was slowly being alleviated as our ships were sweeping out the mines that we had laid in North Vietnam's harbors eight months earlier. By the time the North's violations became public knowledge the mines were gone as were we.

Gen. Tran Van Tra went back to Hanoi to explain their problems to the party leaders. Their men had been beaten badly, were exhausted and their units were in disarray. Losses had been severe and replacements few in numbers. Ammunition and foods were equally scarce, and the few remaining local VC wanted to abide by the peace agreement.

Remembering their failures at TET in 1968, Tra wanted to wait awhile before they embarked on another major attack. The party leaders in Hanoi did not agree.

They wanted to strike before Thieu could complete his two year plan of counterattacks and mopping up of the remaining VC. The Party directed Tra to commence small attainable battles to keep the ARVN busy. That would enable the North to begin the huge logistical effort for their next offensive. Following their orders, he began organizing for the road ahead.

In America the Congress was being run by the anti-war and left wing branch of the Democratic Party. *Their agenda was to prevent any further U.S. action in Indochina, despite Pres. Nixon's veto's or promises.*

On June 4, 1973 the Senate voted to stop all funding for any military activity in Indochina. The Case-Church Amendment **was attached to a State Dept. Authorization bill,** and blocked any further funding for Vietnam, Cambodia or Laos unless specifically approved by the Congress.

How tragically ironic that those secretive and ruinous politicians that created and expanded this damaging foreign policy and war now took steps to prevent any stabilizing action that had been created with so much loss.

(Obama did the same thing in Iraq when he took over in 09.)

The freedom of South Vietnam had already been paid for in vast quantities of wealth and our most precious resource, our sons and daughters. But those efforts were ignored as the latest batch of scheming politicians decided to abandon the region.

Pres. Nixon had wisely insured that as much equipment and supplies as possible was given to the South before we left. Almost 1 billion dollars worth of used equipment, supplies and aid had been turned over. He was under no illusions that the communists would keep the peace. (He was also being undercut by the break-in and cover-up at the Watergate Complex the year before.)

With the removal of all U.S. personnel it fell to the South Vietnamese people to continue the fight for their freedom. The heavy communist losses in equipment and personnel the prior spring had curtailed NVA activity in the South. The aerial beating taken by the North in December and the shutting down of their supply system stopped all of their actions.

Continued counterattacks by the ARVN had recovered about 15% of the land taken by the NVA in the spring. Buoyed by their victories against the NVA at An Loc, Kontum and Quang Tri City, the troops and commanders of the ARVN and ARVN Marines fought hard and believed they could hold. Their initial victories in the counterattacks had been made with limited U.S. air support, but after treaty the South was fighting on their own. **By 1973 they controlled roughly 75% of their nation's land, and 85% of the population.**

Middle East

Islamic terrorists were continuing their crimes. On Feb. 22, 1971 Lufthansa Flight 649 was hijacked by Palestinians. Unwilling to face the terrorists West Germany decided to pay the $5 million dollar ransom.

May 8, 1972 Sabena Flight 571 was hijacked by Palestinians who threatened to kill all of the passengers and crew. Israeli commandos stormed the aircraft killing the terrorists. One civilian died and three were wounded. (Two future Israeli leaders were leading the raid, Ehud Barak and Benjamin Netanyahu.)

Fatal Flaws | 543

Then on May 30, 1972 Palestinian and Japanese terrorists stormed LOD airport in Israel. Firing automatic weapons and throwing grenades the terrorists killed 26 and wounded 79 before they were also killed.

During the 1972 Olympics in Munich, W. Germany five Palestinian terrorists broke into the Israeli dorm. Eleven Israeli athletes were murdered as was a W. German policeman, the five terrorists were killed. In retaliation Prime Minister Golda Meir directed Mossad to hunt down and kill all of the members of the Black September terrorist group.

March 1, 1973 Islamic terrorists attacked the Saudi embassy in Khartoum, Sudan.

Ten of the diplomats were taken hostage and three were killed.

In each of the above cases the attacks were well planned and violent.

Days later terrorists setup three car bombs near Israeli targets in NYC.

Israeli Prime Minister Golda Meir was expected on a visit, and the terrorists hoped to kill her if she visited one of the sites. *The NSA decrypted a message from Baghdad to NYC describing the attempt.* Warnings went out and the FBI and PD found all of the bombs in time to disarm them.

Libya nationalized all of the foreign oil firms operating in their lands on Sept 1, 1973. Most of the profits would now go to Col. Mohmar Khadafy a former army officer who took over in a coup the year before.

On September 12 Egypt and Jordan made amends, and the next day Syrian and Israeli jets fought another air battle.

Then on October 6, 1973 the Mideast again exploded into war.

The Arab Nations had been hoping and planning for a multi-national effort to strike at Israel since their humiliating loss in 1967. Their training and planning had been done with such secrecy and coordination that this time Israel was the one caught unprepared. *Israel had an extensive and talented intelligence service, but in their hour of darkest need they were fooled with an elaborate ruse by an Egyptian double agent.*

In 1969 an Egyptian agent had walked in unannounced to Israeli intelligence-officers with copies of secret documents and promises to bring more. His wife was the daughter of Egyptian President Nasser, and he sat at the small table of Egypt's leaders.

This was a coup of unbelievable proportions and the Mossad principals were walking on air. With this agent Mossad could keep appraised of any potential dangers.

From the spring of 1969 onward this spy had convinced the Israeli's that the Arab League was in shambles as was Egypt's military. To back up the ruse documents were constantly presented showing discourse and problems. This deception convinced Israel's leaders that they were safe from attack.

When Nasser died in 1970 Anwar Sadat became President.

Sadat greatly wanted to reverse the disastrous losses from 1967, and it was he who set in motion the latest plans for war. This Egyptian campaign was the brainchild of Gen. Shazly who had been a divisional commander in the Sinai in 67 when Israeli tanks chased them back across the Suez Canal. Crushed by that loss, Shazly envisioned a simple plan to win the day.

Egypt's troops would fight a limited war to recapture the east bank of the Suez. Once the Israeli forts and Suez battlements had been crushed his forces would advance 15 or so kilometers and then dig in. Israeli planes would come screaming in to attack and become trapped within a well planned anti-aircraft missile and canon layout. With the recent weapons given to them by the Russians, Shazly felt the Israeli air force would be decimated within their ambush. They knew the Israeli tanks would also charge across the desert. In his plan they would find themselves in a similar trap facing Russian made T-62 tanks and their new hand held Sagger wire-guided missiles.

By operating in a relatively safe environment the Egyptian's would only advance when they could remain under their missile shield. In this way they could negate the potent Israeli air force and slowly savage the Israeli army. When the time was right the Egyptians would advance and reclaim the entire Sinai. Being such a small nation Israel could not endure a prolonged war. Heavy losses among their citizen-soldiers would break their will and the disruption to their economy would destroy the nation.

It was a viable plan and Sadat approved it.

Back in February 1971 Anwar Sadat had announced to a stunned nation that if Israel moved back 30 miles from the Suez Canal he would reopen the waterway to them and sign a peace agreement with Israel. But at that time the Jewish leaders saw no reason to give anything back unless the Arabs permanently agreed to Israel's right to exist. Terrorist attacks were a constant occurrence in the Holy Land and for Israel to make any lasting peace all of their safety conditions needed to be answered.

With his peace efforts having been rebuffed Sadat directed that war would be used. Gen. Shazly was promoted to Chief of Staff and directed to train their forces.

Politically Egypt had to retake all of the Sinai and Gaza as the Russians had insisted on that outcome if they were going to supply them with their latest weapons.

Pres. Sadat did not want Russian interference so he decided to gamble and expelled the 14,000 Russian troops in Egypt. Those "advisors" were the ones who manned the newest SAM-6 missile sites, flew the Egyptian Mig-25 jets, and operated the electronic jamming and recon aircraft that flew around Israel.

Sadat won his gamble for just three months later Russia promised to send Egypt Mig-23 and SU-20 fighter-bombers and scud missiles. The latter had a range of 150 miles, perfect as a terror weapon upon Israel and quite similar to the V-2 missiles Hitler had sent into England. On Oct 24, 1972 Pres. Sadat gave a speech to his Military Supreme Council and challenged them to win the day.

During the following months the planning and training continued getting the attention of the Israelis. In early April 1973 the "spy" told his Israeli handlers that war was imminent. May 15 would be the day of the attack. For weeks the Israeli leaders conferred and debated the report, finally deciding that they had to call up the country's reservists. On May 7 the major call-up was announced to the nation. Tens of thousands of citizen-soldiers left homes and jobs to man the outposts and bring up their war fighting equipment. The operation was called *Blue-White*, and cost the Israeli State an estimated $35 million dollars. But war did not come.

The Arab forces simply continued their training programs that seemed to be threatening but were not. Israel remained in their heightened state of alert for three months finally drawing down their forces in September 1973. In Egypt their Intel people noted and watched with satisfaction the initial alarm and political fallout as the Zionists finally returned to their lives.

So well plotted were the Arab war plans, that even the Jewish Sabbaths and election cycle had been programmed into their attack. The Israeli's holiest Sabbath of Yom Kippur was on Oct 6, and their elections were set for Oct 28. That same month the tides and nights were also favorable for an attack. And October was also the month of Ramadan, a sacred Muslim time of fasting.

No one would suspect an attack was coming.

(Every Democracy has one major weakness, when the politicians must vie for votes and not upset the voters. This trick had been used successfully before although in America in 1972 Nixon had not fallen for it.)

During April 1973 Pres. Sadat had secretly met with Syria's Hafez al-Assad to personally discuss Egypt's upcoming war plan. Assad had adeptly consolidated his power and rebuilt his military with massive aid from Russia. Assad used "donations" to undertake numerous public works projects to help his people, but he arrested, tortured, imprisoned and murdered anyone who got in the way. Assad was a clever man, and a good negotiator. Unlike most of the autocrats in the Middle East, Assad did not squander his nation's assets on a lavish lifestyle.

Happy with the plans he saw Assad stated that he would join in the attack. But Assad insisted that Egypt had to advance deeper into the Sinai to draw away more of Israel's tanks and planes. Being that Syria shared a common border Assad was fearful that Israel would send their strongest forces against him first. Sadat desired and needed Syria's participation, so he agreed to the change.

But this political move was destined to destroy Egypt's battle plan and forces because it was the opposite of what Gen. Shazly had planned for.

When Pres. Sadat returned to Egypt Gen. Shazly complained and tried to stop the change but was overruled. On August 23 the final secret meeting of the Egyptian and Syrian commanders was made. Their plans were gone over once more and all was agreed to. October 6, 1973 would be the day Israel would be destroyed.

Soon after Sadat visited Jordan to make amends.

One Israeli Intelligence officer did see the attack coming.

Major Shabati Brill had developed his own photography drone by attaching a camera to a small model plane. Flying the model while with his family "on holiday", he obtained good shots of the Egyptians in training. From the images he obtained and the "intelligence chatter" he was going through he realized that an attack really was imminent. But his superiors refused to listen to his warning because they had been wrong in May.

Along the Golan Heights the Syrian Commander had been slowly increasing the number of tanks being deployed, and most of them were the lethal T-62s. Mobile SAM batteries were also moving up near the border and many of those were recent arrivals from Russia. In Egypt there were now five infantry divisions "training along the Suez."

Then on Sept 13th the Syrians aggressively attacked a flight of Israeli *Phantom* jets trying to perform a recon mission over the Golan Heights. The Syrians lost a dozen planes to the superior pilots and American made jets of Israel. Gen. Shazly was convinced their operation was now imperiled. Surely Syria would retaliate and Israel would prepare for further attacks.

But Syria's Assad complained in public but did nothing further. That air battle actually worked to the Arab League's advantage. The Israeli Intel principles looked at the continuing Syrian and Egyptian activity and somehow convinced themselves that it was just a "reaction over the air battle".

Only Major Brill identified and spoke of how this activity had been ongoing since August 7. But like the British Intelligence officers who spoke up before operation *Market Garden* in 1944, those superiors again refused to listen and eventually forced them out.

(And just like in 1944, those bureaucrats were able to save themselves despite killing thousands of their countrymen.)

To further the illusion that the Egyptians were falling apart Gen. Shazly had the Egyptian papers print articles that quoted "government sources" in which the Russian advisors were complaining about the ineptness of the Egyptian troops.

Picking up on these unsubstantiated reports the *Washington Post* and *NY Times* both reported on those failures and the pending collapse of Arab unity.

In addition to weapons and munitions, the Russians also provided a revolutionary river fording technique. (This system was the same one as the Soviets would use if/when they invaded Western Europe.) Bridge sections were premade and rapidly assembled from the far shore. As the sections were added the bridge advanced into the water towards the enemy's side of the river. Like a Lego set the bridge sections were added at an incredible rate of one per minute. In less than thirty minutes a bridge could be constructed across the Suez, and Shazly planned to build 25 separate ones!

Once across the Suez the Egyptian Army units needed to go through the massive sand walls that the Israeli's had built. Once again a young engineer provided a solution.

They would use industrial fire-pumps to shoot large, high pressure water streams into the sand walls. The water streams would quietly carry away the sand and provide the access routes the Egyptian units needed to get through the sand wall.

(The fire pumps came from West Germany.)

On September 25 in a secret meeting King Hussein of Jordan met with Israeli Prime Minister Golda Meir. Hussein spoke of a clandestine meeting held in Cairo on the 12th. That meeting was addressing the issue that "Arab patience was at an end".

The King explained all of the Egyptian training programs that were still ongoing were actually preparations for war, and that he told the Syrians and Egyptians he wanted no part of another war.

Meir was rattled for sitting in her office was an Arab Monarch warning her of an imminent attack by the surrounding Arab nations. Meir spoke with her Intelligence and Military principals, and implausibly they dismissed the King's warnings. They stated that they knew who the King's sources were and they put all of their trust in the "In-law".

Within 24 hours the King's warnings were marginalized and then dismissed.

On the night of Sept 29-30 the CIA also sent a war warning to Israel.

It too was dismissed.

And then Major Brill found what he felt was incontrovertible proof.

The Syrians had moved two fighter squadrons to an advance base closer to Israel. They had left the safety of their hardened Soviet built hangers so they could be in position for their initial attack. If they were worried about an Israeli first strike they would have stayed in their northern bases and shelters surrounded by SAM missiles.

But again his superior Col. Porat dismissed him and his claims.

Israel actually had one more intelligence ace up their sleeve, a secret listening device that had been buried deep in the sand outside of Cairo. The battery powered device was attached to the Egyptian phone and cable connections, and when activated could listen in on all types of communications. Because they were battery powered they could only be activated in extreme emergencies.

As the Israeli principals began to get disturbed about all of the recent warnings those devices were supposed to have been used. The Director of Intelligence thought that Col. Porat had ordered their activation, but he did not because no order had been issued to him to do so. Thus another solid source was missed.

Not until October 5th did the Israeli leaders finally grasp what was happening. All military leaves were canceled and their Air Force and 7th Armored Brigade were placed on full alert. The 7th Armored was tasked to reinforce the two tank battalions that had been sent (two weeks earlier) to defend the Golan Heights. But moves on maps and on paper are not actual events, not until men and women make it so.

And by that point Israel was out of time.

At 2:00 PM on the 6th the thunder of hundreds of Egyptian canons began firing towards the Israeli fortifications along the Sinai. Syrian jets began bombing the defenses on the Golan Heights. Along the Suez the Egyptians sent 100,000 men, 1850 artillery pieces, 1550 tanks and hundreds of other vehicles into battle.

Manning the Israeli forts on the Suez were 436 soldiers and 3 tanks.

Their main reserve force of 277 tanks and artillery were based 20 miles back.

This Arab onslaught was well planned and massive. Hundreds of Arab jets flashed across the sands bombing and firing as they went. Russian made missiles were launched and landed with their 1,000 lb payloads. In the first few minutes over 10,000 shells landed on the Israeli forts in the Sinai.

At 2:20 Egyptian infantry and commando units were sent across the Suez to hold the ground the bridges would occupy. The German made water pumps also went across and began their well rehearsed destruction of the sand walls. Advance teams went deeper into the desert to take up their hidden firing positions. They carried with them the Soviet *Sagger* anti-tank missiles. Those missiles took just two minutes to setup and were ready to be used. The firing team needed to keep the missile sights on the target as thin wires relayed firing instructions to the missile as it flew. Dozens of the advancing Israeli tanks were blown up by these hidden teams and their armored counterattack was driven back. The Suez forts fell quickly.

(The Sagger was yet another example of Russian spies stealing an American invention almost as soon as we had made it.)

The vaunted Israeli Air Force had still not gone airborne, and when they finally did at 4PM it was a scratch mission that was just thrown together.(??)

Flying blind across the Sinai desert they were facing the new Russian SAM-6 missiles.

At that time there was no counter-measures tuned to the SAM-6 frequency and twelve Israeli Phantoms were lost before the jets even got across the desert.

In just three hours the Egyptians had bridged, breeched and crossed the Suez with 30,000 troops! During that first night all of the bridges would be in place and more forces would be in the Sinai setting up their traps.

In the Golan area there were 45,000 Syrians with 1400 tanks. Facing them were just 5,000 Israeli's armed with 100 canons and 177 tanks. High on the Golan Heights the Israeli's had setup a secret electronic listening post, *Mutzav 104*. The site was packed with the latest American spy/communication equipment tuned on Syria. The platoon of specialists from Major Brill's unit 848 manned the outpost that was designed to withstand artillery and bombing.

But at 2:55 PM four Russian made MI-8 helicopters brought in teams of Syrian commandos. They attacked the bunker manually and after hours of fighting the heavy blast doors were blown off. All of the Israeli's inside the post were killed.

The incredible booty of hi-tech American spy and communications hardware was inspected, disassembled and taken by the Russians.

(This unexpected assault was similar to the German attack on Fort Eben Emal in Belgium in 1940.)

By 3PM two columns of Syrian tanks were inside Israel. The Russian made tanks were equipped with infrared targeting systems, thus the Syrian tanks could see and attack in the coming darkness. A small Israeli tank unit sacrificed themselves and was able to keep the Syrians out of the town of Kuneitra and away from the bridges that spanned the Jordan River. But it was clear that come the dawn the Syrians would be back in force.

In a moment of fear or a just a failure to plan, the Syrians did not send commando or sapper units in with the tank units. Dismounted men could have crept around during the night similar to the work done by NVA sappers in Vietnam. They would have been able to destroy many of the remaining Israeli tanks which were operating for the most part alone. *That incredible Fatal Flaw in their plan enabled the Israeli's to stay alive and counterattack come the dawn.*

Gen. Shazly was told that the first of his tank bridges was operational at 11:30PM. Quickly 200 T-62 tanks would be across along with hundreds of other vehicles.

By dawn it was expected that all of the heavy bridges would be up and operational.

The Israeli tank division that had been held back in reserve for just such an eventuality had tried three times to reach the forts at the Suez. But Egyptian anti-tank teams had crossed over and setup their anti-tanks guns and missile traps.

During that first day of fighting the Israeli's had lost 180 of their 290 tanks.

Israeli casualties were high, and thus far the Egyptians had lost only 300 men. The battle to cross the Suez had been won.

During the next dawn the Israeli Air Force launched the expected missions to try to stop the Egyptians. Their initial raids hit the Egyptians hard but none of the planes returned for further attacks. Gen. Shazly was puzzled and worried. Numerous Egyptian antiaircraft units had been wiped out as had four of their airfields. If the Israelis had learned how to defeat the Soviet SAM's his forces would be unable to survive.

Unknown to him the dire circumstances in the Golan Heights required all available help. There was not a single Israeli tank left to protect the El Al route to Galilee. With no plan to guide them the redirected Israeli pilots flew low concentrating their attacks on groups of enemy armor that were just plodding along.

Rather than push on into the settlements and finding possible cover the Syrian tank crews actually left their vehicles and hid when the jets arrived. Dozens upon dozens of valuable armored vehicles were lost in the continual air attacks on the stopped columns. (This failure was a command failure. Where were the Syrian leaders?? Where was their air force and anti-air units) Those initial battles were costly for Israel's Air Force as they had already lost over 10% of their jets. Later that day a few more Israeli tanks arrived and they continued to hold the road to Kuneitra.

Israeli reinforcements had also begun arriving in the Sinai and soon there would be more than 600 tanks ready to fight. Why the Egyptian planes did not try to interrupt this effort was another command failure for as soon as those tanks entered the battlefield the tide would turn.

On the 8th the Israeli counterattack in the Sinai began but the Israeli commanders were at odds with each other and their planned attack failed. As was expected by the Egyptians, the sparring Israeli commanders had sent their tanks right into the prepared killing zones the Egyptians had setup. More losses occurred and as dusk began to approach the Israeli forces wisely pulled back. Tomorrow was another day.

In the north the Syrians were using artillery to attempt to destroy what remained of Israel's defense force. But still a small number of die hard troops were keeping them at bay. *Early in the morning of the 9th Moshe Dayan began discussions with the Prime Minister about using their secret weapons called Temple. Dayan was asking for permission to arm missiles and jets with nuclear weapons.*

Their final plan was that if Israel was destroyed, so would all of their enemies' cities. (The same atomic plan we used.) Golda Meir sadly approved the preparations.

It would take a day to accomplish. Meir sent a desperate message to Pres. Nixon asking for arms. Though his cabinet was torn over the idea, Nixon ordered a full package of aid and 550 planeloads of modern weapons arrived in Israel.

The Arab nations had secretly fielded a massive force of over 1 million men, 5,000 tanks, 5,000 artillery pieces and over 1,000 planes. Thousands of Egyptian anti-tank teams armed with RPGs or Sagger missiles prowled the desert.

Besides the SAM-6 antiaircraft missiles the Russians also sent SAM-7 mobile systems. These fired 4 or 8 rockets at a time at a passing jet increasing the chances of a hit. Hundreds of their excellent tracked 23mm four barreled canons called ZPU 23-4 completed the fatal mix. Russia had spent a fortune outfitting those armies, but the weapons of war are not the only statistic. Training, motivation and leadership are actually more important. The U.S. had learned this in Vietnam, and the Arab armies would soon learn this lesson too.

At 0900 on the 9th the Syrian artillery batteries again struck. Over 100 Syrian tanks moved against 17 Israeli ones. By 1130 only seven Israeli tanks remained when reinforcements finally arrived. As the armored battle continued into the afternoon the disheartened Syrians abandoned their tanks and ran away. The Syrians had also run out of SAMs. Soon the Israeli jets would be bombing Damascus.

(With their infrared capable tanks the Syrians should have made all of their attacks in the dark. The one night attack they made on the 7th did well, but it was on a small scale.)

In the Sinai the squabbling Israeli commanders again launched disjointed attacks losing another 50 tanks. But the Egyptians had not advanced or taken advantage of the Israeli failures. And unnoticed an Israeli recon patrol had found a seam between the two Egyptian armies. In their command bunker the Israeli principals argued on what to do. Some wanted peace as things stood while some wanted to recklessly attack. Golda Meir was worried that the superpowers would intervene and Israel would lose everything in the peace. She advocated attacking to end the war.

By the next morning more Israeli reinforcements had arrived at the Golan Heights. The reduced strength Israeli 7th armored brigade would now attack into the Syrian units. By the 12th they were slowly advancing into Syrian territory as the poorly led forces from Damascus fell apart.

In the south Gen. Shazly was being told to advance deeper into the desert.

Shazly warned that their gains would be eliminated for the Israeli air force was still too strong, but his bosses would not listen. Syria was demanding help to draw off the Israeli armored units.

Unseen the Israeli nuclear weapons had been silently removed. There was no longer a chance of their country being defeated. In their southern command post talks began to center on a plan to "cross" the Suez and attack into Egypt. At the same time the Egyptians were sending all of their reserves across the Suez Canal to aid in the new offensive plan. (Despite Gen. Shazly's objections.) This time Israeli intelligence learned of the moves and alerted the general staff.

Now the Israelis could plan smart and await their enemy.

It would be the Egyptian tanks that ran into a killing zone.

At 6:15am on the 14th over 2,000 tanks faced each other in the Sinai.

(This was the largest tank battle since Kursk in 1943.) Egyptian artillery began the attack followed by Russian made rockets and then the T-62 tanks. An hour later over 100 Egyptian tanks were burning out in the sand. By noon the entire offensive had been stopped costing the Egyptians over 250 tanks. As they retreated the Israeli jets gave chase against the wounded army destroying another 60 tanks. The Prime Minister approved their plans to attack across the Suez the next night.

To the north the Israelis had stopped 15 kilometers inside the Golan Heights, at the old borders of Syria. The Syrians had lost over 1200 tanks and were incapable of any further aggression. The Israeli's could have continued on untouched, but stood down.

In the Sinai Gen. Arial Sharon, (a similar personality to Patton), was tasked to lead the counterattack across the Suez. Silently the Israelis moved through the night and they stumbled into a huge supply depot of the Egyptian Second Army. While that fight was going on Israeli paratroopers began to cross the Suez in rubber boats. By morning of the 16th just 27 Israeli tanks and 2,000 troops were across the canal.

Sharon's brigade had lost almost half of their force during the confusing night battles. He decided to shelve the original battle plan and just continue ferrying small units across. They would attack at will, shoot-up any rear units encountered and head towards Cairo. His superiors disagreed but Sharon refused to stop. By noon his HQ was also across the canal with 50 tanks. More debates and battles were held and on the evening of the 18th the first Israeli bridge was across the Suez. Thus reinforced their units began attacking anything in range. The war would go on for three more days, but the Arab forces were crushed.

On the morning of the 22nd the UN Security Council passed Resolution #338, that a ceasefire would go into effect at 6:52 pm.

The war had cost the Arabs over 11,000 dead with another 15,000 wounded. Israel had lost over 2,800 dead and almost 9,000 wounded.

One fact that most people do not know was that the U.S. and Russia had almost joined the fight. Who can say how that would have ended.

Russia's leaders had been completely stunned at the reversal of fortunes in the Mideast. They were asked by the Arabs to help, and Russian paratroops were sent to an airfield in the Caucuses and their transports prepared to take off.

Warned of this pending communist effort, President Nixon called Brezhnev on the Hot Line and told him that war with America would begin if the Russians sent any troops to the region. Pres. Nixon had the 82nd Airborne Division put on immediate standby for deployment to the war zone and the entire 6th Fleet was ordered to deploy to the eastern Mediterranean.

The Soviets then sent 26 of their submarines into the eastern Mediterranean as a first strike capability. Our naval forces were hard pressed to stay in position to sink them if war came. And in addition to their conventional forces, both sides began moving nuclear weapons into the region. **U.S. Forces were put on a full worldwide alert. Convinced that Nixon was not bluffing the Russians again backed down.**

America

Watergate was the name of a Washington D.C. hotel.

As stated before on June 17, 1972 five burglars were arrested attempting to plant hidden microphones in the offices of the Democratic National Committee.

President Nixon and his team were upset about the June 1971 illegal publication of the classified Pentagon Papers. Even though he was not implicated in any of the material, Nixon and his Administration had worried that revelations contained therein could have been harmful to the ongoing peace negotiations.

Nixon did not try to stop the publication and allowed the paper to continue the articles. But the President felt that a potential anti-government plot may have been involved and authorized David Young and aide Egil Krogh to investigate, regardless of cost. Those two men setup a team called the "plumbers", which had a former CIA and FBI agent on board. They compiled a list of Nixon's "enemies", and eventually their continued activities became illegal ending with the break-in and arrest mentioned above.

Nixon denied any knowledge or the existence of the team, (which was true), but the trail quickly led from the two aides back to two senior White House staff, Haldeman and Ehrlichman. At that point the President should have come clean to the public by firing those involved and moving on. Instead he was loyal to his people and tried to cover-up the problem which made things exponentially worse.

Subpoenas were issued and it was learned that Nixon had been made aware of the team a few days after the arrest. Smelling a chance for political blood, (Alger Hiss, Impoundment Articles, Vietnam), the Congress began holding publicized hearings.

The Democratic Congress was vehemently anti-war, and completely against everything Nixon had done over the past years in Vietnam. They were no longer working with the President on any matters of national concern. As stated earlier they cut all funding to Indochina and imposed restrictions on the use of military forces.

On October 12, 1973 the Congress passed the War Powers Resolution Act. That law would limit Presidential authority to using U.S. Military forces for only 60 days. Any longer time frame than that the Congress would have to approve. (I agree.)

Nixon felt that this was unconstitutional, and vetoed it.

The Congress overrode him on Nov 7. *(During the above time frame the Yom Kippur War was ongoing with the threat of a Superpower confrontation. The War powers Act could have caused an issue if Russia had come in.)*

After the Middle East War ended the OPEC nations in the Middle East protested the United States support of Israel by enacting an oil embargo. Sales of oil were sharply curtailed to any nation that aligned itself with Israel. *"When the Arab Lands captured in the 1967 war were evacuated", then the embargo would end.*

This was the first time in modern memory any league of nations had restricted global trade as a way to force a political goal and they set a dangerous precedent.

The modern world was dependent upon oil for its energy needs and this act would greatly affect America and the West. Had those nations tried this type of embargo against Russia the Soviets would have invaded and crushed them. But against the Democracies this measure was timidly addressed with economic and political goals.

To reduce our use of oil and its main byproduct of gasoline, speed limits were reduced on all expressways. By the end of the month Nixon was forced to enact the Emergency Petroleum Act of 1973. With winter coming to the northern latitudes the reduction in oil supplies would become dangerous. By Nov 30, 1973 gasoline prices rose sharply as the embargo began to take hold. In a month gas-lines would form as cars waited for hours to be able to purchase a few gallons. Later on an odd/even day schedule was used to try to reduce the gas lines. (Those lines were a major shock to a nation that had never known that type of restrictions.)

Great Britain was hit so hard it was reduced to a three day work week, and in December gas rationing began. The developing world suffered from the effects the worst, for those nations were least able to afford the price spikes.

(Disturbingly high profit levels rose at many U.S. Oil companies as they were not just passing along the price increases from OPEC.)

With the Yom Kippur War ended major changes occurred. The Israeli's conducted an internal investigation, sacking three of their senior officers for failing to do their duty. Meanwhile the useless politicians and those with political allies escaped unharmed. Golda Meir would resign from office in 1974.

Egypt and Syria would never be able to field such large military forces again. And that changed the balance of power in the Mideast.

(Once more the arms of the West had outperformed the Soviet ones.)

In April 1974 Pres. Sadat would end his country's reliance on Soviet support and weapons. (The Arab hardliners would turn solely to terror tactics to hurt the Israelis.) Realizing that war could not rectify their problems Sadat looked to America for a chance at peace.

During his last world tour in June 1973 Pres. Nixon promised to repair the relations between Egypt and America. He promised to help Egypt reach their goal of providing nuclear energy which would give them the electricity they needed to modernize. Nixon's overtures enabled future Presidents Ford and then Carter to negotiate a peace between Egypt and Israel. Egypt would become an ally.

Nixon also met with Syria's Assad and talks of restoring relations were held. **But after Nixon left office no further advances on that premise were followed.**

Because of that failure Syria remained a troubled nation with a dangerous ruler who continued to use terrorism and death to damage his neighbors.

(Pres. Nixon also made a final stopover in Russia. He and Brezhnev held their third summit and their discussions centered on restoring peace to the world.)

And with all of those issues on the front pages **Islamic terrorism returned**.

On November 25, 1973 KLM Flight 861 was hijacked by three Palestinians.

On December 17, 1973 the PLO sent terrorists to attack Rome's airport. Pan Am Fl 110 suffered 34 killed with 22 wounded, while a nearby Lufthansa flight was hijacked and taken to Athens. They suffered 2 killed and 2 wounded.

For months the Watergate hearings and court proceedings filled the daily press and televised news reports. Democrats in the House began looking at impeachment proceedings. They were led by Peter Rodino and one of the many assistants was a Hillary Rodham and Bernie Nussbaum. (Rodham was fired by her boss for lying and being dishonest in handling legal proceedings.) Both would be back.

President Nixon rightfully resigned on August 9, 1974 rather than prolong the pain to the Nation and himself. One of his last acts was to sign a law sending aid to S. Vietnam. Only $200 million of the promised aid actually reached them.

Though the media and liberals would claim him the worst of our Presidents, it was not so. His deft and creative Foreign Policies enabled him to end a terrible war begun and run by deceptive liberal politicians. *Our military forces and his war ending actions gave S. Vietnam a chance at freedom.* Pres. Nixon began the movement to control nuclear weapons, (SALT), reduce superpower tensions, and his initiatives allowed Communist China to rejoin the world of nations and set the stage for future accomplishments.

None of our enemies could comprehend his resignation over such a trivial issue. Nixon's loss to the nation and to world affairs would not be felt right away. **But his absence and the political collapse in America that followed set the stage for a decade of problems with the communists and allowed the Islamic Extremists to come to power.**

Gerald Ford was a moderate congressman who had become Vice-President a few months earlier. (Former V.P. Spiro Agnew had failed to report $29,500 additional income while he was Governor of Maryland in 1967. Agnew was hit with a charge of income tax evasion and he resigned on Oct 12, 1973.)

*For a short while some of the Democrats conjured up a chance to actually take over the White House. Prior to Ford's swearing in if Nixon "left office" for any reason then Democratic Speaker of the House Carl Albert would have become president. (*Major Democrats like Bella Abzug from NYC and Ted Sorenson one of JFK's speechwriters pushed hard for the takeover.)

Ford took the oath of office but had no mandate to be president, he was a fill in. As such he had no political capital to use in running the country. One of his first problems was the desire by many to indict Nixon for the attempted cover up. The former president had to go to court over scores of nonsensical lawsuits that were designed to bankrupt and dishonor him. Rather than prolong the nation's darkness Ford pardoned Nixon.
Liberals and activists hated that decision, but in looking at the situation was it worth the time to pursue?

(It was not like Nixon had been corrupt as in the Teapot Dome or Truman's five-percenter scandals. He had not lied under oath or attempted witness tampering as Bill Clinton did in 1997, nor had he leaked government secrets and perjured about it, or spied for enemy nations like so many are doing now.) His pardon ended the Watergate episode, and the world kept turning.

In early 1974 the OPEC nations began withdrawing their petro-dollars from the banks in the West in a further effort to hurt them. But on March

13, 1974 the OPEC nations decided to end their boycott. *They had reaped a $100 Billion dollar windfall from the 300% price increase.*

One major result of the increased energy costs was a dangerous surge in inflation as the price of oil affected all aspects of the West's economies.

President Ford warned in a September 1974 speech that the continuing price increases associated with the oil crisis would threaten the world's economy for decades.

It was vital for the United States to reach its goal of energy independence.

But no concrete plan was ever researched or enacted by our failing government. Not then, and not now forty years later!

During the last months of 1974, Israel, Syria and the PLO operating out of southern Lebanon would fight many small battles. In October an Arab League Summit promised to send billions of dollars in aid from the Oil profits to the Arab countries that had fought against Israel. The League also recognized the PLO as the sole representative of the Palestinians. Yasir Arafat was their leader and he addressed the U.N. wearing a pistol. (He never should have been allowed into the building.)

He condemned Israel and demanded a Palestinian State.

Many of the diplomats supported him and his murderous efforts.

It is a recurring travesty that the Arabs had refused to partition the land back in 1947 when the United Nations tried. Had they agreed back then, they would have had a Palestinian State and western aid to help them get started. Their failure to do so resulted in the wars and terrorism that followed.

No effort to help the Palestinian people had ever been made, or assistance offered by the Arab nations prior to that time. And no such offers had come in since 1947!

Even after the Yom Kippur War was over the nations in the region still could not agree to donate some of their lands to enact that needed outcome. Imagine if Egypt, Jordan, Israel and Saudi Arabia could each give up a small section of land to create a new nation called Palestine. That would give those people a home and a future which all people deserve. (That same scenario should also be done to create Kurdistan from Turkey, Iraq and Iran.)

And the Islamic terrorism continued.

On February 7, 1974 Palestinians attacked the Japanese Embassy in Kuwait.

On April 11, 1974 a PLO attack into Israel killed 18 and wounded 16. Israel retaliated and bombed six villages in southern Lebanon harboring the PLO terrorists. Additional attacks occurred on both sides.

September 8, 1974 TWA Flight 841 to NYC was destroyed by a bomb in the cargo hold

Eighty eight were killed as the PLO and Abu Nidal used a suicide bomber in the attack.

Asia

In spite of the thawing of relations and the gains they had made because of Pres. Nixon's earlier efforts, Communist China began to smuggle vast amounts of arms into the South. Without that covert aid the North could not have invaded again.

With Nixon gone from power the communist enemy became emboldened.

China was always looking for an easy grab. They saw the political weakness in America and seized the Paracel Islands from S. Vietnam in mid January 1975. Tests had shown that oil could be present around those islands. Like Japan, China had no oil of its own. And like Japan of 1941, China reached out and took it. Weeks later Mao ordered another "cultural revolution". (The last one started in 1965 had killed over twenty five million people in the demented communist orgy of purging dissidents.)

To help the Cambodian's hang on after we had left Pres. Nixon had ordered an airlift to get supplies to them. Pres. Ford had continued the effort and the airlift would work through a front company called Bird Air. By mid-1974 they had delivered over 450,000 tons of supplies to Phom Penh.

In late 1974 terrible events began to unfold, the first was the resignation of Nixon.

Then in Feb 1975 the communists were finally able to block the Mekong River stopping all shipping. The U.S. Congress had stopped sending any more supplies. As a result of those factors the Cambodian Army was unable to hold off the 100,000 communist attackers. Soon after Communist artillery began shelling the capitol causing hundreds of casualties among the innocent civilians. As the fighting grew worse the U.S. Embassy ordered the evacuation of all our citizens and personnel on April 12. **On April 17, 1975 the communist Khmer Rouge captured the city and the war in Cambodia ended. The killing did not.**

Not since the days of the Mongols had a nation been subjected to such barbarity. An insane despot named Pol Pot became the head of the communist regime that took over. He insisted he would remake the nation into an agrarian state. All of the educated people, government workers and "undesirables" were herded out of the cities and murdered outright or placed in work camps. Millions of innocents died terrible deaths at the hands of yet another communist regime.

Into 1978 the murderous and destructive Cambodian regime of Pol Pot was still seeding their Killing Fields. They released a report stating that there had actually been over 200,000 Communist troops secretly operating in NE Cambodia during the Vietnam War years.

Across the border S. Vietnam faced the same perils. With the ending of the American war effort and the Paris Peace Accords life in S. Vietnam returned to a sense of normalcy. President Thieu had made many democratic improvements to his country. His Land to Tiller program had reduced tenant farming from 60% down to 7%. Farm output had risen dramatically and the economy in the South had begun to improve.

There was still fighting in the outlying provinces as the ARVN forced the NVA out from some distant areas, but for the most part the war was over. The VC had mostly been uncovered and eliminated, and they too desired peace.

Our Embassy was still active and there were over 6,000 Americans working in the South. Some were military advisors, some were CIA, some were contractors brought over to keep the infrastructure working. Most were State Dept. employees working a normal posting in a foreign land.

As stated earlier U.S. aid to South Vietnam had been cut greatly reducing the South's fuel and ammo supplies. The 1973 Oil Embargo had quadrupled the price of oil, and within a few months began causing even more severe restrictions on ARVN fuel supplies. (Eleven of their air force units had to be disbanded for lack of fuel.) With the drastic reduction in our aid and the exit of many of the humanitarian organizations corruption in South Vietnam resumed. That drained away resources from their continuing struggle to remain free.

At the same time the NVA were regaining their strength, freed from all American interference. Hanoi knew that the people in the South still did not want to join them, so their preparations for forced inclusion had continued, but they did not attack. *After what had happened to them in 1972, the North Vietnamese feared Nixon. If he had remained in office the North would not have resumed the war.*

But after Nixon resigned things began to change for the worse.

And as their problems and dangers increased President Thieu slowly fell away from the principals of Democracy that had started to take hold.

In late 1974 the U.S. State Dept issued a special report that North Vietnam had infiltrated an additional 170,000 troops into the South. Accompanying those forces were over 400 tanks and vast amounts of supplies.

The report warned of an imminent attack by the NVA!

As hard as it is to believe our own media continued to create the illusion that our efforts and those of the South had been brutal and oppressive. In rebuttal Newsweek columnist Ken Crawford wrote that this was the first war in which our media were more friendly to our enemies than to our allies. Coverage of the South was still tainted.

Anti-war Americans Jane Fonda and Ramsy Clark were given celebrity status for their false statements that we were the oppressors in Vietnam and that our POWs had been given good treatment. As stated earlier Fonda had visited a POW camp and met with many of our prisoners in a photo op for the communists. *A few of the captured pilots tried to get a list of the POWs to her and she turned them in! Two of those American prisoners were beaten to death after she left.* And during the war numerous American colleges had sent aid packages to the enemy. They were discovered in NVA supply caches. (All of those involved should have been arrested and imprisoned for treason.)

NVA General Tran Van Tra had examined the NVA failures from TET and the Easter Offensive and developed a new plan of action. As deputy commander his forces were going to strike the ARVN redoubts quickly, and prevent the ARVN aircraft from flying. Air power had been decisive in 1972 despite the presence of SAM units in the NVA attacks. This time they would shut it down. If they struck rapidly and well, America would not be able to intervene in time.

Only Le Duc Tho was against the plan preferring to wait until 1976.

Their re-supply from China and Russia had ended and it was doubtful any more would be coming. Tho wanted to be cautious and continue their current slow and steady pace. Party Secretary Le Duan approved a compromise plan to just attack Phuoc Long province adjacent to Cambodia.

Months of never ending fighting against the NVA forces remaining in their Northern and western provinces had continued to drain away at the ARVN units. Much of the NVA gains from the 1972 invasion had been recaptured by the ARVN.

(Most of their best units were deployed in I Corps, leaving the rest of the South weaker.) Lack of spare parts and ammo was severe with stockpiles at just 20% of the 1972 levels. By late 1974 desertions also began to reduce the effectiveness of the ARVN.

Then in mid-December 1974 NVA troops attacked into South Vietnam. They captured Route 14 by Christmas, and on January 6, 1975 their 8,000 man force captured the capital of Phuoc Binh after another savage bombardment by artillery and rockets. Again thousands of civilian casualties were caused in the attacks.

This was the NVA's first major accomplishment in almost three years.

Those NVA attacks were in clear violation of the Paris Peace Accords. There was almost no reaction from our government, and there was no reaction from the United Nations. This was a clear case of a communist nation invading a free and separate state, but the UN had become polarized and ineffectual.

In those recent battles the ARVN air attacks had not been as effective due to the strong NVA anti-air defenses that had been brought forward. The NVA had learned much in the past years and Russia had supplied them with the same anti-air weapons they had given Egypt. Pres. Thieu was stunned by the lack of reaction from America. Nixon had promised we would come back if the NVA attacked.

Pres. Ford met with Brezhnev at Vladivostok, while Kissinger met the Chinese in Beijing. Neither diplomatic attempt made any headway to try to reign in the N. Vietnamese. With Nixon gone both communist nations knew Saigon was doomed. (Seeing the weakness in America, China was secretly rushing aid to the Khmer Rouge, while Gen. Viktor Kulikov went to Hanoi with promises of more aid.)

Encouraged by the positive events from the recent attacks, Le Duan recommended more aggression. Their next target was to be Ban Me Thuot in the Central Highlands. Senior NVA General Van Tien Dung had replaced Gen. Giap and was mindful of how poorly his plans had been in 1972. This time he concentrated his forces in the jungles of the Central Highlands and hoped to split the South in two by driving towards the coast before the May monsoons began. Speed was his main asset and he wanted to defeat the ARVN before they could react.

On March 1, 1975 four NVA divisions attacked into the III Corps region north of Saigon. Those NVA divisions besieged Ban Me Thuot and captured it on March 11. Watching the lack of reaction from America additional strong NVA attacks began striking in I Corps. Again all of those communist attacks were in direct violation of the Paris Peace Agreement.

Nonelected Pres. Gerald Ford had no mandate to act, and the Democratic Congress was still smiling over their "apparent political victory". They would not honor any prior pledge from former President Nixon. But their political win was an empty shell for with Nixon's removal from office and the general malaise in the Congress our government left the world stage to its own ending. But when international power is in the equation a vacuum is not tolerated,

"For There are Tigers in This World,"
and They are Always Watching.

Part of the lack of judgment and vision from the Congress of the 1970s was caused by the failed leadership of the 1960s. First those poor leaders of the 60s moved from one crisis to another. Then they undermined and eliminated an "allied regime" because it did not match with their desired liberal ideals of how a modern society should exist. Next they committed vast sums of our national wealth and our children to shore up the weak regimes that took over.

Those same leaders consistently mislead the public as they moved us into a war which none of our citizens wanted or asked for. Then they insisted we were winning the war as they closed their eyes to the truth. Lyndon Johnson and his Administration lost their will and their credibility when the heavy fighting of TET began in January 1968. Nixon won the election in their turmoil, and the American center stood by him and gave him time to obtain a peace. It took four more years to get that peace but the liberals and antiwar members in Congress turned completely against our Foreign Policy efforts and sabotaged all of America's interests for the rest of the decade.

By this point in time the North Vietnamese had created over 12,000 miles of roads which formed the Ho Chi Minh Trail. It was truly a remarkable achievement.

During the war they had moved almost a million troops and logistic personnel down the trail. And they had transported 1,200 prisoners northward, (SOG, Commando, Recon, Aircrew and ARVN from Lam Son 719.) Over 1,770,000 tons of supplies and arms had also traveled the Trail, culminating in their takeover of S. Vietnam.

The reduction in the South's air assets and artillery was now observed and became a fatal weakness. Pres. Thieu ordered his units to abandon the highlands and protect the coastal areas. Forced to use the time honored plan of trading space for time the ARVN was trying to withdraw and regroup. ARVN General Pham Van Phu cowardly saved himself as the mixed column of 200,000 ARVN troops and refugees tried to move down the mountainous road without any command or organization. In a typical display of poor leadership no one else stepped up to take command. And as was typical of the savage NVA, they shelled the slow moving column mercilessly killing thousands of innocent civilians.

Observing the lack of offense or defense, NVA attacks in I Corps moved quickly with refugees filling those roads too. With this string of reversals Pres Thieu wrongly ordered a redeployment of all of his northern forces at the same time. This withdrawal was not well planned nor organized which resulted in mass confusion and panic. The populace was justifiably terrified of the communists and civilian traffic crowded the roads which prevented any organized movement or counterattacks by the ARVN units. Discipline fell apart as desertions increased so the soldiers could care for their families.

Hue fell on March 25, 1975. More than a million refugees were on the roads heading for Da Nang when NVA long range rockets ripped into that city. Again thousands upon thousands of innocents were slaughtered in the needless attacks. Desperate to escape civilians and soldiers jammed the airports, docks and beaches hoping to find a way out. Many thousands more died as Da Nang fell too.

The ARVN Marine Division was split up with half trying to save Da Nang while the other half protected Saigon. Their northern unit was eventually overwhelmed by two NVA Divisions and they were annihilated in the closing battles.

(Cambodia was collapsing at this time.)

At the U.S. Embassy military advisors and CIA officers repeatedly warned Ambassador Martin to began evacuating the Embassy and all American personnel. There were dozens of thousands of S. Vietnamese that had worked with us that also needed to be evacuated. Martin refused any such talk or planning, calling it defeatist!

Watching the disintegration of the ARVN Gen Dung was told to press on. He had his NVA units in the III Corps area re-directed to attack towards Saigon.

All that stood between them and victory was the ARVN 18th Div.

Never considered one of the ARVN best, the 18th held the city of Xuan Loc from April 9 to the 23. The NVA hammered them nonstop with heavy artillery and rockets, and used frontal attacks with three divisions. Before they were finally overrun in the human wave assaults, the 18th killed over 5,000 NVA troops.

In the northern areas the modern mechanized NVA forces moved freely and quickly across the numerous battlefields overrunning the collapsing ARVN units.

As was the proven concept in armored attacks, it was vital to hit them before they could organize a defense.

In Saigon the U.S. Embassy suddenly had a serious problem on their hands. Ambassador Graham Martin had refused to believe the reports that the ARVN were falling apart. He had delayed the civilian evacuations until this last minute.

Almost a hundred thousand aid workers and South Vietnamese Nationals were suddenly placed at great risk. Should the NVA envelop the country those people would be captured and most would be murdered.

One of Martin's reasons for procrastinating was the belief that we, meaning our government would not let the NVA win. (Martin's fatally flawed evacuation mistakes echoed those of Sir Shenton Thomas at Singapore in 1942.) Behind his back State and Military officers had already started an underground railroad type endeavor were evacuating thousands of S. Vietnamese. Another group setup an evacuation route using commercial shipping at Saigon's port. Another officer had the S. Vietnamese Navy assemble their ships for a similar mission. Packed with thousands of desperate civilians and military refugees the ships were sailed to the Philippines.

On April 23 Xuan Loc was overrun by 40,000 NVA troops. That placed them just 35 miles from Bien Hoa airfield and Saigon. Commercial airlines had been hurriedly brought in and carried thousands to safety in the few days before the airport began being shelled. Once the NVA began shelling the airfields near Saigon it closed off the only major way out of the country. *(On the last day an airliner carrying hundreds of orphaned children was blown up just before takeoff. All were killed.)*

After that horrible disaster the airfields were closed and adhoc helicopter evacuations were begun around the city. Marine helicopters picked up over 8,000 more from the embassy rooftop and courtyard. All were ferried out to aircraft carriers in the S. China Sea. A mistake in the timing left 420 S. Vietnamese stranded inside the Embassy. *Because of the evacuation delays thousands upon thousands of South Vietnamese loyal to their nation and America were left behind.*

(One of those left behind referred to the sounds of the helicopter airlift as; *The Dream In The Wind.* He would spend years in a Communist labor camp before escaping and making his way to America.)

Chaotic scenes filled the airwaves as the country was being overrun. The U.S. Congress did nothing to help or try to prevent this from happening and the last U.S. helicopter flew off with the Marine Embassy Guards on April 30. In and around Saigon ARVN units desperately attempted to hold on. After the brutal fighting less than 250 of the ARVN Marines escaped from the communists. That was probably a common fate for all of the ARVN ground units.

ARVN helicopter units were able to save themselves by flying out to sea and landing upon our ships. TV images of those few dozen soldiers saving themselves and their families made many in the audience angry. But what would you have done?

Hours after the last flight left Saigon the NVA captured the city and South Vietnam became just another domino, as had Cambodia.

(Watching these events on television I remember the cold, dejected feelings that coated that time frame. All of our efforts, all of the cost, all of those wonderful people we lost, gone in a failed endeavor. Our military did not lose Indochina, our corrupt and arrogant politicos did.)

Also left behind in Saigon were the embassy files, just like in Korea in 1950.

The communists went through the papers finding everyone who had worked for us or the South Vietnamese Government. Thousands of those dedicated civilians were murdered by the communists. Multiple dozens of thousands went to work camps where more died from forced labor, starvation, disease and neglect.

Over the following months hundreds of thousands of refugees from South Vietnam became "boat people" as they franticly left their country and the vicious communists on any sea craft they could get. (Similar to the Cuban refugees.) Those poor souls were abandoned and left to their fates floating in the South China Sea. More than 600,000 of them would perish.

The Vietnamese refugee crisis became just another horrible human tragedy as many countries in the region refused them entry. And America's caring liberals also turned their backs on them.

After watching those disastrous events our Democratic controlled Congress even rejected Pres. Ford's request for funds to resettle the 150,000 Vietnamese refugees that our forces had picked up. Religious and charitable groups helped fund the relocations.

Throughout the rest of 1975 the patented communist control plan was in full swing. The economies of Cambodia and S. Vietnam would be devastated crippling the futures of millions. Similar to the events in Singapore in 1942, the nation's traders who were mostly ethnic Chinese were ironically persecuted. They were stripped of all of the processions, property and businesses as over two hundred thousand were rounded up and expelled, those who survived.

Religion once such an integral part of life in South Vietnam and a key factor in convincing JFK to oust Pres. Diem was attacked by the communists in an effort to eradicate all of it, Christian and Buddhist.

In Saigon over a million city dwellers were sent into the country for re-education. Their corrupt western ways would be sweated out of them in forced labor camps. Again thousands would die unseen in the camps.

More S. Vietnamese died during the communist takeover and peace than had perished in the war!

(Again the media never commented on that fact, but as Lenin once said, "Facts can be such stubborn things.")

William Colby the CIA Director would sadly remark;

"In an ironic twist the communists initiated their war against Diem by following Mao's principals of a People's War using subversion and deceit.

The French and Americans responded wrongly to the communist effort by trying to fight a conventional war mirroring WWII and Korea.

In the early 1970's President Thieu had partly succeeded in rebuilding his country. He had defeated the "peoples' war policies" by implementing the effective Phoenix Program and by his Democratic reforms that actually helped the people of South Vietnam.

But in the end he lost the war to the Communists who invaded in a conventional mechanized military assault.

It wasn't a barefoot S. Vietnamese peasant in black pajamas who captured the Presidential Palace.

It was a Russian T-62 tank, built in the Soviet Union, shipped to Haiphong in a Russian ship and manned by a North Vietnamese crew." (59)

Yet even today America's liberals and leftists will tell you it was a "civil war".

END BOOK 2

Index

B

Bay of Pigs, 301-07, 315, 336, 346, 352, 363, 378, 539
Berlin, 3-6, 50, 61, 67-69, 113, 181, 212, 217, 224, 254, 314-21, 323-25, 334, 350, 354, 358, 370, 431

C

Cambodia, 11, 48, 73, 232, 248, 252, 281-83, 290, 299, 329, 332, 338-39, 245, 378, 392, 406, 409, 413, 427, 430-31, 443-44, 447-49, 462, 467, 476, 481, 490-95, 500-10, 514-15, 526-28, 532, 539-41, 559-61, 546-66
CCF Communist Chinese Forces, 26-27, 32-37, 105-07, 116, 134, 159, 162-90, 193-97, 205-16, 229, 524
Chiang Kai-shek, 24-33, 36-38, 43, 47, 71-73, 81, 99, 101-05, 109-12, 274, 324, 335, 342, 380, 387
China, 4, 13, 19, 24-36, 39-48, 51-54, 57, 61-62, 68-73, 80-81, 89-91, 94-96, 99-108, 112-116, 123-24, 127-33, 148-52, 155-61, 167-68, 185, 197-99, 205-08, 213-16, 223-24, 229-35, 243-47, 250-51, 264-68, 270, 281, 285-89, 299-300, 306-08, 334-35, 342-45, 350-51, 364 66, 385-87, 390-92, 398-403, 425, 432-33, 445-47, 459-62, 483-87, 494-95, 499-02, 511, 524-28, 532-33, 538, 557, 559-62
Chosin Reservoir, 163, 167-68, 173, 177, 189, 194, 492, 510
Chou En-lai, 32-33, 37, 107, 150, 155, 216, 233, 398, 525
Cuba, 8, 62, 244, 266, 280, 287-88, 291-96, 299-306, 314-16, 325-29, 334, 346-64, 370, 378, 394, 433, 458, 499 501, 539, 566
Cuban Missile Crisis, 346-64

D

General Douglas McArthur, 42, 93-96, 104-09, 111-14, 117-24, 127-38, 140-53, 156-72, 174-77, 184-85, 188-89, 191-93, 195-97, 201, 211, 213, 301, 331, 432, 440, 465, 474
Dwight Eisenhower, IKE, 4, 11, 17, 28, 87, 93, 103, 128, 194, 213-14,

217-19, 225-33, 237-39, 242-59, 262-68, 270, 275-82, 287, 290-304, 310, 313-18, 326, 343, 356, 381, 387, 430, 538-39

E

Egypt, 7, 64-66, 215, 227-28, 242, 256-59, 262-65, 275-77, 327, 364, 454-56, 497, 501, 512-13, 543-58, 562

G

Gemal Abdel Nasser, 215, 227-28, 257-59, 263-66, 275-77, 327, 364, 454, 513, 543-44
George Marshall, 17, 25, 27-38, 52-63, 68-76, 83, 94, 123, 128, 148, 158, 168, 175-77, 208, 223, 237, 243, 297, 430

H

Hanoi, 11, 45-48, 200, 229, 232, 251, 254, 272, 282-83, 290-91, 309, 331, 378, 392, 398, 401-02, 406-11, 415, 419-20, 431, 453, 459, 464, 474, 492-94, 503-05, 515, 525-27, 530-32, 535-37, 541, 560, 562
Harry Truman, 3-5, 8-10, 16- 20, 22-24, 26-32, 34-38, 45, 50-62, 67-85, 88-89, 94, 97-105, 108, 112-19, 120-28, 132-34, 140, 148, 157-60, 167-70, 175, 183-88, 191-201, 209-12, 215, 219-26, 231, 240-44, 256, 264-66, 277, 281, 296, 312, 315-17, 334, 344, 352, 373, 386, 390, 397, 406, 420, 432, 459, 461-62, 487, 511, 538-39, 557

Henry Kissinger, 489-90, 497, 503-05, 511, 524-25, 529, 532-35, 538, 562
Ho Chi Minh, 10-11, 43-48, 89, 94, 99-100, 107, 233-34, 250-52, 282-83, 391, 329, 332, 345, 397, 402, 405-07, 410-13, 421, 424-26, 433, 441-46, 463, 471, 494, 500
Hue, 290, 377, 387, 472-75, 564

I

Iran, 13, 21-22, 27, 34-36, 51, 61, 94, 103, 116, 240-43, 256-59, 293, 334, 356, 376, 426, 513, 558
Islamic Fundamentalists, 6, 215, 228, 240-42, 257, 275-77, 310, 376, 456, 497-99
Israel, 65-66, 84, 228, 256, 262-66, 275, 327, 454-56, 497-98, 512-13, 542-58

J

John Kennedy, JFK, 51, 232, 249, 255, 267, 288, 293-328, 330-36, 340-46, 349-54, 356, 359-63, 366, 370, 376-78, 381-90, 394, 397, 406, 414, 459, 517, 539
John Vann, 332-33, 337-41, 345-46, 366-79, 384, 387, 390, 405, 410-11, 431, 436-37, 441, 459, 464-67, 471-72, 478-79, 488-90, 493, 495-96, 500, 529, 531
Josef Stalin, 3, 5, 9, 12-15, 19, 21-26, 33-39, 49-52, 54-61, 68-71, 74, 77, 82, 86-88, 95-96, 99-101, 104-07, 109-111, 116-17, 128, 138-39, 155-58, 183, 191, 194, 208, 210, 214-15, 243-45, 253,

231, 266, 269, 286, 312, 314-17, 334, 362, 382

K

Khe Sahn, 284, 371, 393, 449-52, 467-69, 473, 476-78, 493, 541-15, 527-28
Kim il Sun, 69, 94-95, 105-06, 113, 138, 150, 155, 254

L

Laos, 11, 48, 73, 205, 229, 232, 248, 252, 281-91, 297-301, 305-09, 311-16, 323-24, 331-32, 336, 344-45, 370, 377-80, 392-93, 398, 403, 406, 409, 413, 421-24, 427, 441-42, 447-50, 460, 469-70, 476-78, 481, 492, 503-06, 510, 514-17, 521, 526-28, 539-41
Le Duc Tho, 43, 503-05, 529, 532, 534-35, 561
Lin Biao, 36, 71, 162-63, 524
Lyndon Johnson, LBJ, 78, 197, 215, 232, 251, 265, 295, 320, 323, 330, 336, 389-96, 400-10, 412-20, 423, 426-68, 433, 438, 444, 448, 451, 456, 463-64, 469, 474-85, 488, 492, 510-11, 517, 530, 539, 563

M

Manchuria, 13, 22-27, 32-39, 61, 71-72, 79, 95-96, 106, 133, 154-59, 163, 167-70, 175, 194, 197, 211, 220, 432, 461, 489, 494
Mao Zedong, 26, 31-32, 36, 71-72, 89, 99, 105-08, 134, 155-57, 165, 192-94, 266, 285-86, 289, 334, 392, 398, 403, 447, 483, 489, 495, 502, 517, 524-27, 559, 567

Marshall Plan, 55-61, 72-74, 83, 87-88, 98, 117, 224, 246, 253, 257, 320, 334
General Mathew Ridgeway, 28, 140-41, 175, 177, 184, 192-99, 205-09, 213-14, 221-22, 231-22, 237, 298, 310, 324, 373, 379, 401, 432
Maxwell Taylor, 214, 238, 291, 297, 305, 315, 318, 323-28, 331, 336, 346, 350-53, 370-71, 374, 378-81, 384-86, 390-98, 401-03, 406-08, 410-13, 416, 420, 435, 439, 482, 485
Moscow, 14-16, 43-44, 50-55, 61, 68, 79, 81, 84, 88-90, 99, 105-06, 109, 113, 117, 124, 254, 258, 260-61, 276-77, 289, 307, 347, 351, 355-60, 363, 382, 403, 445, 486, 504, 524-26, 533
Mohammed Mossadegh, 241-42, 257

N

NKPA, N. Korean People's Army, 102-110, 114-18, 122-29, 132-39, 141-49, 151-57, 160-65, 169, 173-75, 180, 189-90, 194, 205-09, 211, 432, 462, 470, 538
Ngo Dinh Diem, 10, 44, 234-35, 245, 248-51, 274, 283-85, 290-91, 298-99, 312, 323-25, 329, 332-33, 339, 341-45, 369-70, 373-74, 377-78, 381-88, 391-92, 566-67
North Korea, 22, 38, 61, 71, 89, 95-96, 101-06, 108-10, 112-20, 126, 132-35, 149-53, 155-64, 166-68, 170-81, 184-90, 208-09, 211-14, 220, 239, 250, 254, 281, 329, 392, 432, 445, 448, 461, 470-72, 494, 531

O

General Oliver Smith, 98, 141, 144-46, 166, 169-72, 174-82, 185, 187-89, 193-95, 222

P

Philippines, 8, 91, 96, 100-03, 112, 116, 129, 140, 231, 235, 244-45, 249, 285, 291, 300, 324, 329, 365, 565

Pusan, S. Korea, 40, 110-111, 119, 122-23, 126-43, 146, 151-53, 158, 162-63, 190, 218, 432

R

Richard Nixon, 51, 77-78, 256, 280-81, 287-89, 293-94, 301, 304, 313, 382, 388, 449, 482, 485, 488-89, 491-506, 508-14, 517-21, 524-31, 533-42, 545, 551-57, 559-63

Robert Kennedy, RFK, 295, 306, 328, 346, 350-54, 359-62, 381, 386, 479, 482-85

Robert McNamara, Sec. Defense, 296, 300, 310, 313, 322, 325, 330, 333, 336, 339-40, 343-40, 349-52, 357-62, 370, 374, 381, 384-86, 388-401, 404, 407-10, 415, 420-23, 432-42, 444, 450-51, 459, 463-66, 479, 482, 485, 521

S

Saigon, 9, 11, 46, 201, 251, 284, 299, 311, 329-32, 339, 366-68, 377, 380, 387-88, 397, 403, 405, 409, 411-16, 424, 430, 436, 441, 444, 449, 465-67, 472-75, 478, 487-92, 503, 506, 509, 528, 534, 562-69

Seoul, S. Korea, 109, 111, 114-15, 118, 141-42, 145-48, 152, 155-57, 160, 162, 169, 184-85, 192-96, 203-05, 221, 470, 473, 475

South Korea, 13, 27, 34, 38-42, 69-70, 72-73, 93-98, 100, 103-110, 115-143, 148, 151-57, 194-98, 201-05, 209, 212, 214, 217-222, 231, 233-36, 308, 373, 395-97, 406, 431-36, 447, 461, 481, 487-89, 525, 538-39

Syria, 8, 64-65, 256, 264-65, 270, 275-77, 327, 376, 454-55, 498, 513, 543, 545-52, 555-58

T

Truman Doctrine, 55-56, 88-89, 117, 224, 334

U

United States, 1, 13, 23, 42, 45, 50, 91-92, 102-04, 117, 121, 189, 201, 217, 219, 249, 262, 289, 345, 376, 387, 524, 555, 558

USMC Unites States Marine Corps, 98, 128-31, 141-44, 153, 166, 174, 178-80, 186-89, 192-95, 222, 238, 291, 298-300, 308, 395, 414, 423, 434-35, 439, 442, 450-53, 467-68, 529

W

Washington D.C., 15-17, 23, 32, 35-39, 42, 67, 71, 80, 86, 103, 108, 112-13, 119-21, 148, 157, 166-70,

191-94, 205-07, 230, 251, 277, 287, 290, 304, 307, 323, 336, 344-46, 360, 369, 381-85, 389-90, 399-402, 406, 411, 424, 430, 440, 457-59, 465-66, 470, 489-90, 506, 520, 547, 554
General William Westmoreland, 391-393, 398, 403, 408, 411-12, 415-16, 420-26, 429-31, 434-44, 448-51, 454, 463-69, 473-78, 481-82, 527
General Wilton Walker, 124, 127-28, 132, 135-36, 140, 146, 149-53, 155, 162-65, 172-75, 184-85, 192

V

VC, Viet Cong, 250, 282-84, 290, 297, 312, 324-25, 330-32, 337-42, 345-46, 366-71, 375, 379-80, 383-88, 392, 398, 403-05, 409-13, 416-23, 426, 432-39, 441, 446-67, 471-75, 478-79, 487-93, 496, 501-04, 516, 522-23, 528, 541, 560
Venona Project, 14-15, 18, 31, 74, 78-82, 199, 224-26
Vietminh, 45-48, 64, 101, 159, 200, 229-34, 250-52, 274, 282-84, 374, 392, 411, 464

S

Soviet Union, 4, 12, 15-16, 26, 33, 60, 82, 101-02, 199, 220, 253, 259, 264, 268, 277, 288, 309, 348, 254, 445, 495, 499, 567
Spies, 13-16, 25-29, 74, 78-79, 83-85, 90, 102, 113, 183, 190, 198-99, 214, 223-26, 245, 268, 309, 315, 367, 381, 389, 494-95, 515, 533, 549

References

About Face by Colonel David Hackworth and Julie Sherman Simon and Schuster 1989
A Bright Shining Lie Neil Sheehan Random House 1988
Acceptable Loss Kregg P. Jorgenson Ballantine Books 1991
A Fellowship of Valor by Col. Joseph H. Alexander The History Channel and Lou Reda Productions Harper Collins Publishers 1997
A History of the 20th Century Martin Gilbert W. Morrow and Co. 1997
A History of the Twentieth Century Volumes Two and Three by Martin Gilbert William Morrow and Co. 1998
Alien Wars by Gen. Oleg Sarin and Col. Lev Dvoretsky Presidio Press 1996
Ambush Valley by Eric Hammel Pacifica Press 1990
American Caesar by William Manchester
American Cruisers of World War II by Steve Ewing 1984
America's Tenth Legion by Shelby Stanton Presidio 1989
America's Tenth Legion Shelby Stanton Presidio Press 1989
A Rumor of War by Philip Caputo H. Holt and Co. 1977
Battle for Hue by Keith William Nolan Presidio Press 1983
Battle For Korea Robert J. Dvorchak and The Associated Press Combined Books 1993
Battles in the Monsoon by S.L.A. Marshall Morrow 1968
Beyond the Wild Blue by Walter J. Boyne St. Martin's Press 1997
Black Berets and Painted Faces by Gary A. Linderer Doubleday Books 1991
Black Book of Communism by Stephane Courtois Harvard University Press 1999
Blind Mans Bluff Sherry Sontag and Christopher Drew Public Affairs 1998
Blood Tears and Folly by Len Deighton Harper and Collins 1993
Breakout by Martin Russ Penguin Books 1999
Chronicle of the Twentieth Century by Time Life Books 1990

Colder Than Hell by Joseph Owen Blue Jacket Books 1996
Cold War by James R. Arnold and Roberta Wiener ABc-Clio 2012
Conflict: The History of the Korean War by Robert Leckie Putnam 1962
Covert Warrior Warner Smith Presidio Press 1996
Cruisers an Illustrated History by Antony Preston 1980
Days of Infamy by Michael Coffey and A&E Television Hyperion 1999
Death in the A Shau Valley by Larry Chambers Ivy Books 1998
Death Valley by Keith William Nolan Presidio Press 1987
Dereliction of Duty H.R. McMaster Harper Collins 1997
Everything We Had by Al Santoli Random House 1981
Fatal Flaws Book 1 by Capt. Richard A. Meo ret. FDNY Xlibris.com 2014
Fatal Victories by William Weir Archon Books 1993
FDR's Last Year by Jim Bishop William Morrow and Co. 1974
Fire in the Streets by Milton Vorst Simon and Schuster 1979
Firepower-Air Warfare by Chris Bishop Chartwell Books 1999
From A Dark Sky by Orr Kelly Presidio Press 1996
From Hiroshima to Glasnost by Paul Nitze Weidenfeld & Nicholson 1989
General of the Army by Ed Cray WW Norton and Co. 1990
George C. Marshall by Forrest C. Pogue Viking Press 1987
German Weapons of World War II by Chris Bishop and Adam Warner Chartwell Books Inc. 2001
Goodbye Darkness by William Manchester Little & Brown 1979
Good to Go by Harry Constance and Randall Fuerst W. Morrow and Co. 1997
Green Berets in Vietnam by Shelby L. Stanton Presidio Press 1985
Guests of the Ayatollah by Mark Bowden Atlantic Monthly Press 2006
Hell in a Vey Small Place by Bernard Fall J.B. Lippincott 1966
History of United States Naval Operations in World War II Volumes I-XIV by Admiral Samuel Elliot Morrison Castle Books 1960
History's Worst Decisions by Stephen Weir Metro Books 2008
I Led Three Lives by Herbert Philbrick McGraw Hill 1952
Incursion by J.D. Coleman St. Martin's Press 1991
Infamy by John Toland Anchor Publishers 1982
In The Arena by Richard Nixon Simon and Schuster 1990
Into Cambodia by Keith William Nolan Presidio Press 1990
Into Laos by Keith William Nolan Presidio Press 1986
Jane's Battleships of the 20th Century by Bernard Ireland and Tony Gibbons Harper Collins Publishers 1996
JFK and Vietnam by John M. Newman 1992
Journey Among Warriors Col. Victor Croziat USMC ret. White Mane Publishing 1997
Jungle Dragoon by Paul D. Walker Presidio Press 1999

Kennedy's Wars by Lawrence Freedman Oxford Press 2000
Khe Sanh: Siege in the Clouds by Eric Hammel
MacArthur's War by Stanley Weintraub The Free Press 2000
Making of a Quagmire David Halberstam Random House 1965
Marine Sniper by Charles Henderson Berkley Books 1986
Memoirs of Harry Truman Vol. 1 & 2 Doubleday 1955-56
Never Without Heroes by Lawrence C. Vetter Jr. Ivy Books 1996
No End Save Victory Essays by Ambrose, Carr, Keegan and Manchester 2001
No Shining Armor by Otto J. Lehrack University Press 1992
One Bugle No Drums by William Hopkins Algonquin Books of Chapel Hill 1986
On War by Carl von Clausewitz Princeton University Press 1976
Operation Buffalo by Keith William Nolan Presidio Press 1991
Operation Tuscaloosa by John J. Culbertson Ivy Books 1997
Phantom Warriors Book 1&2 by Gary A. Linderer Ballantine Books 2001
Platoon Leader by James R. McDonough Random House 1985
Pleiku Dawn of Helicopter Warfare by J.D. Coleman St. Martin's Press 1988
Presidents Under Fire by James R. Arnold Orion Books 1994
Recondo by Larry Chambers Ivy Books 1992
Reflections of a Warrior Franklin D. Miller Presidio Press 1991
Reluctant Warrior by Michael C. Hodges Ballantine Books 1996
Ringed in Steel Micheal D. Mahler Presido Press 1986
Ripcord by Keith William Nolan Ballantine Books 2000
Russia and the West Under Lenin and Stalin by George Keenan Little, Brown & Co. 1960
Secrets of the Vietnam War Lt. General Phillip Davidson Presidio Press 1990
Semper Fi Vietnam Edward F. Murphy Presidio Press 1997
Shield of the Republic by Michael T. Isenberg St. Martins Press 1993
Silent Warrior Charles Henderson Berkley Books 2000
Six Days in June by Eric Hammel McMillan Publishing 1992
SOG by John L. Plaster Simon and Schuster 1997
Special Men by Dennis Foley Ivy books 1994
Steichen at War by Christopher Phillips 1981
Strategy For Defeat by Admiral U. S. G. Sharp Presidio Press 1978
Street Without Joy by Bernard Fall Stackpole Books 1963
Summons of the Trumpet by David Palmer Presidio Press 1977
Sun Tsu's Art of War by General Tao Hanzhang Sterling Publishing Co. 1987
Tactical Genius in Battle by Len Deighton and Simon Goodenough Phaidon Press 1979
Tanks in the Wire by David B. Stockwell Daring Books 1989
Target Patton by Robert K. Wilcox Renemy Publishing 2008

TET Offensive by James R. Arnold Osprey Books 1990
The 1ˢᵗ Cav in Vietnam Shelby Stanton Presidio Press 1987
The 1950s by Richard A. Scwartz Facts on File Inc. 2003
The Battle for Pusan by Addison Terry Presidio 2000
The Best and the Brightest by David Halberstam Random House 1969
The Blood Road by John Prados John Wiley and Sons 1998
The Dying President
The Eve of Destruction by Howard Blum Harper Collins Publishers 2003
The Eyewitness History of the Vietnam War 1961-1975 by George Esper and the Associated Press Ballantine Books 1983
The French Betrayal of America by Kenneth R. Timmerman Crown Forum 2004
The Generals by Thomas E. Ricks Penguin Press 2012
The Giants by Richard J. Barnet Simon and Schuster 1977
The Great War by Jay Winter and Blaine Baggett Peguin Studio 1996
The Haunted Wood by Allen Weinstein and Alexander Vassiliev The Modern Library 1999
The Illusion of Peace by Tad Zulc Viking Press 1978
The Last Parallel by Martin Russ Rhinehart and Co. 1957
The Last Stand of Fox Company by Bob Drury & Tom Clavin Publishers Group 2009
The Linebacker Raids by John T. Smith Arms and Armor Press 1998
The Lost Peace by Alan Goodman Hoover Institute 1978
The Magnificent Bastards by Keith William Nolan Presidio Press 1994
The McNamara Strategy and the Vietnam War by Gregory Palmer Greenwood Press 1978
The Memoirs of Richard Nixon by Richard M. Nixon Sidgwick and Jackson 1978
Then and Now by Tad Zulc William Morrow and Co. 1990
The Pentagon Papers by Neil Sheehan Bantam Books 1971
The Price of Peace by Lawrence Freedman Henry Holy 1986
The Real War Richard M. Nixon Warner Books 1999
The Rise and Fall of an American Army by Shelby L. Stanton Presidio Press 1985
The River and the Gauntlet by S.L.A. Marshall The Battery Press 1955
The Ten Thousand Day War by Michael Maclear Thames Methuen 1981
The Timelines of History by Bernard Grun Simon & Schuster 1991
The U.S. Navy An Illustrated History by Nathan Miller American Heritage and The U.S. Naval Institute 1977
The Victors by Stephen E. Ambrose Simon and Schuster 1998
The War Managers by Douglas Kinnard Avery Publishing 1985

Fatal Flaws | 579

The Weekly Standard periodical
This Kind of War by T. R. Fehrenbach Brassey's 1963
Tim Page's Nam Thames and Hudson Press 1983
To Bear Any Burden by Al Santoli Abacus 1986
Treachery by Bill Gertz Crown Forum 2004
Treason by Ann Coulter Three Rivers Publishers 2003
U.S. Marine Corps Aviation Peter B. Mersky N&A Publishing 1983
US News and World Report periodical
Venona: Soviet Espionage and the American Response NSA and CIA 1996
Victor Six David Christian and William Hoffer McGraw Hill 1990
Victory and Deceit by James F. Dunnigan and Albert A. Nofi William Morrow and Company 1995
Victory and Deceit James F. Dunnigan and Albert A. Nofi William Morrow and Company 1995
Vietnam, a History Stanley Karnow & PBS Television 1983
Vietnam at War by Phillip B. Davidson Sidgwick and Jackson 1988
Vietnam A Visual Encyclopedia Philip Gutzman PRC Publishing 2002
Vietnam Decisive Battles by John Pimlott Barnes and Noble Books 1990
Vietnam Decisive Battles by John Pimlott Barnes and Noble Books 1990
Vietnam the Naval Story by Frank Uhlig Naval Institute Press 1986
Vietnam Witness by Bernard Fall Prager Press 1966
War in Korea by D. M. Giangreco Presidio Press 1990
Warships From Sail to the Nuclear Age by Bernard Ireland Hamlyn 1978
Warships of the 20th Century by Christopher Chant Tiger Books 1996
We Were Soldiers Once and Young by Lt. Gen. Harold G. Moore and Joseph L. Galloway Randon House 1992
We Were There Vietnam edited by Hal Buell Tess Press 2007
What If by Robert Crowley Essays by Carr, Lucas, Ambrose, Keegan Puntam 1999
White House Years by Henry Kissinger Little & Brown 1982
World War 2 by Life Magazine 2001 Edited by Richard B. Stolley Bulfinch Press 2001
World War II a 50th Anniversary by The Associated Press 1989
WWII by the Editors of Time Life Books 1989 Time Life Books
Yeager by Gen. Chuck Yeager Bantam Books 1985

Video Documentaries

American Experience: Harry Truman
>LBJ PBS 1991
>FDR PBS 1994
>Nixon PBS 1990
>Ronald Reagan
>General Douglas PBS 1999
>MacArthur

Blood and Oil	Mary Callaghan 2006
Century of Warfare	The History Channel 1994
Chosin	Brian Iglesias
Citizen King	PBS
Cold War The Series	2012
Fires of Kuwait	IMAX
First to Fight: The Marines	The Military Channel 2008
Freedom Riders	The American Experience
Frontline, the Al Qaeda Files	PBS
George Marshall and the American Century	2007
Great Blunders of WWII	The History Channel
History Rediscovered Why We Fight Series	Frank Capra

581

Horror in the East	The BBC 2001
Inside 9/11	
Israel's War History	2009
Korea	The History Channel 2005
Korea, The Forgotten War	2010
Korean War Stories	by PBS
Lawrence of Arabia: The Battle for the Arab World	PBS 2003
Lessons of Darkness	by Herzog
Medal of Honor	PBS 2008
Modern Warfare the Series	
Nobody Listened, Castro	
Race in America	PBS
Secrets of the Russian Archives	History Channel
Six Days in June	Levi Eshkol
Stealth Technology by the History Channel	
The 50 Years War Israel and the Arabs	PBS 1998
The Atomic Café	1982
The Berlin Airlift	by PBS
The Century of Warfare	The History Channel 1994
The Forgotten War	
The Korean War	The History Channel
The Last Days in Saigon	PBS
The Manhattan Project	The History Channel 2002
The Secret War Series	The History Channel 2012
The Vietnam War	by The History Channel
The Vietnam War	The History Channel 2008
The War Zone: The Series	
The World at War	The BBC 1974
Vietnam A Television History	PBS American Experience 1983
Vietnam a Television History	PBS

Vietnam in HD	The History Channel 2011
Vietnam The Ten Thousand Day War	PBS 1998
War File: The Series	
Warplanes of WWII	The History Channel
Winston Churchill: the History Channel	
World War I	

Source Notes

Page 9	History of the 20th Century	page 712
	Then and Now	page 53
Page 10	Then and Now	pages 61-62, 96-99
Page 11	Then and Now	pages 41-42, 59-60
	Time Life Books, WWII	pages 444-447
	Cold War	pages 91-92
Page 12	History of the 20th Century	pages 724
	Cold War	pages 91-92
Page 13	Presidents Under Fire	pages 193-95
	Then and Now	pages 63-67, 118
	Shield of the Republic	pages 422-25
Page 15	Target Patton	Pages 400
	Cold War	Pages 250
	A Bright Shining Lie	Pages 168-70
Page 16	Storm Landings	Pages 190
	Then and Now	Pages 83-85, 114-15
Page 17	Then and Now	Pages 75, 107-10
	Days of Infamy	Pages 223
	History of the 20th Century	Pages 766
	Cold War	Pages 215-17
Page 18	Target Patton	Pages 236-38

585

	Secrets of the Russian Archives video	
Page 19	Haunted Wood	Pages 10-11, 44-49, 94-109, 124, 148
	US News &World Report 2/3/03	
Page 20	Giants	Pages 107
	Haunted Wood	Pages 10-11, 44-49, 94-109, 124, 148
Page 22	Target Patton	Pages xi-xix, 1-14, 20-21, 155-57, 200-02, 208-13, 234-37, 393-404
Page 23	History of the 20th Century	Pages 714, 735
	Hiroshima to Glasnost	Pages 29-45
Page 24	Cold War	Pages 69-70, 217-19
	Then and Now	Pages 101-02
	The Real War	Pages 73
	History of the 20th Century	Pages 714, 735
Page 25	Then and Now	Pages 101-03
	Shield of the Republic	Pages 130-36, 165
	Hiroshima to Glasnost	Pages 23-24
Page 26	History of the 20th Century	Pages 713
	Shield of the Republic	Pages 165
Page 27	Then and Now	Pages 87
	History of the 20th Century	Pages 712-13
Page 29	The Generals	Pages 2-39, 110-115
Page 30	General of the Army	Pages 555, 557-60
Page 31	General of the Army	Pages 557-61
	Target Patton	Pages 251-53
Page 32	Shield of the Republic	Pages 126-28
	General of the Army	Pages 558-62
Page 33	General of the Army	Pages 564-66

Page 34	Days of Infamy	Pages 224-25
	General of the Army	Pages 592
	Then and Now	Pages 98-102
	History of the 20th Century	Pages 737
	Cold War	Pages xxiii
Page 35	What If	Pages 377-86
	History of the 20th Century	Pages 737-38
Page 36	What If	Pages 385-86
	General of the Army	Pages 575-85
Page 37	What If	Pages 349-351
Pages 38-9	This Kind of War	Pages 18-28
Page 40	History of the 20th Century	Page 717
	This Kind of War	Pages 18-28
Page 41	Vietnam, A History	Pages 122-27
	Dereliction of Duty	Page 33
Page 42	Vietnam, A History	Pages 144-47
	Secrets of the Vietnam War	Pages 124
Page 43	Vietnam: A History	Pages 147-52
Page 44	Vietnam: A History	Pages 147-56
	History of the 20th Century	Pages 800-01
	Cold War	Pages 87
	Time Life Books WWII	Pages 480-81
Page 45-6	Then and Now	Pages 91-94
Page 46	Days of Infamy	Pages 226
	Time Life Books WWII	Pages 460
	The Real War	Pages- 48
Page 47	In the Arena	Pages 184-87
Page 48	The 1950s	Pages 7
	General of the Army	Pages 594-96
Page 49	General of the Army	Pages 594-96, 599, 601-06, 608-12
Page 50	History of the 20th Century	Pages 739-40

Page 51	History of the 20th Century	Pages 809-10
	Then and Now	Pages 150, 155
	Cold War	Pages xxiv, 71-73, 199-200
Page 52	Treason	Pages 84-86
Page 53	Shield of the Republic	Pages 133-37
	General of the Army	Pages 640-45
Page 54	History of the 20th Century	Pages 812-13
	General of the Army	Pages 644-46
Page 55	Giants	Pages 16-17
	Time Life Books WWII	Pages 464
	The Real War	Pages 74
	Shield of the Republic	Pages 132-38
	Cold War	Pages 201-02
Page 56	Then and Now	Pages 127-28
Page 57	General of the Army	Pages 661-63
	History of the 20th Century	Pages 747-49, 815-16
Page 58	The 1950s	Pages 6
	Then and Now	Pages 120-22
	History of the 20th Century	Pages 788-91, 815
Page 59	Then and Now	Pages 122-23
	General of the Army	Pages 646-47
	Time Life Books WWII	Pages 456-57
Page 60	History of the 20th Century	Pages 816-18
	What If	Pages 360-63
	The Cold War	Pages 200
Page 61	This Kind of War	Pages 23
	History of the 20th Century	Pages 817-18
Pages 62-63	Time Life Books WWII	Pages 468, 482
	What If	Pages 377-92
	General of the Army	Pages 632-38
Page 65	Target Patton	Pages 135-38

Page 66	General of the Army	Page 629
Page 67	Treason	Pages 19, 22, 76-77
	What If	Pages 806-11
	American Experience - Ronald Reagan	
Pages 68-69	What If	Pages 801-11
	The 1950s	Pages 51-52
	Target Patton	Pages 133-54, 243-50
	Haunted Wood	Pages 103-06, 339-42
	Treason	Pages 40, 45
	Shield of the Republic	Pages 41, 56
Pages 70-71	Treason	Pages 46, 64-68
	Target Patton	Pages 139-40, 246-51
	Haunted Wood	Pages 21, 38-48, 153-60, 218, 283-91
Pages 72-73	I Led Three Lives	Pages 238-60
	Weekly Standard	November 2012
	Then and Now	Pages 96
	Target Patton	Pages 133-54, 252-53
	Haunted Wood	Pages 103-06, 339-42
	Hiroshima to Glasnost	Pages 9, 21
	In the Arena	Pages 248-50
Page 74	History of the 20th Century	Pages 832-34
Page 75	Shield of the Republic	Pages 138-41
	The Generals	Pages 120-22
	What If	Pages 357-58
Page 76	Time Life Books WWII	Page 458
Page 77	Weekly Standard	June 25 2012
Pages 78-80	Then and Now	Pages 113, 118-19
	Time Life Books WWII	Pages 468, 474, 478
	The Cold War	Pages 1-2
Pages 82-83	This Kind of War	Pages 284-96

	Time Life Books WWII	Pages 471-73
	Shield of the Republic	Pages 148-51
Pages 84-86	Days of Infamy	Pages 224-28
	Vietnam; A History	Pages 174-75
	The Cold War	Pages 89
	History of the 20th Century	Pages 770, 846-52, 857-65, 907-09
	General of the Army	Pages 676-78
	Alien Wars	Pages 88
Pages 88-90	Giants	Pages 107-09
	Shield of the Republic	Pages 140, 150, 156-59
	Hiroshima to Glasnost	Pages 98-99
	Then and Now	Pages 155-56, 162-63
	This Kind of War	Pages 32
	MacArthur's War	Pages 12-17
	Weekly Standard	November 2012
Pages 91-94	MacArthur's War	Pages 17-22, 24-26
	Then and Now	Pages 163-64
	History of the 20th Century	Pages 844-45
	Alien Wars	Pages 59-60
	Secrets of the Russian Archives Video	
Pages 96-97	MacArthur's War	Pages 33, 35
	Then and Now	Pages 168-69
	This Kind of War	Pages 46
Page 98	Target Patton	Pages 237
Page 99-100	This Kind of War	Pages 28, 54-56
Pages 101-02	This Kind of War	Pages 57-60
	MacArthur's War	Pages 41, 49
	Shield of the Republic	Pages 177-79
Pages 103-04	General of the Army	Page 689
	History of the 20th Century	Pages 871-75

Pages 105-06	History of the 20ᵗʰ Century	Pages 872-73
	MacArthur's War	Page 69
	Shield of the Republic	Pages 180-83
Pages 107-08	Fellowship of Valor	Pages 252-55
	Shield of the Republic	Page 146
	One Bugle No Drums	Page 23
Pages 110-12	Shield of the Republic	Page 182-187
	MacArthur's War	Page 89-93
Pages 113-14	MacArthur's War	Page 95-99
	This Kind of War	Pages 158
	Shield of the Republic	Pages 188-190
Pages 116-17	MacArthur's War	Pages 108, 111, 118, 123-124
	America's Tenth Legion	Pages 319-320
Pages 118-19	MacArthur's War	Page 106-107
	Fellowship of Valor	Pages 270
	America's X Legion	Pages 70
Pages 124-25	This Kind of War	Pages 163, 181
Pages 126-27	MacArthur's War	Page 168-169
	This Kind of War	Pages 163, 184
	Shield of the Republic	Pages 206-208
Pages 128-29	MacArthur's War	Page 175-179
	This Kind of War	Page 186
	Alien Wars	Page 63
	General of the Army	Page 694
Page 131	MacArthur's War	Pages 184-185, 188-194
	History of the 20ᵗʰ Century	Pages 895-896
Page 132	Then and Now	Pages 466-467
	Hiroshima to Glasnost	Pages 109-110
	The 1950's	Page 385

Pages 133-34	MacArthur's War	Pages 200-205, 210-211
Pages 135-36	MacArthur's War	Pages 210-214
	One Bugle No Drums	Pages 71-73
	America's X Legion	Pages 162-63, 169, 175-177, 179-80
	The Generals	Pages 140
Pages 137-38	MacArthur's War	Pages 216-218, 220
	The Generals	Pages 152-155
	America's X Legion	Pages 163, 183-184
Pages 139-41	The Generals	Pages 137-140
	America's Tenth Legion	Pages 189-190
	MacArthur's War	Pages 226-228
Pages 142-43	The Generals	Pages 138-140
	America's Tenth Legion	Pages 196-198
	Breakout	Pages 184
	Battle for Korea	Page 108
	The River and the Gauntlet	All
Pages 144-47	America's Tenth Legion	Pages 197, 207-211, 217-223
	Breakout	Page 198
	General of the Army	Pages 701-703
Pages 148-49	America's Tenth Legion	Pages 238-240, 247, 268-271
	Fellowship of Valor	Page 294
	Battle for Korea	Page 139
Page 150	MacArthur's War	Pages 250-260
	The Haunted Wood	Pages 176-196
	The 1950's	Page 53
	History of the 20th Century	Pages 894-895
Pages 151-54	MacArthur's War	Pages 246-249, 265-267
	Battle for Korea	Page 142

Pages 155-56	MacArthur's War	Pages 266, 280-288
	Shield of the Republic	Pages 217-218
	This Kind of War	Pages 251-253
	America's Tenth Legion	Pages 258-261, 294-295
	Colder Than Hell	Pages 120-28
Pages 157-58	Fellowship of Valor	Pages 303-304, 313
	MacArthur's War	Page 285
	Battle for Korea	Page 172
	The Generals	Pages 135-175
Pages 159-60	Alien Wars	Page 79
	The Generals	Pages 177-191
	About Face	Page 816
Page 161	This Kind of War	Pages 271-272
	MacArthur's War	Pages 336, 373
Page 162	The 1950's	Pages 54, 94
	Target Patton	Pages 242-243
Page 163	Vietnam; A History	Pages 177-178, 182-185
Pages 164-66	This Kind of War	Pages 284-285, 290-93, 298-307
	History of the 20th Century	Pages 876-877
	About Face	Pages 358-361
Pages 167-68	This Kind of War	Pages 313, 360-361, 422-423
	Battle for Korea	Pages 218-219, 231
Pages 169-70	Shield of the Republic	Pages 230, 234
	Mustang	Pages 225-226
	This Kind of War	Page 364
Pages 171-73	This Kind of War	Pages 366-386, 414
	Battle for Korea	Page 239
Page 174	In the Arena	Page 225
	The Cold War	Page 116

Fatal Flaws | 593

	Giants	Page 91
Pages 175-76	Then and Now	Pages 184-187
	This Kind of War	Pages 290, 443
	MacArthur's War	Pages 326-327
	The Cold War	Pages xxvi-xxiii
Pages 177-78	This Kind of War	Pages 453-456
	Shield of the Republic	Pages 281-283
Pages 179-81	Shield of the Republic	Pages 266-271
	The Generals	Pages 168-175
Pages 181-83	Treason	Pages 32, 64-66, 97, 104
	The 1950's	Pages 52-53, 81, 94-95, 179-181
	The Haunted Wood	Pages 316-317
Page 184	The Cold War	Page 58
	Rise and Fall- Great Powers	Page 393
Pages 185-86	The Blood Road	Pages 1-5
	The Best and Brightest	Pages 137, 142-143
	Vietnam; A History	Pages 188-195
	The Cold War	Pages 89-91
Page 187	Shield of the Republic	Pages 588-591, 607-610
	The Best and Brightest	Pages 139, 144
	Vietnam; A History	Pages 197-199
	A Bright Shining Lie	Page 172
	What If	Pages 391-393
Pages 188-89	In The Arena	Pages 299-300
	The Best and Brightest	Pages 145, 147
	This Kind of War	Pages 453-456
	Vietnam; A History	Pages 200, 215-217
	Target Patton	Page 400

Pages 190-91	Shield of the Republic	Pages 257-266, 290-304
Page 192	About Face	Pages 644-665
	The Generals	Pages 203-214
	Vietnam; A History	Page 360
Page 193	Shield of the Republic	Pages 617-620, 695-698
	History's Worst Decisions	Pages 131-135
Pages 194-95	History's Worst Decisions	Pages 160-162
	Then and Now	Pages 208-211
	The 1950's	Page 94
	Hiroshima to Glasnost	Pages 127-137
Pages 196-97	Shield of the Republic	Pages 777-780
	Then and Now	Pages 204-211, 213-214
	Kennedy's Wars	Page 125
	Rise and Fall- Great Powers	Page 390
Pages 198-99	Shield of the Republic	Pages 355-374, 424, 475, 666
Pages 199	Then and Now	Page 177
	The 1950's	Page 212
Pages 200-02	Then and Now	Pages 207-208
	The Blood Road	Page 38
	Vietnam, A Visual Encl.	Pages 107, 136
Page 203	Rise and Fall- Great Powers	Pages 414-426
	Vietnam, A Visual Encl.	Pages 136-38, 224-25
	A Bright Shining Lie	Pages 136, 139-40
	Vietnam; A History	Pages 221-223
	The 1950's	Page 266
	The Cold War	Pages 239-240
Page 204	The 1950's	Page 264
	Then and Now	Page 186

	A Bright Shining Lie	Pages 173-174
	Hiroshima to Glasnost	Pages 163-164
Pages 205-06	Hiroshima to Glasnost	Pages 160, 164-168
	History's Worst Decisions	Pages 168-172
	Then and Now	Pages 220-224
Pages 207-08	Shield of the Republic	Pages 698-701
	Then and Now	Page 211
Pages 209-10	Then and Now	Pages 188-194
	The Cold War	Page 240
	The 1950's	Pages 279-280
Pages 211-13	Shield of the Republic	Pages 705-709
	The 1950's	Pages 279-281
	The Real War	Page 79
	Rise and Fall- Great Powers	Page 424
Pages 215-16	The Cold War	Pages 45-46
	Giants	Page 80
	The 1950's	Pages 313-314
	Then and Now	Pages 18, 215-221
	Then and Now	Pages 196, 263
Pages 216-18	Shield of the Republic	Pages 659, 671-72, 675-79, 720-50
	Then and Now	Pages 197-98
	The 1950's	Page 315
Pages 219-20	Vietnam; A History	Pages 224-227
	A Bright Shining Lie	Pages 183-184
Pages 221-22	Shield of the Republic	Pages 711-719
	The 1950's	Pages 351-353
	Then and Now	Pages 223-224
Pages 123-24	Then and Now	Pages 295-298
	The Cold War	Pages 78-79
	Hiroshima to Glasnost	Pages 167-171
Pages 224-25	The 1950's	Page 353

	In The Arena	Pages 177-181
Pages 226-28	The Cold War	Pages 19-21
	SOG	Pages 18-19
	Vietnam, A Visual Encl.	Pages 83, 226
	Vietnam; A History	Pages 236-239
	The Blood Road	Pages 9-18
Pages 229-30	The Cold War	Pages 133-135
	History's Worst Decisions	Pages 183-185
	Kennedy's Wars	Pages 287-293
Pages 230-31	Shield of the Republic	Pages 777-781
	Black Book of Communism	Page 651
Pages 232-33	Secrets of the Russian Archives Video	
	The Cold War	Pages 190-93
	The Blood Road	Pages 15-18, 21-24
	Vietnam, A Visual Encl.	Pages 89-90
	Then and Now	Page 234
Pages 234-35	A Bright Shining Lie	Page 196
	Vietnam; A History	Pages 237-239
	Then and Now	Page 233
	Black Book of Communism	Page 650
	The Cold War	Pages 9-11, 44-45
Pages 236-37	Shield of the Republic	Pages 752-754
	Then and Now	Page 240
	In The Arena	Pages 27-28
	What If	Pages 806-810
	The Best and Brightest	Page 454
Pages 237-38	Kennedy's wars	Pages 126-127
	The Best and Brightest	Pages 12, 26-29, 39
	Hiroshima to Glasnost	Pages 180-182
	Dereliction of Duty	Pages 2-8
Pages 238-40	The Blood Road	Pages 23-27, 32-33

	JFK and Vietnam	Pages 5-7
	The Generals	Pages
Pages 240-41	Vietnam A Visual Encyl.	Page 10
	The Blood Road	Pages 33-37
	Dereliction of Duty	Pages 6-7
	JFK and Vietnam	Pages 9-15
Pages 242-44	Shield of the Republic	Pages 788-792
	Dereliction of Duty	Pages 29-32
	Then and Now	Pages 247-249
	SOG	Page 22
	Kennedy's Wars	Pages 123-148
Page 245	Kennedy's Wars	Pages 147-49
	Hiroshima to Glasnost	Pages 183-184
Pages 246-47	Kennedy's Wars	Pages 123-146, 299-303
	Shield of the Republic	Pages 792-793
	JFK and Vietnam	Pages 14-19
Page 248	Secrets of the Red Files	Video
Pages 249-50	Shield of the Republic	Pages 752-756
	Kennedy's Wars	Pages 302-304
Pages 250-51	Kennedy's Wars	Pages 45-50
	The Cold War	Page 239
	Then and Now	Pages 235-237
Pages 251-52	Shield of the Republic	Pages 793-794
	Kennedy's Wars	Pages 51-59, 64-72
	The Best and Brightest	Page 76
	Hiroshima to Glasnost	Pages 185-187
	Rise and Fall Great Powers	Pages 428-430
Page 253	Kennedy's Wars	Page 150
	The Blood Road	Page 67
Pages 254-56	Kennedy's Wars	Pages 65-71, 73, 151
	Hiroshima to Glasnost	Pages 197-99

Pages 257-58	Rise and Fall Great Powers	Pages 401, 423-426
	The Generals	Pages 201-203, 215
	Kennedy's Wars	Pages 94, 96-104
	Hiroshima to Glasnost	Pages 205-207
Pages 258-61	The Best and Brightest	Pages 76-77, 135, 150-151, 156, 173, 175, 184
	A Bright Shining Lie	Page 195
	American Heritage	November-1989
	Vietnam; A History	Page 247
	The Blood Road	Pages 41-42, 46-47
	The Generals	Pages
Page 261	Then and Now	Pages 239-243
	The Cold War	Pages 13-14
Pages 262-63	The Cold War	Page 46
	Then and Now	Page 250
	Shield of the Republic	Pages 795-797
Pages 263-64	Vietnam A Visual Ency.	Page 238
	JFK and Vietnam	Pages 208-215, 217-219, 223-228
Pages 265-67	The Generals	Pages 224-229
	The Best and Brightest	Pages xiv-xv
	The Blood Road	Pages 27-31
	JFK and Vietnam	Pages 204-207
	A Bright Shining Lie	Pages 51, 58-59
Pages 267-68	Kennedy's Wars	Pages 249-256
Pages 269-70	Vietnam A Visual Ency.	Pages 227-228
	A Bright Shining Lie	Pages 59, 67
	About Face	Pages 417, 480-481
	Dereliction of Duty	Pages 15-22
	In The Arena	Page 273
Pages 270-72	A Bright Shining Lie	Pages 64, 89-92, 111, 317

	Then and Now	Pages 238-239
	About Face	Pages 675-685
	JFK and Vietnam	Pages 232-235, 240-259
Pages 273-75	The Blood Road	Pages 48-50
	A Bright Shining Lie	Pages 135-143, 310-311
Pages 275-77	A Bright Shining Lie	Page 290
	Vietnam; A History	Pages 255-257
	The Best and Brightest	Page xiv
	The Blood Road	Page 50
	JFK and Vietnam	Pages 267-280, 288-296
	Shield of the Republic	Pages 757-767
Pages 277-80	Shield of the Republic	Page 798
	Then and Now	Pages 237, 251-252
	Dereliction of Duty	Pages 24-25
	Kennedy's Wars	Pages 157-160, 164-169, 173-174
Pages 280-82	Shield of the Republic	Pages 800-803
	Kennedy's Wars	Pages 174-179, 184-185
	Hiroshima to Glasnost	Pages 214-222
	Then and Now	Page 253
	Blind Mans Bluff	Pages 40-41
Pages 283-85	Kennedy's Wars	Pages 193-195, 197, 202-207
	Shield of the Republic	Page 809
Pages 286-88	Kennedy's Wars	Pages 208-219
	Shield of the Republic	Pages 812-815, 818
Pages 289-91	Kennedy's Wars	Pages 219-224, 230, 234
	Shield of the Republic	Pages 818-820

	Secrets of the Russian Archives Video	
	Blind Mans Bluff	Page 47
Pages 291-92	Then and Now	Pages 279-280
	Hiroshima to Glasnost	Pages 240-242
Pages 292-94	Vietnam; A History	Pages 267-269
	A Bright Shining Lie	Pages 317-318
	SOG	Pages 23-25
	The Best and the Brightest	Page 178
Pages 295-96	A Bright Shining Lie	Pages 277, 283-284
	The Best and the Brightest	Pages 179-180, 184
	Vietnam Decisive Battles	Pages 24-31
Pages 297-98	A Bright Shining Lie	Pages 314-316
	The Real War	Page 102
	Then and Now	Page 239
	The Blood Road	Pages 57-60
	Vietnam A Visual Ency.	Page 392
	Target Patton	Pages 232-234
Pages 299-300	The 1st Cav in Vietnam	Pages 24-36
	The Blood Road	Pages 51-60
	JFK and Vietnam	Pages 298-309
	A Bright Shining Lie	Pages 326-327
	The Best and the Brightest	Pages 186-188, 202
Pages 301-03	A Bright Shining Lie	Pages 335-339, 341-342
	JFK and Vietnam	Pages 3, 317-323, 328-331
	The Best and the Brightest	Pages xv, 267, 370
Pages 304-05	A Bright Shining Lie	Pages 346-350
	The Best and the Brightest	Pages xv, 267, 370
	Then and Now	Page 265
	Vietnam A Visual Ency.	Page 208

Page 305	U.S. News and World Report 2/13/02	
Pages 306-08	The Best and the Brightest	Pages 208, 257, 277-281, 370-376
	A Bright Shining Lie	Pages 362-363
	About Face	Pages 712, 731, 831
	Vietnam; A History	Pages 284-288
	Dereliction of Duty	Page 39
	Secrets of the Vietnam War	Page 122
	JFK and Vietnam	Pages 321-333, 372-375, 387
Pages 309-10	The Best and the Brightest	Pages 297-299
	A Bright Shining Lie	Pages 368-375
	In The Arena	Page 71
	JFK and Vietnam	Pages 411-415, 419-420
	Then and Now	Pages 242-243
Pages 311-12	A Bright Shining Lie	Pages 373-377
	Vietnam; A History	Page 320
	JFK and Vietnam	Pages 433-435, 443-46, 449, 457-60
	Then and Now	Pages 266-268
	Vietnam A Visual Ency.	Page 209
	The Men Who Killed Kennedy	Video
Pages 313-14	The Best and the Brightest	Page 350
	Dereliction of Duty	Pages 50-53, 63-67, 71-75,
	Then and Now	Pages 264-268
	About Face	Pages 712, 731, 831
	A Bright Shining Lie	Page 376
	Vietnam; A History	Page 329
Pages 315-16	The Generals	Pages 231-240, 254-255

	Dereliction of Duty	Pages 36-44, 62-68, 87-88
Pages 317-18	Dereliction of Duty	Pages 67-69, 89-91, 105-106, 111-18
	Vietnam; A History	Page 362
	The Generals	Pages 255-256
	The Blood Road	Pages 80, 88
	SOG	Pages 30-32, 35
Pages 319-20	Dereliction of Duty	Pages 127-128
	The Blood Road	Pages 123-125
	Then and Now	Pages 267-270
	A Bright Shining Lie	Pages 378-379
	Vietnam; A History	Pages 357-362, 371-374
	The Best and the Brightest	Pages 418-420
	The Generals	Page 256
	U.S. News and World Report	12/2005
	Presidents Under Fire	Pages 205-208
Pages 321-22	The Best and the Brightest	Pages 415-419, 483-485
	Vietnam; A History	Pages 357-362, 376-377
	The Blood Road	Pages 71-75, 90
	Dereliction of Duty	Pages 143-145
Pages 322-24	Vietnam; A History	Pages 377, 395-396, 400-409
	Presidents Under Fire	Pages 212-215
	The Blood Road	Pages 91-93
	A Bright Shining Lie	Pages 381-383
	Then and Now	Page 200
	Vietnam; Decisive Battles	Page 38
	Dereliction of Duty	Page 172

Pages 325-26	Dereliction of Duty	Pages 194-197, 212-229
	Vietnam; A History	Pages 330-334, 401, 412
	The Blood Road	Pages 94-98, 129-131
	Vietnam A Visual Encyl.	Page 403
	Secrets of the Vietnam War	Pages 161-163
	SOG	Pages 34-35
Pages 327-28	Dereliction of Duty	Pages 218-230
	Vietnam A Visual Encyl.	Pages 148, 209
	Vietnam; A History	Pages 413-415
	The Best and the Brightest	Pages 512, 516-517
	The Linebacker Raids	Pages 149-151
	Presidents Under Fire	Pages 213-217
Pages 329-30	Presidents Under Fire	Pages 224-225
	Dereliction of Duty	Pages 245-271
Pages 331-32	The Cold War	Pages 55-56
	About Face	Page 460
	Then and Now	Page 292
Pages 332-33	Vietnam A Visual Encyl.	Page 86
	Vietnam; A History	Pages 420-425
	Vietnam; Decisive Battles	Page 43
Pages 334-36	Vietnam A Visual Encyl.	Page 405
	Vietnam; A History	Pages 420-439
	The Best and the Brightest	Pages 585-587
	Dereliction of Duty	Pages 283-286
	The Blood Road	Pages 123-125
Pages 336-37	Dereliction of Duty	Pages 304-315
	Hiroshima to Glasnost	Pages 258-261
Pages 337-38	The Blood Road	Pages 116-121, 146-149
	Vietnam Decisive Battles	Pages 40-47
	The 1st Air Cav in Vietnam	Pages 37-54

Fatal Flaws | 605

	Vietnam A Visual Encyl.	Pages 371-373
Pages 338-39	Then and Now	Pages 292-293
	Recondo	Pages 205-208
Pages 341-44	We Were Soldiers Once and Young	
	The Blood Road	Pages 146-149
	Pleiku; Dawn of Helicopter Warfare	
	Vietnam Decisive Battles	Pages 48-59
	Presidents Under Fire	Pages 225-228, 239-242, 245
	The Generals	Page 315
	The 1st Air Cav in Vietnam	Pages 45-64
	The Blood Road	Pages 148-149
	About Face	Pages 198-199, 486-489, 634
Pages 344-45	SOG	Pages 40-42
	The Blood Road	Pages 150-161
	The Generals	Pages 257-259
Pages 345-47	The Best and the Brightest	Pages 604-609, 615-616
	Presidents Under Fire	Pages 233-235
	About Face	Pages 597-598
	The Generals	Pages 261, 269-274
	Vietnam; A History	Pages 438-440
Pages 347-49	Vietnam A Visual Encyc.	Pages 70-71, 218-219
	The Cold War	Page 79
	The Blood Road	Pages 224-227
	About Face	Pages 494-495, 508, 516
	Vietnam; Decisive Battles	Pages 60-71
	The Generals	Pages 263-266
Pages 350-51	Vietnam; A History	Pages 440-443

	Hiroshima to Glasnost	Pages 263-265
	A Bright Shining Lie	Pages 620-628
	The Blood Road	Pages 185-187
	Vietnam Decisive Battles	Page 72
Page 351-52	A Bright Shining Lie	Page 629
	Vietnam Decisive Battles	Pages 72-83
	Vietnam A Visual Encyc.	Pages 173-174
	A Fellowship of Valor	Pages 328-329
Pages 352	A Bright Shining Lie	Page 651
Pages 353-54	About Face	Pages 518-525
	SOG	Pages 57-59
	Vietnam Decisive Battles	Pages 72-83
Pages 354-55	Death Valley	Pages 203-204
	Then and Now	Page 293
Pages 355-56	The Blood Road	Pages 181, 190-192
Pages 356-57	About Face	Pages 531-533, 737
	In The Arena	Page 291
Pages 357-60	Vietnam Decisive Battles	Pages 96-107
	Khe Sanh Siege in the Clouds	
	Presidents Under Fire	Pages 253, 255-56
	Operation Buffalo	Pages ix-39
	A Bright Shining Lie	Pages 642-649
Pages 360-61	Operation Buffalo	
	Vietnam Decisive Battles	Pages 116-127
	Vietnam A Visual Encycl.	Page 83
	Presidents Under Fire	Page 256
Pages 361-63	Then and Now	Pages 281-284
	Road to 9/11	Video
	Blood and Tears	Video
Page 364	Detroit	Video
	Race in America	Video

Fatal Flaws | 607

Pages 364-66	About Face	Pages 484-485, 624-635
	The Generals	Pages 274-284, 317-320
	Strategy For Defeat	
	The Best and the Brightest	Pages viii-ix
Pages 366-69	The Blood Road	Pages 195-198
	About Face	Pages 547-579
	Vietnam; A History	Pages 486-489, 503-508
	A Bright Shining Lie	Pages 683-684
Pages 369-70	A Bright Shining Lie	Pages 694-696
	About Face	Pages 609-610
	The Blood Road	Pages 233-238
	Vietnam; A History	Pages 542-543
Pages 370-73	A Bright Shining Lie	Pages 700-702
	About Face	Pages 611-613
	The Generals	Page 238
	The Blood Road	Pages 237-239, 244-246
	Vietnam Decisive Battles	Pages 116-126
Pages 374-75	Secrets of the Russian Archives	Video
	Hiroshima to Glasnost	Pages 271-272
Pages 375-77	Vietnam Decisive Battles	Pages 116-139
	Khe Sahn Siege in the Clouds	
	The Blood Road	Pages 245-246, 249-252
	A Bright Shining Lie	Pages 706-709
	TET Offensive 1968	
	Vietnam; A History	Pages 525-528
Pages 377-78	Vietnam Decisive Battles	Pages 116-139
	Khe Sahn Siege in the Clouds	

	Six Silent Men	Pages 40-44
	TET Offensive 1968	
	1st Air Cav in Vietnam	Pages 115-131
	Vietnam; A History	Pages 525-540
	A Bright Shining Lie	Pages 706-709
	The Blood Road	Pages 249-252, 255-257
Pages 378-80	Vietnam; A History	Pages 529-536, 549-552
	The Generals	Pages 286-291
	Tanks In The Wire	
	1st Air Cav In Vietnam	Pages 125-150
	Vietnam A Visual Encyc.	Pages 211, 229
Pages 381-83	Vietnam; A History	Pages 546-548
	A Bright Shining Lie	Pages 722-723
	Secrets of the Vietnam War	Pages 180-186, 268
	Strategy For Defeat	
	Presidents Under Fire	Pages 270-273
Pages 383-86	The Best and Brightest	Pages 657-658
	The Men Who Killed Kennedy	Video
	The Killing of RFK	Video
Pages 386-88	Then and Now	Pages 109-111, 164-165, 289-292
	The Cold War	Pages 27-28, 179-181,
Page 387-89	Vietnam A Visual Encycl.	Pages 303-304
	Incursion	Pages 25-26
	About Face	Pages 711-715, 767
	Vietnam; A History	Pages 582-584
	A Bright Shining Lie	Page 730-731
	Secrets of the Vietnam War	Pages 155-157
	In The Arena	Page 292
Pages 389-91	Incursion	Pages 6-35

	1st Air Cav in Vietnam	Pages 153-160
	Incursion	Pages 6-35, 61-72
Pages 391-92	About Face	Pages 700-705
	The Blood Road	Pages 288-295
	SOG	Pages 233-236, 239-241
	Incursion	Pages 121, 125-126
	About Face	Pages 700-705
Pages 392-93	In The Arena	Pages 292-293
	Linebacker Raids	Pages 44-45
	Vietnam; A History	Pages 636-639
	Rise and Fall of Great Powers	Pages 398-400
Pages 393-94	SOG	Pages 240-243
	A Bright Shining Lie	Pages 732-735
	The Generals	Pages 320-323
	Incursion	Pages 62-63
Pages 396	Then and Now	Pages 321-323
Pages 397	Incursion	Pages 80-90, 112-15, 140-56
	A Bright Shining Lie	Page 735
Pages 397-98	Then and Now	Pages 195-196
	Rise and Fall of Great Powers	Pages 395-397
Pages 398-400	Incursion	Pages 12-13, 188-190
	Vietnam; A History	Pages 589-591
Pages 400-01	SOG	Pages 244-249
	Incursion	Pages 214-18, 220-25 240-48
	1st Air Cav in Vietnam	Pages 168-176
Pages 402-03	Vietnam A Visual Encycl.	Page 202
	Linebacker Raids	Pages 45-46
	In The Arena	Pages 340-341
	Shut Up And Sing	Page 36

Fatal Flaws | 609

Pages 404-06	SOG	Pages 247-250	
	Incursion	Pages 249-262	
	1st Air Cav in Vietnam	Pages 178-190	
	About Face	Page 734, 766	
	Vietnam A Visual Encycl.	Pages 86-87	
	The Best and Brightest	Pages 611-612	
Page 406	Vietnam; A History	Pages 625-627	
Pages 406-08	Then and Now	Pages 312-314, 318-321	
Pages 408-11	Vietnam A Visual Encycl.	Page 222	
	Vietnam Decisive Battles	Pages 148-159	
	SOG	Pages 323-325	
	The Blood Road	Pages 317-25, 335-60 363-65	
Pages 411-14	U.S. News and World Report	May 1994	
	In The Arena	205-207, 245, 282	
Pages 414-16	Vietnam A Visual Encycl.	Pages 68-69, 85, 94, 184, 304, 314	
	Vietnam Decisive Battles	Page 148, 183	
	Vietnam; A History	Page 602	
	A Bright Shining Lie	Pages 732-733	
	The Real War	Pages 39-41	
	The Blood Road	Pages 340-350	
	The Generals	Pages 324-326	
	Platoon Leader	Pages 229-240	
Page 416-18	Then and Now	Page 328	
	In The Arena	Pages 12-16, 205-07, 282	
	U.S. News and World Report	May 1994	
Pages 418-19	The Blood Road	Pages 368-371	
	The Linebacker Raids	Pages 50-53	
Pages 419-424	The Linebacker Raids	Pages 52-54, 58-60, 90-103, 110-15	

	About Face	Pages 562, 812-813
	Vietnam Decisive Battles	Pages 160-179
	The Blood Road	Pages 370-372
	Blind Mans Bluff	Page 161
	Vietnam a Visual Encycl.	Page 229
Pages 424-25	The Cold War	Pages 144-146
	Treason	Page 193
	In The Arena	Pages 254-256
Pages 425-429	In The Arena	Page 293
	The Linebacker Raids	Pages 124-134, 161-163
	Vietnam a Visual Encycl.	Page 423-424
	Strategy For Defeat	Page 258
Pages 429-431	Treason	Page 215
	About Face	Page 818
	Vietnam Decisive Battles	Page 180
	Vietnam a Visual Encycl.	Page 422
	Vietnam; A History	Pages 654-659
Pages 431-436	Eve of Destruction	Pages 90-100
Pages 436-440	Eve of Destruction	Pages 98-102
	In The Arena	Pages 335-336
	Your Government Failed You	Page 6
	Blind Mans Bluff	Page 171
Pages 441-442	Strategy For Defeat	Page 263
	Vietnam Decisive Battles	Page 183
Pages 442-444	In The Arena	Pages 20-22, 40-42
Pages 445-446	The Real War	Page 108, 115
	Strategy For Defeat	Page 263-265
	Vietnam A Visual Encycl.	Page 86, 213
Pages 447-448	The Real War	Pages 115, 119
	Strategy For Defeat	Page 265
	Vietnam A Visual Encycl.	Pages 98

Pages 448-452　Vietnam A Visual Encycl.　　Page 422
　　　　　　　　The Blood Road　　　　　　 Pages 373-375
　　　　　　　　The Real War　　　　　　　　Page 124
　　　　　　　　In The Arena　　　　　　　　Pages 254-256,
　　　　　　　　　　　　　　　　　　　　　　340-346

　　　　　　　　Vietnam Decisive Battles　　Pages 180-187
　　　　　　　　The Last Days in Saigon　　 Video
　　　　　　　　Vietnam; A History　　　　　Pages 660-669

Direct Quotes

1.	Page 2	This Kind of War by T.R. Fehrenbach	Page 84
2.	Page 4	Then and Now by Tad Zulc	Page 97
3.	Page 23	Shield of the Republic by Micheal T. Isenberg	Page 165
4.	Page 29	The Generals by Ricks	Page 555
5.	Page 30	The Generals by Ricks	Page 555
6.	Page 34	Days of Infamy by Micheal Coffey	Page 225
7.	Page 37	What If by Cowley	Page 386
8.	Page 41	This Kind of War by T.R. Fehrenbach	Page 84
9.	Page 53	General of the Army by Cray	Page 595
10.	Page 53	General of the Army by Cray	Page 599
11.	Page 55	The Great War by Winter	Page 344
12.	Page 55	This Kind of War by T.R. Fehrenbach	Page 84
13.	Page 55-56	History of the 20th Century by Gilbert	Page 809
14.	Page 60	History of the 20th Century by Gilbert	Page 812
15.	Page 67	History of the 20th Century by Gilbert	Page 816
16.	Page 102	The Giants by Richard J. Barnet	Page 108
17.	Page 120	This Kind of War by T.R. Fehrenbach	Page 84
18.	Page 121	This Kind of War by T.R. Fehrenbach	Page 59
19.	Page 150	One Bugle No Drums by Hopkins	Page 23
20.	Page 155	This Kind of War by T.R. Fehrenbach	Page 181

21.	Page 157	MacArthur's War by Stanley Weintraub	Page 175
22.	Page 163	MacArthur's War by Stanley Weintraub	Page 211
23.	Page 168	MacArthur's War by Stanley Weintraub	Page 216
24.	Page 188	The Generals by Ricks	Page 167
25.	Page 197	This Kind of War by T.R. Fehrenbach	Page 271
26.	Page 201	This Kind of War by T.R. Fehrenbach	Page 284
27.	Page 202	Vietnam; A History by Karnow	Page 177
28.	Page 203	This Kind of War by T.R. Fehrenbach	Page 290
29.	Page 207	This Kind of War by T.R. Fehrenbach	Page 292
30.	Page 208	Battle for Korea by Assoc. Press	Page 231
31.	Page 218	Shield of the Republic by Isenberg	Page 234
32.	Page 218	Shield of the Republic by Isenberg	Page 283
33.	Page 220	This Kind of War by T.R. Fehrenbach	Page 453
34.	Page 222	This Kind of War by T.R. Fehrenbach	Page 453-56
35.	Page 200	Shield of the Republic by Isenberg	Page 266
36.	Page 234	The Best and the Brightest by Halberstam	Page 145
37.	Page 241	Then and Now by Tad Zulc	Page 209
38.	Page 243	Shield of the Republic by Isenberg	Page 777
39.	Page 254	From Hiroshima to Glasnost by Nitze	Page 163
40.	Page 288	Shield of the Republic by Isenberg	Page 781
41.	Page 314	Shield of the Republic by Isenberg	Page 793
42.	Page 318	From Hiroshima to Glasnost by Nitze	Page 197
43.	Page 346	Shield of the Republic by Isenberg	Page 798
44.	Page 349	Kennedy's Wars by Freedman	Page 160
45.	Page 351	This Kind of War by T.R. Fehrenbach	Page 84
46.	Page 380	The Best and the Brightest by Halberstam	Page xv
47.	Page 386	The Best and the Brightest by Halberstam	Page 286
48.	Page 386	Secrets of the Vietnam War by Davidson	Page 122
49.	Page 388	In the Arena By Richard Nixon	Page 71
50.	Page 390	JFK and Vietnam by Newman	Page 459
51.	Page 390	A Bright Shining Lie by Neil Sheehan	Page 376

52.	Page 392	Vietnam; A History by Stanley Karnow	Page 329
53.	Page 394	Dereliction of Duty by McMaster	Page 62
54.	Page 400	Vietnam; A History by Stanley Karnow	Page 374
55.	Page 424	A Rumor of War by Philip Caputo	
56.	Page 466	A Bright Shining Lie by Neil Sheehan	Page 701
57.	Page 494	The Blood Road by John Prados	Page 290
58.	Page 529	Vietnam A Visual Encyclopedia	Page 229
59.	Page 567	The Real War by Richard Nixon	Page 124

Maps not to scale

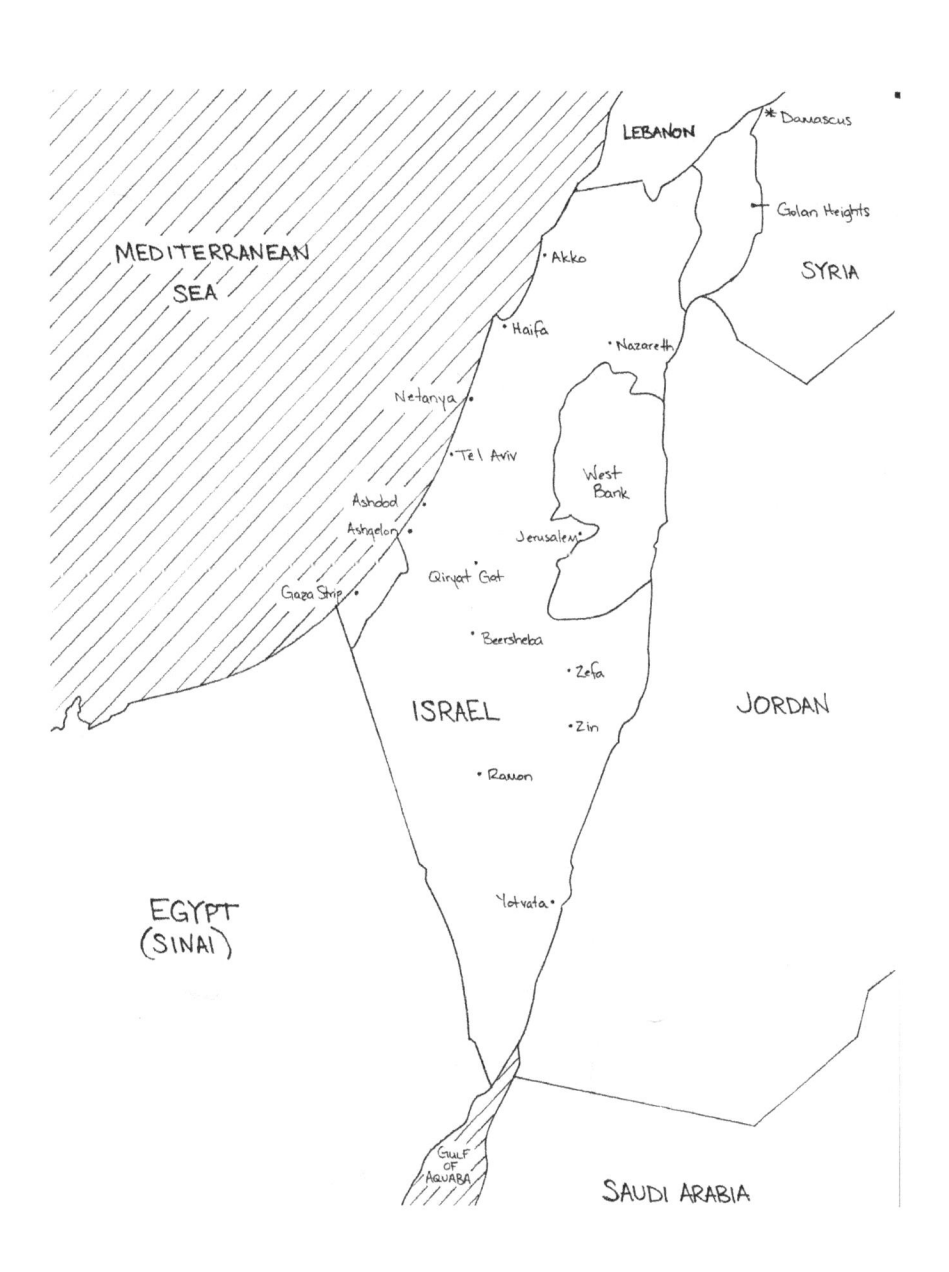

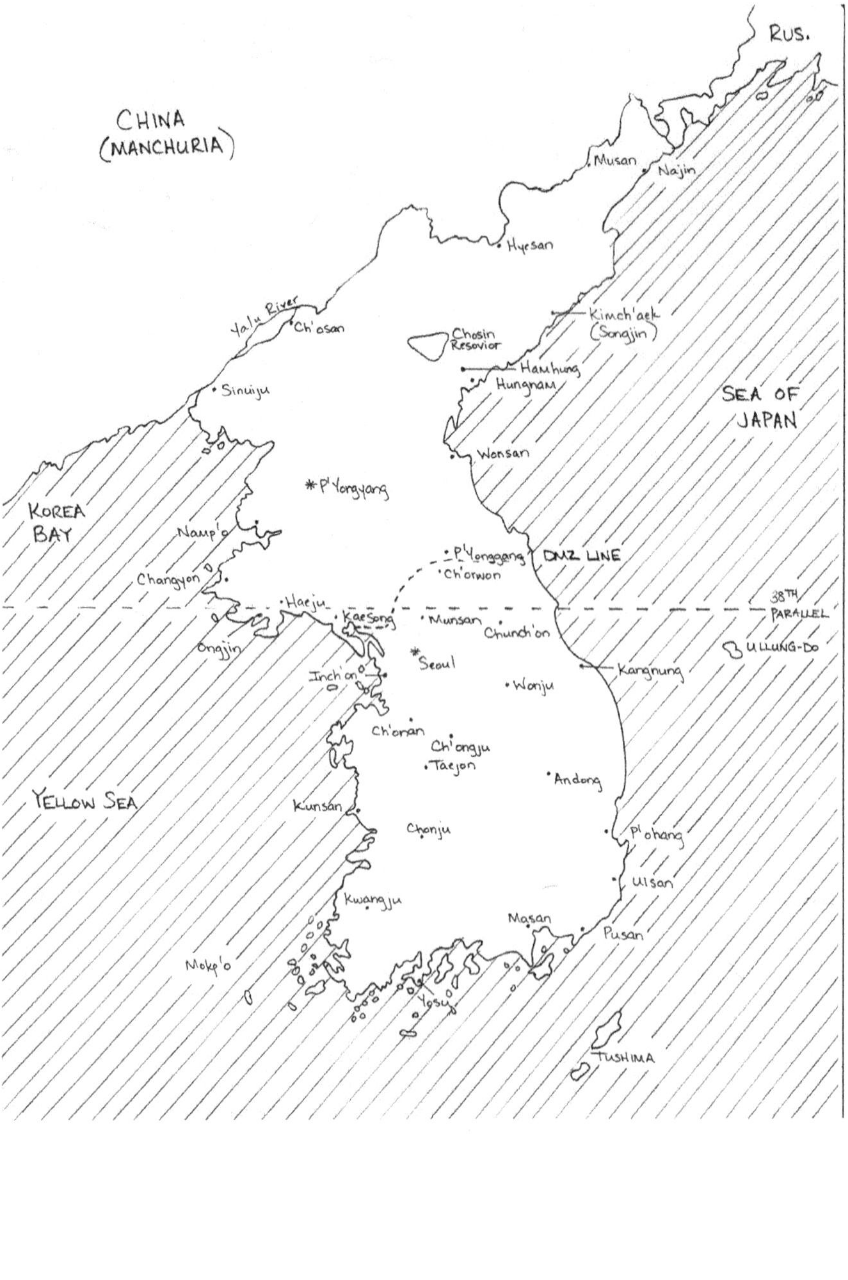

RUS.
CHINA
(MANCHURIA)
Musan
Najin
Hyesan
Yalu River
Ch'osan
Chosin
Resovior
Kimch'aek
(Songjin)
Hamhung
Hungnam
Sinuiju
SEA OF
JAPAN
Wonsan
P'Yongyang
KOREA
BAY
Namp'o
P'Yonggang
DMZ LINE
Ch'orwon
Changyon
38TH
PARALLEL
Haeju
Kaesong
Munsan
Chunch'on
Ongjin
ULLUNG-DO
Seoul
Inch'on
Kangnung
Wonju
Ch'onan
Ch'ongju
Taejon
Andong
YELLOW SEA
Kunsan
Chonju
P'ohang
Ulsan
Kwangju
Masan
Pusan
Mokp'o
Yosu
TUSHIMA

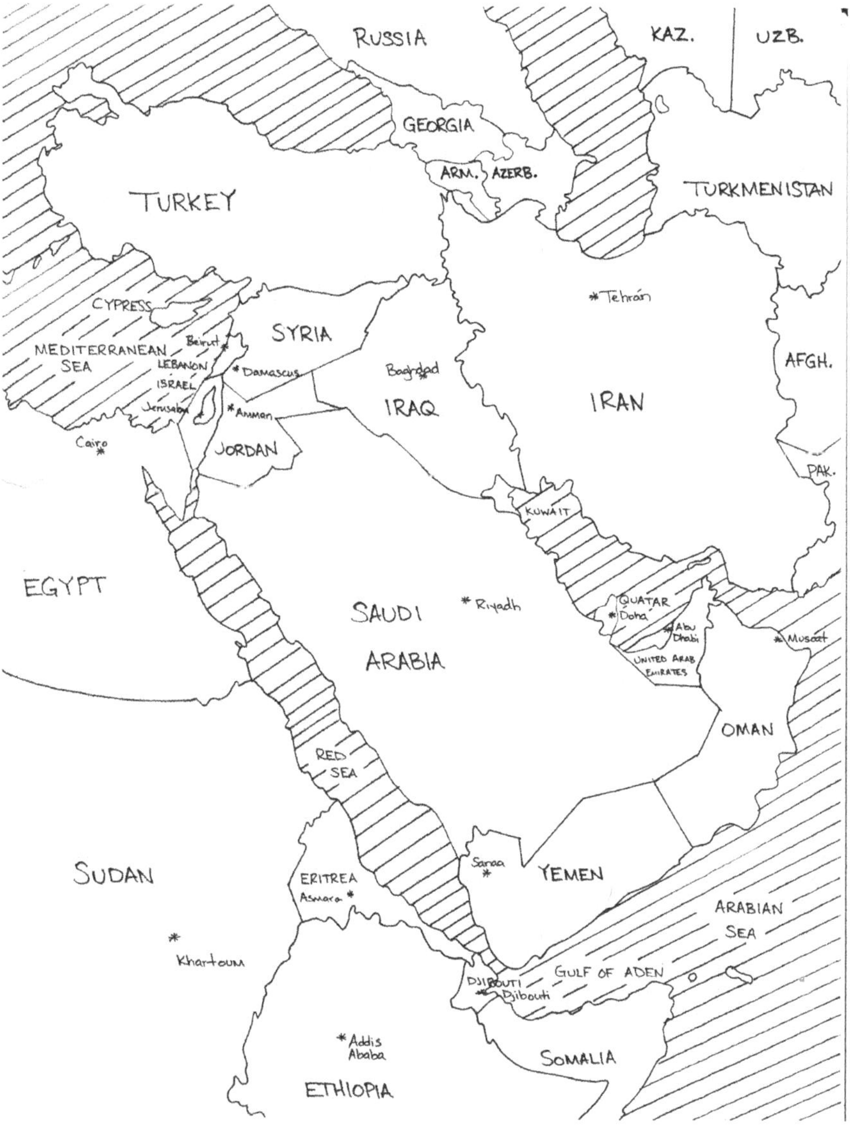
RUSSIA
KAZ.
UZB.
GEORGIA
ARM.
AZERB.
TURKMENISTAN
TURKEY
CYPRESS
MEDITERRANEAN SEA
Beirut
LEBANON
ISRAEL
Jerusalem
Damascus
SYRIA
Amman
JORDAN
Cairo
Baghdad
IRAQ
Tehran
IRAN
AFGH.
PAK.
KUWAIT
EGYPT
SAUDI ARABIA
Riyadh
QUATAR
Doha
Abu Dhabi
UNITED ARAB EMIRATES
Muscat
OMAN
RED SEA
Sanaa
YEMEN
SUDAN
ERITREA
Asmara
Khartoum
ARABIAN SEA
GULF OF ADEN
DJIBOUTI
Djibouti
Addis Ababa
SOMALIA
ETHIOPIA

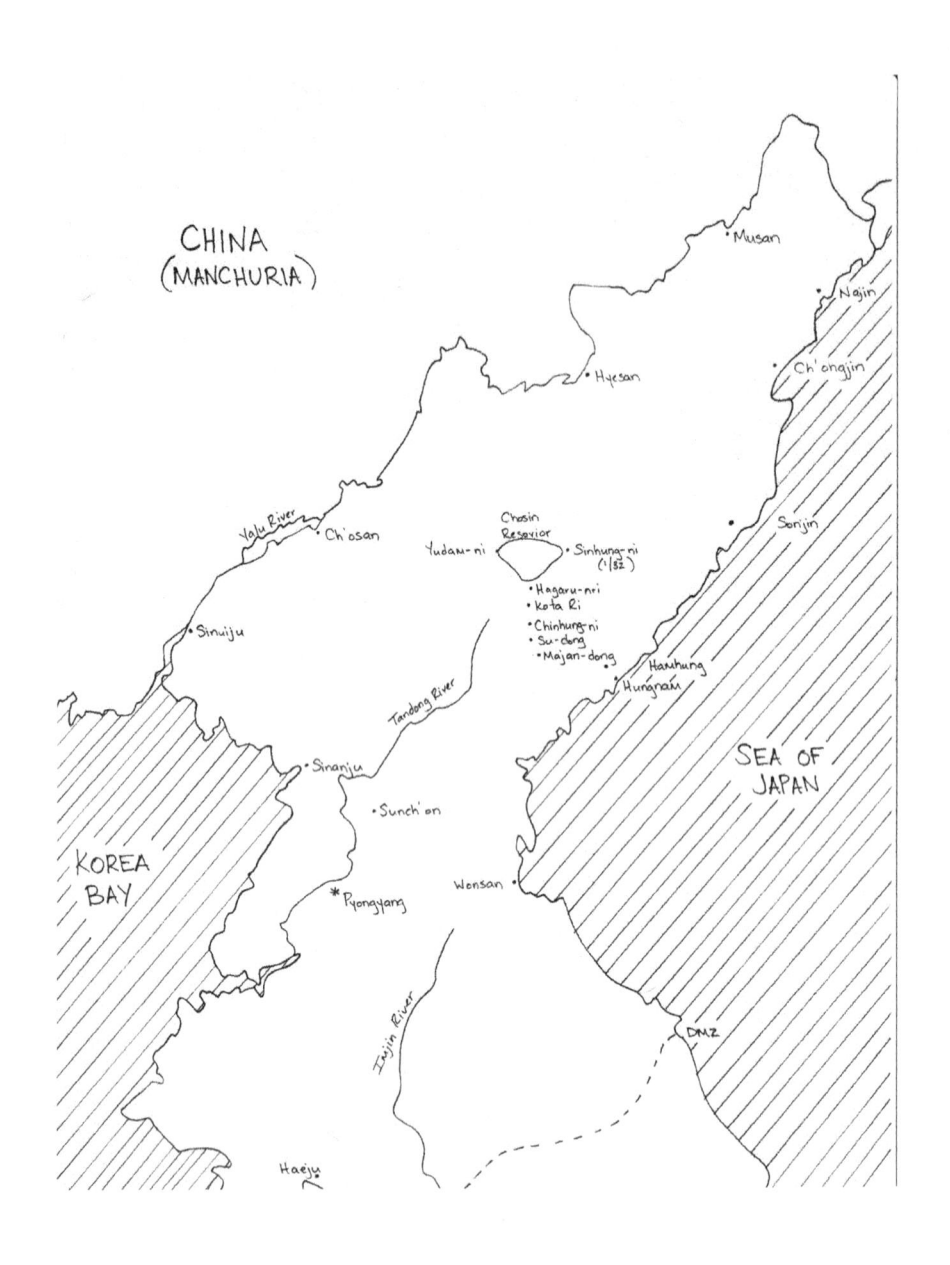

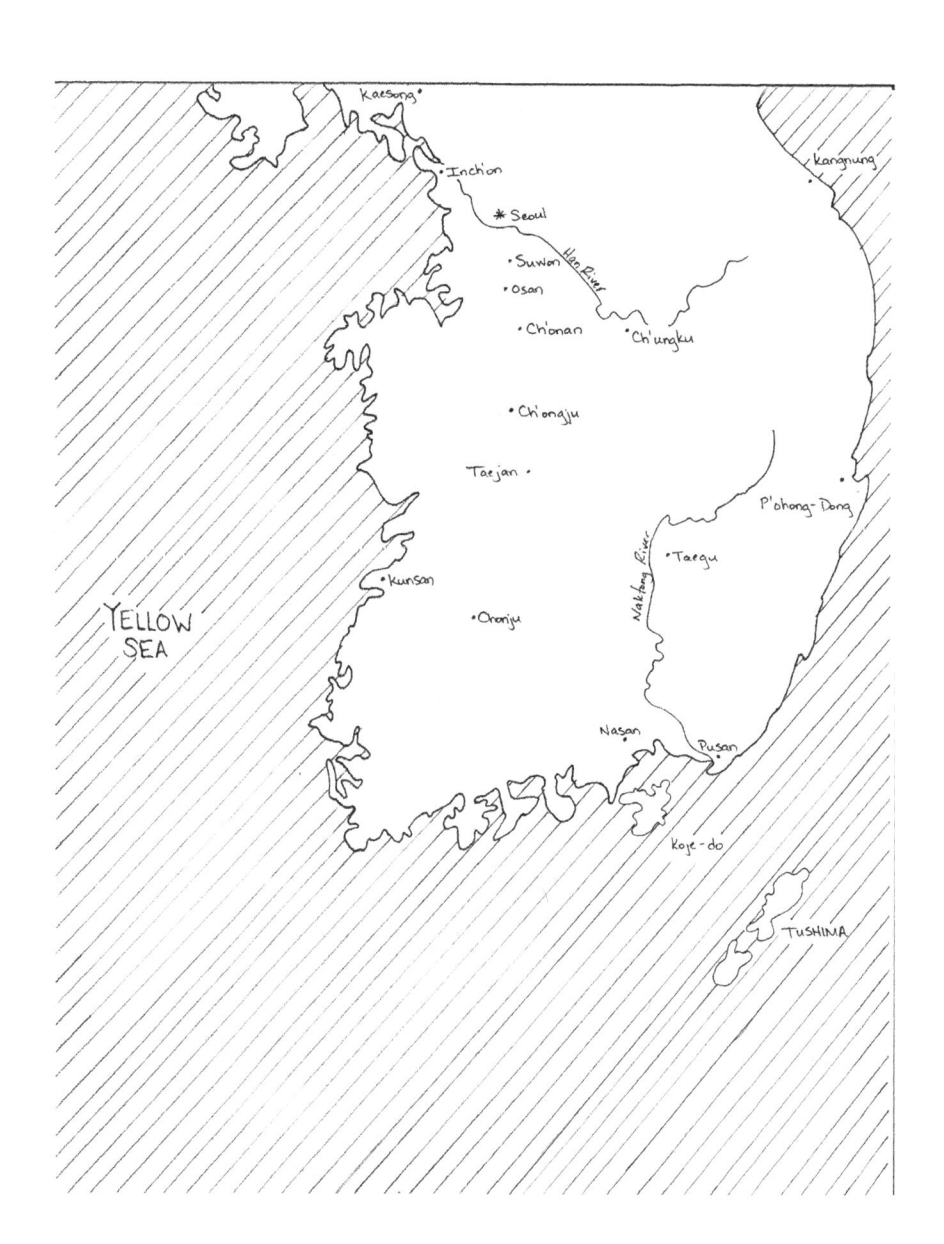

Author Bio

Born in New York in the late 50s. Graduated High School in 1975. Nominated to US Naval Academy and accepted into USMC Platoon Leader Class. Graduated from Oswego College BA in Biology. Accepted into the Fire Dept of New York 1980, and attended John Jay College for Fire Science. Served in the FDNY until 2003, retiring as a Captain. Originally published My Turn on the Firelines in 2009 with Trafford Publishing. Updated in 2014 and available with MRK Publishing. A newly edited and expanded edition was completed with MRK Publishing in 2014. Speaker and presenter on 9/11 issues, and owner of a painting and decorating company in Florida.